Le Morte d'Arthur

Sir Thomas Malory's

LE MORTE D'ARTHUR

King Arthur and the
Legends of the Round Table

A RENDITION IN MODERN IDIOM BY
Keith Baines

WITH AN INTRODUCTION BY
Robert Graves

DECORATIVE ILLUSTRATIONS BY ENRICO ARNO

756543

BRAMHALL HOUSE

NEW YORK

Copyright © MCMLXII by Keith Baines
Library of Congress Catalog Card Number: 62-14302
All rights reserved.
This edition is published by Bramhall House
a division of Clarkson N. Potter, Inc.
c d e f g h
Manufactured in the United States of America

For Anna

Preface

The edition on which this rendering of Malory's *Le Morte d'Arthur* is based is the Winchester Ms. edited by Eugène Vinaver and published by Oxford (The Clarendon Press), 3 vols., in 1947; also in the Oxford Standard Authors series, 1 vol., in 1954. It is important to distinguish this edition from the Caxton Ms. known popularly through the Everyman edition, differing as it does both in content and layout.

The purpose of this book is to provide a concise and lucid rendering of *Le Morte d'Arthur* in modern idiom for the benefit of those students and general readers who wish to obtain a firm grasp of the whole, but lack the time and enthusiasm necessary to perform this task for themselves.

My procedure throughout has been to retell each tale "in my own words," clarifying those episodes which, for the purpose in hand, seemed obscure, and condensing those which seemed prolix. I am aware that to do this places an unusually heavy premium on the translator's judgment, and far from supposing my own to be infallible, would plead only that my reading of the original has been assiduous, and my drafts for the present rendering innumerable.

I do undertake to have made no deliberate omission of circumstantial fact, no deliberate distortion of action or character, and to have added no material of my own invention.

While hoping that readers will enjoy this book in its own right, I wish to emphasize that I would regard it as an impertinence to try to echo Malory's own grand manner—let alone to attempt a rival masterpiece. Hence I would ask readers to regard this book as a supplement to the original—an endeavor to bridge the gulf which separates Malory's age and idiom from our own.

For ease of reference I have adopted the same table of contents as that of the original, but with simplified headings. Also, I have chosen what appealed to me as the most characteristic of variant spellings of personal and place names, and simplified them only slightly. At the request of my publishers I have added an Appendix summarizing the actions and relationships of the principal characters.

I should like to make acknowledgments to my wife and mother for their persistent faith in me; to Robert and Beryl Graves for their generous help and encouragement; to my publishers for their endurance and sympathy. Finally, my thanks to the Clarendon Press for permission to quote from the various "Inscriptions" in the text; and here I should like to pay tribute to the manifest excellence of Eugène Vinaver's editing of the Winchester Ms.

K.B.

Deyá, Majorca, 1959–1961

Contents

Introduction

Sir Thomas Malory led a life of adventure, much of it seemingly discreditable to his chivalrous ideals. He inherited an estate at Newbold Revell in 1433 and, three years later, served at the siege of Calais with a train consisting of a single lancer and two archers. In 1445 he became a Member of Parliament for Warwickshire, yet in 1450 not only tried to ambush and murder the Duke of Buckingham, but broke into Coombe Abbey, where he robbed and insulted the abbot. He was also charged with forcing one Henry Smyth's wife, stealing cattle on a large scale, and highway robbery. For these misdemeanours he served eight periods of imprisonment, and twice escaped—in July, 1451, swimming the moat of Coleshill prison; in October, 1454, making an armed breakout from Colchester Castle. In 1462 he fought for King Edward IV against the Scots and French, but presently went over to the Lancastrian rebels. In 1468 the King excluded him from a general pardon, whereupon he appears to have been imprisoned at Newgate until his death three years later. There he wrote *Le Morte d'Arthur,* which Caxton published on July 31, 1485. Caxton, who suppresses Malory's authorship, claims to be acting on the plea of many nobles and gentlemen who thought that "King Arthur should be remembered among Englishmen before all other Christian kings"; he himself believed that the gallant and virtuous deeds of the Round Table knights deserved permanent record.

Malory's sources were several Norman-French romances and an English alliterative epic, *Morte Arthur.* The French had used the legends of Arthur as a formal tapestry on which knights forever jousted, fought, succoured damsels, and slew monsters; each tale was almost drowned in rhetoric and reiteration. Malory, however, by a judicious choice of episodes, built up something like a coherent history of Arthur from his curious birth to his dramatic death. Even so, *Le Morte d'Arthur* remains an enchanted sea for the reader to swim about in, delighting at the random beauties of fifteenth-century prose rather than engrossed by the plot. John Milton once had the notion of turning it into a verse epic, but afterward chose a Biblical theme as the easier option, and two hundred years more went by before Tennyson exploited some of Malory's more dramatic incidents in *Idylls of the King*. Tennyson did not dare present the "bold bawdry and open manslaughter" of the Round Table knights to a Victorian public; instead, he credited them with Protestant moral sentiments foreign to their nature.

The Arthurian legend, a strange web of history, saga, and religious myth woven in the Dark Ages, had grown stranger still since the Norman Conquest, when Bretons in the train of King William combined their own bardic traditions of King Arthur with those that they found current in Wales—for the Bretons were of Welsh origin and spoke the same language. Through their influence Arthur soon became the favourite fictional character of the Norman-French *trouvères,* a peg on which to hang fine conceits of Chivalry and Courteous Love.

The original Arthur, as Sir John Rhys first suggested, and as Messrs. R. G. Collingwood and Geoffrey Ashe have since proved beyond reasonable doubt, was a heroic British cavalry general named Arturius. A hundred years after the Roman legions had evacuated Britain, he halted the pagan Saxon invaders with their Pictish and Anglian allies, fighting ten main battles, and in 517 won a decisive victory at Mount Badon which gave him possession of London. Early annalists do not make Arthur a king, but *Dux Bellorum* ("Leader of Wars") and *Comes Britanniarum* ("Count of the Britains"), meaning commander in chief. King Uther Pendragon ("Chief Dragon"), who figures as his father in some accounts, seems to have been a hereditary Captain-General of the Roman forces in North Britain. The title refers to a red silk dragon with a wide-open mouth, serving not only as a standard but as a wind sock that helped archers to correct their aim. This dragon, now the national emblem of Wales, had been brought to Britain all the way from China by way of the Byzantine Empire.

Arthur based his strategy on defensive dikes, reconditioned hill forts, and mounted commandos. Though he and his men professed themselves Christians, certain lives of British saints hint that he incurred the Church's dislike when he financed his antipagan war by sacrilege. He fell in 538, at the Battle of Camlan, near Glastonbury, which was both the seat of an ancient pagan cult and a Christian shrine associated with St. Joseph of Arimathea. There his knights secretly buried him. The Saxons took heart, regained Salisbury in 550 and London in 571, and by 623 had forced the British back into Wales.

This historical sequence is obscured in *Le Morte d'Arthur*. According to the first book Malory wrote, "Arthur and Lucius," Arthur fought wars that gave him dominion over Britain, Ireland, and France, and finally made good his ancestral claim to the Roman Empire. Here the historic Arthur, as *imperator* of the Roman-British forces fighting the Saxons, has been confused with the Spanish-born general Maximus, who in 383 was acclaimed *Imperator* ("Emperor") by the legions in Britain. Maximus led a large force across the Channel, seized Paris, and established an imperial court at Trèves. Later, Spain and Africa submitted to him. In 387 he reinforced his army with British recruits, and in 388 took Rome, but was then defeated at Aquileia and beheaded by his rival Theodosius. The Bretons, whose bards, like the Welsh, prophesied Arthur's second coming and vengeance on the Saxons, are descended partly from the survivors of Maximus' forces, partly from refugees who fled to Brittany after Arthur's death.

Ireland has been added to Arthur's empire in "Arthur and Lucius," on the strength of another Welsh bardic tale which describes Bran the Blessed's expedition from Wales to Ireland in vengeance of his wronged sister Brangwen. Bran was an ancient British hero with whom the bards identified Arthur, perhaps because Bran bore the title *Arddu* ("the Dark One," pronounced *Arthū*) and had a shrine at Glastonbury. Bran, whose emblem was the raven, had been defeated by his twin Beli in a certain "Battle of the Trees," and his head buried on Tower Hill, London, where ravens are still protected as a good-luck charm. "Arthur's Bosom," or "Arthur's Bower," to which the soul of Sir John Falstaff went, seems to be the northern paradise from which, according to prophecy, Arddu would one day return.

Had Arthur not been a cavalryman as well as a hater of Saxons, the Norman knights who broke King Harold's Saxon footmen at Hastings would never have celebrated him. In ancient Rome, armoured infantry ruled the battlefield, using cavalry as mere flank support—until the Battle of Adrianople (A.D. 378), when charges of Gothic lancers broke the Emperor Valens' Roman legions. This reversed the tactical postion: cavalry became the main arm. The code of chivalry (which means "cavalry") is Gothic in origin, though later modified by Italian, Byzantine, Celtic, Arabic, and other influences. Medieval knights were freemen; their base-born serfs, or infantry ("children"), fought on foot; and this social difference between the two arms persisted in Europe until machine guns and barbed wire robbed the cavalry of serious tactical importance. Chivalry is now on the wane, and not to everyone's regret. For though *caballero* still means "gentleman," and no Spanish boy of good birth would dare ride a donkey or perform menial tasks, the English phrase, "cavalier fashion," recalls the heartless arrogance which hard-riding gentlemen often showed the lower classes, and which is implicit in *Le Morte d'Arthur.* The highly artificial romances drawn upon by Malory were those that Cervantes' Don Quixote took in so literal a sense that his wits turned. Reading of knights who wore modern armour, fought according to an antique code, were constantly beset by medieval sorcerers, and had absurd encounters with pre-Christian monsters and giants, he tried to emulate their feats.

Pitched battles, even in *Le Morte d'Arthur,* are always so vaguely described that no strategic or tactical system can be deduced from them, except a customary concealment of reserves under the shade of trees. We are told only how this knight or that unhorsed his opponent, or helped a fallen comrade to remount. After a welter of conventional language— "feinting and fointing and sore strokes"—comes a parenthetical "five thousand were slain," and, as in Homer's *Iliad,* where chariotry ruled the battlefield, no mention can be found of the base-born fighter. Malory eschews realistic detail. All villages and cities are fair, all towers strong, all abbeys white-stoned, all chapels little. Nor are even the principal characters defined physically. We learn nothing of King Arthur but that he had grey eyes, or of Sir Launcelot and Sir Tristram but that they were big men. Though certain ladies may be "passing fair," their faces, figures, and colouring cannot be guessed. We are given no relief of domestic or political scenes while the knights joust, fight, love, hunt, make merry, and perfunctorily attend mass. Many of them seem to spend their entire lives on guard at some bridge or lurking in an enchanted castle from which to charge out upon the unwary. A few fishermen and shepherds appear as background characters, but there is a conspicuous lack of artisans, merchants, shopkeepers, and other working folk. Food and arms are simply "obtained"; no money changes hands, except in the form of mass-pennies and once when Queen Gwynevere finances an expedition in search of the crazed Sir Launcelot, her lover.

The Round Table is Christian in name only. Extramarital unions abound, nor does any slur attach to the offspring unless born in incest like Sir Modred. Sir Galahad and Sir Torre, for instance, are both blameless bastards, and at the end of long adventures we find Sir Tristram and Iseult living in adulterous ease at Sir Launcelot's castle, Joyous Gard, with Arthur's and Gwynevere's full assent. It would dishonour a knight to repudiate an extramarital union, and Malory is sympathetic towards women who suffer from illicit love pangs. Thus Gwynevere comforts Iseult when she complains that Sir Tristram has married the King of Brittany's daughter, remarking that noble knights are often tricked into marriage but after a while weary of their wives and come back to their first loves.

Nor may knights always forgive their enemies: they must avenge slain kinsmen. A typical Arthurian blood feud begins with King Lot's death at the hands of King Pellinore. Sir Gawain (a hotheaded but endearing character) kills King Pellinore. In reply, King Pellinore's son, Sir Lamerok, seduces Queen Margawse. Sir Gawain and his brother kill Sir Lamerok. Sir Lamerok's cousin, Sir Pynel, tries to poison Sir Gawain but another knight eats the apple by mistake. . . .

Malory's own life may, therefore, have been consistent with the ethics of *Le Morte d'Arthur*, especially if Henry Smyth's wife was not really "forced," as Henry Smyth claimed, and if Malory had inherited a grudge against the Duke of Buckingham. The Round Table knights clearly despised abbots (unwarlike creatures, often of base·birth) and, when away from their own rich earldoms and dukedoms, lived off the land, commandeering whatever they might need. Hermits were a different matter, many of them being ex-knights ensconced in comfortable manors and glad to entertain their former comrades. Sir Launcelot himself ended as a hermit.

In Welsh legend, Arthur fights the mythical giant of St. Michael's Mount (Malory takes over this incident in "Arthur and Lucius"), also the Great Cat of Losane and the terrific Twrch Trwyth (in Latin, the *Porcus Troit*), and sails in his magic ship *Prydwen* to harry a pagan Hell from which, in pure Bronze Age style, he carries off an enchanted caldron. He is buried in the Isle of Avalon (or Glastonbury), where the monks later disinter his gigantic bones from an oak-coffin burial which dates him about 1500 B.C. However, the inscription on the coffin, in monkish Latin, states that "Arthur King of the Britons and his wife Gwynevere lie here." Giraldus Cambrensis saw this coffin, and so did Edward I. Yet an ancient

Welsh Triad insists that Arthur's grave will never be found, and this corresponds with a legend current in various parts of South Wales: that he lies asleep in a cave with a golden crown on his head, whence he will emerge only to rescue his "honey isle" from foreign oppression. For the Scots, King Arthur occupies a hidden cave in the Eildon Hills, whence he will emerge only when someone finds and blows the trumpet he lost in his last battle thereabouts. The same legend is current in Sicily and Majorca, brought there by the Normans. And as a child I was taken to the top of a hill near Snowdon and told that this was where the usurping Modred dealt King Arthur his mortal wound, and that when seven church steeples could be seen from there, and when a pair of twins, a boy and a girl, went looking for lost lambs on a Sunday afternoon, they would find King Arthur's dinted crown rolled away under a bush of bracken.

In the Middle Ages, Arthur was the object of deep and sincere belief. Caxton writes in his preface:

. . . in hym that shold say or thynke that there was never suche a kyng callyd Arthur myght wel be aretted grete folye and blyndenesse, for there be many evydences of the contrarye. Fyrst, ye may see his sepulture in the monasterye of Glastynburye; and also in *Polycronycon,* in the fifth book the syxte chappytre, where his body was buryed and after founden and translated into the said monasterye. Ye shal se also in the story of Bochas, in his book *De Casu Principum,* parte of his noble actes, and also of his falle. Also Galfrydus, in his Brytysshe book, recounteth his lyf. And in dyvers places of Englond many remembraunces ben yet of hym and shall remayne perpetuelly, and also of his knyghtes: fyrst, in the abbey of Westmestre, at Saint Edwardes shryne, remayneth the prynte of his seal in reed waxe, closed in beryll, in which is wryton PATRICIUS ARTHURUS BRITANNIE GALLIE GERMANIE DACIE IMPERATOR; item, in the castel of Dover ye may se Gauwayns skulle and Cradoks mantel; at Wynchester, the Rounde Table; in other places Launcelottes swerde and many other thynges.

The best, in fact, that we can do with King Arthur is to accept him as a national obsession, and his paradoxes as peculiarly insular. He was anointed king by an archbishop and wore a cross on his shield, yet his sponsor was Merlin the Enchanter, begotten on a nun by the Devil himself, and according to the Taliesin poems in *The Red Book of Hergest*, "erudite druids prophesied for Arthur."

Why this assemblage of authenticated religious relics, as though Arthur had been Jesus Christ; and Launcelot, Peter; and Gawain, John the Evangelist? The truth is, Arthur had long been converted into a counter-Christ, with twelve knights of the Round Table to suggest the Twelve Apostles, and with a Second Coming. For while the seigneurial class consented to fight for the Cross as an emblem of Western civilization, the ascetic morality preached by Jesus did not appeal to them in the least. Jesus' grave warning that "he who lives by the sword shall perish by the sword" was read as a joyful reassurance to the true knight that if he always observed the code of chivalry, he would die gloriously in battle and be translated to a Celtic Paradise in the twinkling of an eye. Moreover, the Western conception of personal honour could not be reconciled with humility, turning the other cheek, and leaving God to avenge injuries. The concept of knight-errantry would have made poor sense in Israel. I recall no distressed damsels in the entire Bible, the heroes all being national deliverers, not individual adventurers. When an ancient Israelite fought in God's name, he fought ruthlessly: thrusting women through the belly with his javelin, dashing the little ones against stones, and smiting non-combatants with the edge of his sword—churlish behaviour for which an Arthurian knight (unless engaged in a blood feud) would have had his spurs lopped off by the common hangman. And the Israelite was realistic about yielding to superior force in allowing himself to be led away captive; not so the true knight. Sir Accolon would have killed Arthur with

> . . . many grete strokes, and for the moste parte every stroke Accolon gaff wounded him full sore. And always King Arthur loste so much blood that hit was marvayle he stode upon his feete, but he was so full of knighthode that he endured the payne. And his swerde braste at the cross and felle on the grasse among the blood, and when he saw that, he was in grete feare to dye.

However, he would not yield:

> . . . for I promised by the feythe of my body to do this batayle to the uttermoste whyle my lyff lastith, and therefore I had liver to dye with honour than to lyve with shame. . . .

So Arthur fought on with shield and sword pummel, until the Damsel of the Lake disarmed Sir Accolon by magic, whereupon Arthur won the advantage, but generously spared Sir Accolon's life.

Sir Launcelot's love for Gwynevere is altogether unchristian. He loved her truly and was found "togyders abed with her in her chamber." Later he rescued Gwynevere from the fire to which she had been condemned by Arthur "and kept her as a good knight should." After Arthur's death, he repented as a matter of form, "endured in grete penaunce syx yere, and then dyed."

> And so after mydnyght, ayenst day, the Bysshop that was hermyte, as he laye in his bedde aslepe, he fyl upon a grete laughter. And therwyth al the felyshyp awoke and came to the Bysshop and asked hym what he eyled.
>
> "A, Jesu mercy!" sayd the Bysshop, "why dyd ye awake me? I was never in al my lyf so mery and so wel at ease."
>
> "Wherfore?" sayd syr Bors.
>
> "Truly," sayd the Bysshop, "here was syr Launcelot with me, with mo angellis than ever I sawe men in one day. And I sawe the angellys heve up syr Launcelot unto heven, and the yates of heven opened ayenst hym."

Arthur, of course, had no right to complain of Sir Launcelot; he had himself begotten Sir Modred on King Lot's queen in her husband's absence, similarly claiming that he could not resist the pangs of true love—though, according to some writers, she was his own aunt; and to others, his sister.

Malory's tales vary in treatment and interest. "King Arthur" is a muddled, lively book, and Merlin an imposing enchanter, though he anticipates every main event by prophecy, sometimes twice repeated. Queen Morgan le Fay (the Celtic battle-goddess Morgana, here figuring as Arthur's sister) makes a successful villainess. But nobody would guess from the absurd campaigns in "Arthur and Lucius" (one major battle and three skirmishes) that the author had ever taken the field himself. "Sir Launcelot du Lake" must have provided enjoyable entertainment for a mead-sodden baron sprawled before a great hall fire in wintertime, with rushes on the floor, arms and armour hung on the walls, draughts rustling the arras, and a page slowly spelling out the tale—which consists of some twenty horseback duels in succession. Malory's reading public demanded duels and tournaments with no less insistence than the television public now demands horsy Westerns. "Sir Gareth," a similar tale, is enlivened by a sharp-tongued damsel who continues to scorn the overvirtuous hero, though his fighting fame spreads; he has been riding incognito, and she mistakenly despises him as of base birth. Chivalrous incognito provides four fifths of Malory's minor plots and several of his major ones, notably Balan and Balin, Arthur and Accolon, Tristram and Launcelot, Gawain and Uwayne, Palomides and Lamerok. These pairs are all good comrades or kinsmen who, after nearly killing each other, weep for dismay on recognizing a familiar face behind the visor.

"The Book of Sir Tristram of Lyoness" does contrive to present Tristram and Iseult as illustrious lovers, though readers may feel disappointed when Sir Tristram and his rival Sir Palomides, so often interrupted by accidents from fighting to the death, are at last tamely reconciled. Sir Palomides ("The Maidens' Castle," "The Round Table," and "Sir Palomides") is one of Malory's few well-rounded characters. Sir Dynadan ("Sir Tristram's Madness and Exile") is another: he castigates Sir Tristram and Sir Launcelot for their obsession about fighting, and acts as a useful butt in "The Tournament at Surluse," the only humorous episode in the entire work.

Malory takes little trouble with the quest of the Holy Grail ("The Tale of the Sangreal"), which contains Christian miracles, far-fetched glosses on the Old and New Testaments, and numerous sermons preached by maudlin hermits. He clearly has no desire to emulate Sir Galahad's virginal purity, and Professor Loomis has shown that Corbenic, or Carbonek, the Grail castle, was named after the pagan *Cor Benoit* ("Blessed Horn"), a magic cornucopia belonging to Arthur's mythical double, Bran the Blessed. *Cor* got misread as *cors* ("body") and taken to mean the Body of Christ, or Host, laid in the Grail (*graduale*), the Virgin Mary's Communion Cup, which was said to have been brought there by St. Joseph of Arimathea, an ancestor of King Pellinore's.

"Launcelot and Elaine" and the Launcelot and Gwynevere tales carry conviction. "The Healing of Sir Urry" lists one hundred and two names of Arthur's courtiers, soon to be disbanded, but contributes little to the story. The last tale, which gives its title to the whole collection, is well written and justly famous.

Keith Baines here renders *Le Morte d'Arthur* in readable form, removing all of the idle rhetoric but faithfully preserving the sequence of events. This workmanlike task should earn him general gratitude, since of the numerous educated people who profess to have read Malory, few indeed could give a straightforward account of any tale except perhaps the last. The fact is that late medieval English prose style was based on *amplificatio*—the embroidering of a simple statement to the point where it almost ceased to make sense—and on the practice of lulling the ear with hypnotic rhythms. The story was regarded as of lesser importance.

—Robert Graves

Deyá, Majorca

The Tale of King Arthur

1. MERLIN

King Uther Pendragon, ruler of all Britain, had been at war for many years with the Duke of Tintagil in Cornwall when he was told of the beauty of Lady Igraine, the duke's wife. Thereupon he called a truce and invited the duke and Igraine to his court, where he prepared a feast for them, and where, as soon as they arrived, he was formally reconciled to the duke through the good offices of his courtiers.

In the course of the feast, King Uther grew passionately desirous of Igraine and, when it was over, begged her to become his paramour. Igraine, however, being as naturally loyal as she was beautiful, refused him.

"I suppose," said Igraine to her husband, the duke, when this had happened, "that the king arranged this truce only because he wanted to make me his mistress. I suggest that we leave at once, without warning, and ride overnight to our castle." The duke agreed with her, and they left the court secretly.

The king was enraged by Igraine's flight and summoned his privy council. They advised him to command the fugitives' return under threat of renewing the war; but when this was done, the duke and Igraine defied his summons. He then warned them that they could expect to be dragged from their castle within six weeks.

The duke manned and provisioned his two strongest castles: Tintagil for Igraine, and Terrabyl, which was useful for its many sally ports, for himself. Soon King Uther arrived with a

21

huge army and laid siege to Terrabyl; but despite the ferocity of the fighting, and the numerous casualties suffered by both sides, neither was able to gain a decisive victory.

Still enraged, and now despairing, King Uther fell sick. His friend Sir Ulfius came to him and asked what the trouble was. "Igraine has broken my heart," the king replied, "and unless I can win her, I shall never recover."

"Sire," said Sir Ulfius, "surely Merlin the Prophet could find some means to help you? I will go in search of him."

Sir Ulfius had not ridden far when he was accosted by a hideous beggar. "For whom are you searching?" asked the beggar; but Sir Ulfius ignored him.

"Very well," said the beggar, "I will tell you: You are searching for Merlin, and you need look no further, for I am he. Now go to King Uther and tell him that I will make Igraine his if he will reward me as I ask; and even that will be more to his benefit than to mine."

"I am sure," said Sir Ulfius, "that the king will refuse you nothing reasonable."

"Then go, and I shall follow you," said Merlin.

Well pleased, Sir Ulfius galloped back to the king and delivered Merlin's message, which he had hardly completed when Merlin himself appeared at the entrance to the pavilion. The king bade him welcome.

"Sire," said Merlin, "I know that you are in love with Igraine; will you swear, as an anointed king, to give into my care the child that she bears you, if I make her yours?"

The king swore on the gospel that he would do so, and Merlin continued: "Tonight you shall appear before Igraine at Tintagil in the likeness of her husband, the duke. Sir Ulfius and I will appear as two of the duke's knights: Sir Brastius and Sir Jordanus. Do not question either Igraine or her men, but say that you are sick and retire to bed. I will fetch you early in the morning, and do not rise until I come; fortunately Tintagil is only ten miles from here."

The plan succeeded: Igraine was completely deceived by the king's impersonation of the duke, and gave herself to him, and conceived Arthur. The king left her at dawn as soon as Merlin appeared, after giving her a farewell kiss. But the duke had seen King Uther ride out from the siege on the previous night and, in the course of making a surprise attack on the king's army, had been killed. When Igraine realized that the duke had died three hours before he had appeared to her, she was greatly disturbed in mind; however, she confided in no one.

Once it was known that the duke was dead, the king's nobles urged him to be reconciled to Igraine, and this task the king gladly entrusted to Sir Ulfius, by whose eloquence it was soon accomplished. "And now," said Sir Ulfius to his fellow nobles, "why should not the king marry the beautiful Igraine? Surely it would be as well for us all."

The marriage of King Uther and Igraine was celebrated joyously thirteen days later; and then, at the king's request, Igraine's sisters were also married: Margawse, who later bore Sir Gawain, to King Lot of Lowthean and Orkney; Elayne, to King Nentres of Garlot. Igraine's daughter, Morgan le Fay, was put to school in a nunnery; in after years she was to become a witch, and to be married to King Uryens of Gore, and give birth to Sir Uwayne of the Fair Hands.

A few months later it was seen that Igraine was with child, and one night, as she lay in bed with King Uther, he asked her who the father might be. Igraine was greatly abashed.

"Do not look so dismayed," said the king, "but tell me the truth and I swear I shall love you the better for it."

"The truth is," said Igraine, "that the night the duke died, about three hours after his death, a man appeared in my castle—the exact image of the duke. With him came two others who appeared to be Sir Brastius and Sir Jordanus. Naturally I gave myself to this man as I would have to the duke, and that night, I swear, this child was conceived."

"Well spoken," said the king; "it was I who impersonated the duke, so the child is mine." He then told Igraine the story of how Merlin had arranged it, and Igraine was overjoyed to discover that the father of her child was now her husband.

Sometime later, Merlin appeared before the king. "Sire," he said, "you know that you must provide for the upbringing of your child?"

"I will do as you advise," the king replied.

"That is good," said Merlin, "because it is my reward for having arranged your impersonation of the duke. Your child is destined for glory, and I want him brought to me for his baptism. I shall then give him into the care of foster parents who can be trusted not to reveal his identity before the proper time. Sir Ector would be suitable: he is extremely loyal, owns good estates, and his wife has just borne him a child. She could give her child into the care of another woman, and herself look after yours."

Sir Ector was summoned, and gladly agreed to the king's request, who then rewarded him handsomely. When the child was born he was at once wrapped in a gold cloth and taken by two knights and two ladies to Merlin, who stood waiting at the rear entrance to the castle in his beggar's disguise. Merlin took the child to a priest, who baptized him with the name of Arthur, and thence to Sir Ector, whose wife fed him at her breast.

Two years later King Uther fell sick, and his enemies once more overran his kingdom, inflicting heavy losses on him as they advanced. Merlin prophesied that they could be checked only by the presence of the king himself on the battlefield, and suggested that he should be conveyed there on a horse litter. King Uther's army met the invader on the plain at St. Albans, and the king duly appeared on the horse litter. Inspired by his presence, and by the lively leadership of Sir Brastius and Sir Jordanus, his army quickly defeated the enemy and the battle finished in a rout. The king returned to London to celebrate the victory.

But his sickness grew worse, and after he had lain speechless for three days and three nights Merlin summoned the nobles to attend the king in his chamber on the following morning. "By the grace of God," he said, "I hope to make him speak."

In the morning, when all the nobles were assembled, Merlin addressed the king: "Sire, is it your will that Arthur shall succeed to the throne, together with all its prerogatives?"

The king stirred in his bed, and then spoke so that all could hear: "I bestow on Arthur God's blessing and my own, and Arthur shall succeed to the throne on pain of forfeiting my blessing." Then King Uther gave up the ghost. He was buried and mourned the next day, as befitted his rank, by Igraine and the nobility of Britain.

During the years that followed the death of King Uther, while Arthur was still a child, the ambitious barons fought one another for the throne, and the whole of Britain stood in jeopardy. Finally the day came when the Archbishop of Canterbury, on the advice of Merlin, summoned the nobility to London for Christmas morning. In his message the Archbishop promised that the true succession to the British throne would be miraculously revealed. Many of the nobles purified themselves during their journey, in the hope that it would be to them that the succession would fall.

The Archbishop held his service in the city's greatest church (St. Paul's), and when matins were done the congregation filed out to the yard. They were confronted by a marble block into which had been thrust a beautiful sword. The block was four feet square, and the sword passed through a steel anvil which had been struck in the stone, and which projected a foot from it. The anvil had been inscribed with letters of gold:

WHOSO PULLETH OUTE THIS SWERD OF THIS STONE AND ANVYLD IS RIGHTWYS KYNGE BORNE OF ALL BRYTAYGNE

The congregation was awed by this miraculous sight, but the Archbishop forbade anyone to touch the sword before mass had been heard. After mass, many of the nobles tried to pull the sword out of the stone, but none was able to, so a watch of ten knights was set over the sword, and a tournament proclaimed for New Year's Day, to provide men of noble blood with the opportunity of proving their right to the succession.

Sir Ector, who had been living on an estate near London, rode to the tournament with Arthur and his own son Sir Kay, who had been recently knighted. When they arrived at the tournament, Sir Kay found to his annoyance that his sword was missing from its sheath, so he begged Arthur to ride back and fetch it from their lodging.

Arthur found the door of the lodging locked and bolted, the landlord and his wife having left for the tournament. In order not to disappoint his brother, he rode on to St. Paul's, determined to get for him the sword which was lodged in the stone. The yard was empty, the guard also having slipped off to see the tournament, so Arthur strode up to the sword, and, without troubling to read the inscription, tugged it free. He then rode straight back to Sir Kay and presented him with it.

Sir Kay recognized the sword, and taking it to Sir Ector, said, "Father, the succession falls to me, for I have here the sword that was lodged in the stone." But Sir Ector insisted that they should all ride to the churchyard, and once there bound Sir Kay by oath to tell how he had come by the sword. Sir Kay then admitted that Arthur had given it to him. Sir Ector turned to Arthur and said, "Was the sword not guarded?"

"It was not," Arthur replied.

"Would you please thrust it into the stone again?" said Sir Ector. Arthur did so, and first Sir Ector and then Sir Kay tried to remove it, but both were unable to. Then Arthur, for the second time, pulled it out. Sir Ector and Sir Kay both knelt before him.

"Why," said Arthur, "do you both kneel before me?"

"My lord," Sir Ector replied, "there is only one man living who can draw the sword from the stone, and he is the true-born King of Britain." Sir Ector then told Arthur the story of his birth and upbringing.

"My dear father," said Arthur, "for so I shall always think

of you—if, as you say, I am to be king, please know that any request you have to make is already granted."

Sir Ector asked that Sir Kay should be made Royal Seneschal, and Arthur declared that while they both lived it should be so. Then the three of them visited the Archbishop and told him what had taken place.

All those dukes and barons with ambitions to rule were present at the tournament on New Year's Day. But when all of them had failed, and Arthur alone had succeeded in drawing the sword from the stone, they protested against one so young, and of ignoble blood, succeeding to the throne.

The secret of Arthur's birth was known only to a few of the nobles surviving from the days of King Uther. The Archbishop urged them to make Arthur's cause their own; but their support proved ineffective. The tournament was repeated at Candlemas and at Easter, and with the same outcome as before.

Finally at Pentecost, when once more Arthur alone had been able to remove the sword, the commoners arose with a tumultuous cry and demanded that Arthur should at once be made king. The nobles, knowing in their hearts that the commoners were right, all knelt before Arthur and begged forgiveness for having delayed his succession for so long. Arthur forgave them, and then, offering his sword at the high altar, was dubbed first knight of the realm. The coronation took place a few days later, when Arthur swore to rule justly, and the nobles swore him their allegiance.

King Arthur's first task was to re-establish those nobles who had been robbed of their lands during the troubled years since the reign of King Uther. Next, to establish peace and order in the counties near London. Meanwhile he appointed Sir Kay as Seneschal; Sir Badouin of Brittany, Constable; Sir Ulfius, Chamberlain; and Sir Brastius, Warden of the North, from the river Trent upward.

The most formidable of King Arthur's enemies lived in the north and west of Britain; and toward the end of a year, King Arthur rode with his retinue to Caerleon, in the west. There he proclaimed a tournament on Pentecost to celebrate the first anniversary of his reign.

It was reported that six kings were approaching with retinues varying from four to seven hundred knights. They were: King Lot of Lowthean, King Uryens of Gore, King Nentres of Garlot, the King of the Hundred Knights, King Carados, and the young King of Scotland. Arthur was pleased and sent messengers with gifts to greet them.

The messengers returned with the news that the six kings had refused his gifts, and were marching on Caerleon in order to make war on him. Arthur withdrew to a strong tower with five hundred picked knights and plentiful provisions, so that when the six kings arrived and laid siege to the tower, he was able to defy them.

Merlin appeared on the fifteenth day of the siege, and the six kings all gathered round him. "Why," they demanded, "has the British throne fallen to this underling, Arthur?"

"Sires," Merlin replied, "Arthur is your rightful king: he is the son of King Uther Pendragon and Igraine, formerly wife to the Duke of Tintagil——"

"A bastard! A bastard!" the kings all cried at once.

"Not so," said Merlin. "Arthur was conceived by Igraine three hours after the death of the duke; thirteen days later King Uther made Igraine his queen. And I must warn you that Arthur is destined to greatness: I prophesy that he will win homage, not only from you, but from monarchs in many other lands as well."

Although some of the kings were awed by this speech, others sneered, and King Lot accused Merlin of being a false prophet. However, they all agreed to parley with Arthur, and pledged themselves to his safety. Merlin advised Arthur to show no fear of the six kings, but to remember that he was their rightful lord.

Arthur was attended at the parley by his chief dignitaries: the Archbishop of Canterbury, Sir Badouin, Sir Brastius, and Sir Kay; but beneath his robe he wore a coat of double mail. Arthur was as uncompromising in his answers as the six kings were hostile in their questions, and before long both sides withdrew angrily—Arthur to his tower, where he prepared to withstand another siege.

Merlin warned the six kings that Arthur would defeat them; he then advised Arthur that while he need have no fear for the outcome of the battle, he should delay the use of his miraculous sword until it seemed that he was losing. Merlin then vanished; meanwhile three hundred knights, who had deserted the six kings, now offered to fight for Arthur.

At the start of the battle King Arthur won the initiative, and distinguished himself even above Sir Badouin, Sir Brastius, and Sir Kay. But then King Lot, King Carados, and the King of the Hundred Knights made a surprise attack on him from the rear. As Arthur wheeled to repel them he was unhorsed, and King Lot struck him to the ground. Four of Arthur's body-guard rushed to his rescue and remounted him. Arthur knew that this was the moment to draw the miraculous sword. Its brilliance had the effect of dazzling his opponents, and Arthur slaughtered with zest. The commoners, who had been watching the battle with eager curiosity, now stampeded onto the field, and with clubs and staves helped Arthur to conclude the battle in a rout. Merlin appeared once more, and warned Arthur against pursuing them any further.

King Arthur returned to London and held a council of war. His advisors, confident that they were strong enough as they stood, were silent. Still doubtful, Arthur proposed sending for Merlin, and this was done. Merlin was able to tell the council that four more kings and a duke had joined the alliance of the six kings, and that to defeat them Arthur would now need more cavalry.

"How should we raise them?" asked one of the barons.

"Send two messengers to France to seek the alliance of King Ban of Benwick and King Bors of Gaul. They are together at present, and besieging, though unsuccessfully, their common enemy King Claudas. You must pledge your aid in return for theirs."

Merlin's suggestion was adopted; Sir Ulfius and Sir Brastius were charged with written and verbal messages for the two French kings. The two envoys, after crossing the channel, were riding toward the city of Benwick when they were accosted by eight knights. In the name of King Arthur of Britain, Sir Brastius demanded the envoy's right of free passage to Kings Ban and Bors of Benwick and Gaul.

"That you shall not have," said one of the knights, "because our allegiance is to King Claudas, in whose name we now take you prisoner, unless you prefer to be killed."

"Not on your life!" said Sir Brastius.

Two of the French knights couched their spears and charged, only to find themselves flung from their horses as Sir Ulfius and Sir Brastius received them. The envoys continued their journey, and two by two the French knights attacked them; but each pair was likewise defeated, so that all eight were bruised, if not seriously injured.

Sir Ulfius and Sir Brastius were received at King Ban's court at Benwick by Sir Lyonses and Sir Pharyaunce, who welcomed them warmly on hearing that they had come from King Arthur, and at once escorted them to Kings Ban and Bors. The two kings read the letters, and with one accord accepted the alliance. Sir Ulfius and Sir Brastius then told the two kings the story of their encounter with the eight knights; the kings were shocked, because the knights had formerly been friends of theirs.

After an excellent feast, and being loaded with gifts, more than they could carry, Sir Ulfius and Sir Brastius returned to King Arthur and reported that Kings Ban and Bors would arrive in Britain by Allhallowmass.

King Arthur proclaimed a feast and tournament for Allhallows, prepared a royal reception for the two kings on their arrival, and arranged to meet them himself ten miles from London. The three kings were served at the feast by Sir Kay, Sir Lucas, and Sir Gryfflet. When the feast was over and they had washed, the kings and their noblewomen (who were to act as judges) resorted to the royal pavilion which had been erected on the jousting field for the occasion. It was the size of a hall and had been richly hung with many-colored silks and gold cloth.

Seven hundred knights had assembled for the tournament, and were divided into two parties, British and French. The first combat was between Sir Gryfflet and the French knight, Sir Ladynas. They couched spears, dressed their shields, and galloped together. Both men and horses were flung to the ground when they met; the horses were seriously injured and the men knocked unconscious. When they had recovered, Sir Lucas brought them fresh horses, and both knights further distinguished themselves in the course of the tournament.

The combats that followed were: Sir Kay with five British knights against six French knights; Sir Ladynas against Sir Gracian, both French knights, and Sir Kay against Sir Placidas, a French knight. Sir Kay was victorious until he met with Sir Placidas, who unhorsed him. Sir Kay's followers were furious at this, and five of them galloped across the field to attack the French knights. King Arthur tactfully called the tournament to an end.

Prizes for the tournament were awarded by King Arthur with Kings Ban and Bors, to Sir Kay, Sir Lucas, and Sir Gryfflet, after evensong and supper. The three kings then retired for a council of war with Merlin, Sir Ulfius, Sir Brastius, and Gwenbaus, a clerk who was a brother to the French kings. They debated until late that night and all the following morning before settling their plans.

Merlin, with a ring of King Bors' as a warrant, traveled to France with Sir Gracian and Sir Placidas in order to raise troops. They were given a warm welcome on their arrival and questioned about the purpose of the kings' visit to Britain. Merlin replied with such persuasiveness that soon fifteen thousand men had volunteered to fight King Arthur's cause. When he had secured provisions for this number, Merlin marched them

all to the coast, where, dismissing the infantry, he embarked
for Britain with the ten thousand cavalry. Sir Gracian and Sir
Placidas had been commissioned by Kings Ban and Bors to remain in France and marshal the defenses of their kingdoms
against the attacks of King Claudas.

Taking advantage of a secret route, Merlin led his cavalry
from the port at Dover to the forest of Bedgrayne (in the
north of Britain), where he stationed them together with the
supplies. He then returned to London, where the three kings
awaited him, and was congratulated on his success.

King Arthur, in the meantime, had raised an army of ten
thousand, and Merlin escorted him, with Kings Ban and Bors,
to the cavalry camp at Bedgrayne. When the armies met, they
settled down merrily together, British and French. As a precaution against spies, Merlin suggested that every knight south
of the river Trent should carry a token of Arthur's, and this
was done.

The eleven kings, who had sworn to overthrow King Arthur
and avenge their defeat at Caerleon, had joined forces north of
Bedgrayne. Their total strength was fifty thousand cavalry and
ten thousand infantry. Their names were as follows: King
Brandegoris of Strangor; King Clarivaunce of Northumberland; the King of the Hundred Knights; King Lot of Lowthean
and Orkney; King Uryens of Gore (the father of Sir Uwayne);
King Idres of Cornwall; King Cradilment; King Angwyshaunce
of Ireland; King Nentres of Garlot; King Carados; and the Duke
of Canbenet.

The eleven kings advanced upon Bedgrayne, halting briefly
to besiege the castle of Bedgrayne, which was one of Arthur's
strongholds. Two nights before the armies met, the King of the
Hundred Knights had a prophetic dream in which all his castles
and towns were shaken by a terrible tempest and then carried
away by a flood.

Meanwhile, the enemy movements were reported to Arthur
by his patrols, and he sent a party to lay waste the land which
lay ahead of them.

When the enemy was within striking distance, Merlin suggested to Arthur a night attack. So, leaving his army in readiness in the open country, Arthur, with a picked company, crept
through the forest and into the heart of the enemy camp. He
had started hacking down the commanders' tents as they slept
before the enemy guards discovered him and ran through the
camp shouting, "To arm! my lords, to arms!"

The camp sprang to life and the eleven kings succeeded in

fighting their way into the open country; their armies straggled onto the field, and ten thousand were killed by dawn, when Arthur withdrew.

Merlin advised Arthur that his best chance of success lay in concealing Kings Ban and Bors, with their army of ten thousand, in the woods, since their presence was as yet unsuspected by the enemy. He should then confront the enemy, whose strength was still fifty thousand, with his own army of twenty thousand, and do his utmost to tire them before signaling Kings Ban and Bors to break their ambush.

Both armies drew up on the field, and the eleven kings felt duly confident when they saw how greatly they outnumbered Arthur. Battle was joined when Sir Ulfius and Sir Brastius charged with three thousand cavalry, and, surprising the enemy with the force of their attack, killed many of them. Sir Ulfius was then attacked by King Clarivaunce and the Duke of Canbenet, and knocked off his horse; however, he continued to fight on foot. Sir Brastius attacked first the duke, whom he felled with a single blow, together with his horse, and then King Clarivaunce, with whom he fought until both men and horses were thoroughly gored.

Kings Brandegoris, Idres, and Angwyshaunce attacked Sir Gryfflet and Sir Lucas, and unhorsed them both. Sir Kay attacked King Nentres, and, winning his horse, gave it to Sir Gryfflet, and then, with the same spear, charged King Lot and wounded him. The King of the Hundred Knights attacked Sir Kay, and, unhorsing him, remounted King Lot, who thanked him. Sir Gryfflet overcame Sir Pynel and remounted Sir Kay with his horse.

Likewise, King Lot remounted King Nentres with Sir Meliot's horse; the King of the Hundred Knights remounted King Idres with Sir Gwyniarte's horse, and King Lot remounted the Duke of Canbenet with Sir Clarivaunce' horse. The eleven kings, all being now remounted, swore their revenge.

King Arthur galloped into the melee; in the course of the battle he was to win enduring fame for his formidable qualities on the field. Although the eleven kings were already famed for their valor, none was to prove superior to Arthur at Bedgrayne.

Seeing that Sir Ulfius and Sir Brastius were both in peril—fighting on foot and being constantly fouled by the horses' legs—King Arthur charged King Cradilment, and bringing him to earth, seized his horse and led it to Sir Ulfius, saying as he did so, "My friend, you have need of this." And Sir Ulfius thanked him.

Then the King of the Hundred Knights attacked Sir Ector, and remounted King Cradilment with his excellent horse. King Arthur, who dearly loved Sir Ector, and knew the pride he had taken in this horse, charged King Cradilment again, and this time cut clean through both helmet and skull with his sword, and the blow finished in the horse's flank, so that both crashed to the ground. Sir Ector was then remounted by Sir Kay, who struck down King Morganoure, and Sir Brastius was remounted by Sir Ector, who struck down Sir Kardens.

Sir Gryfflet was defending Sir Lucas, who lay wounded and in danger of being trampled on, against fourteen enemy knights who had singled him out for destruction. Sir Brastius came to his aid and first killed one of the knights with a blow through the helmet and then disabled two more by hacking off their arms. Sir Gryfflet beheaded still another, whose horse he gave to Sir Lucas, whom he urged to take revenge for the wounds he had suffered.

Sir Lucas first revenged the death of Sir Maris by striking down King Angwyshaunce, and then killed two knights in order to remount Sir Gwynas and Sir Bloyas.

The noise of the battle grew louder as both sides redoubled their efforts, and was heard by Kings Ban and Bors, who prepared to break their ambush. King Arthur, meanwhile, was relieved to see that all his knights were mounted once more.

Sir Lucas, Sir Gwynas, Sir Bryaunte, and Sir Bellias engaged with Kings Lot, Nentres, Brandegoris, Uryens, Idres, and Angwyshaunce, and with the help of Sir Kay and Sir Gryfflet, kept them on the defensive. King Arthur, fearing a deadlock, fought his way through twenty enemy knights, all of whom he killed, to King Lot, whom he wounded on the shoulder, thereby forcing him to retire.

Sir Ulfius, Sir Ector, and Sir Brastius attacked the Duke of Canbenet, King Clarivaunce, King Carados, and the King of the Hundred Knights, and pressed them so hard that they too were forced to retire.

King Lot addressed his fellow kings: "I believe our only chance of winning this battle is to divide. Let the King of the Hundred Knights, King Angwyshaunce, King Idres, the Duke of Canbenet, and me, with a command of ten thousand, return at once to the battle and fight King Arthur until we are both at the point of exhaustion. Then the remaining six kings, with their command of twelve thousand, can return to the battle freshly, and rout them."

The eleven kings agreed to this, and King Lot returned, with

THE TALE OF KING ARTHUR

his command, to the battle. He was met fiercely by Sir Phary-aunce and Sir Lyonses, who attacked King Idres and would have killed him, had not King Angwyshaunce come to his rescue.

At this moment King Bors galloped onto the field at the head of his company. "God save us!" said King Lot in dismay, "here comes King Bors with his whole army!"

"How did he come here?" asked the King of the Hundred Knights.

"It was Merlin's doing," one of the knights replied.

"Well, I shall go and fight with him, but stand by, for I may need your help," said King Carados.

"God's speed!" said his fellow kings.

King Carados galloped his men to within bowshot of Sir Bleobris, King Bors' godson, who was acting as standard-bearer. "Now," said King Bors, "we shall see what stuff these men from the north are made of," and led his cavalry into the attack.

King Carados met them bravely, but was soon struck to the ground by King Bors, who would have killed him, had not the King of the Hundred Knights come to his rescue.

King Ban, resplendent in his armor of green and gold, now appeared on the field at the head of his company.

"Aha!" said King Lot, "here comes the brother, King Ban. It seems that whichever way we turn we shall not escape today."

King Lot was right: Kings Ban and Bors, with their army as yet untired, were fighting with terrible effect. Again and again the army of the eleven kings closed its ranks, only to have them broken by a fresh attack. King Lot was moved to tears as his men kept falling or were chased from the field.

King Ban fought with the King of the Hundred Knights, and in a furious exchange of blows, both horses were killed, and the King of the Hundred Knights finally stunned. King Ban likewise overcame King Morganoure. He continued to fight on foot, and when, some hours later, King Arthur found him, he was surrounded by a tangle of corpses, wounded and bleeding, and set on by the enemy from all sides. However, he still kept them at the point of his sword. King Arthur, himself bespattered with gore and unrecognizable, killed one of the enemy knights, and, giving the horse to King Ban, said: "My friend, revenge yourself well for your injuries."

The eleven kings were now fighting in such close formation that none could break through, in spite of the destruction of

their army all about them. King Arthur, King Ban, and King
Bors, tired from the previous night's fighting, withdrew at last
to a little stream. "Shall we never defeat these kings?" Arthur
said angrily.

"Sire," King Ban replied, "they are renowned for their valor,
and are fighting as kings should. Had you won their allegiance,
you would love them for it."

"But they are my sworn enemies, so I cannot," said Arthur.

"That was proved at Caerleon," said King Bors, "and certainly it is a shame to see what fine men have fallen today because of their mischief."

Meanwhile, King Lot was holding a conference. "My lords,"
he said, "our army is being destroyed. Let us dismiss the footmen; they can take refuge in the forest, for now they are only
a drag on the cavalry. We must then fight in close order, and
the penalty of death to anyone who breaks it! In this way only
shall we survive."

The eleven kings agreed, and so, righting their harness and
choosing new spears, they formed up. They looked as firm as
trees, and even Arthur could not but admire their dauntless
bearing.

Forty of Arthur's knights volunteered to attack them, and
amongst the forty were the following: Lyonses, Pharyaunce,
Ulfius, Brastius, Ector, Kay, Lucas, Gryfflet, Marrys, Gwynas,
Bryaunte, Bellaus, Morians, Flaundres, Annesians, Ladynas,
Emerause, Caulas, Graciens, Bloyse, and Colgrevaunce.

Both parties dressed their shields, leveled their spears, and
charged. The fighting was grim and furious. Kings Arthur,
Ban, and Bors galloped into the thick of it, and soon their
horses were up to their fetlocks in blood, and trampling the
wounded. But the eleven kings were not to be overthrown, and
Arthur was forced to retire once more to the little stream.

Merlin appeared before him on a great black charger. "Will
you never have done?" he cried, "Of the sixty thousand who
fought against you today, only fifteen thousand survive. It is
time to call a halt, or the wrath of heaven will be upon you.
You will not overcome the eleven kings today, and I warn you
that if you resume the battle, it will turn in their favor. So have
done! return to your camp, and reward your men as they deserve. I prophesy that for three years these kings will not
trouble you."

Kings Ban and Bors departed, and Merlin said to Arthur,
"The eleven kings have more troubles on hand than they know

of: The Saracens have invaded their kingdom and already have laid siege to the castle of Wandesborow, so you need fear them no longer. When you have gathered the spoils, divide them equally between yourself and Kings Ban and Bors. They deserve no less, and in this way you will secure their friendship."

King Arthur did as Merlin suggested, and Kings Ban and Bors likewise divided their spoils amongst their followers.

Meanwhile, Merlin paid a visit to his old master, Bloyse, who lived in Northumberland, and gave him a full report of the battle. In this way Bloyse was able to keep a written record of Arthur's adventures, from his birth to his death. Then Merlin returned to Arthur, who was now resting at the castle of Bedgrayne.

It was at Candlemas that an outlandish figure accosted Arthur; he was clothed in a russet gown, black sheepskin, and huge boots. In one hand he carried a bow and arrows, in the other some wild geese.

"Sire," he said, "make me a gift."

"And why," said Arthur, "should I make a gift to a ruffian like you?"

"Sire," the ruffian replied, "it would be better for you to make me a gift than to lose the treasure you buried beneath the battlefield."

"Who told you about this treasure?" Arthur asked in alarm.

"Merlin," the other replied. At this Kings Ban and Bors both smiled, but Arthur was thoroughly confused.

"Sire," said King Ban, "do you not realize that this ruffian is Merlin himself?" And for a long time Kings Ban and Bors teased Arthur about how Merlin had deceived him.

Since the battle of Bedgrayne, many noblemen had come to pay homage to Arthur. One day a young noblewoman appeared on behalf of her father, Lord Lyonors, and her name was Sanam. Arthur was overwhelmed by her beauty, and this pleased her. That night she gave herself to him, and thereby conceived a child named Borre, who was to be one of the Knights of the Round Table.

At this time, Arthur's friend King Lodegreaunce was being besieged by King Royns of West Britain. He sent a message to Arthur appealing for aid, and Arthur responded at once. Within a few days, together with Kings Ban and Bors, he had marched his army of twenty thousand to Camylarde, and there, in a pitched battle, defeated King Royns, killing ten thousand of his men and routing the rest. King Lodegreaunce gave a feast in honor of his allies and it was then that Arthur first met Gwynevere, King Lodegreaunce' daughter, and fell in love with her.

Before leaving Bedgrayne, Kings Ban and Bors had commissioned four of their knights—Pharyaunce, Anthemes, Gracian, and Lyonses—to return to France and protect their kingdoms of Benwick and Gaul. They now received news that King Claudas had broken through and was ransacking them at will, so they prepared to leave without further delay. Arthur offered to go with them.

"No," said King Ban, "you have enough on your hands in Britain just now, and with the spoils we have won here we should be able to raise an army large enough to defeat King Claudas. Only if we fail will we call on your help."

At the leave-taking of the four kings Merlin appeared, and prophesied that within two years Kings Ban and Bors' enemies would all be defeated by Arthur, and that the eleven kings would fall to two brothers, Sir Balan and Sir Balin.

The eleven kings, meanwhile, had marched the remnants of their army to Surhaute, in King Uryens' territory. They were resting there, and having their wounds treated, when the news reached them of the Saracen invasion and the siege of Wandesborow.

"Is there no end to our disasters?" King Lot asked bitterly. "And I suppose that if we had not fought against King Arthur, he would now be helping us as he did King Lodegreaunce."

At a council of war it was decided to defend their kingdoms jointly, stationing their forces at strategic points from Cornwall to the north, and basing King Nentres with four thousand cavalry at Wyndesan—an alliance which was to prove effective for three years, and enable them to defeat Kings Royns and Nero. Throughout this period they continued to enlarge their army, in the secret hope that one day they might avenge their losses at Bedgrayne.

When Arthur had returned to Caerleon, Margawse, King Lot's wife, came to his court on an official visit, accompanied by a large retinue and her four sons: Gawain, Gaheris, Aggravayne, and Gareth. Her secret purpose was to spy on Arthur, but soon she found herself in love with him, and he with her, so they became lovers. They lived together for a month and the bastard Sir Modred was conceived. Arthur was unaware that Margawse was his mother's sister.

When Margawse left, Arthur dreamed that his whole kingdom was overrun by griffins and serpents, that he succeeded in driving them out, but in doing so received the most terrible wounds. Arthur awoke with fear in his heart, and ordered his household to make ready for a hunt in order to divert his gloomy thoughts.

They soon saw a large white hart, and Arthur at once gave chase. The hart was unusually fleet, and when Arthur had outdistanced the rest of the hunt, he continued for several hours through the forest in lonely pursuit. Each time he drew within range of the hart, it somehow managed to elude him; finally, his horse, which had become badly winded, dropped dead beneath him.

A passing woodman offered to bring him a fresh horse, and Arthur accepted gratefully. He then sat down by a wellhead, worried and thoughtful. Suddenly he heard an uncanny noise, and looking up saw a beast, of indescribable monstrosity, go to the well and drink. The noise seemed to come from the belly, and was like the yapping of thirty hounds in pursuit of their quarry; it ceased only when the beast was drinking. Soon it lumbered off into the forest again, and Arthur fell into a troubled sleep.

He was awakened by a knight. "Sire, forgive my interrupting your thoughts or your dreams, but could you tell me if you have seen an unusual beast pass by?"

"I have, certainly," Arthur replied; "what on earth is it?"

"It is the Questing Beast and I am King Pellinore; it is my destiny to pursue this beast and either run it to earth or lose my strength. But just now I have lost my horse and must find another one."

"Sire," said Arthur, "why not abandon your quest for a year, and let me pursue this beast?"

"You cannot, and you would be a fool to try. The succession, if I fail, falls to my nearest of kin, Sir Palomides."

At this moment the woodman reappeared with a horse. King Pellinore leaped onto it, and said to Arthur, "God bless you for the horse!"

"I might yet challenge your right to it," King Arthur replied.

"As you will; I can always be found here at the well. As it happens, though, this is one of my own horses." And with that King Pellinore departed.

Arthur was brooding, when a boy of fourteen walked up to him. "Sir, why do you look so thoughtful?" he asked.

"I am thoughtful because of what I have seen," Arthur replied.

"That I know," said the child, "just as I know all of your thoughts; and I can tell you that you are a fool, because thoughts will change nothing. Also I knew King Uther, your father, and Igraine, your mother, who was formerly married to the Duke of Tintagil——"

"You liar!" Arthur shouted angrily, "you are too young to know any of these things. Begone with you!" The child made off into the forest, and almost at once an old man appeared. His face looked kindly and wise, and Arthur trusted him. "Sire, why are you looking so thoughtful?" the old man asked.

"For many reasons," Arthur replied. "Just now a child was here who claimed to know my father——"

"He did," said the old man, "and he knew much more than that: for instance, that lately you took for a lover Margawse, your mother's sister; that your kingdom will fall to the child she bears you, and that you will die at his hands in battle. His name will be Sir Modred."

"Then who are you to tell me such things?"

"Merlin," the other replied.

"A magician you certainly are," said Arthur. "But I do not like the idea of being killed in battle."

"You are more fortunate than I. At least you will die gloriously, whereas I shall be buried alive, treacherously."

While they were talking, the woodman had returned with a horse for Arthur. Merlin retrieved his own horse from the forest where he had hidden it, and they rode together to Caerleon. Once there Arthur summoned Sir Ulfius and Sir Ector.

"I must know the secret of my birth," he said. "Please tell me."

"Sire, King Uther was your father, and Queen Igraine is your mother," Sir Ulfius replied.

"So Merlin tells me; but I shall not believe it until Igraine tells me so herself."

A message was sent to Igraine, inviting her to the court, and Arthur prepared a splendid reception for her. Igraine arrived with a large retinue and with her beautiful daughter, Morgan le Fay. In the course of the banquet held in her honor, Sir Ulfius rose from his chair and addressed the queen.

"You are the vilest woman on earth," he said, "and a traitor to the king's person."

"Beware!" said Arthur; "those are dangerous words."

"And with my life I will prove them," said Sir Ulfius.

"Queen Igraine has been too cowardly to acknowledge in public that King Arthur is her son, and hence the rightful heir to the British throne. The result has been that his subject princes, supposing that Arthur is only a pretender, have defied his sovereignty and continue to make war on him."

"I am only a woman," said Igraine; "will no gentleman defend me? You, Merlin, and you, Sir Ulfius, know under what circumstances my child was conceived. You know also that Merlin took him from me the moment he was born, and from that moment to the present day, I swear, I have known nothing of what became of him, not even his name."

"Then Merlin is the culprit," said Sir Ulfius.

Arthur took Merlin by the hand and asked, "Is this my mother?"

"Sire, it is," Merlin replied. Then Sir Ector came forward and bore witness to his having fostered Arthur at King Uther's command. Arthur was convinced of the truth at last. He took Igraine in his arms and kissed her tenderly; and for a week, mother and son celebrated their reunion.

One day a squire arrived at the court, supporting his master, Sir Myles, who had been mortally wounded. He described to Arthur how he had been attacked by King Pellinore at the well, and then begged that he should be buried, and that one of Arthur's knights should avenge his death. After the burial a squire named Gryfflette pleaded with Arthur to make him a knight; he was the same age as Arthur.

"You are too young to be a knight," Arthur said gravely.

"Sire, but I beg you," said Gryfflette.

"It would be a shame," said Merlin, "to lose Gryfflette. He will make an excellent knight when he is older, but at the moment he would be no match for King Pellinore."

"I will make you a knight," said Arthur, "if you will swear not to joust with King Pellinore more than once, and then return to me."

"I swear it," said Gryfflette; so Arthur dubbed him.

Sir Gryfflette ran happily to his armor, and when he was clad and mounted, set off at a gallop for the well. He found there a brilliantly decorated pavilion, and outside it a horse, already harnessed. A multicolored shield hung from a tree, and resting against it was a spear. Sir Gryfflette struck the shield a ringing blow, and it fell to the ground. King Pellinore appeared at the entrance to his pavilion. "Sir, why do you strike my shield?" he asked.

"Because I wish to joust with you," Sir Gryfflette replied.

"You are but newly knighted, and too young," said the king. "Tell me, where do you come from?"

"I come from the court of King Arthur, and still I mean to joust with you."

"Very well, then; but I am reluctant to do so," the king rejoined.

The two knights met at full gallop: Sir Gryfflette's spear was broken, and the shaft driven deeply into his side; he lost consciousness and fell to the ground. King Pellinore swiftly ran over to him and loosened his armor. Sir Gryfflette recovered his wind slowly, and when he had done so, King Pellinore lifted him gently onto his horse. "God's speed, young knight," he said.

At King Arthur's court Sir Gryfflette collapsed once more; however, he was placed in the hands of a surgeon by whose skillful treatment the wound was eventually healed.

Meanwhile, twelve aged ambassadors had come from Rome, and in the name of the Emperor Lucius, demanded tribute. "Since you are only ambassadors," Arthur said, "we shall not put you to death for your insolent words; but tell your Emperor that if he tries to win tribute from us, that will be his fate."

The ambassadors withdrew angrily, and Arthur himself was doubly grieved: by the Emperor's message and by Sir Gryfflette's injury. He decided to avenge Sir Gryfflette secretly, so he commanded the chamberlain to take his horse and armor to the outskirts of the city at dawn the following day.

When Arthur was armed and mounted, he instructed the chamberlain to await his return, and then galloped off toward the well. He had not gone far when he saw Merlin being chased by three ruffians; he galloped up to them and the ruffians fled in terror.

"Your magic did not save you that time," said Arthur.

"It could have," Merlin replied, "had I so wished, whereas your anger will certainly not save you from the superior strength of King Pellinore, whom you are about to challenge."

Merlin accompanied Arthur to the well, and when they arrived they found King Pellinore seated outside his pavilion. "Sir," said Arthur, "it would seem that no knight can pass this well without your challenging him."

"That is so," said King Pellinore.

"I have come to force you to change this custom of yours, so defend yourself!"

They jousted three times, each time breaking their spears,

until the third time, when Arthur was flung from his horse. "Very well," said Arthur, "you have won the advantage jousting; now let us see what you can do on foot." King Pellinore was reluctant to dismount and lose the advantage he had won; however, when Arthur rushed at him boldly with drawn sword, he grew ashamed and did dismount.

They fought until both collapsed from pain and exhaustion; their armor was splintered and the blood flowed from their wounds. They fought again, until Arthur's sword broke in his hand. "Now," said King Pellinore, "you shall yield to me, or die."

"Not so!" Arthur shouted as he sprang at him, and grabbing him around the waist, threw him to the ground. Arthur was unlacing his helmet when, with a sudden fearful effort, King Pellinore overturned Arthur and clambered on top of him. King Pellinore had loosened Arthur's helmet and raised his sword to strike off his head when Merlin spoke.

"Hold your hand!" he said; "you will endanger the whole realm. You do not realize who it is you are about to kill."

"Who is it, then?"

"King Arthur."

Hearing this, King Pellinore feared that he would receive little mercy from Arthur if he spared him—so he raised his sword once more. Merlin adroitly put him to sleep with a magic spell.

"You have killed him with your magic," said Arthur hotly. "I would rather that my whole realm were lost, and myself killed; he was a magnificent fighter."

"He is more whole than you are," Merlin replied. "He will not only live, but serve you excellently: It is to him that you will give your sister in marriage, and she will bear two sons— Sir Percivale and Sir Lamerok—who will be two of the most famous of the Knights of the Round Table."

They mounted, and Merlin led the way to a hermit, who treated Arthur's wounds, and in whose dwelling they rested for three days. They resumed their journey, which was to the Lake of Avalon, and as they were approaching the lake, Arthur said, "How sad that I broke my magic sword!"

"You shall have another one," Merlin replied.

Just then Arthur saw that in the center of the lake the surface was broken by an arm, clothed in white samite, and that the hand grasped a finely jeweled sword and scabbard.

"That is the magic sword Excalibur," said Merlin, "and it will be given to you by the Lady of the Lake, who is now crossing the water in her bark. She comes from her castle, which is hewn in the rock, and more beautiful than any earthly dwelling. You must address her courteously, and do as she directs you."

The Lady of the Lake appeared before them. "My lady," said Arthur, "I beg you to make me a gift of the sword Excalibur."

"King Arthur," she replied, "Excalibur shall be yours, if you consent now to granting me whatever gift I shall ask of you in my own time."

"I swear," said Arthur, "whatever gift is in my power to grant."

"Even so," said the Lady of the Lake. "Now use my bark and row yourself to the sword, and take it, together with the scabbard."

Arthur and Merlin tethered their horses to two trees, and boarded the bark. When Arthur had taken the sword and scabbard the arm disappeared into the water.

On the homeward journey they repassed King Pellinore's pavilion, and Arthur asked Merlin why King Pellinore was not there. "He has been fighting Sir Egglame, and has chased him nearly all the way into Caerleon," Merlin replied.

"What a pity!" said Arthur. "Because now that I have this beautiful sword I should like to fight him again, and perhaps this time have my revenge."

"That you shall not do," said Merlin. "King Pellinore is already tired from his fight with Sir Egglame. To win would bring you no honor, to lose would be to increase your shame. And lose you might, because he is still stronger than you are."

"I will do as you advise," said Arthur, as he examined his sword once more, admiring its beauty and temper. "Tell me," said Merlin, "do you prefer the sword or the scabbard?"

"The sword," said Arthur.

"You are a fool," said Merlin. "The scabbard is worth ten of the sword, because while you wear it, regardless of how seriously you are wounded, you will lose no blood."

They were drawing close to Caerleon when they passed King Pellinore; he appeared not to see them. "Why," asked Arthur, "did King Pellinore not speak to us?"

"Because he did not see us," Merlin replied. "I cast a spell over him; had he done so, you would not have escaped so lightly."

When Arthur and Merlin arrived at the court, they were questioned eagerly on all that had happened; and when the story was told, Arthur's knights rejoiced in the boldness of their king.

Meanwhile, a messenger had arrived from King Royns of West Britain. King Royns claimed to have fringed a mantle with the beards of the kings he had defeated; the fringe required but one half-grown beard to complete it: namely, Arthur's. Arthur could yield it, or otherwise have his whole kingdom laid waste, and himself be beheaded.

"Surely," said Arthur, "this is the most barbaric and despicable message ever sent to a king! Tell King Royns I owe him no homage and that before long he will be kneeling before us and begging for mercy."

The messenger departed and Arthur asked if any of his knights knew King Royns. Sir Naram replied, "I have seen him. He is an intrepid warrior, but overbearing as a king."

"Well," said Arthur, "we shall soon discover him."

On Merlin's advice, in order to destroy his bastard son Modred, Arthur commanded that, on pain of death, all babies of the nobility born on May Day were to be brought to the court. Arthur then set them adrift in an unmanned vessel, which eventually foundered. However, the plan failed, for the wreck was discovered by a yeoman who clambered aboard and found a lone survivor, whom he took into his care; and this was the baby Modred.

Meanwhile, King Royns had received King Arthur's reply, and prepared to fulfill his threat.

2. BALIN, OR THE KNIGHT WITH THE TWO SWORDS

King Royns of West Britain, upon receiving Arthur's indignant refusal to pay homage, had raised a large army, and was now marching on Arthur and laying waste all before him.

Arthur was in London when he received news of the invasion; at once he let cry a general call to arms, and summoned his nobles to Camelot for a council of war. The council was interrupted by a young noblewoman who had begged admittance to Arthur, claiming that she had a message for him from the Lady of Avalon.

The young noblewoman, as soon as she stood before Arthur, drew aside her gown and revealed a handsome sword and scabbard, hung from her girdle. "My lady," said Arthur, "a sword is hardly becoming to one of your sex. Please tell me why you wear it."

"Because of an enchantment," she replied, "the sword can be drawn only by a knight of matchless courage and virtue, and such am I seeking. Lately I was at the court of King Royns, but every one of his knights failed. Now I have come to you, because your knights are praised for their excellence even above his."

"I will set an example to my knights by being the first to make the attempt," said Arthur, "though I make no claim myself to such excellence."

Seizing the hilt of the sword in one hand and the scabbard in the other, Arthur strained to his utmost to draw them apart, but to no avail.

"The sword will be drawn without effort by the knight I am seeking," said the young noblewoman. "But there is one further condition: that both his mother and father shall be of noble lineage."

"Very well," said Arthur, "let come forward who will!"

But Arthur's knights hung back. None felt that he could fulfill these exacting conditions, and none wished to be shamed by failure, so they all remained in their places. The young noblewoman burst into tears. "Surely," she said, "amongst yours, the most celebrated knights in Christendom, there is one who is worthy?"

"I am ashamed that none will come forward," said Arthur.

There was one knight present, however, who had been released from jail to witness the unusual scene; and this was Sir Balin, whom Arthur had imprisoned six months earlier for killing a cousin of his while jousting. Sir Balin was raggedly dressed and dared not reveal himself before the assembly, so he waited until the young noblewoman, still weeping, had left the hall and passed into the courtyard; there he addressed her.

"My lady," he said, "I ask you not to judge me by the poverty of my attire, but to allow that it may serve to conceal a knight who is not unworthy. In short, will you try me in drawing the sword?"

"And why should you succeed where others have failed?" she retorted. "But then, since none here has had the courage even to try, I suppose you may as well."

Balin seized the hilt of the sword, and lightly withdrew it

from the scabbard. He examined the sword and rejoiced; it was the most beautiful that he had ever held.

Meanwhile King Arthur and his nobles had gathered around, astonished at Sir Balin's success, and several of the nobles were secretly envious. "Sire," said the young noblewoman to Arthur, "this knight will become famous before he dies," and then to Sir Balin: "Sir, please give me the sword again."

"Now that I have won this sword," said Sir Balin, "nothing will part me from it."

"It is for your sake and not mine that I ask you," said the young noblewoman. "If you keep it you will fight to the death with the man you love most."

"Still, I would rather chance my fate," said Sir Balin; and so the young noblewoman departed sorrowfully.

Sir Balin had sent his squire for his horse and armor, and was preparing to leave the court, when Arthur spoke to him: "Sir Balin, you must be angry with me for having imprisoned you; I understand now that I was wrongly informed. If it pleases you, remain at the court, and I will advance you to the barony."

"Sire, I thank you," Sir Balin replied. "I could not ask for a better liege. No praise of mine could equal your generosity; but still I beg you to let me go."

"As you will, then," said Arthur, "although it saddens me to lose you. Please know that if you return, my offer remains."

Overhearing this conversation, several of the barons muttered angrily among themselves that Sir Balin had won the sword by a trick, and was not worthy of such distinction. Just then, however, the Lady of Avalon, mounted on a richly harnessed palfrey, rode up to Arthur.

"Sire," she said, "I now demand the gift you swore to when I gave you the magic sword."

"My lady," said Arthur, "what is the name of the sword?"

"Excalibur."

"Then name the gift."

"I demand the head of the knight who won the sword just now, or the head of the woman who gave it to him. Either will do, for he killed my brother, and she was the cause of my father's death."

"Since I am a Christian king I may grant you neither," said Arthur, "so please ask me for something else."

"I will accept nothing else," the lady replied. Thereupon Sir Balin, who had witnessed the conversation, swiftly drew his sword and beheaded her.

"You criminal!" Arthur shouted, "this lady was our bene-factress. How dared you kill her in my presence, in my court, where—whatever her demands—she was entitled to my protec-tion?"

"Sire," said Balin, "I considered that. But our benefactress not only caused my mother to be burned to death, in addition she enticed many an innocent knight to a shameful death by means of her magic."

"Whatever your reasons, you should have forborne in my presence," said Arthur. "Now understand that you are exiled from this court forever."

Taking the lady's head, Sir Balin called his squire, mounted, and rode from the court; his squire followed.

"Now," said Sir Balin to his squire, "take this head and ride with it to my kinsmen in Northumberland. Tell them my news: how I was released from prison, won the sword, and killed my deadliest enemy."

"I am troubled that you treated King Arthur as you did," said the squire.

"What I shall do," Sir Balin replied, "is to ride to King Royns of West Britain and challenge him: if he does not kill me first, I shall kill him. He is King Arthur's greatest enemy, and in that way I shall regain his friendship."

"And where shall I meet you next?" asked the squire.

"At King Arthur's court." So they parted.

Meanwhile Arthur buried the Lady of Avalon, and mourned for her. Then Sir Launceor, a vain and boastful knight from Ireland, who had long been jealous of Sir Balin, approached Arthur and offered to avenge his wrong on Sir Balin. Arthur gave his assent.

Then Merlin appeared at the court. Arthur told him all that had happened, and Merlin replied: "It grieves me that Sir Balin won the sword, because he is a noble-hearted knight who will yet render you good service. The young noblewoman is utterly evil: by mischance her brother killed her betrothed, so she begged from the Lady of Avalon an enchanted sword, such that it could be drawn from its sheath only by a courage-ous knight, who, under the enchantment, would challenge and kill her brother, and then himself be destroyed."

Sir Launceor overtook Sir Balin as he was riding through the hills of the borderland.

"I have come to avenge the wrong you did to King Arthur," he said, "so defend yourself!"

"You may repent it," Sir Balin replied as he couched his spear.

They rode at each other: Sir Balin's shield was splintered by Sir Launceor's spear, but his own spear drove clean through Sir Launceor's shield, through his hauberk, and into his body; Sir Launceor fell from his horse's cropper, and was dead before he reached the ground.

Not realizing that he was dead, Sir Balin had leaped from his horse, drawn his sword, and was standing over him thus, when a young noblewoman appeared on a slender palfrey. The moment that she saw Sir Launceor lying dead, she dismounted and threw herself upon him, uttering the most heartbroken cries.

"You have killed two hearts with one body, two bodies with one heart," she said, and then, seizing Sir Launceor's sword, pierced her breast and fell dead next to her lover.

Greatly moved, Sir Balin mounted his horse, and was heading for the forest when he saw his brother, Sir Balan, riding toward him. As soon as they met, they flung off their helmets and kissed.

"How fortunate!" Sir Balan exclaimed. "I heard from a knight at the Castle of the Four Stones that you had been released from prison, and I was coming to meet you."

Sir Balin told his brother all that had happened, and they both grieved over the death of the lovers.

"Since you are going to challenge King Royns," said Sir Balan, "I will come with you. Being your brother, it is right that I should throw in my lot with yours."

In the meantime a dwarf from King Arthur's court had noticed the dead bodies. "Whose work was this?" he asked the brothers.

"Mine," said Sir Balin.

"King Arthur will never forgive you," said the dwarf, "and the knight's kin will search you out and revenge him, no matter how far you flee."

"I do not fear them," said Sir Balin, "but I curse my fate, that by ill chance I should once more have caused offense to King Arthur. Because of the maiden, I shall forever put the service of her sex foremost."

While they were talking, King Mark of Cornwall rode by, and seeing the knight and the maiden, also asked for their story. When he had heard it, he declared that he would search for a tomb worthy of them.

Sometime later, when King Mark had returned with a tomb, Merlin appeared. "On this spot," he said, "will occur the most desperate battle between the two most ardent lovers of all time, namely Sir Launcelot du Lake and Sir Tristram; but they will not kill each other." He then inscribed their names on the tomb in letters of gold.

"You must be a prophet," said King Mark, "and yet you look strangely uncouth. Please tell me, who are you?"

"When Sir Tristram has found his paramour," Merlin replied, "you shall know my name, and learn from me many matters which will not be to your liking." Then Merlin spoke to Sir Balin. "It is a disaster that you were unable to save the maiden."

"Alas!" said Sir Balin, "she was too quick for me."

"In consequence, you will strike the most fateful blow since that struck at our Saviour: three kingdoms will be laid waste for twelve years, and an honorable king incurably wounded."

"If this is true," said Sir Balin, "I would prefer to take my life now, to prevent it. . . ."

But Merlin had vanished; so the two brothers took their leave of King Mark, who asked Sir Balin his name.

"Call him the Knight of the Two Swords," Sir Balan replied.

King Mark departed for Camelot; Sir Balin and Sir Balan were heading west for King Royns', when they were again confronted by Merlin, who in another disguise deceived them both until he told them where they were going, for what purpose, and offered them his advice. Merlin then led them to a wood where they rested until midnight.

"Now," said Merlin, "you will need courage: King Royns is approaching with a bodyguard of sixty knights; he has sent another twenty in advance to warn Lady de Vaunce that to-night he will sleep with her."

As the party drew close to them, Sir Balin whispered to Merlin: "Which is King Royns?" and Merlin pointed with his staff.

"There," he said.

Drawing their swords, Sir Balin and Sir Balan rushed out from their ambush and attacked King Royns with such force that before long he sank to the ground, severely wounded. The bodyguard set on them from all sides, but proved no match for the brothers' skillful swordplay: forty were killed and the remainder fled. Returning to the wounded king, Sir Balan dragged off his helmet while Sir Balin stood over him with raised sword, prepared to cut off his head.

"Good knights, spare me, I beg you!" said King Royns. "By my death you will gain nothing; alive I am worth a good ransom."

"Very well," said Sir Balin; and then the brothers bound him firmly to a horse litter.

The following day King Royns was conveyed by Sir Balin and Sir Balan to the palace guard, and by the palace guard into the presence of King Arthur. King Arthur had been forewarned by Merlin of King Royns' capture.

"Welcome to our court!" said King Arthur to King Royns. "Pray tell me: how have you come?"

"A painful way," said King Royns from his litter. "I was captured by the two hardiest knights living. They are brothers, and one of them is known as the Knight of the Two Swords."

"I am greatly indebted to them," said Arthur. "I wonder who they could be."

"Sir Balin and Sir Balan," Merlin replied.

"I certainly did not deserve this from Sir Balin," said Arthur, "whom I exiled from my court forever."

"He will serve you yet," said Merlin. "But tell me, is your army in readiness to meet an invasion? King Nero, King Royns' brother, is now advancing upon you in strength, and tomorrow you will have to give battle."

King Arthur, with only ten battalions, met King Nero's huge army on the plain of Terrabyl. However, King Arthur's commanders, Sir Kay, Sir Hervy, Sir Balin, and Sir Balan, fought with such verve that his men were inspired, and defeated King Nero, killing the greater part of his army on the field. King Arthur himself killed twenty knights and maimed another forty.

While the battle was in progress, Merlin appeared before King Lot on the Island of Orkney and, knowing that King Lot had pledged his aid to King Nero, and that in the next battle between King Arthur and King Lot one of them was destined to die, beguiled him with stories until a messenger arrived reporting the defeat of King Nero.

"You have tricked me, Merlin," King Lot exclaimed. "What shall I do now? Make a treaty with Arthur, or attack him?"

"Attack him," said Merlin, knowing that King Lot would now be the one to die.

King Lot's grievance against Arthur had been aggravated by the birth of the bastard Modred, resulting from Arthur's union with Lot's wife. So he now advanced upon Arthur, determined to accomplish his revenge at last. His army was led by the eleven kings who had been his allies in the battle of

Bedgrayne, and they too were bent on revenge. Meanwhile, King Pellinore, as well as Sir Balin and Sir Balan, had volunteered to fight for Arthur.

When battle was joined, both sides fought for many hours with equal determination, and neither was able to gain the advantage. Then King Pellinore attacked King Lot and killed him, by first spearing his horse so that he fell, and then splitting his helmet and skull with his sword. The eleven kings and their armies were severely shocked, and some of King Lot's men started to flee from the field. Taking advantage of their weakness, King Arthur led an attack which ended in the massacre of the eleven kings and their entire army.

Arthur buried the eleven kings together in one tomb, and King Lot in a separate one, in the church of St. Stephens at Camelot. King Lot's widow attended the burial with her four sons, Gawain (who was later to avenge his father's death), Gaheris, Aggravayne, and Gareth; King Uryens and his wife, Morgan le Fay, were also present at the burial.

At King Arthur's request, Merlin made bronze candle-holders, overlaid with gold, each representing one of the eleven kings in an attitude of defeat; and then one of Arthur, brandishing his sword in an attitude of victory, to be set above those of the eleven kings. The candles were to burn in the church, night and day.

When Merlin had completed the work, he prophesied to Arthur the extinction of the candles after Arthur's death, which was to be at the hands of Sir Modred in the Battle of Salisbury; the accomplishment of the quest of the Holy Grail by knights of the Round Table; the forthcoming theft of Arthur's sword by the woman he trusted most; and in the immediate future, the fateful blow to be struck by Sir Balin. Finally the birth of King Uryens' son Sir Bagdemagus, who would be Arthur's cousin-german.

"And where are King Pellinore, Sir Balin, and Sir Balan now?" Arthur asked. "For I would wish to have such excellent knights always by me."

"King Pellinore and Sir Balin you will see shortly, but Sir Balan has left your court forever," Merlin replied.

A few days later, Arthur fell sick, and as he lay in his pavilion, a grief-stricken knight rode toward him. "Sir," said Arthur, "please tell me: what grieves you?"

"Nothing that you can cure," the knight replied, and rode on his way toward the castle of Meliot. Next, Sir Balin rode by, and seeing Arthur, dismounted and greeted him.

"Sir Balin," said Arthur, "I request that you bring to me a knight who is riding toward Meliot; he is grief-stricken, but refuses to tell me the cause."

"Sire," Sir Balin replied, "I will bring him to you—as a prisoner if he does not come of his own free will."

Sir Balin rode into the forest and found the knight in the company of a young noblewoman. "Sir," he said, "I am commanded by my liege, King Arthur, to bring you to his court. If you refuse, you will have to accept my challenge."

"I am reluctant to accept either," the knight replied. "But supposing I come with you: will you pledge your life to my safe conduct?"

"Readily," said Sir Balin; so he and Sir Harleus (which was the knight's name) left the young noblewoman and rode toward the court. They had just reached Arthur's pavilion when Sir Harleus was transfixed by a spear from an invisible rider.

"This is the work of Sir Garlot," he said, as he lay dying. "Take my horse, which is better than yours, and avenge my death."

Sir Harleus was buried and mourned ceremoniously by Arthur, and his tomb was inscribed with his name and that of his murderer, Sir Garlot. Meanwhile, Sir Balin had returned to the young noblewoman, and when he had given her the shaft of the spear which had killed her paramour, they set off together in search of the invisible knight.

They had not ridden far when they came upon Sir Peryne de Mounte Belyarde, who had been hunting. Sir Peryne hailed them, and then noticing their looks of consternation, inquired the cause. On hearing their story, he offered to accompany them, and all three rode on together. However, just as they were riding past a hermit's dwelling, Sir Peryne was attacked and killed by the invisible Sir Garlot. "Alas!" said Sir Balin, "I now have two deaths to avenge."

The hermit assisted in the burial of Sir Peryne, and inscribed his name on the tomb, together with that of Sir Garlot. In the morning a fresh inscription had appeared on the tomb, in letters of gold, which stated that Sir Gawain would revenge his father's death on King Pellinore.

Continuing their search, Sir Balin and the young noblewoman rode up to a substantial castle. Sir Balin entered first, and had just passed through the portcullis when it closed behind him. Thereupon half a dozen knights set upon the young noblewoman with their swords, wounding her liberally.

Sir Balin leaped from the castle wall, and was driving them off furiously, when one of the knights cried out:

"Sir, hold your hand for a moment: the lady of the castle is sick and can be cured only by receiving a silver basin full of the blood of a maiden princess. Hence it is our custom to draw blood from every young noblewoman who passes by."

Hearing this, the young noblewoman graciously offered her blood, which, however, failed to cure the lady (who was destined to remain sick until receiving blood from Sir Percivale's sister). Sir Balin and the young noblewoman rested overnight in the castle, and were entertained hospitably.

For three days and two nights they continued their journey without further incident. On the third night, however, while they were dining with a gentleman who had offered them hospitality in his comfortable manor, they heard strange cries issuing from another room. In answer to Sir Balin's inquiry, the host replied:

"It is my son: he has been wounded by Sir Garlot, a knight who rides invisibly; and I have been advised that he can be cured only by blood drawn from Sir Garlot's own body."

"Sir Garlot," said Sir Balin, "is the very knight for whom we are searching. Have you any knowledge of his whereabouts?"

"Yes," said the gentleman. "King Pellam of Lystenoyse has proclaimed a feast for fifteen days from now, which is to be attended by all the nobles of his realm, together with their ladies or betrothed; and at·this feast you will find Sir Garlot."

"Then let us ride together to the feast," said Sir Balin, "and I can promise you the blood you need to cure your son."

Sir Balin, the young noblewoman, and the gentleman arrived at King Pellam's court on the day of the feast. They were cordially received, and ushered first to the cloakrooms and thence into the banqueting hall. Sir Balin was requested to leave his sword in the cloakroom, but managed to excuse himself from doing so on the grounds that this was not the custom in the court from which he had come.

Once he had taken his seat at the banqueting table, Sir Balin asked his neighbor if he knew Sir Garlot by sight.

"I do," his neighbor replied. "He is the black-faced knight sitting on the far side of the table. He is the most remarkable knight living, because he rides invisibly."

Meanwhile Sir Garlot had noticed Sir Balin staring at him. He rose from his seat, and coming over to Sir Balin, slapped him across the face with the back of his hand.

"You are here to feast," said Sir Garlot, "so get on with it."

"Sir, this is not the first time you have wronged me," Sir Balin said quietly; and then, seemingly in one movement, sprang up from his seat, drew his sword, and cleft Sir Garlot's head from crown to jaw. Next, taking the spear shaft from the young noblewoman, he plunged it deeply into Sir Garlot's body, and blood flowed from the wound.

"This spear looks better in the body of its owner than it did in the body of the innocent knight he murdered," said Sir Balin, and then to the gentleman, "and now you can take a cupful of blood to cure your son."

Meanwhile King Pellam and his knights had hastily armed, and were surrounding Sir Balin. "You have killed my brother," said King Pellam, "and surely you shall die for it."

"Avenge him yourself," Sir Balin replied.

King Pellam struck at Sir Balin's head; Sir Balin raised his sword to ward off the blow, and the sword was sheared off at the hilt. Breaking free from his assailants, Sir Balin ran fleetly from room to room in search of a weapon, with King Pellam in close pursuit. He found none until he came to an eerie room, richly furnished and containing a bed on which lay an embalmed corpse covered with a gold cloth. A finely wrought spear had been placed on a small, gold-topped table with silver legs. Sir Balin seized the spear just in time to strike King Pellam as he charged at him.

There followed a tremendous roaring sound as the walls of the castle collapsed, killing everyone within except Sir Balin and King Pellam, both of whom lay in a trance. The spear with which Sir Balin had struck King Pellam was the spear which had pierced the body of Jesus as He hung from the Cross: it had been brought to Britain by Joseph of Arimathea, whose corpse it had been that lay on the bed, and from whose kin King Pellam was descended. The result of this blow, as Merlin had prophesied, was that the three adjacent kingdoms were laid waste for a period of twelve years, and King Pellam's wound remained open until Sir Galahad, many years later, cured him.

Merlin appeared three days later and roused Sir Balin from his trance. "You must go from here," he said.

"And what of the young noblewoman?" Sir Balin asked.

"She is dead," Merlin replied.

Sir Balin said good-bye to Merlin, whom he was never to see again, and rode through the ruined landscapes and desolate cities of the three kingdoms. Everywhere people were dead or

dying, and those who were able to speak said accusingly:
"Knight of the Two Swords, this is your doing; but vengeance
will be done!"

At last Sir Balin rode clear of these lands, and eight days
later came to a castle in a thickly wooded valley. In the castle
grounds was sitting a grief-stricken knight.

"Sir," said Sir Balin, "tell me the cause of your grief, and
perhaps I can find a remedy for it."

"Sir, please leave me to my grief," the knight replied.

Sir Balin withdrew a little, and as he did so overheard the
knight saying to himself: "Alas, my lady, that you gave me
this sword and failed to keep our tryst: for now I shall kill
myself with it." As he drew the sword, Sir Balin ran back and
stayed his hand.

"Who are you, that you cannot leave me in peace?"

"Sir Balin, the Knight of the Two Swords. But why not tell
me where your lady is to be found, and we will seek her out."

"Then you are the most famous knight living! I will tell
you, my name is Sir Garnysh of the Mount. I was born of
poor parents, and won my knighthood and my lands on the
battlefield. My lord is the Duke of Harmel, whose castle lies
six miles from here, and it is his daughter whom I love, and
who, until now, loved me."

They rode together to the castle, and when they arrived Sir
Balin offered to search for the duke's daughter. He searched
through every room in the castle without finding her, and then
passing into the garden found a small arbor, where, lying
beneath a laurel tree, was the young noblewoman, in the arms
of the foulest-looking knight he had ever seen. They were
both asleep, and covered by a cloth of green samite. He returned to Sir Garnysh, told him what he had seen, and led
him to the lovers.

Sir Garnysh was unable to control his grief when he saw
them, and broke into violent sobs; then, drawing his sword,
beheaded them both with a single blow.

"Sir Balin, what you have shown me makes me more heartbroken than I was when I first decided to kill myself," he said.

"I hoped you would take courage when you saw how
your lady had betrayed you, and harden your heart against her;
for that is how I should have felt."

"I loved her more than my life," said Sir Garnysh, and driving his sword through his own body, fell dead beside them. Not

wishing to be held responsible for the three dead bodies, Sir Balin rode swiftly and sadly away.

Three days later he came to a stone cross bearing an inscription in gold letters:

IT IS FOR NO KNYGHT ALONE TO RYDE TOWARD THIS CASTEL.

However, Sir Balin rode on, and then a gray-bearded old man appeared. "Sir Balin, turn back! you will overreach yourself," he warned him, and then vanished. After this there was a dismal horn blast. "That horn sounds for me," thought Sir Balin. "So be it if it is my fate; I am not dead yet."

He was welcomed at the castle by a hundred knights and ladies, amid dancing, song, and revelry. Then the lady of the castle greeted him: "Knight of the Two Swords, you will have to fight the Knight of the Island, for that is our custom here."

"A sorry custom," said Sir Balin.

He armed wearily, and as he was doing so a knight brought him a shield. "Take this shield," he said; "it is larger than yours and you will need it." Sir Balin took the shield, but when he had reached the island and was mounting, a lady whispered, "Sir, it is a shame your shield has no device; your friends will not recognize you."

"And I should be ashamed to turn back now," Sir Balin replied.

A knight in red armor, with red harness to match, was riding across the tournament field toward Sir Balin. For a moment Sir Balin thought that it was his brother, Sir Balan, but then, noticing that his shield bore no device, supposed he was wrong.

They couched spears and thundered together, and both men and horses were stunned by the collision. The Red Knight was the first to recover, and rushed at Sir Balin with drawn sword. Sir Balin rose just in time to defend himself. A fierce battle ensued.

By the second respite, the armor and hauberks of both had been hacked to pieces, and blood was flowing abundantly from their wounds. Sir Balin glanced up at the tower, and noticed that the ladies of the castle had crowded to the windows and were watching them eagerly.

They resumed the fight. Many hours had elapsed since they started, and they were now thrusting and slashing at each other's half-naked bodies, and even the hardiest of the spectators was aghast at their terrible endurance. At last the Red Knight collapsed, mortally wounded, and, immediately after him, Sir Balin.

"Sir," Sir Balin gasped, "you are the most formidable knight I have ever fought. Please tell me: what is your name?"

"Sir Balan, brother to Sir Balin," the Red Knight replied.

"Alas!" said Sir Balin, and fainted.

Sir Balan crawled up to him and pulled off his helmet, but his brother's face was so wounded and bloody as to be unrecognizable.

Sir Balin came to. "My dear brother," he said, "we have killed each other, and our story will be told after we are both dead."

"When I came to this castle," said Sir Balan, "I too had to fight the Knight of the Island. I won and was forced to take his place. The same would have happened to you: so whichever of us had come first, the result would have been the same. There was no hope for us."

The lady of the castle came up to them, accompanied by four knights and six ladies, and Sir Balin told her they were brothers, and begged that they should be buried in the same tomb. The lady promised to do this, and both she and her companions wept when they heard their story. Sir Balin died after both received extreme unction, and his brother a few hours later, at midnight. The lady kept her promise and buried them in the same tomb, but only Sir Balan's name was inscribed, since Sir Balin's was not known.

Merlin appeared on the morning after the burial, and first completed the inscription:

HERE LYETH SIR BALIN LE SAVEAGE: KNYGHT OF THE TWO SWERDES WHO STRUCK THE DOLOROUS STROKE.

Then he made an enchanted bed, which was to drive every sleeper out of his wits, until Sir Launcelot lay on it and broke the spell. Next he made a new hilt for Sir Balin's sword, and handing it to a nearby knight, asked: "Sir, would you please draw this sword from its scabbard?" The knight tried, but was unable to do so. Merlin laughed.

"This sword is enchanted," he said, "and will be drawn only by Sir Launcelot and his son Sir Galahad. Sir Launcelot will kill the man he loves most with it, as Sir Balin did, and the man will be Sir Gawain."

Merlin took the sword again, and inscribed his prophecy on the hilt. After this he built an enchanted iron bridge from the island to the mainland, which only knights of unexampled purity would be able to cross. He then set the scabbard of the sword on the mainland, and the sword in a marble block, midstream, with the blade and hilt rising above the surface of the water. Sir Galahad was to discover first the scabbard, and then the sword, when it had floated downstream to Camelot, where he was to win it.

Merlin then returned to King Arthur, and told him what had befallen Sir Balin and Sir Balan.

"Alas!" said Arthur, "those two brothers were the finest knights I have ever known."

3. TORRE AND PELLINORE

It was natural that King Arthur, having sought Merlin's advice during the early years of his reign, while enforcing his sovereignty over the petty kings of the north and west of Britain who had challenged his right to the succession, should again seek Merlin's advice in the matter of marriage, which his loyal barons were urging upon him now that peace had been established.

"Certainly a king should marry," said Merlin. "But tell me, is there already a lady who has captured your heart?"

"There is," Arthur replied. "The daughter of my friend King Lodegreaunce of Camylarde. I mean, of course, the incomparably innocent and beautiful Gwynevere."

"She is certainly as beautiful as one could wish, and if indeed you are set on making her your queen, I suppose that you must do so, although many more as beautiful, and more happily destined, could be found."

"Why do you say that?"

"Because Gwynevere is destined to love Sir Launcelot, and he her, and many disasters will result from their love. However, provide me with a royal escort and I will go to King Lodegreaunce and tell him that you are in love with Gwynevere and would like to marry her."

King Lodegreaunce was overjoyed when Merlin disclosed the purpose of his visit. "What greater honor could I receive," he said, "than that so illustrious a king as Arthur should choose my daughter for his queen?"

Instead of the usual lands or riches for a wedding gift, King

Lodegreaunce decided to give King Arthur the Round Table which he had received from King Uther, and to place under Arthur's command the hundred knights who served him. This would leave empty at the table fifty seats, which had belonged to knights who had been killed or captured in King Lodegreaunce' service in the course of the years.

When Merlin and his escort, with the Round Table, and accompanied by Gwynevere and the hundred knights, returned to Camelot, he was received by Arthur with unabashed delight; and orders were given to prepare for the royal wedding and the coronation of Gwynevere.

Merlin then scoured the country for suitable knights to occupy the empty seats at the table, and found twenty-eight, who were sworn in to Arthur's service by the Archbishop of Canterbury. When the ceremony was over it was seen that each place at the table was now marked in gold letters with the name of the knight to which it belonged; but two places were left blank, and the one between them was marked: SIEGE PERELOUS.

King Arthur had issued a proclamation that on the day of the feast all reasonable petitions would be granted, and the first to take advantage of this was Gawain, King Lot's son, who begged to be knighted. Gawain was Arthur's nephew, and he readily assented. The next was a poor cowherd called Aryes, who came to make the same request on behalf of his son Torre, who accompanied him.

"This is a large request for you to make," said Arthur. "Please tell me your name, and whose wish it is that your son should be knighted: yours or his."

"Sire, my name is Aryes the cowherd; I have thirteen sons, and they all work for me willingly enough but this one, Torre. Since he was a child he would have none of it, but was always practicing with the sword or shooting with the bow, or running off to watch tournaments."

Arthur looked carefully at Torre. He did not resemble his father in any way; he was large, well built, of fine features and fearless expression, about eighteen years of age.

"I should like to see his brothers," said Arthur. They were sent for, and when they were all together before Arthur, he noticed how they all resembled their father but Torre.

"Have you a sword?" Arthur said to Torre.

"Sire, I have," Torre replied.

"Then give it to me, kneel down, and request to be knighted." Torre did so and Arthur dubbed him. At this moment Merlin appeared.

"Merlin," said Arthur, "I have knighted this young man Torre. Have I done wisely?"

"You have," Merlin replied. "You may not be aware of it, but he is King Pellinore's son."

"How so," asked Arthur, "when Aryes the cowherd claims to be his father?"

"Send for his mother," Merlin replied.

Sir Torre's mother was a mature and handsome housewife, and she answered Merlin's question without hesitating.

"Sire, one day before I married, and while I was still a maid, I went down to the cowshed to milk the cows. A stern-looking knight rode up, and persuaded me, with a little force, to the act of love. It was then I lost my maidenhead, and Torre was conceived. The knight took my greyhound and said that he would keep it to remind him of me."

"I wish that it had been otherwise," said Aryes, "but it explains why Torre is so different from me."

"You dishonor my mother," Sir Torre said to Merlin.

"That is not so," Merlin replied, "since you were conceived before your mother was married, and since your father, King Pellinore, is an important king. Rather, you should be honored, for at this court you may well win advancement and fame."

"Well, that is something," said Aryes, and left with his family. King Pellinore arrived at the court the next morning, and was delighted to discover his bastard son, now a knight.

At last the day of the feast arrived, and the royal wedding and the coronation of Gwynevere took place in the church of St. Stephens, and were conducted with befitting solemnity by the Archbishop of Canterbury. When it was over, King Arthur with his queen and their suite repaired to the Round Table for the banquet.

"Tell me, Merlin," said Arthur, "why those two seats are blank, and why the one between them is marked: SIEGE PERELOUS."

"Sire, because it would be death for any but the appointed knight to sit at the Siege Perelous, and only a little less disastrous at the unmarked seats on either side. The knight who shall sit at the Siege Perelous has not yet been born; the names of the knights who shall sit at the other two seats will appear when they arrive at the court. However, I suggest that King Pellinore, as the senior knight present, should take the seat adjacent to them."

Sir Gawain, who had been knighted that morning, was furious when he heard this, and whispered to Gaheris, his brother,

who was acting as his squire, "Why should King Pellinore be
so honored? You know that he killed our father at the battle
of Terrabyl. Well, with this good sword of mine, I am going
to avenge his death."

"But not now," said Gaheris, "not at King Arthur's own
table. We must bide our time; anyhow, I want to avenge his
death myself as soon as I am knighted."

The banquet was nearly over, and the guests about to rise
from their seats, when Merlin addressed the company at large:
"My lords and ladies, pray keep your seats, for you are about
to witness an unusual event."

And just as he spoke, a white hart galloped into the hall, pursued by a white brachet and thirty pairs of black hounds. The
brachet kept snapping at the hart's haunches, and finally succeeded in tearing off a piece of flesh. The hart made a tremendous leap and, in doing so, overturned a knight who was sitting
at one of the side tables. The knight jumped up, seized the
brachet, and made off with her.

Almost immediately a young noblewoman rode into the hall
on a white palfrey. She was sobbing with anger and dismay, and
rode straight up to Arthur. "Sire," she cried, "summon the
knight who has stolen my brachet at once, for I cannot be without it."

"I may not summon him now," Arthur replied.

Next, a knight appeared, fully armed and riding a powerful
charger. He rode up to the young noblewoman and, despite her
screams, seized her around the waist, threw her across the
withers of his horse, and galloped out of the hall again. Arthur
was relieved that the hubbub was over; however, Merlin spoke
up once more.

"Sire, you cannot let these matters rest here. It would go ill
for your marriage, and your court would be dishonored."

"Very well," said Arthur. "Sir Gawain, I request you to retrieve the hart; you, Sir Torre, to retrieve the brachet, and capture or kill the knight who stole her; and you, King Pellinore,
the lady, and capture or kill her captor. None of you is to return to the court before your quest is accomplished."

Sir Gawain and Gaheris were the first to set off, and they galloped through the forest until they came upon two knights
fighting each other on foot. Sir Gawain rode his horse between
them. "What is your quarrel?" he cried.

Both knights looked up sheepishly. "We were fighting," said
one of them, "to prove which of us is the bigger, and should
therefore be the one to pursue a white hart which ran by a short

time ago. It came from the direction of King Arthur's court, and we thought that one of us could win fame by chasing it down. We are brothers."

"That is a silly quarrel indeed," said Sir Gawain, "and now either you will have to accept my challenge, or go to King Arthur and yield to him, saying that you are prisoners of the knight on the quest of the white hart. But tell me first, what are your names?"

"Our names are Sorlus and Bryan of the Forest. We will be your prisoners rather than fight any more, we are so weary."

Sir Gawain and Gaheris could still hear the yapping of the hounds in the distance, and so they turned eagerly to their quest once more. Coming to a river they were challenged by a knight on the further bank. "Sir, you may not pursue the white hart without first fighting me," he shouted.

Sir Gawain swam his horse across the river. They jousted and Sir Gawain threw his opponent off his horse at the first encounter, and demanded that he should yield. "Not until we have fought on foot with our swords," said the knight.

"Please tell me, what is your name?" Sir Gawain asked him.

"Sir Alardyne of the Outer Isles."

Sir Gawain drew his sword and with one stroke chopped clean through Sir Alardyne's helmet and skull. "That was a fine stroke for a young knight," said Gaheris appreciatively.

The brothers galloped off again in pursuit of the hart, and were soon joined by three pairs of greyhounds who slipped out from the undergrowth. Together they pursued their quarry until it fled into a castle; the greyhounds raced in first and made their kill in the hall.

Sir Gawain and Gaheris arrived at the entrance to the hall in time to see a knight emerge from an inner room and set about the greyhounds with his sword. He killed two of them and the remainder fled.

"Alas, my white hart!" the knight exclaimed, "gift that you were from my sovereign lady; but at least you shall not go unavenged."

He withdrew to the inner room and a moment later reappeared in full armor. "Sir," said Sir Gawain, "why kill the greyhounds, whose nature it is to devour their quarry? Why not try to kill me instead?"

"I will," said the knight.

They fought, and both were severely wounded before Sir Gawain sent his opponent reeling to the ground with a blow on the helmet. He begged Sir Gawain to spare his life.

"I will not," Sir Gawain replied. "You killed my grey-hounds."

"For those I can surely make amends," said the knight.

But Sir Gawain felt no mercy and dragged off his helmet. He was just poised to behead him when the knight's lady appeared and threw herself between them. Unable to restrain the blow, Sir Gawain beheaded the lady. He was completely dismayed.

"Arise, I grant you your life," he said to the knight.

"I think little of your mercy now," the knight replied, "since with your cowardly stroke you have killed my lady, who was far more dear to me than my own life."

"In truth, it was you I meant to kill," said Sir Gawain. "But go now to King Arthur: tell him what has befallen you, and say that you are a prisoner of the knight on the quest of the white hart. Before you go, please tell me, what is your name?"

"Sir Blamoure de la Maryse," the other replied.

Sir Blamoure strapped the two greyhounds to his horse, one on either side of the saddle, and departed for Camelot. Sir Gawain and Gaheris meanwhile prepared to rest overnight in the castle. Sir Gawain started to disarm.

"What, would you disarm here?" asked Gaheris. "Surely we must be surrounded by enemies."

No sooner had he spoken than four knights in full armor rushed into the hall and attacked them.

"You should be ashamed," one of them shouted, "that you, a newly made knight, have already dishonored the order of knighthood by killing a lady. However, you need expect no mercy from us."

Sir Gawain and Gaheris fought desperately, but were no match for their attackers. Soon Sir Gawain received a crippling wound in the arm, and they were both at death's door when four ladies appeared and begged the knights to spare their lives.

They spent the night bemoaning their fate, as prisoners in one of the castle cells. Sir Gawain was particularly troubled by his arm, and feared that he had lost the use of it. In the morning one of the ladies came to them.

"Good knight, what cheer?" she said.

"No cheer," Sir Gawain replied.

"The fault is your own," she said, "but please tell me your name and from whose court you have come."

"Sir Gawain, son of King Lot of Lowthean and Orkney, and of Margawse, sister to King Arthur. I am a knight of the Round Table, and King Arthur is my liege."

The lady was impressed. "Since you are related to King Arthur," she said, "I will intercede on your behalf with the four knights."

Sir Gawain and Gaheris were released soon afterward, on condition that Sir Gawain should bear the corpse of the lady on his own body throughout the journey to Camelot, and that he should report to Arthur truthfully all that had occurred. He was allowed to take the hart's head as proof that he had accomplished his quest.

King Arthur and Queen Gwynevere listened attentively to Sir Gawain's account of his adventures, and when he had finished, Queen Gwynevere rebuked him sternly, commanding that henceforth he should always spare those who begged for mercy, and always put the service of ladies foremost. Sir Gawain swore on the gospel to do so, and so ended his first quest.

Sir Torre had set off on the quest of the brachet, and had not ridden far through the forest when a dwarf appeared before him and struck his horse on the nose with his staff, so that the horse started backward by a spear's length.

"Why did you do that?" Sir Torre demanded.

"Because no knight may ride this way without first fighting my masters," the dwarf replied.

"I am on a quest and have no time for idle jousting," said Sir Torre; but the dwarf blew on his horn and two knights appeared from their pavilions.

Sir Torre jousted and fought with each in turn, and overcame them both. "What are your names?" he demanded.

"Sir Phelot of Langeduke," said one.

"Sir Petipace of Winchilsee," said the other.

"Go then to King Arthur, and say that you are prisoners of the knight on the quest of the knight with the white brachet."

They left, and the dwarf asked Sir Torre, "Sir, will you grant me a wish?"

"Ask and you shall have it," Sir Torre replied.

"May I now serve you instead of those two rascally knights whom you just defeated? If you accept me, I can lead you to the lady who now has the white brachet."

Sir Torre accepted the dwarf, and they rode together through the forest until they came to two pavilions hard by a priory. Outside each was a shield, one red and one white. Sir Torre dismounted, gave his spear into the keeping of the dwarf, and looked first into the pavilion with the white shield; there he saw three maids asleep on a paillasse. He then looked

inside the other pavilion and saw a lady asleep, and by her
the white brachet. He seized the animal, despite its furious
barks, and strode out of the pavilion with it.

By the time that Sir Torre had given the brachet to his
dwarf and remounted, the lady and her three maids had
emerged from their pavilions. "Sir, why do you take my brachet?" the lady cried.

"My lady, I am obliged to, since my liege King Arthur has
commanded me to bring it to his court."

"Beware, then, for I shall be avenged by a knight who will
prove more than your match," she replied.

"By the grace of God I shall suffer such adventures as He
shall provide," said Sir Torre, and rode away with the dwarf
toward Camelot. It was already dusk, and Sir Torre asked
the dwarf if he knew of a lodging nearby. "Only a poor hermitage," the dwarf replied.

The hermit, however, made them welcome, gave fodder to
their horses, and provided a frugal supper for Sir Torre and
the dwarf. They left early in the morning after hearing mass
and receiving the hermit's blessing. They rode for many miles
through the forest and then were confronted by a handsome
knight, fully armed and mounted on a fine charger.

"Sir, you must yield to me the brachet which you have
stolen from my lady," he demanded of Sir Torre.

Sir Torre refused, and they fought. The jousting brought
both horses and men to the ground, and there followed a long
and savage sword fight in which the armor and hauberk of
each were hacked to pieces. At last, when both were thoroughly bloodied and gasping, the knight, whose name was Abellyus,
fell faint. Sir Torre pressed his advantage and sent him staggering to the ground with a final blow on the helmet.

"Now yield," he said.

"Never, while there is breath in my body, and while you
have the brachet," Sir Abellyus replied.

At this moment a lady galloped up to them on a palfrey and
cried out aloud to Sir Torre.

"My lady, what can I do for you?" Sir Torre responded.

"In the name of King Arthur, grant me my wish."

"Name it and it shall be granted."

"May God reward you!" she said. "It is that you kill this
treacherous knight before you."

"I am loath to do that," said Sir Torre. "Surely, if he has
wronged you, he can make amends?"

"He cannot. He killed my brother in front of my eyes. My

brother was the better knight, and they were fighting only for sport. For half an hour I knelt in the mire before Abellyus, pleading for my brother's life, and then he beheaded him. If you do not grant my wish I shall shame you before King Arthur and all of his court."

Sir Abellyus grew frightened when he heard this, and at once began begging for mercy. "It is impossible now," said Sir Torre, "for me to go back on the promise I made to this lady; if you had only yielded in the first place, I should not have to kill you."

Sir Torre then seized his helmet and dragged it off, but Sir Abellyus managed to struggle free and fled into the forest. Sir Torre gave chase, and soon returned bearing the knight's head.

"Sir," said the lady, "would you allow my lord and me to give you lodging for the night?"

"I would gladly," Sir Torre replied. "Both my horse and I have fared badly since we left Camelot."

The lady and her husband, a handsome elderly knight, entertained them hospitably at their comfortable manor, and both men and horses were at their ease. They took their leave in the morning after hearing mass and breaking their fast. The lady asked Sir Torre his name. He told her, and how he had been newly knighted, and what his quest had been.

"Good knight," said his host, "do please remember us when you are in this part of the country again, and know how welcome you will always be at our poor manor."

Three days later, Sir Torre, with his dwarf, arrived at Camelot, and was received joyfully at the court by King Arthur and Queen Gwynevere. Sir Torre had left poorly equipped for his quest, supplied with an old suit of armor by Arthur, and a very old courser by King Pellinore; but now, when he had described his adventure, Merlin praised him so highly and prophesied such distinction for him in the future that Arthur rewarded him with an earldom. So ended Sir Torre's first quest.

King Pellinore, who had been commanded to bring back the young noblewoman (whose name was Nyneve), had set out at the same time as Sir Torre. He rode through the forest and came to a valley where he found another young noblewoman seated with a wounded knight in her arms. On seeing King Pellinore she cried out aloud:

"Good knight, for the love of Jesus, help me, I beseech you!"

But King Pellinore was so eager in the pursuit of his quest

that he did no more than salute the young noblewoman (whose name was Alyne) and continue on his path. Alyne cursed him bitterly when he had passed, praying to God that when he was most in need, he too should be denied all succor. The knight, her lover, died in her arms a few hours later, and Alyne, crazy with grief, killed herself with his sword.

Further along the valley, King Pellinore came upon a laborer and, halting his horse, asked if he had seen a knight with a captive lady.

"I have," the laborer replied. "The knight was challenged by one of two brothers, whose pavilions you will find further down the valley, and who claim to be her cousins. They were fighting when I left, and if you ride fast you should find them still there."

"I thank you," said King Pellinore, and galloped away.

King Pellinore found the knights still fighting, and Nyneve standing by the two pavilions, together with the two squires. He rode straight up to Nyneve.

"My lady, I am commanded by my liege, King Arthur, to bring you to his court."

"Sir," said one of the squires, "you will have to challenge the two knights who are already fighting for her, if she is to accompany you."

"That is fair," said King Pellinore, and rode up to the two combatants, who were fighting on foot, and drove his horse between them. "What is the cause of your quarrel?" he demanded.

Sir Meliot, Nyeve's cousin, replied first. "Sir, I am fighting to protect my kinswoman (she is my aunt's daughter) against this knight who has taken her by force, and against her will."

"Sir," said Sir Outelake, her captor, "I won the lady by force of arms, and by force of arms I shall keep her."

"That is a lie," said King Pellinore. "I was present when you made off with her; we were banqueting and none had the chance to challenge you. But now I am commanded by King Arthur to bring her back with me to the court, so I challenge you both."

Sir Outelake accepted the challenge, and then suddenly thrust his spear into King Pellinore's horse and killed it. King Pellinore managed to leap clear, and Sir Outelake said:

"Now we can fight on an equal footing."

"You shall pay for that thrust," King Pellinore replied, and drawing his sword, killed Sir Outelake with a single stroke, which

split open his head. Sir Meliot at once knelt before [ ]
nore and yielded.

"Sir, I will not fight with a knight of your prowess,'
"but I beg you not to dishonor my cousin."

"As I am a true knight you need have no fear for [ ],
King Pellinore replied, "but now I am in need of a horse, so
I will take Sir Outelake's."

"Sir, if you will do me the honor of lodging with me tonight,
I will give you a horse that I promise will please you more."

"I will gladly accept," said King Pellinore.

Sir Meliot regaled King Pellinore and Nyneve with excellent food and wine, and they spent the evening merrily
together. In the morning Sir Meliot gave King Pellinore a
splendid bay courser, and they exchanged names before leave-
taking. Sir Meliot also gave his brother's name, which was
Sir Bryan of the Isles.

"I wonder that your brother did not offer to fight for Nyneve," said King Pellinore.

"My brother is an excellent knight, but he will fight only
when he is challenged, or when he is absolutely certain that
the cause is a just one."

"Why not bring him to King Arthur's court?" said King
Pellinore. "You both would be most welcome."

"I thank you; we will come together one day," Sir Meliot
replied.

King Pellinore and Nyneve departed for Camelot. They
were riding through a rocky valley, where the path was strewn
with stones, when Nyneve's horse stumbled and threw her. She
fell heavily on her arm, bruising it painfully, and fainted. When
she came to she begged that they should rest a while, so they
both lay beneath a tree and slept until dusk. King Pellinore
then prepared to continue the journey, but Nyneve said:

"In this light we shall not know whether we are riding forward or backward."

King Pellinore agreed, and so they settled down to bivouac
for the night, and King Pellinore disarmed. A little before
midnight they were awakened by the sound of two horses approaching from opposite directions. King Pellinore hastily re-
armed, and warned Nyneve to keep silent. The two riders met
within earshot of them, one from the direction of Camelot, one
from the north. They hailed each other.

"What news from Camelot?" said one.

"Bad news," the other replied. "I have just been spying on

King Arthur's court, and I have to report to my chieftains in the north that he now has the flower of the chivalry at his command, in the fellowship of the Round Table. There is good reason for their fame, and I fear that we shall never break them."

"As for that, I cannot agree. I have in my wallet a deadly poison, and at Arthur's court we have a sworn accomplice, who, for the immense rewards that my chieftains have offered, will administer it to Arthur willingly enough."

"Then you must beware of Merlin; with his devil's craft he always seems to find out what is going on."

"I do not fear Merlin," the other replied, and with that they parted.

King Pellinore and Nyneve continued their journey in the morning, and came to the well where Alyne had besought King Pellinore's aid. Of Alyne, all that remained now was her still beautiful head, with its long golden hair; of her lover, a mangled corpse, for they had been preyed upon by wild animals. King Pellinore was overwhelmed by remorse. "Alas! that I did not save them," he said.

"Why do you complain now?" asked Nyneve.

"Because she was young and beautiful, and it was in my power to save her, but I was too eager to accomplish my quest."

"Then why not take the remains of the knight to the nearest hermitage and have him decently buried, and yourself bear the head of the lady to King Arthur's court?"

They did this, and King Pellinore rewarded the hermit by allowing him to keep the knight's armor. They arrived at Arthur's court at noon on the same day and were received by the king and queen, who commanded King Pellinore to recount, under oath, all that had happened to him. When he had come to the end of his story the queen rebuked him for deserting the young noblewoman.

"Ma'am, I repent it," said King Pellinore.

"You have cause to," said Merlin, "for the young noblewoman, whose name was Alyne, was your own daughter by the Lady of the Rule; the knight, Sir Myles, was her betrothed, and they were on their way to Camelot to serve King Arthur, when he was treacherously attacked by Sir Lorayne. Now, it is ordained that you yourself shall be deserted by the man you have trusted most, at the moment of your death."

"May God show His mercy yet," King Pellinore responded.

King Arthur, now that the three quests were accomplished, established each of the knights of the Round Table with suffi-

cient lands and wealth to maintain the dignity of the fellowship;
and every time the feast of Pentecost came round, the oath was
renewed, which was: only to fight in just causes, at all times to
be merciful, at all times to put the service of ladies foremost.

4. THE WAR WITH THE FIVE KINGS

When King Pellinore, Sir Torre, and Sir Gawain had returned from their quests, Merlin fell deeply in love with Nyneve, whom King Pellinore had brought back to the court, and
who had formerly served the Lady of the Lake. Wherever
Nyneve went thereafter, Merlin followed, and Nyneve was at
first pleased by this, for she wished to discover from Merlin
the secrets of his magical crafts.

One day Merlin spoke to Arthur and told him that he was
leaving his court forever, because he knew that now his own
destiny, which was to be buried alive, was close at hand. He
then prophesied to Arthur the main events of his life, and
warned him never to part with his sword Excalibur or its
magical sheath; for Merlin knew that the woman Arthur most
trusted secretly hated him, and was planning to steal Excalibur
in order to bring about his destruction.

"Surely," said Arthur, "with your foreknowledge and magic
you can avert your own destiny?"

"That is not so," Merlin replied.

Merlin and Nyneve left Camelot together, and in the course
of their journey Merlin used every means in his power to persuade Nyneve to the act of love; but Nyneve had no intention
of losing her maidenhead to Merlin, and before long she forced
him to swear not to use his magic as a means of overcoming
her.

They traveled first to the court of King Ban at Benwick, in
France. King Ban was at war with his most formidable enemy,
King Claudas, and so Merlin spoke to his beautiful wife,
Elayne, and her young son, Launcelot. Elayne complained to
Merlin of the great damage done to them by King Claudas.

"Do not lose heart," said Merlin, "for within twenty years

your son Launcelot will inflict such a defeat on King Claudas
that all Christendom shall hear of it. Sir Launcelot and his son
Sir Galahad are destined to become the two most famous
knights of all time."

"And shall I live to witness their fame?" asked Elayne.

"You shall, and for many years afterward," Merlin replied.

Merlin and Nyneve took their leave of the queen, returned
to Britain, and then made their way slowly to Cornwall. As
they traveled, Merlin revealed to Nyneve many secret and
wonderful places, known only to himself and his initiates. But
Nyneve, growing weary of Merlin's persistent attentions, began to seek for a means by which to be rid of him. Finally,
when they had reached Cornwall, Merlin showed Nyneve a
secret underground cave, the entrance to which was closed by
an enchanted rock. Nyneve begged Merlin to move the rock
and lead her into the cave. Merlin did so, and Nyneve, instead
of following Merlin, replaced the rock, thereby imprisoning
him forever, and fulfilling his prophesied end. Nyneve herself eventually returned to King Arthur's court.

King Arthur, meanwhile, after holding a feast at Camelot,
had made his headquarters at Carlisle, where he received the
news that five kings, leading a formidable army, were invading
his lands. The kings were: the King of Denmark, the King of
Ireland, the King of Sorleyse, the King of the Isle of Lontayse,
and the King of the Vale.

"Alas!" said Arthur. "Since I was crowned king I have not
had one month of peace; and yet I cannot allow my loyal subjects to suffer these barbarous invaders."

First, King Arthur wrote to King Pellinore and begged him
to raise an army and come to his aid; then he let cry a general
call to arms, but many of his barons, resentful of being con-
tinually at war, failed to respond. Finally, Arthur spoke to
Gwynevere and asked her if she would consent to accompanying him on the campaign to give him fresh heart.

"My lord," she replied, "you know that my one desire is to
be with you, whether it is in peace or in war."

It was with a very small army, and only the most loyal of
his knights, that Arthur and Gwynevere marched north to meet
the invaders. They made their camp in the forest just below
the river Humber while waiting to be joined by King Pellinore.
However, their movements were observed by an enemy knight,
a brother to one of the five kings, who at once returned to them
and advised that they should attack Arthur without delay.
"For," he said, "Arthur's army is bound to increase, but now it

is so small that you might well defeat him." The five kings accepted this counsel, and at once started on a series of forced marches from the west of Britain to the river Humber, in the north.

One night when Arthur, in order to please Gwynevere, and Sir Gawain had disarmed, in spite of the timely warnings of Sir Kay, the alarm was raised of an enemy attack. "Alas!" said Arthur, "we have been betrayed." And just then a knight, himself seriously wounded, burst into the royal pavilion, and said with his last breath:

"Sire, we are lost: your army has been slaughtered in its sleep. Only flee, and save yourself and your queen."

At once, King Arthur, Queen Gwynevere, Sir Gawain, Sir Gryfflet, and Sir Kay, all of whom were now fully armed, slipped out of their pavilion, mounted their horses, and galloped to the banks of the Humber. There they found the waters raging as the result of a tempest.

"Now," said Arthur, "we have to choose between the fury of the waters and the fury of the enemy: which shall it be?"

"I would rather die in the water than at the hands of your enemies," said Gwynevere.

Just then, however, Sir Kay noticed that they had been pursued by the five kings, who were unaccompanied and charging at them with leveled spears. "Let us meet the five kings and overthrow them," he said as he pointed them out.

"That would be foolhardy," said Sir Gawain, "for we should be but four against five."

"If each of you will undertake to kill one of them, I will promise to kill two," said Sir Kay.

With that, he couched his spear and met the charge of the first of the kings, and killed him with a single thrust. King Arthur, Sir Gawain, and Sir Gryfflet followed, and each killed his man; Sir Kay then killed the last of the kings with his sword, chopping through both helmet and skull.

"That was well done," said Arthur to Sir Kay, "and I shall not forget you for keeping your brave promise."

King Arthur and his companions then set Queen Gwynevere on a bark, for she was still determined to return by water; and she too praised Sir Kay for his valor. "Sir, whatever woman may fail to recognize your worth, please remember that I shall always value you for keeping your promise today as a knight should."

Once the queen had embarked, Arthur and his knights returned to their camp and told the survivors how they had killed the five kings. "And now," said Arthur, "let us rest until morning. I believe that when the enemy hear the news of their disaster, they will be so dispirited that we shall be able to make short work of them."

King Arthur's judgment proved correct, and that morning they massacred the bewildered army of the five kings, to the number of thirty thousand. When the battle was over, Arthur humbly offered a prayer of thanksgiving for so easy a victory against such overwhelming odds, and then sent a message to his queen to rejoin him.

King Pellinore, having advised Arthur of his approach by a messenger, arrived the next day, and together they celebrated the victory. Arthur found that he had lost only two hundred men in all, eight of whom had been knights of the Round Table. On the site of the battle, Arthur founded an abbey, which he named the Abbey of the Beale Adventure. Meanwhile Arthur's enemies in the north and the west, hearing the news of the defeat of the five kings, were seriously discouraged.

When King Arthur had returned to Camelot, he asked King Pellinore for his advice on replacing the eight knights whom he had lost from the fellowship of the Round Table.

"Sire," King Pellinore replied, "I would advise that you take four of the older knights and four of the younger. For the older I would suggest King Uryens, who after all is married to your sister Morgan le Fay; Sir Hervyse de Revell, Sir Galagar, and the King of the Lake. For the younger knights I would suggest Sir Gawain, Sir Gryfflet, Sir Kay, and then either Sir Bagdemagus or Sir Torre. I may not recommend Sir Torre to you personally because he is my own son, but I would ask you to let his deeds speak for him."

Arthur agreed to King Pellinore's choice, and included Sir Torre in preference to Sir Bagdemagus. Consent was then obtained from Arthur's council and the knights installed in their seats; when this was done the name of each knight duly appeared at his place inscribed in gold letters.

Sir Bagdemagus, however, was furious at the preference given to Sir Torre, and at once left the court with his squire, determined not to return until he had won equal distinction. Riding through the forest he came upon a stone cross, and dismounted to offer up a prayer; as he did so his squire saw that a message for him had been inscribed on the cross in gold letters, which instructed him to meet and overcome one of the Round Table knights before returning to the court.

They continued their journey, and soon Sir Bagdemagus was vouchsafed the sight of a herb so holy that subsequently it was seen only by knights on the quest of the Holy Grail. Sometime later they came upon the cave in which Merlin was buried, and hearing his cries, Sir Bagdemagus tried to release him; but the stone was so large that a hundred knights together could not have moved it. Hearing his attempts, Merlin told him that the stone was enchanted and could be removed only by her who had replaced it, namely Nyneve.

Sir Bagdemagus continued on his adventures, and in time achieved the fame that he desired and was appointed a knight of the Round Table; but that is another story.

5. ARTHUR AND ACCOLON

It happened one day when King Arthur was chasing a hart, that he and two of his companions, King Uryens and Sir Accolon, being better mounted, outstripped the rest of the hunt by ten miles or so before their horses fell dead beneath them. King Uryens suggested that they should all go on foot in search of the nearest lodging; but the hart continued to limp along just ahead of them, weary as it was by now, and foaming at the mouth. They followed it to the shore of a lake, where it was set upon and killed by a brachet and some hounds. Arthur blew on his horn, and then flayed and quartered the beast.

Moored at the shore of the lake was a much decorated barge, hung with silk awnings down to the water line. Arthur looked inside and, seeing no one, suggested that they should rest in the barge overnight. It was now dusk, and as the three of them boarded, a hundred torches miraculously appeared, to illuminate the painted decks and richly furnished cabins. Then, as from nowhere, twelve maidens appeared, and, kneeling before Arthur, one of them addressed him by his royal title and begged that he and his companions should accept their hospitality, which, she promised, would be of the best. The maidens ushered them to the dining saloon, and as soon as they were seated at the long dining table, served them a veritable banquet of delicate meats and wines. When they were done, each of the knights was led to a well-appointed cabin to take his rest; and each, as soon as he lay on his couch, at once fell into a deep and enchanted slumber which lasted until morning.

King Uryens awoke to find himself in the arms of his wife, Morgan le Fay, at his quarters in Camelot. Since it had been a two-day ride from Camelot to the barge, he realized that his return could only have been made by means of an enchantment.

King Arthur awoke to find himself in a dark dungeon among some twenty fellow prisoners who complained bitterly of their fate. It was explained to him that some of the prisoners had been there for as long as eight years, in the course of which time eighteen had died from starvation and neglect.

In answer to his question as to the cause of their imprisonment, Arthur was told that the lord of the castle, Sir Damas, was a wicked knight who had wrongfully taken possession of his brother's estates after the death of their father. His brother, Sir Outlake, was an honest knight and had challenged Sir Damas to settle their differences by means of single combat, but Sir Damas, being too cowardly to accept the challenge himself, had adopted the practice of seizing errant knights and offering them the choice of imprisonment or championing his cause. Sir Damas was so hated that every knight so far had chosen imprisonment.

"May the Lord deliver us!" Arthur responded.

Just then one of the castle maids came to Arthur and, after greeting him, put before him this very choice.

"It is a hard choice to make," Arthur replied. "I should certainly prefer to die fighting rather than by starvation in this dungeon. However, I can only agree to fight if I am provided with a suitable horse and set of armor, and if all my fellow prisoners are released regardless of the outcome."

"That can be promised," said the maid.

"Tell me," said Arthur, "have I not seen you at King Arthur's court in Camelot?"

"No, sir," the maid replied; but she was lying, because in fact she served Arthur's sister, Morgan le Fay.

The maid reported Arthur's words to Sir Damas, who then sent for him, and seeing what an excellent champion he would make, agreed to his conditions, provided that Arthur undertook to fight to the death.

Sir Accolon awoke to find himself overhanging a deep well,

with a fountain in the form of a silver pipe through which the water flowed before splashing down onto a marble block. Realizing that at the slightest movement he would have fallen into the well, Sir Accolon gave thanks to God for his miraculous delivery, swore revenge on the maidens of the enchanted barge, and again prayed that King Arthur and King Uryens had likewise escaped disaster. Just then he was approached by a dwarf with a large mouth and a flat nose.

"Sir," said the dwarf, "I bring you greetings from your lady, Morgan le Fay. She bids you be of good cheer, for at dawn tomorrow you shall fight and overcome a knight whose death shall enable you to become king of the realm, with Morgan le Fay as your queen. In this way the agreement between you shall be fulfilled; and to assure your success she sends you King Arthur's own sword, Excalibur, together with the magic sheath. Fight bravely and all will be yours."

"Now," said Sir Accolon, "I understand the reason for my enchantment; tell your mistress that I send her my love, and that I vow not to fail her."

The dwarf departed, and not long afterward a knight, a lady, and six squires rode up to the fountain and invited Sir Accolon to their manor. Sir Accolon accompanied them on a spare horse, and when they arrived he was welcomed by Sir Outlake, who was the lord of the manor. Sir Outlake was wounded in both thighs as the result of a spear thrust which he had received while fighting a recent engagement, and when a messenger came to deliver Sir Damas' challenge to fight his champion at dawn the following day, Sir Accolon realized that this must be the knight whom Morgan le Fay intended that he should fight in fulfillment of their agreement; and therefore he at once offered to accept the challenge on Sir Outlake's behalf. Sir Outlake thanked him warmly, accepted the offer, and informed the messenger accordingly. Sir Accolon was not aware, however, that Sir Damas' champion was King Arthur.

After hearing mass and breaking his fast, Arthur was provided with a good horse and set of armor. He was about to enter the tournament field when a maid came to him and presented him with a perfect counterfeit of his own sword, Excalibur, and a message from Morgan le Fay: "Your sister sends you this sword for the sake of the love that she bears you." Arthur was completely deceived.

When the two champions met on the field, neither recognized the other; and amongst the spectators there was only one who knew the identities of both, and this was Nyneve. She loved King Arthur, and had come in order to save him if she could, having discovered Morgan le Fay's plot to have him killed.

The battle started with jousting, and at the first encounter both knights and horses crashed to the ground. As soon as the knights recovered, they drew their swords, and a deadly fight began. Before long Arthur suspected that it was his opponent, whose sword was identical in appearance to his, who was wielding Excalibur; for while his own blows were without effect, failing to pierce his opponent's armor, the blows that he was receiving wounded him every time. He became dizzy with pain, and the blood gushed from his wounds, as it would not have done if he had been wearing Excalibur's magic sheath. From both fear and anger he redoubled his efforts, and while he came near to stunning his opponent, each stroke served only to blunt his sword still further.

Sir Accolon was feeling triumphant, as blow for blow Arthur was wounded while he himself was almost undamaged. Several times he tried to taunt Arthur into yielding, but Arthur, in spite of his terrible sufferings, defied him, and Sir Accolon could not but admire his courage. Finally Arthur withdrew a little to recover, and begged leave to take breath, but Sir Accolon pursued him relentlessly and struck him hard on the helmet. Enraged, Arthur returned the blow with such force that his false sword broke at the hilt.

"Now yield, recreant knight!" said Sir Accolon, "or surely I shall kill you."

"Sir, I have sworn to fight to the death," Arthur replied, "and I should rather die a hundred times than break my oath."

"Then die you shall," said Sir Accolon as he rushed at him. The spectators were horrified to see Arthur, wounded and staggering as he was, face his opponent with a broken sword. However, Arthur withstood another tremendous blow on the helmet, and then, pressing his shield against Sir Accolon's body, jabbed him so hard with his broken sword that Sir Accolon reeled back for several paces.

Once more, Sir Accolon brandished Excalibur; but Nyneve, who had missed nothing, and whose heart was bleeding for Arthur, by means of a magic spell made it fly from his hand. Arthur leaped upon the sword where it fell, and the moment he picked it up, knew it for his own. Seeing the sheath still hanging from Sir Accolon's side, he suddenly wrenched it from him, and flung it far from them both.

"Sir, too long have I suffered from my own sword," he said, "but now you shall have a taste of it."

Therewith he dragged Sir Accolon bodily to the ground, tore off his helmet, and struck with all his might. As from a fountain, the blood flowed from every part of Sir Accolon's head: from mouth, ears, eyes, nostrils, and hair.

"And now," said Arthur, "I shall kill you."

"Sir," Sir Accolon gasped, "you have won the right to."

But at that moment, in spite of Sir Accolon's unnatural disfigurement and voice, Arthur thought that he recognized him.

"Sir, please tell me your name and where you are from, and how you came to possess the magical sword Excalibur."

"Sir, I am called Sir Accolon and I come from the court of King Arthur. My paramour, Morgan le Fay, stole Excalibur from King Arthur and gave it to me to assure my success in killing Sir Outlake's opponent, whose death, she maintained, would clear the way for her to kill both her husband, King Uryens, and King Arthur himself, by which means I should then rule over his realm with her for my queen. But the plan has gone sadly astray; and because of your terrible valor, not only shall I never rule, but I doubt if I shall live to see my paramour again. But please tell me, most invincible knight, who are you?"

"King Arthur."

"Alas, my liege! I should have known. I beg you to forgive me, and to believe that although I agreed to your death, I did not know that it was you whom I was fighting."

"Sir Accolon, although you have plotted against my person, I believe that you have spoken the truth, and I forgive you. But my sister Morgan le Fay, whom I have honored more than any living person except for my queen, I shall never forgive; and on her I swear the most terrible vengeance."

King Arthur then summoned Sir Damas and Sir Outlake and revealed to them his true identity and that of Sir Accolon, and how they had come to fight each other. He then proceeded to pass judgment on the two brothers.

"Sir Damas, you have proved yourself to be both cowardly and treacherous, and therefore you shall yield to your brother not only his own rightful estates, together with all their appurtenances, but all of your own estates as well. You shall release and fully compensate all of your prisoners for the damage you have done them. Your brother will provide you with a palfrey each year, and upon that you shall always ride, for only true knights should ride coursers. Finally, if any word of complaint about your behavior ever reaches me, I shall have you summarily executed, so beware!

"Sir Outlake, you are known for an honorable knight, and I charge you to enter my service, where I promise you will find excellent opportunities for winning both fame and wealth."

"Sire," Sir Outlake replied, "it will be an honor to serve such a liege as yourself, and I thank you for your judgment. I am grateful that on account of the wound in my thighs it was not I who fought you today."

"Indeed I should have suffered less if you had," Arthur replied. "Now tell me, how far are we from Camelot, and is there a lodging nearby? For I am much in need of rest."

"Sire, Camelot lies two days' ride from here, but there is a wealthy abbey only three miles hence, where the nuns will take good care of you."

King Arthur then took his leave of the company and, together with Sir Accolon and Sir Outlake, rode to the abbey, where their wounds were skillfully treated by a surgeon, and where the nuns nursed them tenderly. Soon Arthur began to recover, but Sir Accolon died four days later from excessive loss of blood. By Arthur's command his corpse was conveyed to Camelot on a horse litter, and taken into the presence of Morgan le Fay, to whom the bearers delivered this message: "Herewith is a gift from King Arthur to his sister. He informs her that he has recovered Excalibur and its sheath and is aware that she stole it from him."

Morgan le Fay, meanwhile, supposing that Arthur would be killed on the appointed day, had sought for an opportunity of getting rid of her husband, King Uryens. Finding him asleep in his bed one afternoon, she ordered her maid to fetch his sword for her. The maid, however, terrified of her mistress' intentions, went first to Sir Uwayne, their son, and after waking him, warned him to go secretly to his father's chamber, in order to prevent his assassination. Sir Uwayne sped to the chamber, and had successfully hidden himself when the maid, still quaking with fear, delivered the sword to her mistress. Sir Uwayne watched his mother raise the sword to behead the sleeping king, then leaped out from his hiding place and seized her.

"Fiend!" he shouted, "how can I recognize in you the

mother who bore me? And yet were it anyone else I should kill him this instant."

"My son!" she exclaimed, "spare me, I beg you. For one moment I must have fallen prey to the devil's command; but only forgive me, and keep the secret so that our name shall not be dishonored, and I swear that never again shall I be so tempted."

"And I thought it was Merlin who was the one supposed to be born of the devil! Well, after the oath you have sworn, I must agree to take no action this time, and shall say nothing."

It was just after her attempt to murder her husband that Morgan le Fay received the corpse of her mutilated lover. She could barely control her grief at the sight of it; but then, receiving Arthur's message, she was inspired with a cold and merciless anger. Taking good care to hide her feelings, she presented herself to Queen Gwynevere, and begged in her sweetest tones for leave to ride with an escort to Arthur, for whom, she said, she had important tidings.

The queen gave her consent when Morgan le Fay insisted that the tidings were urgent. Summoning her escort, Morgan le Fay then set off for the abbey, determined to do to Arthur what harm she could.

Riding all day and all night, she reached the abbey at noon the next day, and demanded, as Arthur's sister, to be admitted to Arthur at once. While humbly acknowledging her rank, the sisters pleaded that the king was asleep for the first time in three days and three nights.

Morgan le Fay then commanded that none but herself should be admitted to him before he awoke, and was directed to his chamber. She found him asleep with the naked Excalibur grasped in his right hand. Cursing silently, she looked about for the scabbard, and finding it, concealed it beneath her gown before leaving. Morgan le Fay then summoned her escort and rode away from the abbey.

Arthur was enraged when he discovered that Morgan le Fay had succeeded once more in stealing Excalibur's scabbard, and after complaining that he had not been properly watched over, demanded that the two best available horses should be saddled immediately. The sisters excused themselves on the grounds that they could not countermand his sister's orders, and the horses were prepared.

Taking Sir Outlake with him, Arthur set off in pursuit of his sister. They had not ridden far when they came upon a cowherd taking his ease by a stone cross. In answer to Arthur's question, the cowherd replied that he had seen Morgan le Fay, together with an escort of forty men. Arthur and Sir Outlake galloped off again in the direction he had indicated.

When Morgan le Fay saw that she was being pursued by Arthur and Sir Outlake, and that they were gaining upon her, she rode up to the shore of a lake and threw the scabbard into the water; being heavy with gold and jewels, it sank immediately. When this was done she led her escort into a rocky valley, and by means of an enchantment, made the whole party indistinguishable from the rocks.

When Arthur and Sir Outlake entered the valley and found it apparently deserted, they gave up the pursuit and searched about for the scabbard. Failing to find this too, they rode back sorrowfully to the abbey, and Arthur swore again to revenge himself upon his sister.

Morgan le Fay revoked the spell as soon as their pursuers had gone, and asked if any of her men had seen them. "I did," one of them replied, "and Arthur's countenance was so wrathful that, disguised as I was, I shook for fear of him."

"I believe you," said Morgan le Fay.

The party continued on their journey, and before long they came upon two knights, one of whom was leading a horse to which the other was bound hand and foot.

"Sir, what will you do with your prisoner?" asked Morgan le Fay.

"My lady, I shall drown him in the well, for he is guilty of committing adultery with my wife."

"Indeed," said Morgan le Fay, and then to the captive: "Sir, what is your version of this story?"

"The charge is untrue," the knight replied.

"Then tell me, what is your name, and whence have you come?"

"Sir Manessen is my name. I am cousin to the noble Sir Accolon, and King Arthur is my liege."

Thereupon, Morgan le Fay ordered her men to release the prisoner and bind up his captor instead, and drown him in the well. When this was done she said:

"Sir Manessen, do not suppose that it is for your sake that I have saved you, no, but for the sake of Sir Accolon, who is dead, and whom I loved. Now, I bid you, go to King Arthur and tell him that I, his sister, Morgan le Fay, while I am an enchantress, do not fear him; furthermore, that the damage I have done to him so far is nothing to what I will do yet, when the time comes."

In spite of her words, however, Morgan le Fay then prudently led her escort to the country of Gore, where she knew she would be well received and where, should Arthur attack her, she could command several towns and castles in her defense.

6. GAWAIN, UWAYNE, AND MARHAUS

When King Arthur's wounds were finally healed, he left the abbey and returned to Camelot, where he was joyfully received by Queen Gwynevere and the nobles of his court. He recounted all his adventures since he had left, and when he came to disclosing that it was Morgan le Fay who had plotted his death, many of the knights grew indignant and demanded that she should be burnt for her evil sorcery. Then Sir Manessen arrived and repeated to Arthur Morgan le Fay's defiant message.

"Such is the gentle nature of .ny sister," said Arthur. "But do not doubt that when the time comes for my revenge, it will be so terrible that all Christendom shall hear of it."

The next morning a maid arrived at the court, bearing a mantle of magnificent appearance, being wrought throughout with precious stones. Arthur was entranced with it, and the maid said:

"Sire, I bring this mantle to you from Morgan le Fay, who begs you to accept it as a gift; and she promises that you shall be fully recompensed for every offense she has given you."

Before Arthur had time to reply, Nyneve drew him aside and spoke to him privately:

"Sire, I beg you to take my advice and let no man in your court touch this mantle until Morgan le Fay's maid has herself worn it."

"I will do as you advise," Arthur replied, and turning to the maid, commanded her to wear the mantle.

"Sire," she said, "this is a garment intended for a king.

Surely it would be unseemly for a servant such as myself to wear it?"

But Arthur insisted, and the maid put the mantle over her shoulders. She had no sooner done so than she burst into flames, and in a moment was reduced to ashes.

Arthur's rage was terrible to see as he addressed King Uryens, who was standing just by him. "Sire, it seems that my sister, since she became your wife, has determined to destroy me; and I am bound to suspect both you and your son Sir Uwayne of being accomplices. However, since Sir Accolon confessed to me before he died that she was also plotting your death, I will consider you innocent; but your son remains suspect, and I cannot risk the threat to my person which his continued presence at the court must offer. Therefore I now banish him."

Sir Gawain, who was cousin-german to Sir Uwayne, as soon as he heard of Sir Uwayne's banishment declared: "Whoever banishes my cousin banishes me too." And so when Sir Uwayne departed, Sir Gawain joined him, and they rode off into the forest together. Sir Gawain's departure was felt keenly by the other knights of the Round Table; and Gaheris, Sir Gawain's brother, summed up 'he general feeling when he commented: "And now, for the love of one knight, we have lost two."

Meanwhile, Sir Gawain and Sir Uwayne had spent their first night at an abbey, and the next day continued their journey through the forest until they rode onto the grounds of a castle, which was situated in a valley. The castle gate was guarded by two knights, and twelve maids were to be seen busy about their domestic tasks. Before long the cousins noticed that each time any of the maids passed by a certain tree from which was hung a white shield, she would spit at the shield, or else throw dirt at it. Riding up to one of them, Sir Gawain inquired the cause of this curious behavior.

"Sir," the maid replied, "there is here a knight whose name is Sir Marhaus, son of the King of Ireland. Although he is a man of great prowess, he despises the service of our sex, and therefore we revenge ourselves on him in this way."

"But I know Sir Marhaus," said Sir Gawain. "He is a splendid knight; I myself watched him at a tournament where he defeated all comers. I do not believe for one moment that he despises your sex, and that if here he seems to do so, there must be an excellent reason for it."

Sir Gawain and Sir Uwayne withdrew a little, and then saw Sir Marhaus himself ride out from the castle gate. The maids scattered in all directions, falling over each other in their anxiety to escape him, and then one of the guards shouted a challenge. They jousted, and the guard was killed at the first encounter; the second guard repeated the challenge, and was likewise killed. Sir Marhaus then rode up to the shield, which was utterly filthy by now, and said to himself: "At least I have revenged myself for the despoilment of my shield; but take it I must for the sake of my sovereign lady."

He then rode up to Sir Gawain and Sir Uwayne, and asked what had brought them to the castle. They replied that they had come in search of adventure.

"Adventure you shall have in plenty," he replied, "if you will allow me to fetch a new spear."

"I think," said Sir Uwayne, when he had gone, "that he is too good a knight for either of us."

"Nonsense!" Sir Gawain replied. "Anyhow, it would be a shame for us not to joust with him."

"Very well, then," said Sir Uwayne, "I will joust with him first; but if he kills me, you must avenge my death."

Sir Marhaus reappeared and Sir Uwayne jousted with him, with the result that he was flung from his horse and wounded in the left side; his own spear had broken on Sir Marhaus' shield. Then Sir Gawain jousted with him and was also flung from his horse, but immediately he leaped up and, drawing his sword, rushed at his opponent on foot. Sir Marhaus also drew his sword and galloped at Sir Gawain.

"Dismount! or I shall kill your horse," Sir Gawain shouted.

"You speak justly," Sir Marhaus replied, and dismounted.

They fought all day, and during the morning Sir Gawain's strength increased, until at noon it was three times as great as it had been when they started. In after years only six knights were to defeat Sir Gawain at the peak of his strength, and these were: Launcelot, Tristram, Bors, Gaynes, Percivale, and Pelleas.

However, as evening drew on, Sir Gawain's strength began to wane, and all the time Sir Marhaus grew stronger. They were both liberally wounded, and at last Sir Marhaus called a truce.

"Sir, today you have proved that your strength is formidable, but I see now that it is beginning to fail you; since we have no quarrel, I would suggest that we stop before one of us is seriously wounded."

"Sir," Sir Gawain replied, "I thank you for being the chivalrous knight that you are."

Then both of them threw off their helmets and kissed and swore to love each other like brothers. Sir Marhaus invited the cousins to lodge with him that night, and the three of them rode off together.

"Tell me," said Sir Gawain, "how it is that a knight such as you should come to despise the service of ladies?"

"Sir, it is only at the castle we have just left that I shun them; for there they are nothing but a bevy of mischievous witches whose one care is to lure innocent knights into their castle, and then, by depriving them of their manhood, reduce them to pitiful cowards. Elsewhere, I certainly serve ladies as a knight should."

For a week the three knights remained at Sir Marhaus' small priory, while recovering from their wounds. When he discovered that the cousins were related to King Arthur, Sir Marhaus did all in his power to prove himself worthy as their host. At the end of the week, the cousins begged to take their leave, as they were anxious for further adventure.

"Let us not take leave of each other here," said Sir Marhaus, "but rather allow me to accompany you through the forest, which hereabouts is well known to me." For a week the three knights rode through the forest together, and then they came to a part known as the Forest of Arroy.

"Here," said Sir Marhaus, "is a country which no knight ever rode through without meeting some unlikely adventure."

They were riding upstream through a valley, and when they came to the spring they found a well with three noblewomen seated on it. The eldest wore a garland of gold in her hair, and was aged about sixty; the next wore a circlet of gold in her hair, and was aged about thirty; the youngest wore a garland of flowers in her hair, and was aged about fifteen. When the knights and the noblewomen had exchanged greetings, Sir Gawain asked them why they were seated on the well.

"We are waiting for three errant knights whom we shall instruct in the paths of adventure," the eldest replied. "And if each of you will choose one of us, the three couples can set off in different directions, and meet again at this well in a year's time."

"That is well spoken," said Sir Marhaus.

"Since I am the youngest," said Sir Uwayne, "I shall choose the eldest of the ladies, of whose ripe experience and wisdom I stand the most in need."

"For myself," said Sir Marhaus, "I would choose the lady whose age lies between those of the other two."

"And I," said Sir Gawain, "am then left with the lady who is both the youngest and the most beautiful, and whom certainly I would have chosen."

After kissing each other farewell and swearing to reunite at the well in a year's time, the three couples each went their way: Sir Uwayne and his lady to the west; Sir Gawain and his lady to the north; Sir Marhaus and his lady to the south.

At the end of the first day, Sir Gawain and his lady lodged with an elderly knight, who promised that on the following day he would lead them to witness a strange spectacle. When the time came their host led them to a stone cross at the edge of a plain where they met a knight of noble bearing, but seemingly overwhelmed by grief. He saluted them, and Sir Gawain returned the salute, wishing him honor and fame.

"Alas, good knight," Sir Pelleas replied (for that was his name), "the more honor I win, the more cruelly do I have to suffer."

Before he could say anything further, however, ten knights drew up on the plain, and faced them with leveled spears; Sir Pelleas charged at them. He jousted with each of the knights in turn, and without even breaking his spear, flung each from his horse. But when he had done this he dismounted and stood like a statue while they bound him hand and foot, lashed him to his horse's belly, and so made off with him.

"For the love of Jesus!" Sir Gawain exclaimed, "how strange that after overcoming them all he should allow them to do that."

"It is strange indeed," his host assented.

"Sir, I think that you should go to his rescue," said the young noblewoman.

"I think," said Sir Gawain slowly, "that he cannot wish me to do for him what he could have done for himself."

"More probably," said the young noblewoman, "you are afraid to try."

While they were talking a knight and a dwarf rode out of the forest. Both were fully armed except for their helmets; the dwarf had a large mouth and a short nose. A young noblewoman followed almost immediately, and the dwarf said: "Ah! here comes our lady; now why do we not ask the knight at the cross to settle our dispute for us?"

The three of them then rode up to Sir Gawain, and begged him to decide whether the knight or the dwarf should henceforth accompany the young noblewoman. "If I am to judge this matter," Sir Gawain replied, "will you swear to abide by my judgment?"

They all swore to do so, and then Sir Gawain told the young noblewoman that it was she who must choose between them.

"I choose the dwarf," she replied.

And so the young noblewoman and the dwarf rode off together, the dwarf shouting for joy; and the knight rode off alone, groaning dismally. They had no sooner gone than two more knights appeared from the forest, and on seeing Sir Gawain, one of them shouted: "Sir Gawain, of the court of King Arthur, I challenge you."

Sir Gawain couched his spear and they charged at each other. Both were flung from their horses, and so they drew their swords and began to fight on foot.

Meanwhile the other knight addressed himself to the young noblewoman, and suggested that she should leave Sir Gawain and allow himself to become her protector.

"That I will do gladly," she replied, "since Sir Gawain was too cowardly to rescue a knight who, after fighting off ten of his enemies, allowed himself to be taken prisoner by them, strapped shamefully to his horse's belly. Let us go at once while those two are still busy fighting."

For many hours Sir Gawain and Sir Carados, his opponent, tested each other; but in swordplay as in endurance, they seemed to be equally matched. At last, by common consent, they ceased, and Sir Carados invited Sir Gawain to lodge with him for the night; Sir Gawain accepted, and they rode away together.

"Sir, can you tell me," Sir Gawain asked, "what you know of a knight who today, after overcoming ten opponents in jousting, allowed them to carry him off as a prisoner?"

"Sir, I will tell you his story," said Sir Carados. "His name is Sir Pelleas, and as you have seen, he is one of the ablest knights living; but some time ago he had the misfortune to fall in love with the great heiress, Lady Ettarde, who was far too proud to accept him. Instead she proclaimed a three-day tournament with a gold circlet for the prize, to be offered by the winner to the most beautiful lady present.

"Five hundred knights, all of them of renown in this country, competed in the tournament, and Sir Pelleas proved himself the champion beyond all doubt. For three successive days he fought twenty knights each day and defeated them all. He was awarded the prize and at once offered it to Lady Ettarde, although she was by no means the most beautiful woman present; she accepted the circlet but was still too proud to accept Sir Pelleas as her paramour.

"Disregardful of the scorn which her refusal of Sir Pelleas excited among her peers, she then did everything to drive him from the country, but Sir Pelleas was not to be shaken so easily, and he still lodges in a small priory near to the castle, and continues to petition her humbly. Every day she sends her knights to challenge him, in the hope that one day he will be killed, but always, as you saw today, he defeats them, but then allows them to drag him back to the castle in order that he can set eyes on her once again. And today, had he been challenged with the sword, after jousting, you can be sure he would have got the better of them; for such is the quality of the man."

"It is a shame," said Sir Gawain. "Do you think that to-morrow we could seek him out? for I should dearly like to help him."

The next day Sir Gawain and Sir Carados found Sir Pelleas, as grief-stricken as ever, and when they had exchanged greet-ings, he told Sir Gawain the story of his unhappy love, which Sir Carados had told him on the previous day.

"And did I not love her so much," he concluded, "I would prefer to die a hundred times over rather than suffer as I do; but always I hope that one day she will take pity on my suffer-ing, and reward my constancy with as much tenderness as she now shows cruelty. She knows well that her own knights will not easily defeat me, and that willingly I would fight them to the death if in that way my cause could be won."

"Sir, you must not allow your grief to overwhelm you," said Sir Gawain. "Rather let us plan how we might win the lady; for I am here to pledge myself to your aid, and I will undertake anything within my power to bring this about."

"Then tell me, sir, what is your name, and from whose court do you come?"

"My name is Sir Gawain; I am the son of King Lot of Lowthean and Orkney; my mother is Margawse, sister to King Arthur; and King Arthur is my liege."

"My name is Sir Pelleas and I am a lord of the Isles. Sir Gawain, I will gladly accept your help, for I have never loved a woman before, and since you are of royal blood I know that you can be trusted not to betray me. You can see how hopeless my case is: In order to see my lady at all I have to allow her knights to drag me into her presence as a prisoner; and then she abuses me shamefully, and has me flung out again. She will not even keep me as a prisoner."

"Well," said Sir Gawain, "this is what I suggest: that we

exchange armor and that I ride to the castle and tell Lady Ettarde that I have killed you. Then I will teach her to love, winning her first for myself, and, once her heart is unfrozen, you will appear as from the dead. Then, surely, she must return your love for all the suffering that she has caused you."

The two knights swore oaths of loyalty to each other and exchanged their armor. Sir Gawain rode to Lady Ettarde's castle, but before he had reached the pavilions outside, the lady herself caught sight of him and fled. Sir Gawain cried out to her:

"My lady, this is another knight, not Sir Pelleas."

"Then take off your helmet, and show yourself," she replied.

Sir Gawain did so, and when the Lady Ettarde saw him, she invited him into her castle, asked him his name, and whether in fact he had killed Sir Pelleas. Sir Gawain told her his name and swore that he had killed Sir Pelleas.

"Then you are my deliverer," she said. "It is a pity, in a way, for Sir Pelleas was certainly an able knight, but I could never endure for one moment his terrible insistence. Henceforth, good Sir Gawain, please know that I am yours to command."

In the hours that followed, Lady Ettarde did all in her power to please Sir Gawain, and at last he confided to her that he loved a lady who was indifferent to him.

"Indeed, she is to blame," said Lady Ettarde with spirit, "for there can be no woman in Christendom of whom you are not worthy, with your royal blood and noble deeds to recommend you."

"Would you swear, then," said Sir Gawain, "by the faith in your body, to do your utmost to make her mine?"

"Certainly I will swear to do so," she replied.

"Very well, then. Now I must tell you that it is yourself whom I love, and whose indifference I cannot endure; and since you have sworn, I would hold you to your oath."

"I have no choice," Lady Ettarde replied, "and therefore I yield myself to you, gentle knight, to take what pleasure shall be yours."

It was the month of May, and Lady Ettarde had set three pavilions outside her castle: one for three of her knights, with their squires, one for four of her maids, and the third for herself, now to share with Sir Gawain. For three nights and three days Sir Gawain and Lady Ettarde companied in love; but on the third night, as it drew toward dawn, Sir Pelleas appeared in their tent, and watched grimly as the lovers slept in each other's arms. Under his breath he cursed them: "Alas! that ever so false a knight was born," he whispered.

Sir Gawain had sworn to return to Sir Pelleas within twenty-four hours, and Sir Pelleas had waited as day succeeded night, and night day, until, no longer able to contain himself, he had ridden to the castle. First he had seen the knights in their pavilion, then the maids in theirs, and finally he had come to the lovers.

Sir Pelleas thought that his heart would burst for grief and for anger; but at last he left them and rode slowly through the forest for half a mile or so, when he was suddenly overcome by his rage and turned back, resolved to kill them both. Once more he watched them as they lay peacefully in each other's arms, and he whispered to himself: "No! even now I cannot betray the high order of knighthood by killing them in their sleep." And so he rode again into the forest, but again returned, and this time drew his sword. Instead of killing them, however, he placed it naked across their throats; after that, he rode furiously until he came to his own pavilions, where he told his knights and squires all that had happened.

"And now," he concluded, "I am going to lie on my bed, never to rise again. In return for your faithful service, I charge you to divide my possessions amongst yourselves. But when I am dead, you must cut the heart out of my body, and, placing it between silver platters, present it to the Lady Ettarde with these words: 'A gift from Sir Pelleas, who watched you asleep in the arms of your lover, the traitor Sir Gawain.'"

When Lady Ettarde awoke and found the sword, she recognized it at once as belonging to Sir Pelleas, whereupon she roused her lover, saying: "Sir Gawain, this is the sword of Sir Pelleas whom you have betrayed; and if he had been such a knight as you are, he would have killed us both. As it is, I am dishonored in my own household." Sir Gawain made no reply, but strode from the pavilion, mounted his horse, and galloped away.

It so happened that the sorceress Nyneve was riding through the forest not far from Sir Pelleas' pavilions, when she came upon one of his knights wandering on foot, alone and bewildered. She halted to ask him the cause of his distress, and the knight replied that he was grief-stricken on account of his master, Sir Pelleas, whose story he then told her. "Take me to him," she commanded, "and I promise that I will cure Sir Pelleas of his despairing love, and Lady Ettarde of her savage pride."

When Nyneve saw the noble Sir Pelleas lying on his bed, resigned to death, she was deeply moved. First, she cast a spell over him, so that he fell into a deep slumber, and then, commanding that none should wake him until her return, rode to the castle to fetch the Lady Ettarde.

Two hours later when Lady Ettarde, over whom Nyneve had cast another of her spells, beheld the sleeping knight, she exclaimed: "How strange! I seem to see Sir Pelleas as for the first time, and I feel for him such a love as I have felt for no man hitherto; and to think that up to now I found him unendurable!"

"So have the heavens judged you," said Nyneve.

At that moment Sir Pelleas awoke, and seeing Lady Ettarde, was filled with an unconquerable hatred. "Vilest of women!" he exclaimed, "leave me, and may I never set eyes on you again!"

"Sir Pelleas," said Nyneve, "take to your horse and ride from this country if you would find the woman whom you will love, and who will return that love."

"I will gladly do so," Sir Pelleas replied, "since the lady of this country has shown me only evil."

"And now you may thank me," said Nyneve. As soon as Sir Pelleas had given the command for his retainers to follow with his possessions, he and Nyneve rode off together. Before long he discovered that it was she whom he was destined to love, and who was to return that love; and thereafter their lives belonged to each other. As for the Lady Ettarde, she died of a broken heart not long after they left.

Sir Marhaus and his lady, who had taken the southerly route, rode through dense forest all the first day, and that night, coming to a small courtyard, asked the laborer who owned it for lodging. The laborer refused them, but added that if they wished it, he would take them to the duke's castle where they could be certain of being lodged, although at a certain risk to themselves.

"What risk do you speak of?" asked Sir Marhaus.

"That you will discover when you get there."

"Very well, then," said Sir Marhaus, "lead on, for we are both weary, and so are our horses."

The laborer led them along a lane, and an hour later they came to the castle, where he roused the porter and asked if the knight and the lady could stay for the night. "I will ask the duke," said the porter.

"Certainly they can stay for the night," said the duke, "although tomorrow they may repent it."

The porter took a torch and led Sir Marhaus and his lady into the castle, where many knights and ladies greeted them. When their horses had been stabled, they were presented to the duke, who asked Sir Marhaus his name and from whose court had he come.

"My name is Sir Marhaus, and I come from the court of King Arthur."

"That is unfortunate," said the duke, "because I am a sworn enemy of King Arthur, and all his fellowship of the Round Table. Tomorrow you will have to do battle with me and my six sons."

"All together?" asked Sir Marhaus.

"Yes, all together," the duke replied. "Since Sir Gawain killed my seventh son I have been waiting to meet a knight from King Arthur's court and revenge myself on him."

"Tell me, sir, what is your name?" asked Sir Marhaus.

"The Duke of South Marches."

"Ah yes! I have heard of you."

"Tonight you may take your ease in my castle, and you shall want for nothing; tomorrow we shall fight to the death." And with that Sir Marhaus and his lady were led to their chambers.

In the morning, after mass and breakfast, Sir Marhaus armed and rode into the courtyard to encounter the duke and his six sons, who were to prove no match for him. First the duke and his sons all charged Sir Marhaus together, but they succeeded only in breaking their spears on him; next the sons charged at him in pairs, and with the same result. Then Sir Marhaus, starting with the duke, charged at each of them separately, and sent each crashing to the ground, half stunned by the collision. After this, Sir Marhaus swiftly dismounted and rushed upon the duke, who was still dazed, brandishing his sword. He commanded him to yield, but as he did so two of the duke's sons recovered and made at him.

"Sir, command your sons to yield also; otherwise I shall kill you immediately, and all your sons after you."

The duke, aware that Sir Marhaus was capable of making good his threat, yielded at once, and commanded his sons to do likewise. All together, they knelt before him and offered Sir Marhaus their swords by the hilts. Sir Marhaus commanded them to swear allegiance to King Arthur at the next Pentecost.

Sir Marhaus and his lady left the castle, and his next adventure was a tournament held by Lady Vawse, in which he defeated forty knights in combat, and won the prize of a gold circlet worth forty bezants.*

They continued their journey south, and two weeks later came to the castle of the young Earl Fergus, who had only lately come into his inheritance, and who at that time was plagued by a giant who was ravaging his estates and terrorizing his people. The earl welcomed Sir Marhaus to his castle and, before long, told him of the terrible giant.

"Does he fight on horseback or on foot?" asked Sir Marhaus.

"On foot; no horse is large enough to bear him."

"Then I shall fight him on foot."

The next morning Sir Marhaus, with an escort provided by the earl, set off to fight the giant, whom they found sitting beneath a holly tree, his huge iron-bound clubs and battle-axes within easy reach. Sir Marhaus drew his sword, and then raised his shield to defend himself, as the giant struck at him with a club; however, the blow sent the shield flying in fragments from his hand. Sir Marhaus was now in danger of his life, but he fought courageously with his sword, and, not before receiving some terrible injuries from the club, finally succeeded in dismembering the giant's right arm at the elbow. The giant roared and fled through the forest with Sir Marhaus in close pursuit. They came to a river and the giant, with his great height, was able to wade in far out of Sir Marhaus' depth. Sir Marhaus at once ordered his escort to collect some stones, and with these he pelted the giant until he staggered, fell into the water, and was drowned.

Sir Marhaus and his escort rode to the giant's castle and there released twenty-four knights and twelve ladies whom the giant had taken prisoner. Sir Marhaus then helped himself to the castle treasure—enough to make him a wealthy man to the end of his days—and finally returned to the earl's castle. The earl offered Sir Marhaus half his estates in gratitude for his deliverance from the giant, but Sir Marhaus refused on the grounds that he had won sufficient treasure from the giant's castle; however, he remained as the earl's guest for six months while recovering from his wounds.

At the end of the six months, Sir Marhaus and his lady took their leave of the earl. In after years the earl was to serve Sir Tristram, and Sir Tristram was to kill the giant's brother,

*Bezant: a coin originally minted in Byzantium, of varying value, approximately equal to a gold sovereign ($2.80) today.
(Editor's note)

Taulas, in Cornwall. On their return journey, Sir Marhaus and his lady met with both Sir Gawain and Sir Uwayne; and then with four more knights from King Arthur's court, with each of whom Sir Marhaus jousted, and each of whom he overthrew; their names were Sir Sagramour, Sir Ozanna, Sir Dodynas, and Sir Phelot.

Sir Uwayne and his lady had ridden to the west of Britain, and Sir Uwayne's first adventure was a tournament in which he overcame thirty competitors and won the prize of a falcon and a fine white courser with gold trappings. After several minor adventures, Sir Uwayne's lady took him to visit the Lady of the Roch, who at that time was being imposed upon by two brothers: Sir Hew and Sir Edwarde of the Red Castle, who had extorted from her, and were holding by force, estates which formed a large part of her inheritance.

"My lady," said Sir Uwayne, when he had heard her story, "as I am a knight of King Arthur's court, so will I win back your lands for you. If in a parley they refuse to honor their knightly vows, then by force of arms I shall make them to yield to you what is yours."

"May God reward you!" the lady replied.

The brothers were summoned and appeared in the morning in force with a hundred armed retainers. Fearing treachery, the Lady of the Roch would not allow Sir Uwayne to parley with them in the open, but insisted that he should speak to them through the tower window.

In spite of Sir Uwayne's eloquence, the brothers, Sir Edwarde and Sir Hew, remained defiant, and said merely that what they had won they would keep.

"I am here to champion the lady's cause," said Sir Uwayne. "Therefore you must decide between you who is to champion your cause, and settle the matter in single combat."

"That we shall not decide," said Sir Hew, "for if you are to champion the lady, you will have to fight us both together."

"Both together, then," said Sir Uwayne.

Arrangements were made to insure against treachery on either side; and that night Sir Uwayne dined well and took his ease in the castle. In the morning he rode onto the plain and there confronted the two brothers.

First Sir Edwarde and Sir Hew charged Sir Uwayne simultaneously, but both broke their spears on him; then Sir Uwayne charged each separately, and flung each from his horse. Drawing their swords, all three fought like men possessed for the next five hours. The Lady of the Roch, watching anxiously from the tower window, thought again and again that Sir Uwayne must collapse from his wounds. Finally Sir Uwayne killed Sir Edwarde with a stroke that split his head down to the vertebrae. Sir Hew lost courage and faltered, and Sir Uwayne set on him ferociously, and would have killed him too, had he not then dropped to his knees and begged for mercy. Sir Uwayne granted it, and they walked together into the castle.

Sir Hew was heartbroken about his brother's death; he swore to return to the lady all of her estates, and to yield to King Arthur at the next Pentecost. Sir Uwayne was seriously wounded, and for six months remained with the Lady of the Roch while he recovered. Then it was time for him and his companion to retrace their steps to the well.

Sir Gawain, Sir Marhaus, and Sir Uwayne met at the well on the appointed day, and there parted from their ladies (except for Sir Gawain's, who had deserted him earlier). The three knights rode off together and before long were met by a messenger summoning them to King Arthur's court. King Arthur, sadly missing the two cousins, had sent these messengers off a year ago to scour the country for them and repeal the banishment.

And so, twelve days later, Sir Gawain, Sir Uwayne, and Sir Marhaus, who had agreed to accompany them, arrived at the court and were warmly welcomed by King Arthur. Under oath, each recounted his adventures.

At the feast of Pentecost Sir Pelleas and Nyneve also arrived, and were welcomed by King Arthur. The usual tournament was held, and Sir Marhaus and Sir Pelleas proved themselves the champions, whereupon Arthur made them both knights of the Round Table, since two knights had been killed in the course of the year.

Sir Marhaus, in after years, was to fight with Sir Tristram and be killed by him, but not before wounding Sir Tristram so seriously that it was to take him six months to recover in a nunnery. Sir Pelleas was to become one of the four knights to achieve the quest of the Holy Grail. Nyneve, ever anxious for him, was always to prevent his fighting Sir Launcelot, who was to be the most powerful knight of all time. Meanwhile, Sir Pelleas was never able to forgive Sir Gawain for betraying his love for the Lady Ettarde; and often at tournaments, while stopping short of killing Sir Gawain, he would punish him severely on this score.

The Tale of King Arthur and the Emperor Lucius

King Arthur and Gwynevere, his queen, and the knights
of the Round Table were holding a feast at Camelot on the
day when twelve ambassadors arrived at the court with a
message from Lucius, the Roman Emperor. The feast was to
celebrate Arthur's recent victories over the most formidable of
his enemies in Britain and France, and in honor of Sir Launcelot and Sir Tristram.

The ambassadors knelt before Arthur and delivered their
message. It was a demand for the tribute which Rome was
accustomed to levy on Britain as a subject kingdom. Although
Arthur remained silent while the ambassadors spoke, his anger
was betrayed by the expression in his gray eyes, and soon the
ambassadors were trembling for fear of him.

"Sire, we beg you to spare us. In delivering this message we
do no more than obey the commands of our own liege, the
Emperor Lucius."

"Cowards!" said Arthur contemptuously. "If it is my looks
you fear, I can assure you I have warriors in this hall whose
one glance would frighten any of you out of an earldom!"

"Sire, pray be merciful! I admit that it was your stern
countenance that robbed us of our courage for a moment. But
to continue the message: The tribute demanded by our Emperor is in accordance with the statutes laid down by Julius
Caesar, the first Roman to conquer Britain; and it has been
paid by every British monarch since, and without question,
including your own father, King Uther. Therefore we claim

that the Emperor's demand is a just one, and we have to warn you that should you refuse to yield, our imperial armies will invade your kingdom and annex the whole of it to Rome."

"Well spoken! But in spite of your solemn warning I shall first consult my subject sovereigns and councilors of state, and only in seven days' time give you my final decision. Meanwhile you shall be accommodated at our court as befits your rank."

At this there was a commotion among the younger knights of the Round Table, who demanded that the ambassadors should be summarily executed for bearing a message so insulting to their king. Arthur, however, silenced them at once, with the command that the slightest insult or injury to the ambassadors would be punishable by death, and then commanded Sir Clegis to insure their comfort and honorable treatment throughout their stay. Sir Clegis performed his office well, and the ambassadors were greatly impressed by the dignity and wealth of Arthur's court.

Meanwhile, Arthur summoned his councilors and commanded that each should speak freely what was in his mind. Sir Cador of Cornwall spoke first:

"Sire, the Emperor's message pleases me well; for just now we are rested, and a war against Rome would give us the opportunity of winning more wealth, and fresh glory for Britain."

"Sir Cador, I love you for your words," Arthur replied. "And let us now consider the precedents: I have learned from the chronicles of our land that the title of Roman Emperor has in the past been held by us. First by Sir Belyne and Sir Bryne, over a period of a hundred and sixty years between them; then by Constantine, and lastly by Lady Elyneye's son, who also recovered from Rome the Cross upon which our Lord was crucified. These men are our ancestors, and therefore I propose that we can justly reclaim the title for ourselves."

King Angwyshaunce spoke next: "Sire, lead us against Rome, and I will provide an army of twenty thousand. You are the only just king, and under your rule we have prospered. Under Roman rule we suffered ignominiously. Our nobles were ransomed, and when unable to pay the enormous sums demanded, forfeited with their lives."

Then King Little of Brittany: "Sire, defy the Romans, and I will provide an army of thirty thousand. I shall never forget how the Viscount of Tuscany ransomed my knights when I was passing through Point Tremble on a pilgrimage, and how even the Pope refused me redress."

Then Sir Ewayne, a relative of Arthur, who, with his son Idres, ruled Ireland, Argayle, and the Outer Isles:

"Sire, make war on the Romans, and we with our army of thirty thousand will march with you through Lombardy and Melayne, through the valleys of Point Tremble and Vyterbe, into Rome itself, and there vanquish them forever."

Then the young and eager Sir Launcelot: "Sire, I command an army of twenty thousand, and we will readily fight to the death in your service, although my own lands would be the first to suffer from an invasion."

Lastly Sir Badouin of Brittany: "Sire, make war on the Romans, and I swear you my allegiance and that of my army who number ten thousand."

"My lords," King Arthur replied, "I thank you all for this proof of your loyalty; and now I am confident that we can make this proud Emperor repent of his message."

At the end of the seven days Arthur summoned the ambassadors:

"Gentlemen, here is our answer to the Emperor Lucius: that we, with our subject kings of fifteen realms, shall forthwith march upon Rome. We shall march through France and Alemaine, across the Alps, through Lombardy—to shake the walls of proud Milan—and thence to Rome, to make ourselves masters and claim our traditional title of Emperor. And in Rome we shall hold our next feast for the knights of the Round Table.

"For yourselves, these are your instructions: that you shall embark from the port of Sandwich within seven days. Wattling Street is to be your route, and from it you must not depart, but rest at night wheresoever you find yourselves. If you disobey, not all the gold in Christendom will pay your ransoms."

"Sire, this is hard indeed, that we should have to flee without even the security of a safe passage."

"You shall have safe passage," Arthur replied.

The ambassadors accomplished their journey. First Sir Cador accompanied them to Carlisle; thereafter, by changing their horses at every town, they arrived at Sandwich on the seventh day. That night they embarked for France, and once aboard, felt grateful as never before for having escaped with their lives. They rode straight overland to Rome and there delivered Arthur's dispatches to Lucius.

On reading the dispatches Lucius grew speechless with rage, and once again the ambassadors trembled in fear of their lives. At last Lucius managed to speak.

"How can this king dare to defy us—he alone, when every other king throughout Christendom pales at the very mention of our imperial name?"

"Majesty, speaking for ourselves, we would not, for all the realms under your sway, venture to Britain again; we were grateful enough to escape with our lives. Arthur is a most formidable king, his court lacks neither wealth nor etiquette, and in the fellowship of the Round Table he commands a chivalry which is unsurpassed. We believe that his threat to invade Rome and win the title of Emperor for himself, which he claims to have been held by his ancestors, is a very real one. We beseech your majesty therefore to marshal the forces at your disposal in defense of the empire, and especially to man the mountain passes between Alemaine and Lombardy."

"Have no fear," Lucius replied. "Our armies shall not stay at the frontiers, but shall invade and lay waste the whole of France. And for our spearhead, we shall have the Giants of Geen, each one of whom is worth a hundred of the knights of the Round Table."

Lucius then commanded his most experienced ambassadors to negotiate with each of his subject or allied rulers for assistance in the war. The ambassadors set forth to Ambage and Arryke; to Ertayne and Elamye; to the Outer Isles, Arrabe, Egypt, Damask, and Damyake; to the kings of Tars and Turkey; Pounce and Pampoyle and Preter Jones' Land; also to the Sultan of Surre; from Nero to Nazareth, Garesse to Galey, from Cyprus to Macedonia, from Calabe to Catelonde and Portugal.

And the ambassadors did their work well: No less than sixteen kings with their armies mustered beneath the imperial flag, and fifty of the Giants of Geen, who were so huge that no horse could carry them.

Lucius led his armies, which stretched sixty miles in marching order, across the Alps and into France where he captured the castle of Cullayne and garrisoned it with Saracens. He then divided his command and arranged that the two columns should join at Barflete in Normandy, the purpose of this being to enable them to lay waste the greatest possible area as they advanced. Lucius chose for himself the route through Brittany.

King Arthur, meanwhile, had convened a parliament at York, to follow the octave of St. Hilary; and there he announced his intention of making war on Lucius and recovering the title of Roman Emperor. In the course of the debate it was decided to commandeer all ships for the conveyance of the armies abroad from Sandwich in fifteen days. During Arthur's campaign, Sir Constantine was to be chief of the affairs of state, and Sir Badouin his principal adviser. Except for Sir Carados, who was Sir Constantine's father, Sir Constantine was Arthur's nearest of kin.

During the fifteen days while the armies were being mobilized Sir Tristram unaccountably returned to King Mark in Cornwall. Sir Launcelot in particular was furious at this, but was unaware that Sir Tristram was moved to do so by his love for the beautiful Iseult, King Mark's wife.

On the eve of Arthur's departure, Gwynevere was overcome by grief and fainted. Her ladies-in-waiting carried her up to her chamber, and Arthur enjoined Sir Constantine to give her his special care during his absence.

When all his armies were drawn up, and before giving the order to march, Arthur bade farewell to Sir Constantine and announced, in the hearing of all, that should he fail to return from the campaign Sir Constantine was to succeed him to the throne.

The embarkation at Sandwich was impressive for the large number and variety of ships, among them broad-beamed carrack and swift, many-oared galleys; for the thousands of horses, resplendent in their harness; the colored pavilions, gleaming suits of armor, and well-polished weapons. The troops were lined up along the quay beneath their own flags and awaiting grimly the battles that lay ahead; and most conspicuous among them were the knights of the Round Table, all eager to win glory.

The fleet set sail that night, and Arthur, asleep in his cabin, was disturbed by a strange dream. He watched a dragon flying across the sky from the west, and its appearance filled the onlookers with awe. The head shone like blue enamel, the shoulders like gold, the belly like mail, and the tail was multicolored and with jagged points at the edges. The feet were covered with sable and the claws were of gold. From the jaws issued flames at each breath. Meeting the dragon from the east was a terrible bear, huge and black as a storm cloud, with paws staunch as posts, fur shaggy, and gait shambling. As he moved he uttered a dreadful roar.

Twice the dragon attacked the bear, rising up to a tremendous height and then swooping down with outspread claws and fiery breath. The bear resisted the first attack and wounded the dragon with his tusks, so that the blood spurted all over him and down into the sea beneath. But with the second attack the dragon ripped the bear from head to tail, and then burnt him to ashes which were blown away by the breeze.

On waking, Arthur summoned a soothsayer to interpret the dream. "Sire, have no fear. The dragon was yourself, its colors representing those of the armies you lead, and the jagged tail your knights of the Round Table. The bear was some tyrant whom, in the near future, you shall fight and overcome, thereby delivering your people."

It seemed that the soothsayer was to be right, for not long after Arthur had encamped at Barfleet, where he was welcomed by his loyal nobles whom he had summoned at Christmas, a local squire begged to speak to him.

"Sire, I have come to beseech your aid. For seven years now our country has been terrorized by one of the Giants of Geen. In this time he has eaten more than five hundred of our children, and only last night captured the Lady Howell, in spite of her escort of five hundred knights, who were powerless to rescue her. She is the wife of your kinsman, Sir Howell of the Hend; and you can be sure that once he has despoiled her, he will eat her as he has all his other captives. We beg you, therefore, as our sovereign protector, to deliver us."

"Alas! I would give my kingdom to have saved her. But tell me, where is this giant to be found? For certainly I shall challenge him."

"Sire, do you see the hill in the distance with two fires burning at the top? That is St. Michael's Mount, and there you will find the giant. Also more treasure than in all the provinces of France put together."

"Enough!" cried Arthur, "I am already grieved; please speak no more."

Arthur summoned Sir Kay and Sir Bedivere and warned them that they were to make a private pilgrimage to St. Michael's Mount that night, and that they were to be well armed and mounted.

The three knights set out at dusk; Arthur was clad in his jazerant and basinet, and carrying his broadest shield. The birds were still singing as they rode through the beautiful countryside; and when they arrived at the small promontory, they all dismounted and Arthur ordered his companions to await his return. Alone, he strode up the craggy hillside, and was grateful for the mild sea breeze. Soon he reached the first of the fires and saw, not far from it, two wells and a newly dug grave. By one of the wells a widow was seated, and wringing her hands with grief.

"Madam, pray tell me, what is the cause of your grief?"

"Sir, please lower your voice or we will be overheard. I am mourning for the Lady Howell, despoiled and killed last night by the Giant of Geen. But why do you come here, alone and armed as for battle?"

"Madam, I come on behalf of King Arthur and his people to challenge this giant."

"You have no chance: the giant could kill fifty like you with his bare hands. The most powerful kings in the country go in fear of him, and only recently sixteen of them donated their beards as a tribute, in the hope that he would spare their lands and their people. But he simply used them to make a fringe for the coverlet of his bed. He has more wealth than the whole nobility of France, and this coverlet is wrought throughout with precious stones. Your only hope would be to offer him Gwynevere, King Arthur's wife, for it is in the hope of capturing her that he has come to live on the mount. However, tonight his supper is already under preparation: six children are roasting on the spits, turned by three maids. When they are ready he will eat them with spices and wash them down with precious wines. Then he will despoil the maids; they have not more than four hours to live."

"I thank you for your warning, but still I shall challenge him," said Arthur.

"You will find him by the next fire, and God's speed!"

The giant was crouching by the fire to warm his haunches; he was entirely naked, and chewing on a man's leg. As the widow had described it, the children were being roasted on spits turned by the captive maids.

"You murderous freak!" Arthur shouted. "I have come to avenge the Christian children you have gorged yourself on, and their martyred parents, also the Lady Howell. So be ready to die."

The giant glowered. He was more horrible than Arthur could have believed possible, with his fiendish countenance, houndlike fangs, and huge, ungainly body, more than thirty feet tall. Snatching an iron club, the giant rose to his full height and brought it crashing down on Arthur's helmet, which fell to the ground in splinters. Covering himself with his shield, Arthur struck at the giant's head, but failed to reach it. The giant lunged again with his club, but this time Arthur neatly sidestepped him, and with an unexpected thrust, severed the giant's genitals. The giant roared with pain and struck out blindly, but succeeded only in tearing up great clods of earth. Arthur next thrust at his belly, and managed to slit it open so that the nauseous bowels slithered to the ground. Hurling away his club, the giant seized Arthur bodily and threw him, breaking several ribs as he did so. At this a wail of dismay arose from the maids, who flung themselves on their knees in prayer. As the combatants struggled they came to the edge of the hill and started rolling down, over the rough boulders and through the bushes. Arthur managed to draw his dagger, and drove it again and again between the giant's ribs, and by the time they reached the bottom of the slope—at the very point where Sir Kay and Sir Bedivere were still waiting—the giant was dead.

"God save us!" exclaimed Sir Kay. "Our king has been killed by this giant, and now surely it will be our turn."

"Not so!" Arthur shouted cheerfully. "I have just dragged this saint down from his retreat at the top of the hill; but now help me, I pray you."

"What a foul monster it is!" said Sir Bedivere as he extricated Arthur from the dead giant. "If such are the saints in God's heaven I should prefer not to go there."

Arthur laughed. "This saint was certainly near enough to sending me to heaven just now—the worst I have met since I was in Egypt. But now cut off the head and set it on a spear shaft and let your squire, who is well mounted, take it to Sir Howell, who deserves to see it first. After that we can set it on a cairn at Barfleet so that the country people can rejoice. Then would you mount the hill and fetch my sword and shield, also the giant's club and the coverlet lined with beards, for those are the souvenirs I want for myself. For yourselves, take what treasure you will, and the rest we will divide equally among our followers, so that none shall have cause to complain."

When this was done, Arthur and his companions returned to the camp. The news of Arthur's victory spread quickly, and soon people from far and near were hastening to give thanks to Arthur for their deliverance. "Thank the Lord, not me," Arthur replied to them all, and subsequently gave orders for a church to be built on the Mount of St. Michael.

The following morning Arthur struck camp and marched his proud army through the open country, and at nightfall camped in a valley. Two messengers arrived from the Marshal of France and reported to Arthur that Lucius had advanced through Burgandy, laying waste all before him, and that the nobility of Paris had fled in terror to the Rhone valley and the lowlands, and would resist Lucius only if Arthur himself supported them.

Arthur summoned Sir Bors: "Sir, take with you Sir Gawain, Sir Bedivere, and Sir Lyonel, and as many more knights as you think you may need; and ride to the Emperor Lucius and in my name command him to withdraw from France. Warn him that if he refuses he will have to do battle with my armies, which he will not overcome as he has the defenseless civilians of this land in his advance so far."

Lucius had camped in a broad meadow by a stream, and Sir Bors, overlooking the camp from some nearby wood-lands, could not but admire the many-colored silk pavilions, the Emperor's own being marked by a standard bearing the imperial eagle. Sir Bors divided his small army, leaving half in ambush under the command of Sir Lyonel and Sir Bedivere, while with Sir Gawain and the other half, he galloped down to the camp. Riding straight to the Emperor's pavilion, Sir Bors boldly announced himself.

"Majesty, I bring you a message that will displease you. My liege, King Arthur, is marching upon Rome to claim his ancestral title of Roman Emperor. He commands you to withdraw from France, and warns you that if you fail to do so, you will be forced to give battle to Arthur's armies, which will destroy you as easily as you have destroyed the defenseless civilians in your advance through this country so far."

"You deliver your message in accordance with your instructions, doubtless, and certainly it does not please us. Give our greetings to King Arthur and report to him that our imperial armies shall continue their invasion up to the Seine, and beyond: to the banks of the Rhone."

Then Sir Gawain spoke privately to Sir Bors. "The Emperor's words ill become such a coward! I should take more pleasure in fighting him than in ruling the whole of Normandy."

"And I, than in ruling the whole of Brittany and Burgandy," Sir Bors responded.

They were overheard by Sir Gainus, a nephew of the Emperor, who commented: "How these Britons boast! Anyone would think they had the whole world to wager."

Sir Gawain was furious, and drawing his sword, beheaded

him. He and Sir Bors then galloped their men out of the
Roman camp, and across the open country to the woodlands
where Sir Lyonel and Sir Bedivere awaited them. They were
closely pursued by a squadron of Romans, and so they turned
about just outside the woods where Sir Bors met the first of
the Roman knights, one clad entirely in golden armor, and
killed him with a spear thrust through the bowels.

A lively skirmish followed and five thousand of the enemy
were killed, including two distinguished officers: Sir Calle-
borne, who fell to Sir Bors, and Sir Feldenake, who fell to Sir
Gawain. The Romans retreated slowly, and sent a dispatch
rider to warn the Emperor to call out reinforcements. Then
Sir Lyonel and Sir Bedivere broke their ambush, and a further
ten thousand of the enemy were killed before they had reached
their own camp. Once there, however, they were joined by
the reinforcements, and soon the British found themselves in
difficulties, with both Sir Berell and Sir Bors taken prisoner,
so Sir Gawain gave the command to withdraw, and then consulted his fellow commanders.

Sir Idres, the son of Sir Ewayne, was the first to speak up.
"My lords, never, while I command five hundred good men,
will I allow Sir Berell and Sir Bors to be held captive by the
Romans. Further, while I am alive, I would never dare to
confront King Arthur with such shameful tidings."

"Sir Idres, you speak as a knight should," Sir Gawain re-
plied, "and like one worthy of your great father and country.
Very well, then, we shall resume the battle until both Sir
Berell and Sir Bors have been recaptured."

Sir Gawain and his fellow commanders led their men into
battle once more, and in the first fury of their attack, killed
or wounded a large number of the enemy, and took prisoner
many distinguished officers. Sir Gawain recaptured Sir Bors,
and Sir Idres recaptured Sir Berell. But once more the numer-
ical superiority of the Romans enabled them to recover; and
a senator succeeded in seriously wounding Sir Gawain, and
would have killed him had not Sir Idres come to his rescue
and taken the senator prisoner. Sir Gawain then gave the
order to withdraw, and sent a dispatch rider to Arthur to
report the day's work.

Arthur was delighted with the news of the successful skirmish, and with the many prisoners taken, but deeply anxious
about Sir Gawain's wound. As soon as Sir Gawain returned,
Arthur embraced him and wept over him, and swore that

should he fail to recover, he would put to death all the prisoners.

"Sire, I shall certainly recover, and to kill the prisoners would be a shame," Sir Gawain responded. That night Arthur and his fellowship of the Round Table made merry over the exploits of Sir Gawain and his fellow knights.

At dawn the next day Arthur commanded Sir Launcelot to march their prisoners to Paris, and there deliver them into safekeeping. To accompany him, Arthur had also summoned Sir Bedivere, Sir Bors, Sir Bryan, Sir Cador, Sir Clegis, Sir Cloudres, and Sir Clarrus; and among them they were to insure that the prisoners were not recaptured by the Romans. Sir Launcelot set off at once with the prisoners and an army of ten thousand.

Lucius, meanwhile, having received intelligence of the expedition from one of his spies, decided to ambush them at Troyes, whither he sent an army of sixty thousand under the command of the King of Libye, with the Sultan of Surre, the Senator of Sawtre, Sir Edwarde, and Sir Edolf as assistant commanders.

Aware of the likelihood of an enemy ambush, Sir Launcelot halted outside the woods at Troyes, and ordered Sir Cador, Sir Clegis, and Sir Claryon to make a reconnaissance. As soon as the three knights entered the woods they realized that the enemy were present in large numbers, and Sir Clegis was unable to resist shouting a challenge:

"Is there any knight here who dares to encounter a knight of the Round Table?"

"Look who comes, thinking he is going to conquer the world!" shouted an enemy earl, who, however, remained in his place of concealment.

"Coward!" Sir Clegis replied. "It is Sir Clegis, of ancient and noble lineage, who offers this challenge, and it is no idle one."

"Fine words! But this time we shall let you go free," the hidden earl responded.

The three knights then galloped back to Sir Launcelot and reported the estimated number of the enemy, and suggested that they should attack. Sir Launcelot resolved to do so, and was supported by Sir Bors, who added: "Let us win glory for our king, who will reward us with honors and lands; and the devil take the hindermost!"

Sir Launcelot ordered Sir Berell, Sir Bedivere, and Sir

Edwarde to guard the prisoners and, in case of a reverse, to
retire to a small castle and send to Arthur for deliverance.
He then formed up his cavalry on a front of five hundred
and gave the order to attack. He was supported by Sir Hecti-
mer, Sir Jonek, Sir Aladuke, Sir Hammeral, Sir Hardolf, Sir
Harry, and Sir Harygale.

The Romans formed up behind the King of Libye, who galloped out to meet the British and, in the first encounter,
killed Sir Berell with a spear thrust through the throat.

"Alas for my cousin!" said Sir Cador, and dismounting,
took him in his arms and gave him into the keeping of his
men. Then the King of Libye triumphed over him: "There
is one proud knight who will trouble us no more."

"May God help me to overthrow that king!" said Sir Cador.

"He will," Sir Launcelot replied grimly.

Sir Launcelot, Sir Cador, and Sir Bors made three sorties
together, and among them killed a hundred enemy knights.

"Aha! so you have indeed revenged your fellow!" said the
King of Libye.

As the battle grew fiercer, the Romans and their allied
Saracens lost heavily, and at last the King of Libye determined
to redress the balance. First he killed Sir Aladuke, Sir Her-
wade, and Sir Harygale, then seriously wounded Sir Lyonel,
Sir Lovell, Sir Clegis, and Sir Cleremond—and would have
killed the last two had not Sir Launcelot come to their rescue.
It was then that Sir Cador saw his opportunity for revenging
his cousin, Sir Berell, and, charging at the king, dashed out his
brains with a blow on the helmet.

Incensed by the death of his commander-in-chief, the Sultan
of Surre reformed his Saracens for a fresh attack. However,
he was met by Sir Launcelot and Sir Bors, and before long
five thousand Saracens lay dead or dying. Sir Edwarde, a
Roman captain, and two Roman earls were taken prisoner by
Sir Kay; the Senator of Sawtre was taken prisoner by Sir
Cador; and finally the sultan himself by Sir Launcelot. After
that the Romans and Saracens took to their heels, and all were
killed, except for a few who got away in time to take refuge
in a small castle.

It was during this battle that Sir Launcelot first established
his immense renown as a warrior. Although he was young, and
but recently knighted (together with Sir Bors and Sir Lyonel),
no enemy knight had been able to withstand him, and he had
struck awe and wonder into the hearts of his comrades and
the enemy alike.

Once the battle was over, Sir Launcelot collected his dead and sent them under escort to Arthur for proper burial. He then resumed his march to Paris, where he handed over the prisoners, and after refreshing himself with the cool wines of that city, returned to Arthur's camp without further adventure.

Arthur welcomed the returning army with open arms, and embraced each of his knights. "Surely, no king has ever had such knights as I!" he exclaimed.

"Sire," said Sir Cador, "while I think I can say honestly that none of us failed in this expedition, there is one among us who is surely the finest knight living: I mean Sir Launcelot."

"That is true," Arthur replied.

When Sir Cador told Arthur the casualties they had suffered, Arthur wept bitterly, and said:

"You realize that your courage might have been your undoing? That often it is folly not to retreat when you find yourself fighting against overwhelming odds?"

"And yet to retreat may also be folly," said Sir Launcelot; "for it is a shame which surely no knight can outlive."

Both Sir Cador and Sir Bors agreed with Sir Launcelot.

Lucius, meanwhile, was giving audience to a Roman knight who had escaped from the battle at Troyes.

"Majesty," he said, "I beg you to withdraw from France while you may. Whereas we can overrun the civil population easily enough, once we face King Arthur, we find that every one of his knights is worth a hundred of ours."

"For shame!" cried Lucius. "Much as I grieve for my losses, I grieve much more to hear such cowardly words."

Lucius then called a council of war, and it was decided to advance to the valley of Sessoyne, following a powerful advance guard under the command of Sir Leomye.

News of the Emperor's plans reached Arthur through one of his spies, and he decided to forestall him. Arriving at Sessoyne first, he divided his command between himself and Sir Cador, and then disposed the forces so that each of the strategic points should be manned. Arthur was supported by Sir Launcelot, Sir Bors, Sir Marroke, and Sir Marhaus; Sir Cador by Sir Kay and Sir Clegis.

Lucius, as soon as he reached the valley, realized that he was surrounded and, as far as he was able, arranged his forces to correspond with the enemy dispositions. He then addressed his whole command. "Romans, today you will fight a battle in which many of you will die. But remember that the glory of Rome is founded on her armies. Take courage and fight as Romans have always fought, and the day shall be ours!"

Then the eagles were unfurled, the trumpets sounded, and battle was joined.

The first Briton to distinguish himself in the battle was Sir Vyllers, who had sworn to kill the Viscount of Rome. He had been ambushed near enough to the Romans to overhear the Emperor's speech, and the moment the trumpets sounded he charged down upon them, bearing proudly his shield with its dragon device, and, leveling his spear, made straight for the viscount and ran him through. Meanwhile furious volleys of arrows were flying in both directions from the British and Roman archers.

Sir Launcelot and Sir Ewayne both attacked the Emperor's bodyguard, and both succeeded in killing standard-bearers and capturing their standards, which they presented to Arthur. Sir Launcelot had also killed Sir Jacounde, a Saracen noble.

Sir Bors killed three Roman knights, and then one of the ugly Giants of Geen. Arthur, seeing the great effect these giants were having on his army—killing men and horses at a single blow of their clubs—decided to lead an attack upon them. At the first encounter he chopped off a giant's legs at the knees. "You bare-legged churl," he muttered, "now you are more of a size!" He then swiftly beheaded him. Arthur's followers set to with a will: Sir Launcelot, Sir Cador, Sir Kay, Sir Gawaine, Sir Ector, Sir Lyonel, Sir Ascamore, Sir Marhaus, and Sir Pelleas; and within a short time all fifty of the giants were hacked to pieces.

While Arthur now attacked the Roman center, forcing them to the defensive, Sir Kay, Sir Clegis, and Sir Bedivere attacked the flank, and before long five hundred Romans were fleeing before them. Following an engagement with the King of Ethiope, Sir Kay was critically wounded by a common soldier; before sinking to the ground, however, he managed to kill the soldier, saying as he did so: "Now at least you shall not outlive me!"

Seeing their comrade fall, Sir Clegis and Sir Bedivere fought with fresh fury, like greyhounds slaughtering hares; but as soon as they had won a brief respite, they took Sir Kay in their arms and carried him to Arthur.

"My liege," said Sir Kay, "for long I have served you, and now I must die. I beg you, commend me to your excellent queen, Gwynevere; and to my wife, who has never caused me a moment's anger, and ask her to pray for my soul."

"But you must not die!" said Arthur, weeping, and with his own hands withdrew the spear shaft. Then, taking him to his pavilion, he ordered his surgeon to examine the wound. The surgeon was able to report that the bowels, liver, and lungs were all uninjured, and that he might recover. "Now," said Arthur to Sir Kay, "I shall avenge you," and, filled with sadness and rage, returned to the battle. Thirty times Arthur rushed upon the enemy, and each time men and horses fell to the terrible blows he delivered with his sword Excalibur.

Sir Launcelot, Sir Gawain, and Sir Lovell attacked the Emperor's bodyguard, who had formed up a little aside from the main press of the battle. Lucius, seeing Sir Gawain, taunted him: "Welcome sir! If you are looking for trouble you will certainly find it here; and I think you will not for long withstand our person and bodyguard!"

Sir Launcelot, furious at the taunt, rode up to Lucius and struck him on the helmet—a blow which brought the blood streaming down to his feet. Sir Gawain attacked the bodyguard and killed three Saracen princes, and Sir Lovell killed a king and a duke, both famous men.

Lucius and his bodyguard now became the focus of the battle. First, a Roman commander, seeing the danger to his Emperor, led his squadron into the attack and inflicted heavy casualties on the British; and Sir Bedivere was stunned, and would have been killed had not Sir Launcelot and Sir Lovell come to his rescue. Then Arthur, who had been assisting certain of his knights who were more remarkable for their wealth than their valor, decided to leave them to their fate and join the battle around the Emperor. With great skill and daring he rode straight through the bodyguard and up to Lucius, who met him with a sword thrust and wounded him on the cheek. Arthur responded with a blow on the helmet which split open both head and neck, and Lucius fell dead at Arthur's feet.

The most important of Arthur's knights now rallied round him, and before leading them into the final attack, Arthur addressed them as follows: "My lords, in honor of Sir Kay and Sir Bedivere, who have both fallen in this battle, I exhort you not to spare the enemy. Do not for the sake of a ransom take any prisoners, but kill them, kill them all, Christians and heathens alike."

Grimly, Arthur's commanders obeyed their liege, and slaughtered over a hundred thousand of the disheartened enemy; only a few thousands, who fled opportunely, escaped with their lives.

The battle over, Arthur collected and buried his dead, each according to rank, and ordered his surgeons to attend the wounded. Arthur always employed the finest surgeons, and spared no expense to insure that as many as possible of his own wounded should recover. Both Sir Kay and Sir Bedivere were successfully healed.

The enemy dead, apart from the Emperor Lucius, included the Sultan of Surre, the kings of Ethiope, Egypt, and India; seventeen other kings, and sixty Roman senators. Arthur decided to have them embalmed with proper ointments and sixty layers of linen, and then placed in open coffins with their shields on their breasts so that the identity and rank of each should be clearly visible.

When three ambassadors arrived from Rome, Arthur pointed out to them the corpses, now arranged in chariots:

"My lords, please accompany these corpses to Rome, and there tell your Potentate that this is the tribute offered to Rome by King Arthur of Britain; that we believe this sufficient to meet the present demand, and the arrears which have accumulated over the last sixty years. If, however, the Potentate considers it insufficient, we promise faithfully to increase the tribute in kind when we march upon Rome itself, which we shall do in the course of the next few weeks."

The ambassadors departed with the train of corpses, and duly delivered Arthur's message, together with details of the battle in which the Romans and their allies had been so roundly defeated.

Arthur continued his campaign, marching by Lushburne through Flanders, Lorraine, Alemaine, Lombardy, and thence into Tuscany. Throughout each town and country Arthur re-established British dominion, but the first city in Tuscany was well garrisoned, and defied him. He rode out, unarmed, before the city gates, and demanded capitulation; Sir Florens was anxious for his safety.

"Nonsense," Arthur replied. "These Tuscans will never resist a truly anointed king!"

The Tuscans refused to yield and a battle ensued. Arthur won his way through the outer defenses and on to the bridge, but from there was unable to break through the massive fortifications of the town walls. On the advice of one of his subordinates, Arthur withdrew to the outer defenses, in order to devise a more effective siege.

Then Sir Florens warned Arthur that their provisions had
fallen dangerously low, and suggested a foraging party. Arthur
agreed and appointed Sir Florens commander with Sir Gawain,
Sir Wysharde, Sir Walchere, Sir Clermount, Sir Clegis, and a
captain of Cardiff as subordinates.

The party set off, and after riding all day through forests,
over hill and heaths, came that night to a meadow, filled with
flowers, where they camped.

Sir Gawain rose at dawn the next day, and rode off alone
in search of adventure. He had just ridden through a wood
and come to a river when he saw, riding along one of the
banks, a splendid-looking knight accompanied by a page who
carried his spear. The knight's shield was inlaid with gold and
silver and jewels, and the main device was three griffins worked
in sable. Gripping his spear in readiness, Sir Gawain challenged the knight to make known his name and his allegiance.
The knight answered in his native Tuscan, "Robber! proudly
you bear yourself, but your challenge can lead only to your
destruction."

"Sir, proudly you speak; but look to your arms, or else you
will be destroyed." And with that they both couched their
spears and charged.

Both succeeded in driving their spears through the bright
armor of the other, and into the flesh by a hand's breadth.
Then they set to with their swords, and their fury was such
that it seemed as if their helmets were on fire.

Finally Sir Gawain broke through his opponent's shield,
and cutting through the mail of his corslet, exposed both liver
and lungs. The unknown knight then wounded Sir Gawain in
the shoulder, with a blow that penetrated to the bone. He
paused for a moment and warned Sir Gawain that he must
bind the wound immediately if he was not to die from it, as
he was fighting with a magic sword.

"By God!" Sir Gawain replied, "you will not get the better
of me in that way. If you wish to yield, do so, and then only
will I bind my wound."

"Brave knight! I insist that you shall have succor for your
wound; in return you shall make me a Christian, that I may
learn to repent of my evil ways hitherto."

"Sir, happily I shall do as you ask; but pray tell me who
you are, who is your liege, and how you come to be riding
alone on this quest."

"Sir, I am called Sir Priamus, and am heir to the Great
Alexander of Africa and the Outer Isles, an overlord to whom

many kings pay tribute. My father is a great prince, and through him I am related to Ector, to the Duke Josue, and to Judas Maccabeus. In the past my father has often revolted against Rome, invading her territories and striking terror into her armies. But in this war we are allies and I, with my father's consent, am leading a hundred and forty knights. Hitherto I have acknowledged no man my equal, but today, after fighting you, I know better; and so I beg you to tell me your name and your allegiance."

"Sir Priamus, I am no knight, but was brought up to be a humble valet to the noble King Arthur; I cared for his arms and his wardrobe, and those of his barons and earls. However, at Yole, his majesty was pleased to make me a yeoman and give me a hundred pounds, together with horse and armor. And now, if I have served my liege well, I am pleased enough."

"Sir, I pray you tell me your name. I cannot believe that you are only a servant. If Arthur's servants are all like you, what then must his knights be like?"

"Sir Priamus, I will deceive you no longer; and you must not be ashamed of your defeat at my hands, for surely God lent me strength to serve His own purpose. I am called Sir Gawain, son of King Lot of Lowthean and Orkney. My mother is Margawse, sister to King Arthur, and King Arthur himself has made me an earl. I am one of the knights of the Round Table and, in my own land, thought not unworthy of the arms I bear."

"Sir Gawain, your answer pleases me better than if I had won the whole kingdom of Africa, for surely I would rather have been torn to pieces by wild horses than defeated by a mere servant or yeoman-at-arms. But now that we are reconciled, I must warn you of the dangers that beset us. Within hearing distance of your page's horn (so do not let him blow it) lies an army of sixty thousand under the command of the Duke of Lorraine, including his own chivalry, which is the finest in the country. Also are the kings of Sessoyne and Southelonde leading their Saracens; the Duke of the Dutchmen, the Earl of Ethelwolde, Sir Ferraunte of Spain, Sir Cheldrake—and all with their followers. Also some of the Giants of Geen and my own squadron, who will, I trust, change their allegiance as I have, to King Arthur. But it is a formidable army; and should they discover us, they would show no mercy, but hack us to pieces, regardless of what ransom we might offer."

Taking his bearings from the river, Sir Gawain led Sir

Priamus back to the meadow where Sir Florens and his party
were camped. They were all in high spirits until Sir Wycharde,
glancing up, suddenly noticed Sir Gawain's gaping wounds
and, rushing forward, asked him what had happened. Several
of their comrades gathered around and Sir Gawain described
his encounter with Sir Priamus, and warned them of the
danger, close at hand, of the Duke of Lorraine's army. Sir
Gawain and Sir Priamus then disarmed, and the onlookers
were horrified by their injuries; however, Sir Priamus spoke
calmly:

"Good sir, please fetch for us the small vial in my saddle
bag: it contains drops of the four waters of Paradise, whither
we shall all go one day, and which should cure our wounds
within four hours."

Sir Gawain and Sir Priamus first cleansed the wounds with
cold white wine, and then applied the Holy Waters, again
and again, until, as Sir Priamus had asserted, they were healed
completely.

Sir Florens and his whole party now broached a barrel of
wine and sat down to a splendid meal of local game. When
they had done they dispersed to arm, and then, at the sound
of a trumpet, reassembled for a council of war.

At Sir Gawain's request, Sir Priamus described the number
and quality of the enemy, and warned the council of their
determination to recapture him at all costs. When he had finished, Sir Gawain spoke:

"My lords, I urge that we accept this challenge; that not
to do so, in spite of the great enemy strength, would be to
dishonor our king and the fellowship of the Round Table.
However, you, Sir Florens, are our appointed commander,
and in your hands the final decision must rest."

"My lords, Sir Gawain has expressed my own sentiments.
But I appeal to your greater experience in these matters, to
determine whether in following them our action will result
in glory or ignominy."

Then Sir Priamus spoke once more: "My lords, I beg you
to consider that the enemy is formidable both in numbers
and in quality, that they outnumber you by seven to one,
although it is true that part of their number is made up of
servants and yeomen whose worth in a serious battle is but
little."

"Sir Florens," said Sir Gawain, "would you be willing to
advance upon this formidable army with only a hundred
of your knights?"

"Certainly I would," Sir Florens replied. And so the matter was decided.

Sir Florens summoned Sir Florydas, and with a hundred knights advanced at a fast trot to the woods where the enemy was lodged. He was met by King Ferraunte of Farmagos, Spain, at the head of seven hundred cavalry. The two commanders charged at each other, and Sir Florens drove his spear through his opponent's throat and killed him.

"You have killed an anointed king!" shouted Sir Ferraunte's cousin, "and now, surely, you must die for it."

"Advance, heretical wretch," Sir Florens replied.

In this encounter Sir Florens drove his spear through his opponent's stomach, so that the guts came tumbling out, and he too was killed. Immediately, a common soldier in the service of Sir Ferraunte broke out from the ranks, determined to avenge his lord; however, he was met by Sir Richard, a knight of the Round Table, who thrust his spear into the soldier's heart and killed him while he was uttering a horrible roar.

By now many more of the enemy had advanced from the wood, and Sir Florens was surrounded and outnumbered by at least five to one. Undaunted, he and Sir Florydas recouched their spears and charged into the main press of the battle, killing five enemy knights at the first onslaught. Sir Gawain, mounted at the head of his chivalry, was watching the battle closely when Sir Priamus spoke to him:

"Sir Gawain, are not your comrades too greatly outnumbered? Why not allow me to lead a small company to their assistance?"

"Not yet, Sir Priamus; Sir Florens and his knights are yet fresh; indeed many have not fought a proper battle for five seasons. It will be time enough when the rest of the enemy appear, for we know they still have large numbers in reserve." However, just as he spoke, both the Earl of Ethelwolde and the Duke of the Dutchmen advanced with their armies, the earl in the front and the duke at the rear.

Sir Gawain at once gave the alarm, and shouted: "Comrades, fight in good faith and the field will be ours!" He advanced at a gallop, and wherever he attacked the enemy, they fell before him, unable to resist his fury; and before long all the enemy servants and yeomen had fled from the field.

"Ah! Now that pleases me," said Sir Gawain. "The enemy are less by several thousand already, whatever boasts they may have made among themselves."

As the battle developed it became clear that neither the Romans nor the Saracens could withstand the British, and their number of dead and wounded mounted ominously. Of Sir Gawain's comrades, only one, Sir Garrade, fell ignominiously to one of the ugly Giants of Geen, called Jubeance.

Sir Priamus, fighting under his own colors, soon came upon his retinue fighting in the enemy ranks, and led them out of the battle for a parley. He told them of his change of allegiance, and they agreed to join him. A messenger was sent to inform their commander-in-chief, the Duke of Lorraine; and they justified themselves on the grounds that for seven years they had received no bounty.

"Then they can go to the devil; I have no use for such soldiers," was the duke's reply.

Sir Priamus rejoined Sir Gawain, and the Duke of the Dutchmen re-formed his men to attack them. In the course of the fighting Sir Priamus killed the Marquesse of Moyslande; and then Chastelayne, a page from Arthur's court and one of Sir Gawain's wards, killed Sir Cheldrake. One of Sir Cheldrake's companions at once turned on the child and broke his neck with his sword. Both Sir Gawain and Sir Gotlake wept for the valiant page and redoubled their efforts, determined to avenge him. Sir Gawain killed sixty knights, including Sir Dolphin, Sir Hardolf, and a duke, and at last encountered the knight who had killed the page.

"Now for my revenge!" he said as he put him to the sword.

Meanwhile, the British had won the day; and so without further ado Sir Florens returned to Arthur with his party, proudly bearing their spoils, and their many prisoners, among them the lords of Lorraine and Lombardy.

"Sire," said Sir Gawain to Arthur, "here are so many more of the enemy who will trouble us no further."

"Sir Gawain, tell me who is that knight over there, who although a stranger does not appear to be included among the prisoners?"

"Sire, his name is Sir Priamus, and he is a noble knight of this country. This morning we fought; he yielded to me and now wishes to swear his allegiance to you, and to be made a Christian."

Arthur performed the ceremony at once, christening him with the name he already bore; and then, dubbing him a knight of the Round Table, granted him the rank of duke.

The assault on the Tuscan city was now resumed; siege engines were raised and a furious battle followed. At last the

grand duchess appeared before Arthur with her ladies-in-
waiting, and kneeling down, begged him to spare their city
and their lives. Arthur lifted the visor of his helmet, and speaking gently, promised the duchess that if the city surrendered
immediately, all lives would be spared, and redress paid to
each according to rank.

The city keys were handed over to Arthur by the duke's
son, and Arthur made a triumphal entry, wearing his crown
instead of his helmet. The city constables and captains were
sworn in to Arthur, and new wardens appointed to administer
the lands under the city's jurisdiction. The grand duke was
taken prisoner and sent to Dover, but a dowry awarded to
the duchess and her children.

While consolidating his rule in northern Italy, Arthur
assigned the task of besieging the town of Virvyn to Sir
Florens and Sir Florydas; which task they accomplished
swiftly and with success. The troops, as ever, were forbidden to
plunder, and in gratitude the city swore allegiance to Arthur,
and offered a handsome tribute.

Awed by Arthur's successes, the Lord of Milan, on behalf
of his own city, also Pleasance, Petresaynte, and Point Trem-
byll, now hastened to swear allegiance to Arthur and offer a
high annual tribute. He sent ambassadors loaded with silver
and sixty horses to negotiate with Arthur, and his proposals
were accepted.

Arthur continued his march, through Vyterbe to Spollute,
where he reprovisioned his army, and thence to Vysecounte,
where he anticipated he would be met by ambassadors from
Rome. Duly a long train of senators and cardinals arrived,
and begged Arthur to spare their city and swore that in return
they would anoint him Roman Emperor. Arthur accepted
graciously, and allowed them the six weeks necessary to prepare for it; and the coronation was arranged for Christmas
Day.

The ceremony was performed with all due pomp by the
Pope, and was attended by emissaries from throughout the
civilized world. Once anointed Emperor, Arthur dealt with
the more urgent affairs of state, and then decided on the
awards for his knights, who had served him so faithfully
throughout the campaign; and his generosity was such that
none found cause for complaint.

Among the awards, Sir Launcelot and Sir Bors were granted
the realm of the defeated King Claudas; and Sir Priamus the

dukedom of Lorraine, together with a gift of fifty thousand horses which Arthur promised on his return to Britain.

At a conference, the knights of the Round Table now begged Arthur to lead them back to Britain, where they might once more attend to their wives and their estates, from which they had been absent for so long. Arthur agreed to do so, admitting the folly of prolonging the campaign, now that their aims had been accomplished.

Attended by the chief dignitaries of church and state, Arthur departed from Rome, and a few weeks later arrived at Sandwich. In London, at the head of his triumphant army, Arthur was greeted by Gwynevere, his beloved queen, and by all the ladies of the court, who beheld with wonder the magnificent spectacle they presented, illumined as they were with success, and laden with the spoils of war.

The Tale of Sir Launcelot du Lake

When King Arthur returned from Rome he settled his court at Camelot, and there gathered about him his knights of the Round Table, who diverted themselves with jousting and tournaments. Of all his knights one was supreme, both in prowess at arms and in nobility of bearing, and this was Sir Launcelot, who was also the favorite of Queen Gwynevere, to whom he had sworn oaths of fidelity.

One day Sir Launcelot, feeling weary of his life at the court, and of only playing at arms, decided to set forth in search of adventure. He asked his nephew Sir Lyonel to accompany him, and when both were suitably armed and mounted, they rode off together through the forest.

At noon they started across a plain, but the intensity of the sun made Sir Launcelot feel sleepy, so Sir Lyonel suggested that they should rest beneath the shade of an apple tree that grew by a hedge not far from the road. They dismounted, tethered their horses, and settled down.

"Not for seven years have I felt so sleepy," said Sir Launcelot, and with that fell fast asleep, while Sir Lyonel watched over him.

Soon three knights came galloping past, and Sir Lyonel noticed that they were being pursued by a fourth knight, who was one of the most powerful he had yet seen. The pursuing knight overtook each of the others in turn, and as he did so, knocked each off his horse with a thrust of his spear. When all three lay stunned he dismounted, bound them securely to their horses with the reins, and led them away.

Without waking Sir Launcelot, Sir Lyonel mounted his horse and rode after the knight, and as soon as he had drawn close enough, shouted his challenge. The knight turned about and they charged at each other, with the result that Sir Lyonel was likewise flung from his horse, bound, and led away a prisoner.

The victorious knight, whose name was Sir Tarquine, led his prisoners to his castle, and there threw them on the ground, stripped them naked, and beat them with thorn twigs. After that he locked them in a dungeon where many other prisoners, who had received like treatment, were complaining dismally.

Meanwhile, Sir Ector de Marys, who liked to accompany Sir Launcelot on his adventures, and finding him gone, decided to ride after him. Before long he came upon a forester.

"My good fellow, if you know the forest hereabouts, could you tell me in which direction I am most likely to meet with adventure?"

"Sir, I can tell you: Less· than a mile from here stands a well-moated castle. On the left of the entrance you will find a ford where you can water your horse, and across from the ford a large tree from which hang the shields of many famous knights. Below the shields hangs a caldron, of copper and brass: strike it three times with your spear, and then surely you will meet with adventure—such, indeed, that if you survive it, you will prove yourself the foremost knight in these parts for many years."

"May God reward you!" Sir Ector replied.

The castle was exactly as the forester had described it, and among the shields Sir Ector recognized several as belonging to knights of the Round Table. After watering his horse, he knocked on the caldron and Sir Tarquine, whose castle it was, appeared.

They jousted, and at the first encounter Sir Ector sent his opponent's horse spinning twice about before he could recover.

"That was a fine stroke; now let us try again," said Sir Tarquine.

This time Sir Tarquine caught Sir Ector just below the right arm and, having impaled him on his spear, lifted him clean out of the saddle, and rode with him into the castle, where he threw him on the ground.

"Sir," said Sir Tarquine, "you have fought better than any knight I have encountered in the last twelve years; therefore, if you wish, I will demand no more of you than your parole as my prisoner."

"Sir, that I will never give."

"Then I am sorry for you," said Sir Tarquine, and with that

he stripped and beat him and locked him in the dungeon with
the other prisoners. There Sir Ector saw Sir Lyonel.

"Alas, Sir Lyonel, we are in a sorry plight. But tell me, what
has happened to Sir Launcelot? for he surely is the one knight
who could save us."

"I left him sleeping beneath an apple tree, and what has
befallen him since I do not know," Sir Lyonel replied; and
then all the unhappy prisoners once more bewailed their
lot.

While Sir Launcelot still slept beneath the apple tree, four
queens started across the plain. They were riding white mules
and accompanied by four knights who held above them, at
the tips of their spears, a green silk canopy, to protect them
from the sun. The party was startled by the neighing of Sir
Launcelot's horse and, changing direction, rode up to the
apple tree, where they discovered the sleeping knight. And as
each of the queens gazed at the handsome Sir Launcelot, so
each wanted him for her own.

"Let us not quarrel," said Morgan le Fay. "Instead, I will cast
a spell over him so that he remains asleep while we take him to
my castle and make him our prisoner. We can then oblige him
to choose one of us for his paramour."

Sir Launcelot was laid on his shield and borne by two of the
knights to the Castle Charyot, which was Morgan le Fay's
stronghold. He awoke to find himself in a cold cell, where a
young noblewoman was serving him supper.

"What cheer?" she asked.

"My lady, I hardly know, except that I must have been
brought here by means of an enchantment."

"Sir, if you are the knight you appear to be, you will learn
your fate at dawn tomorrow." And with that the young noblewoman left him. Sir Launcelot spent an uncomfortable night
but at dawn the four queens presented themselves and Morgan
le Fay spoke to him:

"Sir Launcelot, I know that Queen Gwynevere loves you,
and you her. But now you are my prisoner, and you will have
to choose: either to take one of us for your paramour, or
to die miserably in this cell—just as you please. Now I will tell
you who we are: I am Morgan le Fay, Queen of Gore; my
companions are the Queens of North Galys, of Estelonde, and
of the Outer Isles. So make your choice."

"A hard choice! Understand that I choose none of you,
lewd sorceresses that you are; rather will I die in this cell.
But were I free, I would take pleasure in proving it against

any who would champion you that Queen Gwynevere is the finest lady of this land."

"So, you refuse us?" asked Morgan le Fay.

"On my life, I do," Sir Launcelot said finally, and so the queens departed.

Sometime later, the young noblewoman who had served Sir Launcelot's supper reappeared.

"What news?" she asked.

"It is the end," Sir Launcelot replied.

"Sir Launcelot, I know that you have refused the four queens, and that they wish to kill you out of spite. But if you will be ruled by me, I can save you. I ask that you will champion my father at a tournament next Tuesday, when he has to combat the King of North Galys, and three knights of the Round Table, who last Tuesday defeated him ignominiously."

"My lady, pray tell me, what is your father's name?"

"King Bagdemagus."

"Excellent, my lady, I know him for a good king and a true knight, so I shall be happy to serve him."

"May God reward you! And tomorrow at dawn I will release you, and direct you to an abbey which is ten miles from here, and where the good monks will care for you while I fetch my father."

"I am at your service, my lady."

As promised, the young noblewoman released Sir Launcelot at dawn. When she had led him through the twelve doors to the castle entrance, she gave him his horse and armor, and directions for finding the abbey.

"God bless you, my lady; and when the time comes I promise I shall not fail you."

Sir Launcelot rode through the forest in search of the abbey, but at dusk had still failed to find it, and coming upon a red silk pavilion, apparently unoccupied, decided to rest there overnight, and continue his search in the morning.

He had not been asleep for more than an hour, however, when the knight who owned the pavilion returned, and got straight into bed with him. Having made an assignation with his paramour, the knight supposed at first that Sir Launcelot was she, and taking him into his arms, started kissing him. Sir Launcelot awoke with a start, and seizing his sword, leaped out of bed and out of the pavilion, pursued closely by the other knight. Once in the open they set to with their swords, and before long Sir Launcelot had wounded his unknown adversary so seriously that he was obliged to yield.

The knight, whose name was Sir Belleus, now asked Sir Launcelot how he came to be sleeping in his bed, and then explained how he had an assignation with his lover, adding:

"But now I am so sorely wounded that I shall consider myself fortunate to escape with my life."

"Sir, please forgive me for wounding you; but lately I escaped from an enchantment, and I was afraid that once more I had been betrayed. Let us go into the pavilion and I will staunch your wound."

Sir Launcelot had just finished binding the wound when the young noblewoman who was Sir Belleus' paramour arrived, and seeing the wound, at once rounded in fury on Sir Launcelot.

"Peace, my love," said Sir Belleus. "This is a noble knight, and as soon as I yielded to him he treated my wound with the greatest care." Sir Belleus then described the events which had led up to the duel.

"Sir, pray tell me your name, and whose knight you are," the young noblewoman asked Sir Launcelot.

"My lady, I am called Sir Launcelot du Lake."

"As I guessed, both from your appearance and from your speech; and indeed I know you better than you realize. But I ask you, in recompense for the injury you have done my lord, and out of the courtesy for which you are famous, to recommend Sir Belleus to King Arthur, and suggest that he be made one of the knights of the Round Table. I can assure you that my lord deserves it, being only less than yourself as a man-at-arms, and sovereign of many of the Outer Isles."

"My lady, let Sir Belleus come to Arthur's court at the next Pentecost. Make sure that you come with him, and I promise I will do what I can for him; and if he is as good a man-at-arms as you say he is, I am sure Arthur will accept him."

As soon as it was daylight, Sir Launcelot armed, mounted, and rode away in search of the abbey, which he found in less than two hours. King Bagdemagus' daughter was waiting for him, and as soon as she heard his horse's footsteps in the yard, ran to the window, and, seeing that it was Sir Launcelot, herself ordered the servants to stable his horse. She then led him to her chamber, disarmed him, and gave him a long gown to wear, welcoming him warmly as she did so.

King Bagdemagus' castle was twelve miles away, and his daughter sent for him as soon as she had settled Sir Launcelot. The king arrived with his retinue and embraced Sir Launcelot, who then described his recent enchantment, and the great obligation he was under to his daughter for releasing him.

"Sir, you will fight for me on Tuesday next?"

"Sire, I shall not fail you; but please tell me the names of the three Round Table knights whom I shall be fighting."

"Sir Modred, Sir Madore de la Porte, and Sir Gahalantyne. I must admit that last Tuesday they defeated me and my knights completely."

"Sire, I hear that the tournament is to be fought within three miles of the abbey. Could you send me three of your most trustworthy knights, clad in plain armor, and with no device, and a fourth suit of armor which I myself shall wear? We will take up our position just outside the tournament field and watch while you and the King of North Galys enter into combat with your followers; and then, as soon as you are in difficulties, we will come to your rescue, and show your opponents what kind of knights you command."

This was arranged on Sunday, and on the following Tuesday Sir Launcelot and the three knights of King Bagdemagus waited in a copse, not far from the pavilion which had been erected for the lords and ladies who were to judge the tournament and award the prizes.

The King of North Galys was the first on the field, with a company of ninescore knights; he was followed by King Bagdemagus with fourscore knights, and then by the three knights of the Round Table, who remained apart from both companies. At the first encounter King Bagdemagus lost twelve knights, all killed, and the King of North Galys six.

With that, Sir Launcelot galloped on to the field, and with his first spear unhorsed five of the King of North Galys' knights, breaking the backs of four of them. With his next spear he charged the king, and wounded him deeply in the thigh.

"That was a shrewd blow," commented Sir Madore, and galloped onto the field to challenge Sir Launcelot. But he too was tumbled from his horse, and with such violence that his shoulder was broken.

Sir Modred was the next to challenge Sir Launcelot, and he was sent spinning over his horse's tail. He landed head first, his helmet became buried in the soil, and he nearly broke his neck, and for a long time lay stunned.

Finally Sir Gahalantyne tried; at the first encounter both he and Sir Launcelot broke their spears, so both drew their swords and hacked vehemently at each other. But Sir Launcelot, with mounting wrath, soon struck his opponent a blow on the helmet which brought the blood streaming from eyes, ears, and mouth. Sir Gahalantyne slumped forward in the saddle, his horse panicked, and he was thrown to the ground, useless for further combat.

Sir Launcelot took another spear, and unhorsed sixteen more of the King of North Galys' knights, and with his next, unhorsed another twelve; and in each case with such violence that none of the knights ever fully recovered. The King of North Galys was forced to admit defeat, and the prize was awarded to King Bagdemagus.

That night Sir Launcelot was entertained as the guest of honor by King Bagdemagus and his daughter at their castle, and before leaving was loaded with gifts.

"My lady, please, if ever again you should need my services, remember that I shall not fail you."

The next day Sir Launcelot rode once more through the forest, and by chance came to the apple tree where he had previously slept. This time he met a young noblewoman riding a white palfrey.

"My lady, I am riding in search of adventure; pray tell me if you know of any I might find hereabouts."

"Sir, there are adventures hereabouts if you believe that you are equal to them; but please tell me, what is your name?"

"Sir Launcelot du Lake."

"Very well, Sir Launcelot, you appear to be a sturdy enough knight, so I will tell you. Not far away stands the castle of Sir Tarquine, a knight who in fair combat has overcome more than sixty opponents whom he now holds prisoner. Many are from the court of King Arthur, and if you can rescue them, I will then ask you to deliver me and my companions from a knight who distresses us daily, either by robbery or by other kinds of outrage."

"My lady, please first lead me to Sir Tarquine, then I will most happily challenge this miscreant knight of yours."

When they arrived at the castle, Sir Launcelot watered his horse at the ford, and then beat the caldron until the bottom fell out. However, none came to answer the challenge, so they waited by the castle gate for half an hour or so. Then Sir Tarquine appeared, riding toward the castle with a wounded prisoner slung over his horse, whom Sir Launcelot recognized as Sir Gaheris, Sir Gawain's brother and a knight of the Round Table.

"Good knight," said Sir Launcelot, "it is known to me that you have put to shame many of the knights of the Round

Table. Pray allow your prisoner, who I see is wounded, to recover, while I vindicate the honor of the knights whom you have defeated."

"I defy you, and all your fellowship of the Round Table," Sir Tarquine replied.

"You boast!" said Sir Launcelot.

At the first charge the backs of the horses were broken and both knights stunned. But they soon recovered and set to with their swords, and both struck so lustily that neither shield nor armor could resist, and within two hours they were cutting each other's flesh, from which the blood flowed liberally. Finally they paused for a moment, resting on their shields.

"Worthy knight," said Sir Tarquine, "pray hold your hand for a while, and if you will, answer my question."

"Sir, speak on."

"You are the most powerful knight I have fought yet, but I fear you may be the one whom in the whole world I most hate. If you are not, for the love of you I will release all my prisoners and swear eternal friendship."

"What is the name of the knight you hate above all others?"

"Sir Launcelot du Lake; for it was he who slew my brother, Sir Carados of the Dolorous Tower, and it is because of him that I have killed a hundred knights, and maimed as many more, apart from the sixty-four I still hold prisoner. And so, if you are Sir Launcelot, speak up, for we must then fight to the death."

"Sir, I see now that I might go in peace and good fellowship, or otherwise fight to the death; but being the knight I am, I must tell you: I am Sir Launcelot du Lake, son of King Ban of Benwick, of Arthur's court, and a knight of the Round Table. So defend yourself!"

"Ah! this is most welcome."

Now the two knights hurled themselves at each other like two wild bulls; swords and shields clashed together, and often their swords drove into the flesh. Then sometimes one, sometimes the other, would stagger and fall, only to recover immediately and resume the contest. At last, however, Sir Tarquine grew faint, and unwittingly lowered his shield. Sir Launcelot was swift to follow up his advantage, and dragging the other down to his knees, unlaced his helmet and beheaded him.

Sir Launcelot then strode over to the young noblewoman: "My lady, now I am at your service, but first I must find a horse."

Then the wounded Sir Gaheris spoke up: "Sir, please take

my horse. Today you have overcome the most formidable knight, excepting only yourself, and by so doing have saved us all. But before leaving, please tell me your name."

"Sir Launcelot du Lake. Today I have fought to vindicate the honor of the knights of the Round Table, and I know that among Sir Tarquine's prisoners are two of my brethren, Sir Lyonel and Sir Ector, also your own brother, Sir Gawain. According to the shields there are also: Sir Brandiles, Sir Galyhuddis, Sir Kay, Sir Alydukis, Sir Marhaus, and many others. Please release the prisoners and ask them to help themselves to the castle treasure. Give them all my greetings and say I will see them at the next Pentecost. And please request Sir Ector and Sir Lyonel to go straight to the court and await me there."

When Sir Launcelot had ridden away with the young noblewoman, Sir Gaheris entered the castle, and finding the porter in the hall, threw him on the ground and took the castle keys. He then released the prisoners, who, seeing his wounds, thanked him for their deliverance.

"Do not thank me for this work, but Sir Launcelot. He sends his greetings to you all, and asks you to help yourselves to the castle treasure. He has ridden away on another quest, but said that he will see you at the next Pentecost. Meanwhile, he requests Sir Lyonel and Sir Ector to return to the court and await him there."

"Certainly we shall not ride back to the court, but rather we shall follow Sir Launcelot wherever he goes," said Sir Ector.

"And I too shall follow him," said Sir Kay.

The prisoners searched the castle for their armor and horses and the castle treasure; and then a forester arrived with supplies of venison, so they feasted merrily and settled down for the night in the castle chambers—all but Sir Ector, Sir Lyonel, and Sir Kay, who set off immediately after supper in search of Sir Launcelot.

Sir Launcelot and the young noblewoman were riding down a broad highway when the young noblewoman said they were within sight of the spot where the knight generally attacked her.

"For shame that a knight should so degrade his high calling," Sir Launcelot replied. "Certainly we will teach him a much-needed lesson. Now, my lady, I suggest that you ride on ahead, and as soon as he molests you, I will come to the rescue."

Sir Launcelot halted and the young noblewoman rode gently

forward. Soon the knight appeared with his page, and seized the young noblewoman from her horse; she cried out at once, and Sir Launcelot galloped up to them.

"Scoundrel! what sort of knight do you think you are, to attack defenseless women?"

In answer the other knight drew his sword. Sir Launcelot did likewise, and they rushed together. With his first stroke Sir Launcelot split open the knight's head, down to the throat.

"Let that be your payment, though long overdue," said Sir Launcelot.

"Even so; he certainly deserved to die. His name was Sir Percy of the Forest Sauvage."

"My lady, do you require anything more of me?"

"No, good Sir Launcelot; and may the sweet Lord Jesu protect you, for certainly you are the bravest and gentlest knight I have known. But pray tell me one thing: why is it you do not take to yourself a wife? Many good ladies, both high born and low born, grieve that so fine a knight as yourself should remain single. It is whispered, of course, that Queen Gwynevere has cast a spell over you so that you shall love no other."

"As for that, people must believe what they will about Queen Gwynevere and me. But married I will not be, for then I should have to attend my lady instead of entering for tournaments and wars, or riding in search of adventure. And I will not take a paramour, both for the fear of God and in the belief that those who do so are always unfortunate when they meet a knight who is purer of heart; for whether they are defeated or victorious in such an encounter, either result must be equally distressing and shameful. I believe that a true knight is neither adulterous nor lecherous."

Sir Launcelot then took his leave of the young noblewoman, and for two days wandered alone through the forest, resting at night at the most meager of lodgings. On the third day, as he was crossing a bridge, he was accosted by a churlish porter, who, after striking his horse on the nose so that it turned about, demanded to know by what right Sir Launcelot was riding that way.

"And what right do I need to cross this bridge? Surely, I cannot ride beside it," said Sir Launcelot.

"That is not for you to decide," said the porter, and with that he lashed at Sir Launcelot with his club. Sir Launcelot drew his sword, and after deflecting the blow, struck the porter on the head and split it open.

At the end of the bridge was a prosperous-looking village, overtopped by a fine castle. As Sir Launcelot advanced he heard someone cry: "Good knight, beware! You have done yourself no good by killing the chief porter of the castle."

Sir Launcelot rode on regardless, through the village and into the castle court, which was richly grassed. Thinking to himself that this would be a good place for combat, Sir Launcelot tied his horse to a ring in the wall and started across the lawn. Meanwhile people were peering at him from every door and window, and again he heard the warning: "Good knight, you come here at your peril!"

Before long two giants appeared, fully armed except for their heads, and brandishing huge clubs. Together they rushed at Sir Launcelot, who raised his shield to defend himself, and then struck at one of the giants and beheaded him. Thereupon the second giant roared with dismay and fled into the forest, where Sir Launcelot pursued him. In a few minutes, Sir Launcelot drew abreast of the giant and struck him on the shoulder with a blow that carried through to the navel, and the giant dropped dead.

When Sir Launcelot returned to the castle, he was greeted by threescore ladies, who all knelt before him.

"Brave knight! we thank you for delivering us. Many of us have been prisoners for seven years now, and although we are all high born, we have had to work like servants for our keep, doing silk embroidery. Pray tell us your name, so that our friends can know who has saved us."

"My ladies, I am called Sir Launcelot du Lake."

"Welcome, Sir Launcelot! It was you alone whom the giants feared, and you alone who could have overcome them. How often have we prayed for your coming!"

"My ladies, please greet your friends for me; and when I pass through this country again, grant me what hospitality you may feel is my due. Please recompense yourselves from the castle treasure, and then insure that the castle is restored to the rightful owner."

"Sir Launcelot, this is the castle of Tintagil, and belonged formerly to the duke of that name. But after his death, Igraine, who had been his wife, was made queen by King Uther Pendragon, to whom she bore Arthur, our present king."

"And so, after all, I know the owner of this castle. My ladies, I bless you, and farewell."

Always in quest of adventure, Sir Launcelot rode through many different countries, through wild valleys and forests, and across strange rivers; and at night he slept where he could, often in the roughest of lodgings. Then one day he came to a well-kept house where the lady offered him the best of hospitality. After supper he was taken to his chamber, which overlooked the front door, and there Sir Launcelot disarmed and fell comfortably asleep.

He was awakened a short time later by a tremendous knocking at the door below, and looking through the window recognized Sir Kay in the moonlight, and three knights galloping toward him with drawn swords. The moment they got to the house, they dismounted and set upon Sir Kay, who turned about and drew his sword to defend himself. Sir Launcelot hastily armed, saying to himself: "If they kill Sir Kay I shall be a party to his death, for three against one is unjust."

He let himself down from the window by means of his sheet, and then challenged the three attackers, whispering to Sir Kay to stand by while he dealt with them. Sir Kay did as he was advised, and then Sir Launcelot, with seven tremendous blows, brought all three knights to their knees and begging for mercy.

"Your lives will be spared if you yield to Sir Kay," said Sir Launcelot.

"Sir, it is surely you to whom we should yield, since we could easily have overcome Sir Kay."

"If you wish to be spared, you will go as prisoners of Sir Kay, and yield to Queen Gwynevere."

Each of the knights then swore on his sword to abide by the conditions of his surrender, and Sir Launcelot knocked once more at the door of the house.

"Why, I thought you were safely in bed," said the landlady, recognizing Sir Launcelot as she opened the door.

"Madam, I was, but then I had to jump out of the window and rescue this comrade of mine."

As they came into the light, Sir Kay recognized Sir Launcelot and thanked him humbly for twice saving his life.

"It was no more than I should have done, but come up to my chamber; you must be tired and hungry."

When Sir Kay had eaten, he lay on Sir Launcelot's bed, and they slept together until dawn. Sir Launcelot woke first, and rising quietly, clad himself in Sir Kay's armor, and then, mounting Sir Kay's horse, rode away from the house.

When Sir Kay awoke, he was astonished to find that Sir Launcelot had exchanged armor with him, but then he realized he had done it so that he should ride home unmolested, while

Sir Launcelot encountered his opponents. And when Sir Kay had taken his leave of the landlady he rode back to the court without further incident.

For several days Sir Launcelot rode through the forest, and then he came to a countryside of low meadows and broad streams. At the foot of a bridge he saw three pavilions, and a knight standing at the entrance to each, with a white shield hanging above, and a spear thrust into the ground at one side. Sir Launcelot recognized the three knights, who were from Arthur's court, as Sir Gawtere, Sir Raynolde, and Sir Gylmere. However, he rode straight past them, looking neither to right nor to left, and without saluting them.

"Why, there rides Sir Kay, the most overbearing knight of all, in spite of his many defeats. I think I will challenge him and see if I cannot shake his pride a little," said Sir Gawtere.

He then galloped up to Sir Launcelot and challenged him. They jousted, and Sir Gawtere was flung violently from the saddle.

"That is certainly not Sir Kay," said Sir Raynolde. "For one thing, he is very much bigger."

"Probably it is some knight who has killed Sir Kay and is riding in his armor," Sir Gylmere replied.

"Well, since he has overcome our brother we shall have to challenge him. But I think it must be either Sir Launcelot, Sir Tristram, or Sir Pelleas; and we may not come well out of this."

Sir Gylmere challenged Sir Launcelot next, and was also overthrown. Then Sir Raynolde rode up to him.

"Sir, I would prefer not to challenge a knight so powerful as you, but since you have probably killed my brothers, I am obliged to; so defend yourself!"

They jousted; both broke their spears and they continued the combat with swords. Sir Gawtere and Sir Gylmere recovered, and attempted to rescue their brother, but Sir Launcelot saw them in time, and using more strength than hitherto, struck each off his horse again. At this, Sir Raynolde, badly wounded as he was, and with blood streaming from his head, picked himself up and once more rushed at Sir Launcelot.

"Sir, I should let things be," said Sir Launcelot. "I was not far away when you were knighted, and I know you to be worthy: therefore do not oblige me to kill you."

"May God reward you!" Sir Raynolde replied. "But speaking both for myself and my brothers, I would prefer to know

your name before yielding to you, because we know very well
that you are not Sir Kay, whom any one of us could have
overcome."

"That is as may be; but I still require that you yield to
Queen Gwynevere at the next Pentecost, and say that Sir Kay
sent you."

The three brothers took their oath, and Sir Launcelot left
them. He had not ridden much further when, coming to a
glade, he found four more knights of the Round Table: Sir
Gawain, Sir Ector, Sir Uwayne, and Sir Sagramour le Desyrus.

"Look!" said Sir Sagramour, "there rides Sir Kay. I will
challenge him."

Sir Sagramour first, then each of the other knights in turn,
challenged Sir Launcelot, and was flung from his horse. Sir
Launcelot left them gasping on the ground, and said to himself as he rode away: "Blessed be the maker of this spear;
with it I have tumbled four knights off their horses." Meanwhile the four knights were picking themselves up and con-
soling each other.

"To the devil with him! He is indeed powerful," said one.

"I believe that it must be Sir Launcelot," said another.

"Anyhow, let him go now; we shall discover when we return
to Camelot," said a third, and so on.

Riding once more through the forest, Sir Launcelot came
upon a black brachet, eagerly pursuing a trail. Sir Launcelot
followed and soon noticed traces of blood. The brachet kept
glancing over its shoulder as if to insure that Sir Launcelot
was still there, and finally came to an ancient castle which
had been built on a green marsh. The brachet led the way
across a shaky bridge and into the hall. A dead knight lay on
the floor. The brachet went up to him and started licking his
wounds, and then a lady appeared, haggard with grief, and
wringing her hands.

"Sir, you have brought me much grief," she said.

"My lady, do not say that, for surely I never set eyes on
this knight before. The brachet led me here. But truly, I am
sorry for your grief."

"Sir, I see now that you are speaking the truth, for the
knight who killed my husband is seriously wounded; nor will
he recover."

"My lady, pray tell me: what was your husband's name?"

"He was called Sir Gylberd the Bastard, and was one of
the truest knights who ever lived; but I do not know the name
of the knight who killed him."

"My lady, may the Lord comfort you in your grief, and farewell!"

Sir Launcelot rode away from the castle, and soon came upon a young noblewoman wandering alone through the forest.

"Sir, I beseech your aid. My brother lies mortally wounded; he is under an enchantment and cannot recover unless I can find a knight brave enough to rescue him. He lately fought with and killed Sir Gylberd the Bastard, who is now in the Chapel Perelous, wrapped in a silken cloth all bloody with his wounds. And it is a piece of that cloth, together with Sir Gylberd's sword, that is needed to cure him."

"My lady, this sounds miraculous indeed. But pray tell me, what is your brother's name?"

"Sir Melyot de Logres."

"Then he is a knight of the Round Table. Certainly, my lady, I will try to rescue him."

"Good knight! Over there is the highway which leads to the Chapel Perelous. I will await you here, and God's speed! I am sure that no other knight than you would have any chance of success."

Sir Launcelot rode to the Chapel Perelous, dismounted, and tied his horse to a small gate. On the chapel wall hung many shields, upside down, and several of them Sir Launcelot recognized. Beneath the shields stood thirty knights, all in black armor and their faces distorted in horrible grimaces. Sir Launcelot raised his shield, drew his sword, and advanced, but not without fear in his heart.

As he approached the chapel doors, the knights drew aside and allowed him to pass. Inside the chapel, which was lit only by one small light, he discerned the corpse, lying wrapped in the silken cloth; he cut off a small piece of it, and as he did so the ground shook beneath him, and he felt fearful once more. Then taking Sir Gylberd's sword, which lay beside him, he made his way hastily out of the chapel. As he was passing through the knights, one of them spoke: "Sir Launcelot, surrender the sword, or else you shall die."

"Sir, whether I am to live or to die, you shall not win the sword by a threat. Fight for it if you wish."

But none of the knights took up the challenge, and Sir Launcelot came to the end of the chapel yard, where he was confronted by a beautiful noblewoman.

"Sir Launcelot, leave the sword behind, or else you shall die," she said.

"My lady, not for the sake of a threat."

"Sir, you are fortunate, for had you relinquished the sword, you would have lost forever the love of Queen Gwynevere."

"It is as well, then, my lady."

"Brave knight, I require that you kiss me once."

"Never, my lady."

"Sir, if you had kissed me you would not have lived long. But alas for me! I built this chapel only for you, and for Sir Gawain, and when he was here he fought with Sir Gylberd and struck off his left hand. But you I have loved for seven years now; and knowing that nothing could shake your love for Queen Gwynevere, I planned to kill you, so that I could at least embalm your corpse and kiss it every day to spite the queen."

"May God preserve me from such sorcery!" said Sir Launcelot, and mounting his horse, left her. The young noblewoman, who was known as Lady Hallews of the Castle Nygurmous, and a famous sorceress, died two weeks later of a broken heart.

Sir Launcelot returned to Sir Melyot's sister, who greeted him with tears of joy. Together they rode to her castle and there found Sir Melyot, bleeding profusely and as pale as death. Seeing them, he struggled to speak and besought Sir Launcelot's aid. Sir Launcelot swiftly dismounted, and first touched him with the sword and then applied the cloth to the wounds. The effect was miraculous: Sir Melyot rose within a few minutes, without a scar.

The three of them made merry that evening, and Sir Launcelot, before taking his leave, suggested that Sir Melyot should seek him out at Arthur's court at the next Pentecost.

Sir Launcelot continued his journey, through valleys and across moors, until one day, passing a castle, he heard bells ringing within the walls. At the same time he noticed a falcon flying toward a high elm tree, where it perched, and then became entangled by the leashes still fastened to its claws. In the meantime a lady had come running out of the castle and, seeing Sir Launcelot, cried out to him:

"Good Sir Launcelot, flower of the knighthood, I beg you to catch my falcon for me. If you do not, my husband will kill me without mercy as soon as he discovers I have lost it."

"My lady, please tell your husband's name."

"Sir Phelot, and his liege is the King of North Galys."

"I must confess, my lady, that I am a very poor climber, and that this tree is high and without many branches. How-

ever, as a knight I am bound to come to your aid, so I will
try."

Sir Launcelot dismounted, and the lady helped him to disarm. He wrapped his clothes in his breeches and climbed
up to the falcon, which he released; and then, by tying the
leashes to a rotten branch, managed to throw it down to the
lady. Suddenly Sir Phelot appeared from a thicket; he was fully
armed and had drawn his sword.

"Sir Launcelot, now I have you as I want you," he said.

"Tell me, my lady, what is the reason for your treachery?"

"My wife has done no more than obey my instructions. You
will now have to descend and meet your death at my hands."

"For shame that you should kill a defenseless man! At least
hand me my sword."

"You shall have neither sword nor armor, Sir Launcelot,
so prepare to meet your death."

"A shameful death, indeed!"

However, looking about him, Sir Launcelot noticed a dead
branch in the form of a spike, so he tore it away from the
trunk, and then made a sudden leap, landing just in front of
his horse. Sir Phelot rushed at him, anxious to kill him at
once; but Sir Launcelot knocked aside his sword with the
spike, and then brought it crashing down on Sir Phelot's
helmet. Sir Phelot staggered beneath the blow, and Sir Launcelot leaped on top of him, bearing him to the ground, then,
wrenching the sword from him, tore off his helmet and
chopped through his neck.

"Alas!" cried the lady. "Why have you killed my husband?"

"It is no more than your treachery deserves," Sir Launcelot
replied. The lady fainted, but Sir Launcelot swiftly armed
himself and rode clear of the castle, afraid that otherwise Sir
Phelot's followers might set upon him, and once away, thanked
God for his deliverance.

Sir Launcelot's next encounter was in a valley where he
saw a knight about to behead a lady with his sword. Seeing
Sir Launcelot the lady cried out to him to rescue her, and
Sir Launcelot drove his horse between them.

"Miscreant! why do you kill a defenseless lady?"

"Sir, this is between my wife and me; and I will not be
interfered with."

"Sir, you shall not kill the lady without first fighting me."

"But my wife has betrayed me."

"That is a lie," said the lady. "I love my first cousin dearly,
and my husband is jealous, but without cause because our love

is innocent. So I pray you, Sir Launcelot, save me, for my husband is without mercy."

"Do not fear, my lady, your husband will have to deal with me first."

"Sir, while you watch over us, I swear to be ruled by you."

The three of them rode on together, with the lady between the two knights. Suddenly the husband said to Sir Launcelot:

"Sir, look behind you; we are being pursued!"

Sir Launcelot did so, and immediately the knight beheaded his wife.

"Traitor!" said Sir Launcelot, and drew his sword to kill him, but the knight slid off his horse and began groveling on the ground and begging for mercy.

"Get up and fight, you coward!"

"Sir, never shall I rise until you have granted me mercy."

"Very well, I will take off my armor, throw away my shield, and you can fight me wearing only my shirt."

"Sir Launcelot, I shall never fight you."

"Then it is a shame that you were ever born! These are my commands, that you shall take the head and body of your murdered wife to Queen Gwynevere, tell her exactly what has happened, and throw yourself on her mercy. Now tell me, what is your name?"

"Sir Pedivere, and I swear now to obey you."

Sir Pedivere rode straight to the queen and told her the truth. She rebuked him severely and commanded him to bear the corpse to the Pope for burial, and never, even while he slept, to remove it from his own body. In obedience to the queen, Sir Pedivere made this pilgrimage, and his wife was duly buried by the Pope, who commanded him to return to Queen Gwynevere. On his return, Sir Pedivere repented truly, and renouncing his knighthood, became a hermit, and subsequently a very holy man.

Sir Launcelot returned to Camelot two days before the feast of Pentecost, and at the court was acclaimed by many of the knights he had met on his adventures.

Sir Gawain, Sir Uwayne, Sir Ector, and Sir Sagramour all laughed when they saw him in Sir Kay's armor, but without the helmet, and readily forgave his joke at their expense.

Sir Gaheris described to the court the terrible battle Sir Launcelot had fought with Sir Tarquine, and how sixty-four prisoners had been freed as a result of his victory.

Sir Kay related how Sir Launcelot had twice saved his life.

and then exchanged armor with him, so that he should ride unchallenged.

Sir Gawtere, Sir Gylmere, and Sir Raynolde described how he had defeated them at the bridge, and forced them to yield as prisoners of Sir Kay; and they were overjoyed to discover that it had been Sir Launcelot nevertheless.

Sir Modred, Sir Mador, and Sir Gahalantyne described his tremendous feats in the battle against the King of North Galys; and Sir Launcelot himself described his enchantment by the four queens, and his rescue at the hands of the daughter of King Bagdemagus.

Finally Sir Belleus and his lady arrived at the court, and at Sir Launcelot's request, Sir Belleus was made a knight of the Round Table.

And thus it was, at this time, that Sir Launcelot became the most famous knight at King Arthur's court.

The Tale of Sir Gareth

It happened one Pentecost when King Arthur and his knights of the Round Table had all assembled at the castle of Kynke Kenadonne and were waiting, as was customary, for some unusual event to occur before settling down to the feast, that Sir Gawain saw through the window three gentlemen riding toward the castle, accompanied by a dwarf. The gentlemen dismounted, and giving their horses into the care of the dwarf, started walking toward the castle gate.

"My lords," Sir Gawain shouted, "we can sit down to the feast, for here come three gentlemen and a dwarf who are certain to bring strange tidings."

The king and his knights sat down at the great Round Table, which provided seats for a hundred and fifty knights; but this year, as in most, several were vacant because their owners had either been killed in the course of their adventures, or else taken prisoner.

The three gentlemen entered the hall, and there was complete silence as they approached the king. All three were richly clothed; and the one who walked in the center was obviously young, but taller than his companions by eighteen inches, strongly built, of noble features, and with large and beautiful hands. He leaned heavily on his companions' shoulders and did not stand up to his full height until he was confronting the king. Then he spoke:

"Most noble king, may God bless you and your knights of the Round Table! I come to ask you for three gifts, and none of them is unreasonable or such as to give you cause to repent. The first of the gifts I will ask for now, the other two at the next Pentecost."

"The three gifts shall be yours for the asking," Arthur replied.

"Sire, today I ask that you shall give me food and drink for twelve months, until the next Pentecost, when I shall ask for the other two."

"My dear son, this is a simple thing to ask for. I have never denied food and drink either to my friends or to my enemies. Can you ask for no worthier gift? For you have the appearance of a man nobly born and bred."

"Sire, for the present I ask nothing more."

"Very well, then; but pray tell me your name."

"Sire, that I cannot tell you."

"It is strange indeed that you should not know your name."

King Arthur then commanded Sir Kay, his steward, to serve the young gentleman with the best fare available throughout the coming year, and to treat him with the courtesy due to a nobleman.

"Sire, that is unnecessary," Sir Kay answered sourly, "for were he of noble birth he would have asked for a horse and for armor. No! he is nothing but a great loafer born of a serving wench, you may be sure. However, I will keep him in the kitchen and feed him until he is as fat as any pig, and the kitchen shall be his sty. And since he has neither name nor purpose, I shall call him Beaumains."

And so Beaumains' companions duly delivered him into the charge of Sir Kay, who lost no opportunity to gibe and jeer at him. Both Sir Gawain and Sir Launcelot were deeply ashamed of Sir Kay's cavalier behavior, and Sir Launcelot spoke his mind:

"Sir Kay, take warning! Beaumains may yet prove to be of noble birth, and win fame for himself and for our liege. You seem already to have forgotten how, in the meanness of your heart, you nicknamed Sir Brewnor 'La Cote Male Tayle,' who afterward made you a laughingstock by dint of his noble deeds."

"As for that, Sir Launcelot, you may forget it; but at least Sir Brewnor sought fame, whereas this lout seeks only food, so there can be no comparing them. You can be sure he is a servant from some abbey, and only came here because they failed to feed him enough."

Throughout the next twelve months, while Sir Kay remained irate and contemptuous, both Sir Launcelot and Sir Gawain treated Beaumains with the greatest courtesy, inviting him frequently to their quarters to dine, and urging him to accept money for his needs. With Sir Launcelot this was due to his habitually gentle nature; but with Sir Gawain it was more, for he had an unexplained feeling of kinship with Beaumains. However, Beaumains always refused them, remaining in the kitchen to work and eat with the servants, and meekly obedient to Sir Kay. Only when the knights were jousting would he leave the kitchen to watch them, or when games were played, then he participated, and by virtue of his natural strength and skill, was always the champion; and only then would Sir Kay take pride in his charge, and say: "Well, what do you think of my kitchen lad now?"

Once more the feast of Pentecost came around, and once more King Arthur and his knights waited for an unusual occurrence before sitting down to the banquet. This time a squire came running into the hall, and straight up to Arthur:

"Sire, you may take your seats at the Round Table, for a lady is approaching the castle, with strange tidings to relate."

As soon as the king and his knights were seated at the table the lady entered the hall, and kneeling before Arthur, begged his aid.

"Lady, pray tell us your story," Arthur responded.

"Sire, I have a sister, of noble birth and wide dominion, who for two years has been held captive by a most audacious and tyrannical knight; so now I beseech Your Majesty, who is said to command the flower of the chivalry, to dispatch one of your knights to her rescue."

"My lady, pray tell me her name and where she lives, also the name of the knight who holds her prisoner."

"Sire, I may not reveal her name or where she lives; I can only plead that she is a lady of great worth. The knight who holds her prisoner while extorting wealth from her estates is known as the Red Knight of the Red Lands."

"Then I do not know him."

"Sire, I do!" cried Sir Gawain. "He is a knight who is said to have the strength of seven men, and I can believe it, because I fought him once and barely escaped with my life."

"My lady," said Arthur, "I can send a knight to rescue your sister only if I know her name and where she lives; otherwise you can have no help from this court."

"Alas! I thought you would not fail me; so now I must resume my search."

But then Beaumains spoke up: "Sire, for twelve months I have eaten in your kitchen; now the time has come for me to ask you for the other two gifts."

"You ask at your peril, Beaumains," said the king.

"The first is that I pursue the quest besought by this lady, for I believe that it is my appointed one. The second, that Sir Launcelot should follow us, and when I have proved myself worthy, make me a knight, for it is only by him, who is peerless among all knights, that I should wish to be sworn into the order."

"I grant you both gifts, Beaumains."

"Sire, you shame me! To send a kitchen boy on such a noble quest! I will have none of it," said the lady, and walked angrily from the hall.

Meanwhile Beaumains' two companions and the dwarf had arrived, leading a fine charger with gold trappings, and an excellent sword and suit of armor; only a spear and shield were lacking. Beaumains armed at once and mounted; and Arthur's knights were astonished to discover him the possessor of such fine equipment and to see how nobly he bore himself, once clad in it. Beaumains returned to the hall, took his leave of Arthur and of Sir Gawain, and then set off after the lady, followed by Sir Launcelot.

Just as they were leaving the court, Sir Kay appeared, fully armed and mounted. "I too am going to follow this kitchen lout," he said grimly.

"Sir Kay, you would do better to remain here," said Sir Launcelot.

But Sir Kay was not to be dissuaded, and he galloped up to Beaumains and shouted: "Well, Beaumains, do you still recognize your master?"

"I know you for the most ungracious knight at the court, Sir Kay, so now beware!"

Sir Kay couched his spear and charged at him. Beaumains, having neither shield nor spear, drew his sword, and as Sir Kay bore down on him, made two rapid strokes. With the first he knocked the spear out of Sir Kay's grasp, and with the second lunged at Sir Kay and drove the sword into his side, wounding him deeply so that he fell to the ground as though dead.

Beaumains dismounted, took possession of Sir Kay's spear and shield, and then remounted and instructed his dwarf to take the spare horse. At this point Sir Launcelot rode up to him, and Beaumains asked if he would like to joust, to which Sir Launcelot agreed.

They drew apart and then galloped together, and the collision sent both men and horses tumbling to the ground. Recovering quickly, both drew their swords and attacked each other with the ferocity of wild boars. Sir Launcelot, who had hitherto been unmatched, was astonished at Beaumains' strength and skill, and felt as if he were fighting a giant rather than an ordinary man. Each succeeded in delivering blows that sent his opponent staggering to the ground, only to recover immediately. After a while, however, Sir Launcelot began to realize that his strength was not equal to that of Beaumains, and fearing an ignominious defeat, called a halt.

"My friend, pray hold off! for we have no quarrel" he said.

"That is true, Sir Launcelot, yet it does me good to feel your strength, though I have not yet fought to my uttermost."

"Then you are matchless: I called a halt just now for fear that I should be shamed into begging for mercy!"

"Sir Launcelot, will you make me a knight?"

"Certainly, but first you must reveal to me your true name, and of whom you were born."

"Sir, if you will pledge yourself to absolute secrecy, I will tell you."

"I shall not betray you."

"My name is Gareth of Orkney; I am Sir Gawain's brother, born of the same parents."

"Gareth, that gladdens my heart, for I guessed that you were of noble birth."

Sir Launcelot then knighted Gareth and left him. Sir Kay was still lying senseless, so he laid him on his shield and brought him to the court, where the other knights, especially Sir Gawain, taunted him without mercy. However, Sir Launcelot excused Sir Kay on the grounds that he was young and ignorant of Beaumains' birth and of his purpose in serving in the kitchen for a year.

Sir Gareth, meanwhile, had ridden after the lady, and as soon as he caught up with her she rounded on him:

"Why do you follow me, you wretched lackey? Your clothes still stink of tallow and grease; and I know from Sir Kay that you are nameless and have to be called Beaumains, and how treacherously you overcame that excellent knight! Now leave me, I command you; have done!"

"Madame, I have come to serve you, and your words shall not deter me."

"Lewd little knave! Well, before long we shall meet a knight who will frighten you back to your kitchen quickly enough."

At this moment a man came running frantically out of the forest.

"My good fellow, what is your trouble?" asked Sir Gareth.

"My lord, six thieves have attacked my master; they have him bound and at any moment will kill him."

"Pray lead me to them."

Sir Gareth killed three of the thieves as soon as they came upon them. The other three fled, and Sir Gareth chased them until they turned about and attacked him fiercely, but before long he had killed them all. Returning to the knight, he released him from his bonds, and the knight begged Sir Gareth to accompany him to his castle, where he would be able to reward him as he deserved.

"Sir, I need no reward for doing as a knight should; and today I have been knighted by the peerless Sir Launcelot, so I am content enough. Pray forgive me now if I return to my lady, whose quest I am pursuing."

Sir Gareth returned to the lady, and she turned on him again:

"Misshapen wretch! What pleasure do you expect me to take in your cumbrous deeds? Now leave me, get back to your kitchen, I say!"

The knight whom Sir Gareth had rescued now rode up to them both and offered them hospitality for the night. It was already dusk, and the lady accepted. At dinner she found herself sitting opposite to Sir Gareth, and protested at once: "Sir, forgive me, but I cannot possibly dine in company with this stinking kitchen knave; why, he is fit only for sticking pigs."

Thereupon the knight set Sir Gareth at a side table, and excusing himself, removed his own place there as well.

In the morning, after thanking their host, Sir Gareth and the lady resumed their journey. Soon they came to a broad stream, and on the further bank were two knights.

"Now," said the lady, "I think you had better fly, and save your bacon."

"My lady, were there six knights, I should not fly."

The first of the knights and Sir Gareth galloped their horses into the stream, and both broke their spears as they collided. They drew their swords, and soon Sir Gareth stunned his opponent with a blow on the helmet, and he fell into the water and was drowned. Urging his horse through the stream, Sir Gareth met the second knight on the far bank; and again, both spears were broken, and again Sir Gareth struck his opponent on the helmet, this time with a blow that killed him outright.

"It is strange," said the lady when Sir Gareth had joined her once more, "that fortune should favor so vile a wretch as you. But do not suppose for one moment that it was either by skill or daring that you overcame those two excellent knights. No, I watched you closely. The first was thrown into the water by his horse stumbling, and so unhappily drowned. The second you won by a cowardly blow when he was not expecting it. However, had you not better turn back now? For the next knight we meet will certainly cut you down without mercy or remorse."

"My lady, I shall not turn back. So far I have fought with such ability as God gave me, and trusting in His protection. My only discouragement has been your own extraordinary abuse."

All day they rode together, and the lady's villainous tongue never ceased to wag. In the evening they came to the Black Land. By a black hawthorne on which was hung a black shield, and by the side of which was a black rock, stood a black standard. Under the tree stood a knight in black armor, who was Knight of the Black Lands.

"Now fly," said the lady to Gareth, "for here is a knight before whom even the brave might tremble."

"I am not a coward, my lady."

"My lady!" shouted the Black Knight, "are you come with your champion from King Arthur's court?"

"Sir, unhappily not! This ill-gotten lout has pursued me from King Arthur's kitchen, and continues to force his odious presence upon me. Purely by mischance, and by treachery, he has overcome a few knights on the way; but I beg you to rid me of him."

"My lady, that I will happily do. I thought for a moment that since he was accompanying you, he must be of noble birth. Now let us see: it would be degrading to fight him, so I will just strip him of his armor and horse, and then he can run back to his kitchen."

"Sir, I shall pass through this country as it pleases me, and whether you will or no. It appears that you covet my horse and my armor. Very well, let us see if you can win them! Now—defend yourself!"

And with that, both knights, in a black rage, galloped thunderously at each other. Both broke their spears, but while Sir Gareth was unharmed, the point of his own spear was embedded deeply in the body of his opponent. They fought with their swords, and for an hour and a half the Black

Knight held out, but then he fell dead from his horse.

Noticing the fine quality of the Black Knight's armor, Sir Gareth stripped him of it, and exchanged it for his own. He then remounted and joined his lady.

"Alas! the lackey still lives. Shall I never be rid of him? Tell me, cockroach, why do you not run off now? You could boast to everyone that you have overcome all these knights, who, entirely through misfortune, have fallen to you."

"My lady, I shall accompany you until I have accomplished my quest or died in the attempt. This, whether you will or no."

Next they came upon the Green Knight, clad in green armor, who, seeing Sir Gareth's black armor, inquired if it were not his brother, the Black Knight.

"Alas! no," the lady replied. "This is but a fat pauper from King Arthur's kitchen, who has treacherously murdered your noble brother. I pray you, avenge him!"

"My lady, this is most shameful; certainly I will avenge him."

"This is slander," said Sir Gareth. "I killed him in fair combat; so now defend yourself!"

The Green Knight blew three times on his horn, and two maids appeared, who handed him his green spear and green shield.

They jousted and both broke their spears, then continued the fight with swords, still on horseback, until Sir Gareth wounded his opponent's horse and it collapsed under him. They both leaped clear and resumed the fight on foot. The Green Knight was powerful, and both were soon liberally wounded. At last the lady spoke up:

"Why, sir, for shame! Does it take so long to dispatch a mere scullery boy! Surely you can finish him off; this is the weed overshooting the corn!"

The Green Knight, deeply ashamed, redoubled his blows, and succeeded in splintering Sir Gareth's shield. Sir Gareth then exerted his full strength, and striking his opponent on the helmet, sent him reeling to the ground, where he unlaced his helmet in order to behead him; and the Green Knight cried for mercy.

"Mercy you shall not have, unless this lady pleads for you," Sir Gareth replied.

"And that I should be beholden to a servant? Never!" the lady replied.

"Very well, sweet lady, he shall die."

"Not so fast, knave!"

"Good knight, I pray you, do not kill me for want of a good word from the lady. Spare me, and not only shall I forgive you the death of my brother, but I will myself swear you allegiance, together with that of the thirty knights at my command."

"In the devil's name! The Green Knight and his thirty followers at the command of a scullery boy! For shame, I say!"

For answer, Sir Gareth raised his sword, and made as if to behead the Green Knight.

"Hold, you dog, or you will repent it!" said the lady.

"My lady's command is a pleasure, and I shall obey her in this as in all things; for surely I would do nothing to displease her."

With that Sir Gareth released the Green Knight, who at once swore him homage.

"My lord," said the lady to the Green Knight, "I deeply regret your wounds, and the unfortunate death of your brother. And now I am in great need. Would you be gracious enough to accompany me through this forest? for indeed it frightens me."

"My lady, have no fears. Tonight you shall both lodge at my castle; and in the morning I will accompany you through the forest."

The two knights and the lady rode to the Green Knight's castle, and as ever, the lady unbridled her flow of invective against Sir Gareth, and once more refused to dine at the same table with him. The Green Knight removed both his own and Sir Gareth's places to a side table, and the two knights ate merrily together. Then the Green Knight addressed the lady:

"My lady, it astonishes me that you can behave in such unseemly fashion before this noble knight, who has proved himself worthier than I—and believe me, I have encountered the greatest knights of my time. He is surely rendering you an honorable service, and I warn you that whatever mystery he pretends concerning his birth, it will be proved in the end that he is of noble, if not royal, blood."

"My lord, you make me sick," the lady responded.

Before retiring to their chambers, the Green Knight commanded thirty of his retainers to watch over Sir Gareth while he slept, and to be on their guard against treachery.

In the morning, after mass and breakfast, the Green Knight accompanied Sir Gareth and the lady through the forest, and when he came to take leave of them, spoke to Sir Gareth:

"Noble knight, please remember that I and my thirty knights are sworn to your service, to command when you will."

"Sir, I thank you; when the time comes, I shall request you to make your allegiance to King Arthur."

"Sir, we shall be ready at all times," said the Green Knight.

"For shame! For shame!" cried the lady.

They parted, and then the lady spoke to Sir Gareth:

"Now, you greasy knave, surely you have run to the end of your leash. Ahead of us lies the Passage Perelous, and it would take a true-born knight, and one of the quality of Sir Launcelot, Sir Tristram, or Sir Lamerok, to pass through this stage of the journey without losing courage. And so I advise you to run for it now!"

"Perhaps, my lady, I shall not run," Sir Gareth replied.

They were approaching a castle comprising a fine white tower, surrounded by machicolated walls and double ditches. Leading up to the gate was a large jousting field, with a pavilion in process of erection for a coming tournament; and hung above the gate were fifty shields bearing different devices. The lord of the castle, seeing Sir Gareth approach with the lady and his dwarf, decided to challenge him, so he clad himself in puce armor, for he was the Puce Knight, and then rode out to meet them.

"Sir, are you not my brother, the Black Knight?" he asked.

"Sir, indeed he is not. He is a nameless servant from King Arthur's kitchen, called Beaumains. Purely by treachery and mischance he has killed your brother the Black Knight, and obtained the allegiance of your excellent brother the Green Knight. I beg you to avenge them, and rid me of his odious presence once and for all."

"My lady, it shall be done," the Puce Knight replied.

They jousted and both horses collapsed, and they continued the fight on foot. After two hours the lady could contain herself no longer:

"Sir, for shame that you should dally so long with a mere scullery boy. Pray do me the goodness to finish him off."

The Puce Knight was duly ashamed, and redoubled his strokes, but to no avail; for Sir Gareth, using only a little more strength, struck him to the ground, then, straddling him, dragged off his helmet to behead him. The Puce Knight pleaded for mercy.

"Mercy you shall not have unless my lady pleads for you."

"Leave him be, Beaumains; he is a noble knight," said the lady.

"Then, my lady, he shall thank you for his life," said Sir Gareth.

The Puce Knight rose, and begged them to accept hospitality in his castle for the night. The lady accepted and that evening they dined well and then went to bed; but as ever she continued to abuse Sir Gareth. Distrusting her, the Puce Knight commanded his sixty knights to keep watch over him while he slept. In the morning, after hearing mass and breakfasting, the lady and Sir Gareth took leave of their host; and before parting the Puce Knight swore his allegiance, and that of his sixty knights, to Sir Gareth, who, as before, said that in due course he would require him to make his allegiance to King Arthur.

They resumed their journey, and by noon had come in sight of a beautiful city. Before it stretched a plain, the grass was newly mown, and many splendid pavilions had been erected. But one in particular caught the eye, being the color of indigo, and arranged about it were armor and equipment of the same color; so also were the adornments of the ladies who passed to and fro.

"Yonder lies the pavilion of Sir Persaunte, the Indigo Knight, and lord of this city. But for one, he is the greatest knight living, and when the weather is good he pitches his pavilions on the plain and spends his time in jousting and tournaments, and other pastimes suitable to the nobility. He has at his command a hundred and fifty knights, and it is his custom to challenge every knight who passes through his terrain. And so now, filthy knave, had you not better think twice and flee, before Sir Persaunte chastises you with the ignominy that you deserve?"

"My lady, if he is noble, as you say he is, he will not dispatch his knights to murder me, but fight with me in single combat; and if he has won honor as you say he has, the greater glory will be mine if I overcome him. Before each combat you yourself chasten me with your abuse; and after each you deny flatly what I have truly accomplished, distorting the event so that it serves only to augment the hatred you bear me!"

"Sir, your courteous speech and brave deeds astound me. I have with my own eyes witnessed what you have already accomplished, and I am becoming convinced that you must indeed be of noble birth. But this time I would save you, so please offer no challenge to the Indigo Knight, for both you and your horse have already suffered much in your previous combats. Up to now we have come safely through this difficult journey, but here we are within seven miles of the castle where my sister is held captive; and to combat the knight who holds her, you will need all your strength, for his is seven times that of ordinary men."

"My lady, I should be ashamed to withdraw from combat with the Indigo Knight now; but with God's grace, we shall be able to continue our journey in two hours."

"Ah Jesu!" exclaimed the lady. "Worthy knight, you must indeed be of noble blood to have borne for so long and with such courtesy the terrible way in which I have reviled you."

"My lady, it would be an unworthy knight indeed who was unable to bear the chastisement of a lady. The anger your insults inspired in me I. turned against my opponents, and so overcame them more readily. Always have I been determined to prove my own worth: I served in King Arthur's kitchen in order to discover who were my true friends, and who my enemies. What my blood may be shall be revealed in due course; but at present I wish to prove myself by my deeds alone. And so, my lady, I shall continue to serve you as I have already."

"I beg you, gentle knight, can you forgive me my terrible words?"

"My lady, you are forgiven; and if formerly anger made me strong, may joy now make me invincible!"

Meanwhile, the Indigo Knight had seen Sir Gareth and the lady approach, and sent a messenger to inquire whether they came in war or in peace. Sir Gareth replied that he offered a challenge only if the Indigo Knight wished to receive one. The Indigo Knight decided to accept the challenge and fight to his uttermost, so he mounted and rode out to meet Sir Gareth.

They charged at each other with equal determination, and both broke their spears into three pieces, while their horses tumbled to the ground.

The sword fight lasted for two hours, and in the course of it Sir Gareth wounded the Indigo Knight deeply in the side; however, he continued to fight bravely. At last, though somewhat loath because of his opponent's bravery, Sir Gareth delivered his crushing blow on the helmet, and the Indigo Knight was sent spinning to the ground. Once more Sir Gareth straddled his opponent and unlaced his helmet to behead him, and the Indigo Knight yielded. The lady at once begged that Sir Gareth should spare his life.

"My lady, that I will gladly do, for he is a noble knight."

"May God reward you!" said the Indigo Knight. "Now I understand well enough how it was that you killed my brother Sir Perarde the Black Knight, and won the allegiance of my other two brothers, Sir Pertolope the Green Knight and Sir Perymones the Puce Knight."

Sir Persaunte then led Sir Gareth and the lady to his pavilion, where he refreshed them with wine and spices, and insisted that Sir Gareth should rest both before and after supper. That evening he summoned his beautiful daughter, who was aged eighteen:

"My daughter, if you would please me, go to Sir Gareth, lie in his bed, take him in your arms and kiss him, and make him welcome as only a woman can."

At her father's bidding, the daughter went to Sir Gareth's bed, quietly undressed, and got in beside him. Sir Gareth awoke when she caressed him, and asked:

"Pray, who are you?"

"Sir, I am Sir Persaunte's daughter, and I come at his command, not of my own free will."

"Are you a maid or a wife?"

"Sir, I am a maid."

"Then God forbid that I should deflower you, which I shall certainly do if you remain. It would be as shameful for me as for your father; so I beg you, return to him." And with that, he kissed her and bade her farewell. The daughter duly returned to her father and told him all that had happened.

"He must indeed be of noble blood," her father responded.

In the morning Sir Persaunte asked the lady where she was leading Sir Gareth.

"To the Castle Dangerous."

"Ah ha! that is where the Red Knight of the Red Lands lives, and holds the Lady Lyoness prisoner, is it not? But tell me, you are surely her sister, Lady Lynet?"

"Sir, that is my name," the lady replied.

"Well, sir, you must prepare yourself for an ordeal, for it is said that the Red Knight has the strength of seven ordinary men. But you will be fighting for a worthy cause, for this knight has held the Lady Lyoness prisoner for two years now. He could at any time have taken his pleasure of her, but he has been waiting for a challenge from one of four knights from King Arthur's court: Sir Launcelot, the most powerful of all, Sir Tristram, Sir Gawain, or Sir Lamerok. And although many other knights have achieved much fame—for example,

Sir Palomides, Sir Safere, Sir Bleobris, Sir Blamoure, Sir Bors, Sir Ector, Sir Percivale, and so on—it is one of these four he wishes to fight. So, now, let me wish you God's speed, and strength for the coming battle."

"Sir Persaunte, would you have the goodness of heart to make my companion a knight? It would please me greatly to see this done before he fights the Red Knight of the Red Lands."

"My lady, I will gladly, if he will accept the order from so simple a man as I."

"Sir, I thank you for your gracious offer, but I have already been knighted by Sir Launcelot, for I wished it to be from no other hands than his. And if you will both swear to keep the secret, I will now reveal to you my name, and of whom I was born."

"We swear," they said together.

"I am Sir Gareth, Sir Gawain's brother, and the youngest son of King Lot of Lowthean and Orkney; my mother is Margawse, King Arthur's sister. But neither King Arthur, Sir Gawain, nor any other at his court, with the exception of Sir Launcelot, knows who I am."

Whilst the two knights and the lady were conversing, Sir Gareth's dwarf had ridden to the Castle Dangerous to tell Lady Lyoness of her sister's approach with a knight from Arthur's court, who was to be her champion.

"Pray, what sort of knight is he?" asked Lady Lyoness.

"A noble knight, my lady; he was knighted by Sir Launcelot," the dwarf replied.

"And pray, how did he come here?"

"By the Passage Perelous, my lady. First he defeated Sir Kay at jousting: he had at that time only a sword, so he won Sir Kay's spear and shield. Then he battled with Sir Launcelot, whom he nearly overcame, and Sir Launcelot knighted him. After that he killed the two brothers, Sir Gerarde and Sir Arnolde le Brewse, who challenged him by a river. Next he killed the Black Knight, and it is his armor he now wears. Finally he won his three brothers, the Green Knight, the Puce Knight, and the Indigo Knight, at whose castle he now is."

"If he has won Sir Persaunte, he must indeed be a powerful knight. Now tell me, what is his name?"

"My lady, that I may not reveal; but he is of royal blood, a son of the King of Orkney."

"Dwarf, you bring good tidings. Now, these are my instructions: Go first to my hermitage nearby, and take with you two flagons of good wine, two loaves, plenty of roast venison and game, two silver flasks, and my precious goblet of gold, inlaid with jewels. Then ride to my sister, give her my greetings, and lead them both to the hermitage. There commend me to the knight and beg him to sup well and sleep well in preparation for tomorrow. Warn him that my captor, the Red Knight, is a powerful and courageous warrior, but that his murderous ways forbid my ever loving him or yielding to him."

The dwarf obeyed his instructions to the letter. Sir Persaunte insisted on accompanying Sir Gareth and the lady part way to the hermitage, and then, wishing Sir Gareth God's speed, took his leave of them. After supper, the dwarf returned to the Castle Dangerous with the precious goblet; but just as he was entering, the Red Knight waylaid him and demanded to know what tidings he brought.

"Sir, Lady Lynet has brought a knight from King Arthur's court to champion her sister."

"Unless it is Sir Launcelot, Sir Gawain, Sir Tristram, or Sir Lamerok, he has little chance!"

"Sir, this knight has won his way through the Passage Perelous."

"Then he is one of those four?"

"No, my lord, but he is of royal blood."

"Then, pray, who is he?"

"Sir, that I may not reveal."

"Well, I care little. He will doubtless pay the same price as his predecessors have."

"Sir, it is a shame to treat supplicant knights as you do," said the dwarf, and departed.

In the morning, after mass and breakfast, Sir Gareth and the lady rode through the forest, and then across a wide plain, to the Castle Dangerous, which stood on the seashore. The Red Knight had pitched his pavilions beneath the walls of the castle, and to one side Sir Gareth noticed a copse of tall trees, and from the branches hung forty knights. They were in full armor, with their swords in their hands, shields, and spurs at their heels. Sir Gareth was horrified.

"Tell, my lady, what is the meaning of this?"

"Sir Gareth, those are the knights who hitherto have attempted to rescue my sister, so take heed! The Red Knight is a formidable warrior, and lord of many marches; but once he has overcome a knight in battle, he always puts him to this murderous end; and that is one reason why no gentlewoman can love him."

"May Jesu preserve me from such a death! Certainly I should prefer to die fighting. But how strange that no knight from King Arthur's court has yet defeated him!"

"My lord, take courage; he is a powerful knight."

The castle moats were formed by two dikes which ran around from the sea. Several ships were at anchor and everywhere were signs of activity. On board the ships, in the Red Knight's pavilions, and from within the castle could be heard the merry sounds of minstrelsy, while lords and their ladies walked upon the castle walls. Just by the gate grew a large sycamore tree, and on this was hung an elephant's horn for those who wished to challenge the Red Knight. Sir Gareth was about to blow it when the lady cautioned him:

"Sir Gareth, do not sound your challenge yet. Until noon the Red Knight's strength increases, after then it wanes, so if you will wait for a little the advantage will be yours."

"My lady, I should be ashamed not to challenge him at his greatest strength." And with that Sir Gareth blew a tremendous blast on the horn.

Immediately knights and ladies came running from all directions, to the castle walls and windows, or out of their pavilions, in order to witness the coming battle. The Red Knight hastily armed, assisted by his earls and barons. One of them laced on his helmet while another buckled on his spurs and a third handed him his blood-red shield and spear. He then mounted, rode out to a small hollow which could be easily viewed from the castle, and awaited his challenger.

"My lord, here comes your mortal enemy, and at the tower window stands your lady."

"Pray, tell me where," asked Sir Gareth.

The lady pointed with her finger, and Sir Gareth looked up and saw a lady whose beauty filled him with awe. She curtsied to him, and then held out her hands in supplication.

"Truly, she is the most beautiful lady on earth. My quarrel could not be better chosen," he said.

"Sir, you may cease looking at the lady, and look to your arms instead. She is not for you, nor shall she be," said the Red Knight grimly.

"Sir, it would seem that although you hold the lady, she is not yours, and therefore your love for her is nothing but folly. Further, I have heard tell that my presence is not displeasing to her; and now that I have seen her and I know that I love her, by the grace of God, I shall win her for myself."

"Sir, are you not warned by the array of corpses hung from the trees—your predecessors, who spoke as you do?"

"No, I am not. Rather am I filled with anger and contempt, and understand well why the lady does not love you. And for myself, I wish only to fight you to the death and put an end to your murderous ways. Nor shall I feel any of that remorse in overcoming you which I have felt in the past for more honorable opponents."

"Sir, make ready—enough of your words!"

They jousted, and both crashed to the ground with such violence, and lay stunned for so long, that the onlookers supposed that they had broken their necks. However, they recovered, and drawing their swords, chopped at each other with heavy, deliberate blows, beneath which one or the other would occasionally stagger. So they fought until well past noon, when they paused for a moment to recover their breath. Both were streaming with blood from their wounds, panting, and momentarily exhausted as they leaned on their shields.

Beneath the steady rain of blows their shields were chipped and their armor and mail had given way in many places; and Sir Gareth soon learned, to his cost, to defend them from the shrewd blows of his opponent. Several times one or the other fell to the ground, half stunned by a blow, whereon the other would leap on top of him; and more than once in the ensuing scuffle they exchanged swords.

At eventide they agreed to rest, and sat on two molehills while their pages unlaced their helmets so that they should be refreshed by the cool breeze. Sir Gareth looked up to the tower, and seeing the lady, was inspired with fresh courage:

"Sir, let us continue; to the death!"

"To the death!" the Red Knight responded.

Despite their many wounds, they continued the fight with fresh vigor, until with two skillful blows the Red Knight first knocked the sword from Sir Gareth's hand, and then sent him spinning to the ground. Leaping on top of him, the Red Knight started unlacing his helmet, when suddenly Lady Lynet cried out:

"Alas! Sir Gareth, your lady weeps with despair, and my own heart is heavy."

Sir Gareth responded with a tremendous thrust of his body and succeeded in overturning his opponent, then, reaching swiftly for his sword, confronted him once more. A new and desperate battle ensued, as each strained to the limits of his strength to overmatch the other. Then it was Sir Gareth who sent his opponent's sword flying from his hand, and following it up with a hail of blows on the helmet, knocked him senseless to the ground, where he sprang on top of him. He had just unlaced his helmet to behead him when the Red Knight cried aloud:

"Most noble knight, I beg you for mercy!"

"Sir, how can I honorably spare you, when you have murdered so many courageous knights who yielded to you?"

"Sir, there was a reason for that, if you will only allow me to tell you."

"Speak on."

"Once I loved a lady whose brethren had all been killed by Sir Launcelot or Sir Gawain; and it was at her bidding that I fought with every knight who passed this way from King Arthur's court, and hung by the neck those whom I overcame. And to this day I have been waiting for either Sir Launcelot or Sir Gawain to mete her final revenge. And to accomplish this purpose, I have been enchanted, so that each day my strength increases until noon, when it is seven times that of other men, after which it wanes again."

Meanwhile the Red Knight's earls and barons had gathered round, and now they threw themselves on their knees and begged Sir Gareth to spare him:

"Sir, surely nothing can be gained by his death, nor can the dead be brought to life again. But spare him and he shall pay you homage, and learn to atone for his misdeeds."

"My lords, for your asking I will spare the Red Knight; and in my heart I can find some room for forgiveness, since what he did was at his lady's bidding. But these are my conditions: that first he shall yield to Lady Lyoness, making full redress for the damage done to her, and then go to King Arthur's court and yield to Sir Launcelot and Sir Gawain, confessing his enmity toward them."

"Sir, I thank you, and will most certainly fulfill your conditions."

For the next ten days, the Red Knight entertained Sir Gareth and the lady in his pavilion, where the lady treated their wounds. Then, in accordance with his oath, he first yielded to Lady Lyoness and then rode to King Arthur's court, where, in the presence of all, he yielded to Sir Launcelot and Sir Gawain, recounting fully his own misdeeds and defeat at the hands of Sir Gareth, whose progress through the Passage Perelous he also described.

"I wonder," said Arthur, "of whose blood he was born,

for certainly he has proved himself a noble knight since he ate in our kitchen."

"Sire, it is no marvel, for such courage and endurance as his surely stem from noble blood," said Sir Launcelot.

"Sir Launcelot, it would seem that you already know the secret of his birth?"

"Sire, I must admit that I do. I demanded to know before making him a knight, but I have been sworn to secrecy."

Sir Gareth, meanwhile, had asked Lady Lynet if he could not see her sister.

"Sir, most certainly you shall," she replied.

Sir Gareth armed and mounted and rode toward the castle, but as he did so, he was astonished to see the gate being closed and the drawbridge raised. Then Lady Lyoness spoke to him from one of the castle windows:

"Go your way, good knight, for you shall not have my love until you have won further fame; therefore you must strive for another year. Return to me then, and I will tell you more."

"My lady, I had not expected such thanks from one for whom I have already striven so hard, and for whom, alas! I was willing to shed the last drop of my blood."

"Worthy knight, be assured that I love you for your brave deeds, and go forth with a glad heart. Soon the twelve months will pass, and, in the meantime, do not doubt that I shall be faithful to you."

Sir Gareth rode into the forest, bitterly unhappy and care-less of direction, his dwarf following. That night he lodged in a humble cottage, but was unable to sleep. He continued his aimless journey all the next day, and that night came to a marsh where, feeling sleepy, he lay on his shield, while his dwarf watched over him.

As soon as Sir Gareth had ridden into the forest, the Lady Lyoness had summoned her brother, Sir Gryngamour.

"My dear brother, I need your help. Would you ride after Sir Beaumains, and when you find an opportunity, kidnap his dwarf? I am in difficulties because I do not know whether or not Sir Beaumains is of noble birth, and until I know, naturally, I cannot love him. But I feel certain that we can frighten his dwarf into telling us."

Sir Gryngamour prepared to do as his sister asked, and cladding himself entirely in black armor, and mounting a black horse, followed them faithfully until they came to the marsh. Then, as soon as Sir Gareth was asleep, he crept up on the dwarf, seized him suddenly, and tucked him under his arm.

However, the dwarf roared lustily, and Sir Gareth awoke in time to see him disappearing in the arms of a black knight.

Arming himself hastily, Sir Gareth mounted and pursued them as best he could, but with great difficulty, owing to his ignorance of the lay of the land. All night he rode across wild moors, over steep hills, and through dense forest, and frequently his horse stumbled, nearly throwing him. But at dawn he came to a woodland path, and seeing a forester, asked him if he had seen a black knight riding that way, with a dwarf behind him.

"Sir, I have. It was Sir Gryngamour, whose castle lies two miles further on. But I should beware of him, for once provoked he is a dangerous enemy."

Meanwhile Sir Gryngamour had taken the dwarf to his castle, where Lady Lyoness was cross-examining him.

"Dwarf, we wish to know the secret of your master's birth; and if you would prefer not to starve in the castle dungeon, you had better tell us. Who was his father, and who his mother, and whence does he come?"

"My lady, I am not ashamed to tell you that my master is Sir Gareth, the son of King Lot of Orkney and Queen Margawse, King Arthur's sister. Furthermore he is such a knight that he will soon destroy your lands and bring this castle tumbling about your ears if you do not release me."

"As for that, I think we need not trouble ourselves," said Lady Lyoness. "But let us go now and dine."

In honor of his sister's visit, Sir Gryngamour had ordered a splendid banquet, so they all sat down and dined merrily.

"My dear sister," said Lady Lynet, "you know I can well believe that your paramour is of noble birth, for throughout our journey through the Passage Perelous, in scorn of what I assumed to be his low birth, I taunted him unmercifully, and never once did he rebuke me. And certainly, as you yourself have witnessed, his feats at arms are unexampled."

At this moment Sir Gareth rode up to the castle gate with his sword drawn, and shouted in a tremendous voice:

"Sir Gryngamour, treacherous knight that you are, deliver my dwarf to me at once."

"Sir, that I shall not," Sir Gryngamour replied through the window.

"Coward! Come out and fight for him, then."

"Very well," Sir Gryngamour said.

"My dear brother, not so fast!" said Lady Lyoness. "I think Sir Gareth could have his dwarf. Now that I know who he is, I can love him, and certainly I am indebted to him for releasing me from the Red Knight. Therefore let us entertain him, but I shall disguise myself so that he will not know me."

"My dear sister, just as you wish," said Sir Gryngamour, and then to Sir Gareth: "Sir, I beg your pardon for taking your dwarf. Now we know that your name, as well as your deeds, commends you, we invite you to accept hospitality at the castle."

"And my dwarf?" Sir Gareth shouted.

"Most certainly you shall have him," Sir Gryngamour replied; and then, accompanied by the dwarf, he went to the castle gate and, taking Sir Gareth by the hand, led him into the hall, where his wife welcomed him.

"Ah, my good dwarf, what a hunt I have had for you!" said Sir Gareth.

Presently Lady Lynet appeared with her sister, who had dressed in all her finery, and disguised herself as a princess. Minstrels were summoned, and amid dancing and singing Lady Lyoness set out to win the love of Sir Gareth. She succeeded, and was herself enraptured by him, so that before long ardent looks and tender words passed between them. Sir Gareth was completely deceived by her disguise, and several times wished secretly to himself that his paramour at the Castle Dangerous were as beautiful and as gracious.

At supper neither of the young lovers could eat, both being hungry only for the looks and words of the other. Sir Gryngamour noticed this, and after supper took Lady Lyoness aside and spoke to her:

"Dear sister, it appears that you love the young Sir Gareth, and certainly his noble blood and valor commend him. If you wish to pledge yourself to him, and I could think of none worthier, I will persuade him to stay at my castle."

"Dear brother, not only is what you say true, but also I am beholden to him more than to any man living."

Then Sir Gryngamour went to Sir Gareth and spoke to him:

"Sir, I could not but observe the semblance of love between you and my sister; and if this should be founded on true feeling on your part, as it is on hers, I should like to welcome you to stay in my castle for as long as it please you."

"Sir, you make me the happiest man on earth; I thank you."

"Good! Then that is arranged; and I can promise you that my sister will be here to entertain you, both day and night."

"Sir, again I thank you. In fact I have sworn to remain in this country for twelve months, and your castle has the advantage that should King Arthur, my liege, wish to find me, he will be able to do so readily."

Sir Gareth returned to Lady Lyoness, and she now revealed to him her true identity, and admitted that it was at her instigation that his dwarf had been kidnapped, so that she could discover the secret of his birth before declaring herself. Sir Gareth was overjoyed, and there followed an exchange of vows and an assignation for the same night in the hall where he would ask to sleep.

When the company dispersed to their chambers for the night, and Sir Gareth rather clumsily made his request to sleep in the hall, neither Sir Gryngamour nor Lady Lynet was deceived; but a comfortable couch was made up for him, with a feather mattress and furs.

Just before midnight Lady Lyoness came to the hall, and throwing off her ermine cloak—her only covering—slipped into bed with Sir Gareth. However, they had no sooner embraced than a knight appeared, strangely illumined, with grim countenance, fully armed and brandishing a huge spear. Sir Gareth jumped out of bed and seized his sword. They fought furiously for a few minutes and first the knight wounded Sir Gareth in the thigh, then Sir Gareth knocked him to the ground and beheaded him, after which he staggered back to the bed and fainted from his wound.

Lady Lyoness cried aloud, and in a moment Sir Gryngamour came running into the hall, and was shocked by the scene that confronted him.

"My dearest sister, I am deeply ashamed that this should have happened. Not for the world would I have wished Sir Gareth to be molested."

"Dear brother, this was certainly none of my doing, for I have pledged myself to Sir Gareth, and he has sworn to be my husband."

Sir Gryngamour and his sister did their best to stanch the wound, which was very deep. Then Lady Lynet appeared; going up to the decapitated knight, she took the head, and covering the exposed flesh with ointment, fixed it back on the trunk. The knight immediately revived, and walked calmly out of the hall.

"My lady," said Sir Gareth, "as ever, it seems that you wish me nothing but evil."

"Sir Gareth, what I do is only for the best," Lady Lynet replied, and departed.

Sir Gareth soon recovered from his wound, and became

so full of joy that he danced and sang wherever he went; and ten days later made another assignation with his lover. This time he took the precaution of setting both armor and sword within easy reach.

Once more the illumined knight appeared, and once more Sir Gareth fought him. His wound broke open, but regardless of this Sir Gareth did not rest until he had not merely beheaded the knight, but chopped his head into a hundred pieces which he threw into the moat below. And once more he retired to the bed and fainted.

Both Sir Gryngamour and Lady Lynet appeared, the latter with the pieces of the knight's head, which she fastened together by means of her magic ointment, and revived the knight as before.

"My lady," said Sir Gareth, "pray, what have I done to deserve nothing but malice from you, since the very day we first met?"

"Sir Gareth, what I do is only for the purpose of preserving your honor, and that of my family," she replied.

A surgeon was sent for to tend Sir Gareth's wound, but he declared that since it was caused by an enchantment, it could heal properly only when the enchantment was revoked.

At Pentecost, each of the knights whom Sir Gareth had overcome went to Caerleon to surrender to Arthur: Sir Pertolope, the Green Knight, with his fifty retainers; Sir Perymones, the Puce Knight, with his sixty retainers; Sir Persaunte, the Indigo Knight, with his hundred and fifty retainers; and Sir Ironside, the Red Knight, with his five hundred retainers.

Arthur's amazement grew as each of the brothers in turn related how he had been overcome by the knight called Beaumains; also Arthur was delighted, for the five brothers had been among his most implacable enemies. Then he noticed that Sir Perarde, the Black Knight, had not come, and the Green Knight went on to describe how Beaumains had killed him in combat; also the two brothers, Sir Arnolde and Sir Gerarde le Brewse, whom Beaumains had killed at the river. The death of the Black Knight was regretted by all, and Arthur promised to make the four remaining brothers fellows of the Round Table as soon as Sir Beaumains returned.

The whole company now sat down to enjoy the banquet, but no sooner were they seated than Queen Margawse of Orkney arrived, attended by her royal suite. Her sons—Sir Gawain, Sir Aggravayne, and Sir Gaheris—at once left their places and knelt down to receive her blessing, as none of them had seen her for twelve years.

When all were seated once more, Queen Margawse inquired after her youngest son, Sir Gareth, and told Arthur frankly that word had reached her that he had been kept in the kitchen for a year in the charge of Sir Kay, who had dubbed him Beaumains and treated him with the utmost disrespect.

It was now clear to Arthur that Beaumains was none other than Sir Gareth, and so he described to his sister how Sir Gareth had come without revealing his identity and asked for the three gifts: to eat in his kitchen, to pursue the quest of Lady Lyoness, and to be knighted by Sir Launcelot.

"Dear brother," said Queen Margawse, "I can well believe it of him, for even as a child he always displayed a remarkable wit, and was wont to go his own way. And perhaps Sir Kay's scornful name is not so inept after all, for certainly since he was knighted he has won great honor by the use of his hands. But now how shall we find him again?"

"I pray you, let me go in search of him," cried Sir Gawain, "for I too was in complete ignorance of the fact that he was my brother."

"I think that will not be necessary," said Sir Launcelot. "Surely our best plan would be to send for Lady Lyoness, who is certain to know his whereabouts."

This was agreed upon, and a message sent to Lady Lyoness, which she received in the presence of Sir Gareth, whose advice she asked before answering it.

"My love, please do not tell King Arthur my whereabouts, but rather go to him and suggest a tournament for the day of the Assumption of Our Lady, and offer your hand as the prize. Should it be won by a knight who is already married, there could be an alternative prize of a gold crown inlaid with jewels to the value of a thousand pounds, together with a white falcon."

Lady Lyoness rode at once to Arthur's court, and in accordance with her lover's wish, refused to disclose his whereabouts, but suggested the tournament as a means of attracting him. Arthur and Margawse both welcomed the suggestion, and it was arranged that Lady Lyoness and the four brothers should rally sufficient knights to match those of the Round Table.

When Lady Lyoness had returned to the Isle of Avalon, where both her own and Sir Gryngamour's castles were situated, and told Sir Gareth of the arrangements for the tournament, he began to complain of his wound:

"Alas, I am afraid that with this accused wound I shall make a very poor showing at the tournament."

"Sir Gareth," Lady Lynet replied, "I will undertake to heal you now; in a fortnight you will be as lusty as ever." And with that she applied some of her magic ointment, and her promise was fulfilled.

Sir Gareth, Sir Gryngamour and his two sisters, Sir Ironside, and Sir Persaunte now discussed their available resources for the tournament, and Sir Gareth said openly that he did not think that the combined followers of the four brothers would be sufficient to match Sir Launcelot and the knights of the Round Table.

"Therefore," he said, "let us rally all your friends from the length and breadth of Britain."

This was agreed upon. Messengers were dispatched, and within the two months that preceded the day of the Assumption of Our Lady, knights who were hostile to Arthur arrived at Avalon from all parts of the country: Sir Epynogres, the prince of Northumberland; Sir Palomides the Saracen with his two brothers, Sir Segwarydes and Sir Safere; Sir Malegryne and Sir Bryan; Sir Grummor Grummorson from Scotland; Sir Carados of the Dolorous Tower and his brother Sir Terquine; Sir Arnold and Sir Gauter, two knights from Cornwall; finally Sir Tristram, who was already one of the most famous knights living, although not yet a knight of the Round Table; and with him came Sir Dynas the Seneschal, and Sir Sadoke.

Meanwhile Arthur had rallied all his knights of the Round Table, together with many of their kin and several of his subject kings and nobles who were eager to represent him. Sir Gawain's kin included Sir Aggravayne, Sir Gaheris, Sir Uwayne, Sir Agglovale, Sir Torre, Sir Percivale, and Sir Lamerok. Sir Launcelot's kin included Sir Ector, Sir Lyonel, Sir Bors, Sir Bleobris, Sir Blamoure, Sir Galyhodyn, Sir Galyhud, Sir Dynadan, Sir Brewnor le Noyre, Sir Sagramour, and Sir Dodynas. Among the kings were the King of Scotland, King Angwyshaunce of Ireland, King Carados, King Uryens, and King Bagdemagus together with his sons, Sir Mellyagraunce and Sir Galahalte. And among his nobles: Sir Brandiles, Sir Uwayne les Avoutres, Sir Melyot, Sir Petipace, and Sir Gotlake.

Both Arthur and Lady Lyoness set out to accommodate and entertain their respective parties on a scale commensurate with the dignity of the occasion, and great quantities of supplies were bought from far and near, overland and across the water.

Sir Gareth was determined to remain incognito throughout the tournament, and begged both Lady Lyoness and Sir Gryngamour not to reveal his identity.

"My lord," said Lady Lyoness, "we shall certainly do as you ask. And now I beg you to wear this ring during the tournament, and to return it to me as soon as it is over. It is a magic ring and enhances my beauty, but for you it has the advantage that it changes the colors of the wearer from red to green, green to blue, blue to white, and so on; also, while you wear it you will lose no blood. So take it as a token of my love, but please be sure to return it."

"My lady, I thank you for it; and certainly my incognito will be an easy matter now."

Just before Lady Lyoness' party set off for King Arthur's court, Sir Gryngamour gave Sir Gareth a bay courser, armor, and a fine sword which his father had won from the Saracens. They arrived on the eve of the feast, and were received splendidly by Arthur, Queen Gwynevere, and Queen Margawse, and that evening the two parties made merry and were entertained by minstrels who had been specially hired.

The tournament started immediately after matins and mass had been heard on the day of the Assumption. The two parties were announced by trumpeters, and the individual combatants by heralds. The jousting matches, which came first, were as follows:

Sir Epynogres versus	Sir Sagramour:	both spears broken.
Sir Palomides "	Sir Gawain:	both unhorsed.
Sir Safere "	Sir Aggravayne:	Sir Aggravayne unhorsed
Sir Segwarydes "	Sir Gaheris:	Sir Gaheris unhorsed.
Sir Malegryne "	Sir Uwayne:	Sir Malegryne's neck dislocated.
Sir Bryan Sir Grummor Grummorson } "	{ Sir Agglovale Sir Torre } :	Sir Bryan and Sir Grummor Grummorson unhorsed
Sir Carados "	Sir Percivale:	both spears broken.
Sir Terquine "	Sir Lamerok:	both unhorsed.
Sir Arnold "	Sir Brandiles:	both spears broken.
Sir Gauter "	Sir Kay:	both spears broken.
Sir Tristram "	Sir Bedivere:	Sir Bedivere unhorsed.
Sir Sadoke "	Sir Petipace:	Sir Petipace unhorsed.

Sir Dynas	versus	Sir Uwayne:	Sir Dynas unhorsed.
Sir Persaunte	"	Sir Launcelot:	Sir Persaunte unhorsed.
Sir Pertolope	"	Sir Lyonel:	Sir Lyonel unhorsed.
Sir Perymones	"	Sir Ector:	both unhorsed.
Sir Ironside	"	Sir Bors:	Sir Bors unhorsed.

Then Sir Gareth rode onto the field, unannounced, and overthrew in turn twelve knights, and the onlookers were filled with wonder as to who this remarkable knight could be, and at his armor, which shone now red, now green, now blue, now white. And the knights whom he overcame were: Sir Bleobris, Sir Galyhodyn, Sir Dynadan, Sir Brewnor, Sir Sagramour, Sir Dodynas, King Angwyshaunce, King Carados, King Uryens, King Bagdemagus, Sir Mellyagraunce, and Sir Galahalte.

King Arthur, curious, and eager to test this unknown knight to the uttermost, summoned Sir Launcelot:

"My good Sir Launcelot, this many-colored knight is indeed valiant: pray, would you enter the field and encounter him?"

"Sire, I would gladly do so, but now that he has already overthrown so many knights, he must be tired; and for me to defeat him in this condition, which I might well do, would mean but little honor for myself, and would rob him of his well-deserved victory. I suspect that his remarkable deeds today are inspired by his love for a lady."

The jousting being done with, both parties now galloped onto the field and commenced an energetic sword fight. The first notable duels were between Sir Ironside and Sir Lamerok, Sir Palomides and Sir Bleobric, and Sir Gawain and Sir Tristram, in which Sir Gawain was unhorsed. Then Sir Launcelot fought Sir Terquine and his brother Sir Carados together, and would have defeated them both had not Sir Gareth come to their aid; however, once he had parted them, Sir Gareth refrained from attacking Sir Launcelot, who thereby guessed his identity.

Sir Gareth then rode into the main press of the battle and overcame five or six of the Round Table knights before encountering his brother, Sir Gawain, whom he also overcame. Meanwhile, Sir Tristram, who had noticed Sir Gareth's exploits, rode over to Sir Ironside and asked him who he might be.

"He is the knight who won his way through the Passage Perelous, overcoming my four brothers and then me in order to release my prisoner, the Lady Lyoness."

"And pray, sir, what is his name?" asked Sir Tristram.

"Sir Gareth of Orkney, Sir Gawain's brother and King Lot's youngest son."

"If he is young now, he will certainly be matchless when he matures."

"There is none better than he," Sir Ironside agreed. Then Sir Persaunte joined them, and the three knights rode over to Sir Gareth and fought by his side.

Not long after, Sir Gareth withdrew from the battle to quench his thirst, and while he was doing so his dwarf took from him his lady's ring, which he forgot to replace when he returned to the battle.

Sir Gareth's armor was in fact yellow, and without his ring it remained so. This was quickly noticed by Arthur, who at once sent heralds to identify the many-colored knight who had puzzled him throughout the tournament. One of the heralds soon rode close enough to read the letters emblazoned in gold on his helmet—"Sir Gareth of Orkney"—and thereupon set up a cry which was taken up by the other heralds:

"The knight in the yellow armor is Sir Gareth of Orkney!"

The moment Sir Gareth heard his identity revealed, he fought his way furiously out of the battle, stunning both Sir Sagramour and Sir Gawain as he did so; then, finding his dwarf, he demanded the ring immediately, and putting it on his finger, galloped into the forest. His brother Sir Gawain, who had recovered, set off in pursuit, but vainly, for Sir Gareth was once more disguised.

When Sir Gareth had successfully eluded his brother, he stopped and asked his dwarf what they should do.

"My lord, I think first you should return Lady Lyoness' ring."

"You are right," said Sir Gareth, and gave the ring to the dwarf, who took it at once to Lady Lyoness.

"Dwarf, where is my lord now?" she asked.

"My lady, he bade me tell you that he will return to you, and in the meantime to keep your vows to him as he will to you."

The dwarf then returned to Sir Gareth, and a violent storm broke over them, with thunder, lightning, and heavy rain. Sir Gareth was extremely weary from the tournament, and so they sought for lodging; but it was not until nightfall that they came to a castle. They rode straight up to the barbican and Sir Gareth begged the porter to let them in.

"Sir, you shall get no lodging here," the surly porter replied.

"Good porter, I beg you to go to the lord or lady of this castle and ask them in the name of King Arthur, my liege, to give me shelter for the night."

Reluctantly, the porter went to the duchess, her lord being absent, and delivered Sir Gareth's message.

"Very well, for the love of King Arthur, admit him," she replied.

The porter lit a torch and led Sir Gareth and the dwarf into the castle, and as they entered Sir Gareth cried aloud:

"My lord or lady, giant or monster or whatever champion may live here, I beg lodging for one night, after which, if I am challenged, I will readily accept."

"Good knight," said the duchess as Sir Gareth approached her, "you speak boldly and as a knight should. Most certainly you shall have lodging for the night, but these are the conditions: that so soon as you meet the duke, who is an enemy of King Arthur and just now absent from the castle, you shall yield to him, and render such service as he requires of you."

"My lady, pray tell me, what is your lord's name?"

"The Duke de la Rowse."

"My lady, I shall yield to the duke and serve him as he requires, provided that service is honorable; otherwise I shall consider I have the right to challenge him, and release myself from my vow by force of arms."

"Sir, you speak justly."

Sir Gareth and the dwarf were led across the drawbridge and into the hall, where their horses were taken from them, and where Sir Gareth disarmed.

"My lady, I shall not stir from your hall tonight; but tomorrow I will gladly accept whatever challenge may be offered me."

The duchess provided Sir Gareth with an excellent supper, and her ladies-in-waiting all admired the hungry knight with his gentle manners, and a lively evening followed, after which Sir Gareth gladly slept.

In the morning, after mass and breakfast, Sir Gareth took his leave of the duchess.

"Sir, be good enough to tell me your name before leaving us."

"My lady, I am called Sir Gareth of Orkney; though by some I am known still as Beaumains."

Then the duchess knew that he was the knight who had rescued the Lady Lyoness.

Sir Gareth continued his journey, and before long came to

a mountain pass where he was challenged by Sir Bendalayne. They jousted and Sir Bendalayne retired to his castle, mortally wounded, and died as soon as he entered. Sir Gareth unwittingly followed the same route, and coming to the castle shortly after Sir Bendalayne, thought to rest himself there. However, he had no sooner gained the entrance than twenty of Sir Bendalayne's followers galloped out and attacked him with their spears. Sir Gareth, who had broken his spear, defended himself with his sword, and ten of his opponents broke their spears upon him. They then retired for a hasty conference, and decided to attack his horse. Sir Gareth managed to leap clear, and raising his shield high, attacked them vigorously and killed sixteen of them; the remaining four fled for their lives.

Sir Gareth then took one of his attackers' horses and rode forward until he came to another castle, where he heard, from within the walls, the sound of women's voices raised high in lamentation. At the entrance to the castle stood a page, and Sir Gareth asked the reason for their lamenting.

"Sir, within the castle are thirty ladies who have all been widowed by the Brown Knight, who is the most formidable and pitiless knight living. So I should advise you to fly while you may."

"Rather will I challenge him," Sir Gareth replied, and at that moment the Brown Knight appeared, and seeing Sir Gareth, couched his spear and charged him without even uttering a preliminary challenge.

Sir Gareth met the charge and drove his spear clean through his opponent's armor and into the body. The Brown Knight's spear broke in his hand, and he fell dead to the ground.

Sir Gareth entered the castle and the ladies warned him to withdraw.

"My ladies, do not fear; I have killed the Brown Knight."

The widows welcomed Sir Gareth as best they could, and he slept in the hall overnight. In the morning at mass he found each of the ladies weeping over the grave of her lost husband.

"My ladies, I beg you, go to King Arthur at the next feast, and say that I, Sir Gareth of Orkney, sent you."

"Sir, we shall do as you command."

Sir Gareth resumed his journey through the mountains until he was challenged by another knight on his path.

"Sir, may I ask your name?" said Sir Gareth.

"The Duke de la Rowse."

"My lord, some time back I lodged at your castle, and made my oath to your lady that when I met you I should yield."

"Ah! So you are the knight who so proudly challenged all comers? Very well then, let us see what you can do; defend yourself!"

Without further ado they jousted and Sir Gareth knocked the duke off his horse. The duke leaped clear and at once challenged Sir Gareth to dismount and fight with his sword. They dueled fiercely for an hour, and then Sir Gareth struck the duke to the ground and prepared to behead him. The duke yielded.

"My lord, you must surrender to King Arthur at the next feast and say that Sir Gareth of Orkney sent you."

"Sir, I am at your command, together with my hundred knights, who shall swear you allegiance."

The duke departed and Sir Gareth stood alone on the mountainside for a few minutes, and then saw a powerful-looking knight galloping toward him with leveled spear. Sir Gareth mounted at once and they thundered together; the strange knight made a skillful thrust and wounded Sir Gareth in the side. They both dismounted and for two hours fought with equal strength and determination; until Lady Lynet, who was sometimes called the Lady Saveage, rode up to them on a mule and appealed to Sir Gareth's opponent:

"Sir Gawain! Fight no longer with your brother!"

Sir Gawain at once threw away his sword and shield and knelt down before Sir Gareth and begged for mercy.

"How is it, sir, that you who just now were so powerful have suddenly yielded to me?" asked Sir Gareth in amazement.

"I am Sir Gawain, your brother; and indeed I have had a long and arduous task in finding you."

Sir Gareth then removed his helmet and knelt before Sir Gawain and begged his mercy. He rose, and they embraced each other and wept, and each insisted that the other had won the duel.

"Dear brother," said Sir Gawain, "I should indeed honor you, for you have won greater fame, and sent more prisoners to King Arthur, than any other knight of the Round Table, with the exception only of Sir Launcelot."

Lady Lynet stanched the brothers' wounds, and then volunteered to fetch King Arthur, who was encamped with his royal suite only two miles away.

As soon as Arthur heard of Sir Gareth's whereabouts he

called for a mount and ordered his whole camp to follow him and to obtain, regardless of cost, provisions for an eight-day celebration. Queen Margawse rode on ahead with Arthur, and when they saw Sir Gareth and Sir Gawain sitting together on the hillside, neither could hold back tears; and there followed a most tender reunion. Soon the rest of Arthur's suite arrived; all made much of Sir Gareth, and the time was spent in feasting and pleasure. By the eighth day both Sir Gareth and Sir Gawain had been cured of their wounds by Lady Lynet, and that day Arthur asked her about her sister:

"My lady, how strange that Lady Lyoness is not with us, considering the extraordinary feats Sir Gareth performed in her honor."

"Sire, I beg you to excuse her, for she is in complete ignorance of Sir Gareth's whereabouts."

"My lady, I beg you then, fetch her."

"Sire, at your pleasure."

Lady Lynet arrived the following morning with her sister, Sir Gryngamour, and his forty knights, and they were accorded a warm welcome by Arthur and his suite; and of all the women present, the Lady Lyoness was certainly the most conspicuous for her peerless beauty and grace. She greeted Sir Gareth, and he her, as lovers do, and then Arthur came up to them and asked Sir Gareth whether he wished the lady for his paramour or his wife.

"Sire, I love her, and her alone."

"And you, my lady, what have you to say?" asked Arthur.

"Sire, Sir Gareth is my first love, and shall be my last; no other could I love or marry, were he king or prince. And should Sir Gareth ask for my hand in marriage, and perhaps he will, I can assure you that with all my heart I should accept him."

"My lady," said Sir Gareth, "my one desire is that you should be my wife, for always I shall love you and you alone."

"My dear lady and my dear nephew, I give you my blessing; and all in my power, as your sovereign, I shall do to protect you."

King Arthur suggested that the wedding should take place on Michaelmas at Kynke Kenadonne, placed as it was on the sea and with a bounteous hinterland. This was agreed, and Arthur departed thither with his suite to prepare for the ceremony, after presenting Lady Lyoness with a valuable gold bracelet.

Sir Gareth returned with Sir Gryngamour and his sisters to

their castle on the Isle of Avalon, and there exchanged rings with his betrothed. He then rode to Kynke Kenadonne and dispatched messengers to rally all the knights he had won in the course of his quests for attendance on his wedding day.

Of all the knights of the Round Table, it was Sir Launcelot who was Sir Gareth's chosen companion; and as he discovered the impetuous character of his brother, Sir Gawain, he came to avoid him, for fear that otherwise he might be provoked to injure or even to kill him.

On Michaelmas Day the Archbishop of Canterbury married Sir Gareth to Lady Lyoness and, at Arthur's request, Sir Gaheris to Lady Lynet (or Lady Saveage), and Sir Aggravayne to their niece, Lady Lawrell. When the triple wedding was over, the knights whom Sir Gareth had overcome arrived with their followers to swear him allegiance, and each volunteered to serve at the banquet: Sir Pertolope as chamberlain, Sir Perymones as chief butler, Sir Persaunte as chief waiter, Sir Ironside as carver, and the Duke de la Rowse as wine waiter. Then the thirty ladies who had been widowed by the Brown Knight all came and knelt before Arthur and swore to do homage to Sir Gareth thereafter. The rest of the day was given over to banqueting and festivity, and throughout the castle the merry minstrels could be heard.

Tournaments were held for the next three days, but at Lady Lyoness' suggestion none of the newly wed knights was allowed to compete. On the first day Sir Lamerok won the laurels, overcoming thirty opponents; and Sir Persaunte was made a knight of the Round Table. On the second day the laurels were won by Sir Tristram, who overcame forty opponents; and Sir Ironside was made a knight of the Round Table. On the third day Sir Launcelot won the laurels, overcoming fifty opponents; and the Duke de la Rowse was made a knight of the Round Table.

As soon as the tournament ended both Sir Tristram and Sir Lamerok disappeared, causing Arthur much displeasure, but the celebrations in honor of Sir Gareth continued for another forty days.

The Book of Sir Tristram of Lyoness

1. ISEULT THE FAIR

It was at the time when King Arthur had established dominion over the whole of the British Isles, over France and Germany and Italy as far as Rome herself, and now commanded, in the fellowship of the Round Table, a chivalry which was unsurpassed, that King Melyodas of Lyoness courted and married Elizabeth, the peerless sister of King Mark of Cornwall.

Melyodas was a knightly king, as attentive to his newfound wife as to the affairs of state, and when, some months later, it was to be seen that Queen Elizabeth was with child, they both found in this great cause for rejoicing.

However, as the time for Elizabeth's confinement drew near, a sorceress, who had for long been in love with King Melyodas, but whose advances had passed unnoticed, decided to capture him for herself by means of an enchantment. Accordingly, one day when he was out hunting, which was his favorite pastime, she singled him out and managed to lure him into her ancient castle, where she held him captive.

When Melyodas failed to return from the hunt, Elizabeth was so distracted by grief that she ran into the forest, accompanied only by one loyal gentlewoman. The violence of her grief, and her exertions as she forced a way through the forest, brought her prematurely to the labors of childbirth; and she threw herself on the ground as she was seized by the first pangs.

The devoted gentlewoman hastened to her aid and a terrible struggle ensued, as all night they attempted to deliver the child; but at last it was born, healthy and sound. Elizabeth offered a prayer of thanks to the Lady of Heaven, and then collapsed with exhaustion and a fever she had caught because of the cold and dampness of the ground.

"My dear companion, recommend me to the king, and tell him that for his sake I have borne his child in circumstances so rude that now I am overcome by them. Beg him to pray for my soul. And you, my little son, you have already killed your mother, so when you come to be of age you must prove yourself a powerful man. I wish you to be named Tristram, which means 'of sorrowful birth'; and I charge my companion to make this my last request to the king."

Thereupon Queen Elizabeth died. Her companion laid her under the shadow of a large tree and then, taking up Tristram, hastened toward the castle for fear that he too might succumb to the fever.

When King Melyodas' barons discovered that the queen was dead, some among them, supposing that the king had also been killed, and with ambitions to usurp the throne, suggested putting Tristram to the sword; but the queen's companion pleaded so justly and with such eloquence for the child that they resolved after all to spare him.

Meanwhile the king had been released from captivity by Merlin, and returned to the court on the day after the queen had died. He was greeted with every appearance of joy by his barons, but when he learned of the queen's death his sorrow was so great that no tongue could describe it. He gave the queen a rich and seemly burial, and christened his son Tristram in accordance with her last wish.

For seven years, while bestowing the utmost care on the upbringing of Tristram, King Melyodas grieved for Elizabeth and remained wifeless. Then he married the daughter of King Howell of Brittany, and in the fullness of time she bore him sons of her own.

While the queen was raising her family, she grew jealous for her children on account of the inheritance which would have fallen to them had it not been for Tristram; and one day she decided to poison him. She mixed some poison and water in a silver goblet and put it in the nursery, trusting that sooner or later he would need to quench his thirst. It happened, however, that her own son was thirsty, and wandering into the nursery, he drank the poison and died.

The queen was heartbroken, but more determined than ever to poison Tristram, so once again she set out the goblet of poisoned water. This time the king, who had suspected nothing and supposed that their son had died by mishap, picked up the goblet to drink just as the queen herself was passing by. She ran up to him, and seizing the goblet, spilled the contents on the floor. The king, suddenly remembering his son's death, grew suspicious, and drawing his sword, shouted at the queen:

"False wretch, what drink was in that goblet? Tell me or you shall die!"

"My lord, I beg you for mercy! It was poison. I wished to kill Tristram in order that my own children should be your rightful heirs."

"Then you must pay the penalty according to the law."

The king's judgment was approved by his barons, and the queen was bound to a stake for burning. Just then the young Tristram knelt before his father and begged that he would grant him his wish.

"It shall be granted," said the king.

"Sire, grant me the life of the queen, my stepmother."

"That is wrongfully asked; and surely, since it was you she wished to poison, you have the best of all reasons for wishing her dead?"

"Sire, I pray to God to show His forgiveness; and in honor of your promise, I beg you to do the same."

"Tristram, since you have my promise, you may go to the fire and release her."

Tristram rescued the queen, but for some time the king could not bear to admit her to his table, or to his chamber at night, and it took Tristram much arduous persuasion to complete the reconciliation. Then the king grew weary of Tristram, and sent him to France to complete his education under the tutorship of a gentleman scholar called Governayle.

After seven years in France, Tristram and Governayle traveled to Cornwall, and when Tristram was eighteen years of age he returned to his father's court. Tristram was now big and handsome and skilled in the arts of barony: in hunting and hawking, music, warfare and the management of arms; and particularly his gift for the harp and his courteous speech won for him the love of all whom he met. The queen, his stepmother, was delighted with him, and, still grateful for his having saved her life, loaded him with gifts.

Not long after Tristram had left Cornwall to return to Lyoness, King Angwyshaunce of Ireland sent a messenger to King Mark demanding the Cornish tribute, which had now lapsed for seven years. King Mark, still unable to pay, returned a message demanding that he should either send a champion to enforce the claim in single combat, or relinquish it altogether.

King Angwyshaunce was at first furious, but then remembering the queen's brother, Sir Marhaus, asked him if he would accept the challenge. Sir Marhaus, a knight of the Round Table, was famous throughout the realm as being second only to Sir Launcelot, the greatest knight of all, and he accepted eagerly.

"Sire, it will be a pleasure for me to serve you. And should King Mark choose for his champion a knight from the Round Table, I shall win great honor for myself in overcoming him."

Sir Marhaus shipped at once to Cornwall, and as soon as he reached the coast, lay to opposite King Mark's castle of Tintagil, and sent a message reiterating the demand for tribute or for a champion to meet him in single combat.

King Mark was much disturbed, aware as he was of Sir Marhaus' fame as a knight, and feeling hopeless of ever finding a champion to match him. Some of his barons suggested Sir Launcelot, but others persuaded him against it, saying that Sir Launcelot would never fight one of his fellows of the Round Table. A proclamation was then made throughout Cornwall offering a rich annuity to any knight who would encounter Sir Marhaus, but none responded.

However, news of King Mark's dilemma reached Tristram in Lyoness, and his association with that country moved him to feel all the more deeply his uncle's distress, and he resolved to speak to his father.

"Sire, is it not shameful that the country of my uncle King Mark should lie in bondage? Were I a knight I should go at once to his aid."

"Tristram, it is indeed a shame, and Sir Marhaus is a champion that none in our country could match."

"Sire, I beg you, give me leave to go to King Mark."

"Tristram, if that is what your conscience dictates, you must go."

While Tristram was making his preparations, he received several piteous letters from Frances, the daughter of the French King Faramon. But Tristram did not return her love, and responded neither to her letters nor to the beautiful brachet she sent as a gift, and sometime later she died of a broken heart.

As soon as he was ready, Tristram rode to Cornwall and presented himself to King Mark; and on all sides he heard people complaining that no knight could be found to match Sir Marhaus.

"Sire, if you will confer on me the order of knighthood, I will fight Sir Marhaus."

"Tell me, who are you and whence do you come?" asked the king.

"My name is Tristram, and I come from the court of King Melyodas, who married your sister, and who reigns over Lyoness."

"Very well; if you wish to be our champion, I will certainly make you a knight."

King Mark at once sent word to Sir Marhaus that he had a young knight who was willing to be his champion. Sir Marhaus replied that his challenge applied only to knights of royal blood, either on the father's or on the mother's side; and so King Mark now asked Sir Tristram to reveal his parentage.

"Sire, I am King Melyodas' son; and your sister, Queen Elizabeth, was my mother."

"Then welcome, my dear nephew!" said the king.

King Mark purchased for Tristram the finest possible horse, harness, and armor, and again sent word to Sir Marhaus, who was delighted that his opponent should be of royal blood on both sides. It was arranged that the combat should take place on a small island where Sir Marhaus' ships lay at anchor.

When Sir Tristram, clad in his magnificent armor, took his leave of the king, the quay was crowded with knights and ladies from the court, yeomen, and commoners; and all wept for pride and grief that so young and noble a knight should set forth to release their land from bondage.

Once on the island, Sir Tristram set his horse and armor to rights with the assistance of his faithful servant, Governayle. On the further shore were anchored the six ships of Sir Marhaus, who himself stood beneath them, fully armed—a grim and commanding figure.

"And now, where is Sir Marhaus?" asked Sir Tristram.

"On the far shore. Did you not see him?" said Governayle.

"Now I can. My good Governayle, sail to King Mark and commend me to him. Do not set foot on the island again until the battle is done, and I am either slain or victorious. If I should die honorably, ask my uncle to bury me where he will; but if I turn coward and fly from my assailant before the battle is done, and then die, I want no Christian burial."

Governayle wept and left him. Then Sir Marhaus rode up.

"Sir Tristram, you are a young knight of noble blood, and I commend you for your courage. But I have fought, and with these arms defeated, not only the greatest knights in the kingdom, but the greatest knights in the world. Be advised, therefore, and return on your good ship whence you came."

"Sir Marhaus, you are a proved knight, and yet your words shall not dissuade me from the cause to which I am pledged. Today I was knighted, and now the time has come for me to prove in combat the royal blood that flows in my veins; and I rejoice that you, my adversary, are of such renown; for should I prove victorious, the honor will be great. And further, I shall free forever the lovely land of Cornwall from the cruel bondage which Ireland anciently forced upon her."

"Sir Tristram, you speak bravely, but will you withstand even three strokes from my sword? It was for my prowess at arms alone that King Arthur chose me for a knight of the Round Table."

First they jousted, and Sir Tristram was wounded in the side. Then they fought with their swords—now with heavy, deliberate blows, now thrusting and feinting, now charging; and so they fought for more than half the day, until both were painfully wounded, and the blood was trickling through the joints in their armor. At last Sir Marhaus began to weaken, and even as he did so, Sir Tristram showed fresh strength and struck Sir Marhaus on the helmet with such force that his sword became lodged in the skull. Three times Sir Tristram tried to withdraw his sword, but failed. Then Sir Marhaus fell on his knees and the sword broke, leaving a fragment still in his skull.

Sir Marhaus flung away his sword and his shield and ran toward his ships, and Sir Tristram cried after him:

"Sir Marhaus, are you not ashamed to so dishonor your kin and the fellowship of the Round Table? For myself I should prefer that we fight to the death, even though I were hacked to pieces."

But Sir Marhaus ignored him and staggered forward, groaning as he went.

"Sir Marhaus, I swear then that I shall take your sword and your shield, and to prove my honor, bear them before King Arthur and your fellows of the Round Table."

Sir Marhaus returned to Ireland and died, for not the most skillful of King Angwyshaunce's surgeons was able to remove the fragment of Sir Tristram's sword from his skull. But after his death his sister, the queen, preserved the fragment carefully for the day when she would be able to accomplish her revenge.

Meanwhile, Sir Tristram was also suffering from his wounds and, once he had cooled down, sank to the ground, bleeding copiously and in great pain.

Then Governayle landed on the island, accompanied by King Mark and several of his barons; they transported him back to the mainland and carried him between them to the castle of Tintagil, where the king summoned the court surgeons.

"May God grant that he live!" said King Mark. "Not for all my lands would I lose my nephew."

For more than a month Sir Tristram lay between life and death, and no surgeon, either of the court or of those King Mark summoned from abroad, was able to cure him. The cause of this was the wound in his side which Sir Marhaus had made with his spear, the tip of which had been poisoned.

At last, however, a woman physician of great fame arrived, and seeing the poisoned wound, said at once that the antidote could be found only in the country from which the poison had come. So a ship was provisioned, and taking with him his harp, and under the care of his gentle servant Governayle, Sir Tristram set sail for Ireland.

By good fortune they sailed into the harbor that lay hard by King Angwyshaunce' castle, and as they hove to, Sir Tristram played hauntingly on his harp, songs that were unknown in Ireland at that time. Word quickly reached the king and queen of his arrival, and they invited him to their court, where the king asked him his name and whence he had come.

"Sire, my name is Tramtrist and I come from the country of Lyoness. My wounds I received while fighting for a lady."

"Then, God willing, you shall have what succor this land can offer," said the king. "But lately I lost in Cornwall the finest knight of this land, Sir Marhaus, who was a knight of the Round Table."

Then the king went on to tell Tristram (who had deliberately reversed his name) how the battle had come about; and Tristram made a semblance of sympathy.

Tristram was put in the care of the king's daughter, Iseult the Fair, who was a skilled physician. She soon discovered the cause of the open wound and applied an antidote for the poison. While Tristram was recovering, he often played his harp. Iseult was enchanted and begged him to teach her to play also, and in the course of their music lessons they fell deeply in love.

It was at this time that Sir Palomides the Saracen came to King Angwyshaunce' court. He too fell in love with Iseult (for she was the most beautiful woman in the land) and offered her many magnificent gifts, and even to become christened if it would please her. Iseult told Sir Tristram of Sir Palomides' gifts, and of his knightly bearing; Sir Tristram grew jealous, and before long there was deadly rivalry between the two knights.

Meanwhile King Angwyshaunce had proclaimed throughout the British Isles and France a tournament in honor of his cousin, the Lady of the Laundis, whom the winner was to wed four days after the tournament, and become lord of all her lands. Iseult brought the news to Tristram, and urged him to compete.

"My lady, I am as yet feeble; and had it not been for your tender care, I should be dead. How then can I hope to joust?"

"Ah, my lord! Will you really not fight? You must know that Sir Palomides has entered, and I am afraid that if you are not competing he will carry off the prize."

"Fair Iseult, I am but a young knight, and my combat with Sir Marhaus was my first and, as you know, has left me sorely wounded. But for your sake I will enter the tournament and encounter Sir Palomides. I ask only this: that I may be disguised, and that none shall know who I am."

"My lord, have no fear. I shall find you horse and armor."

"Then, my love, I am at your command."

On the first day of the tournament Sir Palomides, bearing a black shield, carried all before him. In turn he jousted with Sir Gawain, Sir Gaheris, Sir Aggravayne, King Bagdemagus, Sir Kay, Sir Dodynas, Sir Sagramour, Sir Gunrete, and Sir Gryfflet; and each he overthrew. He became known as the Knight with the Black Shield, and all the knights present dreaded and honored him. Then King Angwyshaunce asked Sir Tristram if he would not compete.

"Sire, alas, my wound is not properly healed yet."

Just then Sir Tristram noticed Hebes le Renownes, the squire who had delivered to him the unwanted letters and brachet from the French princess Frances; the squire also recognized Sir Tristram, and all but fell down in astonishment. Sir Tristram hastily drew him aside and begged him not to reveal his identity.

"Sir, most certainly I shall not do so unless you should wish me to. I have come myself with Sir Gawain in order to be knighted, and were it possible, I should be greatly honored to receive the order at your hands."

"Come secretly to me on the tournament field tomorrow, and it shall be done," Sir Tristram replied.

Meanwhile Iseult, who had been watching Tristram throughout, had noticed the squire's astonishment when he recognized him, and assumed that Tristram must indeed be illustrious in his own country. This pleased her, and increased her love for him.

In the morning Sir Palomides entered the field once more, still bearing his black shield, and overthrew in turn the King of the Hundred Knights and the King of Scotland. Then Iseult led Tristram to the field through a secret postern; she had provided him with a magnificent white horse and white armor, and in the sunlight he appeared like an avenging angel.

Sir Palomides noticed him at once and they jousted, with the result that Sir Palomides was ignominiously overthrown and, as soon as he recovered, fled from the field in shame. The onlookers were filled with wonder as to who this incredible knight might be, and none of the other competitors dared to encounter him, not even Sir Gawain and his nine followers. Iseult was overjoyed.

Sir Tristram then fulfilled his promise and made Hebes a knight; and that day Sir Hebes proved himself worthy of the order, and thereafter was to prove loyal to Sir Tristram.

After leaving the field, Sir Palomides determined to depart secretly from the court; but Sir Tristram, who had been watching him, set off in pursuit, and as soon as he drew level offered a challenge. They fought, and with one blow of his sword Sir Tristram struck Sir Palomides to the ground, and then demanded that he should yield. For fear of his life, Sir Palomides did so.

"Sir Palomides, these are my conditions, that you shall forever forswear paying court to Iseult the Fair, and that for a year and a day you shall bear no arms."

"Sir, I am shamed forever," Sir Palomides replied, and with that he cut off his harness and angrily threw his arms to the ground.

On his way back to the castle Sir Tristram was greeted by a young noblewoman. Recognizing him as the knight who had overthrown Sir Palomides, whom she knew to have overcome the ten knights of the Round Table, the lady asked him if he were not Sir Launcelot, who had won the Dolorous Gard.

"My lady, I am not Sir Launcelot, nor could I match him, unless our Lord, who is all-powerful, should give me the strength to do so."

"Gentle knight, I pray you, put up your visor."

The young noblewoman, who had thought that Sir Launcelot alone could have accomplished what Sir Tristram had, then knew that it was not he; she was nonetheless entranced by Sir Tristram's handsome appearance and bade him adieu.

Sir Tristram re-entered the castle by means of the secret postern, and there Iseult greeted him joyfully. When it became known to the king and queen that it was Sir Tramtrist (as they knew him) who had overcome Sir Palomides, they treated him with even greater hospitality than hitherto; and Sir Tristram spent many happy weeks at the castle with them and with the beautiful Iseult.

One day while Tristram, attended by Governayle and Sir Hebes, was taking a bath which the queen and Iseult had prepared for him, the queen, wandering through his chamber, discovered the sword with the broken edge.

"Alas!" she said to Iseult, "this must belong to the knight who killed my brother, Sir Marhaus."

Iseult was terrified, deeply in love with Tristram as she was, and knowing her mother's cruelty. The queen ran to her chamber and fitted the fragment she had preserved into the sword. Determined to accomplish her revenge at once, she then ran to the bath, with the sword in her hand, and would have killed Sir Tristram on the spot had not Sir Hebes seized her by the arms and taken the sword from her. The queen then ran to the king.

"My lord!" she said, kneeling before him. "The recreant knight who killed my brother, the noble Sir Marhaus, is here."

"Who is he? Where is he?" asked the king.

"Sire, it is Sir Tramtrist, the very knight our daughter has healed."

"Alas! this is sad news, for he is one of the noblest knights I have known. I pray you, leave this matter in my hands."

The king went straight to Sir Tristram's chamber, and found him fully armed and about to leave.

"No, Sir Tramtrist, let us not quarrel. For the love that I bear you, and not to dishonor myself as your host, I will grant you safe-conduct from my court if you will but answer me two questions. Who are you? And did you, in truth, kill Sir Marhaus?"

"Sire, my father is King Melyodas of Lyoness; my mother was Queen Elizabeth, sister to King Mark of Cornwall. She gave birth to me in the wilds of the forest, and died therefrom. Her last wish was that I should be baptized Tristram, and that is my name. I reversed it when I came to your court in order that none should know me.

"I fought Sir Marhaus for the love of my uncle, King Mark, and for the love of Cornwall, where I spent part of my youth; to win fame for myself, and to free Cornwall from the ancient bondage in which you have held her. Sir Marhaus was still alive when he fled from me and took to his ship, and to this day I have his sword and his shield."

"God help me then! Certainly you did as a noble knight should; but I cannot, at the displeasure of my queen and my barony, keep you here."

"Sire, I thank you for your goodness, and pray that when I return to Britain, I may live to serve you yet, in return for the courteous treatment I have received at your hands. Further, I shall always honor your daughter, Iseult the Fair, and be at her command to defend her cause, be it right or wrong. And now, I beg you to allow me to take leave of the queen, your daughter, and the nobles of your court."

"Granted," said the king.

Sir Tristram went first to Iseult the Fair, and told her how it was that he had come to her country, and how it was that he now had to leave, and thanked her for saving his life.

"Gentle knight! your departure fills me with woe, for never have I loved a man as I love you," Iseult responded.

"My lady, I swear by my true name, Tristram of Lyoness, by my father, King Melyodas, and my mother, Queen Elizabeth, that while I live I shall be beholden only to you."

"May God reward you, Sir Tristram; and I swear that for seven years I shall not marry, except by your consent."

Then Tristram gave her a ring, and she gave him one, and he left her weeping as though her heart would break.

Entering the hall, he then cried out before all the barons:

"My lords, the time has come for me to depart for my native land; and I ask you now, if any has cause for complaint against me, to speak up and I shall make him full redress. And if anyone would speak evil of me when I am gone, I ask him to speak it now, and we will settle the matter, man for man."

The barons stood silent, for there was not one who had real cause for complaint, and not one, though several were of the queen's blood and felt her quarrel to be their own, who dared to accept his challenge.

Sir Tristram sailed to Tintagil in Cornwall, and there was welcomed by King Mark, who was rejoicing in his newfound independence. Thence he traveled to his father and the queen in Lyoness, and they granted him a large part of his inheritance, in lands and in wealth. Then, at his request, they gave him permission to return to King Mark.

For many months Sir Tristram lived happily with his uncle, and was much loved by him, but then by mischance they fell out. It happened that both uncle and nephew fell in love with the same woman: the wife of one of the king's barons, Sir Segwarydes. The lady favored Sir Tristram, and although outwardly King Mark and Sir Tristram remained friendly, covertly they were jealous of each other.

One day the lady sent her dwarf to Sir Tristram to make an assignation with him for the following night. As the dwarf was leaving the castle, King Mark waylaid him, and after forcing him to reveal his message, frightened him into secrecy.

Thus it was that as Sir Tristram was riding toward Sir Segwarydes' castle the following night, with his spear at rest, the king, with two of his most trusted knights, charged out of an ambush, and in the course of their attack, wounded him on the chest. Sir Tristram couched his spear and overthrew each of them in turn. Leaving them stunned, he continued on his way toward the castle.

The lady received Sir Tristram at a postern, and after stabling his horse, led him to supper and thence to her chamber. In the warmth of their passion, both Sir Tristram and the lady forgot his wound, which bled freely and stained the sheets. Then one of the servants warned the lady that her lord was within bowshot of the castle, so Sir Tristram hastily armed, and she led him to his horse at the postern, whence he departed.

Sir Segwarydes ascended to his lady's chamber, and there, seeing the disordered state of the bed and the bloodied sheets, realized what had happened.

"Treacherous woman! Tell me who was this knight, and where he has gone; otherwise you shall certainly die for it."

The lady, terrified, admitted at once that it was Sir Tristram, and said that he could not as yet be further than half a mile from the castle. Sir Segwarydes armed and rode hard in the direction of Tintagil until he saw Sir Tristram riding ahead of him.

"Turn, false knight, and defend yourself!" he shouted.

He couched his spear and charged, but the spear broke on Sir Tristram's shield; then he drew his sword and struck out with all his might.

"Sir, pray hold your hand. For the wrong I have done you, I would forbear fighting you," said Sir Tristram.

"Not so! For what you have done, either you or I must die."

Sir Tristram drew his sword and struck Sir Segwarydes on the waist, so hard that he fell to the ground in a faint. Sir Tristram then returned to Tintagil. Sir Segwarydes was later discovered by his retainers, who carried him back to his castle, where he lay for several weeks recovering.

In the weeks that followed, King Mark, Sir Tristram, and Sir Segwarydes all felt cause to be ashamed of their wounds: King Mark for his treachery; although Sir Tristram was ignorant of his having been his principal assailant; Sir Tristram for his adultery; and Sir Segwarydes for his cowardice, for he was too frightened to challenge Sir Tristram a second time. Thus the incident was tacitly forgotten; Sir Tristram and King Mark politely inquired after each other's recovery, but there was no love between them.

One day, when both King Mark and Sir Tristram had recovered from their wounds, Sir Bleobris, brother to Sir Blamoure and cousin to Sir Launcelot, rode into Tintagil and asked the king to grant him his wish. The king was astonished, since he did not know him, but, because he was a knight of the Round Table, agreed to do so.

"Sire, I wish to choose for my paramour the fairest lady at your court."

"Sir Bleobris, I may not deny you; but you choose at your peril," the king replied.

Sir Bleobris chose Sir Segwarydes' wife, and setting her on the back of his squire's horse, rode away. Word soon reached Sir Segwarydes of what had happened, and he set off in pursuit of them.

This cavalier abduction caused feeling to run high at the court; and among the ladies who were aware of Sir Tristram's love for Sir Segwarydes' wife, one in particular rounded on him for failing to go to her rescue.

"My lady, while Sir Segwarydes is the lady's husband, it is not for me to go to her rescue; but should he fail in the attempt, then most gladly will I have ado with Sir Bleobris."

Just then Sir Segwarydes' squire came running in with the

news that Sir Bleobris had overthrown his master, who now lay seriously wounded. King Mark was grieved; Sir Tristram lost no time in arming, and accompanied by Governayle, set off to the rescue.

Sir Tristram had not ridden far when he met his cousin, Sir Andret, who, at the command of King Mark, had set out to bring back to the court two knights of the Round Table who had been riding in search of adventure. Sir Tristram asked him how he had fared.

"Alas, Sir Tristram! they would not listen to my message; instead they both attacked me and I was sadly wounded."

"Good cousin, go your way, and I shall go mine, and perhaps I shall see them and accomplish your revenge for you!"

Within a short while Sir Tristram and Governayle saw the two knights riding ahead of them, and Governayle, recognizing them as knights of the Round Table, advised Sir Tristram against offering a challenge.

"But challenge them I shall, my good Governayle, to avenge my cousin, to win honor for myself, and also because it is a long time since I last fought."

"As you will, then, good master."

As soon as they came within hailing distance of the knights, Sir Tristram asked them whence they had come and what they sought in Cornwall.

"Pray, sir, are you a Cornish knight?" asked Sir Sagramour, with scorn in his voice.

"Sir, why do you ask?" Sir Tristram replied.

"Because Cornish knights lack valor. Why, only just now we encountered one, and in spite of his great words, we soon put him to flight."

"My lords, the knight was my cousin. Perhaps now you will have ado with me; and it may happen that one Cornish knight will defeat two knights of the Round Table."

With that Sir Dodynas, Sir Sagramour's companion, couched his spear and charged at Sir Tristram. However, his spear broke on Sir Tristram's shield, and Sir Tristram, with his own spear, sent Sir Dodynas flying over his horse's cropper, and when he landed he all but broke his neck.

Sir Sagramour was astonished, but he dressed his spear and charged Sir Tristram, with the result that both he and his horse were flung to the ground and he broke his thigh.

"My lords, would you not have more?" asked Sir Tristram. "For surely it is a shame that a Cornish knight, lacking all valor, should overthrow you! Or perhaps among the fellow-

ship of the Round Table there are knights who are somewhat greater than you are?"

"Noble sir, you have proved your words; and now we beg
you to tell us your name and your kin," said Sir Sagramour.

"My lords, you would know my name? Very well, I shall
tell you. I am called Sir Tristram de Lyoness; my father is
King Melyodas, and King Mark of Cornwall is my uncle on
my mother's side."

The two knights now begged Sir Tristram to allow them to
accompany him, but Sir Tristram refused, explaining that he
had next to challenge Sir Bleobris, of their own fellowship.

"God speed you, sir," they both said, as Tristram departed.

Sir Bleobris was riding through a valley when Sir Tristram
overtook him. He was accompanied by his squire, who rode
a small palfrey with the lady behind him.

"Sir, I charge you either to return the lady to the court, or
to deliver her to me," said Sir Tristram.

"Sir, I shall do neither; I have little reason to fear a Cornish
knight."

"And yet, not three miles from here a Cornish knight overcame both Sir Dodynas and Sir Sagramour."

"Sir, you must indeed be powerful, and yet I do not fear
you. Therefore, if you want the lady you must win her."

"Defend yourself!" said Sir Tristram.

They jousted, and both fell to the ground; then for two
hours they fought on foot, until Sir Bleobris staggered backward.

"Gentle knight, hold your hand for a moment and let us
speak."

"Sir, speak on."

"Sir, I beg you tell me your name, and of whom you were
born."

"I am called Sir Tristram; King Melyodas is my father,
and Queen Elizabeth, sister to King Mark, was my mother."

"In truth! you must be the knight who overcame Sir Marhaus
and freed Cornwall, and then overcame Sir Palomides at the
tournament in Ireland, when he had overthrown Sir Gawain
and his nine followers?"

"I am. Now, sir, pray tell me your name."

"Sir Bleobris de Ganys, brother to Sir Blamoure and cousin
to Sir Launcelot du Lake, the greatest of all living knights."

"Sir, for the love of Sir Launcelot I would fight you no
more, for certainly he is the gentlest and bravest of all
knights."

"Good Sir Tristram, let us not fight for the lady. I suggest that, instead, we put her between us and let her choose whom she will."

Now the lady spoke to Sir Tristram:

"Sir, formerly I loved and trusted you more than any man on earth, and my one wish was that you should return that love; but when Sir Bleobris carried me off, you suffered Sir Segwarydes to come to my rescue, and yourself did not stir. Therefore I will now forsake you, as you did me. I choose Sir Bleobris."

Then Sir Bleobris spoke: "Sir, the lady speaks with justice, and yet, for the love I bear you, I would that you took her, rather than that you should suffer any displeasure."

"May Jesu protect me!" said the lady. "For I will not depart with Sir Tristram; and I should not have done so even if he had won me, which he might well have. But Sir Bleobris, I beg you, before you leave this country, take me to the abbey where my lord, Sir Segwarydes, lies wounded."

"My lady," said Sir Tristram, "I thank you for your service, and in future I shall take more care as to what manner of woman I love and trust. For how could I usurp from your rightful lord the honor of rescue? Now, indeed, you have made your quality plain."

Thereupon Sir Tristram departed for Tintagil, and Sir Bleobris and the lady for the abbey where Sir Segwarydes lay wounded. Once there, Sir Bleobris, having accomplished his quest, resumed his journey in search of adventure. Sir Segwarydes was greatly comforted to see his wife again. She told him, and later King Mark, how Sir Tristram had rescued her, and obliged Sir Bleobris to return her to her lord.

King Mark now determined on a means of bringing about Sir Tristram's death. Sir Tristram had told him often of the peerless beauty and grace of Iseult, so he persuaded Sir Tristram that he would have none other for his wife, and begged him to fetch her. Sir Tristram, who still honored his uncle above all men, and who would have been ashamed to decline any adventure, regardless of how perilous, dared not refuse.

Soon a well-found ship was appointed, and escorted by a company of trustworthy knights, Sir Tristram set sail for Ireland. However, he had not sailed for long when a tempest drove him ashore on the coast of Britain, not far from King Arthur's court at Camelot. There Sir Tristram encamped, and set his shield above his pavilion.

A little later two knights of the Round Table, Sir Ector and Sir Morganoure, noticed the camp, and riding up to Sir Tristram's pavilion, knocked on the shield and asked him if he would joust.

"My lords, allow me to arm and I will readily do so," Sir Tristram replied. As soon as he was ready he jousted with each in turn, and overthrew them both. Then they begged Sir Tristram to tell them his name and his country.

"My lords," said Sir Tristram, "I would have you know that I am a knight from Cornwall."

"Alas! that we should have been overthrown!" said Sir Ector. For shame he threw off his armor, and instead of mounting, led his horse toward Camelot.

Then a young noblewoman, evidently in deep distress, rode up to Sir Tristram's pavilion.

"My lady, pray, what is your trouble?" asked Sir Tristram.

"Good knight, I beg you to help me! A most honorable lady charged me to deliver a child to Sir Launcelot, and not far from here a knight waylaid me and kidnaped him."

"My lady, tell me in which direction I should seek this knight."

Sir Tristram rode off in the direction the young noble-woman indicated, and as soon as he came upon the knight, challenged him. The knight turned about to face Sir Tristram, who at once struck him off his horse with his sword. The knight yielded.

"Sir, you shall ride with me and deliver the child to the lady. Now tell me, what is your name?"

"Sir Breuse Sans Pité."

Sir Breuse, although weakened by the blow, managed to remount and, when he had delivered the child, departed. Afterward, Sir Tristram learned that he was a sworn enemy to the knights of the Round Table, and repented that he had dealt with him so leniently.

On returning to his pavilion, Sir Tristram was told by Governayle that King Angwyshaunce was at Camelot, and in need of help.

"Surely," said Sir Tristram, "this is the best news I have heard in seven years; for should I be able to help King Angwyshaunce, he could hardly refuse me his daughter for King Mark. Pray tell me, what is his trouble?"

Governayle explained that the brothers Sir Bleobris and Sir Blamoure had charged King Angwyshaunce with the assassination of their cousin at his court in Ireland. King Arthur had commanded him, on pain of his displeasure and of forfeiting his lands, to present himself at Camelot for trial. However, on the appointed day, King Arthur, together with Sir Launcelot, having been called away to the Joyous Gard, had requested King Carados and the King of Scotland to act in his stead.

On hearing the charge of assassination, the two kings had judged the case in accordance with the law, which was that King Angwyshaunce would have to prove his innocence by force of arms. Either he or an eligible champion, to be found within three days, would have to fight Sir Blamoure (who was regarded as a knight second only to Sir Launcelot, whose cousin he was).

Sir Tristram sent Governayle to fetch King Angwyshaunce, and as soon as they arrived, ran out to greet him. He held the stirrup for the king to dismount, but the king leaped clear, and they embraced.

"Sire, welcome to this country! And should it be that here I can make some return for the hospitality I enjoyed at your court for so long, I should be most pleased."

"Sir Tristram, I thank you. Just now I stand sorely in need of a champion to fight Sir Blamoure, who with his brother Sir Bleobris has brought against me a charge of assassinating their cousin at my court in Ireland. Sir Blamoure is of the hardy kin of Sir Launcelot, and a difficult knight to match."

"Sire, I have already fought with Sir Bleobris, and although I hear that his brother is the hardier, I do not fear him. I will volunteer to be your champion if you will make me two promises: first, that your cause is just; second, that if I am victorious, you will grant me anything reasonable that I ask of you."

"May God be my witness, I should refuse you nothing!"

King Angwyshaunce went straight to the court and told King Carados that he had found a champion. Both Sir Tristram and Sir Blamoure were summoned, and Sir Tristram heard the charge that had been brought against King Angwyshaunce; then preparations were made for the battle. There was much speculation as to who might win, since Sir Tristram had already won great renown. An earnest conversation between Sir Bleobris and Sir Blamoure took place just before the battle:

"My dear brother, when you fight Sir Tristram, whom we know to be a formidable champion, please remember this: that you will be fighting to uphold the honor of our name and of our kin, none less than the peerless Sir Launcelot. Therefore

I pray you, should your strength fail after you have fought to your uttermost, choose to die by the sword rather than utter the shameful word, mercy!"

"May God help me! It shall be so," Sir Blamoure replied.

The two knights entered the field, and couching their spears, thundered together. Sir Blamoure was hurled to the ground. When he had recovered, they both leaped clear of their horses and set to with their swords. They fought with crashing blows, savage lunges, feinting and charging, and the spectators, accustomed as they were to feats at arms, were nevertheless astonished at their unfailing vigor and endurance.

In the end, however, Sir Tristram proved the stronger, and Sir Blamoure, on receiving a tremendous buffet on the helmet, sank to the ground, defeated.

"Sir," he said to Sir Tristram, "I beg you to kill me, for never will I dishonor my name and my kin by uttering the shameful word, mercy!"

Sir Tristram was troubled in his heart as to what he should do, so he walked up to the judges and knelt before them.

"My lords, I beg you to advise me. As you may have witnessed, my honorable opponent is defeated, yet he refuses to yield. For the love of his courage, and of his kin, Sir Launcelot, I would not kill him; but in honor of my charge to King Angwyshaunce I am obliged to do so. Therefore I beg that King Angwyshaunce might pardon him, and spare me from this act."

"For my own part," said King Angwyshaunce, "I would grant Sir Tristram his wish, and I pray that our judges may do likewise."

The kings then summoned Sir Bleobris for his advice.

"My lords, I rejoice that if my noble brother is defeated in his body, he is not defeated in his heart; and I should wish for him, as for myself, that he should die in honor rather than live in shame."

"Then let him live honorably," said the judges, "for such is the wish of his adversary and his champion. And surely you, Sir Bleobris, would not wish otherwise?"

"My lords, as you will," Sir Bleobris replied.

Thereupon Sir Blamoure was lifted from the field and he kissed Sir Tristram and King Angwyshaunce and was reconciled to them both. Then they swore to a bond between them so that neither they nor their kin should ever again enter into combat with each other. Thereafter Sir Launcelot loved Sir Tristram for his knightly and gentle ways.

Sir Tristram accompanied King Angwyshaunce back to Ireland, and the king made it known that Sir Tristram had championed him. He was honored and welcomed by all, but especially by Iseult the Fair, whose love for him became even more ardent than hitherto. Then King Angwyshaunce asked Sir Tristram what it was he had had in mind when he asked that he should be refused nothing reasonable if he proved victorious in the combat.

"Sire, I ask that you shall give me your daughter, Iseult the Fair, not for myself, but for my uncle, King Mark, who wishes to marry her, and to whom I have pledged myself in this matter."

"Alas, Sir Tristram! I had hoped that it would be for yourself that you would ask her hand."

"Sire, in honoring my pledge to my uncle, I betray my own vows to Iseult; but still I have to ask for her hand for him."

"Sir Tristram, you shall have her; and whether you keep her for yourself, or yield her to King Mark, must be a matter of your own choice."

Iseult prepared for her journey to Cornwall, and begged her mother to let her take Brangwayne, whom she loved, as her principal lady-in-waiting. The queen consented, and then summoned Brangwayne and Governayle to her chamber, and giving them a gold flask, commanded them to give it to King Mark and Iseult to drink from on the day of their wedding in order to insure that their love should be fast.

It chanced that when Sir Tristram and Iseult had set sail, and were together in the cabin, they felt thirsty, and Sir Tristram noticed the gold flask and opened it.

"Fair Iseult, let us drink from this flask. I think it must be a noble wine which our servants intended to keep for themselves."

Iseult drank first, and then Sir Tristram, and it seemed to them that they had never drunk a finer wine, so between them they emptied the flask. Thus it happened that if formerly their love for each other had been strong, now it was unassailable. And it was to remain so, for good or for evil, until they died. This was a powerful love potion which the queen had charged her servants to deliver, and one which acted on both body and mind.

The ship touched Cornwall at the Castle Pleure, and there Sir Tristram and Iseult sought lodging for the night. They were received in the castle, but immediately escorted to one of the cells and locked up. Presently a knight and his lady came to visit them.

"Sir, this is surely an uncouth reception for a knight and his lady," said Sir Tristram.

"My lord, it is the custom of the castle; in the morning your lady will be judged, and you will have to fight for your life."

"May God protect me from such savage customs," Sir Tristram replied.

In the morning, Sir Brewnor, the lord of the castle, came to the cell accompanied by his lady and his retainers.

"My lord and my lady," said Sir Brewnor, "this is our custom: First we shall compare our ladies, and she who is the less beautiful shall be beheaded. Then, my lord, we shall fight, and I shall kill you and keep for my pleasure either my lady or yours, according to the judgment."

"You who are named lord of this castle, understand that while I fear no comparison between your lady and mine, I shall by the might of my arms prove mine against all comers," said Sir Tristram, drawing his sword.

"Let us proceed with the judgment," Sir Brewnor replied, and withdrew the veil which his own lady had worn up to then.

"So shall we," said Sir Tristram, and confident of Iseult, turned her thrice about with his sword. It was at once apparent to all, even to Sir Brewnor, that Iseult was the more beautiful.

"How now?" asked Sir Tristram.

"Sir, your lady is the more beautiful, and therefore, when we do battle, I shall win her for myself."

"Not so. Perhaps it is a shame that your lady should lose her head, and yet, has she not connived with you in this evil custom, and thereby caused the death of many a worthy lady and valiant knight? Therefore I shall take some comfort in beheading first her, and afterward you, when I have defeated you on the field." Sir Tristram then beheaded the lady.

The company departed eagerly for the field, where the two knights mounted, set their spears, and jousted, with the result that Sir Brewnor was flung from his horse. However, he waited until Sir Tristram drew near, and then sprang up and killed his horse with a thrust of his sword, and as Sir Tristram fell, leaped after him, hoping to kill him at once.

But Sir Tristram recovered immediately and Sir Brewnor managed to strike only two or three blows before Sir Tristram had his shield before him and was attacking furiously. Notwithstanding his treachery, Sir Brewnor was a powerful knight, and for two hours fought fiercely with Sir Tristram. Then, changing his tactics again, he seized Sir Tristram bodily and threw him to the ground. Sir Tristram, however, who was the strongest knight living, stronger even than Sir Launcelot (who, however, had the better wind), was soon on top of Sir Brewnor, and while he writhed beneath him, unlaced his helmet and beheaded him.

The lords and ladies of the castle ran to Sir Tristram, and after swearing him homage, begged him to stay for a while and free the castle of the odium in which it had stood. Sir Tristram consented, but meanwhile one of the knights had ridden post-haste to Sir Brewnor's son, Sir Galahalte the High Prince, and informed him of what had befallen his father and mother.

Sir Galahalte, accompanied by the King of the Hundred Knights and his entire company, galloped at once to the Castle Pleure to accomplish his revenge. First, Sir Galahalte challenged Sir Tristram to single combat, and they fought for half a day. Then, as his courage began to fail him and his life became endangered, the King and his Hundred Knights all closed around Sir Tristram, who, seeing them, cried out:

"Sir, I thought while we were fighting in single combat that you were an honorable knight; but now I see that you are one who employs accomplices when your courage fails you."

"Sir Tristram, you will have to yield, or else be killed."

"Very well, I yield—not to you, but to your honorable company," said Sir Tristram, and handed him the pommel of his sword. Even as he did so, the King of the Hundred Knights attacked him.

"There is no need," said Sir Galahalte to the king; "my cause is won. In fact it was my father's custom to imprison all who sought hospitality at his castle. Ladies he would compare with his wife, and behead whichever was the less beautiful; knights he always fought, and, until he met my opponent, always succeeded in killing. It is a custom which I myself shall relax."

"A savage custom indeed!" said the king, horrified.

"It seems that you are a noble knight," said Sir Galahalte to Sir Tristram, "and I require that you tell me your name, and what brings you to this country."

"I am called Sir Tristram. My father is King Melyodas of Lyoness; my mother was Queen Elizabeth, sister to King Mark of Cornwall. I was escorting Iseult the Fair, my companion, from King Angwyshaunce of Ireland to King Mark, to whom she is betrothed, when I had the misfortune to encounter first your father and then you."

"Then welcome to our country, Sir Tristram! I shall now permit you to deliver your charge without further interference. But then I require that you shall seek out Sir Launcelot, and abide by him."

"Sir, I thank you for your courtesy," Sir Tristram replied.

News of Sir Launcelot had reached both Sir Tristram and Sir Galahalte at this time, of an incident which had added to his already great renown. He had been riding past the castle of King Carados when he had seen the king riding toward him with Sir Gawain, who was seriously wounded, slung across the saddle.

"How is it with you?" he had asked Sir Gawain.

"Alas, good Sir Launcelot, I am prisoner to this king whom I have just fought; I am seriously wounded, and I beg you to rescue me."

Sir Launcelot had then challenged the king, who, after binding Sir Gawain and flinging him to the ground, had accepted. The king had fought strenuously, but Sir Launcelot had eventually stunned and beheaded him, and then released Sir Gawain. Thus Sir Tristram was eager to seek out Sir Launcelot, and had it not been for his charge, would have done so immediately.

Sir Tristram and Iseult completed their voyage to Tintagil without further incident, and were welcomed by King Mark on their arrival. The king and Iseult were married with due splendor, attended by the lords and ladies of the land, and the wedding was followed by many days of merrymaking, feasting, and tournaments.

When the feast was over, several of the ladies of the court grew jealous of Brangwayne, Queen Iseult's favorite, and decided on a plot to kill her. She was sent into the forest to collect herbs, and there seized and bound hand and foot to a tree. For three days she remained thus, and would certainly have died had not Sir Palomides chanced to see her. He released her bonds and escorted her to a nearby nunnery, where she was able to recover.

Iseult was heartbroken over the loss of Brangwayne, and one night wandered into the forest and came to a well, where she sat down completely overcome by her grief. Then Sir Palomides rode up to her, and she confided in him the cause of her grief.

"Ma'am, if you will grant me my wish, I will restore Brangwayne to you, safe and sound, within half an hour."

The queen was delighted and promised to fulfill Sir Palomides' wish, without giving thought to what it might be. Sir Palomides fetched Brangwayne, who was still fearful for her life until she was greeted by the queen with her customary affection.

"Ma'am, I have now fulfilled my promise; and in due course I shall ask you to fulfill yours."

"Sir, in promising to fulfill your wish, I trusted that as you are a knight, it could not compromise me. Therefore let us go to the king, and before him you shall make it plain."

The three of them then rode to the court, and once before the king Sir Palomides spoke:

"Sire, as you are a true king, I beg you to grant me justice."

"Sir Palomides, what is your case?"

"Sire, lately I met Queen Iseult in the forest and we made this covenant: that if I should restore to her the Lady Brangwayne, the queen should grant me whatever I asked of her. I have fulfilled my promise, and now I require that the queen should fulfill hers."

"Queen Iseult, is this true?" asked the king.

"My lord, it is. I was so anxious to recover Brangwayne that I gave no thought to my promise being used to compromise me."

"My lady, it is justice that you should grant Sir Palomides his wish, whatever it may be, since that was your covenant."

"Sire, my wish is that I take Queen Iseult, and rule her as I please," said Sir Palomides.

"Sir Palomides, take the queen, and face such adventures as shall befall you; for it may be that you shall not enjoy the queen for long."

Thereupon Sir Palomides took the queen by the hand and led her to his horse. Once mounted, he set her behind him and rode away from the castle.

King Mark had given judgment in favor of Sir Palomides in the confidence that Sir Tristram would need little persuasion to rescue the queen immediately. So now he summoned Sir Tristram, and was utterly dismayed to discover that he was out hunting. However, just as he was giving way to despair, one of Sir Tristram's knights presented himself.

"Sire, for the sake of the trust in which you hold my master, Sir Tristram, would you allow me to attempt the rescue of the queen in his stead?"

"Sir Lambegus, may God reward you if you can accomplish it!"

Sir Lambegus galloped away from the castle, and soon overtook Sir Palomides, who asked him if he were not Sir Tristram.

"No, Sir Palomides, I am Sir Lambegus, and Sir Tristram is my master. Were it he, you would certainly have your hands full."

They fought; and before long Sir Lambegus lay on the ground, seriously wounded and unable to rise. Sir Palomides then looked about for Iseult, but found, to his anger and dismay, that she had gone.

Iseult had run into the forest, and finding a well, determined to drown herself. Just in time to save her, a knight called Sir Adtherpe appeared, and hearing her story, offered her asylum in his castle, which stood nearby. Iseult accepted gratefully, and then Sir Adtherpe armed and set off to challenge Sir Palomides.

When it came to the combat Sir Adtherpe was no more able to withstand Sir Palomides than Sir Lambegus had been, and he too soon lay on the ground, seriously wounded and unable to rise.

"Sir, I command you now to fetch Queen Iseult."

"Sir, my wounds prevent me from doing so; but if you follow that path it will take you to my castle, and there you will find her."

Sir Palomides rode along the path, but as he was approaching the castle, Iseult, who was watching from one of the windows, ordered the gates to be shut. Sir Palomides dismounted, set his horse to pasture, and then sat down at the entrance to the castle, completely overcome by chagrin.

Sir Tristram, meanwhile, had returned from the hunt, and learning at the court what had happened, set off at once in pursuit of Iseult and Sir Palomides. First he found Sir Lambegus, and then Sir Adtherpe, and as soon as he had put them in the care of a forester, pushed on to Sir Adtherpe's castle, where he saw Sir Palomides sitting in a state of distraction.

"My good Governayle, pray go and wake Sir Palomides, and tell him to prepare for battle."

It was only when Sir Tristram had ordered him a second time that Governayle succeeded in rousing Sir Palomides from his torpor; even then he did not utter a word, but as one in a dream, prepared his horse, mounted, and couched his spear. They jousted and Sir Palomides was thrown over his horse's tail. He recovered quickly, and for two hours they battled furiously, both inspired by love of the same woman.

Meanwhile, Iseult was watching from a window in the tower, and was deeply troubled by the thought that Sir Palomides might be killed before he was christened, and at last, unable to bear it any longer, ran out to them and begged them to stop fighting.

"My lady, do you wish that I should forever be dishonored? You know full well that I am bound to accept your command," said Sir Tristram.

"My own dear lord, you know full well that I would not wish you dishonored; but I tremble to think that Sir Palomides might die still a Saracen."

"As you will, my lady."

"Sir Palomides, as you love me, I command that in whatsoever country I may be, you shall not be there. And now go to Queen Gwynevere at King Arthur's court, commend me to her, and tell her that throughout King Arthur's realms there are but four lovers: herself and Sir Launcelot; myself and Sir Tristram."

"My lady, it goes hardly with me, but I will obey you," Sir Palomides replied.

The two knights and the queen then took leave of each other and departed, Sir Palomides for King Arthur's court, Sir Tristram and the queen for King Mark's, where they were welcomed with great joy. On his return journey Sir Tristram had called for Sir Lambegus, who for several weeks was to remain disabled by the wounds inflicted by Sir Palomides.

While Sir Tristram was generally loved and honored at the court, there was one knight who was jealous of him and wished him evil. This was his cousin Sir Andret, who now spent his time spying on Sir Tristram and Iseult until the opportunity should arise of betraying them to the king. One night, as he was peering through the castle windows, he chanced to see them together in one of the chambers; he ran at once to the king, and together they burst in on them.

"Traitor! traitor!" shouted the king, as he lunged at Sir Tristram with his sword. However, Sir Tristram was able to seize him by the arms and wrench the sword from his grasp.

"My lords, I command you, kill this treacherous knight!" the king shouted, but none who had followed him would obey. Sir Tristram then chased the king out of the chamber, beating him on the back of the neck with the flat of the sword.

Hastily summoning his men, Sir Tristram then galloped out into the forest and there took refuge; and in the course of the next few days he waylaid and wounded or killed more than thirty of King Mark's knights who ventured outside the castle. Among them were two brothers, the first of whom he beheaded and the second of whom he wounded. He then commanded the wounded knight to bear his brother's head on his helmet to the king. The wounded knight obeyed him, but fell dead as he delivered it.

The king summoned his privy council, and Sir Dynas the Seneschal advised him:

"Sire, in honor, and for renown, Sir Tristram is second only to Sir Launcelot; also he is much loved. Hence to make an enemy of him would be dangerous, especially if he were to swear allegiance to King Arthur, who would doubtless be glad to have him, and then stir up feeling against us. Therefore, your majesty, I recommend that you invite Sir Tristram to return to the court without prejudice."

King Mark agreed; Sir Tristram returned to the court and they were reconciled. There followed a joyful period, when the king and queen, with Sir Tristram and the lords and ladies of the court, all moved into the forest and camped there, to give themselves up to the pleasures of the hunt, games, and jousting.

One day two errant knights rode up to the camp and challenged all comers. King Mark had thirty knights always ready to joust; and Sir Dryaunte, who was the first to try them, overthrew several before he himself was unhorsed. Then his companion, Sir Lamerok de Galys, tried, and overthrew all thirty in turn.

"Sir Tristram," said King Mark, "this is indeed a remarkable knight. I pray you go and joust with him, for it is a shame that he should leave the field unmatched."

"Sire, would it not be a greater shame to rob him of his victory now that both he and his horse are tired? For I do not doubt that, fresh as I am, and with a fresh horse, I should at present overcome him."

"Sir Tristram, I pray you, as you love me and Queen Iseult, go and joust with him."

"Sire, it is against my scruples to do so, but still I am yours to command."

Sir Tristram and Sir Lamerok jousted, and Sir Lamerok was thrown to the ground; he leaped up at once, and drew his sword and shouted:

"Sir, alight at your peril!"

"Sir, I will not fight with you on foot; it was already against my scruples to joust with you."

"Sir Tristram, for so you are called, I can hardly thank you for your scruples now that you have overthrown me; therefore, I pray you, let me prove myself on foot."

"Sir Lamerok, I pray you do not challenge me today, for already I am ashamed of what I have done."

"Sir Tristram, your shame is your own concern, not mine; and if you are worth the honor in which you are held, I require that you accept my challenge, and I shall not fail you."

"Sir, I so love you for your greatness of heart, that nothing will pursuade me to fight you today, while I am still fresh and you are weary; so now I pray you, let be."

"Sir, I shall surely revenge myself for this."

Sir Lamerok and Sir Dryaunte departed; and before long met one of Morgan le Fay's knights, who was on his way to Camelot. In order to discomfort King Arthur, Queen Gwynevere, and Sir Launcelot, Morgan le Fay had devised a special drinking horn, which she had charged this knight to deliver to them. The horn was richly inlaid with gold, and had the property that only women who were innocent of adultery could drink from it without spilling any of the wine.

On hearing this, Sir Lamerok commanded the knight, on pain of death, to deliver the horn first to King Mark, saying that he, Sir Lamerok, had sent it, and charge him to offer it to his queen to drink from; for Sir Tristram's love for Iseult was by now as famous as Sir Launcelot's love for Gwynevere.

The knight did as he was commanded, and not only Iseult, but a hundred ladies of the court, were all obliged to drink from the horn, with the result that only four were shown innocent.

"Alas!" said King Mark, "this is a mischievous horn, for now my queen and all these ladies will have to be burnt at the stake."

However, the lords of King Mark's court at once held a council, and as a result of it, protested to the king against being ruled by the device of a sorceress as notoriously evil as Morgan le Fay; and the king acquiesced. But thereafter Sir Tristram and those lords held both Sir Lamerok and Morgan le Fay in the greatest hatred and contempt.

Meanwhile, Sir Tristram and Iseult, in spite of the dangers that beset them, night after night companied in love in one or another of the castle chambers. And ever, the treacherous Sir Andret sought to betray them. At last he found an opportunity, and, with twelve accomplices, burst in on them while they were lying naked in bed together. They were taken prisoner and locked in two of the castle cells overnight.

The following day, Sir Andret, with the assent of King
Mark, and accompanied by forty knights, led Sir Tristram to
a small chapel built at the edge of the cliffs, to administer
judgment.

"My lords," said Sir Tristram, "this is not how you received
me when I returned with a poisoned wound from my combat
with Sir Marhaus, who, while he lived, was the second greatest
of all knights. By defeating Sir Marhaus I freed you all from
the heavy tribute which you owed to King Angwyshaunce of
Ireland, and freed Cornwall forever from her bondage. But
now it is a different story: I am stricken by love, not for a land,
but for a lady, and so in the meanness of your hearts, you all
set upon me. And you, my cousin, Sir Andret, whose revenge
I accomplished against two notable knights of the Round
Table—this is how you show your cousinly love and gratitude?
And well you know that were it a matter of combat between
us, man for man, it would not be I who would die today."

"False traitor!" Sir Andret replied. "But for all your boasts,
today you shall die." And with that he rushed at Sir Tristram
with his sword.

Sir Tristram, who was bound by the wrists to two knights
who formed his escort, suddenly drew the knights together
and wrenched himself free; then, leaping at Sir Andret, wrested
the sword from his hand, and struck him so hard on the helmet
that he fell groveling to the ground.

The whole bodyguard now set upon Sir Tristram, who, with
his back to the chapel door, killed the first ten who came within
reach of him; but still he was without armor, and seeing how
greatly he was outnumbered, withdrew into the chapel. Then,
climbing onto the chantry, he tore out the bars from the window and leaped through, over the cliffs and down to the beach
below.

The humiliated bodyguard returned with Sir Andret to the
court; but Sir Lambegus, Sir Sentrayle, and Governayle returned secretly to the chapel, and by means of a rope drew
Sir Tristram up the cliff.

"My good Governayle, tell me now, what they have done
with Queen Iseult?" said Sir Tristram.

"Sir, she is confined in a leper's hut."

"Alas, what an ungodly place! But she shall not be there for
long."

Sir Tristram then rescued Iseult and escaped with her into
the forest, where he dismissed all his men but Governayle,
and where they lived together for some time.

Then it happened, when Tristram had been hunting alone in the forest, and had fallen asleep beneath a tree, that a brother to one of the knights whom Tristram had killed chanced to see him, and letting fly with his bow and arrow, wounded him in the shoulder. Sir Tristram leaped up in time to catch the man and kill him.

The tip of the arrow had been poisoned, and so Sir Tristram was in great pain when he returned to the spot where he had left Iseult, only to find her gone. A party of King Mark's, finding her alone and unprotected, had taken her prisoner and led her back to the castle; so now Sir Tristram was doubly grieved, in his heart and in his shoulder.

Meanwhile, Iseult came to hear of Sir Tristram's wound, and being unable to cure him herself, while held captive in the castle, managed to deliver a message to him by means of one of her ladies, a cousin to Brangwayne. She advised him to go to King Howell of Brittany, whose daughter, Isode of the Fair Hands, alone possessed the skill to cure him.

King Howell welcomed Sir Tristram with open arms, not having seen him since he was a boy, and Isode speedily cured his wound. At this time King Howell was being besieged by the Earl Grype, and one day his son, Sir Keyhydyns, who was in command of their defense, was seriously wounded. On learning this, Governayle spoke to the king:

"Sire, why not ask Sir Tristram to go into the field and defend your castle?"

"My good Governayle, I shall do as you suggest."

Sir Tristram, eager to repay his host, at once sallied forth at the head of King Howell's men, and in a tremendous battle himself killed more than a hundred of the enemy, including the Earl Grype. King Howell was overjoyed, and offered to reward Sir Tristram with his entire kingdom, but Sir Tristram refused it.

"Sire, what I have done still leaves me indebted to you, on behalf of what your daughter has done for me."

In the course of the celebrations which followed his triumph, and while much was being made of him by everyone, especially Isode of the Fair Hands, Sir Tristram was so elated that he began to forget, not merely the wound which had caused him to come to France, but also Iseult, who in her love had sent him thither. Thus, when King Howell suggested to Sir Tristram that he should marry his daughter, Sir Tristram agreed; and the wedding followed not long after.

It was on his wedding night, when he lay in bed with Isode and held her in his arms, that Sir Tristram suddenly recalled the full force of his love for Iseult. He was so stricken by remorse, and so bewildered by the foolhardiness which had led him to this marriage, that throughout the night he did no more than embrace and kiss his bride, denying her the gift of love. And she, in her innocence, was astonished that the wedding night should mean no more than this.

Shortly after the wedding a knight called Sir Suppynabyles, who had been traveling in Brittany at the time, returned to Britain, and gave news of the marriage to King Arthur and all at his court. Sir Launcelot was furious.

"For shame!" he said, "that a knight as noble as Sir Tristram should betray his first love—the more so since it was the peerless Iseult. Sir Suppynabyles, I pray you deliver this message to him: 'I, Sir Launcelot, who have loved you more than any knight living for your brave deeds and gentle heart, must now despise you more than any knight living, and henceforth be counted your mortal enemy.'"

Sir Suppynabyles duly delivered the message to Sir Tristram, who was brokenhearted that he should have lost the confidence of Sir Launcelot.

Meanwhile, Iseult had written to Queen Gwynevere, complaining of Sir Tristram's infidelity, and Gwynevere had replied, urging her to take comfort in the knowledge that the most noble knights were the most easily lured into wrongful marriages, but that subsequently they always returned to their first love with even greater ardor than before.

2. SIR LAMEROK DE GALYS

When Sir Lamerok had commanded Morgan le Fay's knight to deliver her testing-horn to King Mark, in order to spite Sir Tristram, he set sail for King Arthur's court, but was soon driven from his course by a storm, and wrecked on a rocky peninsula off the coast of North Wales. The ship's crew were all drowned, but by dint of strong swimming, Sir Lamerok got ashore, and there the local fishermen gave him clothes and looked after him.

The peninsula was known as the Ile of Servage and was ruled by the lord, Sir Nabon le Noyre, who, according to the fishermen, was a giant of a man, savage in his practices and a sworn enemy to King Arthur and his fellowship of the Round Table. Several of Arthur's knights had ventured to the peninsula, and been defeated by Sir Nabon and then torn limb from limb, the last of them being Sir Nanowne le Petyte.

"Alas!" said Sir Lamerock, "he was my cousin; I should dearly like to avenge him before I leave."

"Willy-nilly you shall encounter the lord before you leave, for otherwise we ourselves shall be put to death."

"Very well, I shall tell him that I am from King Arthur's court, and challenge him."

It happened that while Sir Lamerock was still being cared for by the fishermen, Sir Tristram, who had been sailing for pleasure with his wife Isode and her brother Sir Keyhydyns, was driven ashore not far away. His boat was wrecked and Isode injured, so they made their way through the forest as best they could, until they came to a well where they met Sir Segwarydes with a young noblewoman.

"Sir Tristram de Lyoness! Of all knights living, surely it is you whom I should hate the most for coming between my wife and myself. But that is in the past now, and I swear that I could never hate a knight of your noble prowess for the sake of a faithless wife; so let us be friends, and together see what comfort we can find in this wild country."

So saying, Sir Segwarydes led the party to the castle of a lady who had herself been born in Cornwall. The lady warned them of the dangers that beset them, and of the evil practices of the lord of the Ile of Servage.

"My lady," said Sir Tristram, "formerly I fought Sir Marhaus and delivered Cornwall from bondage, then I fought Sir Blamoure and saved the honor of King Angwyshaunce of Ireland, and it was at his court that I defeated Sir Palomides the Saracen. I am known as Sir Tristram de Lyoness, and reasonably I hope to meet the dangers which you have enlarged upon."

The lady made Sir Tristram and his companions comfortable in her castle, and that evening a fisherman begged admittance to tell them of "a noble knight of King Arthur's court, who had been shipwrecked a few days earlier not far from the castle."

"Pray, who is he?" asked Sir Tristram.

"My lords, I do not know."

"Then be good enough to bring him here in the morning," said the lady, and the fisherman departed.

When Sir Lamerok arrived in the morning, attired in fisherman's garb, Sir Tristram recognized him at once, and could hardly conceal a smile; but Sir Lamerock did not recognize Sir Tristram.

"Sir," said Sir Tristram, "I presume that lately you have changed your clothes? for surely I have seen you before?"

"You may well have seen me, for so have all the noblest knights of the Round Table."

"Sir, pray tell me your name."

"I will tell you my name on condition that you tell me yours, for I must know if you are lord of the Ile, Sir Nabon le Noyre."

"I am not Sir Nabon, but his sworn enemy, as you are, and so I shall prove before I leave this ile."

"Sir, you have spoken well, and since we are sworn to the same cause, I will tell you my name: Sir Lamerok de Galys, son to King Pellinore."

"Sir Lamerok, you have spoken the truth, and had you not, I should have known to the contrary."

"Then, pray, who are you that you know me already?"

"None other than Sir Tristram de Lyoness."

"The very knight who refused my challenge at Tintagil?"

"Sir, you had already proved your might when we jousted. You were weary and I was fresh, and that was why I refused your challenge. And in return for this courtesy you caused that evil horn to be delivered to King Mark, and thereby discomforted all but four of the ladies at his court."

"Sir, I would do the same again rather than allow the horn to go to King Arthur's court, which is surely very different from King Mark's."

"Sir Lamerok, you know well that your motive was to spite me; but, thank God! King Mark was prevailed upon to show mercy, so little came of it. Now let us forget our quarrel, and together seek honor in overcoming this tyrant who rules the ile."

"Sir, now I can believe that you are the peerless knight that men hold you to be; and out of your gentleness I beg you, forgive me."

Sir Nabon, in honor of the knighting of his son, had proclaimed a tournament for five days thence. Knights of the realm of Logres were to compete with those of West Britain, and the presence of all knights on the ile was compulsory. On the day of the tournament more than five hundred knights assembled, among them Sir Tristram, Sir Lamerok, Sir Keyhydyns, and Sir Segwarydes; and it was Sir Lamerok who distinguished himself that day. He jousted with and overthrew nearly all of the five hundred, and Sir Nabon's curiosity was aroused.

"Sir," he said, "I ask you to joust with me, for I have never before seen one knight overthrow so many others in one day."

"My lord, I accept your challenge, bruised and weary as I am."

The two knights drew apart, couched their spears, and charged at each other; but Sir Nabon, instead of aiming at his opponent, aimed at his horse's head, and killed it before he came within reach of Sir Lamerok's spear. Then they fought on foot for some time, until Sir Lamerok, weary as he was, began to fall back.

"Sir, because of your feats today I shall spare you, which is not my custom, if one of your companions will offer to fight in your stead."

Hearing this challenge, Sir Tristram at once stepped forward and begged for armor.

"Sir, go to my pavilion yonder, and help yourself," Sir Nabon replied.

Sir Tristram armed to his satisfaction, but did not mount, since Sir Nabon had fouled in the previous jousting.

"Sir, defend yourself!"

At first Sir Nabon and Sir Tristram appeared to be evenly matched, so long did they fight without pause, each delivering and withstanding tremendous blows. Then Sir Nabon withdrew for a moment.

"Sir, pray tell me your name."

"My lord, my name is Sir Tristram de Lyoness; and King Mark of Cornwall is my liege."

"Sir Tristram, you are welcome; for above all other knights I have wished to encounter you, or else Sir Launcelot."

They fought once more and Sir Tristram killed his opponent. Then, running over to his son, he swiftly beheaded him, too. Thereupon all the lords and ladies of the castle knelt before him and begged him to accept suzerainty of the Ile of Servage.

"My lords," said Sir Tristram, "I do not deserve it; I suggest that you offer the suzerainty to Sir Lamerok, whose feats today you have all witnessed."

"My lords," said Sir Lamerok, "it is surely Sir Tristram who deserves it! Therefore I add my voice to yours in begging that he will accept it."

"Then let us give it to a knight who deserves it less than we do," Sir Tristram replied.

By general consent the suzerainty was awarded to Sir Segwarydes, who at once released Sir Nabon's prisoners and set the land to rights. He then returned to King Mark in Cornwall and told everyone at the court of the exploits of the two knights, and his own advancement to lord of the Ile of Servage; but when Iseult heard the news of Sir Tristram, accompanied by his wife Isode, she wept secretly.

Sir Tristram and Sir Lamerok parted in the forest, and Lady Isode set sail with her brother for Brittany, and when she arrived, reported all that had happened to King Howell. Sir Lamerok resumed his journey to King Arthur's court, and riding through a valley came upon a monastery where the monks regarded him with astonishment, and asked him whence he had come. He told them he had come from the castle of the Ile of Servage.

"That is indeed remarkable," said one of the monks, "for this is the first time in twenty years that a knight has escaped from the ile without being either killed or taken prisoner."

Sir Lamerok then related how Sir Tristram had killed the tyrant Sir Nabon, and made Sir Segwarydes lord in his stead.

"Then surely we shall honor Sir Tristram at this monastery."

Sir Lamerok stayed overnight at the monastery, and the following morning continued his journey until he came upon a knight defending himself desperately against four assailants. Sir Lamerok rode his horse between them and demanded to know the cause of their unknightly behavior.

"Sir, this knight is a miscreant."

"I have only your word for it. Now, what has the defendant to say?"

"Good knight, I am no miscreant, and will prove it, man for man, against any of my assailants."

"Do not suppose that we shall put ourselves in jeopardy for your sake," said one of the assailants. "But were King Arthur himself present, you would still have to perish."

"That is a fine boast!" said Sir Lamerok. "But then there are many who will say things behind a man's back which they would not dare to utter in his presence. Now understand, I am one of the humblest of King Arthur's knights, but before long I shall put an end to your boasts."

Thereupon Sir Lamerok drew his sword, and with two strokes killed two of the assailants; the other two fled in dismay.

"Pray, sir, what is your name?"

"Sir Froll of the Outer Isles."

Sir Lamerok and Sir Froll rode on together, and before long saw a magnificent knight clad in white armor riding toward them.

"I must joust again with this knight," said Sir Froll, "for only lately he overthrew me."

"I should advise you not to, for I think he is a knight of the Round Table. But tell me, was it at your instance or his that you jousted?"

"At mine, and I am determined to try again," said Sir Froll; and then he shouted to the knight, "Sir, defend yourself!"

"Very well," the white knight replied, "although I wish neither to jest nor to joust with you again."

They jousted and Sir Froll was thrown to the ground. The white knight continued quietly on his way; but Sir Lamerok rode swiftly after him, and when he had drawn level, asked him if he were not a knight of the Round Table.

"Sir, I will tell you my name on this covenant: that you shall keep it a secret, and tell me your own name first."

"Sir, I am called Sir Lamerok de Galys."

"And I am called Sir Launcelot du Lake."

Thereupon they both threw off their helmets and embraced.

"Sir Launcelot, allow me to serve you."

"Sir Lamerok, God forbid that one of such noble blood should serve me. And just now my quest is one which I must accomplish alone."

"Then God's speed!" said Sir Lamerok, and they parted.

"Tell me, Sir Lamerok, who was that knight?" asked Sir Froll.

"It is not for you to know at this time, or even to ask."

"For your discourtesy I shall take my leave of you."

"As you will. Since you are still alive, you can still choose."

They parted. Three days later Sir Lamerok was riding toward a well where a knight lay sleeping and a young noblewoman watched over him, when he saw Sir Gawain ride up to them, seize the young noblewoman, place her behind his squire and ride away again.

"Sir, I bid you come back!" shouted Sir Lamerok.

"Sir, what would you? I am King Arthur's nephew."

"Then I shall forbear jousting with you; but otherwise, I swear, I would have won the lady."

However, Sir Gawain did turn back, and the knight who had lain sleeping now woke up and challenged him. They jousted and Sir Gawain was overthrown, and the knight recovered his lady. Sir Lamerok now challenged the knight in order to avenge Sir Gawain, which he was obliged to do since they were both fellows of the Round Table.

They jousted, and Sir Lamerok killed the knight at the first encounter. The young noblewoman at once rode to the knight's brother, Sir Bellyaunce the Proud, whose pavilion was pitched nearby, and told him of his brother's death, and together they returned to Sir Lamerok.

"Sir, you have killed my brother Sir Froll, a greater knight than you ever were; and I come to avenge him."

"Sir, what you say was today proved otherwise."

They jousted, both were unhorsed, and then for two hours they fought on foot.

"Sir, I pray you, tell me your name."

"Sir Lamerok de Galys."

"Sir Lamerok, to save your life I killed my sons; now you have killed my brother. Surely I have cause to hate you; so defend yourself!"

But Sir Lamerok at once knelt before him: "Sir, I yield, not because of your strength, but because I am beholden to you."

"Arise, and defend yourself!"

"Sir, I yield, and pray that for the love of Jesu you will forgive me."

"Sir Lamerok, arise and defend yourself; otherwise I shall kill you where you kneel."

They fought again, a bloody battle, and at last Sir Bellyaunce fell faint to the ground. Sir Lamerok threw his shield over his shoulder and asked: "What cheer?"

"Well!"

"Sir Bellyaunce, I still yield to you."

"Sir, you yield where, had our positions been reversed, I should have killed you. I thank you for your gentleness, and beg you, forgive my malice."

Thereupon the two knights threw off their helmets and kissed each other, and Sir Lamerok cared for Sir Bellyaunce until his wounds were healed, then returned to Arthur's court.

3. LA COTE MALE TAYLE

One day a young man came to Arthur's court, knelt before Arthur, and begged to be made a knight. He was well built and well dressed except for his coat, which, although of the finest gold cloth, was in tatters.

"What is your name?" said Arthur.

"Sire, I am called Brewnor le Noyre, and in due course it will be revealed that I am of noble blood."

"The name he really deserves," said Sir Kay, "is La Cote Male Tayle, that is, the evil-shaped coat."

"To ask to be knighted is to ask much," said Arthur. "But tell me, how do you come to be wearing that coat?"

"Sire, it was my father's coat. One day when he had been hunting in the forest, and then fallen asleep, an enemy of his chanced to find him, and hewed him to pieces. This was the coat he was wearing when he was killed, and therefore I have resolved to wear it myself until I have avenged his death."

"Sire," said Sir Lamerok, "do you not remember how Sir Launcelot first came to this court? Surely he was much as this young man is, of large build and noble countenance, but one whose birth was unknown to us; and now he has proved the foremost knight in the world. Therefore I suggest that you grant Brewnor his wish, and make him a knight too."

"That is well said," Sir Gaheris assented.

"Sir Lamerok, at your request, Brewnor shall be knighted tomorrow," said the king.

Early in the morning King Arthur took a party of his knights into the forest to hunt a hart, and La Cote Male Tayle remained with Queen Gwynevere and her suite. Suddenly a lion, which had been held captive in one of the towers, appeared in the hall. The queen fled, begging her knights to rescue her, but they were as frightened as she was, and all fled after her. La Cote Male Tayle alone remained, and drawing his sword, allowed the lion to spring at him, and as it did so, struck off the head.

When Arthur returned from the hunt the queen told him of La Cote Male Tayle's exploit, and Arthur was delighted.

"This certainly augurs well for his future," he said, and thereupon knighted La Cote Male Tayle.

"Sire, I have one more request to make: that henceforth I shall be known to all at the court as La Cote Male Tayle, since that is how Sir Kay has named me."

"Granted!" said Arthur.

Some time later a young noblewoman came into the hall, bearing a black shield with the device worked in white relief and representing a hand grasping a sword. Arthur asked her whence she had come, and for what purpose.

"Sire, I am seeking a knight hardy enough to undertake the adventure of this shield. For long have I borne it; the knight who gave it to me had won it at great peril, and then he died as the result of a combat with another knight. So now I beg that a champion from your court may undertake this quest."

"My lords, is there any among you who will undertake the lady's quest?" said Arthur.

But none came forward. Then Sir Kay picked up the shield and examined it curiously.

"Sir, what is your name?" asked the young noblewoman.

"Sir Kay the Seneschal; my lady, I am well known."

"Sir Kay, I beg you lay down the shield; this quest is for a greater knight than you."

"My lady, I do not choose to go on this quest, nor shall I accompany anyone who does."

There followed a long silence; then La Cote Male Tayle spoke up:

"My lady, only this day I was knighted; and now I would take this shield, and ask you to lead me where you will."

"Sir, what is your name?"

"La Cote Male Tayle."

"Then you are well named, and should you follow this quest your skin will come to resemble your coat."

"My lady, should that occur, at least I should not need to ask you for succor."

Two squires now came into the hall with horse, armor, and two spears, and when La Cote Male Tayle was clad and mounted he took his leave of the king.

"Sir, you have indeed chosen a perilous quest," said Arthur.

"Sire, surely it is my first, and yet I would not fail."

Meanwhile the young noblewoman, whose name was Maledysaunte, had ridden away, and so La Cote Male Tayle galloped after her; but as soon as he drew level, she rebuked him for accompanying her.

Then Sir Kay bade Sir Dagonet, the court fool, to clad himself in armor, take a spear, and joust with La Cote Male Tayle. The fool did so, and was flung from his horse.

"Sir, it is now you who are the fool, for jousting with a fool," said Maledysaunte.

But La Cote Male Tayle continued to accompany her despite

her rebukes. Then they met Sir Bleobris, who offered to joust with him; he accepted and was thrown off his horse. Immediately La Cote Male Tayle leaped up, and putting his shield before him, drew his sword, and challenged him.

"No, sir," said Sir Bleobris, "I shall not fight with you today," and departed.

"Now that you are proved both a fool and a coward, why not return to the court?" asked Maledysaunte.

"My lady, I am grieved enough without your rebuking me! But still I maintain that I am no worse a knight for having been unhorsed by Sir Bleobris."

They continued their journey for another two days, and then La Cote Male Tayle encountered Sir Palomides and, as before, was thrown off his horse.

"Sir, surely it has become absurd for you to accompany me, since the only knight you were able to withstand was Sir Dagonet the fool."

"My lady, I offered to fight both Sir Bleobris and Sir Palomides on foot, and both declined my challenge."

"And why should they so lower themselves as to accept a challenge from a knight who cannot stay on his horse?"

Just then they were joined by Sir Modred, Sir Gawain's brother, and the three of them rode on together until they came to the Castle Orgulus. The custom at the castle was that no errant knight should pass without being challenged, taken prisoner, or yielding his horse and armor.

They were soon confronted by two knights. Sir Modred jousted with one, and was overthrown; La Cote Male Tayle jousted with the other and wounded him, although both came off their horses. La Cote Male Tayle remounted and first charged Sir Modred's opponent, wounding him seriously, and then chased his own opponent into the castle and killed him, whereupon a hundred knights all appeared and set upon him.

Seeing that his horse was endangered, La Cote Male Tayle dismounted, and then, with his back to the door of one of the ladies' chambers, defended himself lustily. Meanwhile, the lady whose chamber it was watched from one of the windows. Entertained by the spectacle of one knight defending himself against a hundred assailants, she left her chamber by another door and stealthily led La Cote Male Tayle's horse to a postern, where she ordered four knights to guard it. She then returned to her chamber, and spoke to La Cote Male Tayle through the window:

"Worthy knight, it is not enough for you to defend yourself

against these hundred knights. If you are ever to leave this castle you will have to fight your way through them to get to your horse, which I have taken to the far side of the castle."

In fury, La Cote Male Tayle redoubled his blows and fought his way through his assailants, killing twelve as he did so. Then, finding his horse at the postern, he killed two of the guards before the other two fled from him. He rejoined Maledysaunte just as she was saying to Sir Modred:

"Doubtless La Cote Male Tayle is now dead or a prisoner."

La Cote Male Tayle then told her and Sir Modred what had taken place at the castle.

"I expect the truth of the matter is that they let you go out of pity for the fool that you are," said Maledysaunte. However, she sent a courier to the castle, who returned with the news that they had supposed him "a fiend from hell, so ferociously did he fight," because they could credit none but Sir Launcelot or Sir Tristram with such power at arms.

Maledysaunte hung her head in shame, and Sir Modred said to her:

"My lady, I think it wrong for you to abuse La Cote Male Tayle as you do. He is as yet a young knight and inexperienced in jousting; all have to learn, and even Sir Launcelot, when he was young, took many a fall. Therefore it means little that La Cote Male Tayle was overthrown by Sir Bleobris and Sir Palomides; and please notice that neither would accept his challenge to fight on foot. For if young knights are weak on horseback, so are they strong on foot, and it has happened that many an older knight has been defeated in this way. Thus it was for a good reason that Sir Bleobris and Sir Palomides both refused to dismount."

Meanwhile, news of La Cote Male Tayle's exploits at the Castle Orgulus had reached King Arthur, and Sir Launcelot, who had just returned to the court, exclaimed:

"By Jesu, it is a shame that so young a knight should have gone on so perilous a quest! Are you not all ashamed? I know well that Maledysaunte has borne this shield a long time in search of a knight hardy enough to undertake the adventure; and I recall that Sir Breuse Sans Pité bore it for a while, but it was won from him by Sir Tristram, just after he fought my nephew Sir Blamoure, who returned it to Maledysaunte once more. Truly, I think I shall follow him, for he may need my help."

Seven days later Sir Launcelot overtook La Cote Male Tayle and Maledysaunte; and when he appeared, Sir Modred left them. Maledysaunte was still taking every opportunity to abuse

La Cote Male Tayle, and when Sir Launcelot defended him she abused Sir Launcelot instead.

Sir Launcelot had not ridden for long with La Cote Male Tayle and Maledysaunte when a young noblewoman delivered a letter to him. The letter was from Sir Tristram, who begged him not to deny him his friendship on account of his default in marrying Isode. He described how his betrayal of Iseult had become apparent to him only on his wedding night, and how then, as thereafter, he had refused her the gift of love. Once more he begged Sir Launcelot to continue to befriend him, and also Isode if ever she should stand in need of succor.

Having read the letter, Sir Launcelot begged La Cote Male Tayle and Maledysaunte to excuse him, while he made his reply; and so he left them. La Cote Male Tayle and his companion continued their journey until they came to the Castle Pendragon, where La Cote Male Tayle was confronted by six knights who all challenged him together. La Cote Male Tayle jousted with the first of them and overthrew him; then the other five charged at him simultaneously, knocked him from his horse, seized him bodily, and dragged him off to the castle as their prisoner.

When Sir Launcelot had written his reply to Sir Tristram, and given the letter to the young noblewoman to deliver, he rode after La Cote Male Tayle and his companion once more. Approaching a bridge he was challenged by a knight, with whom he jousted and then fought until the knight yielded.

"Sir, I pray you tell me your name; for your great strength warms my heart," said the knight.

"Sir, I will do so if you will tell me yours first."

"Sir Neroveus is my name, and Sir Launcelot, who knighted me, my lord."

"And I am Sir Launcelot, so welcome! You have proved yourself a hardy knight in combat."

Sir Neroveus knelt before Sir Launcelot and would have kissed his feet, but Sir Launcelot would have none of it; so he then warned Sir Launcelot to keep clear of the Castle Pendragon, and described to him how La Cote Male Tayle had just been taken prisoner there.

"Then the Castle Pendragon is my objective," Sir Launcelot replied. "For I was accompanying La Cote Male Tayle, and now I must rescue him."

Sir Neroveus remained at the bridge and Sir Launcelot rode forward until he came to the castle, where he was confronted by six knights who all leveled their spears and charged at him in a body. At the first encounter Sir Launcelot knocked one of the knights off his horse with such violence that he broke his back. At the second encounter Sir Launcelot drove his spear clean through the breast of another of the knights, and the spear broke. Sir Launcelot then drew his sword, and the four remaining knights did likewise, and all lashed at him together. With four strokes Sir Launcelot struck all four of the knights off their horses, and wounded each seriously. He then rode into the castle.

The lord of the castle, Sir Bryan of the Iles, was himself a powerful knight, and he now rode forth and challenged Sir Launcelot. They jousted and both their horses crashed to the ground; then they fought with their swords, and only after a tremendous battle did Sir Bryan finally yield to Sir Launcelot.

Sir Launcelot then released Sir Bryan's prisoners: thirty knights and forty ladies from King Arthur's court, among them La Cote Male Tayle and Maledysaunte.

Meanwhile, Sir Neroveus had sent a young noblewoman to discover how Sir Launcelot had fared at the castle. When she arrived she found them all astonished by the knight who had defeated Sir Bryan, and so she revealed to them that it was Sir Launcelot. Sir Bryan, his lady, and the knights whom Sir Launcelot had overthrown at the bridge were delighted that they had been vanquished by none of less renown than he. But Maledysaunte was mortified when she recalled how she had abused Sir Launcelot when he had accompanied her. Sir Launcelot had already left the castle when the young noblewoman sent by Sir Neroveus had arrived, and so now La Cote Male Tayle and Maledysaunte rode after him, and Maledysaunte determined to apologize. After riding two miles they caught up with him.

"Sir, I beg you to forgive me my abuse and evil words; for I know now that you are none other than Sir Launcelot, who, with Sir Tristram, outshines all other knights of this time. For long I have sought you, and I thank God to have found you at last. Sir Tristram I already know, for he won the shield from Sir Breuse Sans Pité and returned it to me."

"My lady, how is it that you have discovered my name?"

"Sir, it was revealed by a lady whom Sir Neroveus sent to the castle to inquire how you had fared there."

"Then she is to blame, also Sir Neroveus for telling her. Now, my lady, I can agree to accompany you only on this covenant: that you cease forthwith to abuse this noble knight, La Cote Male Tayle, who has undertaken your quest. I followed you both because I value him far too much to see him lost on your adventure."

"Sir, God shall be my witness when I tell you that I have abused La Cote Male Tayle not out of hatred and contempt, but out of love and admiration for him. I sought only to dissuade him from my adventure in order that he should not be killed."

"For what you have told me, my lady, I shall henceforth call you not Maledysaunte, but Beaupansaunte."

La Cote Male Tayle, Sir Launcelot, and Maledysaunte followed their road for many miles until it brought them to the country of Surluse, where they came to a fine village, approached by a fortified bridge. The bridge was garrisoned by a large company of knights and yeomen who challenged them as they drew near.

"My lords, we notice that one of you bears the black shield, and therefore only one shall pass at a time."

Sir Launcelot at once volunteered to go forward, but La Cote Male Tayle restrained him.

"Sir, I beseech you, since the black shield is my adventure, to allow me to cross first. If I am victorious, I shall send for you; if I am killed, you shall mourn for me; if I am taken prisoner, you shall rescue me."

"La Cote Male Tayle, go your way, then; and God's speed!" said Sir Launcelot.

La Cote Male Tayle rode forward alone, crossed the bridge, and was confronted by two knights, the brothers Sir Playne de Fors and Sir Playne de Amoris. They jousted, and La Cote Male Tayle struck both from their horses. Then they fought with their swords, and always the two brothers tried to maneuver one on each side of La Cote Male Tayle, but he skillfully kept them before him. The fight was protracted and bloody; but at last La Cote Male Tayle, although himself so wounded that he could barely stand, forced the brothers to yield.

He then chose the best of the three horses, and proceeded to the second fortified bridge, and there he encountered the third of the brothers: Sir Plenoryus. They jousted, their horses fell beneath them, and they fought on foot. Despite his wounds, La Cote Male Tayle fought with unflinching courage; but he was much enfeebled, and after two hours, sank irresistibly to the ground.

Maledysaunte had watched, distraught with fear, and said

to Sir Launcelot: "Surely, this is more than one knight can endure!"

"My lady, it is his first great battle, and certainly his endurance is something to behold."

But once La Cote Male Tayle had sunk to the ground, Sir Plenoryus took pity on him.

"Good knight, do not be dismayed, for had you been as fresh as myself, I should not have withstood you; so now I shall show you the mercy you deserve." And with that Sir Plenoryus led him into the castle, gave him wine, and salved his wounds.

"Sir," said La Cote Male Tayle, when he had recovered, "I pray you go to the first bridge, and there you will encounter a knight far greater than I."

"Pray, what is his name? I take it he is of your own fellowship."

"Sir, I may not reveal his name."

Just then a knight from the garrison shouted up to Sir Plenoryus that he was summoned to deliver up his prisoner or else encounter the knight at the first bridge.

Sir Plenoryus left the castle, mounted, and galloped out to meet Sir Launcelot. They jousted, and when their horses collapsed, fought on foot. Throughout, Sir Launcelot was in the ascendancy. Although Sir Plenoryus was a proved warrior, Sir Launcelot gradually forced him back to the gate, and then he spoke:

"Sir, I know you for a proved knight; but it is now in my hands whether you live or die."

For answer, Sir Plenoryus struck savagely at Sir Launcelot's helmet, whereupon Sir Launcelot redoubled his blows and drove his opponent to his knees, then, dragging off his helmet, forced him to yield.

Returning to the castle, Sir Launcelot met Sir Plenoryus' remaining three brothers: Sir Pyllownes, Sir Pellogres, and Sir Pelaundris. He jousted and fought with and overcame all three. He then released Sir Plenoryus' prisoners, among them King Carados of Scotland, and offered the castle and estates to La Cote Male Tayle.

"No, Sir Launcelot, I would not rob so noble a knight as Sir Plenoryus of his livelihood; rather, let him swear allegiance to King Arthur, and serve him."

"Sir Plenoryus, so it shall be. Go to King Arthur's court at the next Pentecost, and with your five brothers, swear him allegiance; and should there be a vacant seat, I do not doubt that he will make you a knight of the Round Table."

"Sir, as you command," Sir Plenoryus replied.

Sir Launcelot and La Cote Male Tayle remained with Maledysaunte at the castle until their wounds had healed. They were joined there by Sir Kay and Sir Brandiles, and so they all made the homeward journey together. Sir Launcelot gave the Castle Pendragon to La Cote Male Tayle, and appointed Sir Neroveus his bailiff.

At the next Pentecost, Sir Plenoryus and his five brothers duly yielded to King Arthur, and together with Sir Brewnor le Noyre, Sir Plenoryus was made a knight of the Round Table, and both acquitted themselves well. For the most part, Sir Plenoryus served Sir Launcelot thereafter.

Sir Brewnor le Noyre (or La Cote Male Tayle, as he was to be known ever after) married Maledysaunte, and she was thereafter known as Lady Beauvivante.

4. SIR TRISTRAM'S MADNESS AND EXILE

When Sir Tristram returned to King Howell's court in Brittany, the Lady Brangwayne delivered to him several piteous letters from her mistress Queen Iseult, who begged him to come to Tintagil and bring his wife Isode with him, and promised them a hospitable reception. Sir Tristram asked Sir Keyhydyns if he would accompany him on a secret voyage to Cornwall and Sir Keyhydyns agreed to, so they set sail on a small ship, together with Brangwayne and his squire Governayle.

As they were approaching Cornwall they were caught by a storm and driven far off their course, and finally set ashore on the coast of West Britain, not far from the Forest Perelous. Sir Tristram decided to ride in search of the adventures for which the forest was famous.

"My good Governayle, I pray you remain here with Brangwayne for ten days while Sir Keyhydyns and I ride into the forest; if we are not back by then, proceed by yourselves to Cornwall and we will follow in our own time."

When Sir Tristram and Sir Keyhydyns had ridden a mile or so they came upon a powerful-looking knight sitting sadly by a well. His horse was tethered to an oak tree and his squire stood by, holding his own horse, which was loaded with spears.

"Sir, I judge by your horse and your armor that you are an errant knight. Pray, will you joust with us?" asked Sir Tristram.

Without a word, the knight buckled his shield around his neck, jumped on his horse, chose a spear from his squire, and withdrew by a furlong. Sir Keyhydyns asked Sir Tristram if he might joust first, and Sir Tristram said: "Do your best!"

They jousted and Sir Keyhydyns was wounded in the chest, and flung to the ground.

"Sir, that was well done. Will you joust with me now?" asked Sir Tristram.

"Sir, I am ready."

They jousted and Sir Tristram too was thrown. He jumped up, and putting his shield before him, challenged the knight to fight on foot. The knight dismounted and they fought for two hours.

"Good knight," said Sir Tristram, "pray tell me who you are, and whence you come."

"Sir, if you will tell me your name first, I will tell you mine."

"Sir Tristram de Lyoness."

"Sir Lamerok de Galys."

"Well met, Sir Lamerok! I recall how you sent Morgan le Fay's testing-horn to King Mark in order to dishonor my lady Iseult; therefore I say now that one of us must die."

"Sir Tristram, you promised otherwise on the Ile of Servage."

But for answer, Sir Tristram dressed his shield to Sir Lamerok, and they fought until both were exhausted.

"Sir Lamerok, you are the mightiest knight I have fought with yet; therefore let us stop before we are both wounded beyond recovery."

"Sir, I readily yield to your honor and to your greatness," said Sir Lamerok, offering the pommel of his sword to Sir Tristram.

"Sir Lamerok, you yield to me out of courtesy; I yield to you as a knight who has been overcome," said Sir Tristram, offering his sword by the pommel to Sir Lamerok.

"Then let us not yield, but swear friendship," said Sir Lamerok.

They swore; and just as they did so the Questing Beast came by. This peculiar animal had the head of a serpent, the body of a leopard, the buttocks of a lion, and the feet of a hart; and always as it moved a noise came out of its belly like the yapping of twenty pair of hounds. In pursuit of the beast came Sir Palomides, whose quest it was to pursue it while he lived. Seeing Sir Tristram and Sir Lamerok, Sir Palomides jousted with them both, overthrew them both, and resumed his quest.

It sometimes happens that even the greatest knights are overthrown by knights inferior to them. Both Sir Tristram and Sir Lamerok felt this, and were angry with Sir Palomides when he refused to stay and fight with them on foot, where both felt that they could have retrieved their honor. The two knights now carried Sir Keyhydyns on a shield to the cottage of a nearby forester, whom they charged to care for him. Then they rode together through the forest until they came to a stone cross, where they parted.

"Sir Lamerok, if you should meet Sir Palomides, please tell him that I, Sir Tristram de Lyoness, challenge him, and will prove thereupon who is the greater knight."

Sir Tristram returned to Sir Keyhydyns, and Sir Lamerok rode on until he came to a chapel, where he dismounted and set his horse to pasture. A little while later Sir Mellyagraunce, King Bagdemagus' son, also rode up to the chapel, set his horse to pasture, and, unaware that he was overheard by Sir Lamerok, started bewailing his love for Queen Gwynevere.

Next morning Sir Lamerok rode into the forest again, and finding two knights waiting by a thicket, challenged them to joust.

"No sir, we will not joust with you; we are waiting to revenge ourselves on a knight who killed our brother."

"Who was that knight?"

"Sir Launcelot, and we shall kill him when he comes by."

"It may be otherwise and that you two will be killed," said Sir Lamerok, and departed. He had not ridden far when he met Sir Launcelot himself. Sir Lamerok saluted him and asked if he could be of any service.

"I thank you, Sir Lamerok, but not at this time," Sir Launcelot replied.

Sir Lamerok rode back to the two knights who were waiting in ambush for Sir Launcelot.

"Cowards!" he said. "You are a disgrace to the high order of knighthood." He then rode back to the chapel, and found Sir Mellyagraunce still there.

"Sir, I overheard you bewailing your love for Queen Gwynevere yesterday evening. Do you really admire her so much?"

"I admit that I do; and further, I will prove it by force of arms if challenged."

"Very well, I challenge you, for I maintain that Queen Margawse of Orkney is the fairer of the two."

They jousted, and then fought for a long time. Sir Mellyagraunce, however, was not as strong as Sir Lamerok, who remained on the offensive. Then Sir Launcelot and Sir Bleobris rode up to them, and Sir Launcelot drove his horse between them.

"Pray, what is your quarrel? Since you are both knights of the Round Table, you should surely not be fighting?"

"Sir Mellyagraunce was fighting to prove Queen Gwynevere the fairest, and I was fighting to prove Queen Margawse the fairest," Sir Lamerok replied.

"Since Queen Gwynevere is your own queen, should you not fight for her? Now defend yourself, Sir Lamerok," said Sir Launcelot.

"Sir Launcelot, I admit that I am reluctant to battle with you, as I would be with Sir Tristram, for you two have proved yourselves the greatest knights living. Further, I hold that each knight believes his own paramour to be the fairest; how else could it be? And therefore a duel on these grounds is ill-chosen. However, if you are not persuaded, I will endure you for as long as I may."

Then Sir Bleobris spoke up: "Sir Launcelot, does not this knight speak justly? I too have a paramour, who is neither Queen Gwynevere nor Queen Margawse, and I think that of the three she is the fairest. Therefore, I pray you, be friends, and let each honor whom he will."

"Sir Lamerok, I beg your forgiveness; you speak justly."

"Sir Launcelot, we are reconciled."

With that Sir Launcelot and Sir Bleobris rode off together, Sir Mellyagraunce rode off alone, and Sir Lamerok remained at the chapel. Then King Arthur rode up and challenged Sir Lamerok. They jousted and Sir Lamerok was overthrown. Arthur departed, refusing his challenge to fight on foot, and leaving him furious, and not knowing with whom he had jousted.

Sir Tristram, meanwhile, had met Sir Kay riding through

the forest, and in answer to his question, told him that he was from Cornwall.

"Ah ha! You knights from Cornwall have a very poor reputation, I believe," said Sir Kay.

"Well spoken! Pray tell me, sir, who you may be."

"Sir Kay the Seneschal."

"Sir Kay the Seneschal? You, I believe, have the reputation of being a fine knight, but one with a venomous tongue and, it is said, frequently unfortunate in your encounters."

They rode on together until they came to a bridge where Sir Torre, Sir Lamerok's half brother, challenged them. Sir Kay accepted and was overthrown. Then they rode to their lodging, and were later joined by Sir Torre and Sir Brandiles. That evening Sir Tristram listened quietly while his three companions tried to outdo each other in discrediting knights from Cornwall.

In the morning Sir Tristram jousted first with Sir Brandiles and then with Sir Torre and overthrew them both, but refused to tell either his name. They parted and Sir Kay rode after Sir Tristram, who told him that he wanted none of his company; so Sir Kay returned to Sir Brandiles.

"I wonder who that knight can be," said Sir Brandiles.

"Let us try to persuade him to tell us," Sir Kay replied.

Together they rode in search of Sir Tristram, and found him drinking from his helmet at a well. The moment Sir Tristram saw them he laced on his helmet again and challenged them to joust.

"Sir, we come not to joust, but to beg you to tell us your name."

"Gentlemen, I am Sir Tristram de Lyoness, a knight from Cornwall."

"Sir Tristram, well met! Of all the knights in King Arthur's realm, you are the one most loved by the fellows of the Round Table. I pray you, therefore, will you not join us?" asked Sir Brandiles.

"My lords, it is impossible, for I have yet to prove myself worthy of your fellowship."

"Sir Tristram," said Sir Kay, "it is said that you are a proved knight, the greatest living, except of course for Sir Launcelot, who is without peer throughout Christendom or heathendom."

When they had finished talking, Sir Kay and Sir Brandiles and Sir Tristram each went their different ways.

King Arthur had come to the Forest Perelous at the entreaty

of Aunowre, a sorceress who had fallen in love with him. Once in the forest, she invited him to her castle and there tried to persuade him to her bed; but Arthur remained faithful to Gwynevere, and thereafter Aunowre sought to revenge herself.

Sir Launcelot, Sir Kay, and various of Arthur's knights had followed Arthur into the forest; so also had Nyneve, the Lady of the Lake. Being herself a sorceress, she was able to discover on what day Aunowre planned to take her revenge, and sought the aid of either Sir Launcelot or Sir Tristram to defend him. She found Sir Tristram and begged him to accompany her "in order to avert a most terrible calamity."

"My lady, certainly I will help you if I may, but what is the calamity you speak of?"

"King Arthur is endangered."

"God forbid!" said Sir Tristram.

Sir Tristram and Nyneve galloped through the forest together until they came to a castle. Beneath the castle walls three knights were fighting, and a lady stood by them. Sir Tristram and Nyneve galloped up to them, just as one of the knights was struck to the ground by his opponents, who then held him down and unlaced his helmet, while the lady drew the sword from his sheath and prepared to behead him.

"Murderous witch, stay your hand!" shouted Sir Tristram.

Drawing his sword, he killed the two knights, and Aunowre fled.

"Do not let her escape!" said Nyneve, and Sir Tristram galloped after her and chopped off her head.

Nyneve strung the head to her saddle, and Sir Tristram begged her not to reveal his name to Arthur. He then walked over to Arthur and helped him to mount. Arthur thanked him and asked him his name, but Sir Tristram replied only that he was "a poor knight in search of adventure." They rode through the forest together until they saw Sir Ector in the distance. Sir Tristram galloped up to him and they jousted. Sir Ector was overthrown, and Sir Tristram rode back to Arthur and said:

"Sire, yonder is one of your knights who, I am sure, will accompany you henceforth. So now I will take my leave of you, and when we meet again, I trust you will know me for one who is always ready to serve you."

"Alas, sir, I wish that I could know your name."

"Sire, not at this time," said Sir Tristram, and they parted.

Sir Tristram and Sir Lamerok met by a well, and after collecting Sir Keyhydyns, whose wounds had healed, from the forester's cottage, returned to Governayle and Brangwayne, who had remained by the ship. Then they all sailed to Cornwall.

When they landed, Brangwayne suggested that they should ride to Sir Dynas the Seneschal, and this they did. Then Sir Dynas and Brangwayne rode to Tintagil and told Queen Iseult that Sir Tristram had arrived from Brittany, and hoped to see her. Iseult fainted for joy and, when she came to, begged Sir Dynas to bring him to her.

Sir Tristram was led secretly to a chamber appointed by Iseult, and there followed a reunion of the lovers, which was beyond the power of words to describe.

It happened that Sir Keyhydyns, at first sight of Iseult, had fallen deeply in love with her, and subsequently was to die of that love. Meanwhile, he secretly wrote letters and poems to her, so passionate that Iseult was moved by pity to reply to them. But it was to Sir Tristram she went whenever she could find the opportunity.

One day, when both Iseult and Sir Keyhydyns were in his chamber, Sir Tristram discovered the letters which had passed between them.

"My lady, is it not enough that I have deserted my wife, abandoned my lands and my riches, and undertaken many perilous adventures in order that I may live secretly here for the love of you? Now I see by these letters that it is Sir Keyhydyns who would be your paramour. And as for you, Sir Keyhydyns, whom I chose for my companion, did I enter the field and win back your father's kingdom in order that you should repay me by treachery? Certainly I married your sister, Isode, but that was in return for the care she had bestowed upon me, and to this day, I swear, she is still a maid. So now, Sir Keyhydyns, defend yourself!" And with that Sir Tristram drew his sword and advanced upon him.

Iseult fainted. Sir Keyhydyns was terrified and leaped out of the window, since he saw no other means of escape. He landed just by King Mark, who was playing chess.

"In God's name! What caused you to leap out of the window?" asked the king.

"Sire, I was resting by the window, and by mischance was overcome by sleep and fell out."

Supposing that Sir Keyhydyns would betray his presence in the castle, Sir Tristram hastily armed in preparation for his defense. But none challenged him, so he sent Governayle to fetch his horse, and when it was ready for him, rode openly out of the court. At the gate he met Sir Gawain's son, Sir Gyngalyn, who charged at him with his spear and broke it. Sir Tristram, having no spear, struck out with his sword, and catching Sir Gyngalyn on the helmet sent him tumbling to the ground; the impetus of the stroke carried the sword clean through the horse's neck as well.

King Mark, who had witnessed the whole incident, now sent a squire to discover the name of the wounded knight. The squire told the king that it was Sir Gyngalyn, so the king welcomed him to his court, and gave him a fresh horse. Then he asked him the name of the knight he had encountered, but Sir Gyngalyn was able to tell him only that the knight had appeared extremely sorrowful.

Sir Tristram had ridden into the forest, and there he met Sir Fergus, one of his own knights, and to him he complained of his misfortunes so bitterly that he was overcome by his own words, and fainted.

For three days he lay stricken with grief, then he recovered sufficiently to send Sir Fergus to the castle of Tintagil to discover what he could of Iseult. On his way to the castle Sir Fergus met a young noblewoman whom Sir Palomides had sent to inquire of Sir Tristram. When Sir Fergus told her what state Sir Tristram was in, the young noblewoman asked where he was to be found, and then hastened away to help him. When Sir Fergus got to the castle, he was able to discover only that Iseult was ill with grief and had retired to her chamber.

The young noblewoman was determined to comfort Sir Tristram in his distress, but the more she tried to do so, the wilder he became, and at last, unable to endure her condolences, took to his horse and disappeared into the forest. For three days the young noblewoman trailed after him, and when she found him brought food and wine; but he would have none of it.

Once more Sir Tristram escaped and the young noblewoman followed him, and this time they came to the castle where Sir Tristram and Sir Palomides had fought for Iseult. The young noblewoman went to the lady of the castle, told her of Sir Tristram's grief, and begged her aid.

"My lady, I am indeed sorry to hear of Sir Tristram's distress. Let us bring him to the castle and he shall have the best of hospitality. Also he shall have my harp, for he is the finest player living, and taught me while he was here."

Sir Tristram was brought to the castle, but would eat and drink but little, and frequently wandered away. Abandoning horse and armor, he would walk through the forest, tearing up shrubs, or pulling branches from the trees. Sometimes the lady of the castle followed him, playing the harp, and he came to her, and sometimes himself played the harp. So he lived for three months. He became lean; his clothes were torn and left him half naked.

Then he wandered off from the castle and joined company with some herdsmen, who gave him food and drink, and beat him with rods when he offended them. One day they sheared off his hair, giving him the likeness of a fool. And with these herdsmen he lived for six months, remaining in the forest in order to avoid the villages and towns.

Meanwhile the young noblewoman whom Sir Palomides had sent in search of Sir Tristram, and who had tried to care for him, returned to Sir Palomides and told him how Sir Tristram fared.

"Alas," said Sir Palomides, "that so great a knight should lose his wits for the love of a lady! But I shall go in search of him."

Sir Palomides rode into the forest and chanced to meet Sir Keyhydyns, whom Iseult had just exiled. Together they bewept the hopeless love that they both felt for her.

"At least let us prove our love by trying to recover Sir Tristram," said Sir Palomides, and this was agreed upon.

For three days and three nights they rode together in search of Sir Tristram, and then they came upon King Mark, riding alone and unarmed. Sir Palomides recognized him, but Sir Keyhydyns did not.

"Treacherous knight that you are," said Sir Palomides, "do you realize that your jealous spite has brought Sir Tristram to ruin, the greatest knight living? Now defend yourself!"

"For shame! I am unarmed," the king replied.

"You shall have armor and harness from my companion."

"Even so, I shall not defend myself against your wrongful accusation. The cause of Sir Tristram's madness was the letters that passed between Iseult and Sir Keyhydyns; and for myself, I value him as you do."

Thereupon King Mark and the two knights were reconciled, and the king offered them hospitality in his castle; but both refused, Sir Keyhydyns saying that he must sail to Brittany, and Sir Palomides saying that he must ride to the realm of Logres.

One day, while Sir Tristram and the herdsmen were gathered around a well, Sir Dagonet, King Arthur's fool, rode up, accompanied by two squires, and because the day was hot, made to drink from the well. Thereupon Sir Tristram seized hold of each of them in turn and doused them in the well, while the herdsmen roared with laughter. Then he fetched their horses, and when they had mounted, drove them away.

Fool though he was, Sir Dagonet was furious, and after a brief consultation returned with his squires, and together they set about beating the herdsmen with the flats of their swords. Seeing his friends ill-treated, Sir Tristram ran up to Sir Dagonet, dragged him bodily from his horse, and beat him mercilessly. Then, taking Sir Dagonet's sword, he ran up to one of the squires and beheaded him. The other squire fled into the forest and Sir Tristram gave chase, still brandishing the sword. At last, however, unable to find the squire, and coming upon a monastery, Sir Tristram lay down to sleep. The monks discreetly removed the sword, and for ten days fed and cared for him.

Sir Dagonet resumed his journey to Tintagil, and there warned King Mark against going into the forest "on account of the naked and dangerous madman" who had all but killed him.

The king replied, "That must be Sir Matto le Breune, who lost his wits when Sir Gaheris defeated him and rode away with his lady—a sad case, for he was a noble knight."

At this time Sir Andret, Sir Tristram's cousin, decided on a ruse to win Sir Tristram's lands. He persuaded his paramour to declare before the king, and all in the court, that she had seen Sir Tristram die by a well, and heard his last words, with which he appointed Sir Andret his heir.

The king acted shocked and unhappy to hear of Sir Tristram's death; Iseult's grief knew no bounds. She searched through the castle for a sword and then ran with it into the garden. First she prayed:

"Sweet Jesu, have mercy on my soul, for how can I bear to outlive Sir Tristram—my first love and my last?"

Then, driving the sword up to the hilt through the slender trunk of a plum tree, at breast height, she prepared to fling herself on it. But King Mark had been watching her, and now he drew her away and led her to a chamber where he gave orders that she was to be carefully watched. For a long time Iseult lay grief-stricken and on the point of death.

When Sir Tristram left the monastery, he returned to the

herdsmen; and one day when they were all gathered together at the well, the giant Sir Tauleas, feeling tired and thirsty, came and joined them. Fearing Sir Tristram, Sir Tauleas had for the last seven years kept close to his castle, but the false report of his death had encouraged him to wander abroad again.

Next Sir Dynaunte and a lady rode up to the well. Sir Tauleas hid behind a tree while they dismounted and Sir Dynaunte disarmed. Then he stole Sir Dynaunte's horse, rode up to him, and threw him across the withers, intending to behead him.

The herdsmen and Sir Tristram whispered among themselves, urging each other to go to the rescue. Then Sir Tristram noticed Sir Dynaunte's sword, so he quickly reached for it, ran over to the giant, and chopped off his head.

Sir Dynaunte and his companion resumed their journey, and when they reached Tintagil, described their adventure to King Mark, and their rescue at the hands of "a naked madman." The king asked them where it had taken place, and when they told him, decided to see for himself this madman of whom he had heard so much.

In the morning, the king announced a hunt, and himself rode straight to the well, and then blew his horn. When his knights appeared he commanded them to escort the madman to the castle, and to treat him with due care. The knights covered him with their mantles, and when they got to the castle, washed and clothed him and fed him on hot soup; but neither the king nor any of his knights recognized that the madman was Sir Tristram.

When Iseult heard of the madman whom the king had rescued, she went to the garden with Brangwayne to see him. Sir Tristram was resting in the sun, and Iseult said to Brangwayne:

"How strange! He seems very familiar, and yet I do not recognize him."

But Sir Tristram had recognized Iseult, and he turned his head aside and wept. At that moment, Iseult's brachet suddenly bounded forward, and leaping up at Sir Tristram, started joyfully licking his hands and face. It was the brachet which the Princess Frances had given to Sir Tristram many years previously, just as he was about to champion King Mark against Sir Marhaus of Ireland. Sir Tristram had later given the brachet to Iseult, and the brachet had never allowed any other person to go near it.

"My lady!" said Brangwayne, "it is Sir Tristram."

Iseult fainted, and for a long time lay as though dead. Then she recovered and said:

"My own dear lord, Sir Tristram! I thank God that you are still alive. But my love, I fear for you; this brachet will betray you, and as soon as King Mark discovers who you are, he will exile you forever, if he does not kill you. Therefore, I beg you, do not oppose him but go to King Arthur's court, where you are loved. And whenever it is possible for me to see you, I shall do so; for such is the lonely life of a queen."

"My lady, go then. Your love has saved me from great danger."

Iseult left him, but the brachet remained, and when the king and Sir Andret came to see him, it growled at them both.

"Sire, the madman is none other than Sir Tristram," said Sir Andret. "I know that by the brachet."

"Sir, I do not believe it," the king replied, then, turning to Sir Tristram, said: "Sir, I pray you, tell me faithfully who you are."

"So God help me, I am Sir Tristram de Lyoness. Sire, you must do what you will with me."

The king summoned his counselors and urged that Sir Tristram should be put to death; but many were against it, especially Sir Dynas the Seneschal. Then it was agreed to banish him from Cornwall for ten years, and Sir Tristram was made to swear to abide by this.

A ship was fitted out and Sir Tristram was escorted to the harbor by a large number of the barons, some his friends, some his enemies. They were met by Sir Dynadan, whom King Arthur had sent with an invitation to his court for Sir Tristram.

Sir Dynadan offered to joust with Sir Tristram, and having obtained permission from his escort, Sir Tristram did so, and overthrew him. Then Sir Dynadan delivered King Arthur's message, and they agreed to travel together. When they had embarked, Sir Tristram addressed his escort:

"My lords, I bid you greet King Mark and all my enemies for me. Tell them I shall return when I am able to do so. Tell them that I am well rewarded: for fighting Sir Marhaus on the first day of my knighthood and freeing Cornwall from her bondage to Ireland; for my perilous journey to Ireland to fetch Queen Iseult, and my perilous journey back, when I had to fight my way out of the Castle Pleure; for fighting Sir Bleobris to win back Sir Segwarydes' wife and uphold the honor of this court.

"Tell them I am well rewarded for jousting with Sir Lamerok, against my own scruples, but at the pleasure of my liege; for fighting the King of the Hundred Knights and the King of North Galys, who, but for me, would have put Cornwall in bondage again; and that I am well rewarded for killing the great giant Tauleas.

"My lords, it was for my sake that so many of you have been spared by King Arthur's knights of the Round Table, and his is the company I shall now join. Ask King Mark if he remembers the rewards he offered me when I fought the noble Sir Palomides and restored Queen Iseult to him once more. Ask him, because the only reward I know of is my present banishment from his court."

Then Sir Tristram and Sir Dynadan set sail from Cornwall.

When they landed they met Sir Ector and Sir Bors. Sir Dynadan jousted with Sir Ector and overthrew him; Sir Tristram offered to joust with Sir Bors, but Sir Bors refused out of contempt for his Cornish arms.

Then Sir Bleobris and Sir Dryaunte rode up to them, and Sir Tristram jousted with Sir Bleobris and overthrew him.

"Surely," said Sir Bors, "no Cornish knight was ever so valiant as the one here whose armor is decorated with crowns."

Sir Tristram and Sir Dynadan departed. Sometime later as they were riding through the forest they met a young noblewoman who was searching for knights who would be willing to rescue Sir Launcelot. Morgan le Fay had commanded thirty of her retainers to lie in ambush and assassinate him as soon as he passed. The young noblewoman had already found Sir Ector, Sir Bors, Sir Dryaunte and Sir Bleobris, and obtained from them a promise to go to his aid; now she asked Sir Tristram and Sir Dynadan.

"My lady, pray lead us to the ambush," said Sir Tristram.

"Sir Tristram, would you have us encounter thirty knights?" asked Sir Dynadan. "Why, it is impossible; one good knight might account for two or three, but fifteen, never. I shall not acompany you."

"For shame! Surely you can do your part?"

"Not so, unless you will lend me your shield; the name that Cornish knights have for cowardice might save me."

"Sir Dynadan, you shall not bear my shield, not for the sake of the lady who gave it to me; and I warn you that if you abandon this cause now I shall kill you. I ask you only to kill one knight, or if that is too much, then stand by and watch."

"Sir, I will promise only to watch, and to defend myself if necessary," Sir Dynadan replied.

The thirty knights, on their way to the ambush, first met Sir Ector and his three companions; but since their orders were to assassinate Sir Launcelot, they did not challenge them. Then they met Sir Tristram and Sir Dynadan.

"My lords, for the love of Sir Launcelot, I challenge you!" shouted Sir Tristram.

With that he charged, and killed two of them with his spear, then, drawing his sword, killed another ten. Meanwhile, Sir Dynadan did not hold back, but himself accounted for another eight; the remaining ten fled in fear of their lives.

Sir Ector and his companions had followed the thirty knights and witnessed the battle. They now rode up to Sir Tristram, and after praising him, begged him to tell them his name and to join them at their lodging. But Sir Tristram refused to do either, and so that night when Sir Ector and his companions met Sir Launcelot and Sir Colgrevaunce, they were able to tell him only that a Cornish knight and his companion had accomplished an incredible feat of arms in his defense. Sir Launcelot realized at once that it must have been Sir Tristram, and praised him above all other knights living.

Sir Tristram and Sir Dynadan had ridden on through the forest, and when they came to some herdsmen, asked them if they knew where they might lodge.

"My lords, not far from here is a castle where they will lodge you well enough if first you can overthrow the two knights whom you will encounter at the gate."

"To the devil with it! I shall not lodge there," said Sir Dynadan.

"For shame! Are you not a knight of the Round Table?" said Sir Tristram.

Sir Tristram and Sir Dynadan rode to the castle, overcame the two knights who encountered them, entered, and prepared to take their ease. They had both disarmed when Sir Palomides and Sir Gaheris arrived at the gate. Then it was the turn of Sir Tristram and Sir Dynadan to honor the custom of the castle.

"What sort of hospitality is this? Shall we never have a rest?" asked Sir Dynadan.

"To maintain the custom of the castle is the condition of our hospitality here," Sir Tristram replied.

"Alas, that I ever fell into your company!" said Sir Dynadan.

Sir Tristram jousted with Sir Gaheris and overthrew him; Sir Dynadan jousted with Sir Palomides and himself was overthrown. Since the jousting was equal, they had now to fight on foot; but Sir Dynadan refused, saying that he was already bruised from his fall. Sir Tristram laced on his helmet for him and begged him to fight.

"Sir Tristram, I will not. I was already wounded from our fight with the thirty knights when I came here. I have jousted twice since then and am now bruised as well. You rush from one fight to the next like a madman, and I curse that I ever met you. You make me recall the time when I was in the company of Sir Launcelot. He never stopped fighting, and when I left him it took me three months in bed to recover. So may God defend me from the company of two such knights, especially from yours!"

"Very well, I shall fight them both," Sir Tristram replied.

They started to fight, and Sir Dynadan struck halfheartedly at Sir Gaheris and then turned aside, so Sir Tristram dressed himself against them both.

"Not so!" Sir Palomides cried. "This is not fair, Sir Gaheris; you, too, stand aside."

For a long time Sir Tristram and Sir Palomides fought equally, and then Sir Tristram redoubled his blows and forced Sir Palomides to retreat. With one accord Sir Gaheris and Sir Dynadan stepped forward and separated them. They all agreed to enter the castle, except for Sir Dynadan, who cursed their fellowship and rode away. Sir Tristram then begged the lord of the castle to allow them a servant to lead them to another lodging. They soon overtook Sir Dynadan, and were led to a priory, where they were comfortably lodged.

In the morning Sir Tristram rode away, leaving Sir Dynadan at the priory to recover from his bruises. Sir Pellinore, who had also lodged at the priory, and tried without success to discover Sir Tristram's name, then said to Sir Dynadan:

"I shall follow that knight, and if he does not tell me his name I shall certainly kill him."

"I advise you to beware of him," Sir Dynadan replied.

Sir Pellinore galloped after Sir Tristram; they jousted, and he was wounded in the shoulder and flung from his horse.

Sir Tristram left him and rode on through the forest. The next day he met one of the many couriers who had been dispatched throughout Britain to attract supporters for King Carados and the King of North Galys, who were to contest in a tournament to be held at the Maidens' Castle. King Carados hoped for Sir Launcelot as his champion, and the King of North Galys for Sir Tristram. Sir Tristram decided that he would go.

While Sir Tristram was still with the courier he met Sir Kay and Sir Sagramour, and Sir Kay challenged him to joust. Sir Tristram refused, as he wished to be fresh for the tournament.

"Sir, joust with me, or yield like a coward," said Sir Kay.

"Very well, I accept your challenge," Sir Tristram replied. But Sir Kay turned his back on him, so Sir Tristram added: "Sir, I shall take you as I find you."

Then Sir Kay swung around intending to catch Sir Tristram unawares, but Sir Tristram drew his sword and knocked him to the ground, and then rode away. Sir Sagramour followed and challenged him; they jousted and Sir Sagramour was overthrown.

Sometime later Sir Tristram met a young noblewoman who asked him if he wished to win renown by challenging a knight now famous for his wickedness. Sir Tristram was eager to do so and accompanied the young noblewoman for six miles or so, until they met Sir Gawain, who recognized the young noblewoman as one of the ladies serving Morgan le Fay.

"Sir, where are you going with this lady?"

"Sir, I do not know; she leads."

Then Sir Gawain drew his sword and turned on the young noblewoman and said ferociously:

"My lady, tell me where and for what purpose you are leading this knight, or I shall kill you this instant."

"Sir Gawain, I pray you have mercy on me. My mistress, Morgan le Fay, has sent thirty of us into the forest to search for Sir Tristram and Sir Launcelot, and our instructions are to lead them to her castle, where she has thirty knights lying in ambush, who will kill them."

"Now we have it!" Sir Gawain exclaimed. "Who would believe that she is daughter to a king and queen, sister to a king, and herself a queen? Sir, will you come with me and deal with these assassins of hers?"

"Sir Gawain, I shall not fail you."

They rode together to the castle, and then Sir Gawain shouted:

"Queen Morgan le Fay, send out your thirty assassins who have lain in wait for Sir Tristram or Sir Launcelot, and we two will teach them a lesson."

The queen replied, "Sir Gawain, you shall not encounter

my knights today—not because of yourself, but because of your companion, whose Cornish arms we know full well."

Sir Tristram and Sir Gawain rode away from the castle and by chance met Sir Kay and Sir Sagramour, with whom they joined company. A day or two later they came upon Sir Breuse Sans Pité, who with drawn sword was chasing a lady; he had previously killed her paramour.

"You three conceal yourselves," said Sir Gawain, "and I shall go and challenge him."

Then Sir Gawain rode his horse between Sir Breuse and the lady.

"Sir, now you can have ado with me instead of the lady."

They jousted and Sir Gawain was thrown; then Sir Breuse turned his horse and galloped over Sir Gawain, intending to trample him to death, whereupon Sir Tristram charged out of the thicket in which he had been concealed. However, Sir Breuse saw him in time and fled. Sir Tristram gave chase, but Sir Breuse was well horsed and escaped him.

When Sir Tristram gave up the chase he stopped by a well, where he washed and drank, and then fell asleep. While he was still asleep Brangwayne came to the well, and recognized him by his horse, Passe-Brewell. Sir Tristram had kept Passe-Brewell for many years, and during his madness Sir Fergus had kept it for him. Brangwayne was carrying letters for Sir Tristram from her mistress Iseult, and so as soon as he had woken and they had greeted each other, she gave them to him. The letters were poignant for their tenderness and the pain which Iseult felt as the result of their separation.

"My lady, if you will accompany me to the Maidens' Castle where I am to compete in a tournament, I will afterward write letters to Queen Iseult which you can deliver to her."

This was agreed, and then they sought for lodgings. Before long they met an elderly knight, Sir Pellownes, who invited them to stay at his castle, and on the way told them that Sir Launcelot was to command twenty-two Cornish knights at the tournament. Then they all met Governayle, who was pleased to see Brangwayne again.

When they arrived at Sir Pellownes' castle, they heard that Sir Persides, Sir Pellownes' son, had returned after an absence of two years. Sir Pellownes held up his hands and thanked God.

"Sir, I know your son for a good knight," said Sir Tristram.

Sometime later Sir Tristram and Sir Persides met at the castle; both had disarmed and were taking their ease. They greeted each other, and then Sir Tristram told Sir Persides that he came from Cornwall.

"Ah!" exclaimed Sir Persides, "I was once in Cornwall. I jousted at King Mark's court and overthrew ten knights. Then I jousted with Sir Tristram de Lyoness and he overthrew me, and took my lady away, so I shall never forget him."

"I understand that you are now Sir Tristram's mortal enemy," said Sir Tristram. "Do you think that he would be unable to withstand you?"

"No, Sir Tristram is a greater knight than I am, but even so I could never love him."

They were sitting in one of the bay windows of the castle and, as they talked, watching the many knights who came to and fro in preparation for the tournament.

"Tell me," said Sir Tristram, "who is that knight bearing a black shield and riding a black horse?"

"He is one of the greatest knights living."

"Sir Launcelot?"

"No, Sir Palomides the Saracen; he is as yet unchristened."

They noticed that Sir Palomides was greeted respectfully on all sides, and then a squire came to the castle and reported to Sir Pellownes that Sir Palomides had already overthrown thirteen knights.

"My friend, let us put on our cloaks and go and watch what goes on," said Sir Tristram to Sir Persides.

"Let us not go like commoners, but rather let us arm and face our enemies," Sir Persides replied.

Sir Tristram and Sir Persides armed and rode forth from the castle. Sir Palomides noticed them and said to his squire:

"Go to the knight who bears a green shield decorated with a gold dragon, and offer him my challenge. Tell him that I am Sir Palomides."

Sir Persides accepted the challenge and was overthrown. Sir Tristram returned the challenge, but while he was still unprepared Sir Palomides charged him and flung him over his horse's tail. Sir Tristram leaped up furiously and ordered Governayle to repeat the challenge; but Sir Palomides refused, saying that they would meet at the Maidens' Castle tomorrow. Just then Sir Dynadan rode up to Sir Tristram, and seeing his fury, said:

"Sir Tristram, there was never a man so great that he never failed, nor so wise that he was never made a fool of, nor so good a horseman that he never had a fall."

"Nevertheless I shall abide only until I am revenged," Sir

Tristram replied. "But who is the knight with the black shield?"

"I know him well for a knight from West Britain; his name is Sir Bryaunte," Sir Persides replied.

Several knights from West Britain passed, and then Sir Launcelot rode by, bearing a shield with the Cornish device. He sent his squire to challenge Sir Bryaunte.

"Very well, since I am challenged I will do what I can," Sir Bryaunte answered.

They jousted and Sir Bryaunte was overthrown. Sir Tristram was greatly impressed by Sir Launcelot and asked Sir Dynadan who he might be.

"Sir, I would swear that he is of the blood of King Ban, for they are the greatest knights anywhere," Sir Dynadan replied.

Next, Sir Launcelot jousted with two knights from North Galys, Sir Hew de la Mountayne and Sir Madok de la Mountayne, and overthrew them both.

"Certainly," said Sir Tristram, "that knight with the Cornish arms has the best seat on a horse that I have seen yet."

Then the King of North Galys asked Sir Palomides to joust with the knight bearing Cornish arms who had just overcome two of his own knights.

"Sire, I am unwilling to challenge a knight as able as he is before tomorrow, for I do not want to be bruised when the tournament starts."

"Sir Palomides, that knight has offended me. I pray you, joust with him."

"Sire, as you will, though often the knight who offers the challenge is the one who takes a fall."

Sir Palomides sent his squire to offer his challenge to Sir Launcelot, who on learning his name replied that he wished for nothing better, since for seven years he had wanted to encounter Sir Palomides.

"I believe that Sir Palomides will win," said Sir Dynadan.

"And I believe that his opponent will," Sir Tristram rejoined.

They jousted. Sir Launcelot sat his horse like a rock and Sir Palomides' spear broke on him. Sir Palomides, however, received a blow which ran clean through his shield and hauberk, wounding him in the shoulder, and knocking him violently to the ground. Had he remained in the saddle he would have been killed.

"That was what I expected," said Sir Tristram, "from the way in which the knight with the Cornish arms sat his horse."

Sir Launcelot rode to a well in the forest to drink and to rest, but twelve of the knights of the King of North Galys followed him with the intention of disabling him for the tournament. Sir Launcelot had just time to mount and reach for his spear when they were upon him. The first of his assailants he killed with his spear, and broke it; then he drew his sword and killed another three, and wounded several more, before the remainder fled.

Then Sir Launcelot rode to a friend and lodged with him. But his last battle had left him too sore to compete in the tournament for the first day, so he sat with King Arthur on the judges' platform and helped him to decide on the awards.

5. THE MAIDENS' CASTLE

Sir Tristram, Governayle, and Sir Persides took their leave of Sir Pellownes early in the morning on the first day of the tournament. Sir Tristram carried a black shield which he had ordered Governayle to obtain for him so that he should fight unrecognized.

The two contestants at the tournament were the King of North Galys and King Carados of Scotland, and all knights who entered the field joined one or other of their parties. On the first day Sir Tristram and Sir Persides fought for the King of North Galys. In the course of the fighting Sir Persides was overthrown by Sir Bleobris. Then Sir Tristram attacked both Sir Bleobris and Sir Gaheris and overthrew them. They were rescued by the King of the Hundred Knights, and thereafter formed the nucleus of the fighting.

Throughout the tournament Sir Tristram was known as the Knight with the Black Shield. On the first day he brought victory to his party and won the prize himself, and the curiosity of the spectators was aroused by his remarkable feats at arms. However, those few who knew his identity did not reveal it.

Toward the end of the day Sir Dynadan rode against Sir Tristram and received a stunning blow on the helmet.

"Sir," he said, "I know well who you are, and never again shall I ride against you, for I want no more of your stunning blows."

The fighting was brought to a close by King Arthur blowing on his horn, and the contestants dispersed to their pavilions for the night.

On the second day of the tournament King Arthur and his party fought for King Carados. King Arthur's party included the King of Ireland, Sir Launcelot and his kin, King Ban and his kin, Sir Gawain and his kin, and Sir Palomides. Just before the fighting commenced Sir Palomides sent a young noblewoman, the one who had sought Sir Tristram in the forest during his madness, to ask the "Knight with the Black Shield" his identity.

"My lady," Sir Tristram replied, "tell Sir Palomides that he shall know who I am when I have broken two spears upon him; you may also tell him that I am the same knight whom he treacherously overthrew on the evening before the tournament. Now, I pray you, tell me which party he has joined, and I shall join the opposing one."

"Sir, he has joined King Carados' party, together with King Arthur and his knights."

"Very well, then I shall fight for the King of North Galys."

The fighting started with the King of the Hundred Knights charging King Carados and overthrowing him, and with a fierce attack of King Arthur's knights on the knights of the King of North Galys. Then Sir Tristram entered the battle and made havoc among King Arthur's knights, especially King Ban and his party, which included Sir Ector, Sir Blamoure, and Sir Bors.

All were amazed who witnessed Sir Tristram's feats that day, but at one time his audacity led him into serious danger, surrounded by opponents who would have killed him had not the King of the Hundred Knights come to his rescue. Having withdrawn from King Ban's party, Sir Tristram made his next attack on Sir Kay, whom he overthrew, and then, one after another, his followers.

Sir Launcelot, who had been fighting elsewhere in the field, came upon one of the knights whom Sir Tristram had wounded, and asked him at whose hands it had been.

"Sir, it was the Knight with the Black Shield; he fights more like a devil than a man."

Sir Launcelot determined to seek him out, but when he saw Sir Tristram in the thick of the battle, felling a knight with every stroke of his sword, he said to himself: "For the love of Jesu! he is surely the greatest knight I have ever seen. Were I to challenge him now it could only be to my own shame." And with that he withdrew to another part of the battle.

Following his engagement with Sir Kay, Sir Tristram rode up to the King of the Hundred Knights, who together with another hundred knights of King Galys' was attacking Sir Launcelot's party, who although numbering only twenty managed to hold their ground. Sir Tristram could not but admire them.

"Sire," he said to the King of the Hundred Knights, "surely you can win no honor by attacking twenty knights with two hundred, even if you were to kill every one of them, and it seems that they all are prepared to fight to the death. If you do not withdraw, I myself shall join them, for with them lies the greater honor."

"Sir, you shall have no need to join them; your words have struck home, and I shall withdraw," the king replied.

When King Arthur blew on the horn to end the day's fighting, Sir Tristram, who had again won the prize, was nowhere to be found; and so the prize was awarded to the King of North Galys, for whom he had fought. Then there was a tremendous outcry, which could be heard two miles away, from spectators and contestants alike, for the "Knight with the Black Shield." Both Sir Launcelot, who had wished to win his friendship, and King Arthur, who had wished him to join his fellowship, were dismayed. Arthur had also to console his own knights who had lost the day on account of him, and promise them their revenge on the morrow.

Of all who remained on the field, it was only Brangwayne who knew where Sir Tristram was to be found in the forest. Throughout the tournament she had sat next to Queen Gwynevere, protesting that her only purpose in coming to the tournament had been to deliver her messages of good will from Queen Iseult. But now Brangwayne rode into the forest to find Sir Tristram at his pavilion.

On the way she was startled by cries of distress and sent her squire to discover who it could be. The squire followed the sound until he came to a well, where he found a knight bound to a tree and acting to all appearances like a madman. The knight was Sir Palomides. Seeing the squire he made a violent effort and broke free from his bonds, and then made at the squire as if to kill him. The squire fled back to Brangwayne, and as soon as they found Sir Tristram, she told him what had happened.

Sir Tristram armed and rode to the well. As he approached he heard the knight complaining aloud to himself:

"Alas, Sir Palomides, what next? That you should suffer ignominiously this treachery at the hands of Sir Bors and Sir Ector! Truly you have lived too long!"

Then he was seized by a paroxysm of rage and despair and, with many groans and wild gestures, flung his sword into the well. Then he leaped onto the parapet and was about to throw himself after it, when Sir Tristram grasped him firmly by the arms.

"Sir, who are you, to hold me thus?"

"A knight of this forest; I mean you no harm."

"Alas! you have seized upon one who is wild with despair! It seems that wheresoever I meet Sir Tristram, I can win no honor; and yet when he is not there, I stand supreme, unless challenged by Sir Launcelot or Sir Lamerok. But Sir Tristram has defeated me both in Ireland and in Cornwall, and wherever I meet him he puts me to shame."

"What would you do were Sir Tristram here?"

"I would fight him until my wrath had eased. And yet he is the gentlest and most courteous of knights."

"Sir, shall I take you to your lodging?"

"No, I shall lodge with the King of the Hundred Knights, who rescued me from Sir Ector and Sir Bors."

However, Sir Tristram managed to console Sir Palomides and led him to his own pavilion, having first sent Governayle to warn Sir Persides to be careful with him, and Brangwayne to lodge elsewhere for the night. Sir Tristram slept soundly after his day's fighting, but Sir Palomides lay awake until dawn, when he left Sir Tristram's pavilion and joined Sir Gaheris and Sir Sagramour in theirs, as they had been his companions when he entered the tournament.

On the third day of the tournament the fighting opened with the King of the Hundred Knights charging King Carados and overthrowing him, and the King of North Galys charging the King of Ireland and overthrowing him. Then King Arthur and his followers entered the field, remounted the two kings who had been unhorsed, and forced their opponents onto the defensive.

Sir Tristram entered the field and overthrew in turn Sir Palomides and King Arthur.

When King Arthur and Sir Palomides had remounted, King Arthur charged at Sir Tristram and threw him to the ground. Then Sir Palomides galloped down on him, hoping to catch him at a disadvantage. But Sir Tristram neatly sidestepped and, as he passed, leaped up and dragged him by the arm from his horse. Then both drew their swords and fought furiously; however, Sir Tristram proved the stronger, and struck Sir Palomides three tremendous blows on the helmet, saying: "On behalf of Sir Tristram," at each blow. Sir Palomides fell groveling to the ground.

The King of the Hundred Knights gave Sir Tristram a fresh horse, and Sir Palomides charged him again. Avoiding his spear, Sir Tristram seized him by the neck this time, and hauling him clean out of the saddle, held him aloft while he galloped a hundred and fifty feet down the field and then flung him to the ground once more.

Sir Tristram exchanged further blows with King Arthur, with both spear and sword, and then attacked the followers of King Ban and struck down twelve of them. His feats drew tremendous applause from the spectators, and this was heard by Sir Launcelot, who rode up and challenged him.

They jousted, both broke their spears, and Sir Tristram was wounded deeply in the side. Ignoring his wound, Sir Tristram drew his sword, and gave Sir Launcelot three blows on the helmet which caused him to slump forward in the saddle, half stunned. Sir Tristram then left the field and rode into the forest, and Sir Dynadan, who had been watching him, followed. Sir Launcelot remained, and continued to fight formidably.

Once in the forest Sir Tristram unlaced his harness to ease his wounds. Sir Dynadan was horrified and wept, thinking that he must die.

"Do not fear, Sir Dynadan, I am still whole of heart, and with God's help I shall recover," said Sir Tristram.

Just then Sir Palomides came riding toward them, and Sir Tristram realized that he was determined to catch him at a disadvantage if he could.

Sir Dynadan spoke: "Sir Tristram, you are seriously wounded and you must not fight. I will encounter Sir Palomides and do what I can. If he kills me, pray for my soul; but in the meantime withdraw to the safety of a castle."

"Sir Dynadan, I thank you; but do not fear for me: I can still handle him."

Sir Tristram armed and mounted and rode slowly toward Sir Palomides. Sir Palomides halted, while waiting for Sir Gaheris, who had agreed to support him. Sir Tristram then sent his squire forward to challenge him to joust, on the condition that if Sir Palomides was overthrown they should both withdraw, but if Sir Tristram was overthrown, they should fight to their uttermost.

Sir Palomides accepted the condition. They jousted and Sir Palomides was thrown. Then Sir Gaheris arrived, and he too jousted with Sir Tristram and was overthrown.

Leaving Sir Persides and Governayle at his pavilion, Sir Tristram then rode with Sir Dynadan to the castle of an elderly knight called Sir Darras and begged him for lodging. Sir Darras accepted them. He was awaiting the return of his five sons, who were all competing in the tournament.

When Sir Tristram had left the field, Sir Launcelot, with King Arthur by his side, distinguished himself above all the other contestants, and forced the party of the King of North Galys onto the defensive. When the fighting was over it was cried that Sir Launcelot had won the prize, but Sir Launcelot objected:

"Not so! It is surely Sir Tristram who deserves the prize; he was the first on the field and lasted the longest, and for three days his feats have been unexampled."

Everyone present was struck by Sir Launcelot's magnanimity, and praised him for it, but he himself was furious that Sir Tristram had once more escaped from the field without receiving the honor due to him. Then the cry arose from all sides:

"Give Sir Launcelot the prize, and let none dispute it!"

Sir Launcelot rode up to King Arthur, and King Arthur spoke:

"We are all dismayed that Sir Tristram has ridden off the field, for certainly he is one of the noblest knights of all time. And now we can be certain that it was he who bore the black shield; for when he struck Sir Palomides he said, 'On behalf of Sir Tristram!'"

King Arthur, Sir Launcelot, and Sir Dodynas decided to seek Sir Tristram in the forest, and Sir Persides offered to take them to his pavilion. But when they arrived he had gone. Then they learned of the wound which Sir Launcelot had inflicted on him and were filled with sorrow.

"I am more grieved about his wound than about the wounds

which all my knights together have received today," said Arthur.

Then Sir Gaheris reported to Arthur how he and Sir Palomides had followed Sir Tristram and jousted with him at his own request, and Arthur replied:

"It was a shame for Sir Palomides to ride after him when he was wounded. We all know Sir Tristram for one of the greatest knights living—the last three days have given us proof of that. As for his wound, it was honorably received, for when two great knights encounter it is inevitable that one will receive an injury."

Sir Launcelot spoke next:

"Sire, not for the whole of my inheritance would I have wounded Sir Tristram if I had known it was he. But in the heat of battle one may well make a mistake, and as it happened I did not see his black shield. I have many reasons to love him, and only recently I was beholden to him for challenging thirty knights who were lying in ambush for me, and with the help only of Sir Dynadan, defeating them all. One thing is quite certain now, that Sir Palomides shall suffer for his malice when he followed Sir Tristram into the forest."

Then King Arthur called a feast, and his knights continued to praise Sir Tristram.

Sir Palomides, as the result of his last fall at the hands of Sir Tristram, had all but lost his wits. He had remounted and galloped furiously after him. Before long he came to a river, and rashly tried to jump it. His horse lost its footing and both were plunged into the water, and Sir Palomides feared that he would drown. However, he succeeded in swimming ashore; there he sat for a long time, cursing and raving.

Sometime later a young noblewoman rode by. She had been sent by Sir Gawain and his brother to Sir Modred, who was at Sir Darras' castle recovering from a wound given to him by Sir Persides in the course of a duel fought ten days previously, and from which the brothers had rescued him. There followed an acrimonious exchange between the young noblewoman and Sir Palomides, and then she rode on to the castle and reported that a raving madman was sitting by the river.

"My lady, could you describe his shield?" asked Sir Tristram.

"Sir, it was a black shield with a white device."

"Then certainly it was Sir Palomides; I know him well for one of the best knights in the realm."

Sir Darras mounted a small hack, rode to the river, and returned with him to the castle. Sir Tristram, who had recovered from his wound sufficiently to be able to walk, recognized Sir Palomides at once, but Sir Palomides did not recognize Sir Tristram. Sometimes he thought he looked familiar; then he would say to Sir Dynadan:

"If ever I meet Sir Tristram he shall not escape me!"

"It is strange to me that you should say that," Sir Dynadan would reply, "for I have witnessed several encounters between you, and you came off worst every time."

Then Sir Palomides would keep quiet.

King Arthur, meanwhile, still felt great chagrin at the disappearance of Sir Tristram, and rounded on Sir Launcelot for wounding him in their last duel. Sir Launcelot called for a Bible, and then said:

"Sire, I am the last man on earth who would wish to lose Sir Tristram; but in the heat of battle one may easily hurt one's friends as well as one's foes. I say now, let us ten knights swear to search for him, not resting night or day for a year without bringing him to this court."

This was agreed upon, and the ten knights who took this oath were: Sir Launcelot, Sir Ector, Sir Bors, Sir Bleobris, Sir Blamoure, Sir Lucas, Sir Uwayne, Sir Galyhud, Sir Lyonel, and Sir Galyhodyn. They all rode from the castle together, and then parted at a cross, each taking a different route.

Sir Launcelot had not ridden far when he caught sight of Brangwayne galloping full tilt on her little palfrey. He rode up to her:

"My lady, why do you gallop like that?"

"My lord, I am being pursued by Sir Breuse Sans Pité."

"Abide by me, then," said Sir Launcelot, and almost immediately Sir Breuse appeared.

"Coward! Now prepare to die!" Sir Launcelot shouted.

But Sir Breuse recognized Sir Launcelot and fled. Sir Launcelot chased him, but could not catch him, because Sir Breuse, whose practice it was to molest noblewomen, had provided himself with a horse swift enough to enable him to escape from the knights who came to their rescue. Sir Launcelot returned at length to Brangwayne, and she thanked him for her timely deliverance.

Sir Lucas had by chance taken the route which led to Sir Darras' castle, and asked the porter if he could lodge there. The porter asked Sir Darras, who at the time was with his nephew Sir Daname.

"No," said Sir Daname, "he may not lodge here. But tell him that I challenge him to joust."

Sir Daname armed and rode out to meet Sir Lucas. They jousted and Sir Daname was overthrown. Then Sir Dynadan said to Sir Tristram:

"It is a shame that our host's nephew should take a fall outside his own castle."

"I will challenge him!" said Sir Tristram.

First Sir Dynadan and then Sir Tristram jousted with Sir Lucas. Sir Dynadan was wounded in the thigh by Sir Lucas, and Sir Lucas was wounded by Sir Tristram. Then Sir Uwayne rode up, and seeing Sir Lucas wounded, challenged Sir Tristram.

"Sir, pray tell me your name," Sir Tristram responded.

"Sir Uwayne of the Fair Hands."

"Then I should prefer not to joust with you."

"You shall not escape so lightly," Sir Uwayne said.

They jousted and Sir Uwayne was wounded in the side, but not seriously, so he ordered a horse litter for Sir Lucas and conveyed him to the Castle Ganys, of which Sir Bleobris was lord, and which was the rendezvous for the ten knights in the quest of Sir Tristram.

Sir Tristram had returned to the castle, and when he met Sir Daname, had difficulty in restraining him from riding out to kill Sir Lucas in revenge for his fall. Then a young noble-woman arrived with the news that three of Sir Darras' sons had been killed at the tournament by the Knight with the Black Shield, and the remaining two seriously injured.

Sir Darras suspected that the Knight with the Black Shield was Sir Tristram, and went to his chamber to confirm it. Once he had seen the black shield he put Sir Tristram, Sir Palomides, and Sir Dynadan into the castle prison.

Sir Palomides, certain now of Sir Tristram's identity, never ceased to complain against him, but Sir Tristram answered little. He had fallen sick, and in time it became so serious that not only was Sir Dynadan anxious for him, but also Sir Palomides.

Sir Darras had forty kinsmen, and on hearing of the death of his three sons, they all tried to persuade him to put Sir Tristram to death; but Sir Darras refused to do so, and also insured that his prisoners had enough to eat and drink.

Nevertheless, Sir Tristram suffered greatly from his sickness; for whereas a healthy prisoner may live in hope of deliverance, a sick prisoner loses all hope, and in so doing increases his very sickness.

6. THE ROUND TABLE

Several of the ten knights on the quest of Sir Tristram rode to Cornwall, among them Sir Gaheris, King Arthur's nephew. By chance he rode straight to Tintagil, where King Mark entertained him well and asked him the news from Logres.

"Sire, King Arthur is the noblest of kings, and recently he held a tournament at the Maidens' Castle. The greatest knights of the land were present; but one, bearing a plain black shield, distinguished himself above all the others."

"Sir Launcelot or Sir Palomides?"

"No, they were both fighting against the Knight with the Black Shield."

"Then it was Sir Tristram de Lyoness!"

King Mark was mortified to think that Sir Tristram should fight for another king and win honor in another realm, but Queen Iseult was secretly pleased.

Then King Mark proclaimed a feast, and to that feast came Sir Uwayne, and offered a challenge to the knights of Cornwall. At first it seemed that there was none to answer him; then Sir Andret, King Mark's cousin, accepted the challenge.

All was made ready; they jousted, and Sir Andret was overthrown. King Mark was at a loss for a second champion, so he asked Sir Dynas the Seneschal to represent him.

"Sire, I am most reluctant to encounter a knight of the Round Table," Sir Dynas replied.

"And yet, for the love you bear me, I beg you to do so," said the king.

Sir Dynas made ready; they jousted, and he too was overthrown.

"Alas! Have I no knight who will withstand Sir Uwayne?" said the king.

"Sire, for your sake, I will joust with him," said Sir Gaheris.

Sir Gaheris made ready, but as soon as he entered the field Sir Uwayne rode up to him.

"Sir, I know from your shield that you are a knight of the Round Table, and you know from mine that I am. Have you then forgotten our vow: that we do not wittingly enter into combat with one another? Do not suppose that I am frightened of you because I refuse your challenge, but understand that for myself I shall honor my oath. It would seem that you have also forgotten that we are related, since our mothers are sisters."

Sir Gaheris was ashamed and withdrew. Sir Uwayne and the

other knights who had come for the feast each rode on their way. But before Sir Uwayne had ridden far, King Mark, fully armed and accompanied by a squire, suddenly charged at him through a gap in the hedge, overthrew him, and wounded him severely.

By chance Sir Kay found him, and asked what had happened.

"Sir, I hardly know: I was attacked without warning, wounded, and the knight galloped away before I had an opportunity of recognizing him."

Just then Sir Andret rode by, in search of King Mark. "Coward!" said Sir Kay. "I suppose that you are responsible for attacking this knight?"

"Sir, that is not true," Sir Andret responded.

"Shame on the knights of Cornwall anyhow! There never was a good one among them," said Sir Kay.

Sir Andret departed and Sir Kay carried Sir Uwayne to the Abbey of the Black Cross, where he was nursed until his wound had healed.

Sir Kay rode to Tintagil, and arrived just as Sir Gaheris was taking his leave of the king:

"Sire, you brought shame on yourself by exiling Sir Tristram, for had he been here no knight could have withstood him."

The king made a semblance of welcoming Sir Kay, then he asked them both:

"My lords, is one of you hardy enough to venture into the forest of Morrys?"

"Sire, I am ready to undertake the adventure," Sir Kay replied.

Sir Gaheris left the castle immediately, rode into the forest, and then, ordering his squire to warn him of Sir Kay's approach, settled down to wait for him. A short time later Sir Kay arrived.

"Sir Kay, are you wise to ride at the request of King Mark, when we have reason to suspect him of treachery?"

"Sir Gaheris, if you think that, will you accompany me?"

"I shall not fail you."

They rode together through the forest until they came to the Lake Perelous, and waited near the shore beneath a coppice.

King Mark stayed in his castle until midnight, avoiding all but his few close friends. Then he summoned Sir Andret and commanded him to arm and mount as quickly as possible, and clad himself in black armor and mounted a black horse. They left the castle by a postern, and accompanied by two squires, rode to the lake.

Sir Kay saw King Mark first and challenged him. They jousted and Sir Kay was thrown. Sir Gaheris challenged the king and overthrew first him and then Sir Andret.

Sir Gaheris and Sir Kay stood over the king and Sir Andret and ordered them to yield on pain of death, and to reveal their identities.

"It is King Mark of Cornwall, therefore beware what you do; and I am his cousin, Sir Andret."

"The more shame on you for being two such cowardly knights; most certainly you shall not live," said Sir Gaheris.

"My lords, as I am an anointed king, spare my life, and I will make amends."

"Treacherous king that you are, you shall die," said Sir Gaheris, and with that he drew his sword and attacked him, while Sir Kay attacked Sir Andret.

King Mark soon yielded to Sir Gaheris, and kneeling before him, begged for his life and swore by the cross on his sword never again to molest errant knights, also to befriend Sir Tristram when he returned to Cornwall. Then Sir Andret yielded to Sir Kay, who would have killed him for the mischief he had done to Sir Tristram, but for the intervention of Sir Gaheris. Sir Gaheris and Sir Kay rode on to Sir Dynas, knowing that he was still loyal to Sir Tristram.

Sir Dynas had just lost his wife. One day when he was out hunting she had made a rope from some towels and secretly let herself out of the castle, and then, taking with her two brachets, had gone to her lover. Sir Dynas had followed her, challenged her lover, and broken his arm and his leg in the course of combat. His wife had sworn to be faithful to him thereafter; but Sir Dynas, more angered by the loss of his brachets than of his wife, had said:

"No, you had better remain here, for a woman who has proved unfaithful once will prove so again." And with that he had taken the brachets and returned to his castle.

Sir Dynas had no news of Sir Tristram, so Sir Gaheris and Sir Kay rode back to the realm of Logres, where they met Sir Launcelot together with Brangwayne. When they told Sir Launcelot of their adventures with King Mark, he smiled and said:

"It is hard to cure in the flesh what is bred in the bone!" They all made merry that evening; then Brangwayne set off for Cornwall, and the three knights to the country of Surluse to continue their search.

Sir Tristram, Sir Palomides, and Sir Dynadan, meanwhile, were still held prisoner by Sir Darras, and Sir Palomides continued to complain about Sir Tristram.

"Sir Palomides, you surprise me," said Sir Dynadan. "In prison even the wolf and the sheep must abide together; once we are free you can challenge Sir Tristram again, and see what comes of it."

Sir Palomides was quiet for a moment and Sir Tristram spoke:

"Sir Palomides, I have heard much of the ill will you bear me. I do not answer you now, however, for as yet we do not know what our fate as prisoners is to be."

While Sir Tristram was speaking, a maid had appeared:

"My lords, you need not fear for your lives. I myself have heard Sir Darras say that they shall be spared."

They were all cheered by this news, for daily they had expected to be put to death. A short time after this, however, Sir Tristram fell seriously ill, and this was reported by the maid to Sir Darras, who ordered the prisoners to be brought before him.

"Sir, I am sorry for your sickness. I know that you have won great renown; and I would not have it said that I, Sir Darras, allowed you to die in my prison. But you understand that you have killed three of my sons; therefore I can release you only if you swear to befriend the two who still live, and if before going you tell me your name."

"I am Sir Tristram de Lyoness; King Mark is my uncle, and I was born in Cornwall. I killed your sons in fair combat, and had they been of my own kin I could not have spared them; certainly, if I had killed them treacherously I should deserve to die."

"Sir, I know that you have done only as a knight should do, and therefore if you will take the oath I ask, you shall be free."

"Sir Darras, you have done as is natural for a father, and I readily swear to serve both you and your sons," Sir Tristram replied.

Sir Tristram remained at the castle until he had recovered from his illness, and then rode with Sir Palomides and Sir Dynadan to a crossroads in the forest, where they all parted.

Sir Dynadan was the first of the three to meet with adventure. He was riding past a well when he met a young noble-woman in tears.

"My lady, what is your trouble?" he asked.

"Sir, five days ago Sir Breuse Sans Pité killed my brother, and since then has forced me to be his mistress; and I find him the most loathsome man on earth. Therefore, I pray you, deliver me."

"My lady, wait only until he comes."

Sir Dynadan remained by the lady, and sometime later Sir Breuse appeared and challenged him. They jousted, and the result was that Sir Breuse was wounded in the shoulder and fled. The young noblewoman then begged Sir Dynadan to ac-company her to her uncle's castle, four miles away. This he did, and then resumed his ride in quest of adventure.

Sir Tristram, at the end of the first day, chanced to ask for lodging at a castle of which Morgan le Fay was the lady. He was entertained well that night and in the morning went to Morgan le Fay to take his leave of her.

"Sir, understand that you are my prisoner, and you shall not leave this castle until I know who you are and whence you have come," said Morgan le Fay.

"Alas, I have only just been released from prison," said Sir Tristram.

Morgan le Fay was attended by her lover, Sir Hemyson, at the castle, and it became her habit to order Sir Tristram to stand on one side of her, and Sir Hemyson on the other, and then to compare them. This made Sir Hemyson furious, as he felt that the comparison was to his disadvantage, and he had difficulty in restraining himself from running Sir Tristram through with his sword.

One day Morgan le Fay said to Sir Tristram:

"Sir, tell me your name and I shall release you."

"Ma'am, on that covenant I shall do so. I am Sir Tristram de Lyoness."

"Alas! If I had known that you were Sir Tristram you should not have escaped. However, I will keep my word, pro-vided that you enter the tournament which King Arthur has proclaimed at the castle of the Harde Roche, bearing a shield that I shall give you, and fighting as you did at the castle of the Maidens."

"Ma'am, may I see the shield I am to bear?"

The shield was brought. The device showed three figures: a king and a queen and, above them, standing with one foot on the head of each, a knight.

"Ma'am, pray tell me, what is the meaning of this device?"

"The king and queen are Arthur and Gwynevere, and the knight above them is one who holds them both in bondage."

"And who is the knight?"

"Just now I shall not tell you," said Morgan le Fay.

The knight represented was Sir Launcelot, and Morgan le Fay had devised this shield in order to discomfort the three of them, since she was jealous of Sir Launcelot's love for Queen Gwynevere; however, Sir Tristram was unaware of this and agreed to use the shield at the tournament. As soon as he had left the castle Sir Hemyson, Morgan le Fay's paramour, prepared to follow him.

"My lord, I pray you, do not pursue that knight, for I know who he is, and he will kill you," said Morgan le Fay.

"My lady, he is from Cornwall. Sir Tristram alone is to be feared of the Cornish knights, and he at present is with Isode. As for this fellow, do not fear, I will avenge you easily enough."

"My lord, I still beg you to remain here."

Sir Tristram had not ridden far when he heard a knight galloping after him, who, as soon as he was within earshot, challenged him.

Sir Tristram couched his spear and they galloped together furiously. Sir Tristram was unhurt, but Sir Hemyson was flung from his horse and mortally wounded. Seeing that this was so, Sir Tristram resumed his journey and Sir Hemyson's squire unlaced his helmet and asked if he were not about to die.

"I shall live for a little longer; therefore, I pray you, help me onto my horse, and then mount behind me, and in that way we may get back to the castle. I wish to speak to my paramour once again, for I am sick at heart.'

With great difficulty Sir Hemyson's squire brought him to the castle; but the moment they arrived, he fell down dead. Morgan le Fay saw him, wept over him, and buried him. On the tomb she inscribed the legend:

HERE LYETH SIR HEMYSON SLAYNE BY THE HONDIS OF SIR TRISTRAM DE LYONESS.

Sir Tristram met with no further adventures that day, and in the evening lodged with an elderly knight. He asked his host what news he had.

"Sir, only last night Sir Ector de Marys lodged here with a young noblewoman, and she told me that he was the greatest knight living."

"That is not so," Sir Tristram replied, "because I know of four knights who are all better than he is: Sir Launcelot, Sir

Bors, Sir Blamoure, and Sir Gaheris."

"Sir Gawain is surely the better brother?"

"I think not, for I have encountered them both, and found Sir Gaheris the better. But then there is Sir Lamerok, who is as good as any of them with the exception of Sir Launcelot."

"Surely Sir Tristram is as good as any of them?"

"I do not know Sir Tristram," Sir Tristram replied.

And so they talked for the evening, and then went to bed.

The next day Sir Tristram rode to the castle of the Harde Roche and found the tournament already in progress. King Carados and King Angwyshaunce and their knights were fighting against the knights of King Arthur. Bearing the shield which Morgan le Fay had given him, Sir Tristram entered the melee, and his feats soon drew the attention of Arthur and Gwynevere. Both noticed the shield. Gwynevere understood the meaning at once, but Arthur was puzzled and asked aloud what it could mean. One of Morgan le Fay's maids was standing by and she answered him:

"Sire, the shield represents the shame which has fallen upon yourself and Queen Gwynevere."

The maid disappeared before the king could ask her whence she had come, and he was filled with anger and dismay. Meanwhile, the queen whispered to Sir Ector:

"I believe this shield was made by Morgan le Fay in order to expose me and Sir Launcelot, and I fear that she may succeed and that soon I shall be destroyed."

The queen was alarmed because the king never took his eyes off Sir Tristram and the shield. The king was greatly puzzled as to who Sir Tristram might be; for he knew it could not be Sir Launcelot, and believed Sir Tristram to be in Brittany with Isode, since none of his knights had been able to find him in the realm of Logres.

King Carados and King Angwyshaunce gradually retreated before the violence of Sir Tristram's attack. At last King Arthur summoned Sir Uwayne and rode with him to Sir Tristram, demanding to know the meaning of the shield.

"Sir, the shield was given to me by Queen Morgan le Fay, who charged me to bear it at this tournament. What the device means I do not know, but I trust that I bear my charge honorably."

"Sir, if you are worthy to bear arms you should know their meaning. Now tell me, what is your name? Or do you prefer to accept my challenge?" said King Arthur.

"Sir, you shall not know my name and I accept your challenge, although it is a cowardly one; for you are as yet fresh while I have fought all day and am weary."

Sir Tristram and King Arthur jousted, with the result that King Arthur broke his spear and was unhorsed and seriously wounded in the flank. Sir Uwayne tried to avenge him, but with the result that he too was flung violently out of the saddle and seriously bruised.

"My lords, I trust you are satisfied; for I have had enough of jousting for one day," said Sir Tristram.

"Sir," said Arthur to Sir Tristram, "it was from pride that we challenged you; and although we do not know your name, I must admit we have received only what we deserve."

"And from a knight who, by St. Cruse, must be as strong as any living!" Sir Uwayne added.

Sir Tristram departed, and for many days rode in search of Sir Launcelot, but could find him nowhere. One day he came to a castle; on one side was a marsh, on the other a meadow, and in front of the castle ten knights were fighting. As he rode toward them Sir Tristram recognized Sir Palomides, who was defending himself against Sir Breuse Sans Pité and eight of his retainers. Sir Palomides was fighting on foot; he had killed half his assailants' horses and driven the remainder into the fields. Sir Tristram, moved by Sir Palomides' valor, galloped up to Sir Breuse and demanded that he should call off his knights.

"Sir, this knight shall not escape us, so cease meddling and return whence you have come!"

"I warn you, I shall not leave so valiant a knight to be murdered by cowards!" said Sir Tristram.

In order that his horse should not be killed, Sir Tristram dismounted, then drawing his sword, set at the assailants with such good effect that they soon fled. He chased them to the castle, but they managed to enter and close the gates behind them. Sir Tristram then returned to Sir Palomides, who was sitting beneath a tree and nursing his wounds.

"Good knight, greetings!" said Sir Tristram. "Now, I pray you, tell me your name."

"Sir Palomides."

"Sir Palomides, I have rescued you, and now I must challenge you."

"Sir, pray tell me, what is your name?"

"Sir Tristram, your mortal enemy."

"Sir Tristram, it is true that today you have rescued me; and yet your challenge is not just, for you are fresh and I am wounded. Therefore let us swear to an assignation for another day."

"Very well, for two weeks from today at Merlin's stone, in the meadow by the river at Camelot."

This was agreed, and then Sir Tristram asked Sir Palomides how it was he came to be assaulted by Sir Breuse and his retainers.

"Sir, I was riding through the forest when I came upon a lady weeping over her dead lord. I asked her who was responsible for his death, and she told me Sir Breuse, so I promised to accompany her and assist in the burial. I set her on her palfrey, and we were riding past this castle when Sir Breuse attacked without warning, unhorsed me, and then killed the lady. I was deeply ashamed and challenged him; then he called his fellows and they too set upon me."

"I understand you well; and now, although I do not forget our assignation, let us ride together out of this evil country."

They rode together until they came to a well where they could hear the cool water bubbling beneath.

"A drink is just what I need," said Sir Tristram, and dismounted. They were then startled by the sound of a horse neighing, and looking about them saw a huge charger and, not far away, a handsome knight asleep on the ground with his head on his helmet.

"What shall we do?" asked Sir Tristram.

"Awaken him," said Sir Palomides, and, going over to him, tapped his armor with the butt of his spear. Without saying a word, the knight leaped up, laced on his helmet, grasped a spear, mounted, and withdrew to some distance. Then he galloped at Sir Tristram and knocked him clean out of the saddle, wounding him in the side.

The knight withdrew once more, and then charged upon Sir Palomides, and likewise threw him out of the saddle. Then, still without uttering a word, he galloped away into the forest.

"By my faith, he is certainly a strong knight! He has shamed us both, and I shall follow him," said Sir Tristram.

"Very well. I shall remain here and seek out a friend of mine," said Sir Palomides.

"Then farewell; but do not fail me on the day of our assignation. I am afraid that you may, because I am the stronger."

"I do not fear you; but if you follow that knight it may well be that you will fail me on the day of our assignation."

They parted and Sir Tristram rode after the knight. Before long he came upon a lady who lay weeping on the body of a dead knight.

"My lady, pray tell me, who has killed your lord?"

"Sir, a strange knight came riding by, and when he saw my lord he asked him if he were of King Arthur's court; and when my lord replied that he was, the strange knight challenged him, saying that he was an enemy of all the knights of the Round Table. They jousted, my lord was overthrown and killed, and the strange knight rode away."

"My lady, I am sorry for your misfortune. Pray, what was your lord's name?"

"Sir Galardonne, and he would have proved a worthy knight."

Sir Tristram left the weeping lady and continued to pursue the unknown knight, resting only at the most meager of lodgings. On the third day he met Sir Gawain and Sir Bleobris, both of whom were wounded. He asked them what had happened, and Sir Gawain replied:

"Sir, we met a knight riding with a covered shield. He challenged us, and then Sir Bleobris said to me that he looked too strong for either of us. The knight thought he was being mocked and forced Sir Bleobris to accept his challenge, and when he did so, overthrew him. Then it was my turn and the same happened to me. After that he rode away. Alas that we ever met him!"

"He must be the same knight who overthrew Sir Palomides, me, and another knight three days ago," said Sir Tristram.

"I say, let him go," said Sir Gawain. "You can be sure that we shall find him sitting at the Round Table at the next feast."

"All the same, I cannot rest until I have discovered him," said Sir Tristram.

The three knights exchanged names and parted. Sir Tristram rode on until he came to a meadow, where he met Sir Kay and Sir Dynadan.

"What news?" asked Sir Tristram.

"Ill news," Sir Dynadan replied.

"How so? Tell me, for I am following a strange knight."

"What shield does he bear?"

"His shield is covered."

"Ah so! Then he must be the very knight whom we encountered lately. I shall tell you: We were all lodged together in a house belonging to a widow, and when this knight heard that we came from the court of King Arthur, he abused the king, the queen, and our whole fellowship, and challenged us to joust with him in the morning. When the morning came I jousted with him first and was overthrown. When Sir Dynadan saw this he did not attempt to avenge me, but fled; the knight with the covered shield then rode on his way."

After exchanging names Sir Tristram departed and rode through the forest and onto a plain, where he came to a priory. There he rested for six days while Governayle obtained a new set of harness for him from the nearest city. They left the priory early in the morning on the day after Governayle had returned, and met Sir Sagramour and Sir Dodynas, who challenged Sir Tristram to joust.

"My lords, I would prefer not to, because I have an assignation to fight in a few days' time, and I shall have little chance against my opponent if I am wounded beforehand."

"Sir, you shall joust with us all the same," Sir Sagramour replied.

"Since you oblige me to do so, I will," Sir Tristram replied. Sir Tristram jousted with them both, and both were hurled from their horses; then Sir Tristram continued on his way. However, he had not gone far when he heard them galloping after him.

"Surely, it is not long since I overthrew both of you, which was at your request and not mine. What more do you want of me?"

"We have come to seek revenge," said Sir Sagramour.

"My lords, we have already fought at your request, and already I had asked you to forebear because of the duel I have to fight in three days' time. My reason is that I do not wish to be wounded in advance; but understand that if we do fight now, I shall not be the only one to be wounded."

"Whom are you to fight?"

"Sir Palomides."

"By my faith! he is certainly a knight to reckon with. We shall therefore do as you ask if you will tell us your name."

"Sir Tristram de Lyoness."

"Well met, Sir Tristram! We have already heard much of you."

Sir Tristram took his leave of the two knights and rode straight to the meadow at Camelot in which stood Merlin's stone. This was the place where Sir Launceor, Prince of Ireland, had been killed by Sir Balin, and the prince's lover, the lady Columbe, had taken her life in grief for him. And it was where Merlin had prophesied that the two greatest lovers of all time, who would also be the two greatest knights of all time, would fight each other.

When Sir Tristram arrived he looked about for Sir Palomides, but he was not to be seen. Then the strange knight with the covered shield came riding toward him.

"Welcome, good knight, you have kept true to your promise."

Both knights withdrew and then galloped full tilt at each other. The force of the collision sent both knights and horses tumbling to the ground, but the knights leaped up immediately and crossed swords. For four hours they fought without speaking. Their armor and shields became chipped, their harnesses began to give way under the strain, and the blood poured in rivulets from their wounds and stained the ground beneath them.

"I wonder that your master has withstood mine for so long," said Governayle to the other squire.

"And I was thinking the same thing about your master," the other replied.

"For the love of Jesu! it is a shame that two such knights should destroy each other."

And so both squires watched and wept to see their masters engaged in combat. Then Sir Launcelot, who was the knight with the covered shield, paused for a moment and spoke:

"Sir, I pray you, tell me your name. You have fought as no knight I have encountered yet."

"Sir, I am loath to tell any man my name."

"Truly? I have never hesitated to tell mine."

"Then tell me, I beg you."

"Sir Launcelot du Lake."

"Alas! What have I done? You are the man I love most in the world."

"Now, I pray you, tell me your name."

"Sir Tristram de Lyoness."

"Ah Jesu!"

Thereupon both Sir Tristram and Sir Launcelot knelt down, and each offered the other his sword in token of yielding. Then they rose, sat on Merlin's stone, removed their helmets, and kissed each other a hundred times.

Later, as they rode together toward Camelot, they met Sir

Gawain and Sir Gaheris, who were still searching for Sir Tristram.

"You need search no further, for Sir Tristram is with us," said Sir Launcelot.

"Welcome, Sir Tristram! Our quest is at an end. But tell me, how did you come to be here?"

"Sir, I came to fight Sir Palomides by Merlin's stone, and by chance Sir Launcelot appeared there in his stead. I am still wondering where Sir Palomides may be."

They all rode together to Camelot, and when they arrived King Arthur took Sir Tristram by the hand.

"Sir Tristram, welcome to this court!" he said.

Then Sir Tristram described how he had come to Camelot to fight Sir Palomides and had fought the knight with the covered shield, how he had saved Sir Palomides from Sir Breuse, and had been following the knight with the covered shield ever since.

"By my faith, we too were struck down by the knight with the covered shield," said Sir Gawain.

"And so were we," said Sir Kay.

"Then none of you knew who it was?" said King Arthur. "It must have been Sir Launcelot, surely, and it is not the first time he has done that."

"Sire, it was," said Sir Launcelot.

King Arthur then led Sir Tristram to the Round Table and he was welcomed by the queen and the ladies of the court.

"Welcome," said King Arthur, "to a knight who is among the bravest and gentlest living, who is first in the arts of hunting and hawking, first in the measures of speech, and first in the skills of music! Welcome to this court! And now I beg you, grant me my wish."

"Sire, it is granted."

"That you will abide in my court."

"Sire, I have ties in many lands."

"And yet I will keep you to your promise."

"As you will, my liege."

King Arthur searched the empty seats at the Round Table until he came to the one which had belonged to Sir Marhaus, and there was inscribed a new legend in letters of gold:

THIS IS THE SYEGE OF THE NOBLE KNYGHT SIR TRYSTRAMYS.

And so Sir Tristram came to occupy the seat of the knight whom he had fought on the first day of his knighthood, on behalf of King Mark, and to free Cornwall, the land of his birth, from bondage.

7. KING MARK

The honor accorded Sir Tristram by King Arthur excited as much anger and jealousy in the heart of King Mark as love and pride in the heart of Queen Iseult. Both had sent spies to report on all that he had done since his exile, and the news that he was now a knight of the Round Table decided King Mark to kill him if he could.

Accompanied by Sir Bersules and Sir Amaunte, he rode into the realm of Logres and inquired of a passing knight where he might find King Arthur.

"Sir, at Camelot."

"And Sir Tristram, too?"

"Most certainly; he is the most famous knight at the court now. Not only did he win the prize at the Maidens' Castle, but he has since beaten more than thirty of the greatest knights, and even matched Sir Launcelot, who for the love of him brought Sir Tristram to King Arthur. He now sits at the Round Table in the seat formerly occupied by Sir Marhaus."

The knight departed.

"Now I will tell you the truth," said King Mark to his companions, "I have come here to destroy Sir Tristram by whatever means come to hand."

"Sire," said Sir Bersules, "Sir Tristram is the most honorable knight living, and do not suppose that I for one am going to be your accomplice."

"Traitor!" shouted the king, and swiftly drawing his sword, beheaded him.

"Murderer!" shouted Sir Amaunte. "You shall suffer for this: I shall charge you with treason at King Arthur's court."

King Mark would have killed Sir Amaunte too, but he saw that not only he, but the squires too, were against him.

"Very well, charge me; but I ask one thing, and that is, do not reveal my name."

"As you wish."

They parted. Sir Amaunte buried Sir Bersules, and King Mark rode on through the forest until he came to a well, where he sat down to decide whether he would continue to King Arthur's court or return to Tintagil. Before long a knight rode up to the well and also sat down. Unaware of the presence of King Mark, he started complaining bitterly to himself:

"Alas! that I should love Queen Margawse, already the mother of Sir Gawain and Sir Gaheris, and of many more besides."

King Mark walked over to him:

"Sir, I am sorry to hear of your grief. Pray tell me, what is your name?"

"Sir Lamerok—why hide it? for just now I am overcome by my grief. But surely, judging by your accent, you must be from Cornwall? I have heard much of the renegade king there, King Mark. Of how he exiled the great Sir Tristram for loving Iseult the Fair, the most beautiful of all women, and one who surely deserves a better husband than a king so mean and treacherous as he."

"I have not heard of the matter," said King Mark. "But tell me, what is the news hereabouts?"

"There is to be a tournament at the castle of Jagent. The King of the Hundred Knights and King Angwyshaunce, I believe, are going to compete."

Meanwhile, Sir Dynadan had ridden up to them, and hearing King Mark's accent, reviled the king and knights of Cornwall more strongly even than Sir Lamerok had. Then Sir Lamerok offered to joust with King Mark, who tried to refuse, but Sir Dynadan urged him on.

They jousted, and King Mark was hurled over his horse's tail. Sir Dynadan flatly refused to avenge him, and told King Mark that his opponent was Sir Kay.

"Surely, Sir Kay is not so large as he?" said King Mark as he remounted and prepared to follow him.

"Sir, what do you want with me now?" asked Sir Lamerok, when the king had caught up with him.

"To fight with the sword, since you have shamed me with the spear."

They fought on horseback with their swords. At first Sir Lamerok did little more than defend himself, but King Mark lashed at him so furiously that he decided to teach him a lesson, so he struck him about the helmet until he slumped forward in the saddle.

"What now?" asked Sir Lamerok. "Have you had enough? It would be a shame to beat you any harder, feeble knight that you are!"

"I thank you; we are ill matched," King Mark replied.

"You will never match a good knight," said Sir Dynadan.

"Sir, you yourself refused to joust with him."

"You think that shameful? It is not. And you knights from Cornwall would do well to acknowledge that you are less courageous and strong than knights elsewhere and, as I do, leave them alone. But no, instead of that, out of jealousy and foolhardiness you try to match them, with the result that you are a laughingstock. Only one great knight ever came from Cornwall, and that was Sir Tristram."

Sir Dynadan, Sir Lamerok, and King Mark rode on until they came to a bridge leading to a castle. The bridge was guarded by two knights.

"Those are two brothers," said Sir Dynadan, "Sir Alyne and Sir Tryan; and we shall not pass until one of us has jousted with them. Therefore, I say, let the Cornish knight try to prove his valor once more."

The king was ashamed to refuse, so he couched his spear and jousted with Sir Tryan. Both broke their spears; Sir Tryan sent his squire with another spear for King Mark, but he refused to joust again.

Then King Mark and his companions asked for lodging and were escorted across the bridge and into the well-kept castle, where they were welcomed by the lord, Sir Torre. They all made merry that evening until the castle lieutenant, Sir Berluse, appeared and noticed King Mark.

"Sir," he said, "I know full well who you are: King Mark of Cornwall. You it was who murdered my father before my very eyes, and would have murdered me too with your treachery had I not escaped into the woods. For the love that I bear Sir Torre, and not to embarrass your noble companions, I shall refrain from taking my revenge now; but do not suppose that once you have left this castle you will escape me. I may add that it surprises me that knights as honorable as Sir Lamerok and Sir Dynadan should company with you at all, considering the many noble knights you have already murdered."

King Mark did not reply, and his companions, disgusted with him, retired to bed at once. The next morning Sir Lamerok rode off alone and Sir Dynadan accompanied King Mark. They had not ridden far when they were confronted by Sir Berluse and his two cousins.

"Traitor, defend yourself!" shouted Sir Berluse.

"Sir, I recommend that you let him be, for I am accompanying him to King Arthur's court, and therefore at this time am bound to take his part."

"Then defend yourselves!" said Sir Berluse.

Sir Berluse charged at King Mark and overthrew him; then Sir Dynadan couched his spear and overthrew both of the cousins in turn. They all set to with their swords, and Sir Dynadan fought with such vigor that soon the two cousins fled and Sir Berluse was at the mercy of King Mark, who would have killed him had not Sir Dynadan come to the rescue. King Mark and Sir Dynadan resumed their journey, leaving Sir Berluse seriously wounded.

They had ridden three leagues when they came to another bridge guarded by a knight.

"Ah ha! now we shall have to joust with him," said Sir Dynadan.

"Certainly, and it falls to you this time to do so," said King Mark.

Sir Dynadan tried to persuade King Mark to accept the challenge, but King Mark refused. Sir Dynadan jousted with him and was thrown from his horse. He leaped up at once and commanded the knight to fight on foot.

"Sir, the custom here is only to joust," the knight replied.

Sir Dynadan was outraged, and demanded that the knight should tell him his name, for he suspected that it was Sir Torre. However, the knight refused to tell him, so they resumed their journey once more.

"I had supposed," said King Mark, "that the knights of the Round Table were matchless."

"You are a fine one to speak," said Sir Dynadan. "Let us see what sort of showing you can make: I challenge you!"

"I pray you, no! I have but one thing to ask of you, and that is that you do not reveal my name to King Arthur."

"Your behavior is a disgrace, and it astonishes me. I know well now that you are cowardly, treacherous, and a murderer. Had I not prevented you just now, when you had him at a disadvantage, you would have murdered Sir Berluse, who is a far better knight than you. And do not suppose that you will ever win honor and fame by your evil ways."

They continued talking until they met a knight who invited them to lodge with him; for it was his practice to offer hospitality to errant knights, and he especially welcomed those of the Round Table. Sir Dynadan asked his host if he knew the name of the knight who guarded the bridge.

"Sir, indeed I do. He is Sir Torre, and one of the finest knights hereabouts."

"Ah! I thought so," said Sir Dynadan.

While they were talking, six knights of the Round Table appeared in the distance, across the plain. They were: Sir Uwayne of the Fair Hands, Sir Uwayne les Avoutres, Sir Brandiles, Sir Ozanna, Sir Aggravayne, and Sir Modred.

Sir Dynadan was determined that King Mark should joust with them, so he rode with him across the plain, and they found the knights all seated around a well, eating and drinking, their horses tethered, and their arms scattered about them.

"Behold!" said Sir Dynadan, "there are some knights who will surely joust with us."

"God forbid! There are six of them and we are only two," King Mark rejoined.

"I will challenge the first of them," said Sir Dynadan, and couched his spear.

King Mark turned his horse about and fled; when he had done so, Sir Dynadan took his spear from the rest and trotted up to his friends, who greeted him warmly, and asked if he had heard any news of Sir Launcelot or Sir Tristram.

"I have seen neither since I left Camelot," Sir Dynadan replied.

"Pray, who was the knight who fled as you were approaching?"

"The greatest coward alive."

"What is his name?"

"That I do not know."

They all rode together to a castle where they were lodged by an old knight known for his hospitality. There they met Sir Grysflet and Sir Dagonet, King Arthur's fool. Then Sir Dynadan discovered King Mark in one of the chambers, and asked him why he had fled.

"We were too greatly outnumbered. But how did you escape?" King Mark replied.

"They proved to be better friends than I had supposed."

"Who is their leader?"

"Sir Launcelot."

"God forbid! Can one know him by his shield?"

"He bears a silver shield with black bands."

"I pray you, will you accompany me to Camelot?"

"I am unwilling to do so, because you forsook me earlier."

Sir Dynadan left King Mark at the castle and rode after his fellows of the Round Table. When he caught up with them they were all talking of the Cornish knight, and he described how he had deceived him so that he would suppose, by the shield that Sir Modred was bearing, that Sir Modred was Sir Launcelot.

"But alas! I am wounded, and if he follows us I cannot fight," said Sir Modred.

"Then let Sir Dagonet the fool bear Sir Modred's shield and armor, and we shall soon see some sport," said Sir Grysflet.

This was done, and before long King Mark appeared; then Sir Dagonet shouted in a tremendous voice:

"Knight from Cornwall, beware! Now defend yourself."

"Alas, I am undone!" said King Mark to himself, and turning his horse, fled into the forest.

Sir Dagonet pursued him, roaring and raving, and the other knights all galloped after them, laughing so much that they nearly fell from their saddles. They were also anxious that Sir Dagonet should not actually joust with King Mark, since Sir Dagonet was a favorite of King Arthur's.

King Mark rode helter-skelter until he came to a well, where he found a powerful-looking knight armed and mounted. When the knight saw King Mark he said:

"Sir, for shame! Turn about and face your enemy."

"Sir, I pray you, let me pass; my enemy is the greatest knight on earth," King Mark replied.

"Do not fear, I shall stand by you; and unless he is either Sir Launcelot or Sir Tristram, I do not doubt that I shall get the better of him."

King Mark remained, and the knight couched his spear and charged with such violence that Sir Dagonet was thrown far over his horse's tail, and nearly broke his neck. Sir Brandiles came galloping immediately after him and, seeing his fall, shouted:

"Sir, defend yourself!"

The knight met his charge, and Sir Brandiles likewise was flung from the saddle. Sir Uwayne and Sir Ozanna came next.

"Jesu! there is a strong knight," said Sir Uwayne.

And they too were overthrown. Next Sir Grythlet, Sir Aggravayne, and Sir Uwayne les Avoutres rode up. Seeing their three fellows all overthrown, they sent their squire forward to inquire the knight's name and whether he was not from King Arthur's court—"for I believe it is Sir Lamerok," said Sir Grythlet.

"Tell your masters that I am a knight errant as they are, and at this time they shall not know my name. Later they will learn that I am not from King Arthur's court."

The squire returned to the three knights and delivered his message.

"By my faith, he is certainly a strong knight," said Sir Aggravayne. "Well, now it is our turn to encounter him."

All three jousted with the knight, and all three were overthrown, with as much ignominy as Sir Dagonet had suffered. Then Sir Dynadan and Sir Modred (who was without his armor) rode up, and the strange knight rode on his way, followed admiringly by King Mark.

They rode for three miles or so, and not once did the strange knight offer a word in answer to the king's expostulations, but instead rode with his head low, sighing, and giving every appearance of grief. Then they came to a castle, and he ordered a squire to go to the lady of the castle and ask for food and drink, and to say that it was for the knight in pursuit of the Questing Beast.

"Alas!" said the lady, "shall not my son, Sir Palomides, come to visit me?"

And then she wept and fainted for sorrow; but when she had recovered, she gave the squire all that he had asked for. On his way back to Sir Palomides the squire was intercepted by King Mark, whose squire he was, and asked who his companion might be. The squire told him, and the king ordered him not to tell Sir Palomides that he now knew his identity.

Sir Palomides and King Mark refreshed themselves and rested, and before long King Mark fell asleep.

"I do not keep company with sleeping knights," said Sir Palomides, and mounted his horse and rode away.

When Sir Dynadan found his seven fellows all lying on the ground and wounded as a result of jousting with the strange knight, whom he believed to be Sir Lamerok, he promised he would try to find him. He rode off through the forest in the direction the knight had taken, and before long met a huntsman.

"Sir, I pray you, has a knight ridden by just lately, one bearing a silver shield with a lion's head?"

"Sir, I saw such a knight; he took the path over there."

"May God reward you! Once I see his tracks I shall find him easily enough."

Sir Dynadan took the path indicated by the huntsman and before long came to Sir Palomides. He was standing by his horse beneath a tree, had taken off his helmet, and was complaining bitterly to himself:

"Alas! why should I love the peerless Iseult, surely the most beautiful woman on earth? And I am nothing to her—more fool I. And does she not love Sir Tristram, the greatest of all knights? No, in my heart I cannot blame her, and yet I cannot but love her. How hopeless it is! And that Iseult, the most perfect of women, should be married to King Mark, the most cowardly and treacherous of kings—that indeed is a shame!"

Unknown both to Sir Palomides and to Sir Dynadan, King Mark also heard these words. When he had woken and found

Sir Palomides gone, he had followed his tracks and come upon him at the same time as Sir Dynadan. He was now terrified that Sir Dynadan would see him and reveal him to Sir Palomides, so he turned about and rode away as quietly as he could, commanding his men to follow him.

He rode straight to Camelot and found that Sir Amaunte had also arrived and already laid before King Arthur his charge of reason for King Mark's murder of Sir Bersules. A combat took place, and, by mischance, King Mark's spear drove straight through Sir Amaunte's armor and wounded him mortally. King Mark rode from the court immediately, still terrified that Sir Dynadan would discover him to King Arthur.

It happened that two of Queen Iseult's ladies-in-waiting, whom Iseult had sent to Sir Tristram, were present at the combat. They knew Sir Amaunte; and when they saw that he was mortally wounded, they begged King Arthur to be allowed to speak to him. They found Sir Amaunte with the shaft of the spear still in his body.

"My ladies, I die at the hands of King Mark. I fought today to avenge my fellow, Sir Bersules, whom King Mark murdered because neither he nor I would consent to his plans for destroying Sir Tristram. Now I beg you, commend me to Queen Iseult, because I have given my life for the love of her true lord, Sir Tristram."

"Alas!" cried one of the maids aloud so that the whole court could hear her, "what have we here? A noble knight killed in a righteous quarrel by a villain!"

When King Mark's treachery was made known, King Arthur was furious with indignation. Sir Tristram wept for sorrow at the death of Sir Bersules and Sir Amaunte, and Sir Launcelot said to Arthur:

"Sire, I beg you, let me make a prisoner of this evil king."

"Sir Launcelot, bring him to the court, although I may not give you the command to kill him."

Sir Launcelot overtook King Mark three miles from the court.

"Renegade king, I come to take you as a prisoner to King Arthur's court!" he cried.

"Good knight, who are you?"

"Sir Launcelot. Now defend yourself!"

When King Mark saw Sir Launcelot charging upon him with leveled spear he lost all courage and cried: "Sir Launcelot, I yield!" But Sir Launcelot pretended not to hear him. Then, without making any attempt to defend himself, he slithered off his horse and fell to the ground like a sack of potatoes. Once more he cried out:

"Sir Launcelot, spare me, I beg you! Mercy! Mercy!"

"Get up and fight, coward!" Sir Launcelot shouted.

"Sir, I yield. I will never fight you."

"God forbid that I may not avenge Sir Tristram and Queen Iseult, and the two knights you have murdered!"

Sir Launcelot escorted King Mark to King Arthur. King Mark threw himself flat on his face as soon as he was before Arthur, and cried for mercy.

"Renegade that you are, I suppose it is good to see you here as a prisoner, and come to beg for your life," said Arthur.

"Majesty, I am Sir Launcelot's prisoner, and am brought here against my will to beg for my life."

"Sire, do you understand that at all times, as a subject king, you owe me homage, loyalty, and service? And what have you done but commit murder and treason? And now how do you propose to acquit yourself?"

"Majesty, your words are just; and I swear that for all the evil I have done, I shall make full amends."

So spoke King Mark in order to save his life, but with no intention whatsoever of abiding by his humble words. However, King Arthur was deceived, and arranged, with due ceremony, a reconciliation between him and Sir Tristram.

When Sir Palomides had done with complaining of his love for Iseult, Sir Dynadan tried to console him.

"Sir, what is your name?" asked Sir Palomides.

"I am a knight errant as you are; I have followed you for some time, knowing you only by your shield."

"And I am ready to defend that shield."

"No, no! I seek only the pleasure of your company. But tell me, which way are you riding?"

"Wheresoever fortune may lead me."

"Have you encountered Sir Tristram lately?"

"So God help me! no. Only lately I was to fight him to the death by Merlin's stone; but by ill fortune I was taken prisoner that day, together with many others. But when I see him I shall soon make it clear that it was not from cowardice that I failed to appear for our assignation."

"Why, that must have been the day that Sir Tristram fought Sir Launcelot—surely the greatest battle that ever took place between two knights! They fought for over five hours, and all were amazed that they could endure such wounds as they received. Then by mutual agreement they stopped and swore eternal friendship. Sir Launcelot took Sir Tristram to King Arthur's court, and he now sits at the Round Table in the seat which belonged to Sir Marhaus."

"Is not Sir Tristram the larger and stronger of the two?"

"Have you fought with them both?"

"I have fought Sir Tristram, but not, to my knowledge, Sir Launcelot, although he did once overthrow both me and Sir Tristram when we jousted with him."

"Well, let them be. They are certainly the two strongest knights living."

"And yet had I a quarrel with either, I would fight him as readily as I would fight you."

"Sir, I pray you, tell me your name; and then I shall accompany you to Camelot, and there I promise you will win great honor in a tournament that is to be held shortly. Both Queen Gwynevere and Queen Iseult will be there."

"For the love of Queen Iseult I shall go; otherwise I would keep clear of King Arthur's court."

"Sir, tell me your name and I shall be of service to you."

"I am called Sir Palomides, brother to Sir Segwarydes and Sir Safere. We were born Saracens."

"I thank you. Now we shall go to the court, and I promise you will find advancement there."

On their way to Camelot they came to a large, well-built castle.

"I know this castle well," said Sir Dynadan. "King Arthur gave it to his sister, Queen Morgan le Fay, a long time ago, and ever since she has used it to spite him. Every knight who passes is challenged by one, two, or three of her knights; and if he happens to come from King Arthur's court and is defeated, she robs him of his equipment and imprisons him. Especially she tries to capture the greatest of King Arthur's knights, whom he loves the most."

"By my faith, that is a shameful custom for a queen, whether she be Christian or heathen! And without question King Arthur commands the finest chivalry anywhere. I shall certainly challenge these knights of hers, and see if I cannot break every one of them, and put an end to her evil ways."

"And I shall stand by you," said Sir Dynadan.

They rode up to the castle, and then a knight with a red shield galloped up to them, followed by two squires.

"My lords," said Sir Lamerok, for he it was, "I pray you, let me challenge the knights of this castle, for I have come here on this quest. Stand by, and only if I am killed avenge my death."

"God's speed, then, and we shall see how you fare," Sir Palomides replied.

Three knights rode out of the castle. Sir Lamerok jousted with each in turn, and sent each flying out of his saddle. And as they fell, Sir Lamerok's squires led their horses away into the forest. Then Sir Palomides rode up to Sir Lamerok and asked him if he might not join with him in the jousting.

"Sir, I pray you leave this matter to me, and only if I am defeated encounter these knights and avenge me."

Meanwhile the lords and ladies of the castle who were watching from the walls cried out:

"Bravo! Knight with the red shield, you have done well."

A fourth knight rode out from the castle, and Sir Lamerok knocked him so hard that he broke his back as he fell to the ground.

"Ah Jesu!" said Sir Palomides. "The knight with the red shield is surely the finest jouster I have seen."

"He would be a match even for Sir Tristram or Sir Launcelot," said Sir Dynadan.

A fifth knight rode out from the castle, bearing a shield with black and silver bands. He too was flung violently from the saddle, and this time the horse's back was broken by the fall.

Then Sir Palomides rode up to Sir Lamerok again:

"Sir, surely you have undertaken too much for one knight? Allow me to encounter the next while you take a rest."

"Sir, have I not already asked you to leave this matter to me? I do not myself doubt that should there be twenty knights today I could overthrow them all. But if you suppose that I am so weak, why then I will joust with you too."

"Sir, I wish only that you should be spared."

"A more courteous knight than you would forbear to shame me so; now defend yourself!"

Sir Palomides and Sir Lamerok withdrew and then galloped furiously at each other, with the result that Sir Palomides was flung to the ground as all the other knights had been. Then Sir Lamerok cried out to Sir Dynadan to defend himself.

"No, no! Most surely I do not wish to joust with you," Sir Dynadan shouted.

But Sir Lamerok had already leveled his spear at him, so Sir Dynadan met his charge, and was likewise overthrown.

However, Sir Lamerok did not allow his squires to take their horses, as they were both errant knights.

Seven more knights rode out of the castle, and Sir Lamerok overthrew them all, and the lords and ladies on the walls applauded him. Of the twelve knights he had killed four; he made the remaining eight all swear to relinquish the customs of the castle. Finally an unarmed knight emerged and walked up to Sir Lamerok.

"Sir, you have defeated every one of our knights, and we are obliged to yield to you. We are sorry that you ever came here, for we are reluctant to abandon the ancient customs of this castle."

Thereupon the knight left him, and Sir Lamerok called his squires and rode on his way. Then Sir Palomides said to Sir Dynadan:

"I have never been so ashamed in my life! I shall ride after this knight with the red shield and seek my revenge."

"I should let him be. You will win little honor by challenging him now, after all he has accomplished," Sir Dynadan replied.

"However that may be, I cannot rest until I have done so."

"Well, I suppose that I shall accompany you."

"Then you shall see what happens."

They found Sir Lamerok resting by a well in a valley; he had taken off his helmet in order to drink.

"Sir, you may remember me from the castle," said Sir Palomides. "I have come now to seek my revenge."

"Sir, you should be ashamed to challenge me after witnessing the work I have already done today."

"I care nothing for that; I am here to seek revenge."

"Very well, perhaps I shall withstand you once more."

Sir Lamerok laced on his helmet, chose a spear, and mounted.

"No," said Sir Palomides, "I shall not joust with you; for that is not how I shall win."

"Sir, I supposed that knights were accustomed to joust."

"I shall fight as I will," said Sir Palomides, who then, dismounting, drew his sword and dressed his shield to Sir Lamerok.

They fought for an hour before even pausing to take breath, and then resumed with even greater energy, so that it seemed that one or the other would certainly be killed. Splinters flew from their shields and armor until both were hacking at each other's flesh. The sight of his own blood on his opponent's sword drove Sir Palomides to fresh fury, but the wound he had received while jousting reopened, and at last he fell faint.

"Sir, I feel that we have both vindicated our honor. I pray you now, tell me your name."

"Sir, I am unwilling to tell my name to a knight whose challenge was as cowardly as yours, considering that I was already wearied with fighting when we started. However, if you will tell me your own name first, I shall then tell you mine."

"Sir, I am called Sir Palomides."

"And I, Sir Lamerok de Galys; King Pellinore is my father, and Sir Torre my half brother."

Then Sir Palomides knelt before him and begged for mercy.

"Sir, I have dealt outrageously with you today. I beg you to forgive my unknightly conduct in challenging you when you had already fought magnificently against so many opponents."

"Sir Palomides, I know you for one of the finest knights in the realm, and my only regret is that we should ever have fought."

"Sir Lamerok, not for the fairest castle in this land would I forgo the friendship of a knight as great as you. I too regret that we fought, and indeed my wounds are greater than yours, but no matter. Henceforth I shall love you less only than my brother Sir Safere."

"And I you, only less than my brother Sir Torre."

Then Sir Dynadan welcomed Sir Lamerok. Their squires dressed their wounds, and the three knights made their way to a nearby priory for the night.

Meanwhile the seven knights who, with Sir Dagonet, had made a fool of King Mark—Sir Brandiles and his companions —had returned to Camelot and told King Arthur of their exploits, and their defeat at the hands of an unknown knight who had befriended King Mark and whom Sir Dynadan had promised to follow. Then King Mark himself appeared, and one of them asked if he knew the name of the knight.

"My lords, I do. We rode together to a castle and he sent his squire to ask the lady of the castle for meat and drink, and to say that it was for the knight who pursued the Questing Beast. When the lady of the castle heard this, she said, 'Alas! shall not my dear son Sir Palomides come to visit me?' So I suppose that Sir Palomides was the knight."

Sir Brandiles and his companions were well pleased, for they did not like to suppose that they had been overthrown by any lesser knight than he.

Sir Dynadan, Sir Palomides, and Sir Lamerok left the priory in the morning and rode on until they came to a castle where the lord, Sir Galahalte, offered them hospitality. The three knights accepted gladly, and soon were at their ease in the castle.

"Sir Dynadan, what are your plans?" asked Sir Lamerok.

"Tomorrow I shall ride to King Arthur's court."

"For myself," said Sir Palomides, "I shall not ride for three days yet. My wounds still trouble me."

"Then let us all stay here, and ride to the court together," said Sir Lamerok.

"I shall not stay, for I must see Sir Tristram again. I am never content for long without him," said Sir Dynadan.

"Ah ha! So you love my mortal enemy? How then do you suppose that I can trust you?" said Sir Palomides.

"Understand that I love Sir Tristram above all other living knights, and that always I shall serve him," Sir Dynadan replied.

"I also feel like that about Sir Tristram," said Sir Lamerok.

On his way to Camelot the next day Sir Dynadan encountered a knight who challenged him to joust.

"Sir, I shall not joust with you," Sir Dynadan replied.

"Then you shall not pass this way."

"Sir, is it love or hatred that compels you to joust?"

"Love."

"Then it is a hard love, that you thrust home with a hard spear! I pray you, come to King Arthur's court and joust with me there."

"Sir, if you will not joust, I pray you, tell me your name."

"Sir Dynadan."

"Ah! Sir Dynadan: I know you well for a wise and gentle knight, and I love you for it."

"Then we shall not joust?" asked Sir Dynadan, and they both rode on their ways.

King Arthur welcomed Sir Dynadan to his court, as did Sir Launcelot and Sir Tristram and all the other knights, who loved Sir Dynadan for his wisdom and gentleness. Then the king asked him, "What news?"

"Sire, I have seen much, some of which is known to King Mark, but not all."

Then Sir Dynadan described to the king how Sir Lamerok had overthrown the twelve knights at Morgan le Fay's castle, killing four of them and forcing the remainder to swear to relinquish their custom. He went on to describe how both he and Sir Palomides had been overthrown, and how Sir Palomides had afterward challenged Sir Lamerok to a sword fight and would have been killed had not they called a truce and then sworn to befriend each other thereafter.

"Truly? I find it hard to believe that any knight should overcome Sir Palomides so readily," said the king.

"Sire, it happened before my very eyes," Sir Dynadan replied.

"My lords," said Sir Tristram, "I too have encountered Sir Lamerok; and as a man-at-arms I judge him second only to Sir Launcelot."

"Then I pray that he may come to our court," said the king.

"Sire, both Sir Lamerok and Sir Palomides will arrive here shortly," said Sir Dynadan.

King Arthur called a jousting tournament to be held three days later, and it was agreed that Sir Launcelot, Sir Tristram, and Sir Dynadan should not compete, so that Sir Gawain and his brothers should have the chance of winning the prize.

Sir Ector, Sir Gawain's brothers, and Sir Gawain all did well at the beginning of the tournament, and it seemed that the prize would fall to Sir Gawain. Then Sir Lamerok rode onto the field with his two squires, and started overthrowing all comers. He had put a leather cover on his shield, but in the course of the jousting it was ripped off and he was recognized, by those who knew him, by the red device, and a general cry was raised:

"Beware of the knight with the red shield!"

Within a short time he had overthrown Sir Gawain, three of his brothers, and two others of the Round Table knights.

"How now?" said the king to Sir Gawain. "It seems you have taken a fall from this remarkable knight with the red shield. Does anyone know his name?"

"Sire, I do, but just now I may not reveal it," Sir Dynadan replied.

"Sire, it is Sir Lamerok, I know him well," said Sir Tristram.

Sir Gawain jousted with Sir Lamerock for a second time, and was again overthrown. Sir Lamerock jousted with another twenty knights and overthrew them all. He was awarded the prize, and then he trotted away into the forest again, accompanied by his two squires. King Arthur, Sir Tristram, and Sir Dynadan called for hacks and followed him.

"Good knight, well met!" said King Arthur when they had overtaken him.

Sir Lamerok took off his helmet and saluted the king, and then ran to Sir Tristram and knelt before him, clasping his knees, but Sir Tristram bade him rise. Then they all rode together to the court and he was accorded a great welcome.

Sir Gawain, however, was jealous of Sir Lamerok for defeating him at the tournament and winning the prize; he called his brothers together to warn them of the necessity of revenge:

"My good brothers, those whom we love King Arthur hates, and those whom we hate he loves. And we have good cause to hate Sir Lamerok, who is likely to remain our enemy, since we killed his father King Pellinore in revenge for his killing our father King Lot. And now he shames us by courting our mother; therefore, I for one shall seek revenge."

"But how shall we accomplish it?"

"For the moment we will wait and watch."

One day King Arthur summoned King Mark. "Sire, I pray you, grant me my wish," he said.

"Majesty, I am at your command."

"Then go to Cornwall, take Sir Tristram with you, and for my sake, honor and cherish him; he is one of our greatest knights."

"Majesty, I swear by God's name and by yours to do as you command."

"Then swear by the Bible, and I shall forgive you everything."

King Mark swore before the whole court to honor and befriend Sir Tristram, and they shook hands; but oaths meant little to King Mark. They left a few days later, and all at the court felt apprehensive.

"Alas, that my lord Sir Tristram has gone!" said Sir Dynadan.

"Sire," said Sir Launcelot to the king, "surely it was reckless to let them go; for we are all aware of King Mark's treachery."

"Sir Launcelot, it was Sir Tristram's will that they should go."

"So much the worse! for King Mark is not to be trusted," Sir Launcelot said again, and then without further ado armed and rode after them.

"King Mark," said Sir Launcelot, "we at King Arthur's court know well that your word is worth nothing; we know of your treacherous ways and of the murders you have committed. Therefore be warned: should any harm come to Sir Tristram, I myself shall be the first to avenge him."

"Sir Launcelot, are you not content that I swore on the Bible, in the presence of the whole court, to honor and cherish Sir Tristram? How then do you suppose I could break such an oath?"

"Easily, as felons and liars do; for such your conduct has proved you to be. So remember my warning."

Sir Launcelot returned to the court, and for eight days all the knights of the Round Table abstained from feasting and merriment. However, as King Arthur had said, it was Sir Tristram's own wish that they should go; for his terrible love for Iseult burned as fiercely as ever.

King Pellinore had four legitimate sons: Sir Lamerok, Sir Agglovale, Sir Dornar, and Percivale; and one illegitimate son, Sir Torre. On the eighth day after Sir Tristram had left the court, Sir Agglovale accompanied Percivale to King Arthur in order to request that he should be knighted.

"Sir, pray tell me his name and lineage, and why you wish him to be knighted."

"Sire," Sir Agglovale replied, "he is called Percivale. His father is King Pellinore, and therefore he is my brother and Sir Lamerok's."

"Sir Agglovale, for the love of you and Sir Lamerok, Percivale shall be knighted tomorrow."

Percivale was knighted, and that evening, when the knights of the Round Table sat down to dinner, he was directed to a seat next to other of the younger knights. Then one of Queen Gwynevere's maids entered the hall; she was of high birth but had been born a mute. She walked straight to Sir Percivale and took him by the hand.

"Arise, Sir Percivale, and come with me; for you are one of God's chosen," she said.

Sir Percivale was led by the hand to the seat on the right of the Siege Perelous.

"Sir Percivale, this is your appointed seat," she said.

Then she departed, was shriven by the priest, and died. Thereafter Sir Percivale was greatly honored by King Arthur and his fellows of the Round Table.

Meanwhile Sir Gawain and his brothers were still determined to revenge themselves on Sir Lamerok, so Sir Gawain prevailed on Arthur to send for his mother, Queen Margawse. Arthur did so, and accommodated her in a castle nearby. Then, as Sir Gawain had foreseen, Sir Lamerok lost little time in making a tryst with her.

On the night of the tryst Sir Lamerok, unaware that Sir Gaheris was following, rode to the castle, entered by a secret postern, and disarmed in a small parlor. The queen welcomed him to her chamber, but they had not been in bed together for long when Sir Gaheris burst in on them, brandishing his sword. He strode over to the bed, seized his mother by the hair, and beheaded her. Sir Lamerok was shocked as the warm blood of the woman he loved spurted from her mutilated body.

"You, Sir Gaheris, a knight of the Round Table! What have you done? Surely you should have killed me, not the mother who bore you?"

"Sir, yours is the offense natural to man; but you should beware of whom it is you court, for you have put our familty to shame once more. First your father killed ours; that Sir Gawain and I revenged by killing your father. But now in choosing our mother for your paramour you have forced us to revenge ourselves for a second time."

"Sir, it was Sir Balin who killed your father, and his death is as yet unrevenged."

"Sir Lamerok, I should kill you for your villainous words, but that you are naked. Now go from here, and remember that when next we meet I shall kill you. As for my mother, she can shame us no longer."

Sir Lamerok left the castle feeling ashamed and sorrowful, and rode away into the forest determined to avoid King Arthur's court thereafter. Sir Gawain was enraged when he learned that Sir Gaheris had killed their mother but allowed Sir Lamerok to escape. King Arthur and his knights were deeply ashamed of the whole incident.

"Sire," said Sir Launcelot to the king, "these misdeeds much touch us all: the shameful murder of your own sister, and the loss of Sir Lamerok; and I fear that Sir Gawain and his brothers will not rest until they have killed him too."

"Alas!" the king replied, "I valued Sir Tristram and Sir Lamerok more than twenty of any other of my knights put together."

Meanwhile Sir Gawain's brothers, Sir Aggravayne and Sir Modred, were riding in search of adventure. A wounded knight galloped up to them, followed by Sir Dynadan.

"My lords," said the wounded knight, "help me, I pray you; my enemy will kill me otherwise."

Sir Dynadan agreed to stand by while Sir Aggravayne and Sir Modred faced the enemy; and at that moment Sir Breuse appeared and charged first Sir Modred and then Sir Aggravayne and unhorsed them both. He turned his horse and galloped six times over Sir Aggravayne, saying:

"Understand that this is Sir Breuse Sans Pité."

Then Sir Dynadan challenged him, and Sir Breuse was flung from the saddle. The moment he remounted he galloped away, for Sir Dynadan had the reputation of being a formidable man-at-arms once he was roused.

Sir Aggravayne and Sir Modred thanked Sir Dynadan for avenging them, and asked him his name.

"I am Sir Dynadan; did you not know me?"

"Sir Dynadan? The very knight who killed my father!" said Sir Dalan, the wounded knight who had fled from Sir Breuse.

"If I did so it must have been at his own request, or in self-defense," Sir Dynadan replied.

"Even so, I shall avenge him," said Sir Dalan.

First Sir Dalan, then Sir Aggravayne, and then Sir Modred jousted with Sir Dynadan, and he overthrew all three. He rode away. It was to be at the hands of these three knights that Sir Dynadan was to be killed, treacherously, when he rode on the quest of the Holy Grail; and his loss was to be felt by all the knights of the Round Table who loved him for his jests and his gentleness.

Sir Dynadan rode to the castle of the Beale Valet and there found Sir Palomides, who was still recovering from the wound which Sir Lamerok had given him at their last encounter. Sir Dynadan told him how Sir Tristram had returned to Cornwall with King Mark, and Sir Palomides was jealous when he thought of Sir Tristram consorting with the beautiful Iseult, whom he still loved as fiercely as ever.

When Sir Tristram arrived at Tintagil both he and Iseult wrote letters of good will to King Arthur and Sir Launcelot. The letters were delivered by Sir Fergus, a Cornish knight of the Round Table, also by one of Sir Tristram's maids. Arthur and Sir Launcelot wrote replies, and Sir Launcelot warned Sir Tristram to beware of "King Fox," as he called King Mark. Sir Tristram was grateful for the warning; however, when Sir Tristram had read the letter, the maid showed it to King Mark, who at once suspected Sir Tristram of treason.

King Mark asked the maid if she would be willing to deliver

letters from himself to King Arthur on the following day, and the maid agreed to do so. Then she told Sir Tristram of what had happened, and Sir Tristram begged her to show him King Mark's letters before delivering them. The maid promised that she would.

The following day, when the maid went to King Mark to take his letters, King Mark told her that he had changed his mind and had none to deliver. He then commanded one of his own squires to deliver the letters to King Arthur, who was now at Caerleon. The letters made King Arthur feel extremely apprehensive, and subsequently Queen Gwynevere and Sir Launcelot when they too had read them. After many expressions of cordiality, King Mark suggested that they should all meet, since, he added, for himself he was well able to rule both his wife and his knights. He concluded the letter by openly declaring that he suspected Sir Tristram of treason, and henceforth would regard him as his mortal enemy.

King Arthur was dismayed by the veiled suggestion that Queen Gwynevere and Sir Launcelot were unfaithful to him, and recalled the words of his sister, Morgan le Fay, who out of spite had more than hinted at the same thing. He was also dismayed by King Mark's declared enmity to Sir Tristram.

When Sir Launcelot had been shown the letter by Gwynevere he was so upset that he retired to bed. But Sir Dynadan, ever anxious for him, followed, and begged Sir Launcelot to take him into his confidence. Sir Launcelot did so, and then asked Sir Dynadan for his advice.

"Sir Launcelot, King Mark is well known for his treachery, hence no one will take his insinuations too seriously. To reply courteously would be a waste of courtesy; therefore I shall compose a lampoon and teach it to the minstrels at the court, and that shall be our reply to him."

Sir Dynadan composed his lampoon. It was excellent, and told of King Mark's treachery and cowardice since the beginning of his reign. King Arthur and Queen Gwynevere were delighted with it, and it was taught to all their minstrels, who were then given instructions to sing it throughout the realm, and especially in Cornwall.

While the minstrels were wandering abroad to sing Sir Dynadan's lampoon, King Mark was attacked by Sir Elyas of Sessoyne at the head of a large army. King Mark was seriously discomforted: not only was he reluctant to call Sir Tristram to his aid on account of his jealousy of him, but at the time Sir Tristram was resting in Sir Dynas' castle, recovering from wounds which he had received in the course of winning a tournament.

Meanwhile Sir Elyas' army was making havoc in Cornwall, and it was necessary for King Mark to march against him immediately. He made three divisions of his army under the commands of himself, Sir Dynas, and Sir Andret.

An extremely bloody battle ensued. The outcome was that King Mark, Sir Andret, and even Sir Dynas, the ablest of the three commanders, were forced to retreat to within the walls of Tintagil. Ten of the enemy managed to gain the bridge, and four were killed at the portcullis.

King Mark sent a messenger to Sir Tristram to tell him that he was now besieged, and Sir Tristram replied that he still needed a few more days to recover from his wounds. Then Sir Elyas called a parley and demanded that King Mark should surrender. King Mark succeeded in delaying the issue until Sir Tristram had recovered, and then, after receiving a repetition of Sir Elyas' demand, and after a consultation with Sir Tristram, agreed to give battle once more.

Sir Tristram asked the king to give him supreme command, and when he had done so divided the army into six battalions, with Sir Dynas in command of the advance guard.

On the eve of the battle Sir Tristram ordered that all Sir Elyas' ships be burned. When Sir Elyas heard of this he said:

"My comrades, Sir Tristram is determined that none of us shall escape. But have no fear, for great as he is, he cannot be everywhere among us at one time."

In the morning Sir Elyas drew up his army before Tintagil. In battle order, and with its dazzling equipment, it was a splendid sight to behold. Sir Dynas galloped out of the castle and opened the attack, but before long he was forced to fight defensively. Sir Tristram followed and killed two knights with his first spear.

Thereafter both armies were inspired by the feats of their commanders to fight to the uttermost: by Sir Tristram on the one side, who in the course of the fighting unhorsed Sir Elyas; by Sir Elyas on the other side, who unhorsed King Mark.

At the end of the day both armies withdrew, and it was found that King Mark had lost a hundred knights, against two hundred knights lost by Sir Elyas. Neither army was willing to undertake a further engagement. Sir Tristram retired to his chamber, exhausted and with many wounds.

Sir Elyas, dismayed by his losses, now challenged King Mark to find a champion who would fight him in single combat, to decide once and for all whether King Mark should pay tribute, or himself forgo his claim.

King Mark was once more in a dilemma, for he realized

that Sir Tristram was his only possible champion, and that he was already wounded. He called a council of war and put the matter before his barons.

"Sire, there is not one amongst us who could match Sir Elyas," the spokesman replied.

"Alas! had it not been for the might of Sir Tristram we should have lost the battle yesterday; and now we are lost once again if he does not come forward as our champion," said the king.

Sir Tristram was sent for. He appeared in a long gown and asked, "What news?"

"My good nephew, Sir Elyas has challenged us to find a champion who will fight him in single combat and decide the issue between us. We are at a loss, for we know that you are already wounded," said the king.

"Sire, I understand that you wish me to be your champion. Very well, my wounds are still green and give me less pain now than they will in a week's time; therefore I will fight him tomorrow."

A message was sent to Sir Elyas, giving the decision, and a truce established with an exchange of hostages. Both armies drew up on the field in the morning, but only the two champions bore arms.

Sir Tristram and Sir Elyas drew far apart, and then galloped full tilt at each other. Both horses and men were thrown to the ground. They fought with their swords for an hour, and then Sir Tristram began to grow faint. Sir Elyas pressed his advantage and struck again and again while Sir Tristram feebly defended himself. It seemed inevitable to the onlookers that Sir Tristram must lose: he was offering only one stroke to every twenty of Sir Elyas'. The Sessoyne army laughed and cheered; King Mark was in tears.

Sir Tristram heard the laughter and the cheers. Then he thought of Queen Iseult, who was also among the spectators, and realized that if he was killed he would never again set eyes on her. This gave him fresh courage; he raised his shield once more and redoubled his blows. Now it was Sir Elyas who was on the defensive, staggering, half stunned, and the blood spurting from his wounds. And now it was the turn of the Cornish army to laugh and cheer Sir Tristram on.

"Now yield!" said Sir Tristram to Sir Elyas, as he struck him a blow that sent him reeling to the ground. "And yet, you are surely the greatest knight I have fought since Sir Launcelot," he added.

But Sir Elyas was already dead.

King Mark kept a large number of prisoners in compensation for the damage he had suffered during the invasion, and allowed the remainder of Sir Elyas' army to find their way back to Sessoyne as best they could. Sir Tristram was carefully nursed, but King Mark was still more jealous than grateful, and determined to destroy him as soon as possible.

While Sir Tristram was recovering, King Mark held a feast to celebrate the defeat of Sir Elyas, and to this feast came one of King Arthur's minstrels, to sing Sir Dynadan's lampoon. He went first to Sir Tristram and sang it to him.

"By Jesu!" said Sir Tristram when he had heard it, "Sir Dynadan certainly is a good composer, for good or for evil!"

"Sir, dare I sing it before King Mark?"

"Certainly! I shall be your warrant."

King Arthur's minstrel was an accomplished singer, and once he had struck up with his harp he commanded the attention of everyone at the feast. He sang the lampoon straight through; instance after instance of King Mark's treachery and cowardice was enumerated. King Mark was outraged.

"Minstrel, how dare you sing such a scurrilous song before us? Do you not fear for your life?"

"Sire, I sing at the command of the king whose device I wear. You can see for yourself that I come from King Arthur's court."

"Very well, your life shall be spared, but let me see you no more."

The minstrel went again to Sir Tristram and told him what had passed, and Sir Tristram gave him letters for King Arthur and Sir Launcelot. King Mark, meanwhile, was convinced that Sir Tristram was responsible for the lampoon, and swore vengeance.

8. ALEXANDER THE ORPHAN

We have now to tell of King Mark's brother, Prince Bodwyne, who was as much loved and honored as King Mark was hated and feared.

Not long after Sir Tristram had defeated the Sessoynes, a huge Saracen fleet drew up at the harbor near Prince Bodwyne's castle. The prince acted swiftly, determined to save Cornwall from another invasion. On the night of the Saracens' arrival he fired three of his own ships and sent them in among the Saracen fleet, and destroyed it. While the fire was in progress he mustered every available man-at-arms and lay in wait until dawn. He then made a surprise attack on the Saracens who had managed to land, and killed every one of them, to the number of forty thousand.

King Mark was made furiously jealous by his brother's victory and planned to kill him, together with his wife and child. He wrote a letter to the prince in the most cordial terms, inviting him to come to his castle and bring with him his wife and young son, whom he would be seeing for the first time.

Prince Bodwyne, suspecting nothing, arrived at Tintagil with Anglydes, his wife, and Alexander, his son. King Mark received them with every appearance of joy and gave them supper; then he turned on his brother:

"Brother, how is it that you failed to warn me when the Saracen fleet drew up at your harbor? Surely the honor of defending the realm belongs to me?"

"Sire, if I had delayed, my lands and yours would have been overrun."

"Felon and traitor! You know well that all you wished to do was to win honor at my expense. Now you shall pay for it!" And with that the king drew a dagger and killed his brother.

Lady Anglydes cried aloud and fainted. Sir Dynas, Sir Tristram, and Sir Fergus looked on horrified while the king calmly stripped the body and then buried it.

Later Anglydes managed to steal the bloodstained shirt and mantle which her husband had been wearing. Then Queen Iseult warned her that she must escape from the castle immediately if she did not wish that she and her son should also be murdered.

Anglydes and Alexander the Orphan, as he was known thereafter, rode from the castle at once, accompanied by a few brave men who sympathized with them.

King Mark, meanwhile, was roaming from chamber to chamber, sword in hand, determined to kill them. When he learned that they had escaped he commanded Sir Sadoke, on pain of death, to fetch them.

Sir Sadoke overtook them ten miles from the castle and ordered them to return with him.

"Sir, is it not enough that my husband has been murdered? What can you hope to gain from my death and my son's?"

"My lady, we are all grieved by your loss. If you will swear to ride from this country at once, and prevail on your son, when he is of age, to avenge his father's death, I will return without you."

"My lord, it shall be as you require. May God reward you!"

Sir Sadoke returned to King Mark and told him that he had drowned Anglydes and Alexander, and the king rejoiced.

Anglydes and Alexander rode night and day, with scarcely a rest, along the south coast road until they came to the Castle Magowns (now Arowndel) in Sussex, and there they begged for lodging. Sir Bellyngere, the constable of the castle, received them hospitably, and then it was discovered that his wife was Anglydes' cousin, and the castle a part of Anglydes' inheritance.

The years passed and Alexander grew brave and sturdy, and exceeded all his companions in the arts of barony. Then Sir Bellyngere said to Anglydes:

"My lady, Alexander is now a young man of parts. Is it not time he was knighted?"

"Sir, I suggest he be knighted in Lent, on Lady's Day."

"My lady, all will be prepared."

Alexander was overjoyed by the news, and on the appointed day was knighted together with twenty of his companions, all sons of the local nobility. When mass had been heard, his mother spoke to him:

"My son, I give you my blessing, and now that you are a knight I must charge you with the responsibility of redeeming the honor of our family."

With that she drew from her gown the bloodied mantle and shirt in which the prince had been murdered.

"Ma'am, I pray you, what is that?" said Sir Alexander, growing pale.

"My son, those are the garments your father was wearing when he was murdered by his brother, King Mark of Cornwall. And now, as you are a true knight, I charge you to avenge his death."

Anglydes fainted when she had spoken these words. Sir Alexander leaped forward and lifted her in his arms, and when she came to, said:

"Ma'am, so God help me, I shall avenge my father."

The feast was followed by a jousting contest, and Sir Alexander overthrew all twenty of his fellows. Then one of them, out of spite, rode to King Mark at Tintagil and told him what had passed between Anglydes and Alexander when he was knighted.

"Ah! here is treason indeed," said the king. "Whom now can we trust?"

Sword in hand, he ran through the castle in search of Sir Sadoke; but Sir Sadoke saw him coming.

"Beware, King Mark!" he shouted. "I do not fear you, nor do I repent of rescuing Anglydes and Sir Alexander. Prince Bodwyne saved Cornwall from the Saracens, and out of jealousy you murdered him. Now Sir Alexander has grown to be a formidable knight, and may God grant him the strength to avenge his father!"

"God forbid that I should listen to your treason!" King Mark exclaimed, and summoned four of his knights to execute Sir Sadoke on the spot.

Sir Sadoke drew his sword as the knights rushed at him, and killed them all. Then he passed through the castle and rode away without further molestation, for Sir Tristram and his friends sympathized with him.

Sir Tristram, aware that King Mark was plotting to murder Sir Alexander, who was his cousin, wrote a letter advising him to go to King Arthur's court and place himself under the protection of Sir Launcelot. Sir Alexander resolved to do so. Meanwhile, King Mark had summoned the knight who had originally betrayed Sir Alexander.

"Sir, I beg you, remain with us for a time."

"Sire, I am obliged to do so, for I have been banished."

"Then surely we shall give you estates worth double those you have lost."

Sir Sadoke, however, was still at large, and knowing this knight for his betrayal of Sir Alexander, killed him one day when he was riding not far from the castle.

King Mark appealed to Queen Morgan le Fay and to the Queen of North Galys to send their sorceresses abroad to lie in wait for Sir Alexander and kill or capture him by means of their enchantments. He also appealed to Sir Breuse Sans Pité, Sir Malegryne, and other likeminded knights to assassinate him if they found the opportunity of doing so.

Sir Alexander had taken leave of his mother, and set off for London to find Sir Launcelot. He carried with him the mantle and shirt. Before long he lost his way, and chanced to ride into a tournament which was being held by King Carados of Scotland. He competed in the jousting and overthrew

King Carados and twenty of his knights, including Sir Safere,
Sir Palomides' brother, and won the prize.

One of Morgan le Fay's ladies-in-waiting was present at the
tournament, and when it was over, hastened to report to her
mistress the feats of the extraordinary young knight who had
won the prize, adding that he had made each knight whom
he overthrew swear to abandon his arms for a year and a day.

"That is excellent," said Morgan le Fay; "he must be the
very knight I have been waiting for."

Morgan le Fay set out on her palfrey to search for Sir Alexander. She rode a great distance and then set up her pavilion
to take a rest. Soon four knights appeared and she asked them,
"What news?" Two of the knights were armed: Sir Elyas
and Sir Car de Gomeret; two were unarmed: Sir Garaunte
and Sir Gye, both of whom were cousins to Queen Gwynevere.

"My lady, we have all four been overthrown by a young
knight who has lodged at a castle nearby. We supposed it to be
Sir Launcelot, Sir Tristram, or Sir Lamerok, for certainly no
other knight could withstand him."

"My lords, I thank you. He is the very knight I am searching for."

Sir Alexander, meanwhile, when he had overthrown the four
knights, had been summoned by the lady of the castle:

"Sir, I pray you, will you challenge my neighbor, Sir
Malegryne? He has for a long time held me in bondage and
prevented my marrying."

"My lady, if he appears I will certainly challenge him."

Sir Malegryne was sent for, and when he arrived Sir Alexander challenged him. They jousted and Sir Malegryne was
unhorsed. He jumped up at once and drew his sword.

"Sir, I grant that you have won the jousting, but now fight
me on foot, and you will soon discover what manner of knight
I am."

Sir Malegryne was an experienced and cunning swordsman,
and while Sir Alexander struck with great force but frequently
wide, Sir Malegryne struck with deadly effect. Regardless, however, of his wounds, Sir Alexander continued to fight with
fierce energy, and at last Sir Malegryne paused.

"Sir, hold your hand a moment, and tell me your name."

"You shall not know my name unless you first tell me yours,
and what cause you have to hold the lady of this castle in
bondage."

"Sir, for the love of this lady I have already killed ten
knights. And I have killed another ten for sport."

"Sir, yours is the foulest confession I have heard from a knight yet, and it is a shame that you should live any longer. May God be my witness when I say that I shall not withdraw from this battle until one of us is killed."

They fought again, and Sir Alexander, with fresh resolution, struck his opponent to the ground and beheaded him. Then he tried to mount his horse, but fell to the ground in a faint.

"Ah Jesu, give me succor!" he murmured.

At that moment Morgan le Fay rode up. She bade him be of good cheer, and conveyed him on a horse litter to the castle. Sir Alexander had sixteen serious wounds, one of which could have caused his death. Morgan le Fay applied healing ointments immediately, and the following day further ointments to ease the pain. Then the lady of the castle spoke to her:

"Ma'am I pray you help me to wed this knight who has delivered me from bondage."

"My lady, you will see what I can do," Morgan le Fay replied.

When the lady of the castle asked Sir Alexander to marry her, he had already been warned by Morgan le Fay to refuse.

"My lady, I do not wish to marry in this country as yet."

"Sir, I pray you, if you will not marry me yourself, will you give me away to a neighbor of mine, who for many years has been my friend, and loved me?"

"My lady, I will do so gladly."

The neighbor's name was Sir Geryne le Grose, and Sir Alexander duly married him to the lady of the castle.

Then Morgan le Fay gave Sir Alexander a potion which sent him to sleep for three days and three nights, and while he was asleep conveyed him to her own castle, La Beale Regarde. When he awoke she asked him if he wished to be cured.

"Ma'am, most certainly I wish to be cured."

"Then you must swear to remain within the bounds of my castle for one year."

"Ma'am, I swear."

But when Sir Alexander had recovered he repented of his oath, for it prevented him from pursuing his revenge on King Mark. Then a young noblewoman arrived at the castle, and found him brooding on his bed. She was niece to the Earl of the Pace, and a cousin to Morgan le Fay; and by rights the castle was her property.

"My lord, be of good cheer: I have news for you," she said.

"My lady, if only my fortune could change! for I am here a prisoner by my own oath."

"My lord, Morgan le Fay will hold you here until such time as she requires her pleasure from you."

"God forbid! I should cut off my manhood first."

"Then I pray you, be ruled by me, and for your love I shall secure your deliverance."

"Tell me by what means, and my love shall be yours."

"Gentle knight, my uncle, the Earl of the Pace, intended that this castle should be mine. He holds Morgan le Fay in abhorrence, and so I shall ask him to burn the castle in punishment for her evil ways. You will go to a secret postern where I shall await you with horse and armor. Then, in order not to break your oath, you may remain on the castle grounds for a year and a day."

"My lady, you say well."

Thereupon Sir Alexander took her in his arms and kissed her, and at leisure they made love and the lady was rewarded.

The Earl of the Pace, who had spared the castle hitherto on account of his niece, gladly consented to her plan, and when his men had done with firing it, not a stone remained standing. The lady duly met Sir Alexander at the postern, and they took refuge in the garden while the castle burned. When it was all over he announced that he would defend the ground against all comers for a year and a day.

Before long Sir Alexander's challenge came to the ears of Alys La Beale Pilgrim. Her father, the Duke Aunsyrus, was of the blood of King Ban, and therefore related to Sir Launcelot. Because of his pious habit of making a pilgrimage to Jerusalem every third year, he was generally referred to as Aunsyrus le Pilgrim.

Alys was both beautiful and rich. She went to King Arthur's court and announced that she would yield both herself and her inheritance to the knight who would overcome Sir Alexander. She then pitched her pavilion by the site of the ruined castle.

Soon after Sir Sagramour le Desyrus came forward and challenged Sir Alexander. They jousted and Sir Sagramour was unhorsed. Then Alys ran out of her pavilion and caught Sir Alexander's horse by the bridle.

"Good knight, I pray you, show me your face."

"My lady, you shall see."

Sir Alexander lifted his visor.

"Sweet Jesu, I could love no other!" Alys exclaimed.

"My lady, I pray that I may see you."

Alys took off her veil.

"Why, surely I have found my true love! Henceforth, my lady, I shall serve only you."

"My lord, pray tell me your name."

"Sir Alexander the Orphan."

"And I am called Alys La Beale Pilgrim. When we know each other better I will tell you from whose blood I come."

And love burned fiercely between them.

Sir Alexander was next challenged by Sir Harleuse, whom he overthrew, and then by Sir Hewgan, who, after he had been unhorsed, fought him on foot, but would have been killed had he not yielded in time. Sir Alexander made both knights swear to abandon their arms for a year and a day.

Then the lady of the castle, the earl's niece, rode up and told Alys how she had released Sir Alexander from Morgan le Fay.

"My lord," said Alys to Sir Alexander, "it would appear that you are much beholden to this lady."

"My lady, I am."

"My lord, understand that I am of the blood of King Ban, father to Sir Launcelot," said Alys.

"My lady, my father was Prince Bodwyne, brother to King Mark; and I am a cousin to Sir Tristram."

Meanwhile three knights had ridden up to them: Sir Vayne, Sir Harvis, and Sir Peryne. Sir Alexander jousted with all three and overthrew them. They departed when they had sworn to carry no arms for a year and a day. Then Sir Alexander gazed up at his lady, now on horseback, and was dizzied by love.

At that moment the renegade knight Sir Modred appeared, and, seeing the love-struck Alexander, took his horse by the bridle and led it hither and thither to make a fool of him; for Sir Alexander hardly knew whether he was mounted or on foot.

The lady of the castle was furious, and seizing a sword and shield, leaped onto her horse and struck Sir Alexander on the helmet so hard that he was nearly stunned. When he came to, she fled into her pavilion and Sir Modred galloped away into the forest. Then Sir Alexander understood, and was grateful to her for saving him from such shame, and furious that Sir Modred had escaped unscathed. But when he saw Alys they laughed about it.

Every day for the next twelve months Sir Alexander fought: sometimes one, sometimes two, three, or even four knights,

some from King Arthur's court, some from other parts—
more battles than there is space here to record. And at the end
of the twelve months he departed with Alys. Their love never
failed them, and Alys gave birth to a son, Sir Bellengerus le
Beuse, who subsequently was to avenge his father's death.

Sir Alexander never went to King Arthur's court, but he
was known there for one of the strongest knights of his time;
and his death, which was brought about by the treachery of
King Mark, was deeply mourned by them.

9. THE TOURNAMENT AT SURLUSE

Sir Galahalte the High Prince, lord of the country of Surluse
—the home of numerous excellent knights, many of whom
remained in the service of Sir Galahalte—rode one day to
King Arthur, his overlord, to beg permission to hold a
tournament.

"I grant you leave to do so, but I shall not be present,"
the king replied.

"My lord, it would give me great pleasure to be present,"
said Queen Gwynevere.

"My lady, most certainly, and Sir Galahalte shall be your
protector."

"And shall I be accompanied by my chosen knights?" asked
the queen.

"My lady, as you will."

The tournament was proclaimed throughout the realm;
princes, dukes, earls, and barons from all parts rode to Surluse
in order to compete. Queen Gwynevere asked Sir Launcelot
to choose a party of knights, and it was agreed that they
should join with those of the High Prince to hold the challenge
against all comers.

THE FIRST DAY. Both Sir Dynadan and—at the request of
Queen Gwynevere and King Bagdemagus—Sir Launcelot,
fought in disguise. Sir Launcelot jousted with his brother Sir
Ector. At the first encounter both broke their spears; at the
second, Sir Ector was unhorsed. Sir Bleobris, who had been

watching them, struck Sir Launcelot on the helmet with his sword. Sir Launcelot struck Sir Bleobris twice on the helmet and knocked him off his horse. The King of North Galys, who was of the opposing party, charged Sir Launcelot and broke his spear. Sir Launcelot unhorsed him with a blow from his sword.

There followed a fierce engagement between the parties of the King of North Galys and King Bagdemagus. The party of the King of North Galys was the larger, but Sir Launcelot was fighting for King Bagdemagus, and when he entered the melee his opponents fell thick and fast before him.

Sir Mellyagraunce, King Bagdemagus' son, hated Sir Launcelot. When he understood that it was he who was bringing victory to his party he begged one of his companions to attempt killing his horse. King Bagdemagus, meanwhile, aware of his son's hostility to Sir Launcelot, asked Sir Sauseyes to challenge him, and beat him out of the tournament if possible.

Sir Sauseyes duly fought Sir Mellyagraunce and would have beaten him had not one of Sir Mellyagraunce' companions come to his rescue.

Then the High Prince blew his horn to end the day's fighting.

While the tournament was in progress a young noblewoman had gone to the High Prince and told him that one of the competitors, Sir Gonereyes, had appropriated her lands, and begged him to find her a champion. None had come forward; but then, just as she had taken up her glove again and was feeling thoroughly downcast, a squire came up to her.

"My lady, would you be willing to take my advice?"

"Certainly," she replied.

"There is a knight resting beside the monastery; he is the knight who pursues the Questing Beast. Go to him and he will aid you."

The young noblewoman mounted her palfrey, rode to the monastery, and asked Sir Palomides if he would be her champion. He agreed to. She rode back to the High Prince and asked his permission for Sir Palomides to be her champion, and he granted it.

Sir Palomides and Sir Gonereyes entered the field, jousted, and broke their spears. Then they both drew their swords; with his first stroke Sir Palomides knocked his opponent to the ground, and with his second stroke beheaded him. Then Sir Palomides went to supper.

It is told that the young noblewoman loved Sir Palomides

and was his paramour; but also that she was of his kin. Whatever the truth may have been, Sir Palomides disguised himself, wearing as his device a figure of the Questing Beast, and obtained permission from the High Prince to enter the tournament and challenge all comers, with the exception of Sir Launcelot, in honor of the lady, and to relinquish her in the event of his defeat.

THE SECOND DAY. When Sir Palomides entered the field the High Prince was on the wing of the battle line. They galloped at each other and broke their spears. Sir Palomides was flung backward, but managed to keep his feet in the stirrups. Then they drew their swords and fought so strenuously that many other knights left their combats to watch them. The High Prince finally struck a blow on Sir Palomides' helmet, but the helmet was so hard that the sword glanced off and continued through the neck of his horse. When Sir Palomides fell to the ground the High Prince dismounted, apologized for the foul, and begged him to accept his own horse as a gift.

"Sir, I thank you for the courtesy," Sir Palomides replied.

"Now I pray you, sir, keep the lady, for you have won her," said the High Prince.

"My lord, the lady and I will be at your command," said Sir Palomides.

The High Prince was a formidable warrior. He fought next with Sir Dynadan, and when they had broken their spears on each other and set to with their swords, Sir Dynadan realized that his chances of defeating him were negligible.

"Sir, I pray you leave me now, and fight another," he said.

The High Prince rode away, unaware that his opponent had been Sir Dynadan, until one of the knights who had witnessed their duel told him.

"Alas!" said the High Prince, "I must find him again; otherwise, what with his jests and jokes, I shall never hear the end of it."

He turned about and rode up to Sir Dynadan again.

"Sir, in the name of King Arthur, defend yourself!"

"So God help me, I shall fight you no more today," Sir Dynadan replied.

The High Prince jousted next with Sir Mellyagraunce and then with another knight, and with the same spear overthrew them both; he all but killed Sir Mellyagraunce with a thrust in the throat.

Meanwhile, the King of North Galys, with many supporters, was forcing the party of the High Prince to retreat, and it appeared inevitable that they should win the victory. At the last moment, however, Sir Symounde le Valyaunte with forty knights behind him managed to turn the scales. Then Queen Gwynevere and Sir Launcelot blew their horns and the competitors dispersed to their lodgings for dinner.

When Sir Palomides had disarmed he went to the High Prince and begged him to find lodgings for him and his lady. The High Prince did so, but Sir Palomides had no sooner entered than he was challenged by Sir Archade, who wished to avenge the death of his brother Sir Gonereyes, for which Sir Palomides was responsible. Sir Palomides put the matter before the High Prince.

"Sir, let us all eat dinner first; then you may go to the field and prepare yourselves," he replied.

The duel was witnessed by the High Prince, Queen Gwynevere, and Sir Launcelot. Sir Palomides drove his opponent clean over his horse's tail in the jousting, and when he had fallen, himself dismounted and drew his sword. But Sir Archade was unable to rise, so Sir Palomides unlaced his helmet and chopped off his head. The High Prince and his companions then retired to supper.

King Bagdemagus, meanwhile, had sent his son away from Surluse on account of his enmity to Sir Launcelot, of which Sir Launcelot himself was unaware.

THE THIRD DAY. King Marsyll, who had received the island of Pomytayne as a gift from the High Prince, fought with King Bagdemagus and was overthrown; likewise, one of the king's followers who tried to avenge him.

Sir Arrowse and Sir Breuse, together with a hundred knights from Pomytayne, joined the party of the King of North Galys, and attacked the party of Surluse. King Bagdemagus was foremost in the defense of Surluse, and a fierce battle ensued, in which many knights were overthrown and trampled upon by their horses. Sir Gaheris singled out King Bagdemagus and struck repeatedly at his visor; then King Bagdemagus struck him off his horse.

Sir Blamoure fought with Sir Palomides, was overthrown, and when he hit the ground, blood poured from his nose, mouth, and ears. Sir Elys la Noyre, who served Duke Chalence of Claraunce, fought King Bagdemagus, and was thrown from the saddle.

Duke Chalence, Sir Palomides, and King Bagdemagus accomplished the most that day, and King Bagdemagus won the prize. At the feast afterward Sir Dynadan mocked him, and everyone laughed, for Sir Dynadan's jests were without spite.

When the feast was over, a squire bearing four spears went up to Sir Palomides and told him that he was challenged to choose two of them and fight on behalf of his lady.

"I shall not fail," Sir Palomides replied, taking two of them.

The High Prince, Queen Gwynevere, and Sir Launcelot witnessed the duel from the judges' platform. At the first and second encounters both spears were broken. For the third encounter Sir Palomides and his opponent chose heavier spears and Sir Palomides was unhorsed. Just as he fell his opponent's horse tumbled, and his opponent was thrown on top of him. They fought with their swords, and the High Prince and Sir Launcelot agreed that they were two of the finest combatants they had seen. Sir Palomides, however, was gradually forced to retreat. Then the High Prince called a halt.

When they had returned to the castle and disarmed, Sir Palomides' opponent proved to be none other than Sir Lamerok. Sir Launcelot and the queen greeted him warmly, for he was loved and admired by all the members of King Arthur's court, except for Sir Gawain and his brethren. Then the queen made Sir Launcelot promise not to fight any of his fellows of the Round Table while they were at Surluse.

THE FOURTH DAY. Sir Safere, Sir Palomides' brother, arrived at the castle and announced to Sir Palomides that he had killed the Earl de la Plaunche, who had been making war on their father. Then he, Sir Palomides, and Sir Palomides' lady rode to the tournament together. Once on the field Sir Palomides fought Sir Bleobris and Sir Safere fought Sir Ector; after unhorsing each other all four combatants fought on foot for the whole day.

Sir Lamerok encountered in turn the King of the Hundred Knights, the King of North Galys, and King Marsyll, and overthrew them all with his spear. Then with spear or sword he overthrew another thirty knights of their party. Out of respect for his feats Duke Chalence exhorted his men to keep clear of Sir Lamerok in order that he might win the honor which was his due.

The three kings joined forces and attacked Sir Lamerok together; Sir Lamerok darted from one to another, and never failed to hold his ground. The High Prince, Sir Launcelot, and Queen Gwynevere were watching intently, astonished by his prowess.

"I must go to his aid," said Sir Launcelot.

"And I will go with you," said King Bagdemagus.

Sir Lamerok was engaged with thirty knights, and keeping them all at the tip of his sword, when Sir Launcelot and King Bagdemagus rode up to him. Sir Launcelot unhorsed Sir Mador; then, together with his companions, fought so lustily that the three kings and their force were put to flight. Then the High Prince blew his horn and all the knights dispersed to their lodgings.

At the feast that night Queen Gwynevere embraced Sir Lamerok.

"My lord, you have fought well today," she said.

Then the High Prince, Sir Dynadan, and Sir Launcelot all praised him, especially Sir Launcelot.

THE FIFTH DAY. Early in the morning Sir Palomides rode to the castle where King Arthur was staying, and there met Duke Adrawns, King Arthur's uncle. They jousted and the duke was thrown over his horse's cropper. Sir Palomides jousted next with Sir Elyce, the duke's son, then with Sir Gawain and his three brothers, Sir Modred, Sir Gaheris, and Sir Aggravayne, and overthrew them all.

"Alas," said King Arthur, "that a Saracen should overthrow so many of my own kin!"

Just as the king was arming in order to avenge them, Sir Lamerok rode up and challenged Sir Palomides on the king's behalf.

They jousted and both broke their spears. They jousted again with heavier spears and Sir Palomides was thrown back on his horse but not unsaddled. When he had recovered himself he rode back to the tournament field at Surluse, accompanied by his brother Sir Safere and by his lady.

When they had gone, King Arthur rode up to Sir Lamerok and thanked him and asked him his name.

"Sire, although my one wish is to serve you, I see that at present you are surrounded by my enemies."

"Then you must be Sir Lamerok. I pray you, abide by me, and I swear by my crown that none of Sir Gawain's brothers shall harm you."

"Sire, they have wronged us both."

"That is true, for their mother was my sister; but surely you would have been wiser to marry her? After all, you are yourself a prince."

"For the love of Jesu, I shall never forgive them her death; and were they not of your kin I should avenge her."

"Sir Lamerok, I pray you be reconciled to them."

"Sire, I beg your forgiveness, but just now I am by honor bound to fight for the High Prince at Surluse."

Before the day's fighting commenced at Surluse, Sir Palomides and the heathen knight Sir Corsabryne appealed to the High Prince to witness a duel between them. The High Prince consented to do so after dinner. Sir Palomides had challenged Sir Corsabryne on behalf of Princess Baudas, who, hearing of his reputation for chivalry, had sent him her token together with a message promising him herself and her inheritance if he could defeat Sir Corsabyrne who, in default of her returning his love, had kept her in bondage and discouraged all other suitors by pronouncing her a half-wit.

In the course of the day's fighting Sir Dynadan excelled, striking down Sir Geryne and four other knights, among many other remarkable feats. Then the High Prince, who knew and loved Sir Dynadan for his jokes, as everyone who knew him did, said to Sir Launcelot:

"Sir, I pray you go and knock down Sir Dynadan, and bring him before myself and the queen."

Sir Launcelot rode onto the field and struck down a large number of knights and finally Sir Dynadan, whom he disarmed and brought before the High Prince and Queen Gwynevere. The High Prince rocked with laughter, but Sir Dynadan was unabashed.

"My lord, I am not ashamed, for it was only at the hands of that rogue Sir Launcelot that I suffered my defeat."

The High Prince blew on his horn and they all went to dinner, still making jokes at the expense of Sir Dynadan.

When dinner was over they returned to the field to adjudicate between Sir Palomides and Sir Corsabryne, and Sir Palomides placed the token between them. They jousted and both fell to the ground, then leaped up and fought with their swords; and before long the shield, harness, and armor of each were breaking beneath the strain. Then Sir Corsabryne called a halt.

"Sir, I demand that you yield the princess," he said.

Without warning he then struck Sir Palomides on the helmet. Sir Palomides fell to his knees, jumped up in a fury, and returned the blow with such power that Sir Corsabryne was sent spinning to the ground.

"Now yield yourself, or die!" he shouted as he stood astride him.

"I defy you—do your worst," the other replied.

Sir Palomides grasped him by the helmet and chopped off his head. Then a foul smell issued from the body of the heathen as the soul departed, and the corpse was hastily buried in the forest.

The High Prince, Sir Launcelot, and the queen returned with Sir Palomides to the castle, and then the High Prince spoke:

"Sir, today you have been vouchsafed a miracle. I beg you to take warning from the foulness of Sir Corsabryne, and yourself become baptized: all knights will love you the better for it."

"Sir, that is my own wish, but I swore to fight seven battles in the name of the Saviour first."

Then Sir Palomides invited the High Prince and the queen to take supper with him. They did so, together with Sir Launcelot, Sir Lamerok, and other of their companions.

THE SIXTH DAY. After hearing mass the competitors entered the field, and when the horn was blown the fighting commenced. Sir Gaheris overthrew Sir Ossayse of Surluse. Sir Dornar and Sir Agglovale, brothers to Sir Lamerok, jousted with two other knights, and all four were flung to the ground. Sir Lamerok was angry at the downfall of his brothers, he himself having overthrown four knights before even breaking his spear; then with his sword he had struck down several more. Seeing his might, many fled before him. Then he spoke to his brothers:

"Brothers, are you not ashamed to be flung from your horses? For it is on horseback that a true knight acquits himself, and is judged. To fight on foot is a last resort, unless you are charged with treason and obliged to fight to the death, otherwise if you are met with an overwhelming force. So let me see you remain in your saddles hereafter."

Duke Chalence jousted with Earl Ulbawys of Surluse, and both fell from their horses. Duke Chalence was remounted by Sir Ector and Sir Bleobris; Earl Ulbawys was remounted by the King of the Hundred Knights. Then Sir Gaheris attacked the King of the Hundred Knights, and Duke Chalence rode between them. At this point the horn was blown and the competitors retired to dinner.

Sir Dynadan walked into the High Prince's castle halfway through dinner and noticed that the High Prince was looking thoroughly vexed and had only pecked at his fish. Seeing another fish on the sideboard, one with a large head, Sir Dynadan put it between two dishes and served it to the High Prince with these words:

"My lord, it would appear that you are a cousin to the wolves, who disdain fish and will eat only flesh."

The High Prince laughed, and then Sir Dynadan spoke to Sir Launcelot:

"Why, surely it is the devil himself, for when he is about no mortal knight has a chance of winning a prize."

"My lord, you are mistaken," Sir Launcelot replied. "You have only to touch me with that great spear of yours and I am out of the saddle! In future I shall take care to encounter your boisterous self only over a dish of meat."

The High Prince and the queen laughed heartily, and throughout dinner the merriment continued.

THE SEVENTH DAY. When the queen and all the spectators had taken their places, and the judges taken up their positions on the field, the horn was blown and the fighting commenced. Duke Cambynes jousted with Sir Arystaunce and both were unhorsed; Earl Lambayle helped the duke to remount, and then jousted with Sir Ossayse and was overthrown. The King of North Galys jousted with Earl Ulbawys, and the judges feared that they had both broken their necks.

Meanwhile, the High Prince, Sir Launcelot, and Queen Gwynevere were persuading Sir Dynadan to arm and enter the field.

"My lords, I am afraid that if I do so, before long I shall have to encounter one or the other of you."

"Sir, you may set your mind at rest, for we shall sit here in the judges' seats with our shields before us, and should we leave them, you will be able to see that we have done so."

Sir Dynadan entered the field and did well. Sir Launcelot hastily found a substitute for his seat, then armed himself, and put on a maiden's gown above his armor. He rode onto the field and took a spear from Sir Galyhodyn and charged at Sir Dynadan. Sir Dynadan looked up in time to see a maid charging at him with a spear, and to suspect Sir Launcelot, but not in time to escape him, and he was sent crashing to the ground. He was then dragged into the forest by some of the High Prince's servants, stripped, dressed in the gown, and taken thus before the High Prince and the queen, who all but fell down with laughing. "Sir Launcelot, you traitor! Shall I never escape you?" he said.

The horn was blown and the tournament brought to an end. The first prize was given to Sir Launcelot, the second to Sir Lamerok, and the third to King Bagdemagus. There was a feast at the castle that night, and in the morning Queen Gwynevere and Sir Launcelot prepared to leave for King

Arthur's court, and begged Sir Lamerok to accompany them. But Sir Lamerok refused.

"My lord," said Sir Launcelot, "I undertake that King Arthur will protect you from Sir Gawain and his brothers."

"Alas! I can never trust Sir Gawain, and were it not for King Arthur I should hasten to avenge Queen Margawse. As it is I pray you commend me to the king, and assure him that I wish nothing better than to serve him wheresoever the occasion may arise—as lately when I avenged his kin, who are yet my own enemies, against Sir Palomides."

Then Sir Lamerok departed, and the queen and Sir Launcelot wept.

10. JOYOUS GARD

Sir Galahalte the High Prince and King Bagdemagus decided to hold a tournament for the purpose of destroying Sir Launcelot, of whom they were both jealous for having carried off the first prize in the preceding tournament. King Mark heard of their plan and was pleased. By persuading Sir Tristram to enter the tournament in disguise, he hoped that he might be killed in Sir Launcelot's stead.

King Mark was fortunate: Sir Launcelot did not compete, and Sir Tristram was duly mistaken for him by virtue of his size and of the remarkable feats he accomplished. At the agreed moment the High Prince and King Bagdemagus both attacked him with such savage force and cunning that Sir Tristram was seriously wounded, and it was a surprise to the onlookers that he lived at all.

Then King Mark went up to him:

"Good nephew, I am shocked to see you so seriously wounded. I pray you, allow me to be your physician."

"May God reward you!" Sir Tristram replied.

King Mark had him conveyed into the High Prince's castle and there gave him food and drink which contained drugs to send him to sleep. The same night he took him to a castle of his own and locked him in a dungeon, where he left him with instructions to the caretakers to supply him with the necessities of life.

For a long time Sir Tristram remained in prison, and Iseult missed him and grew worried, so she begged Sir Sadoke to go in search of him.

When Sir Sadoke discovered that King Mark had imprisoned Sir Tristram, he persuaded two of his cousins to help him ambush the king just outside Tintagil. The king rode by with four of his cousins and several of the Traitors of Magouns. Sir Sadoke killed all four of the king's cousins and one of the Traitors, but King Mark escaped him, and one of his own cousins was wounded.

Sir Sadoke rode on to the castle of Lyonas, where Sir Tristram was imprisoned, and thence to the castle of Arbray, where he found Sir Dynas the Seneschal. When Sir Dynas heard the news of King Mark's treachery he decided to foment a revolt against him throughout Lyoness.

After escaping Sir Sadoke, King Mark returned to Tintagil, buried his cousins, and then, in fear of a revolt, commanded his armies to stand to. The news of the revolt in Lyoness reached him and he decided on a ruse to divert the rebels. He forged letters from the Pope commanding him, on pain of anathema, to sail to Jerusalem and join a crusade against the Saracens. He had these letters delivered to himself by a disguised courier, and thence to Sir Tristram, and promised to reinstate him if he would lead his army on the crusade.

Sir Tristram refused on the grounds that he would accept no commands from a king so treacherous as King Mark.

Then King Mark forged fresh letters commanding Sir Tristram in person to go to Jerusalem. The letters were delivered to Sir Tristram, and he guessed at once that they were forgeries.

"King Mark was always false, and always will be," he commented.

Meanwhile four of King Mark's guards were brought before the king—one wounded in the neck, one in the trunk, one in the arm, and one in the thigh.

"My liege," said one of them, "I pray you, fly: the whole country is in arms against you."

Then Sir Percivale arrived at Tintagil. He had come to Cornwall to find Sir Tristram, and on hearing that he was imprisoned had rescued him. Sir Tristram had asked him to remain, but

Sir Percivale had excused himself on the grounds that he had to ride to West Britain. He now spoke to King Mark and warned him that his cavalier treatment of Sir Tristram, one of the greatest of all knights, was winning him the hatred and contempt of honorable knights throughout King Arthur's realm.

"What you say is true," King Mark replied, "and yet I cannot help myself, because of his love for Iseult."

"For shame! He is your own nephew and should be above suspicion. Queen Iseult is the most beautiful lady in the land, and Sir Tristram a true knight; therefore you can be sure their love is without sin."

When Sir Percivale had gone, King Mark sent a messenger to Sir Dynas bearing his oath that he himself would lead an army against the Saracens, and begging Sir Dynas to call off the revolt. Sir Dynas believed him and did so. Then King Mark imprisoned Sir Tristram once more on the pretext that he had been seen in company with the queen, and regardless of the oaths of good will which he had sworn to Sir Percivale.

Sir Tristram wrote secretly to Iseult and begged her to find a means to release him, and to fit out a ship so that they could sail away together to Logres. Iseult promised that she would, and wrote to Sir Dynas and to Sir Sadoke telling them what had happened and begging them to imprison King Mark while she and Sir Tristram made good their escape. Sir Dynas and Sir Sadoke promptly did as she asked, and she sailed away with Sir Tristram a few days later.

Four days after their arrival in Logres, King Arthur held a tournament, and Sir Tristram competed. He overthrew fourteen knights of the Round Table; and then Sir Launcelot entered the field, determined to avenge them and not recognizing Sir Tristram, who was fighting incognito. However, Iseult was watching, and sent her ring to Sir Launcelot, who then understood, and, instead of jousting with Sir Tristram, welcomed him warmly.

When the tournament was over, Sir Launcelot led Sir Tristram and Iseult to his castle, the Joyous Gard, which he had won with his own hands, and begged them to treat it as their own. It was a magnificent castle, and equipped for a king and queen; Sir Launcelot commanded his retainers to serve Sir Tristram and Iseult as they would serve him.

Sir Launcelot returned to King Arthur and reported the news of Sir Tristram and Iseult. King Arthur was well pleased, and decided to hold a tournament in their honor at the nearby castle of Lonezep. The tournament was proclaimed throughout the realm: in Cornwall, West Britain, Northumberland, Ireland, Scotland, Gore, Surluse, and Lystenoyse. Some knights rejoiced, but others were apprehensive.

"Sire," said Sir Launcelot, "do you not think that so wide a proclamation may not draw more of our enemies than our fellowship can withstand?"

"Sir Launcelot, so be it! and let the best knights prove themselves once more."

Sir Launcelot then made private arrangements that Queen Iseult should witness the tournament without being in any way in jeopardy.

Sir Tristram and Iseult lived together at the Joyous Gard in that rare state of happiness known only to lovers. Every day Sir Tristram went hunting, and not only was he the foremost huntsman of his time, but he it was who originated many of the terms used in hawking, and the different horn blasts in hunting, from the find to the kill; and for this he has been justly celebrated ever since.

One day Iseult said to Sir Tristram:

"My lord, it troubles me that every day you ride forth unarmed when the forest abounds with knights, some of whom must surely be your enemies."

"My love, I will do so no more."

Thereafter Sir Tristram made one of his squires carry his spear and shield wherever he went. One day toward the end of April he paused by a well while chasing a hart, and saw the Questing Beast. He remained, expecting to see Sir Palomides, whose quest it was. Sir Breuse Sans Pité rode up, and a few moments later Sir Palomides. They all saluted each other. Then Sir Palomides spoke:

"My lords, I have news. Sir Tristram and Iseult have come to this realm, and surely we shall encounter them soon. King Mark imprisoned him twice. The first time he was rescued by Sir Percivale, and the second time by Iseult herself: she managed to persuade Sir Dynas and Sir Sadoke to imprison King Mark while they fled, and King Mark is still in prison. And I tell you, I too love Iseult, and while I live I swear that I shall serve her."

While they were talking a knight had ridden up to them, and couched his spear in readiness for jousting.

"My friends," said Sir Tristram, "who will encounter this knight? I see that he bears the arms of King Arthur's court."

"I have never yet, while pursuing the Questing Beast, refused to joust with an errant knight," said Sir Palomides.

"Very well, and I will stand by you," said Sir Breuse.

The knight from King Arthur's court was Sir Bleobris; he jousted with Sir Palomides and overthrew him. Then he saw Sir Breuse.

"Sir, renegade knight that you are, defend yourself!" he shouted. Then Sir Breuse fled, and Sir Bleobris pursued him through forest and clearing. Sir Breuse soon came upon three knights of the Round Table: Sir Ector, Sir Harry, and Sir Percivale, whose reputation was already widespread.

"My lords," said Sir Breuse, "I pray you help me: I am being chased by the most pitiless and treacherous knight living, Sir Breuse Sans Pité."

"Do not fear, we shall be your warrant," Sir Percivale replied.

Sir Bleobris rode up, and seeing four knights all ranged against him, hesitated for a moment; but pride in the knowledge that he was a knight of the Round Table urged him on. He jousted with Sir Ector and with Sir Percivale and overthrew them both. Then he jousted with Sir Harry and they unhorsed each other. Sir Breuse saw his chance, and galloped up and struck Sir Bleobris repeatedly with his sword as he lay on the ground.

Sir Harry leaped up. "For shame!" he cried.

"Let be!" said Sir Breuse.

"Then defend yourself!"

When Sir Breuse saw that Sir Harry was in earnest, he abstained, and Sir Harry withdrew; then he attacked Sir Bleobris again.

"Traitor!" Sir Harry cried, and began to remount.

Sir Breuse galloped at him and struck him down before he had gained the saddle. Then Sir Percivale arose, and with a shout of "Traitor!" leaped on his horse and chased Sir Breuse into the forest. Sir Harry joined him, but Sir Breuse was well horsed and escaped. When they returned Sir Bleobris asked them:

"Why did you help that miscreant?"

"Why? Who was he?"

"Sir Breuse, the most treacherous knight living."

"Pray, sir, who are you?"

"Sir Bleobris de Ganys."

"My good cousin, forgive me!" said Sir Ector. "I am Sir Ector de Marys."

They repented that they had allowed Sir Breuse to escape them. A moment later Sir Palomides rode up, and seeing Sir Bleobris' shield, said:

"I challenge the owner of that shield, for it was he who lately unhorsed me by the fountain."

"Sir, I am ready; and know that my name is Sir Bleobris."

"And mine is Sir Palomides."

They made ready to joust, for they had long hated each other. Then Sir Ector spoke:

"Sir Palomides, understand that the knight who kills any of our kin dies for it. Therefore, if you have a grudge against us, challenge Sir Launcelot, otherwise Sir Tristram."

"I cannot match either of them," Sir Palomides replied.

"Is there any other knight you cannot match?"

"There was a third, and he was the mightiest knight of his time. I mean the peerless Sir Lamerok de Galys. But now he is dead. After he overthrew thirty knights at a tournament, Sir Gawain and his brothers ambushed and killed him."

Sir Percivale fell from his horse in a faint. When he came to, he said:

"Alas for my good brother! And now I shall never know him except for the greatness by which he is remembered. Surely it is enough that my father King Pellinore should have been killed."

They were interrupted by the arrival of a courier who announced the forthcoming tournament at Lonezep.

One day while Sir Tristram was hunting, Sir Dynadan rode up to him and told him his name and asked Sir Tristram his. Sir Tristram refused to tell him.

"Sir, only lately I saw just such a knight as you must be," said Sir Dynadan. "He was lying asleep by a well, his helmet was by him, and he had a foolish grin on his face; he did not say a word, and I'll wager he was dreaming of his beloved."

"Sir, are you not yourself a lover?"

"No! God forbid that I should meddle in that game."

"Sir, surely a knight's prowess is enhanced by his being a lover?"

"For love, then, I pray you, sir, tell me your name; otherwise defend yourself."

"I shall neither fight with you, nor yet tell you my name."

"Coward!"

"Your challenge is foolhardy."

Just then a knight rode toward them.

"Why, there is the very knight who lay sleeping by the well," said Sir Dynadan.

"I know him well: he is Sir Epynogres, Prince of North-umberland, and an ardent lover if ever there was one. His lady is the Princess of West Britain. Now, sir, I pray you, joust with him, and we shall see if a lover cannot prove his mettle."

Sir Dynadan challenged the knight; they jousted, and Sir Dynadan was overthrown.

"How now? It seems the lover did well," said Sir Tristram.

"Coward! Why do you not avenge me?"

"I pray you, mount, and we will ride together."

"Your company does not please me," said Sir Dynadan, who then remounted and rode away.

"Not so fast!" shouted Sir Tristram. "Perhaps I can give you news of Sir Tristram."

"Sir, you would fly from the very sight of him," said Sir Dynadan, turning away again.

"Who knows but we shall meet again!" Sir Tristram shouted.

Sir Tristram returned to the Joyous Gard and found every-one talking excitedly; he asked what was the news.

"Sir, a resident knight of this castle has just been killed by two newcomers for saying that Sir Launcelot is greater than Sir Gawain."

"That was a poor pretext for killing a knight."

"Sir, if only Sir Launcelot were here! He would soon avenge him."

Sir Tristram rode after the two knights, jousted with them, and overthrew them both. They drew their swords, as if deter-mined to fight to the death.

"My lords, I pray you, tell me your names and from what country you come, and whose court; for I might yet show you mercy. Understand that if we engage with our swords you may well lose your lives."

"Sir, we do not fear to tell you: we are Sir Aggravayne and Sir Gaheris, brothers to Sir Gawain and nephews to King Arthur."

"Then for the love of King Arthur I shall spare you, in spite of your misdeeds. But I beg you to consider that you have won for yourselves an evil reputation throughout the realm. You murdered Sir Lamerok de Galys, a far greater knight than any of you; and I for one repent that I was not present to avenge his death."

"Sir, you would not have outlived him."

"My lords, there are many knights greater than those of your blood."

Sir Tristram turned his back on them and rode toward the

Joyous Gard again. Sir Gaheris and Sir Aggravayne followed him.

"Coward! Defend yourself!" they shouted as they attacked him.

Sir Tristram drew his sword and struck each on the helmet— such blows that both were seriously wounded and fell from their horses.

Sir Tristram returned to the Joyous Gard, and told Iseult all that had happened to him that day.

"My lord, is not Sir Dynadan the knight who composed the lampoon?"

"The same; he is one of the best knights, and certainly the wittiest in the realm."

"Then why did you not invite him to the Joyous Gard?"

"My love, he has come here to find me, and find me he shall; but just now he rehearsed a whole diatribe against lovers."

At that moment a squire came to Sir Tristram and reported that a knight bearing Sir Dynadan's arms had entered the town.

"My lady, Sir Dynadan is here. I pray you, invite him to the castle; he will entertain you well, and I will disappear."

"My lord," said Iseult when Sir Dynadan arrived, "pray tell me what brings you to these parts."

"My lady, I have come in search of Sir Tristram."

"Perhaps he is here, but I have heard no news of him."

"My lady, I never cease to wonder at Sir Tristram, and lovers such as he is. What causes such insensate devotion?"

"For shame! Are you a knight and no lover? The very purpose of a knight is to fight on behalf of a lady."

"God forbid! The sweetness of love is short-lived, but the pain endures."

"Sir, only lately Sir Bleobris fought three knights together for the love of his lady, and won them all in the presence of the King of Northumberland. Now, was not that splendidly done?"

"Certainly he is a great knight, and of the same blood as Sir Launcelot."

"Sir, I pray you: Three knights have wronged me; will you not challenge them on my behalf?"

"My lady, you are the fairest in the land, not excepting Queen Gwynevere; but may God be my witness! I would never undertake to fight three knights on your behalf."

Iseult laughed. Sir Dynadan remained for the night. Sir Tristram came early in the morning, armed, and promised Iseult that he would meet Sir Dynadan and ride with him to the tournament at Lonezep. Sir Dynadan rose later, armed, and set off in search of Sir Tristram. Before long he found him, but still did not recognize him.

"Ah ha! the very coward I met yesterday. I swear that now you shall joust with me, willy-nilly."

"My lord, I am unwilling to do so," Sir Tristram replied.

They jousted; Sir Tristram deliberately missed with his spear, and Dir Dynadan broke his on Sir Tristram's shield. Then he drew his sword.

"Not so!" said Sir Tristram. "What angers you?"

"Coward! You disgrace the order of knighthood."

"Sir, you are a valiant knight; I pray you, allow me to ride under your protection."

"Sir, I never set eyes on so large a knight and so useless. Pray tell me, for what purpose do you carry those huge spears?"

"I shall give them to some good knight at the tournament, perhaps to you, if you excel."

While they were talking an errant knight approached them.

"Sir, I pray you, joust with this knight," said Sir Tristram.

"I suppose that with a companion such as you, it falls to me to do so," Sir Dynadan replied.

They jousted and Sir Dynadan was flung from his horse. He jumped up and drew his sword.

"Sir, do you challenge me for love or for hate?"

"For love; now let us fight."

"Sir, what is your name?"

"Sir Dynadan."

"And mine is Sir Gareth."

Thereupon they greeted each other. Sir Gareth was an honorable knight and kept aloof from his brothers, whose recalcitrance he deplored. Then Sir Dynadan told him about his companion (Sir Tristram) and what a coward he was. Sir Tristram overheard and laughed to himself. At that moment another errant knight rode up to them.

"My lords," said Sir Tristram, "which of you will joust with that knight?"

"I will," said Sir Gareth.

They jousted and Sir Gareth was overthrown.

"Sir, will you not avenge him?" said Sir Tristram to Sir Dynadan.

"Indeed, I shall not; that knight is too strong for me."

"Alas! then I shall have to see what I can do," said Sir Tristram.

Sir Tristram couched his spear and charged. His opponent

was knocked clean out of the saddle and flew high over his horse's tail and landed with a crash. He clambered up hastily and drew his sword.

"Sir, what is your name?" asked Sir Tristram.

"Sir Palomides."

"And who is your greatest enemy?"

"Sir Tristram. When we meet one of us must die."

"Sir, I am Sir Tristram; now defend yourself!"

"Sir Tristram, I pray you, forgive me my evil words. I admit your greatness and hold that all honorable knights must love you therefor. Henceforth I shall serve you, and be always ready at your command."

"Sir Palomides, I know you for an honorable knight who has achieved much. Your words become you if you really have no grudge; but if you have, I pray you let us settle it now."

"My lord, I have none."

"So be it, then."

"My lord," said Sir Dynadan to Sir Tristram, "you have made a fool of me. I came to this country to find you, and even Sir Launcelot refused to tell me your whereabouts."

"Truly? And it is at Sir Launcelot's own castle, the Joyous Gard, that I have been staying."

Sir Tristram, Sir Dynadan, Sir Palomides, and Sir Gareth all rode on together, and were presently before the Castle of Lonezep; before them stretched a wide array of pavilions and tents belonging to knights who had come to compete in the tournament.

"There is a tremendous array," said Sir Tristram.

"Not greater, surely, than that before the Maidens' Castle where you won thirty knights?" asked Sir Palomides.

"Or than the array before the High Prince's castle at Surluse?" asked Sir Dynadan.

"My lords, who won the prize at Surluse?" asked Sir Tristram.

"Sir Launcelot first, Sir Lamerok second."

"Sir Launcelot would surely win the prize if he were present," said Sir Tristram. "But the death of Sir Lamerok grieves me, for he must have been the greatest knight of his generation."

"Do we not all repent his death!" said Sir Dynadan.

"My lords," said Sir Gareth, "although Sir Lamerok died at the hands of my own kinsmen, I too repent his death. They deserve the evil reputation they have won, and since that time I have wished only to disassociate myself from them."

"I was present at the tournament at Surluse," said Sir Palomides, "and I watched Sir Lamerok felling his opponents with sword and spear. None could withstand him at that time, and he won true greatness; but when it was over and he rode from the field, Sir Gawain, Sir Modred, and Sir Aggravayne all set upon him. First they killed his horse, then for three hours they fought on foot; and while Sir Gawain and Sir Aggravayne faced him, Sir Modred attacked from the rear, and he it was who finally killed him with a wound in the back. I learned all this from one of their squires."

"To hear of it makes me feel that my heart will burst," said Sir Tristram. "I dare not go near King Arthur's court for fear that if I set eyes on Sir Gawain and his brothers I will kill them."

"Let us speak of other things," said Sir Palomides, "for grieve as we may, we cannot restore his life to him."

"The more is the pity," said Sir Dynadan. "And I hear that the brothers, with the exception of Sir Gaheris, who is an honorable knight, have sworn enmity to all the knights of the Round Table, and especially to Sir Launcelot and his kin. Fortunately Sir Launcelot knows this, and is careful to keep his kin by him."

"Enough!" said Sir Palomides. "Now let us talk of the tournament. Should not the four of us keep together and withstand all comers?"

"That would be unwise," said Sir Tristram, "for I see by the pavilions that there must be above four hundred knights here already. We should be outnumbered, and I have many times seen knights defeated because they tried to overreach themselves. Bravery should be tempered by wisdom; and for myself, I intend keeping my head."

They rode to the banks of the Humber, and there a ship lay at anchor. The ship had red silk awnings, but everyone aboard seemed muted with grief. Sir Tristram entered the cabin and saw a dead knight, in full armor except for the helmet, lying on a richly appareled bed. The corpse was still bloody from its wounds. Then Sir Tristram noticed a letter lying on the bed, and asked one of the mariners what had happened.

"My lords, the knight who lies before you was a great king, and the letter may be read only by a knight worthy and willing to avenge his death."

"Surely one of us shall undertake this quest," said Sir Tristram, and opened the letter. It read as follows:

"I, Harmaunce, King of the Red City, would be recommended to all errant knights, especially those of King Arthur's court; and I would beg that one of them shall undertake to avenge my death, which was wrought by treason and felony by two of my own brethren whom I raised from privation and obscurity. The knight who avenges me shall be heir to my Kingdom of the Red City and all the castles therein."

"Here is a piteous letter indeed," said Sir Tristram, "and I should undertake to avenge him were I not in honor bound to fight at Lonezep."

"Sir, I will avenge him, or die in the attempt," said Sir Palomides.

"Then the task shall be yours: but return here in seven days' time for the tournament."

"Sir Tristram, I shall be here, unless I am killed or crippled," said Sir Palomides.

Sir Palomides sailed away in the ship. Sir Tristram, Sir Dynadan, and Sir Gaheris came ashore, and were met immediately by a knight who came galloping toward them, armed only with a sword.

"My lords, if you are errant knights, I pray you, follow me to my castle," he said.

"With good will," said Sir Tristram.

The knight led them into his well-kept castle and they all sat down to dinner. Then their host recognized Sir Tristram and turned pale with anger.

"My lord, what ails you?" asked Sir Tristram.

"Sir, I know you now for Sir Tristram de Lyoness, the knight who killed my brother. Therefore be warned, I shall kill you."

"Sir, if I killed your brother, allow me to make amends."

"Sir, his death cannot be amended; so take heed."

Sir Tristram and his companion left the castle after dinner, and soon their host came galloping after them; he was fully armed and bore a white shield.

"Sir Tristram, defend yourself!" he shouted.

They jousted and the knight was thrown over his horse's tail. He jumped up, remounted, and struck Sir Tristram two or three times on the helmet with his sword.

"Sir, I pray you, hold your hand; having eaten at your table I am unwilling to battle with you," said Sir Tristram.

But the knight ignored his warning and attacked Sir Tristram again. Sir Tristram drew his sword and with one blow knocked him off his horse, and blood poured through the lacing of his helmet.

"I am afraid I have killed him," said Sir Tristram.

They rode on, and a little while later met Sir Berraunte,

known as the King of the Hundred Knights, and Sir Segwarydes. It happened that Sir Dynadan had Sir Tristram's helmet slung on his shoulder. This helmet had originally belonged
to the Queen of North Galys, who was Sir Berraunte's
paramour. The Queen of North Galys had given it to Queen
Iseult, who in turn had given it to Sir Tristram.

"Sir, how did you come by that helmet?" asked Sir Berraunte.

"What is that to you?" Sir Dynadan replied.

"I challenge you for the love of the lady whose helmet it is."

They jousted, Sir Dynadan was overthrown, and Sir Berraunte ordered his squire to remove the helmet.

"Sir, that helmet shall be dearly bought," said Sir Tristram.

"Then defend yourself!" Sir Berraunte shouted.

Sir Berraunte was twice knocked off his horse, first by Sir
Tristram's spear, and then by a stunning blow from his sword.

"And now two knights have taken a fall for the sake of that
cursed helmet," said Sir Dynadan.

"Will none of you joust with me?" said Sir Segwarydes.

"I will," said Sir Gareth.

"You may joust on my behalf," said Sir Dynadan.

"Strictly speaking, this should be yours, Sir Dynadan," said
Sir Tristram.

"In a word, I refuse," said Sir Dynadan.

They jousted, and Sir Gareth was overthrown.

"Sir Dynadan, you must avenge him," said Sir Tristram.

"Sir, I refuse," answered Sir Dynadan.

"Then I shall," said Sir Tristram.

Sir Tristram overthrew him, and then returned with his
companions to the Joyous Gard. Sir Gareth was reluctant to
enter, but Sir Tristram pressed him to accept his invitation.
That evening Sir Dynadan rebuked Iseult for giving him Sir
Tristram's helmet, and they all made fun of him.

11. THE RED CITY

Sir Palomides slept while his ship sailed down the river
Humber, and just before dawn came to the sea. On the coast
stood a fine castle, and the sailors woke him.

"Sir, you must rise now and go into this castle."

"With good will."

The sailors gave Sir Palomides a horn; and when he blew on it, knights came running to the castle walls.

"Welcome to this castle!" they shouted.

It was dawn when Sir Palomides entered. He was received hospitably and a variety of meats set before him. But before he had finished eating, cries of lamentation arose all around him.

"Pray, what is the meaning of this?" asked Sir Palomides. "It grieves me to hear such mourning."

He was answered by Sir Ebell:

"Sir, we are mourning, as we ever shall, for King Harmaunce of the Red City, for surely he was the gentlest and liveliest king who ever ruled a poor people. He delighted in all the arts of barony, in the chase, and in the perils of the tournament, and he liked nothing better than to joust with the knights of the Round Table and see them tumbled to the ground. But he was destroyed by his own magnanimity: Two knights whom he raised from the dust, and to whom he gave preference even above his own family, in the end destroyed him. Had he kept to his own family he would today be alive, as wealthy and honored as he ever was."

"Pray tell me the story of his death," said Sir Palomides.

"Sir, the two most powerful knights in the land today are the brothers Sir Helake and Sir Helyus, and they are of common blood. The king adopted them as children and brought them up as his own. As they grew he advanced them beyond all the members of his own family; and as he ruled the Red City, so they came to rule him.

"You know how it is with churls: Give them an inch and they will take an ell, and that is how it was with these two. The king was so influenced by them that all his own family left the court in disgust. Then the two brothers plotted to kill the king and usurp the throne.

"They lured him into the forest one day to chase a red hart, and then ambushed him by a well. Sir Helyus drove his spear right into the king and wounded him mortally. By chance I myself found the king just before he died. He told me what had happened and so I carried him to the river and put him on a ship. He then dictated a letter to me which explained how he had been killed, and in which he begged to be commended to the knights of the Round Table, and offered, as a reward for avenging his death, the rule of the Red City.

"I was to send the ship up the river to Lonezep so that one of the knights at the tournament might undertake the quest. And I can assure you that whoever does so will win the love of all at the Red City."

"Sir, I myself read the letter, and am here to undertake the quest."

"Then you must sail to the Delectable Ile first, near the Red City, for that is the brothers' stronghold, and was built for them by King Harmaunce himself. I shall await you here."

"Whatever happens, hold fast here; for then if I am killed either Sir Launcelot or Sir Tristram will come to avenge me."

Sir Palomides left the castle, and as he approached the ship a knight rode toward him. His shield was on his shoulder and his sword was in his hand.

"Sir, what are you seeking here? The quest of the Red City belongs to me."

"Sir, that may be; and yet when the letter was taken from the king's hand, I was the only knight who volunteered. Therefore I shall undertake the quest or die in the attempt."

"Then we shall see who is the better knight, so defend yourself!"

They fought with their swords for over an hour, and then Sir Palomides struck his opponent to his knees.

"Gentle knight, hold your hand! The quest is yours, but I pray you, tell me your name."

"Sir Palomides, from King Arthur's court."

"Well met, Sir Palomides! But for three knights I would rather be overcome by you than by any knight living. The three are Sir Launcelot, Sir Tristram, and my own cousin, Sir Lamerok. I am called Sir Hermynde de Galys."

"Alas! of those three knights we shall see Sir Lamerok no more."

"How so? Is he dead?"

"Yes, he was killed by Sir Gawain and his brothers."

"God forbid! One against five?"

"One against four. Sir Gareth, the best knight among them, keeps clear of his renegade brothers."

Sir Palomides then told Sir Hermynde how Sir Lamerok's death had taken place. Then they parted, Sir Palomides for the Delectable Ile and Sir Hermynde for the Red City, where he gave forewarning of Sir Palomides' approach, saying that he was Sir Palomides the Saracen, the knight in quest of the Questing Beast.

The denizens of the city rejoiced at the news, and sent a messenger to inform Sir Helyus and Sir Helake.

"Is it Sir Launcelot or any of his kin?" asked one of them.

"Sir, he is not of their blood."

"So much the better, for it is only Sir Launcelot whom we fear."

"It is Sir Palomides, a noble knight, but as yet unchristened."

"Then surely he shall die a Saracen."

Sir Palomides, meanwhile, had arrived at the city, and was admired by all for his strength and comeliness. He was a knight in his prime, and although not a Christian, was deeply regardful of his knightly vows. It was his intention to become baptized when he had conquered the Questing Beast and fought seven notable battles in righteous causes.

Two days later the brothers arrived. They were both noble knights by virtue of their prowess at arms, although inwardly treacherous. At the appointed hour they met Sir Palomides on the field.

"My lords, are you the brothers Sir Helyus and Sir Helake who treasonably killed King Harmaunce?"

"We are the same; and understand, Sir Palomides the Saracen, that by the time we have finished with you, you will regret not having been baptized."

"My lords, I do not believe that the coming battle constitutes any threat to my becoming a Christian before I die."

They drew apart and charged. Sir Palomides drove his spear clean through Sir Helake's shield into his breast and killed him. Sir Helyus had scorned to level his spear at Sir Palomides, but now that he saw his brother dead he shouted: "Defend yourself!" and charged.

This time Sir Palomides was thrown to the ground. Sir Helyus galloped over him two or three times, and then Sir Palomides leaped up, seized Sir Helyus' horse by the bridle, and Sir Helyus was thrown. He jumped up and they crossed swords. They fought for more than two hours without a pause: sometimes one, sometimes the other, sometimes both together would stagger and fall, but always to recover immediately. At last Sir Palomides began to grow faint from his wounds, and at the same time Sir Helyus seemed to grow stronger. Sir Palomides was driven to the very edge of the field, and a great cry arose from the spectators:

"Alas! must Sir Palomides die?"

Sir Palomides heard them. More than a hundred of Sir Helyus' blows had struck home, and he could barely stand. A lesser knight would have collapsed, but Sir Palomides was moved by the mournful cries and asked himself: "Sir Palomides, where is your courage now?" Thereupon he raised his shield and looked at Sir Helyus' visor. Then he struck blow after blow on his helmet, tremendous blows which before long sent Sir Helyus reeling to the ground. Leaping astride him, Sir Palomides tugged off his helmet and with a final blow beheaded him.

The people cheered, and he was borne triumphantly into the city, where the nobles swore him allegiance. Then he was begged to accept the suzerainty of the Red City.

"My lords," Sir Palomides replied, "I beg you to excuse me; but I am in honor bound to return to King Arthur and fight at Lonezep."

The nobles offered Sir Palomides a third part of their estates if he would remain and rule them, but Sir Palomides refused. He returned first to the castle of which Sir Ebell was lieutenant, where he was received with triumphal honors, and thence to Lonezep.

Not finding Sir Tristram at Lonezep, Sir Palomides crossed the Humber and entered the town at Joyous Gard. His arrival was noticed and reported to Sir Tristram, who sent Sir Dynadan to fetch him. They greeted each other joyfully, and Sir Palomides stayed with Sir Dynadan that night.

Sir Tristram and Sir Gaheris arrived early in the morning and got them out of bed, and then they all rode together into the fields and woods to repose themselves. After several hours a knight rode up to them and asked Sir Tristram what knights were lodged at the Joyous Gard.

"I do not know who they are," Sir Tristram replied.

"And who are you? It would appear that you are not errant knights since you bear no armor."

"Whether we are knights or not, I have no wish to tell you my name," Sir Tristram replied.

"Then defend yourself!" said the knight.

He couched his spear and was about to charge Sir Tristram when Sir Palomides galloped up to him, and after wounding his horse with his sword, leaped down to kill the knight where he had fallen.

"Sir Palomides, do not kill him," said Sir Tristram. "He is but a fool. Just take his spear away from him."

The knight groaned as he remounted, and once more asked Sir Tristram his name.

"Sir, understand that I am Sir Tristram de Lyoness."

The knight spurred his horse and galloped away before they had a chance to ask him his name. Then Sir Epynogres galloped up to them.

"Where are you off to?" asked Sir Tristram.

"My lords, I am pursuing the most treacherous knight living. I pray you, tell me, have you seen a knight bearing a shield with a red cover?"

"We encountered such a knight fifteen minutes ago; tell me what is his name."

"Sir Breuse Sans Pité."

"Alas that he ever escaped me! I hate him more than any other knight living," said Sir Palomides.

Sir Epynogres rode off in pursuit of Sir Breuse; Sir Tristram and his companions headed for the Joyous Gard.

"Sir Palomides, you did well in the quest of the Red City; I am glad. Now we must arrange matters for the tournament tomorrow," said Sir Tristram.

Sir Tristram decided to set two pavilions by the well at Lonezep, one for himself and one for Queen Iseult. Sir Dynadan assented, but Sir Palomides was silent, for the very mention of Iseult's name was sufficient to kindle the passion he felt for her. At the entrance to the Joyous Gard he tried to excuse himself, but Sir Tristram took him by the hand and led him in. They sat down to supper with Iseult, and her beauty had such power over Sir Palomides that he was unable to eat.

12. THE TOURNAMENT AT LONEZEP

In the morning Sir Tristram, Sir Palomides, Sir Dynadan, and Sir Gareth armed and accompanied Queen Iseult to the castle of Lonezep. Queen Iseult and her three ladies-in-waiting were all finely appareled; the four knights were all clad in green armor. Sir Tristram was attended by three squires, the other knights by their valets. They had not ridden far when they were observed by Sir Galyhodyn, who was riding to the tournament in company with another twenty knights. Sir Galyhodyn was a king in Surluse, and brother to Sir Galahalte the High Prince.

"My lords," said Sir Galyhodyn, "let us challenge those four knights and win the lady for ourselves."

"Should we not send forward a squire to offer the challenge?" asked one of his companions.

The squire offered Sir Galyhodyn's challenge to Sir Tristram.

"If your lord wishes to win the lady, let him advance with three of his companions; then we shall fight equally," said Sir Tristram.

"Sir Tristram, I pray you, allow me to encounter the four knights," said Sir Palomides.

"As you will," Sir Tristram replied, and then to the squire: "Tell your lord that our companion will encounter four of his number."

Sir Palomides jousted with Sir Galyhodyn and three of his companions and with one spear knocked each violently off his horse. Then six more of Sir Galyhodyn's company came forward.

"Not so fast, my friends!" said Sir Galyhodyn. "Yonder is a powerful knight, and should he exert his full strength you might fare worse than we have."

When Sir Palomides saw that the six knights were not going to joust, he rode back to Sir Tristram.

"Sir Palomides, you have done well," said Sir Tristram.

Sir Tristram, the queen, and their three companions rode on toward Lonezep, but soon met another four knights who prepared to joust with them. They were Sir Gawain, Sir Uwayne, Sir Sagramour, and Sir Dodynas.

"Sir Tristram I pray you, let me joust with them; but if I am overthrown, be sure to avenge me," said Sir Palomides.

"Sir Palomides, may you win all the honor you might wish for!" Sir Tristram replied.

Sir Palomides overthrew Sir Gawain, horse and man, and each of his companion, using a new spear for each. Then he returned to Sir Tristram and they resumed their journey to Lonezep.

Sir Gawain rode up to Sir Galyhodyn.

"I wonder," he said, "who are those knights in the green armor?"

"I only know that the one on the white horse overthrew me and three of my companions," Sir Galyhodyn replied.

"Me and my three companions likewise. I believe it must be either Sir Tristram or else Sir Palomides, and the lady Queen Iseult."

While Sir Gawain and Sir Galyhodyn were talking, Sir
Tristram and his companions had ridden to the well where
their pavilions were pitched; many more pavilions had now
been pitched all around them. Leaving Queen Iseult in the
care of Sir Palomides and Sir Gareth, Sir Tristram, taking Sir
Palomides' white horse, rode with Sir Dynadan to the castle
to hear news of the tournament.

Nearing the castle they heard a horn summons and saw
knights assembling from all directions; they asked one of them
what it meant.

"Sir, it is to summon all those knights who are to fight against
King Arthur and his fellowship of the Round Table. Among
them will be the Kings of Ireland, Surluse, Lystenoyse,
Northumberland, and West Britain."

The assembly was addressed by King Marhault of Ireland,
the son of Sir Marhaus, whom Sir Tristram had defeated when
he was first knighted.

"My lords," he said, "remember this; that King Arthur will
be supported by the flower of his chivalry. Therefore I suggest
that each king or lord fight only on his own behalf, and supported only by his own followers."

Sir Tristram and Sir Dynadan rode next to King Arthur's
camp. Sir Gawain and Sir Galyhodyn recognized them at once
by their green armor and told the king how they had been
defeated by them earlier that day. King Arthur called Sir
Tristram and asked him his name.

"Sire, I beg to be excused from revealing my name at this
time," Sir Tristram replied, and rode away.

Arthur summoned Sir Gryfflet and commanded him to tell
Sir Tristram that he wished to speak to him privately.

Sir Gryfflet duly delivered the King's message.

"Sir, I will return provided that King Arthur does not wish
to know my name."

"Sir, I am sure that the king will not insist upon it."

Together they rode back to King Arthur.

"Sir, I pray you tell me for what cause you will not reveal
your name," said the king.

"Sire, I would not withhold my name without having good
reason for so doing," Sir Tristram replied.

"Even so, perhaps you will tell me which party you are
supporting."

"Sire, at the moment I cannot say; but when I enter the field I
shall fight as my heart dictates, so tomorrow you shall know."

Sir Tristram and Sir Dynadan returned to their pavilions. In the morning all four knights clad themselves in green armor and rode to the field. Several of the younger knights were already jousting. Sir Gareth begged Sir Tristram to give him leave to enter, "for shame of not breaking at least one spear." Sir Tristram laughed as he assented.

Sir Gareth rode into the field and jousted with Sir Selyses, a nephew to the King of the Hundred Knights. They galloped together furiously; both knights and horses were flung to the ground and seriously bruised. The King of the Hundred Knights helped Sir Selyses to remount and Sir Tristram helped Sir Gareth to remount. When they had returned to their pavilions, Sir Gareth removed his helmet; and the queen, seeing his bruises, asked him what he had been doing.

"Ma'am, I received a hard blow, but I trust that I gave as hard a one in return. However, none of my companions troubled to avenge me."

"Surely it was not for any of us to avenge you," said Sir Palomides. "There was not one proved knight on the field, and when your opponents saw you they sent forward a good knight to match you. You both did well and neither need be ashamed. Now rest yourself, and prepare for tomorrow."

"Sir, I trust I shall not fail you when the time comes."

"My lords, which party shall we join tomorrow?" asked Sir Tristram.

"Sir Tristram, since Sir Launcelot and many of the greatest knights of the realm will be fighting for King Arthur, I suggest that we shall win more honor by fighting against him," said Sir Palomides.

"That is well advised; we shall do as you suggest," said Sir Tristram.

They all agreed and then retired to bed.

In the morning Sir Tristram and his companions armed and first accompanied Queen Iseult to the castle where she could watch the tournament from a bay window, herself remaining veiled so that no man should recognize her. Then they rode onto the field and attached themselves to the party of King Carados of Scotland.

King Arthur noticed them and asked Sir Launcelot who they were.

"Sire, I am not certain; but if Sir Tristram is in the locality it will be either he or Sir Palomides, and the lady Queen Iseult."

King Arthur summoned Sir Kay.

"Sir Kay, I pray you go to the Round Table and see how many of our fellowship are missing."

Sir Kay found that ten knights altogether were missing: Sir Tristram, Sir Palomides, Sir Percivale, Sir Gaheris, Sir Gareth, Sir Epynogres, Sir Modred, Sir Dynadan, Sir La Cote Male Tayle, and Sir Pelleas.

"Then we may be sure that some of them will be fighting against us," said the king.

At that moment two knights from Orkney came up to King Arthur: Sir Edward and Sir Sadoke, cousins to Sir Gawain. They asked if they might be the first to joust.

"Certainly, I shall be pleased," Arthur replied.

Sir Edward jousted with King Carados and overthrew him, Sir Sadoke jousted with the King of West Britain and overthrew him, and they were cheered by King Arthur's party. Then Sir Palomides rode onto the field and with one spear overthrew both Sir Edward and Sir Sadoke.

"By Jesu!" said Arthur, "who is the knight in green armor?"

"Sire, you will see him do better yet. Within the last two days I have encountered him; he overthrew me and seven others besides. And he has a companion who is even bigger than he is," said Sir Gawain.

Sir Tristram rode onto the field on a black horse, and with one spear overthrew four more of Sir Gawain's kin. Sir Dynadan and Sir Gareth followed, and each overthrew one knight.

"The knight on the black horse is certainly a formidable jouster," said Arthur.

"Sire, he has not begun yet," Sir Gawain replied.

Sir Tristram next remounted King Carados and the King of West Britain, then, galloping into the melee, accomplished such feats that the onlookers were astonished and his opponents grew wary of him. Sir Palomides, Sir Dynadan, and Sir Gareth likewise inflicted great punishment on King Arthur's party, until they finally withdrew to the castle. The kings and lords of Arthur's party had agreed not to assist each other.

When King Arthur's party had withdrawn, the heralds made a count of the knights who had been overthrown, and found that Sir Tristram had accounted for thirty knights and Sir Palomides for twenty, all of whom were known for their prowess.

"Surely," said Arthur to Sir Launcelot, "we should be ashamed that so many of our knights have fallen to only four of the opposing party. Let us ride onto the field and avenge them."

"Sire, will not our shame be the greater for attacking the four knights now that they are wearied?"

"Sir Launcelot, we must seek revenge. You, I, Sir Ector, and Sir Bleobris will ride onto the field and encounter them."

"As you will, my lord," Sir Launcelot replied.

Sir Launcelot overthrew Sir Tristram (whom he thought to be Sir Palomides), Sir Bleobris overthrew Sir Palomides, Sir Ector overthrew Sir Gareth, and King Arthur overthrew Sir Dynadan. There was a tremendous cheer from the spectators.

It was the custom that knights who failed to remount should fall prisoner to the opposing party. When the King of North Galys saw Sir Tristram on foot he rode up to him, and despite the agreement that each should look after his own, offered him his horse.

"Sir, I do not know whence you come, but your feats today render you more deserving of my horse than I."

"May God reward you! I shall try to win a horse for you as soon as I am mounted," Sir Tristram replied.

Sir Tristram mounted, charged King Arthur, overthrew him, and gave his horse to the King of North Galys. Then King Arthur became the center of a fierce battle as his supporters tried to remount him, and Sir Tristram and his companions attempted to thwart them.

Sir Palomides fought magnificently, but after unhorsing many of his opponents, was himself unhorsed. Sir Tristram, meanwhile, had withdrawn from the field. He returned disguised in red armor, with red trappings for his horse. He remounted Sir Palomides, Sir Dynadan, and Sir Gareth, and together they attacked King Arthur's party with fresh heart. Sir Launcelot, however, now recognized Sir Tristram and withdrew for a rest.

Queen Iseult watched Sir Tristram eagerly, weeping when he withdrew, for fear that he had been wounded, and now laughing and cheering to see him fighting in his red armor with more liveliness than before. Sir Palomides saw her laughing; he felt his strength and courage grow, and fought with renewed valor. In his heart he wished that he could overthrow Sir Tristram and win the queen for himself.

"Sir Palomides is certainly outdoing us all today," Sir Tristram remarked to Sir Dynadan.

"It is his day, all right," Sir Dynadan agreed, but thought to himself that it was all for the love of Queen Iseult.

"It is a shame that he has not yet been christened," said Sir Tristram.

It was while everyone was saying that Sir Palomides should win the prize that Sir Launcelot re-entered the field and charged him. Sir Palomides deflected Sir Launcelot's spear with his sword, and then beheaded his horse. Sir Launcelot tumbled to the ground and there was a furious outcry at this foul. Sir Ector charged Sir Palomides and threw him off his horse, and then Sir Launcelot strode up to him and drew his sword.

"Sir Palomides, your cowardly stroke deserves punishment; so defend yourself!" he said.

"Most noble lord, I beg you for mercy! Today I have fought as I have not fought before and shall not fight again. I know well that I could never match you on equal terms; therefore, I pray you, allow me this one day of triumph."

"Sir Palomides, it is true that today your feats at arms have been unexampled, and I know for whose love it is that you have been so inspired. But let me warn you to keep it a secret from Sir Tristram, otherwise you will suffer for it. And since my own paramour is not present, I am content to allow you your day of triumph."

They parted. Sir Launcelot, despite the attacks of twenty knights, won for himself another horse, and then overthrew in turn the Kings of Scotland, West Britain, Northumberland, and Lystenoyse, and another forty knights besides.

Sir Tristram and Sir Palomides were remounted by the Kings of Ireland and of the Streyte Marchis, and they too continued to fight vigorously. Then King Arthur blew his horn to end the day's fighting, and the prize was awarded to Sir Palomides. Everyone praised him as they returned to their lodgings, but Sir Launcelot said to King Arthur:

"Sire, Sir Palomides certainly fought well today, and without once taking a rest or changing his clothes, but I am sure that one of his companions will outdo him before the tournament ends."

Sir Palomides, Sir Gareth, and Sir Dynadan were delighted to discover that the knight in the red armor who had rescued them was none other than Sir Tristram. Sir Tristram commanded Sir Dynadan to accompany Queen Iseult, but when they arrived at the pavilions Sir Dynadan rounded on him:

"What in the devil's name was wrong with you today? While Sir Palomides was going from strength to strength you were dawdling about like one in a dream; therefore I call you a coward!"

"Sir Dynadan, no knight living has yet called me a coward.

It is true that I took a fall from Sir Launcelot, but he is the greatest knight of all, as well as being the most courteous."

Sir Tristram was angry with Sir Dynadan, but Sir Dynadan had spoken as he had only out of jealousy for Sir Tristram's reputation.

"Truly," said Sir Palomides, "Sir Launcelot is the most courteous knight. Today he forgave me even after I had fouled him, and allowed me to win the prize. When the tournament is over I shall serve him."

And so they talked on, about kings and knights and their feats at arms. It was said at that time that no ten knights together accomplished half of what was accomplished by Sir Launcelot and Sir Tristram, neither of whom had ever been known to fail in a quest, provided that it was a worthy one.

Sir Tristram, Queen Iseult, Sir Palomides, and Sir Gareth left early the next morning for the tournament field, while Sir Dynadan remained asleep in his bed. They were observed by King Arthur from one of the windows of his castle.

"Sire," said Sir Launcelot, "there rides the most beautiful lady in the land, with the exception only of Queen Gwynevere."

"What is her name?"

"Queen Iseult."

"Let us arm, and we will ride up to them," said the king.

When they had armed and were riding out of the castle, Sir Launcelot spoke again:

"My lord, I am not sure that Queen Iseult's companions will be pleased by our sudden appearance. They are formidable knights, and you may well be risking your life."

"As for that, I will risk it," said the king.

Soon they caught up with the queen and her companions.

"God save you, madam," said the king.

"My lord, you are welcome," she replied.

King Arthur gazed at Queen Iseult in wonder, and then Sir Palomides spoke to him:

"Sir, surely it is most discourteous to appear so suddenly before a lady; I pray you, withdraw."

But the king ignored him and continued to stare at Iseult. Sir Palomides was enraged, and couching his spear, charged at Arthur and knocked him off his horse. Then Sir Launcelot said to himself:

"Alas! it seems that I shall have to encounter both Sir Palomides and Sir Tristram, for avenge my liege I must."

With a shout of "Defend yourself!" he charged Sir Palomides and overthrew him. Then he was challenged by Sir Tristram.

"Sir, reluctant as I am, I must defend the honor of my liege.

I beg you to understand that my reluctance is based on love and not on fear; and should you be overthrown, I beg you to take it in good part," said Sir Launcelot.

Sir Tristram then realized both from his speech and his bearing that it was Sir Launcelot, and that his companion was King Arthur. So he cast aside his spear and remounted Sir Palomides. Sir Launcelot remounted the king and they departed.

"May God forgive us!" said Sir Tristram to Sir Palomides. "Do you understand now that it was King Arthur whom you so rudely challenged? and that Sir Launcelot was his companion? Surely I shall never forget Sir Launcelot's courteous words, for he always forbears combat when it is not called for, and always from fighting me in particular. Yet when he is roused he is without equal, and a hundred knights could not stand against him if the honor of his king were involved."

"Sir, I would never have believed it of King Arthur to appear so suddenly before errant knights and their lady," said Sir Palomides.

"There is no matter of knightly courtesy which may not be learned from King Arthur," Sir Tristram replied.

"Well, what is done cannot be undone."

When Sir Tristram had accompanied Iseult to the castle, he entered the field and the horn was blown for the fighting to commence.

As on the first day, the first to joust were two of Sir Gawain's kin from Orkney, Sir Uwayne and Sir Lucas. Sir Uwayne unhorsed the King of Scotland, Sir Lucas jousted with the King of West Britain; both broke their spears and both were unhorsed. Sir Lucas was remounted by his companions, then both he and Sir Uwayne were overthrown by Sir Tristram. Sir Palomides and Sir Gareth each overthrew two of their companions.

"Those knights have started well," said King Arthur.

"Sire, you will see them do better yet," Sir Launcelot replied.

Several more of the knights from Orkney entered the field, and Sir Tristram said to Sir Palomides:

"How do you feel today? Will you do as well as yesterday?"

"I shall not; I feel weary and bruised," Sir Palomides replied.

"I am sorry, for I should like to have you by me," said Sir Tristram.

"Sir, you will have to ask someone else," Sir Palomides replied, but he was anxious only to deceive Sir Tristram.

"Sir Gareth, you perhaps will stay by me?"

"Sir Tristram, I shall not fail you," Sir Gareth replied.

Meanwhile, Sir Palomides had ridden into the melee and was fighting as strenuously as hitherto; Sir Tristram noticed him.

"Sir Palomides is avoiding my company," he said to himself as he stood watching him.

"Sir Tristram," said Sir Gareth, "do you recall Sir Dynadan's words yesterday when he called you a coward? He spoke thus only out of love for you, and because he is jealous for your reputation. Surely you are not going to stand aside and allow Sir Palomides to win all the honor today as well as yesterday? Although that, I know, is what he wants."

"Sir Gareth, you are right. I shall enter the fighting and see if I too cannot win some praise."

Sir Tristram entered into the thick of the fighting, and before long the knights of Orkney were falling fast before him. The spectators cheered and his praise was on everyone's lips.

"How now?" said Sir Launcelot to the king; "did I not warn you that the knight in green armor was formidable? And I will tell you, it is none other than Sir Tristram."

"That I can believe, for he is certainly more powerful even than Sir Palomides," the king replied.

Meanwhile, Sir Palomides was weeping for chagrin. King Arthur, accompanied by the King of North Galys, Sir Launcelot, Sir Ector, Sir Bleobris, and Sir Bors, now entered the field, and among them they forced the party of the King of Scotland to retreat. They were cheered by the spectators, and Sir Tristram and Sir Gareth alone stood their ground. Sir Launcelot was careful not to enter into combat with them.

"Is it Sir Palomides who has lasted for so long?" asked Arthur.

"Sire, it is Sir Tristram, and for myself I shall avoid encountering him. Sir Palomides is yonder; see how he stands, like one in a dream. You can be sure that he is full of envy because Sir Tristram has won all the honor."

"Then he is a fool to fight with him instead of against him —not that he would have a chance against Sir Tristram, who is by far the greater knight," said Arthur.

Sir Tristram had ridden back to his pavilion and found Sir Dynadan still asleep.

"Wake up!" shouted Sir Tristram, "you ought to be ashamed to sleep while your companions are fighting on the field."

"What would you have me do?" asked Sir Dynadan.

"Arm yourself and accompany me back to the tournament."

"It is well that I slept. I see by your armor that you have withstood many blows. Had I been with you, I would doubtless have taken as much punishment as I did yesterday."

"Stop joking and ride with me to the field," said Sir Tristram, as he changed into black armor.

"What are you doing? You must be mad, or has something aroused you at last? All of yesterday you behaved like one in a dream."

"Follow me, and if I am unhorsed come to my rescue."

They rode together to the field. Both Queen Iseult and Sir Palomides had watched Sir Tristram ride back to his pavilion, and now, for different reasons, both anxiously watched his return. Observing that Sir Tristram was disguised, Sir Palomides decided on a plan to get the better of him. He rode up to a knight who lay wounded beneath a thorn tree at some distance from the field, and begged him to exchange armor.

"Sir, I shall be honored to do so," the knight replied.

Sir Palomides clad himself in the knight's armor, which shone like crystal or silver, and returned to the field, where he was unrecognized by either King Arthur's party or his own.

Sir Tristram had just unhorsed three knights when Sir Palomides couched his spear and charged him. Sir Tristram received his charge and both broke their spears. Then, as they drew their swords, a tremendous battle started between them. Sir Tristram, who did not recognize Sir Palomides, was surprised by his strength, and angry because he feared that by the time they had finished he would not be fit for any further encounters. Queen Iseult had watched Sir Palomides exchange armor, was infuriated by his treachery, and wept for Sir Tristram. Then a knight rode up to Sir Launcelot:

"Sir, I pray you, challenge the knight in the black armor—he has all but defeated the knight in the silver armor."

Sir Launcelot galloped up and drove his horse between them.

"Sir, I pray you, allow me to encounter your opponent," he said to Sir Palomides, not recognizing either him or Sir Tristram.

Recognizing Sir Launcelot, Sir Palomides assented readily, hoping that Sir Tristram might be defeated at last. Sir Launcelot and Sir Tristram fought for a long time, and Queen Iseult wept for sorrow. Then Sir Dynadan saw them, and recognizing them both, said to Sir Gareth:

"We must go and rescue Sir Tristram; he is fighting Sir Launcelot and he has already done enough for one day."

First Sir Gareth attacked Sir Launcelot with his sword, and then Sir Dynadan charged him with his spear and sent both man and horse tumbling to the ground.

"For shame!" cried Sir Tristram. "Why attack so good a knight as my opponent when I can hold my ground well enough?"

Sir Palomides charged with his spear and unhorsed Sir Dynadan, and then attacked Sir Tristram while Sir Launcelot attacked Sir Dynadan with his sword. Sir Tristram, anxious to rescue Sir Dynadan, sent Sir Palomides reeling to the ground with a blow on the helmet, and then attacked Sir Launcelot, whereupon Sir Dynadan shouted aloud:

"My lord Sir Tristram, take your horse!"

"Ah Jesu!" said Sir Launcelot, "I did not recognize you in your black armor, Sir Tristram; otherwise nothing would have induced me to fight you. I pray you, forgive me."

"Sir Launcelot, once more I have to thank you for your courtesy," Sir Tristram replied.

The horn was blown to end the day's fighting. Those of King Arthur's party declared that Sir Launcelot had won the prize; those of King Carados' party declared that Sir Tristram had. Then Sir Launcelot insisted that Sir Tristram should take it, and this was agreed upon.

Sir Tristram, Sir Dynadan, and Sir Gareth accompanied Queen Iseult back to their pavilions. Sir Palomides, still in his silver armor, rode with them.

"Sir, none of us here is in need of your company; I pray you, leave us," said Sir Tristram.

"Sir, until such time as the knight I serve has discharged me, I shall remain in his company," Sir Palomides replied, and then Sir Tristram realized who it was.

"Sir Palomides, I had always supposed you to be a loyal knight; but now I understand how it was today that by disguising yourself and obtaining the assistance of Sir Launcelot you planned to kill me."

"Alas! are you then Sir Tristram?" asked Sir Palomides.

"I am, and well you know it!"

"How is it, then, that you bear the arms of the King of Ireland?"

"I won them from Sir Marhaus, a noble knight if ever there was one. He was still alive when he fled from me, but he died in the hands of a false physician."

"My lord, I supposed that you had joined King Arthur's party, and that was why I also changed parties."

"Very well, then, I forgive you," said Sir Tristram.

Once at the pavilions they disarmed, washed, and sat down to supper. Sir Tristram noticed that Queen Iseult was unusually pale and quiet, and would not so much as glance at Sir Palomides.

"My lady, what ails you?" he asked.

"My lord, I pray you, do not be angry with me, but how can I sit and sup equably with the treacherous coward who tried to kill you today? I mean Sir Palomides, of course. I saw everything that happened: how he watched you leave the field and return in black armor, how he exchanged armor with a wounded knight who lay beneath a thorn tree, and how then he treacherously attacked you. It was when Sir Launcelot came to his aid that I was seriously frightened, for I was sure that between them they would kill you; and it is quite clear that that is what Sir Palomides wished."

"Madam, I may not contradict you, and yet by my knighthood I swear that I did not recognize Sir Tristram," said Sir Palomides.

"Sir, I could wish that you had not attacked me so strenuously, but nevertheless I forgive you," said Sir Tristram.

Queen Iseult hung her head and was silent.

Then two knights, in full armor, strode into the pavilion.

"My lords," said Sir Tristram, "if you wish to encounter us, can you not wait until we are on the field, instead of disturbing us at our meal?"

"Not so, my lord," one of them replied, "for we come not to challenge you, but to pay our respects to Queen Iseult and to Sir Tristram."

"Then, I pray you, take off your helmets and be recognized."

"As you wish, my lord."

The two knights removed their helmets, and then Sir Dynadan said aside to Sir Tristram:

"My lord, do you realize that they are King Arthur and Sir Launcelot?"

"Madam," said Sir Tristram to Queen Iseult, "I pray you, arise, for here is our liege, King Arthur."

King Arthur kissed the queen, Sir Launcelot and Sir Tristram embraced, and then the queen asked the king and Sir Launcelot to disarm; and they all sat down merrily together.

"Madam," said King Arthur, "I have often heard of your great beauty, and now I can see for myself that it is not exaggerated. Sir Tristram is already well known to me as one of the greatest knights living, and therefore I rejoice that you should bear him company."

"Sire, you are very gracious," they both replied.

Then they all talked of the tournament.

"I wonder," said the king to Sir Tristram, "why you joined the opposing party."

"Sire, I was persuaded to do so by Sir Dynadan and Sir Gareth, your own nephew."

"Sire," said Sir Gareth, "my back is broad enough to take the blame, but surely it was Sir Tristram's own decision."

"Sire, I deeply repent that Sir Tristram ever brought me to this tournament, for I am sorely wounded as a result of it," said Sir Dynadan, and they all laughed.

"Pray tell me," said the king to Sir Tristram, "who was the knight who attacked you so spitefully?"

"My lord, he sits at this table."

"What, Sir Palomides?" asked the king.

"My lord, none other," said the queen.

"Indeed! And I had always supposed him to be an honorable knight."

"Sire, I did not know Sir Tristram; he was disguised," said Sir Palomides.

"That is true," said Sir Launcelot, "I did not recognize him myself."

"Why then did he change parties?"

"Perhaps he too did not wish to be recognized," said Sir Launcelot.

"My lords, I have forgiven Sir Palomides, and I should be sorry to lose his fellowship," said Sir Tristram.

Sometime later the king and Sir Launcelot left, and they all retired to bed. But Sir Palomides could not sleep; instead he wept and groaned the whole night through.

In the morning, however, Sir Tristram found him asleep, and said to Sir Dynadan and Sir Gareth:

"Treat Sir Palomides gently, for I see that he has been weeping, probably because of the rebukes he received from the queen and me."

It was time to go to the tournament, so they awoke Sir Palomides. When they had all clad themselves in red armor, they accompanied Queen Iseult to the castle and then rode onto the field. The horn was blown three times to announce the commencement of fighting.

Sir Palomides jousted with two knights of King Arthur's

party—Sir Kaynes and another—and overthrew them both. Having broken his spear on the second knight, Sir Palomides drew his sword and attacked more of his opponents with such vigor that the spectators applauded.

"Sir Palomides is certainly a strong knight," said King Arthur.

Just then Sir Tristram galloped onto the field, and with one spear unhorsed four knights of King Arthur's party, the first of whom was Sir Kay the Seneschal. He then drew his sword and won even greater applause than Sir Palomides, who was henceforth ignored.

"How now?" said Sir Launcelot to King Arthur. "There surely is a knight who knows how to play his part."

"It seems that they will both distinguish themselves today," the king replied.

"Sir Palomides is ever jealous of Sir Tristram, and tries to outdo him; and yet Sir Tristram is so innocent of heart that he does not realize it," said Sir Launcelot.

Sir Dynadan and Sir Gareth galloped onto the field next (they both were to do well that day), and then King Arthur and Sir Launcelot. Sir Tristram unwittingly overthrew King Arthur and Sir Launcelot tried to remount him, but was prevented from doing so by Kings Carados and Marhault, who attacked him in force, determined that both should be taken prisoner. Sir Launcelot fought back furiously, and his opponents grew wary of him.

Sir Ector attacked Sir Palomides—first with his spear, which broke, and then with his sword, and sent him crashing to the ground. He then offered Sir Palomides' horse to Sir Launcelot, but Sir Palomides leaped up and was in the saddle in a moment.

"Why, then, take the horse, for surely you deserve it," said Sir Launcelot.

Sir Ector brought Sir Launcelot another horse.

"May God reward you!" said Sir Launcelot.

When Sir Launcelot had remounted he overthrew four knights with his first spear, and then helped King Arthur to remount. A fierce engagement followed, in which it is said Sir Launcelot overthrew thirty knights altogether. But King Arthur's knights were greatly outnumbered and, notwithstanding their valor, were hard pressed. Sir Tristram saw this and summoned Sir Palomides, Sir Gareth, and Sir Dynadan.

"My lords, see how valiantly King Arthur and his knights are fighting! But he is hard pressed and he is our liege, therefore I say that we should go over to his side and help him."

"We shall do so," said Sir Gareth and Sir Dynadan.

"As you will," said Sir Palomides; "but for myself, I shall remain with the party I joined in the first place."

"That is out of envy of me, so God help you!" said Sir Tristram.

They parted. Sir Tristram and his companions joined King Arthur, and together they drove the opposing party from the field, Sir Launcelot overthrowing King Carados and the King of West Britain, King Arthur overthrowing Sir Palomides, and the remainder all doing their part.

"Alas!" said Sir Palomides, "now my reputation is lost."

With those words he rode from the field and through the forest until he came to a well, where he dismounted, disarmed, and started weeping and raving like a madman.

Once more there was indecision as to whether Sir Launcelot or Sir Tristram had won the prize. Each insisted that the other had, but in the end they agreed to share it. Sir Ector and Sir Bleobris accompanied Sir Tristram and Queen Iseult back to their pavilions.

Sir Palomides was still raving by the well when the Kings of Scotland and West Britain rode by.

"Alas, that so noble a knight should be so distraught!" said one of them.

Together they helped Sir Palomides to rearm and remount, and then rode with him to Sir Tristram's pavilion, where Sir Palomides begged them to await him.

"Sir Tristram, are you there?" he shouted.

"My lord, it is Sir Palomides," said Sir Dynadan.

"Sir Palomides, will you not enter?" asked Sir Tristram.

"I defy you, traitor!" said Sir Palomides, "and were it still daylight I should kill you with my own hands for what you did to me today. As it is, take heed, for when the time comes I shall not spare you."

"Sir Palomides, had you remained with us today, you would have won further honor, instead of shame. However, I thank you for your warning, and certainly I shall be wary of you in the future."

"Recreant!" shouted Sir Palomides, and departed.

In the morning Sir Tristram, Sir Ector, Sir Bleobris, Sir Dynadan, and Sir Gareth accompanied Queen Iseult over sea and land to the Joyous Gard, where they all made merry for a week. King Arthur returned to Camelot.

Sir Palomides rode with the two kings, complaining all the

while, for he was brokenhearted by having to part not only from Queen Iseult, but also from Sir Tristram, whom he loved in spite of his jealousy of him.

At the end of the week Sir Ector and Sir Bleobris took their leave of Sir Tristram, Queen Iseult, Sir Dynadan, and Sir Gareth and, loaded with gifts, rode to Queen Gwynevere, who was convalescing in a castle by the sea. She asked them whence they had come and they told her.

"How are Sir Tristram and Queen Iseult?" she asked.

"Truly, madam, as Sir Tristram is matchless for his courage and courtesy, so is Queen Iseult for her beauty and high spirits."

"For the love of Jesu! I have heard so much of Queen Iseult that had I myself but a small part of her qualities I should count myself blessed. Alas! that I was sick during the tournament, for never again, I suppose, will there be an opportunity for witnessing such an array of famous knights and ladies."

Sir Ector and Sir Bleobris then described the tournament, and how on the first day the prize had been won by Sir Palomides, on the second by Sir Tristram, and on the third by Sir Launcelot.

"Pray tell me, who of the three did best?" asked the queen.

"Madam, Sir Launcelot and Sir Tristram. Sir Palomides is a great knight, but he is always jealous of Sir Tristram, and toward the end of the tournament he lost the honor he had won by fighting against him."

"Then Sir Palomides will never win true renown," said the queen, "because for every honor that an envious man wins, he will be twice dishonored. And whereas an honorable knight is loved by all, an envious knight will be forever shunned."

13. SIR PALOMIDES

Sir Palomides slept in company with the Kings of Ireland and Scotland, but in the morning took his leave of them. The King of Scotland gave him many precious gifts; the King of Ireland gave him a fine courser and commanded one of his men to serve him. Both kings begged Sir Palomides to remain with them, but Sir Palomides refused them and departed.

He rode at random through the forest until noon, when he came upon a handsome knight who lay wounded by a well and was weeping.

"Good knight, I pray you, tell me the cause of your grief, and then I will tell you the cause of mine, and I am sure you will agree that mine is a hundredfold worse than yours."

"Sir, I pray you, tell me your name first; for should you be of the fellowship of the Round Table, you shall never know my name, come what may!"

"Sir, I am called Sir Palomides. My father is King Asclabor, and my brothers Sir Safere and Sir Segwarydes. We were born Saracens, but each of my brothers, though not I, is now christened."

"Sir Palomides, you are welcome. I am called Sir Epynogres, Prince of Northumberland. Now let us sit down and hear each other's complaints."

Sir Palomides dismounted, tethered his horse, sat down, and began.

"My lord, my misfortune is to love the most beautiful woman on earth: Queen Iseult, wife to King Mark of Cornwall."

"Sir, that is folly indeed, for is not Sir Tristram her paramour and Sir Tristram the greatest knight living?"

"No man knows that better than I do! I have spent this last month in their company, but now, alas! I have lost forever the chance of Queen Iseult's love, and Sir Tristram and I have become mortal enemies."

"Pray tell me, has Queen Iseult ever given any sign that she returns your love? Have you ever companied with her?"

"Alas no! She loves me no better than the world does. Lately she gave me the most terrible rebuke. I deserved it, but it has left me brokenhearted; and for the same cause I have lost the confidence of Sir Tristram. Yet it was in their company, and for the love of the queen, that I accomplished feats at arms greater than ever before; and this serves to increase my grief at losing them."

"My lord, your sorrow is but little compared to mine. I won a lady, we loved one another, and then I lost her. Her father was an earl; I met him returning from the tournament at Lonezep, accompanied by two knights. For the love of his daughter I challenged and killed him, together with one of his companions; the other fled from me.

"That night I companied in love with his daughter, here by

this well. But in the morning a hardy knight called Sir Hellyor le Prewse rode up and challenged me to fight for her. We fought first on horseback and then on foot, with the result that I was wounded and left for dead, and he rode off with my lady. Now you will understand that my grief is far greater than yours."

"Sir, you speak the truth; and since there is no cure for my grief, I promise I will try to win your lady for you or else die in the attempt."

Sir Palomides set Sir Epynogres on his horse and led him to a monastery where he could recover from his wounds. Then he walked into the grounds and lay in the shade of a tree. Soon a knight bearing Sir Ector's shield rode up, at the head of ten more knights who appeared to be in his service, and they too rested in the shade. A little later Sir Hellyor appeared; he was bearing a green shield embossed with a white lion, and leading a lady on a palfrey. The knight with Sir Ector's shield galloped up to him and challenged him to fight for the lady.

"Sir, upon my life I will defend her!" Sir Hellyor replied.

They fought furiously for an hour or so, and then Sir Hellyor surrendered. Sir Palomides walked up to the lady and asked her if Sir Epynogres was not her paramour.

"Alas that we ever met!" she replied. "For his sake I have lost my honor, for mine he has lost his life."

"Not so, my lady: Sir Epynogres still lives. He is in the monastery, so let me lead you to him."

"I rejoice! He is still living?" she said.

At that moment the knight who had defeated Sir Hellyor rode up to them.

"Sir, what will you do with my lady?" he demanded.

"Sir, I shall do as I please with her," Sir Palomides replied.

"Sir, you have me at a disadvantage, for I have only just finished one battle; but for all your boasts, unless you happen to be Sir Launcelot, Sir Tristram, or else Sir Palomides, I shall make you pay dearly for her."

They fought on foot for an hour. Sir Palomides was astonished by his opponent's strength and good wind. Finally he paused for a moment.

"Sir, I pray you, tell me your name," he asked.

"Sir, only if you will do likewise."

"I shall."

"I am called Sir Safere. My father is King Asclabor; Sir Segwarydes and Sir Palomides are my brothers."

"And I am Sir Palomides!"

The brothers threw off their helmets and knelt down and

kissed. Sir Epynogres, meanwhile, hearing the clash of swords, had walked from the monastery to see if Sir Palomides was in need of assistance. When Sir Palomides saw him he took the lady by the hand and led her to him. Then Sir Epynogres and the lady kissed and wept for joy.

"My good lord and fair lady," said Sir Safere, "I see now that it is a shame that you were ever parted. May Jesu give you His blessing!"

"May God reward you, gentle knight!" Sir Epynogres replied, "and you, too, Sir Palomides, for rescuing my paramour."

Sir Epynogres asked Sir Palomides and Sir Safere if they would accompany him to his castle.

"My lord, you are badly wounded; certainly we will do so," Sir Palomides replied.

They all rode to Sir Epynogres' castle, and spent the evening merrily together.

Sir Palomides and Sir Safere left in the morning and rode at random until after noon, when they came to a castle from within which they could hear loud cries of lamentation. They rode up to the gate, where an old man was saying his prayers and counting his beads; then one of the knights in the courtyard saw them and recognized Sir Palomides.

"My lords!" he cried, "here is the very knight who killed our liege at the tournament of Lonezep."

His companions all ran for their armor, and before long Sir Palomides and his brother were surrounded by sixty knights.

"Sir Palomides, we know you well, for it was you who killed our liege at Lonezep; therefore we have no choice but to avenge him."

Sir Palomides and his brother stood back to back and managed to hold off their assailants for two hours, but finally they had to yield and allow themselves to be imprisoned in one of the castle dungeons.

Within the next three days they were tried by twelve knights. Sir Palomides was found guilty and Sir Safere not guilty. Sadly, the brothers took leave of each other.

"My dear brother," said Sir Palomides, "do not weep for me. If it is my fate to die a shameful death after all, so be it, and we must resign ourselves."

Sir Safere departed. The next morning Sir Palomides was bound hand and foot, trussed beneath the belly of an old nag, and, with twelve knights for an escort, led toward the Castle Pellowness for execution. On the way they passed the Joyous

Gard where one of the retainers, recognizing him, asked what was happening.

"My good friend," Sir Palomides replied, "I am to be executed for killing a knight at Lonezep. Alas that ever I parted company with Sir Tristram, for he would have rescued me. However, commend me to him, and to Queen Iseult, and beg them to forgive me if I have trespassed. Also, I pray you, commend me to King Arthur and his fellows of the Round Table."

The knight wept as he heard Sir Palomides' words, and as soon as he had finished, galloped to the castle and told Sir Tristram what had happened.

"Although I have good cause to be angry with Sir Palomides, I shall not allow so great a knight as he is to be shamefully executed," said Sir Tristram, and summoning two squires, armed and set off to rescue him.

Meanwhile, Sir Palomides and his escort had come to a well, where they found Sir Launcelot drinking from his helmet, having tethered his horse to a tree. Sir Launcelot allowed them to pass, and only then noticed that the prisoner was Sir Palomides.

"For the love of Jesu! what has happened? I must go to his rescue," he said to himself, and, arming hastily, rode after them.

"My lords, what is your purpose concerning your prisoner?" he asked.

"Sir, we advise you not to meddle with us. We are leading our prisoner to the death that he deserves," one of them replied.

"Very well, my lords: I shall rescue him; so defend yourselves!" said Sir Launcelot.

Sir Launcelot sent the first four knights crashing to the ground with his spear; the remainder he wounded or killed with his sword. Then, releasing Sir Palomides from his bonds, he set him on the best of the knights' horses and they rode together toward the Joyous Gard. On the way they met Sir Tristram, who, not recognizing Sir Launcelot because of the green shield he bore, challenged him to joust. Sir Launcelot recognized Sir Tristram, however, and then Sir Palomides shouted:

"My lord Sir Tristram, I pray you do not joust with this knight; he has just fought twelve knights and rescued me."

Sir Tristram took his spear out of rest and trotted up to them.

"My lord," said Sir Palomides, "I am deeply grateful to you for venturing to my rescue when I caused you such great offense; but now it has been accomplished by my companion here."

"Good knight, whence do you come?" asked Sir Tristram.

"Sir, I am a knight errant."

"I pray you, tell me your name."

"Sir, I beg to be excused; and now that you two have found each other I shall ride on my way."

"For the love of Jesu! I pray you, sir, accompany us to my castle, and stay overnight," said Sir Tristram.

Sir Launcelot acquiesced. They rode together to the castle, where they stabled their horses and disarmed. Sir Tristram and Queen Iseult embraced Sir Launcelot joyfully when they recognized him, and Sir Palomides knelt down to thank him. Sir Launcelot lifted him to his feet again.

"Sir Palomides," he said, "I am certainly not the only one who would rescue so noble a knight as yourself; for have you not won renown throughout the realm?"

Sir Launcelot remained at the castle for four days, during which time there was much merrymaking, and then departed with Sir Ector and Sir Dynadan. Sir Palomides remained for two months, but his love for Queen Iseult was as fierce as ever. He grew thin and began to pine.

One day he wandered alone into the forest, and coming to a well, looked at his reflection in the water.

"For the love of Jesu!" he said to himself, "what does this mean? I look like a wraith, I who was always said to be one of the handsomest of knights. And why should I go on living, famished for love as I am?"

Thereupon he lay down by the well and started composing a ballad about himself, Sir Tristram, and Queen Iseult, which he sang in a loud, clear voice.

It happened that Sir Tristram was also in the forest, chasing a hart; and passing near to the well, he heard Sir Palomides' singing. He stopped to listen and grew furious. Resisting the urge to kill him on the spot, he trotted up to him.

"Sir Palomides, I have heard your ballad and now I understand the treason that is in your heart. Were you armed I should kill you."

"Sir Tristram, it is true that since I first set eyes on Queen Iseult I have loved her; and probably, like Sir Keyhydyns, I shall in the end die of that love. Also it is true that my love for the queen has inspired those feats at arms for which I have become famous; were it not for her I should have remained the most modest of knights. But it is also true that my love for her has never been returned, and therefore it is nothing to me now whether I live or die, and were I armed I would gladly fight you to the death."

"Sir Palomides, your treason is truly spoken."

"Sir Tristram, are not all men and all women free to love whom they will? You cannot deny a person the right to love, and therefore I say that I am innocent of treason. Furthermore, whereas you have for long rejoiced in your love for the queen, my own has passed unrewarded, and ever shall."

"We will fight to the death!" said Sir Tristram.

"My lord, I could not wish to die in a better cause, or at the hands of a nobler knight."

"Sir Palomides, when shall it be?"

"In fifteen days from now, in the meadow that lies beneath the Joyous Gard."

"For shame! Cannot we fight tomorrow?"

"No, my lord. Lately I have languished, and I need time to recover my strength."

"Very well, then. But I seem to recall that we had such an assignation before, when I had rescued you from Sir Breuse Sans Pité, and that you failed to honor it."

"My lord, on that day I was held prisoner. But this time we shall surely meet."

"So God help me! we had better," said Sir Tristram, and departed.

Sir Palomides armed himself and rode to King Arthur's court, where he obtained the services of four knights and four sergeants-at-arms, and then returned to the Joyous Gard. On the fifteenth day he rode to the place appointed for the assignation, taking with him the four sergeants and four knights as witnesses. He then sent word to Sir Tristram that he was ready for him.

The squire found Sir Tristram in bed. He had been wounded three days previously while hunting, by an archer who had accidentally shot him through the thigh, and with the same arrow killed his horse. For the three days Sir Tristram had been inconsolable, and had suspected Sir Palomides of treachery.

"My lord, Sir Palomides awaits you on the field," said the squire.

"Tell your master that not for all the gold in King Arthur's castle would I avoid fighting him were I able. But alas! I am not. Three days ago I received this wound in my thigh, which, you can see for yourself, is six inches deep. Were I whole I should already be in the field. As it is, tell Sir Palomides that as soon as I have recovered I shall search for him throughout the realm and battle with him to the death, as agreed in our assignation."

The squire returned to Sir Palomides and delivered Sir Tristram's message.

"Truly I am glad," he said, "for I should not have come out well from this battle. Sir Tristram is the hardiest knight living, with the exception only of Sir Launcelot."

Sir Palomides rode away in search of adventure; and a month later Sir Tristram set off in pursuit of him, but throughout the summer failed to find him. However, Sir Tristram met with so many adventures, and acquitted himself so well, that his fame began to surpass even that of Sir Launcelot, whose kinsmen grew jealous. They decided among themselves to waylay him if they could; but then news of their plots reached Sir Launcelot, and he summoned them.

"My lords, it has come to my ears that you are plotting to get rid of Sir Tristram. I wish you to understand that I regard him as the noblest knight òn earth, and anyone who wishes him harm as my personal enemy, whom I would not hesitate to destroy on Sir Tristram's behalf, even if he were of my own kin."

The fame of Sir Tristram's exploits reached Cornwall and Lyoness, and his relatives there sent him letters and treasure to help in the maintenance of his estates. And Sir Tristram, whenever he found an opportunity, returned to Iseult at the Joyous Gard, for the love between them never ceased.

14. LAUNCELOT AND ELAINE

It is said that on the Whitsun before Sir Galahad was born, a hermit appeared at King Arthur's court just as Arthur and his knights had sat down at the Round Table for their annual feast, and asked why the Siege Perelous was empty. King Arthur replied:

"It is death for any but the appointed knight to sit at the Siege Perelous."

"Who is the appointed knight to be?" the hermit asked.

"As yet we do not know."

"Then I shall tell you. The appointed knight is to be conceived and born this year. He shall sit in the Siege Perelous, and he shall win the Holy Grail." And with these words the hermit departed.

When the feast was over Sir Launcelot rode away from the court in search of adventure, and came eventually to the castle of Pointe Corbyn, which was distinguished by a fine tower, and below which lay a small but picturesque town. The inhabitants welcomed him.

"Welcome Sir Launcelot, flower of the knighthood! You have come, and you will rescue us."

"Pray, what is the meaning of this?" asked Sir Launcelot.

"Sir, for five years now an unhappy lady has been imprisoned in the tower, in a chamber where she is perpetually scalded by boiling water. Sir Gawain was here lately, but it was not in his power to rescue her."

"It may not be in my power to rescue her."

"Sir Launcelot, we know that it is."

"Then lead me to her."

Sir Launcelot was led to a chamber whence the steam issued forth fiercely the moment the iron door was unlocked. Within was a young noblewoman, of great beauty and quite naked. It was her beauty which has caused her present distress, for it had aroused the jealousy of Queen Morgan le Fay and the Queen of North Galys. Five years previously they had imprisoned her thus by means of an enchantment which was to endure until the greatest knight on earth should come to her rescue. Sir Launcelot took the lady by the hand and led her out of the chamber. Clothes were brought for her, and when she was fully appareled Sir Launcelot thought that she was the most beautiful lady he had ever beheld. Then she spoke to him:

"Sir, I pray you, will you accompany me to the chapel, where we may worship?"

"My lady, lead on and I shall follow you."

After their thanksgiving Sir Launcelot and the young noblewoman found themselves surrounded by people of all estates:

"Sir, now that you have delivered the lady, you must deliver us from the serpent in the tomb."

"For the love of God, and for the love of yourselves, I shall accomplish what I can."

Sir Launcelot took up his shield and was led to the tomb, which had been inscribed with gold letters:

HERE SHALL COM A LEOPARD OF KING'S BLOOD AND HE SHALL SLE THIS SERPENTE. AND THIS LEOPARD SHALL ENGENDER A

LYON IN THIS FORAYNE COUNTREY WHYCH LYON SHALL PASSE
ALL OTHER KNYGHTES.

The tomb was opened and a horrifying serpent, breathing
fire from its mouth, slithered out. After a long and painful
fight Sir Launcelot killed it. Then a knight rode up to him.

"Sir, I pray you, tell me your name," he said.

"Sir Launcelot du Lake."

"Sir, I am King Pelles, a descendant of Joseph of Arimathea,
and ruler of this country."

The king embraced Sir Launcelot warmly, and then led him
to his castle to dine. When they were all seated in the hall, a
small dove appeared at the window. In its beak was a gold
censer from which came a most fragrant and concentrated odor
of spices, and suddenly the table was laden with every con-
ceivable variety of meat and wine. Then a young noblewoman,
bearing a gold vessel in her hands, appeared, and the king knelt
down before her and prayed.

"In the name of the Lord! what does this mean?" asked Sir
Launcelot.

"Sir, this is the richest gift on earth—the Holy Grail; and
when it passes through King Arthur's court the fellowship of
the Round Table will be dispersed for a season, while his
knights go in search of it."

Sir Launcelot remained with the king, who was all the time
secretly preoccupied with finding a means to persuade Sir
Launcelot to get his daughter Elaine with child. It had been
prophesied that the son she would bear him, Sir Galahad, would
be the purest knight of all time and win the Holy Grail. Then
the famous enchantress, Lady Brusen, came to the king and
advised him.

"My lord, you must understand that Sir Launcelot loves
only Queen Gwynevere. Therefore, I pray you, on pain of my
life, allow me to arrange matters for you. I ask you to send
Elaine, accompanied by twenty-five knights to the castle of
Case."

The king did as he was asked and Lady Brusen cast her
spells. Sometime later a friend of Sir Launcelot's appeared
before him, bearing a ring which Sir Launcelot recognized
as belonging to Queen Gwynevere.

"I pray you, tell me, where is the queen?" asked Sir Launcelot.

"Sir, she awaits you at the castle of Case, which lies not
five miles from here."

Sir Launcelot rode to the castle and was received by various

persons whom he recognized as belonging to Queen Gwynevere's suite. He asked for the queen and was led to one of the
castle chambers, where he found her lying in bed. Lady Brusen
entered the chamber, gave him a goblet of wine, and then
disappeared. Sir Launcelot drank the wine, and then his desire
for the queen grew irresistible. He threw off his clothes and
made love to her until dawn.

Elaine was delighted (for she it was) and knew that Sir
Galahad had been conceived. At dawn Sir Launcelot rose from
the bed and opened one of the windows, all of which had been
closed, and as the light of day entered the chamber, so his
enchantment ceased. He looked at Elaine, who still lay on the
bed.

"Alas!" he said to himself, "what have I done now? It
seems that I have already lived too long!"

Then he drew his sword from its sheath.

"Traitress!" he shouted.

Elaine rose naked from the bed and knelt before him.

"Sir, as you are of royal blood, I pray you have mercy
upon me! Also upon your own child who is now nourished in
my womb, and who, it is prophesied, will become a knight
without peer in any country or age."

"Tell me, who are you?"

"Princess Elaine, daughter of King Pelles."

"My lady, I forgive you."

Sir Launcelot took her in his arms and kissed her. Elaine
was not only of royal blood, but young, beautiful, and clever.

"But I shall revenge myself on the enchantress Lady Brusen
when I find her," said Sir Launcelot; "for surely a knight was
never so subtly deceived!"

"My lord, I beseech you, bear me no ill will, but come to
see me when you may. In compliance with my father's command I have fulfilled the prophecy by which I was enjoined to
bear your child, and in so doing I have surely yielded to you
the greatest gift which it is in the power of a young noblewoman to bestow, namely, my maidenhead. Therefore, I
pray you once more, do not hold me in contempt."

Sir Launcelot armed, gently took his leave of Elaine, and
then returned to the castle of Corbyn. In due course the child
was delivered, christened Galahad, and thereafter carefully
nurtured. Sir Launcelot himself had been christened Galahad
before the Lady of the Lake renamed him.

Not long after Galahad was born, Sir Bromell, a lord of the
land, begged Elaine to marry him.

"My lord," Elaine replied, "my heart already belongs to another, to the greatest knight living."

"My lady, who may he be?"

"Sir Launcelot."

"Then I shall kill him."

"My lord, you may try, but not treacherously."

"My lady, I shall keep this castle for a year and a day, and hope to encounter him."

One day Sir Launcelot's nephew, Sir Bors, rode up to the castle. Sir Bromell challenged him, they fought, and Sir Bromell surrendered.

"Sir, I shall spare your life only if you yield to Sir Launcelot next Whitsun," said Sir Bors.

"My lord, I swear to do so," Sir Bromell replied.

Sir Bors rode into the castle, where he was received by King Pelles and Elaine, and welcomed warmly when they heard that he was Sir Launcelot's nephew.

"Sir Bors, we wonder that Sir Launcelot has never returned to our castle. He was here only once," said Elaine.

"My lady, for the last six months he has been held prisoner by Queen Morgan le Fay."

"Alas!" said Elaine.

Sir Bors could not take his eyes off the child Elaine held in her arms, his likeness to Sir Launcelot was so striking. Elaine noticed this.

"Sir, I pray you, understand that this is Sir Launcelot's son," she said.

Sir Bors wept for joy and prayed that the son might prove as great a knight as the father. Thereupon a white dove flew in through the window, carrying in its beak a gold censer which smelt fragrantly of spices. Miraculously, meat and wine appeared on the table. Then a maiden bearing the Holy Grail entered.

"Sir Bors," she said, "understand that this child is Galahad, who shall sit at the Siege Perelous, and win the Holy Grail. He shall not only equal his father Sir Launcelot, he shall surpass him."

The whole company knelt down and prayed. Then the dove and the maiden vanished. Sir Bors addressed the king:

"Sire, in respect of the wonderful happenings here I should rename your castle the Castle of Adventure."

"Sir Bors, you speak wisely. Furthermore, I believe that only a knight of exceptional courage and piety could ever hope to win honor here. Lately Sir Gawain was here, and he achieved nothing."

"Sire, will you grant me leave to sleep in your castle to-night?"

"Sir, you may do so, but at your own peril. I advise you to go to confession first."

Sir Bors shrove to the priest; his life had been chaste but for one incident, when he had begotten his illegitimate son, Helyn le Blanke, on the daughter of King Brandegoris.

Sir Bors was now led to a chamber with many doors. He looked through each of them, and then asked to be left alone. Without disarming, he lay on the bed and waited. First a light appeared, and at the same time an illuminated spear which wounded him in the shoulder and then disappeared. Next a knight came through one of the doors and challenged him.

"Sir, I am already painfully wounded, but I shall not fail you," Sir Bors replied.

They fought fiercely for a long time; then the knight withdrew to another chamber, rested himself, and returned. They fought again; this time Sir Bors maneuvered his opponent away from the door and forced him to yield.

"Sir, what is your name?" he demanded.

"Sir Bedyvere of the Streyte Marchis."

"You must yield to King Arthur next Whitsun, and say that Sir Bors de Ganys sent you."

Sir Bedyvere departed and Sir Bors lay down to rest. Before long, arrows started flying through the windows and doors, and wounding him in exposed places. Then a monstrous lion appeared and Sir Bors beheaded it.

Next an ugly dragon, and an old, fierce leopard entered the chamber and fought each other. Sir Bors thought that he could discern the words "King Arthur" inscribed in gold letters on the dragon's head. Finally the dragon spewed up a whole brood of young who turned on the parent and devoured him.

When this had happened an old man with two adders round his neck came in, sat down, and sang a ballad about the coming to Britain of Joseph of Arimathea. Then he addressed Sir Bors:

"Sir, you shall meet with no further adventure at this castle, and you must go now. You have done well, and in time to come you shall do better."

The old man left him and the white dove reappeared, still carrying in its beak the gold censer with its fragrant odor of spices. Then a sage entered, accompanied by four children. In one hand he carried a gold censer, in the other the Spear of Vengeance.

"Sir Bors, go now to your cousin Sir Launcelot and tell him all that has happened to you. Tell him also that, although in body he is the greatest knight on earth, because of his defilement many knights shall surpass him spiritually."

Sir Bors was about to leave when four poorly robed gentlewomen passed through his chamber and into the next, which was now brilliantly illumined, and in which stood an altar supported by four silver columns. The four gentlewomen knelt before the altar next to a man whom Sir Bors supposed to be a bishop. Above the bishop's head a silver sword was suspended, of such brightness that Sir Bors was dazzled. Then he heard a voice:

"Go now, Sir Bors, you are not yet worthy of this precinct."

Sir Bors retired to bed for the remainder of the night. In the morning, after describing the miracles he had witnessed to King Pelles, who rejoiced in them, he set off for Camelot to tell Sir Launcelot.

News of the birth of Galahad had reached King Arthur's court, and Queen Gwynevere had been furiously jealous of Elaine, and terribly angry with Sir Launcelot. However, when he described to her his enchantment, she forgave him. King Arthur, meanwhile, had been in France and won from King Claudas the greater part of his kingdom. On his return he invited all his subject and allied kings and princes to a feast to celebrate his victory. When Elaine came to hear of the feast she begged her father for permission to attend.

"My child, it pleases me well that you should go to the feast. But I wish you to be splendidly arrayed, as befits your rank. Therefore, I pray you, spare no expense; you have only to ask, and whatever you need you shall have."

When the time came Elaine arrived at King Arthur's court in due splendor with a suite of a hundred, which included Lady Brusen, ten ladies-in-waiting, and twenty knights. She was greeted by King Arthur, Sir Tristram, Sir Bleobris, and many others of the court, and admired by them all. Sir Launcelot alone would neither greet nor speak to her, for he was ashamed of what had passed between them. Elaine was brokenhearted and consulted Lady Brusen.

"How can I endure Sir Launcelot's coldness?" she asked.

"Peace, my lady! Tonight, I promise you, you shall sleep in his arms."

"Ah! that is what I want more than all the riches on earth."

"Then leave it to me, my lady."

Meanwhile, all at the court were speaking of Elaine's beauty, and Queen Gwynevere decided to receive her. Outwardly the two ladies made much of each other, but in their hearts both were distrustful. King Arthur commanded that the chamber next to the queen's should be prepared for Elaine. Then the queen summoned Sir Launcelot.

"My lord, I require that you shall come to my chamber tonight when I send for you. Otherwise you will spend the night with Elaine, your newfound paramour."

"Madam, you know that I was under an enchantment when I begot Galahad, and that I supposed that it was you who lay in my arms."

The arrangement between Sir Launcelot and the queen was discovered at once by Lady Brusen by means of her magical powers; she told Elaine.

"Alas! what shall we do now?" asked Elaine.

"My lady, leave it to me. Sir Launcelot shall suppose that I am the messenger and that you are the queen."

When all in the castle had gone to bed, Lady Brusen disguised herself and appeared before Sir Launcelot.

"My lord, are you awake? The queen requires that you shall go to her chamber."

Sir Launcelot, wearing only his nightshirt, picked up his sword and followed Lady Brusen to Elaine's chamber, where, supposing her to be the queen, he got into bed with her and did as lovers do.

While Sir Launcelot and Elaine lay happily in each other's arms, Queen Gwynevere lay tossing and sleepless. Her most trusted maid, whom she had sent to fetch Sir Launcelot, had reported that his chamber was empty.

"False knight! What has become of him?" the queen had asked.

Exhausted by the labors of love, Sir Launcelot at last fell asleep, and in his sleep started crying for the queen. She heard him from her chamber, and being familiar with his habit of talking in his sleep, coughed loudly. He awoke, recognized the cough, and realized what had happened. Leaping out of the bed, he ran into the corridor, where he found the queen awaiting him.

"Traitor! So easily have you deserted me?" said the queen.

Sir Launcelot fell to the ground in a faint and the queen left him. When he came to, still mad with grief, he ran to a bay window and jumped out. He was still wearing only his nightshirt; he landed in some thorn bushes which tore his hands and face as he struggled through them, and finally ran from the castle, where none was to hear of him for the next two years.

Meanwhile Elaine had gone to the queen:

"Madam, what have you done? Do you understand that our lord Sir Launcelot is now lost to us both forever? By his cries, and by the look I saw on his face when he ran to you, I know that he has lost his reason. And you are responsible for this; you should never have rebuked him. Surely, for yourself you have an incomparable king, such as is vouchsafed to no other woman on earth, and yet you covet my lord Sir Launcelot, and in so doing bring dishonor on yourself, on King Arthur, and on him. For myself, I love Sir Launcelot truly, to him I yielded my maidenhead, and now I nurse his child Galahad, who is destined to become the greatest knight of all time."

"Princess Elaine, you shall leave this court in the morning, and only at your peril shall you ever again seek Sir Launcelot."

Elaine left in the morning, accompanied by Sir Bors and King Arthur with a hundred of his knights. She confided to Sir Bors all that had happened during the night.

"What will become of Sir Launcelot now?" he asked.

"Alas! I do not know."

"It is certain that between you you have destroyed a great knight."

"Surely it is the fault of the queen, who covets him for herself, and who drove him out of his reason by her rebuke. I saw the madness come over him when he ran to her. For myself, I have tried only to please him."

"My lady, you must divert the king for as long as possible, and I will ride in search of Sir Launcelot."

"Sir, I will do what I can, for I would rather die than that he should suffer."

"My lady," said Lady Brusen, "you must let Sir Bors go now; but I warn you that Sir Launcelot is mad, and that nothing less than a miracle can save him."

Sir Bors first rode back to the court, where he found Queen Gwynevere with Sir Ector and Sir Lyonel. The queen wept when she saw him.

"Madam, it is too late for weeping now; Sir Launcelot is lost beyond recovery. And I ask you, what shall we do? we who are of his kin and who have honored him above all men on earth for his courage and courtesy, and who have always depended on him for succor."

"Alas!" said both Sir Ector and Sir Lyonel.

The queen fainted. When Sir Bors had revived her she knelt

before the three knights and begged them to search for Sir Launcelot and spare no pains nor expense in his recovery.

Sir Bors, Sir Ector, and Sir Lyonel left the castle, the queen gave them treasure, and for three months they rode from country to country, through forest and wilderness and waste land, but without discovering any trace of him. One day they met Sir Mellyon de Tartare with whom Sir Bors was already acquainted.

"My friend, where are you riding?" he asked.

"To Camelot."

"Then, I pray you, tell King Arthur that so far we have failed to find Sir Launcelot."

Sir Mellyon rode to Camelot and delivered Sir Bors' message. Twenty-three knights, including Sir Gawain, Sir Uwayne, Sir Sagramour, Sir Agglovale, and Sir Percivale volunteered to search the realm for him. The king gave them treasure, and the queen her blessing.

All this time Sir Launcelot himself wandered alone and mad, naked but for his nightshirt, and with no knowledge of where he was going.

Once they had arranged a suitable rendezvous, the knights rode off in pairs. Sir Percivale and Sir Agglovale rode first to their mother. The queen was alone in her castle, and wept when she saw them.

"Welcome, my dear sons! Of the four sons left to me when King Pellinore was killed by Sir Gawain, only you two are still alive. And not once since the noble Sir Lamerok was treacherously killed by Sir Gaheris have I been glad of heart. I pray you, therefore, stay with me at the castle."

"Madam, we may not. As we are of royal blood on both sides, so must we fulfill our obligation to win honor for our name."

"Alas! must I then languish here, to be blown away by the wind, or to melt in the rain? Surely my bereavement deserves some consideration!"

The queen sobbed with dismay throughout their visit, and when the time came for them to depart, fainted in the court. However, when she came to, she sent a squire after them to give them her blessing.

The squire set off, and at nightfall begged for lodging at a castle. He was received by the lord, Sir Goodwyne, who asked whence he came and whom he served.

"My lord, I serve Sir Agglovale and his mother, the queen."

"Then because of Sir Agglovale you shall be killed, for he it was who killed my brother."

The squire was dragged into the court and killed, and the next morning taken to the chapel for burial. Sir Percivale and Sir Agglovale rode by the chapel as the burial was taking place, and seeing the dead squire, inquired of one of the women what had happened.

"My lords, it was a shameful death! It was done at the command of Sir Goodwyne, who said that the squire's master, Sir Agglovale, had killed his brother."

"May God reward you! I am Sir Agglovale, and I shall avenge him."

Sir Percivale and Sir Agglovale entered the castle and ordered the porter to announce them. Sir Goodwyne armed and descended.

"Which of you is Sir Agglovale?" he demanded.

"I am. I have come to ask you why you killed my mother's squire."

"I killed him because you killed my brother, Sir Gawdelyne."

"I killed your brother because of his treachery both to knights and to ladies. Now I shall avenge my squire, so defend yourself!"

Sir Agglovale fought Sir Goodwyne and Sir Percivale fought Sir Goodwyne's retainers. Sir Percivale was an excellent swordsman, and soon several of the retainers lay dead or dying, and the remainder would not venture near him. Sir Agglovale and Sir Goodwyne fought ferociously for a long time, but eventually Sir Goodwyne was stunned. Sir Agglovale leaped on top of him, dragged off his helmet, and chopped off his head.

After removing the dead squire to a monastery, the two brothers resumed their search for Sir Launcelot. Then one night, when they were resting at the Castle Cardycan, Sir Percivale got up quietly and spoke to Sir Agglovale's squire.

"Wake up! We are going to ride away together."

"My lord, your brother will kill me."

"Have no fear: I shall be your warrant."

They rode together until after noon, when they came upon a knight who had been chained to the stone pillar of a bridge.

"Sir, I pray you, release me."

"Sir, for what cause were you bound thus?" asked Sir Percivale.

"My lord, my name is Sir Persydes and I am a knight of the Round Table. I was riding in search of adventure and last night lodged at a castle ruled by a lady. She required me to become her lover and I refused; then she commanded her men to bind me thus."

"Sir Persydes, since you are a knight of the Round Table I shall release you."

Sir Percivale drew his sword, and with one stroke cut through the chain and part of Sir Persydes' hauberk, wounding him slightly in the process.

"By Jesu! that was a good stroke; had the chain not been there you would have killed me."

Sir Persydes was no sooner released than a knight from the lady's castle came galloping toward them.

"Beware! This knight will attack you," said Sir Persydes.

"He may do so," said Sir Percivale.

Sir Percivale met the knight's charge and flung him over the parapet of the bridge. The knight would have drowned in the river below but for a small craft into which he fell. Sir Persydes accompanied Sir Percivale to the castle, where Sir Percivale demanded that Sir Persydes' servants be restored to him. This was done, and then the lady of the castle appeared.

"Madam, if I had not more important matters on hand, I should oblige you to change your lewd and murderous customs!" said Sir Percivale.

The two knights then rode to Sir Persydes' castle, where they rested overnight. In the morning, before parting—Sir Persydes for Camelot, Sir Percivale to continue his search for Sir Launcelot—Sir Percivale asked Sir Persydes to deliver a message for him to King Arthur.

"Sir, I pray you, tell King Arthur and my brother Sir Agglovale how I rescued you, and that I shall not return to the court until I have news of Sir Launcelot. Also, I pray you, tell Sir Kay and Sir Modred that I have not forgotten the contempt they showed me when I was knighted, and that before I return, I intend winning greater fame than either of them has so far achieved."

Sir Persydes delivered Sir Percivale's message to the king, and then Sir Agglovale spoke:

"My brother certainly left me rudely enough."

"And yet you may be sure that he will prove to be a noble knight," said Sir Persydes; then to Sir Kay and Sir Modred:

"My lords, Sir Percivale says that he has not forgotten your contempt of him; and he swears that by the time he returns to this court he will have won more fame than either of you has won so far."

"He may swear that, but he seemed an unlikely enough knight when he departed," said Sir Kay.

"I believe," said King Arthur, "that he will prove a noble knight, and one worthy of his brethren."

Sir Percivale, meanwhile, continued to ride through the forest. He rode for a long time and then met a knight with a broken shield and a broken helmet. They jousted, and Sir Percivale was flung from the saddle. He leaped up at once, and drawing his sword, challenged the knight to fight to the death.

"Sir, you would fight more?" said the knight.

Both drew their swords and fought fiercely for half the day with scarcely a pause. Sir Percivale had great strength and endurance, but his opponent was the more experienced swordsman. Sir Percivale was the first to speak:

"Sir, I pray you, hold your hand a moment. Our quarrel is not serious, and you are certainly the strongest knight I have fought so far. I would like to know your name."

"Sir, never before have I been so wounded, although I have fought with the greatest knights of my time. I am a knight of the Round Table and my name is Sir Ector de Marys, brother to Sir Launcelot."

"Alas! and I am called Sir Percivale de Galys. I was seeking Sir Launcelot, but now I am mortally wounded; at your hands I must die."

"Not so! for it is I who am mortally wounded, and at your hands I must die. I pray you, therefore, ride to a monastery and bring a priest that I may make peace with the Saviour. And when you go to King Arthur's court and find Sir Launcelot, do not tell him that you killed me, for that would make him your mortal enemy. Say rather that I met my death in the course of searching for him."

"Sir Ector, you have spoken of that which cannot be. I am so wounded that I cannot rise to my feet; how, therefore, should I take to my horse?"

Then they wept for themselves and each other.

"This will not help us," said Sir Percivale, and knelt down and prayed devoutly. He was not only one of the strongest knights living, but also one of the most pious.

As Sir Percivale prayed, the Holy Grail appeared, with fragrant odor, and both were miraculously healed. Sir Percivale was just able to discern the immaculate maid who bore the Grail. Then Sir Ector also knelt down, and they both offered a prayer of thanksgiving.

"For the love of Jesu! what does this mean?" asked Sir Percivale.

"Sir, we have been vouchsafed the Holy Grail, wherein are contained drops of the blood of our Lord Jesu. But only a holy man may see the grail or the maid who bears it."

"May God forgive me then, for I thought I saw a maid dressed all in white who bore the Grail in both hands; and at that moment my wounds were healed," said Sir Percivale.

The two knights mended their harness as best they could and rode forward together to search for Sir Launcelot; and all the time they talked of their adventures and the wonders which had befallen them.

When Sir Launcelot had leaped through the window and run from King Arthur's castle, he wandered alone for many days through the forest, living on wild berries and spring water, and at the mercy of the weather, for he was protected only by his nightshirt. Eventually he came to a pavilion pitched in a meadow. From a nearby tree hung a white shield and two swords, and against the trunk of the tree rested two spears. Sir Launcelot took one of the swords and struck the shield with it again and again, so that the whole meadow was filled with the sound, as though ten knights were all fighting at once.

Then a dwarf emerged from the pavilion and attempted to wrest the sword from him. Sir Launcelot took hold of the dwarf by the shoulders and flung him to the ground with such violence that he all but broke his neck. The dwarf cried for help.

A knight dressed in a scarlet robe with fur trimmings walked out of the pavilion, and seeing Sir Launcelot was out of his wits, spoke gently to him:

"Sir, I pray you, lay down the sword, for surely what you need is rest and warm clothes."

"Sir, come near me and I shall kill you!" said Sir Launcelot.

The knight withdrew to the pavilion, armed, and returned to Sir Launcelot, determined to get the sword from him by force if necessary. Sir Launcelot knocked him to the ground with a blow that brought the blood streaming from his ears, nose, and mouth, then ran into the pavilion, lay on the bed, and fell asleep.

The knight's lady had been lying on the bed. When she saw Sir Launcelot she jumped out, covered her nakedness with a smock and ran outside to find her lord. When she saw him lying as though dead she burst into tears. However, the knight came to, and asked weakly what had become of the madman; "for surely I have never in my life before received such a blow," he said.

"My lord," said the dwarf, "mad he certainly is, but I suspect that formerly he was a knight of great renown. In fact, he closely resembles Sir Launcelot, whom I saw at the tournament at Lonezep."

"God forbid that so great a knight as Sir Launcelot should have fallen into such straits. But whosoever he is, I shall care for him."

The knight's name was Sir Blyaunte, and his brother, Sir Selyvaunte, lived nearby in the Castle Blanke.

"Go to my brother," said Sir Blyaunte to the dwarf. "Tell him what has happened; ask him to come and to bring with him a horse litter."

The dwarf did as he was commanded, and before long Sir Selyvaunte rode up with a horse litter and accompanied by six men. Sir Launcelot was lifted on the feather bed to the horse litter and taken to the castle, where he was securely bound. When he awoke he was given food and drink and proper clothes, and thereafter carefully tended. He soon recovered his health and his good looks, but not his wits, and for eighteen months remained thus.

Then one day, while riding through the forest, Sir Blyaunte met Sir Breuse Sans Pité and his brother, Sir Bartelot. The brothers attacked him savagely and, before long, feeling faint from his wounds, he fled to the castle.

Sir Launcelot was standing at his window and saw Sir Blyaunte being pursued by the two brothers, who were still lashing at him with their swords. With a tremendous effort, and some hurt to himself, Sir Launcelot broke free from his bonds and ran out of the castle through a postern. With his bare hands he dragged Sir Bartelot from his horse, and then, seizing his sword, struck Sir Breuse on the helmet and sent him crashing to the ground. Seeing what had befallen his brother, Sir Bartelot picked up a spear and charged Sir Launcelot, but Sir Blyaunte rode up and cut off his hand with his sword. Then Sir Breuse and his brother fled.

When Sir Selyvaunte saw how his brother had been rescued by Sir Launcelot, both he and his brother offered up a prayer of thanks for their having given him succor during his madness. They commiserated with Sir Launcelot for the wounds he had suffered in freeing himself from the fetters, and promised to bind him no more. Sir Launcelot remained happily with them for the next six months.

One day a boar hunt drove near to the castle. The boar was huge and fierce, and none of the hounds could hold it. Then Sir Launcelot noticed that one of the huntsmen had tethered his horse to a tree, left his spear beside it, and his sword in the saddle. Sir Launcelot ran out of the castle, mounted the horse, and galloped after the boar.

He came upon it resting its haunches against a stone, just outside a monastery. He charged with his spear, but it broke into three pieces on the boar's hide. Then the boar charged him, and after ripping out the horse's heart and lungs, wounded Sir Launcelot deeply in the thigh as he fell. Sir Launcelot drew his sword and with one stroke beheaded the boar.

A monk leaving the monastery saw Sir Launcelot's wound and offered to salve it, but Sir Launcelot threatened him with his sword. The monk continued on his way until he met a knight with a large number of his retainers.

"Sir, hard by our monastery lies a noble knight who has been wounded by a boar. I pray you, assist me in bringing him into the monastery so that I may cure him."

Sir Launcelot, now too feeble to resist, was put into a cart, together with the dead boar, and taken into the monastery, where the monks tended his wounds. The wounds healed, but Sir Launcelot refused all nourishment, grew thin, and, losing his wits again, one day ran out into the forest.

By chance his wanderings brought him once more to the city of Corbyn. But his appearance had grown so wild that he passed unrecognized, and beggars and children pelted him with filth and stones. He fled to the castle, where he was rescued by the knights and squires, who, seeing the wounds on his body, supposed that at some time he had been a knight. They gave him clothes and a straw bed by the castle gate, and threw him food, though none would venture near him.

It was at this time that King Pelles' nephew, Castor, asked the king to knight him. The king promised to do so on the feast of Candlemas. When the day came Sir Castor found that he had a number of gowns to dispose of. He summoned the court fool, that was Sir Launcelot, and gave him a red gown. Once dressed in it, Sir Launcelot appeared the most handsome man at the court; however, before long he wandered out again and lay down by a well in the garden to sleep. Then Elaine came into the garden to romp with her maids, and one of them discovered him.

"Keep this a secret," said Elaine to the maid, "and lead me to him."

They walked over to the well, and Elaine recognized Sir Launcelot and wept. Telling her maids that she was sick, she ran into the castle and spoke privately to her father.

"Dear father, I need your help, otherwise my happiness must be destroyed forever."

"My child, what is it?" asked the king.

"Sire, Sir Launcelot lies asleep in the garden by the well; and he is mad."

"I cannot believe it! But you must leave him to me," said the king.

The king summoned his four most trusted retainers, and together with Elaine and her attendant Lady Brusen, went to the well to see Sir Launcelot. Lady Brusen spoke:

"Sire, he has lost his wits, and if he is rudely awakened he might do anything. I shall put a spell over him so that he remains asleep for an hour."

When Lady Brusen had cast her spell the king ordered everyone out of the castle, and then Sir Launcelot was carried to one of the tower chambers where the Holy Grail was kept. He was laid down before it, a holy man uncovered the Grail, and Sir Launcelot's reason returned to him.

When he awoke he groaned and sighed, and then, seeing King Pelles and Elaine, grew ashamed and confused.

"For the love of Jesu! tell me how I came here," he asked.

"My lord," said Elaine, "when you came to our castle you had lost your reason. You were not recognized, and we kept you here as a fool. Then one of my maids discovered you sleeping by the well and led me to you. I thought I recognized you, so we brought you to this chamber, where, by virtue of the Holy Grail, your reason has been restored."

"God help me, then! How many know of my madness?"

"My father and I and Lady Brusen," Elaine replied.

"Then I pray you, keep it a secret. As it is, I am too deeply ashamed ever to return to my own country."

Sir Launcelot lay recovering for a further fortnight, and then spoke to Elaine once more:

"Fair lady, you have caused me great suffering, of which you must be aware. I was discourteous when I drew my sword on you after you had yielded your maidenhead to me and conceived Galahad. And yet was this not done by sorcery and against my wish?"

"My lord, what you say is true."

"Then I pray you, persuade your father to find a castle wherein I may dwell. For shame forbids my ever returning to King Arthur's court."

"My lord, I live only to serve you, and readily would I die in the same cause. I shall certainly ask my father for a castle, and I am sure that he will refuse me nothing."

Elaine went at once to the king with Sir Launcelot's request.

"My child," the king replied, "we are honored to have one of Sir Launcelot's blood as our guest. If it is his wish to live in our country he shall have the castle of Blyaunte, and twenty of our most beautiful maids shall serve him. And I pray that you will abide with him there, and you shall be served by twenty of our noblest knights."

Elaine returned to Sir Launcelot and reported King Pelles' resolution. Then Sir Castor, the king's nephew, came up to him and asked him his name.

"Sir, I am called Le Shyvalere Mafete, that is to say, the knight who has trespassed."

"Sir, I supposed you to be Sir Launcelot, for surely I have seen you before."

"Sir, it is discourteous of you to say so. If I had wished to reveal my name I should have done so; as it is, what do you suffer from my discretion? Therefore, be warned that if in the future our paths should cross, you will pay for this."

Sir Castor knelt down before him.

"Sir, I pray you, forgive me, and I swear that never shall I reveal your name while you are in this country."

Sir Launcelot forgave him.

Then King Pelles escorted Sir Launcelot and Elaine to the castle of Blyaunte, and with them rode the twenty knights and twenty ladies who were to serve them. The castle was built on an island in the middle of a beautiful lake, and Sir Launcelot called it the Joyous Ile, and while he lived there was known as Le Shyvalere Mafete. Sir Launcelot ordered for himself a shield, all of sable, and in the center a silver device representing an armed knight kneeling before a queen. Once each day he turned his eyes toward the realm of Logres and thought of King Arthur and Queen Gwynevere, and wept.

One day the news reached him of a tournament to be held at a castle only three leagues distant from Joyous Ile. Sir Launcelot summoned a dwarf:

"Go to the tournament, and before the knights depart, announce that I, Le Shyvalere Mafete, challenge all comers and that the knight who defeats me shall win a fair lady and a falcon."

When the tournament was over, five hundred knights altogether took up Sir Launcelot's challenge, and it is recorded that in the space of three days he overthrew them all, and then held a great feast.

While the feast was in progress Sir Ector and Sir Percivale rode up to the Joyous Ile, but could find no means of crossing the lake. Then they saw one of the ladies of the castle, and Sir Percivale called out to her and asked who dwelled there.

"My lords, a peerless lady lives here, Princess Elaine, and with her a matchless knight who calls himself Le Shyvalere Mafete."

"How did the knight come to this country?"

"He came here a madman, and was chased by beggars and children through the city of Corbyn; then he was taken in at the castle and his reason restored to him by virtue of the Holy Grail. He will fight only before noon; but if you would come to the castle, go to the far shore, and there you will find a boat to take you across."

When they came to the boat Sir Percivale said to Sir Ector:

"I pray you, let me cross first, for it would be wrong for us both to challenge him at once."

"Do as you will, and I shall await you here," Sir Ector replied.

Sir Percivale crossed the lake and spoke to the porter:

"Tell your lord that an errant knight would joust with him."

When the porter returned he led Sir Percivale to the jousting field where the lords and ladies of the castle were to watch the battle. Sir Launcelot rode onto the field. They jousted and both were flung from the saddle. Then for two hours they fought fiercely with their swords, wounding each other severely, while the chips flew from their armor and shields. Sir Percivale was the first to speak:

"Sir, I pray you, tell me your name, for I have never before encountered so strong a knight as you."

"Le Shyvalere Mafete; and now, I pray you, tell me your name."

"Sir Percivale de Galys; King Pellinore was my father, and Sir Lamerok and Sir Agglovale my brothers."

"Alas! I have fought a knight of the Round Table, and at one time I was of your fellowship."

"Sir, by the order of knighthood I pray you now, tell me your true name."

"Sir Launcelot du Lake, son of King Ban."

"Sir Launcelot, I beg your forgiveness. For two long years I have sought you; and across the lake is your brother, Sir Ector, who also has sought you. Once more I pray you for forgiveness."

"Sir Percivale, I forgive you readily."

Sir Ector was sent for, and when he arrived the brothers embraced and wept. Then Princess Elaine greeted them and told them all that had happened to Sir Launcelot since he had been in her country.

Throughout the two years of Sir Launcelot's madness, Sir Bors and Sir Lyonel had also been searching for him. They failed to find him, but by chance rode to the castle of King Brandegoris, where Sir Bors was well known for having gotten a child on the king's daughter fifteen years previously. When Sir Bors saw his son, Helyn le Blanke, he was pleased with him and spoke to the king:

"Sire, I wish to take my son Helyn to King Arthur's court."

"Sir Bors, is he not too young?" asked the king.

"Sire, I would have him at King Arthur's court, which is the most celebrated in all Christendom."

Helyn le Blanke's departure caused great sorrow at King Brandegoris' castle, but he was received joyfully by King Arthur and made a knight of the Round Table, which honor he subsequently justified.

One day Sir Ector and Sir Percivale asked Sir Launcelot if he would not return with them to King Arthur's court.

"My lords, my disgrace forbids my ever doing so," Sir Launcelot replied. Then Sir Ector spoke:

"Sir Launcelot, you are my brother, and I love you as I love no other man on earth. And I would never attempt to persuade you to anything dishonorable. But as it is, King Arthur, Queen Gwynevere, and all the knights of the Round Table lament your absence and pray for your return. You must know that you are regarded as the greatest knight living, and that Sir Tristram alone has a comparable reputation, so why not return with Sir Percivale and me? I would add that Queen Gwynevere cannot have spent less than twenty thousand pounds on the attempt to recover you."

"My good brother! I will return with you," Sir Launcelot replied.

When all had been made ready for their departure, Sir Launcelot took his leave of King Pelles and of Elaine, who was brokenhearted.

"My lord," she said, "I pray that on Pentecost our son Galahad shall be made a knight."

"For the love of Jesu, I hope that he will prove worthy,"
said Sir Launcelot.

"My lord, but for one, he shall prove the worthiest of his
kin."

"That will be worthy enough."

Fifteen days later Sir Launcelot and his companions arrived
at Camelot. Sir Launcelot was welcomed with open arms by
King Arthur, Queen Gwynevere, and all the fellows of the
Round Table. Then Sir Ector and Sir Percivale related the
story of Sir Launcelot's madness, of his sojourn at Point
Corbyn and at the Joyous Ile, of how he had named himself Le
Shyvalere Mafete and challenged and overthrown five hundred
knights in the space of three days. Queen Gwynevere wept
throughout this recital; but when it was over, she was joyous
as she had not been since before Sir Launcelot's madness.

"For the love of Jesu!" said Arthur, "I wonder, Sir Launcelot, what caused your madness? I suspect it was your love for
the fair Princess Elaine, by whom it is said you have a son
called Galahad, who is predicted to win great fame."

"Sire, whatever folly I have committed has come home to
roost," Sir Launcelot replied.

The king said no more, but all Sir Launcelot's kin knew
well for whose love it was that Sir Launcelot had lost his
reason. Then a feast was held in his honor, and all the lords
and ladies of the court rejoiced in Sir Launcelot's return to
Camelot, and in his recovery of his reason.

15. CONCLUSION

During the period of Sir Launcelot's madness, Sir Tristram
had accomplished deeds for which he had become celebrated
as the greatest knight in the realm. Returning one day to the
Joyous Gard, he was greeted by Queen Iseult with the story of
Sir Launcelot's cure by virtue of the Holy Grail, of his recovery by King Arthur and Queen Gwynevere, and of the
feast which they planned at Camelot to celebrate it.

"Alas! that there should ever have been a quarrel between Sir Launcelot and Queen Gwynevere," said Sir Tristram.

"My lord, the queen told me in a letter all that had happened; but thank God he is recovered at last."

"My lady, let us prepare ourselves and go to the feast."

"Sir, if I accompany you to Camelot, you will be overburdened with challenges on my behalf by the many aspiring knights who will be there."

"Then, my love, let us remain here together."

"Not so! for by so doing you will bring shame upon me. You are now the most honored knight in the land, and were you absent from the feast, would not all the lords and ladies at the court say: 'How now? Where is our noble Sir Tristram? See how he hides in his castle with his lady, passing his time in hunting and hawking when he should be at the feast, in order that we may all see and acknowledge him. Is it not a shame that Queen Iseult was ever born, or that he was ever knighted, let alone that he should love her, and she withhold him from the honor which is his due?'"

"My lady, I know now that your counsel has sprung from your heart; it moves me and I shall do as you ask. But I shall go unaccompanied and unarmed, taking with me only my spear and my sword."

Queen Iseult insisted that four knights should see Sir Tristram on his way, but within half a mile he dismissed them. A mile further on he found Sir Palomides, and another knight who lay at his feet, seriously wounded. Sir Tristram repented of being unarmed.

"Sir Tristram! We have now the opportunity of settling our long-standing grievances," said Sir Palomides.

"Sir Palomides, hitherto there has been no Christian knight from whom I have fled; and in the future it shall not be said that I fled from a Saracen."

Sir Tristram charged Sir Palomides with his spear and broke it on his armor; then, drawing his sword, struck him six times on the helmet. Sir Palomides stood still, astonished by Sir Tristram's foolhardiness. "If he were armed," he said to himself, "I should never overcome him. As it is, if I kill him I shall be disgraced wherever I go!"

Then Sir Tristram spoke: "Coward! Why do you not fight? I can defend myself."

"Sir Tristram, I should dishonor myself by killing you while you are without armor, although I know well enough how great are your strength and courage."

"You are chivalrous!"

"I pray you, answer me a question."

"I shall answer truthfully."

"Sir Tristram, if you were armed and I were naked, would you challenge me?"

"Sir Palomides, I grant you that I would not. Therefore, although I do not fear you, depart from me if you will."

"Sir Tristram, I too refuse to fight at an unfair advantage; therefore I will leave you."

"Sir Palomides, I wonder that so worthy a knight as yourself should not be christened."

"As for that, I swore many years ago that I would not become christened until I had fought seven battles, and now I have one to go. But often enough I have felt drawn by the love of Jesu, and of his Holy Mother, Mary."

"If you need but one battle, let it be now. I will ask the knight whom you defeated to lend me his armor." Then Sir Tristram went over to the knight and asked him his name.

"Sir, I am a knight of the Round Table, and my name is Sir Galleron of Galway."

"Sir Galleron, I am sorry for your injuries; but I pray you, lend me your armor, for I wish to fight the knight who defeated you."

"Sir, you shall have my armor, but I warn you that your opponent is formidable. I pray you, tell me your name."

"Sir, I am Sir Tristram de Lyoness, and the other knight is Sir Palomides the Saracen, brother to Sir Safere."

"It is a shame that so noble a knight should be unchristened."

"Either one of us may die, but I swear that he shall be christened first," Sir Tristram replied.

Sir Galleron was large, well built, and a knight of considerable prowess. In spite of his wounds he stood up and helped Sir Tristram into his armor. Then Sir Tristram and Sir Palomides jousted, with the result that Sir Palomides broke his spear and was flung to the ground. He jumped up and for two hours they fought with their swords. Although fearful of Sir Tristram's strength, Sir Palomides stood his ground bravely, and when, as on several occasions, he had been forced to his knees, he always recovered, and succeeded in wounding Sir Tristram in return.

Finally Sir Tristram was provoked to anger by Sir Palomides' resilience, and increasing the power of his blows, he first wounded him seriously in the shoulder and then struck the sword out of his hand. Sir Palomides glanced sorrowfully at his sword, knowing that if he tried to retrieve it Sir Tristram would behead him.

"How now?" asked Sir Tristram. "It is now you who are at a disadvantage as I formerly was. But it shall not be said that I am less generous than you; therefore take your sword and we will call the battle at an end."

"Sir Tristram, for myself I would gladly have done with this battle, for I do not believe that my offense is so great that we may not be reconciled. You are offended by my love for Queen Iseult, but you must allow that I have at all times dealt honorably with her, and offered no disrespect to her person. For my offense to you, surely I am sufficiently punished by the wounds I have received today; and likewise your offense to me is annulled. Therefore, I pray you, forgive me, and at the next church I shall confess and be christened, after which we could ride together to King Arthur's court."

"Very well, we shall do as you suggest, and may God forgive the ill will I have borne you. Take your horse and we will ride to Carlehylle, which lies only three miles hence, and you shall receive the sacrament from the bishop there."

Sir Galleron accompanied Sir Tristram and Sir Palomides to Carlehyll, where the bishop filled his holy vessel with water, blessed it, and then confessed and baptized Sir Palomides. Sir Tristram and Sir Galleron were his godfathers.

The three knighfs then rode to Camelot, where they were received joyfully by King Arthur, Queen Gwynevere, and the fellows of the Round Table, and Sir Palomides was congratulated on his baptism.

And it was at this feast that Sir Galahad first came to Camelot and sat at the Siege Perelous. Afterward all the knights dispersed. Sir Tristram returned to Queen Iseult at the Joyous Gard, and Sir Palomides rode off in pursuit of the Questing Beast.

The Tale of the Sangreal

1. THE DEPARTURE

One Pentecost when King Arthur and his knights of the Round Table had assembled at Camelot, heard mass, and were about to start their feast, a young noblewoman rode into the hall, dismounted, and knelt before Arthur. She had ridden fast and her horse was sweating copiously.

"God bless you, my lady!" said Arthur.

"Sire, I pray you, tell me if Sir Launcelot is here."

"My lady, he is," said Arthur, and pointed him out to her. The young noblewoman went up to him.

"Sir Launcelot, on behalf of King Pelles, I greet you; and I request that you will accompany me into the forest."

"My lady, whence do you come, and for what purpose do you require me?"

"My lord, I come from King Pelles' castle. When we reach our destination you shall know for what purpose you are required."

"My lady, I shall accompany you."

Sir Launcelot commanded his squire to bring him his horse and armor, and then Queen Gwynevere spoke to him:

"Sir Launcelot, must you really abandon us at the feast?"

"Madam," said the young noblewoman, "Sir Launcelot shall return to you by tomorrow dinner time."

"Sir Launcelot shall incur my displeasure if he is away any longer," said the queen.

Sir Launcelot accompanied the young noblewoman through the forest and into a wide valley, where they came to a nunnery. They dismounted and were welcomed. Then Sir Launce-

lot was led to the abbess' chamber, where he disarmed. Asleep
on a bed lay his two cousins, Sir Bors and Sir Lyonel; he awoke
them and they greeted each other joyfully.

"How is it that you have come here, instead of attending
the feast at Camelot?" asked Sir Bors.

"I was brought here by a young noblewoman, but for what
purpose I am as yet unaware."

Just then Galahad entered the chamber, escorted by twelve
nuns, all of whom were weeping. Galahad was remarkable for
his nobility of bearing and comeliness of person.

"Sir," said one of the nuns to Sir Launcelot, "we bring you
this child who hitherto has been our charge, and pray that now
you will confer upon him the order of knighthood, for you
alone are worthy to do so."

Sir Launcelot thought he had never seen a young man of
such extraordinary physical beauty and dovelike modesty.

"Is it his own wish that he should be knighted?"

"My lord, it is," said the nuns, and Galahad assented.

"Then in honor of the high feast he shall be knighted," said
Sir Launcelot.

Sir Launcelot spent the evening companionably, and at dawn
knighted Galahad.

"May God make you as virtuous as He has made you
beautiful!" said Sir Launcelot. "Now, I pray you, will you
accompany me to the court of King Arthur?"

"Sir Launcelot, at this time, no," Sir Galahad replied.

Sir Launcelot, Sir Bors, and Sir Lyonel rode together to
Camelot, where they met the king and queen and fellows of
the Round Table returning from morning mass, and were
welcomed by them.

When they came to seat themselves at the Round Table for
dinner they discovered a number of fresh inscriptions in gold
letters round the Siege Perelous:

HE OUGHT TO SITTE HYRE

and:

HERE OUGHT TO SITTE HE

and:

FOUR HONDRED WYNTIR AND FOUR AND FYFFTY ACOMPLYSSED
AFTIR THE PASSION OF OURE LORDE JESU CRYST OUGHTE THYS
SYEGE TO BE FULFYLLED.

"Here indeed is a miracle!" said all the knights as they beheld
it.

"Surely," said Sir Launcelot, "this means that today the
appointed knight shall sit at the Siege Perelous?"

Then the king commanded that the place should be covered with a silk cloth, and they all took their seats for dinner.

"Sire," said Sir Kay the Steward, "is it right that we should break our ancient custom by sitting down to dinner before a miracle has occurred?"

"Surely not!" said Arthur. "My pleasure at the return of Sir Bors and Sir Lyonel put it out of my mind for a moment."

Just as the king was saying these words, a squire came up to him:

"Sire, I bring news of a miraculous happening."

"What is it?" asked Arthur.

"Sire, where the river passes your castle a stone is floating, and into the stone a sword has been thrust."

"I will go and see it," said the king.

The king, accompanied by his knights, walked down to the river, where they saw a block of red marble floating in the water. Into the marble had been thrust a finely made sword, the jeweled hilt of which bore an inscription in gold letters: NEVER SHALL MAN TAKE ME HENSE BUT ONLY HE BY WHOSE SIDE I OUGHT TO HONGE AND HE SHALL BE THE BESTE KNYGHT OF THE WORLDE.

When the king had read the inscription he said to Sir Launcelot: "Sir, surely as you are the best knight in the world, so is this your sword."

"Sire, I know that this is not my sword and that I am not the best knight in the world. Further, if any but the rightful owner should touch the sword, he will receive from it a wound from which he may never recover. And with the coming of the best knight in the world will start the quest of the Holy Grail."

"My good nephew," said the king to Sir Gawain, "I pray you, try the sword."

"Sire, I beg to be excused," Sir Gawain replied.

"Sir Gawain, as you love me, I command you to try."

Sir Gawain grasped the sword by the hilt and tugged at it, but he could not move it.

"Thank you," said the king.

"Sir Gawain," said Sir Launcelot, "you shall now receive from this sword a wound for which even the finest castle in the realm would be an insufficient reward."

"Sir Launcelot, it was not for me to disobey my liege."

King Arthur repented of his command, and asked Sir Percivale.

"Sir Percivale, for the love that you bear me, would you try the sword?"

Sir Percivale, out of a feeling of fellowship for Sir Gawain, was willing enough to try. He tugged at the hilt, but like Sir Gawain, was unable to move the sword. No other knight could be persuaded to make the attempt.

"Sire," said Sir Kay, "now that you have witnessed a miracle, you may go to dinner."

King Arthur and his companions returned to the Round Table. When they were seated, and the younger knights had served them, the doors and windows of the hall suddenly closed, as if of their own accord, and yet the hall remained light. All were silent, and then the king spoke:

"My lords, today we have already witnessed one miracle; now it would appear that another is to follow."

An ancient and holy man entered the hall. He was dressed in white, and accompanied by a young knight who was clad in red armor and carried a scabbard, but no sword, and no shield.

"My lords, peace be with you!" said the old man, and then to King Arthur:

"Sire, I bring to you this young knight. He is of royal blood both through his father and through his mother, and he is descended from Joseph of Arimathea, and he shall accomplish the greatest undertaking of your realm."

"Sir, you are welcome to this court; and so is the young knight," Arthur replied.

The old man removed the young knight's armor, and then gave him a mantle trimmed with ermine to wear above his red silk tunic.

"Sir, accompany me," said the old man, and leading the knight to the Siege Perelous, he removed the cloth which covered it. A fresh inscription had appeared:

THYS YS THE SYEGE OF SIR GALAHAD THE HAWTE PRYNCE.

"Sir Galahad, this is your seat," said the old man.

Sir Galahad sat down, and then spoke:

"Sir, I pray you, go your way now, for you have fulfilled your commands to the letter. And I ask you to recommend me to my grandfather, King Pelles, and to my lord, King Pecchere, and to say that I shall visit them as soon as I may."

The old man left the hall, and accompanied by twenty squires, rode from the castle.

The knights of the Round Table all marveled at the appearance of Sir Galahad, and at his intrepidity at sitting in the Siege Perelous. But they assumed that it must be in accordance with God's will.

"Surely this must be the knight who shall win the Holy Grail, for none but he could sit at the Siege Perelous with impunity," said one.

"On my life I will swear that he shall win fame," said Sir Bors.

Sir Launcelot, meanwhile, was gazing at his son and filled with joy, as all his fellows praised him. Soon the news of his arrival reached the queen, and when she was told of his resemblance to Sir Launcelot she said:

"I shall go to the Round Table and see for myself. He may well be Sir Launcelot's son Galahad, for did not Princess Elaine bear him a child after she had brought him to her bed by means of an enchantment?"

When the queen had seen the inscription she said to Sir Gawain:

"Good nephew, now we have Sir Galahad amongst us, and he shall bring honor to our court, as Sir Launcelot foretold."

Then the king spoke to Sir Galahad:

"Sir, we welcome you to this court where, it is said, many of our knights will be inspired by your example to pursue the quest of the Holy Grail, which you alone shall achieve."

The king took Sir Galahad by the hand and led him to the miraculous sword embedded in the marble block which still floated in the river. The queen and her ladies followed them.

"Sir, our greatest knights have failed to win this sword," said King Arthur.

"Sire, this is my sword and not theirs; and that is why an empty scabbard hangs by my side." So saying, Sir Galahad lightly withdrew the sword from the marble, and put it in his scabbard.

"May God grant you a shield!" said the king.

"Sire, this sword belonged to Sir Balin le Saveage, who fought his brother, Sir Balan, to the death after he had struck the dolorous stroke which wounded King Pelles and ruined three kingdoms. To this day King Pelles' wound is open, and so it shall remain until the time comes for me to heal him."

At that moment a young woman on a white palfrey galloped up to them and asked for Sir Launcelot.

He answered for himself: "I am here, my lady."

"Sir Launcelot," said the young noblewoman, weeping, "how changed is everything with you since this morning!"

"My lady, what do you mean?"

"Sir, only this morning you were the greatest knight on earth, and now anyone who said that would be telling a lie! It has been proved by the miraculous sword that there is now a knight who is greater than you are. This is what I have come to tell you, and what you must remember."

"My lady, I have always known that I am not the greatest knight," Sir Launcelot replied.

"My lord, of sinful knights you are still the greatest," said the young noblewoman; then to the king:

"Sire, Nacien the hermit sends you this message: that you are to be vouchsafed the greatest honor of any British monarch, for today you and your fellowship shall savor the Holy Grail."

With those words the young noblewoman galloped away.

"My lords," said the king, "never again shall our complete fellowship be assembled at this castle, for soon you shall depart on the quest of the Holy Grail, from which some of you shall not return. Therefore let us go to the jousting field and hold our last tournament, so that when we are dead, men shall remember us by it."

King Arthur had also a secret reason for calling this tournament. He supposed that Sir Galahad was unlikely to return from the quest of the Holy Grail, and he wished to test his powers by matching him against his fellows of the Round Table.

At the request of the king and the queen, Sir Galahad entered the field clad in a jazerant and helmet, and carrying a spear; but he refused a shield. Sir Galahad overthrew all but two of his opponents, the two being Sir Launcelot and Sir Percivale. Then the queen asked him to raise his visor so that she could examine his features.

"Now I can believe that he is Sir Launcelot's son," she said, "because of the striking resemblance of their features; hence his prowess at arms should not surprise us."

"Madam, should Sir Galahad really be so great a knight?" asked one of the ladies-in-waiting.

"He should, for he is of royal blood on both sides, and through Sir Launcelot eight generations from our Saviour, through Princess Elaine, seven."

That evening the Holy Grail passed through Camelot. After hearing evensong at the great monastery, King Arthur and his knights had sat down at the Round Table for supper. Suddenly they were disturbed by peals of thunder which shook the whole castle, then they were all struck dumb by a dazzling sunbeam, seven times brighter than any they had seen before. The spirit of the Holy Ghost descended upon them, and each was beatified. Then the Holy Grail entered the hall. It was covered with white samite and none could discern the maid who bore it, but each smelt the fragrant odor of spices; and miraculously, before each knight appeared the meat and drink of his own choice. The Grail disappeared as inexplicably as it had appeared, and the knights found that they were able to speak again. King Arthur offered up a prayer of thanksgiving and then addressed the fellowship:

"Surely we should thank our Lord Jesu Christ for the blessing He has bestowed upon us this day at the high feast of Pentecost."

"My lords," said Sir Gawain, "by virtue of the Sangreal each has received the meat and wine of his choice, but none has seen the Grail itself. Therefore I make this vow: to set off in search of the Holy Grail tomorrow and not to return for at least a year and a day without seeing it more clearly, but to accept it as in accordance with God's will if this is not vouchsafed me."

When Sir Gawain had finished speaking, many of the knights of the Round Table made similar vows, and King Arthur was deeply distressed.

"Alas!" he said to Sir Gawain, "what have you done? Shall not our fellowship of the Round Table be irremediably broken? A fellowship I have loved better than my own life, and one which is surely unique for its peerless knights, many of whom will now ride away in search of the Holy Grail, never to return! How can I be reconciled to the dissolution of so close a fellowship, and of the ancient customs by which we have been held?"

The king wept as he spoke, and Sir Launcelot tried to comfort him.

"My liege, in the end death must claim us all; then how more gloriously could we die than on such a quest?"

"Sir Launcelot, it grieves me to hear you talk so!" said the king.

When the news reached the queen and the ladies of the court, they too were utterly dismayed, for many besides the queen had their lovers among the knights of the Round Table, and feared to lose them forever.

"Alas! that my lord the king should allow them to go," said the queen.

Many of the ladies resolved to accompany their knights, and this was agreed among them, but then the hermit Nacien came to the court with an announcement that destroyed their hopes.

"My lords, those of you who have sworn to go on the quest

of the Holy Grail must leave your ladies behind you. For this high purpose each of you must labor alone, and I warn you that none who is not cleansed of his sins shall behold the mysteries of our Saviour."

When the hermit Nacien had gone the queen spoke to Sir Galahad:

"Sir Galahad, is it true that Sir Launcelot is your father?"

Sir Galahad did not reply.

"You need not be ashamed, for is not Sir Launcelot of royal blood, and the greatest knight living? The resemblance between you is certainly striking."

"Madam, if you, as many others, are aware that Sir Launcelot is my father, why do you ask me?" Sir Galahad replied.

That night Sir Galahad was given the honor of sleeping in King Arthur's bed. The king himself could not sleep for sorrow, and at dawn went to Sir Launcelot and Sir Gawain, who had risen to attend early mass.

"Sir Gawain," said the king, weeping, "have you not betrayed me? For now our whole fellowship is to disperse, and yet you will never pity me as I do you who are to ride forth on this quest. And you, good Sir Launcelot, I pray you, advise me, for I would that this quest were at an end."

"My liege, your knights could not be expected to break their vows."

"I know it well, and yet there is no joy that could now lighten my sorrow."

The king and queen went to mass. They were followed by Sir Launcelot, Sir Gawain, and the fellows of the Round Table, who went in full armor except for their helmets and their shields. When mass was over they all returned to the castle, and it was to be seen that every one of the hundred and fifty knights of the Round Table was to pursue the quest of the Holy Grail. There was much weeping and lamentation as they prepared for their departure.

In order that her sorrow should not be seen, Queen Gwynevere had retired to her chamber, whither Sir Launcelot came after searching unsuccessfully for her in the hall.

"Sir Launcelot, have you not betrayed me? For I shall surely die if you leave me thus," she said.

"My lady, I pray you, do not be displeased with me, for I shall return to you as soon as I may honorably do so."

"Alas, I sigh for you! But may He who died on the Cross for all mankind protect you and your whole fellowship!"

Sir Launcelot returned to his companions, who awaited him, and together they rode through the streets of Camelot, which were lined with people of all estates who wept as they watched their departure.

That evening Sir Launcelot and his companions arrived at a city and were given hospitality by Sir Vagon of Vagon Castle, an elderly knight who made them welcome. In the morning the fellows bade adieu to one another, and each set off in the direction of his own choice.

2. THE MIRACLES

Sir Galahad, still without a shield, rode for four days through the forest without meeting any adventure, and then came to an abbey built of white stone. The monks greeted him respectfully and led him to a chamber where he was saluted by two of his fellows of the Round Table, King Bagdemagus and Sir Uwayne. When he had disarmed they went together down to supper.

"My lords, may I ask what brought you here?" said Sir Galahad.

"Sir, we were told of a shield which is kept here, and which no knight may bear but at his peril. Tomorrow I shall ride forth with it."

"For the love of God!" Sir Galahad exclaimed.

"Sir, if I fail, will you bear the shield after me?"

"Sire, I will, for I have no shield."

In the morning when the three knights had heard mass, a monk took the shield from behind the altar and gave it to King Bagdemagus. It was white, and the device a red cross.

"My lords," said the monk, "I must warn you that this shield is intended only for the greatest knight on earth, and that any other knight who bears it does so at his peril."

"I do not suppose that I am the greatest knight on earth," said King Bagdemagus, "but I shall adventure forth with the shield, and perhaps it will please Sir Galahad to remain here until he has news of me."

"Sire, I will abide here," said Sir Galahad.

King Bagdemagus set off, accompanied by a squire who was to report his adventures to Sir Galahad. They rode for two miles and entered a valley in which stood a hermitage. A knight in white armor, and riding a white horse, galloped toward them with leveled spear. King Bagdemagus encountered him, with the result that he broke his spear, was wounded deeply in the shoulder, and flung from his horse. The white knight dismounted and took King Bagdemagus' shield.

"Sir," he said, "you suffer from your own foolhardiness; this shield can be borne only by a knight who is without peer." Then he spoke to the squire:

"I pray you, take this shield to Sir Galahad, whom you left at the abbey, and give it to him with my greetings."

"Sir, what is your name?" asked the squire.

"It is not for any man on earth to know my name."

"Then for the love of our Lord, I pray you, tell me why no man may bear this shield but at his peril."

"This shield belongs to Sir Galahad alone."

The squire asked King Bagdemagus if his wound was serious.

"In truth, I do not know whether I shall escape with my life," the king replied.

The squire helped him to mount, they rode slowly back to the abbey, and the king was put to bed, where, it is said, he lay for a long time recovering from his wound.

"Sir Galahad," said the squire, "the knight who wounded King Bagdemagus commanded me to give you his greeting, and to give you the white shield, which belongs to you alone."

"Blessed is my fortune!" said Sir Galahad.

When Sir Galahad had armed, mounted, and slung the shield about his neck, Sir Uwayne asked if he could accompany him.

"Sir Uwayne, I must go unaccompanied, except by the squire."

They parted. Sir Galahad rode to the hermitage, where he exchanged greetings with the white knight.

"Sir, I pray you, tell me the history of this shield," said Sir Galahad.

"Sir, thirty-two years after the Passion of our Lord Jesu Christ, Joseph of Arimathea, who had taken our Lord down from the Cross, set forth from Jerusalem with a large party of his kinsmen, and traveled to the city of Sarras. At the time, King Evelake was about to fight a decisive battle against his cousin King Tholome le Feyntis, who, at the head of his Saracens, had invaded his lands.

"Joseph went to King Evelake, and after revealing to him the mysteries of the Holy Trinity, persuaded him that only by adopting the True Faith could he hope to gain the victory in the forthcoming battle.

"King Evelake was convinced. He entered the battle bearing a shield which he had specially ordered. He kept the shield covered with a cloth until the moment of his greatest danger; then he removed the cloth and the enemy fell back and were defeated. It was a white shield, and the device was a representation of our Lord Jesu on the Cross.

"In the course of the fighting one of King Evelake's soldiers had one of his hands cut off. The king bade the soldier touch his shield in good faith, and when the soldier did so, his hand was made whole again.

"Sometime later the figure and the cross vanished from the shield. No one could explain it, but it was then that King Evelake, together with most of the citizens of Sarras, became baptized.

"Joseph of Arimathea decided to leave Sarras, and King Evelake insisted on accompanying him, so they traveled together to Britain. On their arrival they were thrown into prison by a pagan suzerain. There they would have remained but for a man named Mondramas, who, aware of Joseph's fame, led an army against the suzerain, defeated him, and delivered Joseph and King Evelake. Thereupon the Britons became Christianized.

"Not long after this, Joseph was led to his deathbed. King Evelake stood by him and wept sorrowfully.

" 'Joseph, for the love of you I left my own kin and my own country. Now that you are about to leave this world, I pray you give me some token of remembrance.'

" 'I will do so: bring me the shield you bore in the battle against King Tholome.'

"Joseph was bleeding copiously from the nose, and when the shield was brought to him, he allowed the blood to flow onto the shield in the form of a cross. Then he spoke again:

" 'This cross you shall have in memory of the love that I bear you. Whenever you look upon it you shall remember me, and always shall this cross remain as fresh as it is now. No other knight than you shall wear this shield about his neck, except at his peril, until the time comes for Sir Galahad to wear it. Sir Galahad will be the last of my lineage.'

" 'I pray you, where shall I put this shield in order that Sir Galahad may find it?'

" 'Sire, after your death Nacien the hermit will keep it, until the day Sir Galahad finds it, fifteen days after he has been knighted.'

"And so it is that in the same abbey where you found this shield lies Nacien the hermit."

And with those words the white knight vanished.

Then the squire dismounted and knelt before Sir Galahad and begged that he might be allowed to accompany him until he was made a knight.

"Were I permitted a companion, it would be you," Sir Galahad replied.

"Sir Galahad, I pray you then, will you make me a knight now? And I swear by the grace of God that I shall prove a worthy one."

Sir Galahad agreed to do so, and they rode back to the abbey, where they were greeted joyfully.

Then one of the monks asked Sir Galahad to accompany him to a tomb wherein was a fiend. Sir Galahad, in full armor except for his helmet, accompanied him, and as they approached the tomb a voice cried out from within:

"Sir Galahad, servant of Jesu! depart, otherwise I shall have to return whence I came."

Sir Galahad approached fearlessly and lifted the cover of the tomb. Dense smoke issued forth, and then the fiend leaped out. He was a terrifying figure, in the likeness of a man. Sir Galahad crossed himself, and the fiend spoke again:

"Sir Galahad, I see that you are encircled by angels and that I may not touch you!"

Then Sir Galahad saw in the tomb the body of a man in full armor, with a sword by his side.

"Good brother," he said to the monk, "let us remove this body from the graveyard, for surely he was a heretic."

This was done. They all returned to the abbey, where Sir Galahad disarmed, and then another of the monks came up to him and explained what had happened.

"Sir Galahad, the figure which lay on the body represented the reign of evil on earth. There was a time when sin was manifest, when even father and son did not recognize each other, and then it was that the Almighty God descended in the living flesh of a virgin."

"I believe you," Sir Galahad replied.

The next morning Sir Galahad knighted the squire who had accompanied him to the hermitage. When he had done so he asked him his name and lineage.

"Sir, I am called Melyas de Lyle, and I am the son of the King of Denmark."

"Then in honor of your royal blood, let your conduct be a mirror to all chivalry."

"Truly, sir. And since it is you who have knighted me, it is seemly that I should ask you for my first gift."

"Ask, Sir Melyas, and it shall be granted."

"Sir Galahad, I pray that I may accompany you on the quest of the Holy Grail."

"Sir Melyas, you shall," Sir Galahad replied.

Sir Melyas ordered his men to bring him his horse and arms, and when he was ready he set off with Sir Galahad. They rode together for a week, and then came to a stone cross which bore the following inscription:

NOW YE KNYGHTES ARRAUNTE WHICH GOTH TO SEKE KNYGHTES ADVENTURYS, SE HERE TWO WAYES: THAT ONE WAY DEFENDITH THE THAT THOU NE GO THAT WAY, FOR HE SHALL NAT GO OUTE OF THE WAY AGAYNE BUT IF HE BE A GOOD MAN AND A WORTHY KNYGHT. AND IF THOU GO ON THE LYFFTE HONDE THOU SHALL NAT THERE LYGHTLY WYNNE PROUESSE, FOR THOU SHALT BE SONE ÀSSAYDE.

"I pray you, Sir Galahad, allow me to take the route to the left, for I would prove my strength."

"Sir Melyas, I believe that my own chances of surviving those perils would be greater."

"My lord, I pray you, allow me to take that route."

"In the name of the Lord, do so if you will," Sir Galahad replied.

Sir Melyas followed the route through the forest for two days and then came to a meadow, where he found a timber lodge. Within the lodge he could see a chair on which rested a finely wrought gold crown, and beside the chair the ground had been spread with a cloth upon which were set many kinds of meat.

Sir Melyas was not hungry, but he coveted the crown, so he took it and rode on his way. However, he had not ridden far when a knight came galloping up to him.

"Sir, relinquish the crown, and defend yourself!"

"Ah Jesu! defend your newly made knight!" said Sir Melyas.

The two knights encountered at full gallop and Sir Melyas was flung from his horse with a wound in the left side. His opponent picked up the crown and rode off with it, while Sir Melyas lay on the ground, unable to rise. Then, by chance, Sir Galahad rode by.

"Sir Melyas, you are wounded? Surely you should have taken the other route!"

"Sir Galahad, I pray you, do not leave me to die in this meadow, but take me to an abbey where I may receive extreme unction."

"Sir Melyas, I will do so. But who wounded you thus?"
At that moment a voice cried out from the forest:
"Knight, defend yourself!"
"Sir, charge at your peril!" Sir Galahad replied.
Two knights attacked Sir Galahad in rapid succession. The
first Sir Galahad unhorsed, wounding him in the shoulder and
breaking his spear as he did so. The second he met with his
sword; and when the knight had broken his spear on his armor,
Sir Galahad cut off his left arm. Both knights fled, and Sir
Galahad turned once more to Sir Melyas.

The spear shaft was still buried in Sir Melyas' side, so Sir
Galahad lifted him onto his own horse, mounted behind him,
and rode gently to the nearest abbey. The monks led him to a
chamber, laid him on a bed, and gave him extreme unction.
Then he spoke to Sir Galahad:
"Now I can accept death when God wills it."
So saying, he withdrew the spear shaft and fainted. An old
monk, who formerly had been a knight, examined him carefully.
"By the grace of God I can cure him in seven weeks," he
said.
Sir Galahad rejoiced, and remained at the abbey for three
days, after which Sir Melyas assured him that he would
recover.
"Then I will leave you, for I, like all my fellows, must proceed on the quest of the Holy Grail."
"Sir Melyas," said one of the monks, "it was out of pride
that you set forth in search of the Holy Grail, and out of pride
that you parted from Sir Galahad at the stone cross and chose
the left-hand route. It is written that the left-hand route is for
sinners, and the right-hand route for the righteous, and soon
you fell: when you coveted the crown and stole it. The wound
that you received was in punishment for your sins of pride
and covetousness. Both sins were embodied in the two knights
who attacked Sir Galahad, but, because he is without sin, he
overthrew them, so you must remember in future not to disgrace the high order of knighthood."
"My lord Sir Galahad, as soon as I have recovered I shall
search for you," said Sir Melyas.
"May God speed your recovery!"
Sir Galahad departed, and for many days rode hither and
thither, uncertain which direction he should take. Then he
came to a deserted chapel on a mountainside, and not having
heard mass that morning at Abblasowre, where he had stayed

overnight, he decided to enter and offer up a prayer for guidance. When he had prayed, a voice answered him:

"Go now, adventurous knight, to the Maidens' Castle, and change their evil customs."

Sir Galahad thanked God and rode on again. Before long he came to the valley of the Severn; beside the river he saw a strong, well-moated castle. While he was looking at the castle an old man came by, and after they had exchanged greetings Sir Galahad asked him what the castle was called.

"Sir, it is the Maidens' Castle, and it is of evil repute, therefore I advise you to turn back."

"Sir, I may not turn back," Sir Galahad replied.

After checking his arms and putting his shield before him, Sir Galahad rode on toward the castle. He was met by seven young noblewomen.

"Sir, you ride at your peril, for you will have to cross the water," said one of them.

"My ladies, why should I not cross the water?" said Sir Galahad, and rode on again. Then he was met by a squire:

"Sir, the knights in the castle defy you to enter, unless you first tell them your purpose."

"My purpose is to change their evil customs."

"Sir, you undertake too much."

"So be it. Now go your way," Sir Galahad replied.

The squire entered the castle, and then seven knights emerged; they were brothers.

"Sir, defend yourself, for we promise to kill you," said one of them.

"My lords, do you all intend fighting me at once?"

"We do!"

Sir Galahad met their charge with his spear and sent the first knight flying out of the saddle. The remaining six broke their spears on his armor. Then Sir Galahad drew his sword and struck out with such force that they all fled from the field.

An old man in a monk's habit came up to him: "Sir, here are the keys of the castle."

Sir Galahad opened the gates and entered. The passages were crowded with people, all of whom acclaimed him loudly.

"Welcome to our deliverer!" they shouted.

Then a lady came up to him: "My lord, I must warn you that the knights who fled from you will return tonight and resume their evil customs."

"My lady, what should I do?" asked Sir Galahad.

"Sir, you must blow on this horn, which can be heard two

miles away and which summons all those knights whose lands
are held by the castle, and you must make them swear to revert to the customs which they held before these evil times."

The lady gave Sir Galahad the horn, which was of ivory inlaid with gold, and departed. Sir Galahad blew on the horn,
and then sat down to wait.

Before long a priest came up to him: "Sir, it is seven years
since the seven brothers came to this castle and killed the Duke
Lyanowre, who owned it, and his eldest son. Then they made
free not only with the castle treasure and tributes, but also with
the duke's daughter. She prophesied that one day a knight
would come who would deliver the castle, and so they have
since imprisoned or killed every visiting knight, and violated
every visiting maiden. That is why it is known as the Maidens'
Castle."

"I pray you tell me, is the duke's daughter still here?"

"Sir, she died three nights after she was violated. Since then
they have made free with her young sister, who has suffered
much, as have so many young noblewomen here."

Meanwhile the knights had assembled in answer to the horn
summons. Sir Galahad made them swear allegiance to the duke's
younger daughter, and to revert to the customs of former times.
Then a messenger arrived with the news that Sir Gawain, Sir
Gareth, and Sir Uwayne had killed the seven brothers.

"That is good," said Sir Galahad, and armed and departed.

When Sir Gawain had ridden away from Camelot on the
quest of the Holy Grail, he came by chance to the abbey where
Sir Galahad had found his shield. He followed in his footsteps to
the abbey where Sir Melyas lay wounded, and when he heard
of Sir Galahad's adventures, decided to ride in search of him.

"Sir," said one of the monks, "he will never accept your
fellowship."

"Why not?" asked Sir Gawain.

"Because you are wicked and he is blessed."

While they were talking Sir Gareth rode up to the abbey
and exchanged joyful greetings with Sir Gawain. They left
the abbey and before long met Sir Uwayne. The three knights
rode on together, and Sir Uwayne declared that so far he had
met with no adventures.

"Neither have we," said Sir Gawain.

By chance they rode toward the Maidens' Castle and were
observed by the seven brothers whom Sir Galahad had just
put to flight.

"Since we have been put to shame by one of King Arthur's knights, let us revenge ourselves on these three knights, who are also of King Arthur's court," said one of the brothers.

Sir Gawain, Sir Gareth, and Sir Uwayne met the charge of the seven knights and killed every one of them. Then they rode on to the Maidens' Castle, but finding that Sir Galahad had already left, decided that each should search for him separately.

Sir Gawain came to a hermit at evensong and asked him for his blessing. The hermit gave it to him, and then asked him who he was.

"I am Sir Gawain of King Arthur's court, and I am riding on the quest of the Holy Grail."

"Sir, I pray you, tell me, are you in a state of grace?"

"Lately I was told by a monk that I am wicked."

"Sir, I can believe you," said the hermit. "For many years now, since you were first knighted, you have followed the path of sin; otherwise you and your two companions would not have killed the seven knights. Sir Galahad, who is a virgin and without sin, overcame them all singlehanded, but without killing them, which his virtue forbids unless it is really necessary.

"You must understand that the Maidens' Castle represents the imprisonment of souls before the Incarnation of our Lord Jesu Christ, and the seven knights the seven deadly sins which held sway at that time. And in his deliverance of those within the Maidens' Castle, Sir Galahad was acting in the likeness of our Lord Jesu, who in taking upon himself the sins of the world delivered the souls of men to heaven. Now, Sir Gawain, for your sins you must do penance."

"Father, what penance shall I do?"

"As I shall direct you."

"No, good father, for a knight in the course of his adventures surely suffers enough in body and in soul."

"As you will," said the hermit, and thereafter held his peace.

In the morning Sir Gawain blessed the hermit and left him. He had not ridden far when he met Sir Gryfflet and Sir Agglovale. They rode together for four days without meeting any adventure, and on the fifth day each took a separate route.

Sir Galahad, after leaving the Maidens' Castle, came to a waste land where he met Sir Launcelot and Sir Percivale, neither of whom recognized him. Sir Launcelot jousted with him and was flung to the ground. Then Sir Percivale jousted with him, and received a sword blow on his helmet which knocked him off his horse, and would have killed him had not the sword swerved on the inner core of the helmet.

The jousting had taken place not far from the dwelling of an elderly recluse, and when she saw what had happened, she cried out to Sir Galahad:

"God be with you, peerless knight! I believe that if Sir Launcelot or Sir Percivale had recognized you they would not have been so anxious to challenge you."

Sir Galahad spurred his horse and galloped away, not wishing to be discovered by Sir Launcelot or Sir Percivale, both of whom followed him a short way, but were unable to catch him.

"Let us return to the recluse," said Sir Percivale; "perhaps she can tell us which way he is going."

"Do as you will," said Sir Launcelot.

Sir Percivale rode back to the recluse. Sir Launcelot galloped away, and rode at random across the waste lands until nightfall, when he came to a stone cross which, in the failing light, he thought to be of marble. Hard by the stone cross was an old chapel. Sir Launcelot tethered his horse to a tree, and in the hope of finding company, walked up to the chapel. The door, although partly broken, held fast and he could not enter. Inside, he could see an altar covered by a fresh silk cloth, on which stood a silver candlestick with six candles all burning. Sir Launcelot longed to go into the light, but he could not, so he returned to his horse and unharnessed it. Then he disarmed himself and lay down on his shield to sleep.

Between waking and sleeping he saw two white palfreys approach the cross and stop by it. The palfreys bore a litter on which lay a wounded knight, and Sir Launcelot heard him say:

"Sweet Jesu, when shall I see the Holy Grail and be cured? Surely, lying on this litter, I have suffered for long, for a trespass which was not great."

Thereupon the silver candlestick with the six candles moved mysteriously toward the cross, and at the same time a silver table bearing the Holy Grail appeared before the knight. Sir Launcelot recognized the Grail, having seen it before in King Pelles' castle. The wounded knight lifted both hands and spoke again:

"Sweet Lord, I pray you that as you are present in this Holy Vessel, so will you cure me of my malady!"

So saying, he knelt before the Holy Grail and kissed it, and thereupon was cured.

"My Lord, I thank You for Your mercy," he said.

Sir Launcelot wished that he too could rise up and kiss the

Holy Grail, but because he was in mortal sin he was powerless to do so. He repented bitterly of his failure, and subsequently was to be despised for it by his fellows. The Holy Grail, the silver table, and the silver candlestick all moved away as mysteriously as they had come, and then the knight who had been healed kissed the stone cross and was helped into his armor by his squire.

"My lord, are you healed?" asked the squire.

"I thank God that I am, through the power of this Holy Vessel. But I wonder that this sleeping knight should remain powerless when such a miracle has been vouchsafed."

"Probably because he is in mortal sin," the squire replied.

"Then he is indeed ill-fated, for I think he is one of the knights of the Round Table, all of whom have set off on the quest of the Holy Grail."

"Sir," said the squire, "your armor is complete except for the helmet and sword. Should you not take those belonging to this knight?"

The knight took Sir Launcelot's helmet and sword, also his horse, which was better than his own, and rode away.

When they had gone Sir Launcelot awoke thoroughly and wondered if he had not been dreaming; then he heard a voice:

"Sir Launcelot, you are harder than a stone, more bitter than wood, and more barren than a fig tree. Go hence, for you are not worthy of this holy place!"

These words pierced Sir Launcelot to the very heart, for he knew them to be true. He arose, weeping and cursing, and when he found that his sword and helmet and horse were no longer by the cross, he knew that he had not been dreaming.

"So am I brought to shame!" he said to himself. "When I sought only worldly fame, none could gainsay me, whether my quarrel was right or wrong; but now that I search for holy things, by my sins I am disqualified."

Sir Launcelot sat sorrowing until the first cockcrow, and then, feeling somewhat comforted, rose and walked from the cross. Before long he came to a hermitage. The hermit was hearing mass, and when it was over Sir Launcelot knelt before him and begged him to hear his sins.

"I will do so willingly," said the hermit, and then asked Sir Launcelot if he were not of King Arthur's court.

"In truth I am. My name is Sir Launcelot du Lake, and hitherto my name has been honored. But now all that has changed, and I am the most wretched of knights."

"Sir, surely you have greater cause to give thanks to God

than has any knight living; for has He not given you strength, beauty, and seemliness in excess of any knight living? To God you owe your worldly fame, and yet you have presumed to enter His precincts and to discover His mysteries when you are in a state of mortal sin. He does not appear in the flesh and blood in the Holy Grail before sinful eyes, unless it is to shame the beholder. Therefore be warned: God is against you, and against Him none can avail!"

Sir Launcelot wept when he heard these words.

"Good father, what you say is true."

"Then I pray you, my son, confess your sins."

"Father, for fourteen years I have committed a sin of which I have never been cleansed; now to my shame I will confess it."

Then Sir Launcelot told the hermit of his love for Queen Gwynevere.

"For all these years," he continued, "I have loved her, and fought for her alone, caring nothing for God, and failing to thank Him for my victories. I wished only to win the queen's love and praise. I ask you now to counsel me."

"Sir, in honor of your knighthood, you must forswear the queen forever."

"By the faith of my body I will do so," said Sir Launcelot.

"Sir, if your heart is in accord with your speech, you shall win greater renown than ever before."

"Good father, I pray you, expound the meaning of the words spoken to me at the cross."

"Sir, you are one of the most gifted of men, and one of the most sinful. God, in His love for you, has granted you these gifts; but you, in the hardness of your heart, have not returned that love. You have not used those gifts in the furtherance of His glory; no, you have used them only in the furtherance of your sin. Therefore you are harder than stone: neither water nor fire can soften your sin, nor may the Holy Ghost enter you.

"As well as courage and beauty you have intelligence: you can distinguish between good and evil; you know well what conduct is pleasing to God, and how His love could enfold you. But you shun that love, by your sins you shut Him out, and in sin there is no sweetness; therefore you are more bitter than wood.

"When our Lord Jesu preached to the people in Jerusalem He found that they were hardened in their sins and would not allow His love to enter them. He wandered out of the town and came to a fig tree whose leaves grew copiously but which was barren of fruit. He cursed that tree for its likeness to the people whose souls were made barren by sin. And so it was with you, Sir Launcelot: In the presence of the Holy Grail His mysteries were denied you, for in soul you are as barren as that fig tree."

"Father, I shall repent my sins," said Sir Launcelot.

The hermit gave Sir Launcelot penance and bade him remain at the hermitage until the following day, when, he promised him, he should be given his horse, helmet, and shield.

3. SIR PERCIVALE

When Sir Launcelot galloped away across the waste lands in search of Sir Galahad, Sir Percivale returned to the hermitage and knelt before the window in order to ask the recluse if she had any news of him. The recluse opened the window and asked him what he wanted.

"Madam, I am a knight of the Round Table, and my name is Sir Percivale de Galys."

The recluse smiled, for she was his aunt, and welcomed him in. They spent the evening companionably, and in the morning Sir Percivale asked her about Sir Galahad.

"Why do you ask about him?"

"Madam, I wish to accomplish my revenge, for he overthrew me in jousting."

"It would appear that you are as anxious to meet your death as was your father."

"Madam, do you know me?"

"I do, I am your aunt. Do not be deceived by my present poverty, for I can tell you that I am far happier now than I was as the possessor of great riches and known as the Queen of the Waste Lands."

Sir Percivale wept.

"My dear nephew, have you news of your mother?"

"Madam, I dream of her often, but I do not even know whether she is alive or dead."

"Shortly after you left her, your mother shrove to the priest and died."

"God rest her soul! I suppose that death must come to us all sooner or later. But I pray you tell me about the knight who bore the white shield. Is he not the same who wore red armor on Whitsunday?"

"The same. He is miraculous and no knight will ever overcome him. Merlin devised the Round Table as a symbol of the wholeness of virtue, and the fellows, whether Christian or heathen, have always counted themselves blessed. So much so that many of them, like you, have deserted their families without feeling any sense of remorse.

"When Merlin prophesied that the quest of the Holy Grail would be accomplished by fellows of the Round Table, he was asked by whom it would be, and he replied: 'By three white bulls, two of whom shall be virgins, the third of whom shall be chaste, and the third shall surpass his father in strength and endurance as the lion surpasses the leopard.'

"He was then asked if he would ordain a special place for this knight, and he devised the Siege Perelous. And that was where the knight in the red armor, who bears the white shield, sat last Whitsunday: namely Sir Galahad."

"Madam, I shall seek Sir Galahad, not in order to revenge myself, but in order that he may lead me. I pray you tell me where he may be found."

"My dear nephew, you must ride first to the Castle of Gooth, where his cousin lives. You can stay there tonight, and ask the cousin if he has news of him. If he has none, you must ride on to the Castle of Carbonek where you will find the Maimed King, and there you will certainly hear news of Sir Galahad."

Sir Percivale took leave of his aunt, and they both wept as he did so. He rode until after evensong, when he came to a castle where he heard a clock chiming and where he was given hospitality for the night. In the morning he went to the monastery to hear mass.

The priest was already officiating, but behind the altar Sir Percivale could see a bed overlaid with rich cloths of silk and gold, and beneath them a prostrate figure. At the consecration the figure rose from the bed. It was an ancient man, who looked as if he had lived through several centuries. He wore a gold crown on his head, but was otherwise naked to the waist. His trunk, arms, and head were all covered with terrible wounds. He stretched out his hands and cried:

"Lord Jesu Christ, forget not your servant!"

During the rest of mass the ancient man knelt and said the orisons, and when it was over the priest touched him with the holy icon. Then the ancient man asked that his crown should be placed on the altar.

Sir Percivale asked his neighbor who he was.

"Sir, you must have heard of Joseph of Arimathea, who brought the gospel to this country, and suffered great persecution? Well, he was accompanied throughout his mission by King Evelake, whom Joseph had converted in the city of Sarras where he ruled. Thereafter King Evelake's ruling passion was to enter into the mysteries of the Holy Grail; he was so persistent that eventually God himself became angry and all but blinded him. Then the king prayed for mercy: 'O Lord, have mercy upon me and grant me life until I am kissed by my own kinsman of the ninth generation, who, it is ordained, shall achieve the quest of the Holy Grail.'

"When the king had finished his prayer he heard a voice which said: 'King Evelake, your prayer has been heard and your wish granted, and when you are kissed your sight shall be restored and your wounds healed.'

"And so this holy king has lived for four hundred years, but it is said that at this very moment the knight who shall kiss him and cure him is present at this court.

"Now, sir, I pray you tell me who you are, for it would seem that you are a knight of the Round Table."

"Sir, I am called Sir Percivale de Galys."

"Sir Percivale, you are welcome!"

Sir Percivale then took his leave of his hosts and continued his journey. At noon he entered a valley where he met twenty men-at-arms leading a dead knight on a horse litter. They asked Sir Percivale whence he had come.

"My lord, I come from King Arthur's court."

"Kill him! Kill him!" they all shouted.

Sir Percivale overthrew the first of his assailants with his spear, but then he was unhorsed and would certainly have been killed had not Sir Galahad suddenly appeared and galloped into the melee. With a few tremendous blows he struck several of the assailants cold to the ground, and the remainder fled from him in terror. He chased them into the forest, and Sir Percivale, who realized it must be Sir Galahad, shouted after him:

"Good knight, I pray you return to me, that I may thank you."

But Sir Galahad was soon out of sight. Sir Percivale ran after him, shouting as he ran, but being on foot had no chance of reaching him. Then he met a yeoman riding a hack and leading a huge black charger.

"My friend, as I am a knight, so shall I serve you if you will but lend me your black charger so that I may overtake the knight who just now rescued me."

"Sir, I may not; my master would kill me if I lent this charger to any man."

"Alas! the knight will escape me."

"Sir, a horse would become you well; but this one you would have to take by force."

"My friend, that I will not do."

The yeoman continued on his way and Sir Percivale sat sorrowfully beneath a tree. Before long, however, a knight rode past Sir Percivale; he was well armed, and mounted on the very charger which the yeoman had been leading. A moment later the yeoman galloped up to Sir Percivale, and asked him if he had seen the knight.

"Truly I have; but what would you have me do?" asked Sir Percivale.

"Sir, I pray you take my hack and try to recover the charger for me; otherwise my master will kill me."

Sir Percivale rode after the knight and challenged him. The knight charged Sir Percivale, killed the horse beneath him, and galloped away, ignoring Sir Percivale's challenge to fight on foot. In disgust Sir Percivale threw down his helmet, shield, and sword, saying as he did so: "Unhappy and wretched knight that I am!"

For a long time he sat sorrowing and then fell asleep. He was awakened at midnight by a strange lady who spoke to him urgently:

"Sir Percivale, what are you doing here?"

"Madam, I am doing neither good nor evil here."

"Sir, swear to obey me, and you shall have my horse to take you where you will."

Sir Percivale gave her his oath.

"Remain here and I will fetch my horse."

In a moment the lady returned with a huge, inky black charger, magnificently harnessed. Sir Percivale mounted and galloped away. The charger traveled as no mortal beast could have done: Within an hour they covered what ordinarily would have been a four-day journey, and came to a shore, beyond which the sea was raging.

The charger galloped up to the very edge of the sea, and then Sir Percivale realized that it was not a horse, but a fiend determined to destroy him. He resolutely made the sign of the cross on his forehead. The charger reared and threw him, then plunged into the waves, seeming to cry as he did so, and the waves seemed to burn after him. Sir Percivale knelt down and gave thanks to God for his deliverance, and passed the remainder of the night in prayer.

Sir Percivale found that he was on a rocky island with the sea all around him, and for company none but wild beasts. He walked into a valley and there saw a huge serpent carrying a young lion in its jaws. A moment later the parent lion appeared and with a roar attacked the serpent. Thinking that the lion was the more natural beast, Sir Percivale went to its aid and before long killed the serpent with a blow from his sword.

The lion showed every sign of gratitude and friendship that a beast can show to a man, and when Sir Percivale stroked it, fawned like a spaniel. Sir Percivale threw off his armor and rested until noon. Then the lion departed with the whelp and Sir Percivale prayed to God to give him strength to endure in His service. As if in answer to his prayer, the lion returned, and that night they slept side by side.

Sir Percivale had a strange dream. He saw two ladies; one was young and mounted on the lion, the other was old and mounted on the serpent. The younger one spoke first:

"Sir Percivale, my lord sends you his greeting, and warns you that tomorrow you shall fight the most powerful champion in the world. If he overcomes you, you will not only lose your life, you will be disgraced for all eternity."

"Madam, pray tell me, who is your lord?"

"My lord is the world's greatest lord," she replied, and disappeared.

Then the lady on the serpent spoke to him:

"Sir Percivale, you have offended me without cause."

"Madam, surely I have offered you no offense?"

"Sir, you killed my serpent while he was taking his prey. That serpent I nourished and loved and he served me well. Furthermore, the lion was not yours to defend."

"Madam, I killed the serpent because the lion is the gentler beast; what otherwise should I have done?"

"I require that you shall make amends, and yourself serve me."

"Madam, I must refuse you."

"No! Do you not understand that when you pledged yourself to Lord Jesu Christ you pledged yourself to me? Therefore when I find you unprotected I shall take you for my own."

Thereupon the lady on the serpent vanished.

Sir Percivale awoke feeling troubled in mind and enfeebled

in body. Before long a ship sailed to the shore. The awnings within and without were of white samite, and at the helm stood an old man who was wearing a priest's surplice.

"Sir, welcome to this island," said Sir Percivale, as he boarded the ship.

"God keep you! Whence have you come?" said the old man.

"Sir, I have ridden from King Arthur's court on the quest of the Holy Grail. But I wonder now if I shall ever escape from this wilderness."

"Have no fear. Acquit yourself like a true knight and no enemy shall destroy you."

"Sir, I pray you, tell me whence you have come."

"I have come from a foreign country, and I am here to comfort you."

"Sir, I pray you, explain the dream I had last night," said Sir Percivale, and related it to him.

"The younger of the ladies was the new church, born of the Passion of our Lord Jesu Christ. For love, she came to you to warn you of the battle which you shall fight."

"Against whom shall I fight?" asked Sir Percivale.

"Against the most terrible champion in the world; and if you fail, even as she warned you, you shall be shamed forever.

"The lady who rode the serpent was the old church and her real reprimand was not for killing the serpent, but for killing the fiend who, in the shape of a charger, carried you to the waters. By your faith, when you made the sign of the cross you killed him. And when she required that you should serve her, she meant that you should renounce your faith."

The priest then commanded Sir Percivale to disembark and, when he had done so, sailed away. Sir Percivale returned to the rock where the lion awaited him.

At midday a ship was driven to the island as though by a tempest. Sir Percivale ran to the shore to meet it, and saw that it was hung with black silk awnings. He was greeted by a richly clothed lady of great beauty, who asked him what had brought him to the island "wherein he was likely to remain forever and die of hunger."

"My lady," Sir Percivale replied, "I serve Him in whose service I shall not be permitted to die: for whosoever knocks shall enter, and who asks shall have. He hideth not from those who seek Him."

"Sir Percivale, do you recognize me?"

"My lady, who taught you my name?"

"I know you better than you think. Lately I came from the

Waste Forest, where I met the Red Knight who bears the white shield."

"Ah, my lady, if only I could meet him!"

"Sir, swear by your knighthood to place yourself at my command and I shall bring you to him."

"My lady, I swear."

"Now I will tell you: I saw the Red Knight chasing two other knights through the Waste Forest and into the water of Mortayse, where they fled in terror of him. He rode in after them and they were drowned; but, because of his great strength, he was able to make his way to the shore again."

Sir Percivale thanked her, and she asked him if he had eaten lately.

"My lady, I have eaten no meat for three days and three nights; but I have been sustained by the words of a holy man who was here."

"Sir Percivale, be warned; he was an enchanter and a multiplier of words. Believe him and you will die of hunger on this rocky island, and then fall prey to the wild beasts. And that would be a shame for a knight so young and seemly as you are."

"My lady, I pray you tell me who you are, that you should proffer me such kindness."

"I am she who was the richest in the world, and who now is disinherited."

"My lady, how did that come about?"

"I will tell you. My lord was the greatest in the world, and I his finest ornament. Of this I became perhaps a little too proud, and what I said to him one day displeased him. He drove me from his presence and banished me forever from my inheritance. He is pitiless, and neither I nor my sympathizers could ever move him. Now, gentle knight, I must plead for succor from all who, like you, are courteous, upright, and strong, and ask them to help me recover my lost dominion. Sir, I pray you, as you are a knight of the Round Table, and sworn to help ladies in distress, do not refuse me! Further, I promise you that those who already serve me find, in that very service, reward for their labors."

Sir Percivale promised her what aid was in his power to give, and she thanked him. The sun was now at its zenith and the lady commanded that her pavilion should be pitched on the shore.

"Sir," she said, "rest yourself during the heat of the day."

Sir Percivale thanked her; she took his helmet and shield

and he lay down and slept. He awoke long after noon, and asked the lady if she could provide him with meat.

"Sir, you shall have all you need," she replied.

In a moment a variety of choice meats and a heady wine were set before him. Sir Percivale ate and drank, and as he was warmed with the wine, he began to think his companion the most enchanting lady on earth. He begged to become her lover. For a long time she refused him, though gently and without discouragement; then, when his passion was at its fiercest, she exacted a promise from him:

"Sir Percivale, I shall not yield to you unless you swear me an oath of implicit obedience; and this you must swear by your knighthood."

"My lady, I swear it!"

"I pray you now, gentle knight, do with me as you will. And please know that of all men on earth, it is you whom I most desire."

The lady commanded two of her squires to make a bed in the middle of the pavilion. Then she unclothed herself; Sir Percivale did likewise, and they lay naked together. But at that moment Sir Percivale saw a red cross burning on the hilt of his sword. He remembered the words spoken by the holy man on the previous day, and he made the sign of the cross on his forehead.

Immediately the whole pavilion was whirled away in a cloud of black smoke. Sir Percivale flung himself onto his knees in terror.

"O sweet Lord Jesu! by your grace you have delivered me from evil." So saying he looked toward the ship: the lady was about to embark and she turned to him for a moment:

"Sir Percivale, you have betrayed me!"

Once she had embarked the ship sailed away furiously, the winds roared, and the waves burned in its wake. Sir Percivale watched it sorrowfully, drew his sword, and plunged it into his thigh. Blood poured from the wound.

"O Lord, accept this offering; for surely the very flower of my virginity would have been lost."

Utterly abject, Sir Percivale bound his wound with a strip torn from his shirt, dressed himself, and sat down on the desolate shore.

Toward noon the hermit returned in his ship. When Sir Percivale recognized him he fainted for shame; but when he had recovered, ran up to the ship and saluted him.

"How have you fared since I departed?" asked the holy man.

"Father, I was tempted by a lady," said Sir Percivale, and then told the whole story of what had passed.

"Did you not recognize the lady?" asked the holy man.

"Only as one who had been sent to shame me."

"Sir, it was Lucifer himself; you should have known it—the very same as the old woman who rode the serpent."

Then the holy man told Sir Percivale how the Lord had disinherited Lucifer, "the most beautiful of the angels," for his sin of pride, and how, had it not been for God's grace, Sir Percivale himself would have been won by Lucifer.

"Now, Sir Percivale, you must take heed, for you have been warned," and with those words the holy man vanished.

Sir Percivale boarded the ship and sailed away from the island.

4. SIR LAUNCELOT

Sir Launcelot remained for three days with the hermit to whom he had shriven. Then the hermit gave him his horse, helmet, and sword, and Sir Launcelot departed. At noon he came to a small chapel, and inside was a hermit dressed all in white.

"God save you!" said Sir Launcelot.

"God keep you, and make you a good knight!" the hermit replied.

Sir Launcelot dismounted and entered the chapel. Inside he saw the corpse of a very old man dressed in a white shirt.

"Sir," the hermit said, "for a hundred years the deceased was a holy man; then he broke the vows of his order, otherwise he would not have been wearing a white shirt when he died."

The hermit led Sir Launcelot to the inner sanctuary, put a stole about his neck, and, taking a Bible, made invocatory gestures over it. In a moment a hideous fiend appeared; it was so dreadful that even the bravest of men would have quailed before it.

"And why," said the fiend, "do you so torment me?"

"I wish to know whether the deceased is saved or damned," said the hermit.

"He is not lost but saved!" said the fiend in a terrible voice.

"How can that be when he died in a garment which his order forbade?"

"Not so," said the fiend. "He was of noble blood, and the time came when his nephew, Sir Aguaurs, quarreled with the Earl de Vale. Sir Aguaurs saw that the earl was more powerful than he was and begged his uncle to help him. The uncle did so, and between them they forced the earl and three of his vassals to yield to them.

"The uncle returned to the chapel here, but the earl, in defiance of his oath, sent two of his nephews to avenge him. They arrived during mass, at the consecration. They waited until the mass was over and then attacked him with their swords. But such was the sanctity of the hermit that the steel would not cut into his flesh, for he who serves the Lord truly is protected by Him.

"Next they made a great fire, stripped off the hermit's clothes, and peeled the very hairs off his back.

" 'Understand,' said the hermit, 'that it is not in your power even to singe my skin.'

" 'Well, we shall certainly try,' one of them replied.

"They dressed him in a white shirt and cast him into the flames, where he remained all day and was not burnt. The nephews left and I came in the morning and found him dead, but neither his shirt nor his skin was singed. Then I took him from the fire and laid him where he is now.

"That is all; and I pray you let me go, for I have told you the truth."

The fiend departed in a tempest, and both Sir Launcelot and the hermit rejoiced that the deceased was not damned. Sir Launcelot remained with the hermit overnight. In the morning they spoke again.

"Sir, are you not Launcelot du Lake?" asked the hermit.

"Father, I am."

"What do you seek in this country?"

"The Holy Grail."

"Sir, seek it you may, but were it here before you, you would have no more power to see it than a blind man has to see a bright sword. Certainly you are the greatest knight on earth, and were it not for your sin you would be the first to see it."

Sir Launcelot wept.

"Tell me, have you shriven since you set forth on your quest?"

"Father, I have."

The hermit and Sir Launcelot then buried the dead man.

"Father, I pray you counsel me," said Sir Launcelot.

"My son, take the hair of the hermit and place it next to your skin; it will enhance your virtue. While you are on the quest of the Holy Grail, abstain from meat and wine; and whenever you have the opportunity, go to mass."

At evensong Sir Launcelot took his leave of the hermit, and after putting the hermit's hair next to his skin, departed. He had not ridden far through the forest when he met a young noblewoman riding on a white palfrey.

"Sir, where are you riding to?" she asked him.

"My lady, I ride as fortune leads me."

"Sir Launcelot, I can tell you that you are nearer to your goal now, and more ready to perceive it, than you were formerly."

"My lady, where may I lodge tonight?"

"Sir, tonight you shall find no lodging, but tomorrow you shall be well cared for."

Sir Launcelot blessed the young noblewoman and rode on. Soon he came to a cross, where he dismounted, set his horse to pasture, disarmed himself, and lay down to sleep.

In his sleep Sir Launcelot had a vision of a man wearing a gold crown and surrounded by stars. He led seven kings and two knights up to the cross, where they all knelt down and raised their hands in prayer:

"Sweet Father, we beseech you, visit us, and give unto each according to his deserts."

Thereupon the clouds flew open and an ancient man descended in a company of angels. He blessed all but one of the knights, calling each his faithful servant, but to the one he said:

"You have profaned the gifts I bestowed upon you in wars which you fought for your own vainglory and to win pleasure in the world. You have fought against me, and so now you shall be confounded unless you restore to me those gifts."

In the morning Sir Launcelot resumed his journey, and the vision remained clearly in his mind. At midday he met the knight who had been healed by the Holy Grail when he himself had lain powerless, and who had taken his horse, helmet, and sword.

"Knight, defend yourself!" said Sir Launcelot.

They couched their spears and galloped together. Sir Launcelot's opponent was flung to the ground with such violence that he all but broke his neck. Sir Launcelot then exchanged horses, leaving the one given to him by the hermit tethered to a tree for the benefit of his opponent when he recovered himself.

At dusk Sir Launcelot came to a hermitage, where he exchanged greetings with the hermit.

"Sir, whence do you come?" asked the hermit.

"Father, I come from King Arthur's court. My name is Sir Launcelot du Lake, and I am riding on the quest of the Holy Grail. But I pray you, expound a vision which I had last night."

Sir Launcelot then related it.

"Sir, here you have the story of your lineage: The seven kings and the two knights are the descendants of Joseph of Arimathea, who, forty years after the Passion of our Lord Jesu Christ, preached of King Evelake's victories over the infidel. The first was the holy man Nappus; the second was the holy man Nacien; the third was Hellyas le Grose; the fourth Lysays, and the fifth Jonas. Jonas left his own country and went to West Britain, where he married Manuell's daughter and thereby became the King of Gaul. His son, who was named Sir Launcelot, was your grandfather, and as great a knight as you are now; and his son, King Ban, was your father, who was the last of the seven kings.

"You, Sir Launcelot, are the eighth descendant, but you are not of their fellowship; and Sir Galahad, your son, is the ninth, and he is represented by the lion because he shall surpass all earthly knights. Of earthly knights you are the most remarkable, both for your virtues and your sins, and you, above all other knights, should give thanks to God for the gifts with which He has endowed you."

"Father, you say that the most virtuous of all knights is my son?" said Sir Launcelot.

"That you should know, for did you not in the flesh company in love with Elaine, King Pelles' daughter? And did she not bear Sir Galahad? And did he not sit at the Siege Perelous at the last feast of the Pentecost? You should therefore openly acknowledge that Sir Galahad is your son. Further, I warn you, never encounter him in battle, for he will defeat you, as he would any other knight."

"Holy father, should not Sir Galahad intercede for me with our Lord, so that I may not again fall into sin?"

"Sir Launcelot, you already benefit from his prayers on your behalf; but you must remember that neither father nor son may bear the other's sins, for it is ordained that each man must himself bear his own burden."

The hermit and Sir Launcelot took supper together and then lay down to rest. All night Sir Launcelot was tormented by the hair of the deceased hermit, but he bore it meekly. In the morning he heard mass, armed, and departed.

Sir Launcelot rode through the forest and came to a plain on which stood a fine castle, and before it was an array of silk pavilions in many different colors. Five hundred knights were drawn up before the pavilions preparatory to fighting a tournament. They were divided into two parties, those from the castle being mounted on black horses and clad in black armor, those from the pavilions being mounted on white horses and clad in white armor.

They fought, and soon the white knights gained the ascendancy. Sir Launcelot galloped in among them and fought for the black knights. With Sir Launcelot's help the black knights recovered and forced the white knights to the defensive. Then Sir Launcelot's strength began to fail; the white knights gave him no respite, and eventually dragged him from the field and set him down too badly winded to offer any further resistance. The white knights returned to the field and defeated the black knights.

"Blessed is the Lord that now you are of our fellowship, and shall no longer escape us!" said one of the knights to Sir Launcelot, and departed.

"Alas!" said Sir Launcelot to himself, "never before have I been so shamed on the battlefield!"

Sorrowfully, Sir Launcelot mounted and rode through the forest. Several hours later he found himself in a deep valley, and finding it impossible to ascend the slopes of the mountain, set his horse to pasture and lay down to sleep beneath an apple tree. Then it seemed that an old man came up to him.

"Sir Launcelot, how ill is your faith, that once more and so readily you fall into error!" he said, and vanished.

When Sir Launcelot awoke he remounted and rode down the valley until he came to a small chapel. Through the window he could see a recluse kneeling before the altar. She called him into the chapel and asked him whence he had come. Sir Launcelot told her, and then described the tournament and his vision of the old man, and begged her to explain them to him.

"Sir Launcelot, your worldly renown can avail you nothing in matters of the spirit, and the outcome of the tournament you fought in proves it. The black knights of Argustus, whom you unerringly supported, were those bound to earthly sin; the white knights of Eliazar, King Pelles' son, were those who, free of sin, acted in a state of grace.

"And so it is with King Arthur's knights who have ridden on the quest of the Holy Grail. For the nature of this quest is the challenge of evil which each knight must transcend in order to participate in the holy mysteries which God shall vouchsafe to the righteous. Those of his knights who are virgins and blessed are as those white knights; those who are sinful, as the black knights.

"You have been warned, Sir Launcelot, by the holy man in your vision, and by God Himself, that you do not belong to the blessed; that you will fight only in the cause of evil to gain worldly ends, to assuage your own pride and vainglory, and those things are not worth a pear!

"If you do not renounce your evil ways, which are now proved, and for which God has punished you, you shall surely end in the deepest pit of hell, where your worldly glory will avail you nothing. Therefore, Sir Launcelot, I urge you, repent!"

Sir Launcelot took dinner with the recluse, and afterward blessed her and rode on his way. Through the valley he came to the turbulent river called Mortayse; with fear in his heart but calling for God's blessing, Sir Launcelot crossed the waters.

Then he met a black knight riding on a black horse. Without uttering a word, the black knight killed Sir Launcelot's horse and then rode on his way. Taking up his helmet and shield, Sir Launcelot gave thanks to God for the encounter.

5. SIR GAWAIN

From Whitsun to Michaelmas Sir Gawain rode alone on the quest of the Holy Grail, and failing to meet with any adventures, began to grow weary. Then he met Sir Ector de Marys.

They greeted each other joyfully, and he too complained that neither he, nor some twenty of his fellows whom he had met in the course of his journey, had met with any adventures.

"I wonder what has befallen your brother, Sir Launcelot," said Sir Gawain.

"I have heard no news of him, nor have I of Sir Galahad, Sir Percivale, or Sir Bors," Sir Ector replied.

"Let them be!" said Sir Gawain. "Those four knights are without peer, although Sir Launcelot would be the greatest of them were it not for his sins. But none of them would be grateful for our company on this quest; and if they should fail, most certainly we should."

Sir Gawain and Sir Ector rode together for over a week and then, one Saturday, came to an ancient and ruined chapel. Resting their spears against the door, they entered and found it deserted. They knelt down and prayed, then sat in two of the pews and talked for a while; they both felt discouraged and before long fell asleep. In their sleep, both had visions.

Sir Gawain saw a flowery meadow in which was set a feeding rack. Wandering about the meadow were a hundred and fifty bulls, all of which were black except for three. Of the three two were completely white, and tied together by two cords; the third was white except for one black spot. The three bulls remained meekly in the meadow, but the black bulls ran hither and thither, and seemed to say among themselves, "Let us go elsewhere for our pasture." Some left the meadow and did not return; others did return, but always looking lean and exhausted.

Sir Ector saw himself and his brother Sir Launcelot seated in two chairs. They descended from the chairs and mounted two horses, and one said to the other, "We shall now seek that which we shall not find." Then a man appeared who stripped and beat Sir Launcelot and then dressed him in knotted clothes and set him upon an ass. Sir Launcelot rode on the ass to a well, dismounted, and tried to drink; but as he did so, the water sank. Sir Launcelot then returned to his chair. Sir Ector supposed that he himself rode to a rich man's house and, when he entered, found a wedding in progress. A king was present, and he said to Sir Ector, "Knight, there is no place for you here." Sir Ector then returned to his chair.

When they awoke, Sir Gawain and Sir Ector related their visions to each other. Then Sir Ector said:

"In truth, I shall not be happy until I have heard news of my brother."

While they were talking, an arm appeared before them, moved slowly across the chapel, and vanished. Over the arm lay a bridle, and in the hand was clasped a bright-burning candle. Then from nowhere a voice spoke:

"Knights both: these symbols have failed you, hence you shall not achieve the quest of the Holy Grail!"

"Sir Ector, have you heard?" asked Sir Gawain.

"Sir Gawain, I have. Now let us find a holy man who will explain these mysteries, for it seems that we labor in vain," Sir Ector replied.

They left the chapel, took their horses, and rode along a valley until they met a squire.

"Sir, can you direct us to a hermit?" asked Sir Gawain.

"My lords, up on the mountain is a humble dwelling in which lives Nacien, the holiest man in this land. But I warn you that you will have to go on foot, for the way is too rough for your horses."

Sir Gawain and Sir Ector continued along the valley, but before long met a knight who challenged them to joust.

"For the love of God! I have not jousted but once since I left Camelot. I pray you, let me encounter him," said Sir Gawain.

"Sir Gawain, I should like to joust with him myself," said Sir Ector.

"Avenge me if I am overthrown," said Sir Gawain.

Sir Gawain and the unknown knight couched their spears and galloped together. Both broke their shields and were flung from their horses, Sir Gawain with a wound in his left side, his opponent with Sir Gawain's spear thrust clean through his body and coming out at the further side. Sir Gawain rose and drew his sword, but the other knight continued to lie on the ground, disabled by his wound.

"Sir, you must yield or I shall kill you," said Sir Gawain.

"Sir, I have already received my mortal wound; therefore I pray you take me to an abbey where I may make my peace with the Creator."

"Sir, I know of no abbey hereabouts," said Sir Gawain.

"Lift me onto your horse and I will direct you."

Sir Gawain lifted him onto his own horse, mounted behind him to give him support, and rode gently to the abbey. The knight was disarmed and given extreme unction, then he asked Sir Gawain to withdraw the spear shaft. Sir Gawain asked him his name.

"Sir Gawain, I come from King Arthur's court as you do, and am one of your sworn fellows of the Round Table. My father is King Uryens and my name is Sir Uwayne. I too have ridden on the quest of the Holy Grail; but now, may God forgive us! I shall be remembered only as one who was killed by his own brother."

"Alas!" said Sir Gawain.

"Sir, do not repent! I could wish to die at the hands of no nobler knight than you. But I pray you recommend me to King Arthur and to our fellows of the Round Table."

Sir Gawain wept; so also did Sir Ector. They withdrew the spear shaft from Sir Uwayne's body and, when he had given up the ghost, buried him as befitted a prince. On his tomb they inscribed his name and the manner of his death.

Sorrowfully, Sir Gawain and Sir Ector left the abbey and rode to the foot of the mountain, where they tethered their horses and then climbed to the abode of Nacien the hermit. They found a small chapel and next to it a small courtyard in which grew the roots upon which the hermit lived. Nacien greeted them and asked them what had brought them there.

"Father, we wish to be confessed," said Sir Gawain.

"My son, I am ready."

First Sir Gawain and then Sir Ector told the hermit of his vision, and what had befallen them since.

"Sir Gawain, the feeding rack was the Round Table, the bulls the fellows of the Round Table, and the flowery meadow a representation of the patience and humility upon which true chivalry is founded. The black bulls were those knights in whom sin is still uppermost; the two white bulls who were tied together were Sir Galahad and Sir Percivale, who are virgins, sinless and humble. The white bull with the black spot was Sir Bors, who sinned but once and has since remained chaste.

"The black bulls who sought distant pastures and who failed to return or, if they did return, came lean and exhausted, were those knights who set off on the quest of the Holy Grail and were too impatient or proud to receive their absolution first. As a result they wandered only into the waste lands, where they were killed or exhausted; for so it shall be with your fellows. Many shall meet their death at each other's hands, and the few who return will be astonished when they do so.

"Of the three white bulls, the one with the spot shall return, but the other two shall not."

Nacien spoke next to Sir Ector:

"Sir, the chairs upon which you and Sir Launcelot sat represented the high estate to which you are heirs, and from which you descended. The fruitless search was your quest for the Holy Grail, which neither of you shall achieve. Sir Launcelot allowed himself to be humiliated, dressed in knotted garments, and set upon an ass, as a penance for his sins, the ass being the beast of humility chosen by our Lord Jesu Christ. Sir Launcelot knelt by the well and tried to drink the waters thereof, and the waters withdrew from him—which means that Sir Launcelot desired the grace of God, and to enter into His mysteries. But because for twenty-four years he served the devil, for twenty-four days he shall have to do penance. The grace of God was withdrawn from him, and in the presence of the Holy Grail he was impotent. When the twenty-four days have passed he will return to Camelot and describe a part of his adventures at the court.

"Now I will explain the miracle that befell you in the chapel: The arm was the charity of the Holy Ghost, the bridle signified abstinence; for he who is in a state of grace is held close so that he does not fall into sin again. The bright-burning candle was the light of our Lord Jesu Christ.

"When the voice spoke and said that these tokens had failed you, the meaning was that lacking charity, virtue, and faith, you shall not achieve the Holy Grail."

"Father, you have certainly made these mysteries clear to us," said Sir Gawain. "Now I pray you, tell us why, since we have ridden on this quest, we have failed to meet with any adventures, when formerly this was not the case."

"My son, the quest of the Holy Grail means other things than killing your fellow men, and those are the adventures to which you and your fellow sinners are accustomed. You yourself have killed many men, and that is one reason why you shall not achieve the Holy Grail. Even Sir Launcelot has abstained from killing on this quest; and were he more stable in mind, he would be the first to achieve it, after Sir Galahad. As it is, however, he shall not, for the Lord knows all. But when he dies, he shall die a holy man."

"Father, it seems that for our sins, we are unworthy of this quest," said Sir Gawain.

"My son, on this quest, not you, nor a hundred like you, could win anything but shame."

On hearing these words Sir Ector and Sir Gawain took their leave of the hermit, but he called after them:

"Sir Gawain, it is a long time since you were made a knight, and never since have you served your Maker. You are like an old tree: The leaves, the fruit, the sap are all withered, for with those you served the devil; now all that you can offer to God is a dry husk."

"Father, I would speak with you further, but my companion has already gone," Sir Gawain replied.

"My son, you would do better to remain and hear my counsel."

But Sir Gawain left him and rode with Sir Ector until they came to a forester's house, where they received hospitality. They set off again in the morning, and it was to be a long time before they met with any adventures.

6. SIR BORS

When Sir Bors left Camelot he met a holy man riding on an ass. The holy man recognized Sir Bors as one of the knights errant who had set off on the quest of the Holy Grail. They greeted each other.

"Who are you?" said the holy man.

"Father, I am one who seeks the Holy Grail. I pray you, counsel me."

"Only a knight who is peerless can win the Holy Grail. I advise you to confess."

They rode together to a small hermitage, where the holy man suggested Sir Bors should remain for the night. Sir Bors confessed, and when he had received absolution they made their supper of bread and water.

"My son, partake only of bread and water until you sit at the table whereon the Holy Grail is set."

"Willingly, father; but how do you know that I shall find the Holy Grail?"

"My son, I know it well, also that you shall sit there in company with but few of your fellows."

"Whom God shall send shall be welcome!"

"Now I pray you unclothe yourself, for instead of your shirt I shall give you to wear a garment of chastisement."

The holy man was confident of Sir Bors because he knew

that he had only once sinned in the flesh, when he got with child the daughter of King Brandegoris. Sir Bors donned the garment, which was a red coat to be worn until he had accomplished the quest, armed, and took his leave of the hermit.

He had not ridden far when he saw a large bird perched on a withered tree. Below it were its young, starved and about to die. The parent bird plunged its beak into its breast, and as the blood flowed from the wound the young birds drank and their life was renewed. Then the parent died. The meaning of this was clear to Sir Bors and he rode on his way.

At evensong he came to a well-kept castle which boasted a fine tower. He was received by an ardent and beautiful young noblewoman, who entreated him to sup with her. Sir Bors accepted, and a splendid supper was served, with a variety of choice meats and wines. But Sir Bors, in remembrance of the holy man's instructions, called for bread and water, made sops, and ate only that.

"My lord, does the meat not please you?" asked his hostess.

"My lady, I am forbidden it."

Not wishing to discomfort him, the young noblewoman refrained from further comment, and after supper they talked of different matters. Then a squire appeared.

"Madam, your sister warns you that tomorrow you shall forfeit your castle and estates to her unless you can find a knight who will encounter her champion, Sir Prydam le Noyre."

"Alas!" said the young noblewoman, "must I lose the last of my inheritance, without justice and without cause?"

"My lady, may not I protect you?" said Sir Bors.

"My lord, I will tell you. At one time King Anyause was our overlord. He fell in love with a gentlewoman older than myself, and of evil nature. When he granted her estates, she began to abuse her power and put to death many of my own kinsmen. The king came to hear of this and dispossessed her, and granted the estates to me. But then he died; and from that time, this gentlewoman has conducted a war of conquest on what is properly my demesne. She succeeded in killing the greater number of my men, and in turning the rest against me. Now I have only this castle; and it seems that tomorrow, for want of a champion, I must lose this too."

"My lady, what manner of man is Sir Prydam le Noyre?"

"My lord, he is the most redoubtable warrior in the land."

"My lady, I pray you send him word that I accept his challenge. On behalf of God and of yourself, I will defend your just cause."

When the squire had departed with this message, Sir Bors and his hostess talked pleasantly until it was time to retire. In accordance with the vows he had taken when he started on his quest, Sir Bors slept on the floor instead of on the bed; and that night he was vouchsafed a vision: He saw two birds, one large and white as a swan, one smaller and black as a raven. The white bird spoke first:

"Good knight! Sustain me and I shall yield to you the greatest riches on earth; and in my own likeness you shall be made white."

The white bird vanished and the black bird spoke:

"Good knight! Serve me, and my blackness shall prevail against all that is white."

The black bird departed. Then he found himself in a chapel in which a chair had been set. On one side of the chair grew a rotten tree, on the other two flowers, like white lilies, but they grew so close that they seemed to strangle each other, and their brightness was fading. A holy man walked up and touched both flowers so that they sprang apart. Immediately each flower multiplied and then bore fruit. The holy man spoke:

"Succor is given to the flowers, for they can be saved, but not to the tree, for that is already rotten."

"Sir, it seems that the tree has perished," said Sir Bors.

"Good knight, you must be on your guard when like circumstances befall you," said the holy man, and vanished.

When Sir Bors awoke he crossed himself, dressed, and went to mass at the chapel, where he met his hostess. After mass he armed, and she begged him to take some breakfast.

"My lady, not until I have done with the battle."

Sir Bors mounted and rode with the lady and her suite to the field where her antagonist awaited her.

"Madam, you have done wrong to usurp the lands which King Anyause gave to me; and yet I should prefer that our champions did not fight."

"Madam, you shall not choose, unless it is to withdraw your champion."

An agreement was made that the lady whose champion prevailed should take possession of all the disputed lands. Then Sir Bors and Sir Prydam drew apart for the combat.

They charged together and both broke their spears and were deeply wounded. At the second encounter their horses collapsed beneath them and they continued the battle on foot with their swords.

Sir Prydam was a brave and skillful fighter, and both had

received many grave wounds before he began to feel faint. Sir Bors redoubled his blows, and when Sir Prydam fell to the ground, tore off his helmet and beat his bare face with the flat of his sword, urging him meanwhile to yield.

"Gentle knight! for the love of God do not kill me, and I will swear allegiance to your lady."

Sir Bors granted him his life, and then the old gentlewoman and her followers fled from the field. Next, Sir Bors summoned all those nobles whose lands were held by the castle and obliged them too to swear allegiance to the lady. When all was set to rights the lady offered Sir Bors a reward for his services, but he refused it and departed.

He rode all day, and that night lodged with a lady of his acquaintance. Early the next morning he set off again, and at noon met with an adventure. Coming to a crossroads in the forest, he saw his brother Sir Lyonel bound naked to a horse and being beaten with thorns by two knights. Sir Lyonel suffered his torment in silence, although blood was trickling from more than a hundred wounds.

Sir Bors was about to go to his rescue when he saw a young noblewoman being dragged into the thick of the forest by a knight. The young noblewoman was crying out piteously, "O Holy Virgin, I pray you protect your own!" Then she saw Sir Bors:

"Good knight! as you believe in our Saviour, and as you honor your knightly vows, I pray you deliver me!"

Sir Bors wept when he saw her, and raised his eyes to heaven. "Alas!" he said to himself, "must I suffer my own brother to be killed, or this maid to be violated? Either way leads me to unendurable shame! O Jesu, whose creature I am, I pray you guide me, and if I deliver the maid, grant that my brother shall not be killed!" Then, riding up to the knight, he said:

"Sir, on pain of death, deliver the maid!"

The knight set down the young noblewoman and dressed his shield. Sir Bors charged at him and drove his spear through the knight's shoulder and sent him tumbling to the ground; then, as he withdrew his spear, the knight fainted.

"My lady, your deliverance!"

"My lord, I pray you accompany me to my castle."

Sir Bors did so.

"My lady, who was this recreant?" he asked.

"Sir, he is my cousin. A fiend must suddenly have possessed him, for never before have I had cause to charge him with treachery. But I thank you for my deliverance, else we should have been stigmatized, and the lives of five hundred knights would have been forfeited."

While they were talking they were met by twelve of the lady's knights. She described to them how Sir Bors had rescued her, and they urged him to be presented to her father.

"My lords, I thank you, but my quest leads me elsewhere," Sir Bors replied.

He rode off at once in search of his brother, but for a long time could find no trace of him. Then he met a man appareled in a priest's frock, and riding a pitch-black horse.

"My lord, for what do you search?" he asked.

"Sir, I seek my brother whom I saw being beaten by two knights."

"Sir Bors, do not repent, but your brother is dead."

Whereupon the priest led Sir Bors to a corpse which lay in the undergrowth, and which, mutilated as it was, resembled Sir Lyonel. Sir Bors fell to the ground in a faint, where he lay for a long time before coming to.

"My dear brother, now you are dead and never again shall there be joy in my heart! From Him whom I serve I must ask guidance."

So saying, Sir Bors lifted the corpse onto his horse, and then asked the priest to lead him to a chapel where he might bury him.

"Come, there is one nearby," said the priest.

They buried Sir Lyonel in a marble tomb in a small, crumbling chapel which had been built beneath a strong tower.

"We will hold the burial service tomorrow; let us now repair to our lodging," said the priest.

"Sir, are you a priest?" asked Sir Bors.

"I am."

"Then I pray you, explain to me a dream which I had last night," said Sir Bors, and recounted it.

"Sir, I shall explain part today and part tomorrow. The white bird betokens a lady who loves you dearly for what you are and for what you have done; neither for the love of God nor for fear of your own scruples should you refuse her. To win her would not be to lose your virginity, for that is already lost, nor to achieve fame, for that you have already won, but to win her for her own sake, and thereby to release Sir Launcelot from peril. Because you rescued a maid who was nothing to you, your noble brother has died; now Sir Launcelot is endangered, so it behooves you to consider painstakingly the choice that lies before you."

"Father, there is nothing on earth I would not yield in order that Sir Launcelot should be saved."

"My son, the choice lies with you."

They rode to the tower and there they were received hospitably by many fine knights and ladies. Sir Bors was disarmed and given to wear a mantle trimmed with ermine. In the warmth of his welcome Sir Bors began to forget his sorrow, and then he was presented to the lady of the castle. She was of striking beauty, and more richly clothed and prinked than Queen Gwynevere herself.

"Sir Bors," said one of the courtiers, "this is the lady to whom we have sworn allegiance; and surely she is the most wealthy and the most beautiful heiress on earth. We would have you know that she chooses you alone for her paramour."

Sir Bors was abashed. The lady overwhelmed him with protestations of her love, and of the earthly riches which would be his if he accepted her. With much difficulty Sir Bors refused her, bound irrevocably as he was by his vows of chastity.

"Alas my lord! you would refuse me?" asked the lady.

"Madam, there is no lady but that I should refuse her; and just now, while my brother lies dead, surely it is unkind to entreat me."

"My lord, for your strength and your comeliness I have loved you long and ardently, and now I cannot believe that you will refuse to accompany me to my bed!"

"Madam, I cannot."

"Sir Bors, you refuse, and my life must be forfeit! Come, and I will show you."

So saying, the lady led twelve of her gentlewomen up to the battlements, where they stood on the very edge, prepared to leap.

"Sir Bors, good knight! have mercy upon us! Yield to our lady or else we must all leap to our death, and surely you will be shamed forever."

Sir Bors was aghast at the sight, for these ladies were all beautiful and richly clothed; and yet he was not without prudence, and determined that rather they should lose their souls than he his.

All at once they leaped, and Sir Bors crossed himself. Immediately there was a thunderous din as the castle collapsed and vanished, and wild fiends rushed hither and thither with shrill cries. Sir Bors raised his hands to heaven and prayed:

"Sweet Father, by Your grace I endure and am saved."

Sir Bors rode forth once more; he heard a clock chime, and came to an abbey built within high stone walls. He was received kindly by the monks, who saw that he was a knight of the Round Table riding in quest of the Holy Grail. They led him to a chamber and disarmed him.

"My brothers, I pray you, let me consult a priest," said Sir Bors.

He was led to the abbot and described his adventures.

"My son, I do not know who you are, yet you seem young to be of such strong faith. It is late now and you must repose yourself. Tomorrow I shall advise you."

The monks took good care of Sir Bors that night, and in the morning led him again to the abbot, to whom Sir Bors described the whole circumstances of his journey.

"My son, the Lord showed Himself to you in the likeness of a bird. His Passion and the bleeding from His heart were shown by the bird wounding its breast in order to succor its young. The withered tree was the world which bears fruit only as God wills it.

"Then the Lord was represented by King Anyause, and His church by the young noblewoman for whom you fought against the champion of the old church—the old woman who constantly assaults us with the powers of darkness and evil.

"The black bird was the power of the new church, which shall prevail in the end; the white bird was the old church: white without and corrupt within, for the servants of the devil are hypocrites.

"The priest on the black horse was a fiend in disguise. He censured you for saving the virgin and he lied to you in saying that your brother had died, for he lives still. Then, knowing your tender heart, he led you to the castle where Lucifer himself was disguised as the beautiful heiress who tried to tempt and then to coerce you into sin. Above all, the devil wished to circumvent your achievement of the Holy Grail.

"Now you must understand that the rotten tree in the chapel was your brother Sir Lyonel, who is a murderer and one who has desecrated his vows to the high order of knighthood. The two white lilies whose closeness threatened their sheen were the knight and the maid, both virgins whom you rescued from sin.

"Hence in turning from the rotten tree to the maid you did as one should in the true service of our Lord."

The abbot blessed Sir Bors, who departed. That night he was lodged by an old lady, and the next morning rode on until he came to a castle which stood in a valley. A yeoman came galloping by and Sir Bors greeted him.

"Pray tell me, shall I meet with any adventure in these parts?"

"Sir, you shall. A tournament is to be held beneath this very castle."

"Who will the combatants be?"

"The Earl of Playns is to lead a party against Sir Hervyn, who is nephew to the lady of the castle."

Sir Bors hoped that his brother or at least some of his fellows of the Round Table might be present at the tournament. He rode to a hermitage on the edge of the forest to ask for lodging, and found, sitting at the chapel door, his brother Sir Lyonel.

Sir Bors dismounted and greeted him joyfully.

"Good brother! How did you come here?"

"Sir Bors, surely no knight was ever so heartlessly deserted by his own brother. For all the love that you bear me, I might have been beaten to death! And why? To protect the virtue of a young noblewoman whose name you did not know, and who could have meant little to you. But now I shall punish you as you deserve, so defend yourself!"

Sir Bors knelt before his brother and begged for mercy.

"Mercy you shall not have; rather shall I kill you as I would any common felon or traitor. You are unworthy of our noble father King Bors de Ganis, and of all who come from his house. Now mount your horse, otherwise I shall not scruple to trample you underfoot."

Sir Bors, although not frightened of Sir Lyonel, felt that as he was his elder brother, he should love and respect him, so once more he knelt down.

"Good brother, for the sake of the love that is between us, I pray you have mercy and do not kill me."

Ignoring his words, Sir Lyonel, who was now mounted, galloped straight over him, trampling him underfoot as he had threatened. Sir Bors was seriously wounded and collapsed. Sir Lyonel leaped off his horse and was about to behead him with his sword when a hermit came running out of the chapel and threw himself between them.

"Good knight, have mercy on your noble brother, and save yourself from sin!"

"So God help me, I shall kill you too if you thwart me!" Sir Lyonel replied.

"Sir, rather that you should kill me, for my life is nearly over, than your brother who yet has much to accomplish."

"Very well, then."

Sir Lyonel beheaded the hermit, dragged his body clear of his brother, and was about to behead him, too, when Sir Colgrevaunce, a knight of the Round Table, galloped up to them. Seeing what was about to happen he leaped off his horse, and taking Sir Lyonel by the shoulders, hauled him away from his brother.

"For shame!" he cried. "You would kill Sir Bors, your own brother? and one of the greatest knights living?"

"Hold off, or I shall kill you too!" said Sir Lyonel, brandishing his sword and making for Sir Bors again. Sir Colgrevaunce leaped between them.

"Sir, you shall not kill him without first fighting me."

"As you will, then!"

They fought furiously. Both were powerful knights, and before long blood was flowing freely from their wounds. Sir Bors recovered consciousness and tried to rise but was unable to, so he remained sitting on the ground. "Alas!" he said to himself, "if my brother dies I should avenge him and I cannot, so I shall be shamed; equally shall I be shamed if Sir Colgrevaunce dies, for he is fighting to protect me."

Meanwhile Sir Colgrevaunce had seen him recover and spoke:

"Sir Bors, cannot you come to my aid? For my quarrel is only to save your life."

"Neither of you can be warrant for the other, for I shall kill you both," said Sir Lyonel.

Hearing these words, Sir Bors, with a great effort, rose to his feet and put on his helmet. Then Sir Colgrevaunce cried out:

"Sir Bors, permit me to die in your stead, for you are a more worthy knight than I."

Then Sir Lyonel struck him to the ground, and Sir Colgrevaunce spoke his last words:

"Sweet Jesu! have mercy upon my soul. My heart is torn that I must die here in a just cause, while yet I am unconfessed."

Sir Lyonel beheaded him, and then, like a fiend, rushed upon his brother and with a tremendous blow struck him to the ground once more.

"Good brother, if we kill each other, surely God will punish us for our sin?" said Sir Bors.

"So God help me, you shall have no mercy!" Sir Lyonel replied.

Sir Bors rose to his feet and drew his sword:

"Sir Lyonel, I do not fear you; I fear only God. But now you have killed a gentle hermit and a noble knight. I pray that God will forgive me for defending myself in this unseemly quarrel."

Sir Bors was about to strike his brother when a voice from nowhere cried out: "Sir Bors, fly from your brother, otherwise he shall die at your hands." Then a brilliant flame burned between them, scorching their shields, and both brothers fell to the earth in a faint. When they came to, the voice spoke again:

"Sir Bors, go hence; leave your brother, for Sir Percivale awaits you."

Then Sir Bors spoke: "For the love of God, forgive me if I have trespassed."

"May God forgive you, and I shall gladly," Sir Lyonel replied.

Sir Bors rode to an abbey which lay hard by the sea. He was received by the monks and led to a chamber where he lay down to rest. Then he heard a voice that said, "Go to the sea." Sir Bors crossed himself, armed, and made his way out of the abbey through a break in the wall. When he came to the sea he saw a ship with awnings of white samite, at rest on the strand.

With an inward prayer for guidance, he boarded the ship, which slid miraculously into the waters and seemed to fly over the waves, but it was too dark for Sir Bors to see, so he lay down and slept until morning.

When he awoke he saw Sir Percivale lying beside him, in full armor except for his helmet. He woke him and Sir Percivale was astonished and asked him who he was, and how he came to be there.

"Sir Percivale, do you not know me?"

"Sir, I do, but surely it was a miracle that brought you here."

Sir Bors took off his helmet and they embraced. Then each recounted to the other the story of his temptations, and how he came to board the ship.

Meanwhile the ship sailed on and they comforted each other, and spent much of their time in prayer. Then Sir Percivale said:

"Now only Sir Galahad is missing."

7. SIR GALAHAD

When Sir Galahad had rescued Sir Percivale from the twenty knights he rode through a waste forest wherein he met many adventures of which little is known. Then he came to a castle where a tournament was in progress. It was soon clear to him that the knights of the castle, who were fighting at the castle gates, were unable to hold their own against the visiting party, and he decided to go to their aid.

Galloping into the melee, he overthrew the first of the assailants with his spear, which broke as he did so, and then drawing his sword lashed about him with such good effect that soon the assailants were forced to withdraw. Among them were Sir Ector and Sir Gawain, both of whom had recognized Sir Galahad and wished to avoid him. Sir Ector succeeded but Sir Gawain did not, and received a terrible wound in the head from Sir Galahad's sword, which continued by its own momentum into the withers of the horse, and brought both to the ground. Sir Ector came to his rescue and led him out of the battle.

"And so," said Sir Gawain, "Sir Launcelot's prophecy has been fulfilled; for did he not say that any knight who touched the sword in the rock would receive from it a fatal blow? And certainly I have never before been so wounded."

"Sir Gawain, I believe that your quest is now at an end, but that mine is not," said Sir Ector.

"I shall seek no further," said Sir Gawain.

He was taken into the castle, disarmed, and laid on a richly covered bed where a surgeon attended him. Sir Ector remained with him until it was ascertained that the wound would heal.

As soon as he had beaten back the assailants, Sir Galahad withdrew from the battle and rode away through the forest until nightfall, when he lodged at a hermitage which lay in sight of the castle of Carbonek. He had not been asleep for long when a young noblewoman knocked at the door of the hermitage and asked the hermit, Sir Ulphyne, if she might speak with him. Sir Ulphyne woke Sir Galahad and led him to the young noblewoman.

"Sir Galahad, I pray you arm and follow me. I shall lead you within three days to the highest adventure that can befall a knight."

Sir Galahad armed and mounted and followed the young noblewoman, who galloped ahead on her palfrey, until they came to a castle which lay near to the sea at Collybye. The walls of the castle were high, strongly built, and encircled by running water. They were welcomed by the lady of the castle.

"My lady, will you and your companion remain with us until tomorrow?"

"No, madam, only until my lord has dined and slept a little."

When Sir Galahad awoke he armed by torchlight, and before leaving was presented by the lady of the castle with a richly made shield. The young noblewoman led him to a ship which lay to at the shore, and where they found Sir Percivale and Sir Bors already aboard.

"Welcome, Sir Galahad, for long have we awaited you!"

Taking with them their bridles and saddles, but leaving their horses, Sir Galahad and the young noblewoman crossed themselves and boarded the ship. Mysteriously, the ship slid into the sea, the wind rose, and they were blown across the waters.

At dawn Sir Galahad removed his helmet and embraced his fellow knights, and each related his adventures.

"God Himself must have led you through your temptations," said Sir Galahad, "and led you to this ship. For myself, I would never have found it but for the lady who led me here."

"Alas that Sir Launcelot is not with us! for with him we should feel complete," said Sir Bors.

"If God had willed it, it would have been so," said Sir Galahad.

By now they were many leagues from Logres and approaching two rocks where a natural whirlpool made landing impossible. Hard by lay another ship.

"Our quest now takes us to the second ship," said the young noblewoman.

The ship was deserted, but on the prow was an inscription: THOU MAN WHYCH SHALT ENTIR INTO THYS SHIPPE, BEWARE THAT THOU BE IN STEDEFASTE BELEVE, FOR I AM FAYTHE. AND THEREFORE BEWARE HOW THOU ENTIRST BUT IF THOU BE STEDFASTE, FOR AND THOU FAYLE THEREOF I SHALL NOT HELPE THE.

"Sir Percivale, do you know who I am?" asked the young noblewoman.

"My lady, surely I have not seen you before?"

"Then I will tell you: I am your own sister, daughter to King Pellinore, and you are the man I most love. Now I pray you, board this ship only if your faith in the Lord is absolute, for He will not suffer on board His ship any whose faith is not perfect."

Sir Percivale rejoiced within himself when he knew that it was his own sister who counseled him.

"Dear sister, I shall board the ship; and if my sins prove me false, I will gladly perish."

Sir Galahad crossed himself and embarked first, the young noblewoman followed, then Sir Bors and then Sir Percivale. They examined the ship closely and wondered at the marvelous craftsmanship with which it had been finished. Then Sir Galahad found a sumptuous bed on which lay a silken crown and a sword partly withdrawn from its sheath.

The pommel of the sword was of solid stone, gleaming with many colors, and in each color resided a particular virtue. The hilt was composed of two bones, one from a snake known as the Fiend's Serpent, a native of Calydone, with the power that no hand that ever held it should weary or receive any injury. The second bone was from a fish known as the Ertanax, which is found in the Euphrates when it floods, and possessed the power that the holder could address himself to the matter in hand without thought of sorrow or joy in himself, and also without ever wearying. On the sword was an inscription:

THERE SHALL NEVER MAN BEGRYPE ME, THAT YS TO SEY, THE HANDYL, BUT ONE; AND HE SHALL PASSE ALL OTHER.

"In God's name, I shall try to grip the sword," cried Sir Percivale.

He tried but failed; likewise Sir Bors; then Sir Galahad tried and succeeded. Immediately a second inscription appeared on the blade in letters of blood:

LAT SE WHO DARE DRAW ME OUTE OF MY SHEETH BUT IF HE BE MORE HARDYER THAN ONY OTHER, FOR WHO THAT DRAW-ITH ME OUTE, WETE YOU WELLE HE SHALL NEVER BE SHAMED OF HYS BODY NOTHER WOUNDED TO THE DETHE.

"I would draw this sword, but for fear of offense I shall not," said Sir Galahad.

"My lords," said the young noblewoman, "the withdrawal of the sword is forbidden to any but you. This ship and this sword were at Logres when King Labor and King Hurlaine were fighting an engagement at sea. King Labor was the father of the Maimed King; King Hurlaine was born a Saracen but later became a good Christian.

"King Hurlaine got the worst of the battle and fled to the ship. King Labor followed him, and as he boarded, King

Hurlaine picked up the sword and killed him with a blow that clove clean through the helmet.

"This was the Dolorous Stroke which brought a pestilence to both kingdoms. No grass or corn or fruit but withered and would not grow again, no waters but became empty of fish; and the two kingdoms together became known as the Waste Lands.

"However, when King Hurlaine discovered the sharpness of the sword, he returned to the ship for the scabbard, and when he found it, thrust the sword home. No sooner had he done so than he died at the foot of the bed, which proves that no man ever drew this sword but was maimed or killed. He lay here long, for no man would dare approach him; then a maid came and cast him out."

When the young noblewoman had done, the three knights examined the scabbard and girdle. The girdle was badly worn, and seemed unworthy of the sword and scabbard. The scabbard was of snakeskin, and bore an inscription in gold letters:

HE WHYCH SHALL WELDE ME OUGHT TO BE MORE HARDY THAN ONY OTHER, IF HE BEARE ME AS TRULY AS ME OUGHT TO BE BORNE. FOR THE BODY OF HYM WHICH I OUGHT TO HANGE BY, HE SHALL NAT BE SHAMED IN NO PLACE WHYLE HE IS GURDE WITH THE GURDYLL. NOTHER NEVER NONE BE SO HARDY TO DO AWAY THYS GURDYLL, FOR HIT OUGHT NAT TO BE DONE AWAY BUT BY THE HONDIS OF A MAYDE, AND THAT SHE BE A KYNGIS DOUGHTER AND A QUENYS. AND SHE MUST BE A MAYDE ALL THE DAYES OF HIR LYFF, BOTH IN WYLL AND IN WORKE; AND IF SHE BREKE HIR VIRGINITE SHE SHALL DY THE MOSTE VYLAYNES DETH THAT EVER DUD ONY WOMAN.

"Sir Galahad," said Sir Percivale, "I pray you turn the sword over so that we may see the inscription on the other side."

Sir Galahad did so; it was blood red in color and the inscription in black letters:

HE THAT SHALL PRAYSE ME MOSTE, MOSTE SHALL HE FYNDE ME TO BLAME AT A GRETE NEDE. AND TO WHOM I SHOLDE BE MOST DEBONAYRE SHALL I BE MOST FELON. AND THAT SHALL BE AT ONE TYME ONLY.

"Good brother," said the young noblewoman, "forty years after the Passion of our Lord Jesu, the hermit Nacien, brother-in-law to King Mordrayns, was born on the Ile of Turnance, which lay fourteen days' journey from King Mordrayns' realm.

"It happened that this ship lay to in the rocky harbor

which was Nacien's birthplace, and that he boarded the ship and found the bed and the sword which are before us now, and that he remained in the anchored ship for eight days. On the ninth a tempest drove the ship away to another rocky island where dwelled a terrible giant. As Nacien came ashore the giant attacked him, and he ran back for the sword which now lay naked by its sheath, grateful to have a weapon with which to defend himself. However, the sword broke as soon as he raised it.

" 'Alas!' he said, 'that which I have most praised I must now most blame.'

"He threw down the pieces, leaped overboard, and attacked and killed the giant. He then returned to the ship and was blown away again, this time to the Porte of the Perelous Roche, where he met King Mordrayns in another vessel, where fiends had been busy trying to draw him into evil.

"They greeted each other and described their adventures. Then the king told Nacien that he must have been in mortal sin for the sword to have broken in his grasp, and, taking up the pieces, placed them together so that the sword was made whole again. He put it on the bed and a voice spoke to them:

" 'Leave this ship before you fall into deadly sin; otherwise you shall not escape it, and shall perish.'

"They transferred themselves to the other ship, but while they were doing so Nacien tripped, fell headlong on the deck, and was wounded in the heel by the sword. The voice spoke again:

" 'This wound you shall suffer for your transgression; you have handled a sword of which you are unworthy.' "

"For the love of God!" said Sir Galahad, "you have certainly proved the truth of the inscription!"

"My lords," the young noblewoman continued, "the next to handle the sword was King Pelles, a righteous king and a true bulwark of the church.

"He lived in a castle near to the sea. One day when he was out hunting he lost all his hounds, and all his knights but one. Together they came to the sea and found the ship. King Pelles read the inscription on the prow and, because he was free of sin, embarked. His companion dared not follow him.

"When King Pelles found the sword, he drew it part way from the sheath, as you yourselves found it; then a spear came as from nowhere and wounded him in both thighs. Those wounds have remained open to this day, and that is why King Pelles, your grandfather, is known as the Maimed King."

The three knights next examined the bed, and soon noticed that three of the spindles supporting the canopy were of different colors: blood red, snow white, and emerald green. These colors were natural to the wood and had not been painted on.

"My lord," said the young noblewoman, "when Eve gathered apples from the tree, for the eating of which both she and Adam were to be cast out of Eden, she also took one of the boughs, which delighted her for its freshness. Having no box in which to keep it, she planted the bough in the ground, and God willed that it should grow into a tree. And because Eve was a maid at the time, the tree grew white.

"Then God came to Adam and commanded him to love Eve and enter her in the flesh and procreate his kind. Adam took Eve as she lay beneath the tree which she had planted, and their son Abel was conceived. While Adam and Eve engaged in the act of love, the tree grew green, and for many years remained that color.

"Then, beneath the tree, Cain slew Abel, and the color changed again, this time to red, the color of Abel's blood.

"All the other plants withered and died but this tree alone, which grew large and strong and was the most beautiful tree in the land. So it remained until the time of Solomon, who was King David's son.

"Solomon was wise and knew the virtues of all the trees and all the stones, the courses of the stars, and many other things besides. But he was cursed with an evil wife, and because of her, wrote scornfully of women in his books. Then, one day Solomon heard a voice which said:

" 'Solomon, do not succumb to the sorrow that a woman has brought to you, for of your own lineage shall be born a maid who will bring to men a hundred times greater joy than you have sorrow.'

"When Solomon understood these words he cursed himself for a fool, and before long was able to verify them in an ancient text. Then the Holy Ghost revealed to him the coming of the Virgin Mary, and Solomon asked if she would be of his lineage.

" 'She shall not,' the voice replied, 'but the last of your lineage shall be a knight as holy as the Duke Josue, your brother-in-law, and he shall remain a virgin. Now have I dispelled your doubts.'

"Solomon rejoiced, and searched unremittingly for a text to support these tidings, but could find none. Then his wife came to him and he recounted the message spoken to him by the voice. His wife grew convinced that she would discover who the knight would be.

" 'My lord,' she said, 'let us build a ship of the most durable wood of any tree on earth.'

"Solomon summoned his shipwrights and commanded them to build the ship. When it was done, his wife spoke to him again:

" 'My lord, in honor of the knight who is to be your scion and to surpass all other knights in the virtues of chivalry, let us prepare for him the sword which is the sharpest of all swords, namely, that which belonged to your father King David, and which at present is kept in the temple. For this sword let a new pommel be made, of precious stones so subtly wrought that they shall appear as one stone of many brilliant colors. Then let it be fitted with hilt, sheath, and girdle, all of great splendor. The girdle I myself shall make.'

"Solomon commanded that this should be done, and when the ship and the sword were ready his wife gave orders for a bed covered with rich silk coverings to be placed in the ship. On this she placed the sword, the sheath, and the girdle, which she herself had made from hemp.

"When the king came to see it all, he was greatly disturbed:

" 'Surely we have nothing as worthy as this, and yet how shall we know what knights a maid shall bring hither?'

"Solomon's wife next ordained an imperishable cloth for the ship's awnings, and then summoned a carpenter to the tree beneath which Abel had been slain.

" 'Carve out of this tree as much wood as you will need to make a spindle,' she commanded.

" 'Madam, this is the tree planted by Eve, the first mother.'

" 'Do as I command, or else you shall be killed.'

"Blood oozed from the tree as the carpenter cut it. He faltered, but the queen commanded him to continue, and when he had taken a sliver she commanded him to take slivers from the white tree and from the green tree. These were shaped into spindles to fasten the canopy to the bed, and then Solomon was brought to see the work.

" 'No man on earth, only God, shall know the secret of this wonderful work; but as yet we have to discover the meaning thereof.'

" 'My lord, it may be that we shall discover the meaning sooner than you suppose,' the queen replied.

"That night as Solomon slept he saw angels descend upon the ship and sprinkle it with water from a silver vessel. Then one of them made the inscription on the sword, and another the inscription on the prow which Solomon read:

"THOU MAN THAT WOLTE ENTIR ME, BEWARE THAT THOU BE FULLE IN THE FAYTHE, FOR I NE AM BUT FAYTH AND BELYVE.

"Then Solomon was ashamed and dared not to enter the ship, and as he stood and watched, it slid down to the sea and moved across the waters. Meanwhile a voice spoke to him:

" 'Solomon, the last knight of your lineage shall sleep on the ship's bed.'

"Then Solomon awoke and told his wife of his marvelous vision."

For a long time the three knights gazed in wonder at the three spindles. Then Sir Percivale lifted the silken cover and found a wallet containing a letter with an account of the origin of the bed and of the ship.

"I wonder," said Sir Galahad, "where we shall find a gentle-woman who will make a new girdle for the sword."

"My lords," said Sir Percivale's sister, "I have here a girdle for the sword."

So saying she drew from a box a girdle made of fine gold thread, set with precious stones and fitted with a gold buckle.

"My lords, as a woman of the world I gloried in my hair, but when I knew that I was ordained for this quest, I had it shorn off and made the girdle."

"My lady, you have saved us a well-nigh impossible search," said Sir Bors.

The young noblewoman attached the girdle to the sheath, and then the knights asked her what name should be given to the sword.

"The sword is the Sword of the Straunge Gurdyls, and the scabbard the Mover of Blood, for no man in whom the blood flows shall see that part of the sheath which was made from the Tree of Life."

"Now, Sir Galahad, in the name of Jesu you must gird yourself with the sword," said one of his companions.

The young noblewoman set the girdle about his waist and Sir Galahad gripped the hilt.

"My lords, this sword belongs as much to you as to me. I grip the hilt that we may all take courage in the adventure before us. And for myself, if I die while holding this sword, I care not, for I should die holding her who is the most precious Virgin of all time. And you, my lady, by whose convening we have come so far, I shall serve hereafter."

Sir Galahad and his companions then returned to their former ship. A wind arose and the ship flew across the waves once more. All night they sailed, and were without food. In the morning the ship ran ashore off the coast of Scotland, opposite the castle of Carteloyse. As they landed they were greeted by one of the ladies of the castle:

"My lords, if you come from King Arthur's court, take warning: you shall soon be attacked."

They continued toward the castle, and were met by a squire:

"My lords, are you from King Arthur's court?"

"We are."

"Then you shall repent of it."

As they approached the castle they heard a horn blast from within, and a young noblewoman came up to them:

"My lords, turn back! For in this castle death awaits you."

"My lady, we shall not turn back. He whom we serve, and who delivered us from the rocks, shall deliver us from all evil," Sir Galahad replied.

Meanwhile ten knights had appeared, and dressed their spears against them.

"My lords, yield or you shall die!" they shouted.

"Our yielding shall cost you dear," said Sir Galahad.

The ten knights from the castle charged. First Sir Percivale, and then each of his companions, struck a knight to the ground and mounted his horse; the three of them then chased their assailants into the hall of the castle, where they dismounted. A tremendous battle followed, in which Sir Galahad and his companions were attacked on all sides by the numerous knights of the castle. Miraculously they defended themselves, and before long all the knights of the castle lay dead on the floor. When it was over, each of the three knights felt awed by the carnage.

"I believe," said Sir Bors, "that God would not have given us the strength to kill them had He wished them to live."

"I too believe that He must have made us the instruments of His wrath; for such power surely did not come from ourselves," Sir Galahad replied.

A priest, bearing a vessel of holy wine, entered the hall from one of the castle chambers. The three knights removed their helmets and knelt before him.

"Father, do not fear us; we are from King Arthur's court," said Sir Galahad, and then described the battle to him.

"My sons, you might have lived for as long as the world shall endure, and not have accomplished so much."

"Father, I repent that we have killed them inasmuch as they were Christians," said Sir Galahad.

"My son, do not repent, for they were not Christians. When Earl Hernox, the lord of this castle, first came here, he brought with him his three sons, who were all knighted, and his beautiful daughter. The three sons grew lustful of their sister and, despite her protests, each one of them forced her to lie with him incestuously. The daughter complained to her father, and the three sons all but killed him and then threw him into prison. One of his cousins managed to save his life.

"The three sons turned into veritable Antichrists. They killed all men of holy office and burned down chapels and churches so that the word of God should not be spoken. I confessed the father, and he told me it had been vouchsafed to him that three servants of the Lord should come and mete His vengeance upon those within the castle, and deliver him.

"Therefore, my sons, you have acted only as His servants."

"Father, we could never have killed so many of His enemies without His aid," said Sir Galahad.

The Earl Hernox was released from his cell; and when he came into the hall, by divine revelation he recognized Sir Galahad and spoke to him:.

"Sir Galahad, for long have I awaited your coming! Now, I pray you, take me in your arms, for I wish that my soul should leave my body in the arms of as noble a knight as you are."

"My lord, full gladly," Sir Galahad replied.

Then a voice was heard:

"Sir Galahad, you have avenged the Lord on His enemies. Now go to the Maimed King, for you shall heal him."

The Earl Hernox died, and was buried with the proper rites.

Then Sir Percivale's sister and the three knights rode into the wilderness and found four lions leading a white hart. They followed the lions, who led them into the chapel of a hermitage built in a valley. The hermit was in his priestly vestments and saying mass.

First the hart changed into the form of a man and sat on a pew by the altar. Then three of the lions changed form: one to an eagle, one to an ox, and one to a man; and all four sat by the man who had been a hart. Then they all passed through the

window of the chapel, but the window was not broken, and
again a voice was heard:

"In such fashion did the Son of God enter the womb of the
Virgin Mary, which neither perished nor was hurt."

The three knights and the young noblewoman fell down in
a faint, and when they came to, each felt an extraordinary
clarity. They asked the hermit to expound their vision.

"Pray tell me, what have you seen?" asked the hermit, and
they told him.

"My lords, you are welcome, for you are the knights who will
accomplish the quest of the Holy Grail. The Lord has revealed
Himself to you in the vision of the hart, which by virtue of its
white skin is ever renewed, from old to young again. So did
the Son of God enter into the sinful flesh through the Holy
Virgin, and in the flesh perish, only to rise again in the spirit.

"The four lions were the four evangelists who set down a part
of our Lord's doings when He was on earth. Many times
before has our Lord appeared to men in the guise of the white
hart, but none before you was vouchsafed to know Him. And
probably you shall not see Him again."

Sir Galahad and his companions rejoiced when they understood their vision, and remained with the hermit overnight.
They left in the morning after hearing mass. As they were riding past a castle a knight galloped up to them:

"My lords, I pray you tell me, is the lady who accompanies
you a maid?"

"My lord, I am," Sir Percivale's sister replied.

The knight took her horse by the bridle.

"So God help me, then, you shall not pass without yielding
first to the custom of this castle," he said.

"Sir, hold off! Understand that wheresoever a maid shall go
she shall not be touched," said Sir Percivale.

Meanwhile a dozen knights had galloped up to them from
the castle, and with them a lady who held a silver dish.

"My lords," said the lady, "the young noblewoman must submit to the custom of the castle."

"Madam, what custom do you speak of?" asked Sir Galahad.

"We require that the maid shall fill this dish with her blood,
which we shall take from her right arm."

"My lords, this is a savage custom! And while I am alive I
shall not sanction it," said Sir Galahad.

"Neither shall I!" said Sir Percivale.

"Nor I!" said Sir Bors.

"Then you shall die, for there are no knights on earth who
are a match for us."

Sir Galahad and his two companions drew their swords, and when the twelve castle knights charged, killed every one of them.

Sixty more knights galloped out of the castle.

"My lords, for your own sakes, fly from us!" said Sir Galahad.

"Not so! It is you who should fly, for you shall not escape us, nor shall the maid escape our custom."

They fought until nightfall. Sir Galahad, wielding the Sword of the Straunge Gurdyls, appeared to be everywhere at once, and every knight from the castle who encountered him was struck to the ground as though by divine wrath. Sir Percivale and Sir Bors were likewise inspired and their assailants fell before them, fatally wounded or killed outright.

At nightfall another knight came from the castle to deliver a message:

"My lords, we pray you accept the hospitality of our castle; you have our warrant that your persons shall not be molested. And when you have heard the story of our custom you may be persuaded to respect it."

"My lords, let us go!" said Sir Percivale's sister, "and do not fear for me."

"As you command, my lady," said Sir Galahad.

They were greeted warmly at the castle, and were told the origin of the custom:

"My lords and my lady, this is the truth. Many years ago the lady of this castle, whom we all serve, fell ill, and eventually passed into a coma. No physician could find a remedy for her. Then one came and said that she could be cured only by the blood of a virgin princess. Hence it is our custom to draw blood from every virgin who passes our castle."

"My lords, I shall yield my blood to the good lady," said Sir Percivale's sister.

"Alas! you will die," said Sir Galahad.

"A death worthy of my lineage, and one which, I trust, will bring to an end the bloodshed in this castle."

Sir Percivale's sister and the three knights were treated as guests of honor that night, and all were relieved that a further battle had been avoided. In the morning, after mass, Sir Percivale's sister was brought before the lady.

"Who will let my blood?" she asked.

One of the lady's women came forward and made an incision in her arm. The blood flowed freely, and when the dish was full Sir Percivale's sister blessed the woman and spoke to the lady:

"Madam, I am bleeding to death in order that your life shall be saved; I ask you in your prayers to commend me to our Lord."

Then she fainted. The three knights lifted her up and tried to stanch the wound, but the loss of blood was too great to allow of her recovery. She regained consciousness for a few moments and spoke to her brother:

"Sir Percivale, my good brother! I pray you, when I am dead, do not bury me near this castle, but put my body in a barge at the next harbor and set it adrift. When you come to the city of Sarras to conclude the quest of the Holy Grail, you will find the barge in the moat below the tower. Bury me in the castle which is our spiritual abode, and where subsequently you, Sir Galahad, and Sir Bors shall all be buried."

Sir Percivale wept and promised to fulfill his sister's wish. Then a voice spoke to them:

"Tomorrow at dawn the three knights shall part, until providence brings them together before the Maimed King."

Sir Percivale's sister received extreme unction and gave up the ghost; at the same time the lady of the castle recovered. Sir Percivale wrote an account of his sister's death and placed it in her hand before carrying the body to the barge as she had wished. He covered the barge with a black silk cloth and the onlookers saw it blown out to sea.

As the three knights returned a sudden tempest broke upon them, and, with thunder, lightning, and rain, had carried away more than half the castle by evensong. Then a wounded knight rode up to them, followed by another knight who was accompanied by a dwarf.

"Sweet Jesu! give me succor, for now is my hour of need," cried the wounded knight.

"Stay, for you shall not escape me!" cried his pursuer.

The wounded knight raised his hands and prayed; then Sir Galahad spoke: "For the love of Him whom he has called upon, I shall give him succor."

"Sir Galahad, I pray you allow me to go to his aid, for he is but one knight," said Sir Bors.

"I grant you your wish," Sir Galahad replied.

Sir Bors mounted and set off in pursuit of the two knights. Sir Galahad and Sir Percivale returned to the castle chapel, and prayed all night that Sir Bors might bring his adventure to a successful conclusion. In the morning they left the chapel and found the castle in ruins and all the inmates dead. Then they heard a voice:

"Behold the vengeance of the Lord for the shedding of maidens' blood."

They returned to the chapel and found in the graveyard, which like the chapel was undisturbed by the tempest, sixty graves of young noblewomen who had been killed in order that the lady of the castle should be saved. From the inscriptions they discovered that twelve of them had been princesses. Then they left the chapel and rode into the forest.

"The time has come for us to part," said Sir Percivale, "but I pray that we shall meet again soon."

Both took off their helmets and kissed and then wept as they parted.

8. THE CASTLE OF CARBONEK

When Sir Launcelot came to the turbulent waters of Morayse he felt himself to be in great peril, and in the hope of receiving divine guidance, lay down to sleep. In his sleep a voice spoke to him:

"Sir Launcelot, arise now, arm yourself, and board the first ship that you see."

Sir Launcelot started out of his sleep, and at once felt about him a marvelous clarity. After offering up a short prayer of thanksgiving he armed and set off along the shore. Soon he came upon a ship which was without either sail or oar, but which gave forth an odor of surpassing sweetness.

"Sweet Jesu, surely this surpasses all earthly pleasures!" said Sir Launcelot in wonder.

He boarded the ship and lay on the deck and slept until morning. When he awoke he saw the body of Sir Percivale's sister lying on a handsome bed where Sir Percivale had set her. He took from her hand the letter which Sir Percivale had written and read the account of her birth and of her death.

For a month he remained on the ship, and if you would ask how he lived—as the people of Israel, stranded in the desert, received manna from the Lord, so Sir Launcelot was sustained by the grace of the Holy Ghost.

Then one night as he wandered along the shore, having grown weary of the ship, he heard a horseman approaching. He returned to the ship and a knight galloped up to him, removed the trappings from his horse, and also boarded the ship. They exchanged greetings.

"Sir, I pray you tell me who you are, for my heart warms to you," said the strange knight.

"Sir Launcelot du Lake."

"My lord, you were my beginning on this earth."

"Sir Galahad!"

"Truly."

Father and son embraced, and no tongue could describe how they rejoiced in each other. Sir Galahad recognized Sir Percivale's sister at once and praised her, and then each described to the other his adventures since he had left Camelot. When Sir Launcelot heard the story of the Sword of the Straunge Gurdyls he begged Sir Galahad to draw it from the sheath, and when he saw it he kissed it.

"That is a wonderful story," said Sir Launcelot.

For six months Sir Launcelot and Sir Galahad remained by the ship, living piously and occasionally wandering abroad, where they had many strange encounters with the wild beasts of those regions. Then one Monday a well-mounted knight, clad in white armor and leading a white horse, rode up to them, greeted them in the name of the Lord, and addressed Sir Galahad:

"Sir, the time has come for you to leave your father and the ship and accompany me on the quest of the Holy Grail."

Sir Galahad kissed his father tenderly.

"Good father, I do not know when I shall see you again; I know only that I am moving toward the body of our Lord."

"Pray to the Father that I may still be permitted to serve Him," said Sir Launcelot.

Sir Galahad mounted, and a voice was heard:

"Take heed! You shall not meet until the day of doom."

"Sir Galahad," said Sir Launcelot, "if it is so, let us pray for each other."

"Sir Launcelot, no prayers could touch me so nearly as yours," Sir Galahad replied, and then galloped with his companion into the forest.

A wind rose and blew Sir Launcelot's ship out to sea, and for many months he sailed, not knowing whither he was going, but praying constantly that he might be vouchsafed the presence of the Holy Grail. Then one midnight the ship ran ashore just below where a castle had been built. In the clear moonlight Sir Launcelot was able to see a postern which stood open and which was guarded by two lions. Then a voice spoke to him:

"Sir Launcelot, leave your ship and enter the castle, where in part your prayers shall be granted."

Sir Launcelot armed, and as he approached the postern, drew his sword in case the lions should molest him. Suddenly a dwarf appeared and struck the sword out of his hand, and the voice spoke again:

"Faithless knight! How shall your sword and armor prevail against the will of the Lord?"

Sir Launcelot prayed: "Lord Jesu, I thank You for the reproof! and I thank You for showing me that I may yet be one of Your servants."

After sheathing his sword Sir Launcelot crossed himself and walked between the lions, which threatened but did not molest him, and into the castle.

The gates of the castle were open and the hall deserted. Sir Launcelot passed through the hall and through several empty chambers until he came to one which was closed. He listened, and from within came the sound of a voice singing with unearthly sweetness:

"Joy and honor be to the Father of Heaven!"

Sir Launcelot knelt down and prayed, knowing that he had come to the Holy Grail at last.

"Sweet Jesu, I pray You forgive my many sins! And I pray You take pity on me and reveal to me what is within."

The door opened and an intense ethereal light shone through the castle, more brilliant than all the torches on earth burning together. As Sir Launcelot started forward he heard the voice again:

"Sir Launcelot, enter and you shall repent of it!"

Sadly, Sir Launcelot withdrew, and looked into the chamber. In the center was a silver table, and on it the Holy Grail covered with a cloth of red samite. Above, angels were flying; one held a sacred cross, another a brilliant-burning candle. Before the Grail a priest was performing the consecration of the mass. It seemed to Sir Launcelot that above the priest were three men, and that two of them set the third to rest on the hands of the priest as he raised them, and that the priest held him aloft for the worshipers to behold. Then Sir Launcelot felt that the man must fall. He advanced to the door of the chamber and prayed again:

"Sweet Jesu, surely it will be no sin if I give succor to one who is in need of it?"

He walked toward the priest, but as he drew near to the table he felt himself suddenly burned by a fiery breath. It seemed that his whole head was on fire; he lost all sense of sight, hearing, and speech, and fell down in a swoon. Then he felt himself borne from the chamber, and it was supposed by all who saw him that he was dead.

The following day it was discovered from his pulse that Sir Launcelot was still living, but unable to stir. He was taken to another chamber and laid on a bed. Four days later a holy man came to see him.

"It is God's will that this knight shall live, and in due course He shall restore him. Meanwhile see that he is well tended."

For twenty-four days Sir Launcelot remained prostrate. On the twenty-fifth he awoke, his senses returned to him, and he wept:

"Alas! Why have you awakened me and brought me thus to my sorrow? O Jesu! Who should be so blessed that he could witness Your marvels so hidden from all sinners?"

"Pray, what have you seen?" Sir Launcelot was asked.

"I have seen such things as are beyond the power of the tongue to describe or the heart to recall; and had I not sinned I should have seen much more."

Sir Launcelot was told how he had lain as though dead for twenty-four days and twenty-four nights, and he understood that this must have been in penance for his twenty-four years of sin. Then, just by the bed he noticed the hermit's hair which he had worn for nearly a year, and he felt that his vow to the hermit had been broken.

"What cheer?" he was asked.

"By the grace of God I have recovered. But, I pray you, tell me where I am."

"In the castle of Carbonek, where your quest of the Holy Grail has come to an end, for you shall see it no more."

"I thank God that He has granted me so much; I have done all that an earthly knight could do to deserve it."

Sir Launcelot was brought a fine linen shirt; he put on first the hermit's hair, then the shirt, and on top a scarlet robe. At last his hosts recognized him.

"My lord, Sir Launcelot?"

"My lords, I am."

When King Pelles was told that the knight who had lain as though dead was Sir Launcelot, he came at once to greet him.

They made much of each other, and then the king talked of
his daughter's death.

"Sire, I have rarely seen so young, noble, and beautiful a
princess," said Sir Launcelot.

Sir Launcelot thanked King Pelles for his hospitality and
remained at the castle for another four days. It happened on
the last day, when they all took dinner together in the hall,
that meat and wine appeared before them by a visitation of
the Holy Grail. The doors and windows of the hall had
miraculously closed, when a tremendous knocking was heard
and a voice cried from without:

"Let me enter!"

The king strode over to the door:

"Sir, you shall not enter, for the Holy Grail is here. Go now
to another castle, for surely you are not one who has sought
the Grail, but one who has turned from the service of our Lord
to the service of the devil."

The knight without stormed at the king's words.

"Sir, whence have you come?" asked the king.

"I am Sir Ector de Marys, brother to my lord Sir Launcelot."

"Alas! that I have so dishonored you," said the king, "for
your brother is within."

"So are my shame and my sorrow doubled! And all this was
foretold from our dreams by the hermit Nacien, when Sir
Gawain and I visited him on the hill."

Sir Ector galloped away from the castle, and King Pelles
told Sir Launcelot what had taken place. Sir Launcelot took
up his arms and sadly bade King Pelles adieu, saying that now
he would return to the realm of Logres.

After riding through many lands Sir Launcelot came to the
white stone abbey where King Bagdemagus was buried. He
was warmly received by the monks, and only in the morning,
after hearing mass, did he notice the tomb whose inscription
bore the name of King Bagdemagus and that of Sir Gawain,
who had killed him. Sir Launcelot mourned for the dead king,
and had he died at the hands of any other than Sir Gawain,
would have sworn to avenge him.

"Alas! he will be missed at King Arthur's court," he said
to himself.

Sir Launcelot rode next to the abbey where Sir Galahad
had won his white shield with the red cross, and where he had
exorcised the fiend in the tomb. Then he returned to Camelot.

He was received joyfully by King Arthur and Queen Gwynevere, and he discovered that Sir Ector, Sir Gawain, and Sir

Lyonel had already returned from the quest, but that more than half the knights of the Round Table had lost their lives. He then described his adventures, and those of Sir Percivale, Sir Bors, and his son Sir Galahad, as far as he knew them.

"For the love of God, I wish that those three were here now," said King Arthur.

"Sire, of those three one only will return; the other two you shall never see again," Sir Launcelot replied.

9. THE MIRACLE OF SIR GALAHAD

After much fruitless searching, Sir Galahad found the abbey where King Mordrayns lay wounded. The monks led him to the king when he had heard mass, and the king spoke:

"Sir Galahad, flower of all knighthood, whose coming I have awaited for so long, welcome! I pray you take me in your arms and hold me to your breast, for you alone, true servant of Christ that you are, possess the virginity of the white lily together with the virtue of the burning rose: qualities of the Holy Ghost, by which my flesh shall be made young again."

Taking the ancient king into his arms, Sir Galahad prayed: "Sweet Jesu, I pray You enter me!"

Sir Galahad's prayer was heard and the ancient king's flesh was made young again, before his soul departed from his body.

Sir Galahad gave King Mordrayns a royal burial and then rode forth into the wilderness, where he came to a burning well. It was the power of lust which had caused the water to boil, but the power of Sir Galahad's chastity was greater, and when he touched the well the waters cooled, and thereafter the well bore his name.

Sir Galahad rode next to the country of Gore and came to the abbey where King Bagdemagus lay buried, also the son of Joseph of Arimathea and Simeon. He discovered that in the crypt beneath the minster was a burning tomb, and he asked the brothers why it was so.

"Sir, this miracle shall be brought to an end only by the knight who surpasses all the knights of the Round Table."

"Brothers, I pray you lead me there."

"Willingly."

They descended the steps into the crypt, and as Sir Galahad approached the burning tomb the flames flickered and died. Then a voice was heard:

"Praise be to God! For now this soul is set free from earthly pain and may enter the joys of paradise. I am your kinsman and for three centuries have suffered this fire for my sin against Joseph of Arimathea."

Sir Galahad carried the body into the minster, and lay all that night in the abbey. In the morning he buried his kinsman by the altar, blessed the monks, and departed for the castle of the Maimed King, which he reached five days later.

Sir Percivale meanwhile was following in Sir Galahad's footsteps, only five days behind him, and as he progressed was told of his miraculous deeds. Then, riding out of the forest one day, he met Sir Bors. They embraced and recounted to each other their adventures.

"In eighteen months I have not slept more than ten times in the company of my fellow men," said Sir Bors. "For the rest I have been alone in the wilderness, in the thick of the forest, or up on the bare mountains. But God has always comforted me."

They rode together to the castle of Carbonek, where Sir Galahad had preceded them, and where King Pelles greeted them warmly as knights who were to complete the quest of the Holy Grail.

Then Prince Elyazar brought them the broken spear with which Joseph of Arimathea had been wounded in the thighs. First Sir Bors took the pieces, but swooned when he touched them; then Sir Percivale, but he likewise could not mend them, so he handed the pieces to Sir Galahad, saying:

"Surely you are the one knight on earth who might make this spear whole again."

Sir Galahad took the two pieces and set them together, and at once it was as if the spear had never been broken, so firmly were they forged. It was agreed that the spear should be given to Sir Bors in recognition of his unfailing faith and courage.

At evensong when all the knights of the court were seated in the hall for supper, the spear suddenly appeared above them, huge, and burning with such intensity that many of the beholders fainted. Then a voice was heard:

"Go hence, all those who are unfit to sup at the table of Jesu Christ our Lord; for His servants shall now be fed."

All of the assembled company withdrew from the hall except for King Pelles, his niece, who was still a maid, and Prince Elyazar, also Sir Galahad, Sir Percivale, and Sir Bors. Then nine knights, all armed, entered the hall and greeted Sir Galahad:

"Sir, we have hastened to join you at this holy repast."

"My lords, you are welcome; but whence have you come?" asked Sir Galahad, and they replied that three had come from Gaul, three from Ireland and three from Denmark.

When they were all seated, four gentlewomen brought in a wooden bed which they placed in the center of the hall. On the bed lay an aged and sick man, wearing a gold crown. He addressed Sir Galahad:

"Sir, you are welcome! In fulfillment of the promise made to me, you have come at last to set free my soul from this body which has endured such pain and such anguish for so long, as no other man on earth has. So now I pray you, heal me!"

Then another voice was heard:

"Go hence, those two who are not on the quest of the Holy Grail."

King Pelles and his son departed. Then four angels descended from heaven, and with them an old man wearing the vestments of a bishop and holding in his hand a sacred cross. The angels set the bishop on a chair before the silver table which bore the Holy Grail, and letters appeared on his forehead:

SE YOU HERE JOSEPH THE FIRSTE BYSSHOP OF CRYSTENDOM, THE SAME WHICH OURE LORDE SUCCOURED IN THE CITE OF SARRAS IN THE SPIRITUALL PALAYCE.

The beholders were awe-struck, and the bishop spoke to them:

"My lords, do not marvel, for once I too was an earthly man."

Then a company of angels entered by the door. Two carried candles of wax, another a towel, and a third a spear which dripped blood into a receptacle which the angel carried in the other hand. The candles were set on the silver table, the towel over the Holy Grail, and the spear upright on the Grail.

The bishop went through the motions of the consecration and then lifted a wafer of bread which became in his hands a living child, bright in the face, with which he touched himself before putting it into the Holy Grail. When he had completed the mass he rose, kissed Sir Galahad, and bade him kiss his fellows. Then he said:

"Now, servants of Christ, you shall partake of the flesh which no earthly man has tasted before."

The bishop vanished and all at the table waited in awe for what should befall them, and prayed silently. The figure of our Lord rose from the Grail, made the signs of His Passion, bleeding openly before them, and then spoke:

"Good knights, my true servants, my children: you who have travailed from the life of the flesh to the life of the spirit, from you I shall not hide myself, but reveal to you in part my hidden mysteries! And now you shall partake of the flesh which you have sought."

The figure of Christ took the Holy Grail and offered it in turn to Sir Galahad and to each of his fellows; and that of which they partook was of a holy and marvelous sweetness, such as no tongue could describe. Then the figure of Christ spoke to Sir Galahad:

"My son, do you know what I hold in my hands?"

"My Lord, I do not, unless You tell me."

"You see the dish from which I ate the lamb on Easter day, and this has been your heart's desire. Tonight the Grail shall leave the realm of Logres forever, because the people here have sinned and are not worthy of it. But you shall see it even more clearly than you have seen it today, when you enter the Spiritual Palace in the city of Sarras. Therefore go, with your companions Sir Percivale and Sir Bors, take with you the Sword of the Straunge Gurdyls, and ride until you come to a ship which you will find ready for you. Now, take some of the blood from the spear and anoint the Maimed King on the arms and on the legs, and he shall be healed."

"My Lord, shall not the remaining knights accompany us?"

"No, for I am about to leave you, and I wish that some of my apostles would be here and some at Sarras. I will tell you that two of you shall die in my service and the third bear tidings of what has happened to you."

Thereupon the figure of Christ blessed them and vanished.

Sir Galahad put his fingers on the bloody spear and then touched the Maimed King on the arms and on the legs, and he was healed. He clothed himself, rose from the bed, and uttered a prayer of thanksgiving. Subsequently he joined a monastery of white monks and died a holy man.

At midnight a voice was heard in the hall of the castle:

"My sons—those whom I have chosen, not those who are

only my friends, or yet my enemies—go now as I have bidden you."

In all haste Sir Galahad, Sir Percivale, and Sir Bors took up their armor and prepared to depart. Before they left, the three knights from Gaul, one of whom was the son of King Claudas, begged them to commend them to Sir Launcelot, King Arthur, and his knights of the Round Table.

Sir Galahad and his companions rode for three days and then came to the shore where their ship awaited them. On board they found the silver table and the Holy Grail covered with a cloth of red samite. In reverence to these tokens they all knelt down and prayed, and it was then that Sir Galahad prayed that his soul might be freed from his body. A voice answered him:

"Sir Galahad, your prayer has been heard. Your body shall perish that your soul may live."

Half hearing the voice, Sir Percivale asked Sir Galahad what had come to pass.

"I will tell you: I have longed for the death of my body since we beheld the miracle of the Holy Grail, for then I knew such joy as no man on earth may know, and my soul craves for the Holy Trinity, and every day to behold the majesty of our Lord."

Sometime later Sir Galahad's companions spoke to him again:

"Sir Galahad, are you not named to lie on this bed?"

Sir Galahad lay down on the bed and slept. When he awoke they had come to the city of Sarras, and as they landed they saw the ship bearing the body of Sir Percivale's sister.

"In the name of the Lord! my sister has held her covenant," said Sir Percivale.

Sir Bors and Sir Percivale carried the silver table, and Sir Galahad followed them until they came to the city gates, where they saw a cripple. Sir Galahad commanded him, "Bear this heavy table."

"My lords, I have not walked without crutches for ten years," the old cripple replied.

"Arise in good faith, and forget that you have been a cripple," said Sir Galahad.

The cripple rose and was healed. Together with Sir Galahad he carried the table. News of the miracle spread swiftly through the city; and when the three knights had buried Sir Percivale's sister with the proper rites, they were summoned to appear before the king, whose name was Estorause, and questioned. They told him the true story of the Holy Grail.

King Estorause was descended from a long line of pagans, and was himself a tyrant. He commanded that the three knights be imprisoned in a dungeon.

By the mercy of the Lord, the Holy Grail appeared in the dungeon, and from it the three knights received succor throughout their imprisonment. At the end of the year the king was brought to his deathbed; he summoned the three knights and begged their forgiveness, and they granted it to him.

Thoroughly dismayed, the citizens of Sarras convened a council to appoint a new king. When they had all assembled they were addressed by an unknown voice:

"Citizens! appoint the youngest of the three knights your king, for he shall maintain you, both you and yours."

Sir Galahad was crowned king, on pain of death. When this was done he ordained a chest of gold, set with precious stones, to contain the Holy Grail; and every day at dawn he and his two companions knelt before it and prayed.

On the Sunday following the coronation they found a figure in the vestments of a bishop kneeling before the Grail and saying the mass of our Lady. About the figure angels were flying as they might have about Christ Himself. When the mass was over, the bishop spoke to Sir Galahad:

"Advance, servant of our Lord, and you shall see what you have most wished to see."

Sir Galahad advanced, and soon began to tremble before the unearthly vision. Then he raised his hands and prayed:

"Blessed Jesu! I thank you for giving me what I have desired; and now, if it please you, I pray, may I leave this world?"

The bishop gave to Sir Galahad the Body of our Lord, and Sir Galahad received Him meekly.

"And now, do you know who I am?" the bishop asked.

"I do not," Sir Galahad replied.

"I am Joseph, the son of Joseph of Arimathea, and the Lord has sent me hither to bear you fellowship. I was chosen because you resemble me in two things: you have witnessed the marvel of the Holy Grail, and you are a virgin—as I was, and am."

Sir Galahad blessed and embraced Sir Percivale and Sir Bors and then spoke:

"My lords, I pray you greet my father Sir Launcelot for me, and bid him remember how ephemeral is this earth!"

Sir Galahad knelt down and prayed, and his soul was borne

visibly to heaven by a company of angels. Then a hand appeared and took the Holy Grail and the spear and bore them also to heaven, and no man on earth has seen them since.

Sir Galahad was mourned by Sir Percivale and Sir Bors, both of whom would have been overcome by despair had not they been virtuous men. And he was also mourned by the citizens of Sarras.

Sir Percivale left the city, and adopting hermit's weeds, lived a holy life for a year and two months, and then died. Sir Bors, who had remained in secular clothing, buried him beneath the Spiritual Palace next to his sister and to Sir Galahad, and then shipped to the realm of Logres.

Once in the realm of Logres, Sir Bors rode straight to Camelot, and was received at King Arthur's court with the greatest possible joy. Then King Arthur summoned his scribes, and Sir Bors and Sir Launcelot recounted all their adventures, and those of their fellows, and they were recorded, and the book of the Holy Grail was placed in the library at Salisbury.

Then Sir Bors spoke to Sir Launcelot:

"Sir Galahad sends his last greetings, first to you, and then to all those of the court of King Arthur; and so does Sir Percivale. I buried them both with my own hands in the city of Sarras, and Sir Galahad's last words for you were, 'Remember how ephemeral is this earth!' "

"That is true, and I trust to God that I may avail myself of his prayer." Then Sir Launcelot took Sir Bors in his arms:

"Good cousin, you are most welcome! Please know that whatsoever I may do for you or your kin I shall do while the spirit still burns in this poor body; this I promise you faithfully. Also, dear cousin, while we live, let us two never be parted."

"Sir Launcelot, as you will, so will I," Sir Bors replied.

The Book of Sir Launcelot and Queen Gwynevere

1. THE POISONED APPLE

When all the knights who had survived the quest of the Holy Grail had returned, there was much rejoicing at Camelot. King Arthur was pleased to have his knights by him once more, Queen Gwynevere was especially pleased to have Sir Launcelot by her once more, and Sir Launcelot too was pleased.

In spite of his longing and travail in matters of the spirit, Sir Launcelot knew that he was bound to his earthly love for the queen. Had it not been so he would have surpassed his fellows in the quest of the Holy Grail; but as it was, he returned to the queen with increased ardor, and they spent many hours together as lovers do, both by day and at night.

However, their love did not pass unnoticed at the court, and Sir Aggravayne, being of a vituperative disposition, spoke openly of it. In consequence Sir Launcelot became cautious, and espoused the causes of many young gentlewomen besides that of the queen. But when the queen learned of this she became angry and summoned him to her chamber:

"My lord, it would appear that your love for me is already failing, for I understand that you now champion many gentlewomen besides me."

"My lady, I beg to be excused. I have but lately returned from the quest of the Holy Grail and I cannot altogether forget the holy mysteries, revealed only to those who are chaste in the flesh and in the spirit, and of which I saw something, despite my sins. Nor yet the rebukes I suffered for loving you as I do, which love precluded me from the final mysteries vouchsafed to Sir Bors, Sir Percivale, and Sir Galahad.

"Also, I fear scandal at this court. Already there is talk of us; Sir Aggravayne speaks openly, and Sir Modred bides his time. It is for you, my lady, I am fearful; for whereas I can defend myself at arms or flee, you have to remain here and suffer ignominiously whatever is brought to your door.

"For this reason I espouse the causes of the young gentlewomen who seek my aid. By assuming the part of libertine I allay suspicion of where my true love lies."

Gwynevere wept as she listened, and when Sir Launcelot had finished, spoke angrily:

"My lord, I understand that you are depraved and lecherous; that you disdain my love and, in preference to me, champion the cause of any young noblewoman who appeals to you for aid. So be it! I discharge you from my service and from this court; and do not dare to enter my presence again."

Sir Launcelot was heartbroken as he left the queen, and summoned his nearest of kin—Sir Ector, Sir Lyonel, and Sir Bors—to whom he told everything.

"Good Sir Launcelot, do not be discouraged! Remember that you are the greatest knight living and that many important matters at this court lie in your hands. It is well known that women are inherently changeable, and often repent of their anger. Therefore I suggest that you ride no farther than the hermitage at Wyndesore, where the good hermit Sir Brastius will care for you, and wait there until we have better tidings for you."

"Sir Bors, I thank you; and yet, reluctant as I am to leave the realm, I cannot believe that the queen will restore me to favor."

"Do not say so!" Sir Bors replied. "Queen Gwynevere has many times before been vexed with you and afterward repented it."

"Then I will do as you suggest; and I pray you, good brother, in my absence try to win back the queen for me."

"My lord, I will do what I can for you."

Sir Launcelot left the court, and only his kinsmen knew where he had gone. Queen Gwynevere remained outwardly aloof, and, in order the better to conceal her inward **grief,**

arranged a private dinner party for twenty-four of the Round
Table knights.

The twenty-four knights invited were: Sir Gawain and his
brothers, Sir Gaheris, Sir Gareth, Sir Aggravayne, and their
half brother, Sir Modred; Sir Kay and his kin: Sir Bleobris, Sir
Blamoure, Sir Galyhud and Sir Galyhodyn; the brothers Sir
Bors, Sir Lyonel and Sir Ector; Sir Palomides and his half
brother, Sir Safere; and Sir La Cote Male Tayle. Also Sir
Persalunte and his two brothers Sir Ironside and Sir Brandiles; Sir Madore, Sir Patrise (a knight from Ireland), Sir
Alyduke, Sir Ascamour, and Sir Pynel (a cousin to Sir Lamerok).

Wishing to honor her guests, the queen provided a splendid
banquet with many dainties, including apples especially for
Sir Gawain, whose partiality for them was well known at
the court.

These apples were noticed by Sir Pynel, whose cousin Sir
Lamerok had died at the hands of Sir Gawain, and whose
death he wished to avenge. In consequence, he secretly poisoned several of them before the feast commenced.

When the meat course was over, however, it was not Sir
Gawain but Sir Patrise who, feeling heated with the wine,
first reached for an apple, ate it, and died. The guests all rose
in horror, and yet were hesitant of imputing such an outrage
to the queen. Then Sir Gawain spoke:

"Ma'am, that this feast was prepared for me and my fellows can hardly be denied; also my own fondness for apples
is well known. It seems therefore that I was likely to be killed,
and I fear that your majesty might be proved culpable."

The queen, abashed by the turn of events, could find no
words with which to reply. Then Sir Madore, Sir Patrise's
cousin, spoke:

"My lords, this matter shall not end here. I have lost my
noble kinsman and I am bound by honor to avenge him.
Therefore, majesty, I call you answerable for treason."

The whole company stood in silence, unable to deny the
allegation. The queen was still dumbfounded, realizing how
invidious her position was as hostess. She could only weep,
then she fainted. At once there was a tremendous hubbub
and King Arthur appeared, and when he was told what had
happened he too was grief-stricken and could not speak for
a while. The punishment for treason was burning at the stake,
and the charge of treason could be invoked at that time for
many crimes besides those of plotting against the state.

"My lords," said King Arthur eventually, "this is a most unhappy quarrel, and because I am your sovereign I may not defend my queen. And yet I am convinced that she is innocent, and I cannot bear that she should be burnt at the stake. Therefore I beg that one of you will come forward as her champion. Sir Madore shall name the day, and in battle God shall defend the innocent. Consider, my lords, what ignominy must otherwise befall this court!"

"My liege," said Sir Madore, "I beg you to forgive me; but as you too are sworn to the high order of knighthood, you must recognize that every one of the fellows at this feast must suspect the queen of treason. What say you, my lords?"

None dared to reply.

"Alas!" said the queen, "in God's name I swear that when I prepared this feast I had no thought of treason."

"Sire," said Sir Madore, "I pray you name the day for the battle."

"The battle shall take place fifteen days from now in the meadow that lies outside Winchester. God defend the right; and if no knight comes forward to champion the queen, she shall be burnt at the stake."

"My liege, I am answered," said Sir Madore.

Thereupon the twenty-four knights dispersed, and King Arthur asked the queen what had really happened.

"Jesu help me, I do not know!" she replied.

"I wonder what has become of Sir Launcelot? for he would have championed you."

"My lord, I know only what his kinsmen say: that he has left the realm."

"Alas! then I counsel you to ask Sir Bors to champion your cause on Sir Launcelot's behalf, for I see that none of the twenty-four knights but supposes you guilty, and this brings the most terrible shame on our court."

"Alas for Sir Launcelot!" said the queen.

"My lady, how is it that you have lost him? Surely he is our greatest knight! But go now to Sir Bors and beg him to act on Sir Launcelot's behalf."

The king left, and Gwynevere summoned Sir Bors and begged him to champion her cause.

"Ma'am, I am astonished that you should ask me! for was I not one of your guests, and will not my fellow knights suspect me of collusion? Also, it was you who banished Sir Launcelot from your presence and from this court—Sir Launcelot who worships you and who would lightly have undertaken to champion your cause, whether it were right or wrong. You should be ashamed to put me in so perfidious a position!"

"My lord, I am ashamed. I will try to remedy all that is amiss, but I pray you, counsel me!"

Thereupon the queen knelt before Sir Bors and begged him to save her from being burnt at the stake.

Then King Arthur returned to the queen's chamber. Sir Bors lifted the queen to her feet and spoke again:

"Ma'am you do me the greatest dishonor," he said.

"Sir Bors," said the king, "I pray you have mercy upon the queen, for I am sure that she is innocent. Therefore promise me, for the love that you bear Sir Launcelot and me, that you will champion her."

"Sire, nothing greater could be asked of a knight. If I agree, I shall provoke the enmity of my fellows; and yet for your love and Sir Launcelot's I do agree, provided that no better knight than I comes forward."

"Sir Bors, you swear to this?"

"My liege, I do."

The king and queen both thanked him warmly. Then Sir Bors departed and rode secretly to the hermitage at Wyndesore, where he told Sir Launcelot all that had happened.

"My good cousin, this has turned out well for us! Now I pray you make ready for the battle as arranged, but at the last moment find cause for delay; then I will appear. Sir Madore is a hot-headed knight, and a short delay will make him all the keener for battle."

"Sir Launcelot, it shall be as you say."

When Sir Bors returned to the court, many of the knights censured him for championing the queen; for it was generally held that she was guilty of the death of Sir Patrise. Sir Bors replied to them:

"My lords, are not you ashamed that not only the queen, but also our liege King Arthur, should be so dishonored at his own court? And consider, he is surely the greatest king in all Christendom, and on his part has never failed to honor us, his own knights."

"Sir Bors, we love and honor our king as we should. Our quarrel is not with him but with the queen for destroying his own good knights."

"My lords, this is surely the first time that there has been such an imputation against the queen. Has she not always hitherto watched over us, been bountiful in her gifts and gracious in her manner? How then can we stand by and see her cruelly slain? For myself I do not believe that such a queen as ours could be guilty of Sir Patrise's death; no, rather I suppose it to be due to some treason as yet unsuspected, and that the feast was devised in all innocence. Finally, what grounds had the queen for wishing the death of Sir Patrise?"

Some of the knights were persuaded by Sir Bors' arguments, others remained steadfastly against the queen. On the eve of the battle the queen summoned Sir Bors and asked him if he was still resolved to fight for her.

"Ma'am, I shall not fail you; I shall fight unless by chance a knight better than I should come forward."

"My lord, may I tell the king?"

"Ma'am, as you will."

The queen went to the king and told him.

"My lady, you need not have doubted Sir Bors, for he is one of the noblest knights living, and one of the most upright of men," the king replied.

In the morning all was prepared on the Winchester meadow for the battle, and for the burning of the queen if Sir Madore should prove victorious. The queen was escorted to the meadow by the constable, an iron stake was set up and a fire lit beneath it—for such was the custom, from which none could escape regardless of rank or affiliation. Then Sir Madore and Sir Bors presented themselves to the king as plaintiff and defendant, and swore to settle the charge of treason against the queen by force of arms.

"Now to battle!" cried Sir Madore, "and we shall soon prove who is in the right."

"Sir, I know you for a good knight," said Sir Bors, "and yet I do not fear you, for my trust is in God. In accordance with my oath to the king I shall fight you to the uttermost, unless a better knight than I should proffer himself in the cause of the queen."

"Sir, is that all? Either you will battle with me or you will not: say 'yea' or 'nay.'"

"Sir, let us arm, and before long you shall be answered," Sir Bors replied.

Both knights rode to their pavilions and armed; then Sir Madore rode before the king again and shouted:

"Sire, bid your champion come forth if he dares!"

Sir Bors felt ashamed and rode to the end of the jousting field, and at the very moment Sir Launcelot galloped up to him. He was mounted on a white horse and clad in white armor, and bearing a shield with an unusual device.

"Sir Bors I thank you! I had to ride hard to get here in time, but now I shall undertake the battle for you."

Sir Bors rode to the king and told him that an unknown knight had come to fight in his stead.

"Sir Bors, who may he be?" asked the king.

"Sire, I cannot say, only that he made a covenant with me to fight this battle for the queen. Hence I consider myself discharged."

The king then summoned Sir Launcelot and asked him if he was prepared to fight for the queen.

"Sir, my purpose in coming here is to vindicate your honor and that of the queen and of your court, for you have been greatly dishonored. But I pray you, allow me to undertake the battle without further ado, for when it is over I must ride forth to battles elsewhere."

Neither the king nor the queen nor any of the onlookers recognized Sir Launcelot, and all were astonished by his chivalry; Sir Bors alone knew who he was.

Sir Launcelot and Sir Madore withdrew to the ends of the field and charged at each other. Sir Madore broke his spear and was flung backward off his horse; Sir Launcelot remained in the saddle. Then Sir Madore jumped up, drew his sword, and challenged him to fight on foot.

They fought savagely for an hour, for Sir Madore was a good knight; then Sir Launcelot struck him to the ground. Sir Madore managed to rise again, and wounded Sir Launcelot in the thigh as he did so. Sir Launcelot struck him on the helmet once more and this time held him down while he dragged off his helmet. Sir Madore begged for mercy.

"Sir, I grant you your life on condition that you withdraw your charge from the queen, and that the charge does not appear on the tomb of Sir Patrise."

"My lord, I swear to it."

Sir Madore was led to his pavilion. Meanwhile the queen had been brought to the king and they embraced. Sir Launcelot walked up to the royal stand and knelt before them, and they begged him to take off his helmet and be stayed with a glass of wine. Sir Launcelot removed his helmet and was recognized.

"My lord, may God reward you for what you have done today!" said the queen.

"My king and my queen! your quarrels shall ever be my own, for am I not beholden to you both? You my liege conferred upon me the high order of knighthood, and you my lady have ever honored me; and did you not on the very day when I was knighted save me from shame by retrieving my sword, carrying it in your train, and presenting me with it at the moment of need? Surely then I should be ungrateful not to avert or avenge any wrong that is done to you."

"Good Sir Launcelot, may God reward you for your journey; and I too shall do for you what is consonant with my power."

The queen wept with shame as she beheld Sir Launcelot, and considered with what generosity he had repaid the unkindness she had shown him. Sir Launcelot's kin welcomed him back to the court; and when his own and Sir Madore's wounds had been dressed, there was much rejoicing and festivity at Camelot.

Then it happened that the good sorceress Nyneve, wife to Sir Pelleas, came on a visit to Camelot; and when she was told of the death of Sir Patrise, discovered the truth by means of her magic. The news spread swiftly through the court; and Sir Pynel, the culprit, fled to his own country.

Confidence in the queen was restored; and the whole story of the miscarriage of Sir Pynel's revenge, Sir Madore's indictment of the queen, and the championship of her cause by Sir Bors and Sir Launcelot, was inscribed on Sir Patrise's tomb.

Sir Madore became anxious to recover the good graces of the queen, and Sir Launcelot brought about their reconciliation.

2. THE FAIR MAID OF ASTOLAT

Fifteen days before the Day of the Assumption of Our Lady, King Arthur proclaimed a tournament which was to be held at Camelot on the day of the feast, and in which he, together with the King of Scotland, challenged all comers. On hearing the proclamation, knights, including kings, earls, and barons, hastened to Camelot from all parts of Britain, and among them were the Kings of North Galys and Northumberland, the King of the Hundred Knights, King Angwyshaunce of Ireland, and Sir Galahalte the High Prince.

When King Arthur was about to depart for Camelot the queen announced that she would be unable to accompany him because she felt sick.

"My lady, I am sorry," said the king, "because it is to be the greatest assembly of knights for seven years, excepting only the day of Sir Galahad's departure from this court."

"Even so, my lord, I beg to be excused," the queen replied.

The king felt heavyhearted as he left for Camelot, and it was whispered among his knights that the queen had remained at London in order to be with Sir Launcelot, who had also excused himself from the tournament, saying that he had not yet recovered from his battle with Sir Madore. The king made his first halt at Astolat, that is now called Guildford, and meanwhile the queen summoned Sir Launcelot.

"My lord, is it wise for us to remain here together, while the king and his knights ride to Camelot? Will they not say that you are remaining here for my sake alone?"

"My lady, you have grown wise, and I shall be ruled by you. Tonight I shall rest here, but tomorrow ride to Camelot. However, I shall fight in disguise and against the king, not for him."

"My lord, will you not suffer from the hardy knights of your own kin?"

"My lady, such adventures as God shall ordain, I shall endure."

In the morning Sir Launcelot set off for Camelot, and that night lodged with an old baron, Sir Barnard, at Astolat. It happened that while he was walking in the garden King Arthur saw and recognized him.

"My lords," said the king to his companions, "I have just seen a knight who, I am sure, will compete in the tournament."

"Who may that be?"

"Just now I shall not tell you!" Arthur replied, smiling to himself, and then retired for the night.

Sir Barnard, although he did not know Sir Launcelot, did all in his power to make him comfortable.

"I pray you, sir," said Sir Launcelot, "would it be possible for you to lend me a shield? I wish to ride incognito and my own is too well known."

"My lord, you have the appearance of an excellent knight and therefore I shall help you. My two sons were recently knighted; and the elder, Sir Tirry, was wounded the same day and cannot ride, so you shall have his shield. In return, I ask you to allow my younger son, Sir Lavayne, to ride with you, for I believe that he has the makings of a good knight. Now I pray you, sir, tell me your name."

"Sir, I beg to be excused from telling you my name; but certainly I will take Sir Lavayne with me in return for the shield."

Sir Barnard had also a daughter called Elaine, and the moment she set eyes on Sir Launcelot she fell in love with him, and in the end this love was to prove fatal to her. She begged Sir Launcelot to wear a token of hers at the tournament.

"My fair lady, I have never worn a token at a tournament! You ask me to do what I have not done for anyone before."

But as he spoke, it occurred to Sir Launcelot that because he had never been known to wear a token, this would be the best possible means of insuring his disguise.

"My lady, I will perhaps do as you ask; pray show me the token."

"My lord, it is a sleeve of scarlet cloth embroidered with pearls."

Elaine fetched the token and Sir Launcelot fixed it on his helmet. Then he gave her his shield and begged her to care for it until he returned from Camelot. Sir Launcelot spent the evening merrily with his hosts, and until the time of his departure Elaine watched him constantly and with increasing ardor.

King Arthur rested at Astolat for three days altogether, and then with his party rode on to Camelot where the greatest knights of the land had forgathered for the tournament. Sir Launcelot departed from Astolat on the same day as King Arthur, but when he had taken leave of Sir Barnard and his enraptured daughter, he rode privately with Sir Lavayne; and both bore plain white shields.

The opening of the tournament was announced with a flourish of trumpets. King Arthur entered the royal enclosure accompanied by Sir Gawain (whom Arthur wished to protect from Sir Launcelot), and the two parties drew up on the field: King Arthur's, which was led by the Kings of Ireland and Scotland; and the King of North Galys', which was led by the King of the Hundred Knights, the King of Northumberland, and Sir Galahalte the High Prince.

The fighting started, and before long the King of Scotland had overthrown the King of Northumberland; the King of the Hundred Knights; King Angwyshaunce of Ireland and Sir Palomides the High Prince Sir Galahalte. When these knights had been remounted, fifteen more of the Round Table knights galloped onto the field: Sir Brandiles, Sir Sagramour, Sir Dodynas the Fool, Sir Kay the Seneschal, Sir Lucas the Butler, Sir Bedivere, Sir Aggravayne, Sir Gaheris, Sir Modred, Sir Melyot, Sir Ozanna, Sir Safere, Sir Epynogres, Sir Galleron, and Sir Gryfflet.

Together these knights attacked the party of the King of North Galys and forced them to retreat. Sir Launcelot and Sir Lavayne had been watching the battle from a copse which lay a little behind the dispositions of the King of North Galys.

"See how those good knights deal with their opponents— like so many hounds chasing wild boar!" said Sir Launcelot to his companion. "Now let us see if we cannot discomfit them."

"Lead on, my lord, and I shall do my best," Sir Lavayne replied.

They galloped into the melee, and with his first spear Sir Launcelot struck down Sir Brandiles, Sir Sagramour, Sir Dodynas, Sir Kay, and Sir Gryfflet; and Sir Lavayne unhorsed Sir Lucas and Sir Bedivere. With his second spear Sir Launcelot struck down Sir Aggravayne, Sir Gaheris, Sir Modred, and Sir Melyot; and Sir Lavayne struck down Sir Ozanna. Then Sir Launcelot drew his sword and lashed about him on all sides, and among those who fell beneath his blows were Sir Safere, Sir Epynogres, and Sir Galleron. The knights of the Round Table began to withdraw.

"For the love of Jesu! who is that wonderful knight?" asked Sir Gawain.

"As yet I may not reveal his name," the king replied.

"Sire, from the blows that he deals, and from his horsemanship, I should suppose him to be Sir Launcelot, but I see that he wears a token in his helmet, which Sir Launcelot has never done for any lady."

"Peace, Sir Gawain! We shall see more of him before the tournament is over."

By dint of Sir Launcelot's support the party of the King of North Galys had now reformed, while King Arthur's party had lost its dressing. Sir Bors led eight of his kinsmen in to counterattack; they were Sir Lyonel, Sir Ector, Sir Blamoure, Sir Bleobris, Sir Alyduke, Sir Galyhud, Sir Galyhoden, and Sir Bellyngere. All together they attacked Sir Launcelot; three of them ran their spears into his horse, and Sir Bors drove his spear clean through his shield and into his side, where it broke, leaving the tip embedded in Sir Launcelot's flesh.

As soon as Sir Lavayne saw Sir Launcelot lying on the

ground he galloped up to the King of Scotland, struck him down, and led his horse to Sir Launcelot, whom he helped to remount in spite of the press all about him. Then both took spears; Sir Launcelot unhorsed Sir Bors, Sir Ector, and Sir Lyonel, and Sir Lavayne unhorsed Sir Blamoure.

Feeling that his wound might well be mortal, Sir Launcelot then drew his sword, determined to die fighting. In turn he attacked Sir Bleobris, Sir Alyduke, and Sir Galyhud, and struck each to the ground. Likewise Sir Lavayne struck down Sir Bellyngere, who was the son of Alexander the Orphan.

Sir Bors, Sir Ector, and Sir Lyonel had recovered, and now they attacked Sir Launcelot again, each striking him a blow on the helmet. Sir Launcelot staggered beneath their blows, then struck each in turn and dragged off their helmets, but restrained himself from beheading them.

Thereafter, accompanied by the loyal Sir Lavayne, he continued in the thick of the battle, and, it is said, accounted for more than thirty of the knights of the Round Table, while Sir Lavayne accounted for another ten.

"Sire, I still wonder who is that knight with the red token, for certainly he is a splendid fighter," said Sir Gawain.

"We shall doubtless discover him before he leaves," King Arthur replied, and blew on his horn to end the fighting.

It was announced by the heralds that the knight with the red token had won the prize, and the King of North Galys, with the leaders of his party, rode up to him.

"My lord, may God reward you for championing our cause today; and we pray you, will you accompany us to receive the prize, and the honor which is your due?"

"My lords," Sir Launcelot replied, "if I have earned your praise I have earned it hardly, for I am so wounded that I doubt that I shall live. Therefore I pray you allow me to go my own way, for I am more in need of repose than of honor just now."

Thereupon Sir Launcelot galloped away, groaning as he went. A mile or so from the field he came to a wood, where he drew up and spoke in a feeble voice to Sir Lavayne:

"Good Sir Lavayne, I pray you help me draw this spear tip from my body, for I can bear it no longer!"

"My own lord, I fear that you will die if we do so," Sir Lavayne replied.

"As you love me, so help me do this," said Launcelot, and dismounted.

Together they withdrew the fragment. Blood poured from

the wound and Sir Launcelot shouted with the pain. Then he grew deathly pale and fainted.

"Alas! what shall I do?" said Sir Lavayne.

For half an hour Sir Launcelot lay as though dead. Sir Lavayne turned his head into the wind; then he opened his eyes and managed to speak:

"Good Sir Lavayne, I pray you help me onto my horse. The great Sir Badouin of Brittany lives as a hermit not two miles from here; he has renounced his worldly possessions and is now an excellent physician. He will heal me if it is possible, and if not I will happily die in the hands of my cousin-german, for such he is."

With great difficulty Sir Launcelot was mounted, and blood flowed from his wound throughout their ride to the hermitage. As soon as they arrived Sir Lavayne thundered on the gate.

"For the love of Jesu, open!" he cried.

A child came and asked them what they wanted.

"Go quickly to your master, tell him that a noble knight is here, deeply wounded and in need of succor."

The child returned with the hermit.

"Tell me, is he of the court of King Arthur?"

"Truly I do not know, but today he fought against the knights of King Arthur, and never before have I witnessed such prowess."

"At one time I should have regarded him as my enemy, for I was of the fellowship of King Arthur; but now, thank God! it does not matter. Let me see him."

Sir Launcelot was leaning over the saddle, wan and bleeding. Sir Badouin thought for a moment that he recognized him, but could not be sure because he was so disfigured by his suffering.

"Sir, I pray you, tell me your name."

"Sir, I am an errant knight riding through this realm in search of adventure," Sir Launcelot replied.

Then Sir Badouin recognized Sir Launcelot by an old scar on his cheek.

"Alas, my own lord Sir Launcelot! Should I not have known you?"

"Sir, if you know me I pray you cure me of this pain, regardless of the result, whether I live or die."

"Sir Launcelot, have no doubt; I shall cure you and you shall live," Sir Badouin replied.

Sir Launcelot was carried into the hermitage by two of the servants, disarmed, and laid on a bed. Sir Badouin stanched his wound and gave him some wine to drink, and Sir Launcelot began to look more himself again. In those days many hermits had been men of great wealth and high rank and were well provided to give succor to the wounded, and hospitality to knights errant.

While Sir Launcelot lay between life and death at the hermitage, King Arthur was still at Camelot, presiding over the feast which had been prepared for all those who had entered the tournament. Arthur asked the King of North Galys what had become of "the knight with the red token, who had won the prize." The King of the Hundred Knights replied:

"Sire, we believe he is so wounded that he may not recover, and therefore we shall not see him again."

"Alas! But do you know who he is?" asked Arthur.

"Sire, we do not know either what he is called or whence he has come."

"If he should die it would be my greatest sorrow for seven years. I would readily barter my kingdom to retrieve so great a knight as he is."

"Sire, you know who he is?"

"Whether or no, I pray that our Lord shall grant us some news of him."

They all assented, then Sir Gawain spoke up:

"By my faith! I shall go in search of him, for I have never seen a greater knight in battle. His loss would be a loss to the whole realm, and he cannot have traveled far as yet."

"God help you, good Sir Gawain! and I pray that he has not in the meantime perished by the wayside."

"Sire, I will find him."

Accompanied by his squire, Sir Gawain searched within a seven-mile radius of Camelot, but failed to find him. Two days later King Arthur set off for London. Sir Gawain rode with him, and when they came to Astolat, they chanced to lodge with Sir Barnard.

While he was resting in his chamber the old knight came to him, with his daughter Elaine, to ask him how he did, and about the tournament at Camelot.

"My lord," said Sir Gawain, "two knights outshone all the rest; both carried white shields, and the greater one wore a red sleeve in his helmet. He alone must have sent forty of his opponents tumbling to the ground, and his opponents were all knights of the Round Table."

"I thank God for it! He is my first love and my last," said Elaine.

"My lady, is that so?" asked Sir Gawain.

"It is, my lord."

"Then I pray you, tell me his name."

"Sir, I do not know his name, only that I love him."

"My lady, how did you come together?"

Elaine then explained how Sir Launcelot had lodged with them, borrowed Sir Tirry's shield, and taken Sir Lavayne under his protection, also how he had left his own shield in her care.

"I pray you, may I see the shield?" asked Sir Gawain.

"My lord, accompany me to my chamber and you shall see it," Elaine replied.

"Not so! Surely you can send for it," said Sir Barnard.

The shield was sent for, and Sir Gawain recognized it at once as Sir Launcelot's.

"My lady, you love the greatest knight living, and yet I fear for you," said Sir Gawain.

"My lord, so I believe; but I love him truly, so why should you fear for me?"

"For twenty-four years I have known him, and never before has he worn a lady's token at a tournament; you are much beholden to him. You have my blessing, but you must know that he is wounded, perhaps mortally."

"Alas! I must go to him; where is he?"

"My lady, he was wounded by the man whom he most loves, and who most loves him; and if he should die I cannot tell you how we shall all suffer, for the man you love is none other than the noble Sir Launcelot."

"Dear father, I pray you permit me to ride in search of Sir Launcelot! I shall neither sleep nor eat until I know that he and my brother are safe! and until I know, I cannot be in my right mind. If Sir Launcelot dies, I too shall die."

"My dear child, you shall go to him. I too am sad that so noble a knight should lie in peril of death."

Elaine made ready and set off at once to search for Sir Launcelot, and Sir Gawain rode to King Arthur and told him how he had discovered Sir Launcelot's shield in the keeping of the Fair Maid of Astolat, as Elaine was known.

"This I knew," said the king, "because I saw Sir Launcelot in Sir Barnard's garden when we stayed in Astolat on the way up to Camelot. But I wonder that he wore the maid's token."

"Sire, the maid certainly loves him with all her heart," said Sir Gawain.

Arthur returned with his knights to London, and all at the court were saddened by the news of Sir Launcelot. The queen, however, could hardly contain her wrath, and summoned Sir Bors to her chamber.

"Sir Bors, have you heard how Sir Launcelot has betrayed me?" she demanded.

"Madam, I fear that he has betrayed his own life."

"Sir, he surely deserves to die for his treachery."

"Madam, I pray you do not abuse him."

"And why not? Did he or did he not wear the maid's token at the tournament?" asked the queen furiously.

"Madam, I am sorry to say that he did wear the maid's sleeve, but I do not doubt his loyalty, for I believe that he did so only in order not to be recognized. All his life he has loved no other lady than you."

"Shame on him, I say! And for all his pride he proved a lesser knight than you are."

"Not so, my lady! He overthrew me and eight of my kin, and thirty more knights besides."

"And I heard Sir Gawain say how wonderfully this maid loves him!"

"Madam, Sir Gawain may say what he pleases, but Sir Launcelot is pledged to the service of all ladies, as a knight should be, and he does not favor one above the other. Now I must ask you to excuse me, for I shall ride in search of him wherever he may be. And I pray that he recover!"

Meanwhile Elaine had ridden to Camelot, and there by chance met her brother exercising his horse. She asked him at once for news of Sir Launcelot.

"My dear sister, how did you know that my lord is Sir Launcelot?" Sir Lavayne asked.

Elaine explained, and they rode together to the hermitage. When she saw Sir Launcelot lying pale and lifeless in bed she fainted, and when she came to cried sorrowfully:

"Alas! my lord Sir Launcelot, what has happened to you?"

She fainted again and Sir Launcelot asked Sir Lavayne to bring her to his bed. He took her in his arms and spoke gently:

"My lady, you can hardly cheer me like this! But you are welcome here, and soon, I am sure, my wound will be healed. Now tell me, how did you come to know my name?"

"My lord, Sir Gawain lodged with my father; we showed him your shield and he recognized it."

"Alas! only harm can come of this," said Sir Launcelot and, as he thought about it, realized that Sir Gawain would inevitably tell the queen. He began to dread the consequences.

Elaine nursed Sir Launcelot with great tenderness, watching over him night and day; and it is said that no man ever received from a woman more love and more care. Soon after Elaine's arrival, Sir Launcelot asked Sir Lavayne to go to Camelot and keep watch for Sir Bors.

"Since it was he who wounded me, I am sure that he will be the first to ride in search of me. You will recognize him by a scar on his forehead."

Sir Lavayne rode to Camelot, found Sir Bors, and returned with him to Sir Launcelot. Sir Bors wept when he saw him.

"My lord Sir Launcelot, I am ashamed that a knight such as I should have wounded one as great as you—and the more so when I consider how, when you had me and my kin at your mercy, you spared us. I ask you, can you ever forgive me?"

"My good cousin, you make too much of it! I have only my own pride to thank for my wound, for had I disclosed myself to you it would never have happened. But do not worry; I shall soon recover, so now let us talk of other matters."

Then Sir Bors sat on the bed and told Sir Launcelot how angry the queen was with him

"I feared as much!" said Sir Launcelot, "and yet I only wore the sleeve so that I should not be recognized."

"So I tried to tell the queen, but she would not listen to me. But tell me: this young noblewoman who waits on you, is she the Maid of Astolat?"

"The same, and she will not easily be discouraged."

"But why should you discourage her? Is she not beautiful and well mannered? And I can see for myself that she loves you."

"I am sorry that it is so."

"Well, my lord, she is not the first young noblewoman to break her heart over you."

And so they talked.

Three or four days later Sir Launcelot felt stronger, and Sir Bors told him that King Arthur and the King of North Galys had agreed to compete in another tournament on Allhallowmas.

"Is that the truth? Then I pray you remain with me and we will see if I am not strong enough to enter for it," said Sir Launcelot.

A month passed by. Sir Bors remained at the hermitage while Elaine continued to nurse Sir Launcelot with unfailing love and diligence. No child or wife was ever more sweet to father or husband than was Elaine to Sir Launcelot, and because of this she earned the highest possible praise from Sir Bors.

Then Sir Launcelot, with the consent of Sir Lavayne and Sir Bors, inveigled Sir Badouin and Elaine to go for an excursion into the forest to collect herbs. As soon as they had left, he and Sir Lavayne armed and mounted, complete with shield and jousting spear, to see if his wound would permit of his competing in the tournament.

Once he had couched his spear Sir Launcelot found that his horse was unusually frisky, owing to his several weeks of idleness; and in his endeavors to control both horse and spear, his wound broke open again and bled profusely. He cried out for help, then fainted and fell to the ground.

Sir Lavayne and Sir Bors, with feelings of the utmost remorse, ran to his aid; and Elaine, who had also heard his cry, came running out of the forest. When she saw him pale and bleeding she burst into tears and kissed him. Then she rounded furiously on Sir Bors and Sir Lavayne:

"How dared you to lead him from his bed? If he dies, understand that I shall charge you both with treason!"

Then Sir Badouin returned, and when he saw Sir Launcelot, although he said little, he too was furious.

"Bring him inside!" he commanded.

Still unconscious, and bleeding copiously, Sir Launcelot was carried in and laid on a bed. Sir Badouin applied some herbs to his nose, poured a little water into his mouth, and, when he came to, stanched the bleeding. Then he demanded an explanation of his folly.

"Sir Badouin, I wanted to see if I was yet strong enough to compete in the tournament which King Arthur and the King of North Galys are to hold on Allhallowmas."

"Sir Launcelot, I suppose that your headstrong courage will lead you on until your soul departs from your body! But I pray you, be counseled by me: let Sir Bors compete in this tournament and do what he may. Wait until he returns, and then, by the grace of God, you will be properly healed."

Sir Bors rode to the court and told his news of Sir Launcelot first to King Arthur.

"Thank God that he will live!" the king responded.

Then Sir Bors told the queen, adding:

"Madam, it was for your sake that Sir Launcelot wished to compete in the tournament, and therefore for you that he suffers from this second accident."

"I curse him for the traitor that he is! He may die for all I care," the queen responded.

"Madam, any others who spoke as you do before me or my kin would forfeit their lives! I recall that you have before railed against Sir Launcelot, only to discover in the end that you were unjust and that he is a true knight."

At the tournament on Allhallowmas King Arthur's party was led by the Kings of Scotland, Ireland, and Northumberland, and the party of the King of North Galys by the King of the Hundred Knights and Sir Galahalte the High Prince.

Four of King Arthur's knights distinguished themselves at the tournament: Sir Bors and Sir Gawain, who each struck down twenty of their opponents, and to whom the prize was jointly awarded; and Sir Gareth and Sir Palomides, who accounted respectively for thirty and twenty knights, and to whom the prize would have been awarded had they not withdrawn from the field before the horn was blown to end the day's fighting. It was thought that they had set off together on a quest.

When the tournament was over, Sir Bors returned to Sir Launcelot at the hermitage, and found him on his feet again and virtually recovered. He gave him an account of the tournament.

"I wonder that Sir Gareth should have left without collecting the prize," said Sir Launcelot.

"Except for you, Sir Tristram, and Sir Lamerok, I have never seen a knight overcome so many of his opponents in so short a time. We all were left wondering where he had gone," Sir Bors replied.

"One must love Sir Gareth not only for his prowess, but also for his sweetness—for being forthright and without malice."

The time came for Sir Launcelot to leave the hermitage. He took his leave of Sir Badouin and rode with Sir Bors, Elaine, and her brother to Astolat, where they all lodged once more with Sir Barnard. The next morning Sir Launcelot prepared to leave, and Elaine spoke to him:

"My lord, you are leaving us; I pray you, do not suffer me to die for my love of you."

"My lady, what should I do?" said Sir Launcelot.

"My lord, I wish you for my husband."

"Alas! my lady, I am grateful to you, but I have never wanted to be married."

"Sir Launcelot, will you be my paramour?"

"God forbid that I should so ill reward your father and your brother for the love you have shown me."

"So, my lord, for that love I must die!"

"Do not say so! but forgive me. I could have married before, but would not do so, and will not now. I pray you, give yourself to a worthy knight who will make you a husband, and, in return for the great goodness you have shown me, I will endow you and your heirs with a thousand pounds yearly."

"Sir, it is impossible: unless you can take me for your wife or your paramour, all joy must vanish from my life."

"Fair lady, I may do neither," said Sir Launcelot.

The Fair Maid of Astolat gave a terrible cry and fainted. She was carried to her chamber and put on her bed. When she came to she remained there, sobbing, heartbroken. Before leaving, Sir Launcelot asked Sir Lavayne what he would do.

"My lord, I will remain with you until you drive me away!"

Then Sir Barnard came to Sir Launcelot.

"Sir, my daughter will die for the love of you."

"My lord, I am sorry. Your daughter is beautiful, tender, and gracious, and yet I did not ask for her love, or encourage it. She is a maid still, and I have promised her a bequest if she will marry a worthy knight. Her sorrow pains me, but what else can I do?"

"Good father," said Sir Lavayne, "I believe Sir Launcelot when he says that my sister is still a maid; and also I can understand something of what she feels, for since I first saw Sir Launcelot I too cannot bear to be parted from him."

Sir Launcelot rode with Sir Lavayne to the court where he was welcomed by the king, Sir Gawain, and the knights of the Round Table, except for Sir Aggravayne and Sir Modred. He tried to speak with the queen, but she eluded him.

For ten days the Fair Maid of Astolat remained in her bed, not eating or sleeping but complaining piteously of her love for Sir Launcelot. She grew pale and feeble, and it became clear that she could not live. She shrove to a priest, and when she had done, he begged her to try to forget Sir Launcelot.

"Father, did not my Creator make me of flesh and blood, to love as a woman must love? What sin is there in that? Or have I loved too much? Yet Sir Launcelot is surely a noble knight, also the work of the Creator, so do I not honor Him in my love? Alas! Sweet Jesu forgive me my sins—I cannot believe that they have been great! And I pray take pity on my suffering, wherefrom I must die."

Elaine then called for her father and her brother, Sir Tirry, and begged them to take down a letter as she dictated. When this was done she told them her last wishes:

"Father, I pray that I may be watched over, and when the soul has left my body, this letter placed in my hand while it is yet warm. Then, that I shall be finely appareled, laid on a handsome bed, and put in a barge on the Thames. The barge shall be covered with cloth of black samite and an old man shall row me down the river. So, I pray you, let it be done."

Sir Barnard faithfully followed his daughter's instructions, and for several days the barge hove to on the Thames round about Westminster. Then it was noticed by King Arthur and Queen Gwynevere, and they summoned Sir Kay the Seneschal.

"My lord, this is surely news!" said Sir Kay.

"Sir Kay, go with Sir Brandiles and Sir Aggravayne and bring me word of what is there," the king commanded.

Sir Kay and his companions found the body of Elaine, beautiful in death as she had been in life, and reported to Arthur what they had seen. Taking the queen by the hand, Arthur led her to the barge, and both wondered at the beauty of the maid, and the fineness of her apparel, which was of gold cloth. Then the queen noticed the letter in her hand. They took it and returned to the castle where Arthur commanded a clerk to read it to them. The clerk read as follows:

"Fair lord, Sir Launcelot: Now death has ended the argument of our love and taken me, the Fair Maid of Astolat, who was your lover. I pray that the ladies of the court will lament my death, and that you will bury me and offer the mass-penny, for this is my last request. May God be my witness that I die a virgin; and I beg you, Sir Launcelot, as you are peerless, to pray for my soul."

The assembled company wept as the letter was read, and then the king summoned Sir Launcelot and the letter was read to him.

"Sire, I grieve for the death of this lady. God knows that I did not intentionally lead her to this, as her brother Sir Lavayne will vouchsafe. She was both gracious and beautiful but, alas! she loved too much," said Sir Launcelot.

"My lord," said the queen, "surely you could have shown her some gentleness and saved her life thereby?"

"Madam, the young noblewoman asked me for the two things which I could not grant: that she should be my wife, or else my paramour. For her good will I offered her an annuity of a thousand pounds when she should find a knight worthy of her, but this she refused, swearing that she could love only me. And I could not love her. The heart must be free; it cannot be ordained whom we shall love."

"That is true," said the king, "for the knight who puts his heart in bondage loses himself. Now, Sir Launcelot, it is for you to conduct the burial."

Many of the knights of the Round Table went to see the maid where she lay in the barge. The next day she was given a seemly burial and Sir Launcelot offered the mass-penny. The old man returned up the river with the barge.

The queen summoned Sir Launcelot and begged his forgiveness.

"Madam, this is not the first time that your anger has been ill-founded; and yet, little as you care for my sufferings, I shall abide by you."

Life at the court resumed its normal course. The knights spent their time hawking and tourneying, and toward Christmas, jousting competitions were held with a diamond for the prize. Sir Launcelot entered only the more important tournaments, but Sir Lavayne missed hardly a day on the field and won high praise for his prowess. It was thought that at the next Pentecost he would be made a knight of the Round Table.

3. THE GREAT TOURNAMENT

When Christmas was over King Arthur summoned his nobles and proposed that a tournament should be held on Candlemas Day. It was agreed that the King of North Galys, with the Kings of Ireland and Northumberland, the King of the Hundred Knights, and Sir Galahalte the High Prince, should lead a party against King Arthur and his knights of the Round Table. The tournament was to be contested on the field at Westminster, and when the proclamation was made, many knights began joyfully to prepare for it.

Queen Gwynevere summoned Sir Launcelot: "My lord, I give you warning that you must never again enter a tournament so disguised that your own kin do not know you. For the coming tournament I shall give you to wear on your helmet a gold sleeve of mine, and this you must make known to Sir Bors and his relatives."

"My lady, it shall be done!"

Sir Launcelot tenderly took his leave of the queen, and then summoned Sir Bors, to whom he told her instructions, also that he would be taking Sir Lavayne with him to Wyndesore, where he would rest with the hermit Sir Brastius until the time came for the tournament.

While staying at Wyndesore Sir Launcelot fell into the habit of resting by a well in the forest, where he delighted to hear the fresh spring bubbling, and where sometimes he would sleep.

One day when he was sleeping thus it happened that a lady, whose pleasure it was to go hunting in the forest, accompanied by her women, all armed with crossbows and hunting knives and in command of a good pack of hounds, chased her quarry, a barren hind, to earth at the well, discharged an arrow at it, missed, and hit Sir Launcelot in the buttock. Sir Launcelot leaped up furiously and addressed the huntress:

"Young noblewoman, lady, whichsoever you may be, what devil's craft is this that you practice with your bow?"

"My Lord, I pray you, forgive me! It is my custom to hunt in this forest, and purely by mischance my hand swerved when I shot at my quarry; I did not even know you were by the well."

"Alas! my lady, you have wounded me," said Sir Launcelot.

The lady departed. Sir Launcelot painfully withdrew the arrow, all but the barbed tip, which remained embedded in the flesh, and rode back to the hermitage, where both Sir Brastius and Sir Lavayne were angered by the wound, although without knowing who the culprit was. Sir Launcelot himself was in despair because of the oncoming tournament.

"Alas!" he said, "must I always suffer some misfortune before a tournament?"

The hermit withdrew the arrow tip, stanched the bleeding, and applied the best available remedy for healing the wound quickly. By Candlemas Sir Launcelot was able to ride again, and set off for the tournament with Sir Lavayne, both disguised as Saracens.

The tournament was on a grand scale. The King of North Galys and his supporters, the Kings of Ireland and Northumberland, the King of the Hundred Knights and Sir Galahalte the High Prince each commanded a hundred knights. Likewise King Arthur's supporters: King Uryens, King Howell, King Carados, and Duke Chalens each commanded a hundred knights; and King Arthur himself, two hundred.

Queen Gwynevere, accompanied by several elderly knights who had retired from tourneying, sat on the platform to adjudicate.

The horn was blown and the fighting commenced. The King of North Galys overthrew the King of Scotland, the King of Ireland overthrew King Uryens, the King of Northumberland overthrew King Howell, Sir Galahalte overthrew Duke Chalens; then King Arthur, angry that all his leaders had been overthrown, charged the King of the Hundred Knights, and overthrew him and three more knights after him before breaking his spear.

Sir Gawain galloped onto the field with Sir Gaheris, Sir Aggravayne, and Sir Modred; Sir Gawain overthrew four knights, and each of his brothers one. They were joined by Sir Gareth, Sir Palomides, and the knights of Sir Launcelot's blood, and together attacked Sir Galahalte and his followers. Sir Galahalte, however, managed to hold his ground.

At this point Sir Launcelot and Sir Lavayne galloped onto the field. Sir Bors noticed them and warned his kinsmen and Sir Gareth who they were, and not to attack them.

Sir Launcelot overthrew Sir Gawain, Sir Aggravayne, Sir Gaheris, and Sir Modred; Sir Lavayne encountered Sir Palomides and both were unhorsed. Then Sir Launcelot encountered Sir Palomides and overthrew him, and following him another thirty of the Round Table knights. Meanwhile Sir Bors and his kin kept well clear of them.

King Arthur, angry at the downfall of so many of his followers, commanded ten of his knights to follow him into the attack. The knights he commanded were Sir Gawain, Sir Aggravayne, Sir Modred, Sir Kay, Sir Gaheris, Sir Gryfflet, Sir Lucas, Sir Bedivere, Sir Palomides, and Sir Safere.

Seeing what King Arthur's intention was, Sir Bors spoke to Sir Gareth:

"My lord, I think that Sir Launcelot and Sir Lavayne will be outmatched."

"Sir Bors, I will go to their aid, for I am beholden to Sir Launcelot for knighting me."

"Then I advise you to disguise yourself."

"Sir, I shall do so."

Nearby a knight from West Britain lay wounded. Sir Gareth begged him to exchange armor with him.

"My lord, you are welcome," the knight replied.

Sir Gareth clad himself in the knight's armor and took his shield, which was green, with the figure of a maid embossed on it, and rode to Sir Launcelot:

"Sir, for the love you have shown me in the past I shall now bear you company. You are about to be attacked by King Arthur and ten of his company."

"May God reward you!" said Sir Launcelot.

"Sir, if you will encounter Sir Gawain, I will encounter Sir Palomides, and Sir Lavayne can encounter King Arthur. Then, if we three cleave together, we can hold off the rest."

Sir Launcelot and Sir Gareth overthrew respectively Sir Gawain and Sir Palomides; Sir Lavayne overthrew King Arthur, but was himself unhorsed. Then Sir Launcelot overthrew Sir Aggravayne, Sir Gaheris, and Sir Modred; Sir Gareth overthrew Sir Kay, Sir Safere, and Sir Gryfflet; and when Sir Lavayne was remounted, he overthrew Sir Lucas and Sir Bedivere.

The tournament lasted until nightfall; for while Sir Launcelot and his two companions continued victorious against the knights of the Round Table, King Arthur was reluctant to accept defeat. Sir Gareth, disguised as he was with the green shield of the knight from West Britain, excited much comment by his feats. He accounted for more than thirty of his opponents, and Sir Launcelot himself was greatly surprised, supposing that only Sir Tristram or Sir Lamerok, both of whom were now dead, was capable of such prowess. Sir Lavayne also distinguished himself, striking down more than twenty opponents. Sir Launcelot as ever fought with peerless power and precision.

Throughout the tournament, while King Arthur with Sir Gawain and his brothers engaged Sir Galahalte and his followers, together with Sir Launcelot, Sir Lavayne, and Sir Gareth, Sir Bors and his kin kept clear of them and engaged the King of the Hundred Knights and his followers. Toward nightfall Sir Gawain spoke to King Arthur:

"Sire, have you not noticed how Sir Bors and his kin have kept clear of us while we have been fighting the two knights disguised as Saracens and the knight with the green shield? Surely there must be a reason for this. . . ."

"By my faith!" said Sir Kay, "Sir Gawain is right, and Sir Bors and his kin have done much better than we have."

"Sire," said Sir Gawain, "I believe that the Saracen wearing the gold sleeve is Sir Launcelot, judging by his seat in the saddle and by the lusty blows he delivers, and that his companions are Sir Lavayne and Sir Gareth, who would never fight against Sir Launcelot, since he knighted him."

"Sir Gawain, you speak sensibly; what do you advise?"

"My lord, I think that we should depart to our lodging. Unless we attack each of them with a dozen knights we shall never get the better of them, and there could be little honor in that!"

King Arthur blew his horn, the fighting finished, and the heralds announced that the prize had been won by the knight wearing the gold sleeve, Sir Launcelot having defeated fifty of his opponents, Sir Gareth thirty-five, and Sir Lavayne twenty-four.

Before leaving the field King Arthur sent word to Sir Galahalte that he wished to speak with the knight wearing the gold sleeve. When he had disarmed, the king rode over to them and recognized Sir Launcelot, Sir Lavayne, and Sir Gareth, who had also disarmed, and invited them all to the feast.

"Sir Launcelot, you did not give our fellowship much rest today!" the king added.

At the feast Sir Launcelot told the king how he had been wounded in the buttock by the huntress at Wyndesore; and then the king rallied Sir Gareth about changing parties.

"My lord," said Sir Gareth, "when I saw you lead your ten knights in to attack Sir Launcelot I thought he would need some assistance, and I have been beholden to him since he knighted me."

"Sir Gareth, I have come to know you for a true knight; you have done well today and increased your renown. And, as a knight should, you gave succor to a noble knight who stood in need of it; only a coward would have done otherwise."

The feast continued, with merriment and good will, for in those days true chivalry was well appreciated.

4. THE KNIGHT OF THE CART

It was the month of May, the month when the foliage of herbs and trees is most freshly green, when buds ripen and blossoms appear in their fragrance and loveliness. And the month when lovers, subject to the same force which reawakens the plants, feel their hearts open again, recall past trysts and past vows and moments of tenderness, and yearn for a renewal of the magical awareness which is love.

First a man must love God his Creator, and then, if he is to be ennobled, he must love a woman, for God has created him thus. And that love should be fresh and temperate as the blossoms of May. True love is not cold and barren as the plants are in winter, nor yet is it parched and dizzy as the plants are in summer.

Today, we know, love is commonly as the summer or winter: brief and lewd, or cold and brittle—men cannot love seven nights but they must have their desires. In King Arthur's time this was not so; lovers remained true and fresh for seven years and more, and it was in honor of their ladies that knights bore arms and won glory.

And among such lovers we must speak of Queen Gwynevere, who, because of her unfaltering love for Sir Launcelot, was to end her days honorably and with sweetness.

Early one morning in May, Queen Gwynevere commanded ten of her knights to prepare to ride with her a-Maying. Each knight was to be accompanied by a lady, a squire, and two yeomen, and all were to be decked in silk or other cloth of the freshest green, and decorated with moss, flowers, and herbs. They were to ride into the fields and woods of Westminster, and to return to King Arthur at the court at ten o'clock.

Sir Launcelot was absent from the court at that time, and the ten knights chosen by the queen were Sir Kay, Sir Aggravayne, Sir Brandiles, Sir Sagramour, Sir Dodynas, Sir Ozanna, Sir Ladynas, Sir Persaunte, Sir Ironside, and Sir Pelleas.

It was customary for the queen to ride forth only in a large company of knights, known as the Queen's Knights—knights who were most young, lusty, and eager to win fame, who bore plain white shields. Knights who were killed were replaced at the next Pentecost. Chief of them all, of course, was Sir Launcelot.

The absence of Sir Launcelot, and the small number of the queen's party, were noted by a knight called Sir Mellyagraunce, son to King Bagdemagus. For many years Sir Mellyagraunce had secretly loved the queen, but knowing that he could neither rival Sir Launcelot in her favor, nor overcome Sir Launcelot in combat, had waited patiently for an opportunity to waylay and capture her for his own pleasure.

As it happened, Sir Mellyagraunce had lately been bequeathed a castle near Westminster, so it seemed that fortune had played into his hands at last. Summoning twenty men-at-arms and a hundred archers, he galloped after the queen's party, surrounded them, and himself confronted the queen.

"For shame!" cried the queen, "you a prince, and yet you would betray your father, your fellows of the Round Table, and the liege who knighted you! Have done! I warn you that rather than be dishonored by a traitor such as you, I will take my own life."

"Peace, ma'am! For many years I have loved you; and now that the time has come, I shall take you as I find you."

Then one of the queen's knights spoke up:

"Sir Mellyagraunce, do you not fear to so jeopardize your honor and your person? It is true that at the moment you have us at a disadvantage—we are few and not armed. But do not suppose that in honor of our queen we shall fail to give a good account of ourselves."

"Then defend yourselves as best you may!" Sir Mellyagraunce replied.

The knights of Sir Mellyagraunce charged with their spears and the knights of the queen defended themselves with their swords. A bloody battle followed in which forty of Sir Mellyagraunce' knights were brought to the ground and six of the queen's knights seriously wounded. Sir Brandiles, Sir Persaunte, Sir Ironside, and Sir Pelleas were still on their feet and fighting furiously when the queen addressed Sir Mellyagraunce:

"Sir, I will follow you where you will, on this covenant: that all my knights shall be spared, and that they shall accompany me wheresoever you take me. Fail to do this, and I shall take my own life."

"Ma'am, for your sake I shall spare your knights. You shall all be conducted to my castle."

The queen commanded her knights to cease fighting. Sir Pelleas, a knight justly famed for his indomitable spirit, replied:

"Ma'am, as you command, but we will readily fight to the death for your sake."

At the queen's command the fighting ceased and the wounded knights were helped onto their horses—a piteous sight to behold. Sir Mellyagraunce gave orders that none should stray from the party, for he dreaded that Sir Launcelot might be informed of his misdemeanor. However, the queen managed to speak secretly to one of her pages and commanded him to gallop back to the court at the first opportunity, and inform Sir Launcelot.

The child bided his time, and then galloped off. Sir Mellyagraunce pursued him for a short way but was unable to catch him; then he returned to the queen.

"Ma'am, I see that you wish to betray me to Sir Launcelot; however, I shall arrange an ambush for him."

Sir Mellyagraunce commanded thirty of his best archers to lie in wait for Sir Launcelot and shoot his horse, but to beware of combat with him lest he should defeat them all. The party rode on to the castle. The queen's knights remained by her; and Sir Mellyagraunce, for fear of Sir Launcelot, dared not force his will upon her as he had intended.

The page arrived safely at the court, found Sir Launcelot, and told him all that had happened. Sir Launcelot called for his armor and his horse.

"Alas! would I not have given all my realms in France for the chance of encountering, fully armed, all those recreants!" he said.

Before leaving, Sir Launcelot commanded the page to find Sir Lavayne, tell him what had happened, and follow him to Sir Mellyagraunce' castle. He then rode down to the Thames, made his horse swim across to Lambeth, and then set off at a gallop for the castle. From the field where the battle had taken place, Sir Launcelot followed a trail which led into a a wood, and there the archers challenged him.

"By what right do you waylay a knight of the Round Table?" Sir Launcelot shouted.

"My lord, turn back or we shall kill your horse!"

"Cowards! So you would kill my horse? Why do you not quit your ambush, come forward, and fight? Were you five hundred I should kill you all!"

The archers let fly with their arrows, hitting Sir Launcelot and his horse so that they both fell to the ground; then they fled. Sir Launcelot cursed and tried to follow them, but was prevented by the ditches and tangled hedgerows.

"It is always said that a good man is never in danger except when he meets a coward!" said Sir Launcelot to himself.

He set off for the castle on foot, heavily encumbered by his armor and shield, which he dared not leave behind for fear of further treachery. Then he met a cart laden with wood.

"Good carter! I pray you, take me to the castle which lies not two miles from here."

"Sir, I have come only to fetch wood."

"For whom?"

"For Lord Mellyagraunce."

"It is to his castle that I wish to go."

"Sir, you shall not go with me."

Sir Launcelot strode up to the carter and struck him on the face with the back of his hand. The carter fell down dead. Fearing for his life, the second carter spoke to Sir Launcelot:

"My lord, spare my life and I will take you where you will."

"Drive me to Sir Mellyagraunce' castle," Sir Launcelot commanded.

The carter set off at a gallop, and Sir Launcelot's horse, with forty arrows sticking into it, followed behind. An hour or so later the queen and one of her ladies were standing at a bay window and the lady noticed the cart.

"Madam, you see that knight riding in a cart? I suppose he is going to be hanged!"

"I pray you, where?" asked the queen.

Then she saw them, and at once recognized Sir Launcelot by his shield. His faithful horse followed lamely behind, its entrails hanging to the ground.

"For shame!" said the queen. "I see now what has happened: Sir Launcelot rides in the cart and his faithful horse, which is wounded, follows behind."

She then rounded on her lady for supposing that Sir Launcelot was a knight being led to a shameful death at the gallows. Meanwhile Sir Launcelot had come to the castle gates. He shouted in a tremendous voice, so that all who were in the castle could hear him:

"Sir Mellyagraunce, traitor and coward! Come forth with all your fellows and fight to the death. This is Sir Launcelot du Lake who calls you!"

Thereupon Sir Launcelot opened the gate, struck the porter with his gauntlet, and broke his neck. Hearing Sir Launcelot, Sir Mellyagraunce ran trembling to the queen and threw himself on his knees before her.

"Mercy upon me, good queen! I pray you, protect me."

"My lord, what ails you? I thought that some good knight would come to my rescue, although King Arthur does not yet know of your evil work."

"Ma'am, I would be in your good grace. I pray you allow me to make amends for all that I have done amiss."

"My lord, what would you have me do?"

"Ma'am, intercede with Sir Launcelot on my behalf. Tell him that tonight you shall both be entertained in my poor castle, that tomorrow we shall all ride to Westminster, and thereafter my person and my estates shall be yours to rule."

"Sir, perhaps it is better that you should yield peaceably; I will go and talk to my lord Sir Launcelot."

The queen descended to the inner court where Sir Launcelot stood shouting his challenge: "Traitor! come forth!"

"My lord," said the queen, "what moves you?"

"My lady, how strange that you should ask! Have you not been assaulted and dishonored? I have suffered only the loss of my horse, and yet I shall not rest until I have avenged us both."

"Truly, my lord, there is no need. Sir Mellyagraunce yields his person and his worldly possessions to me. So come, we will enter in peace!"

"Ma'am, if I had known that you should be so readily reconciled to this coward and traitor, I should not have hastened here to your rescue; it seems hardly needed."

"How so, my lord? Do not suppose that I am reconciled to Sir Mellyagraunce out of love for him, no! But our two selves will do better without the noise of further battle."

"Ma'am, only at your command or the king's would I allow Sir Mellyagraunce to escape me thus; although I too would not wish for a scandal."

"Then, my lord, what more do you want, if my command is your pleasure?"

"My lady, you speak well!"

The queen took Sir Launcelot by the hand from which he had removed the gauntlet, and led him to her chamber, where she disarmed him. They found a window with iron bars facing the garden, and agreed that Sir Launcelot should come to the queen that night as soon as everyone in the castle was asleep.

Sir Launcelot then spoke to the queen's knights. He was heartbroken when he saw their wounds, and he told them of the archers' cowardly attack on his horse. They all swore that were it not for the queen's command, Sir Mellyagraunce should not be allowed to escape. Then Sir Lavayne arrived at the castle.

"My lord Sir Launcelot, how is it? I see that your horse is shot with arrows."

"Sir Lavayne, all has been settled, I pray you speak no more of it," Sir Launcelot replied.

Sir Mellyagraunce was careful to see that the wounded knights were properly tended and to provide a good supper for his guests. The queen insisted that the wounded knights should all be placed in an antechamber leading into her own, so that she could tend them during the night if the need arose. Then they all retired, and Sir Launcelot summoned Sir Lavayne:

"My lord, I am going to the queen's chamber; she requires that I speak with her."

"Sir Launcelot, should not I accompany you? We cannot know what treachery Sir Mellyagraunce intends next."

"Thank you, Sir Lavayne, but I must go alone."

Armed with only his sword, Sir Launcelot stole through the castle and into the garden, where he picked up a ladder which he had noticed earlier, and put it up against the wall by the barred window.

Sir Launcelot and the queen talked for some time, and then the queen said:

"My lord, it is a shame that you have to remain outside!"

"My lady, do you wish me to come into your chamber?"

"My lord, I do."

Sir Launcelot grasped the iron bars, and with a sudden effort tugged them free of the stone, cutting his hands to the bone as he did so. Then he jumped lightly into the room.

"Quietly, my lord, the wounded knights are all here!" said the queen, leading Sir Launcelot to her bed.

Disregardful of the blood on his hands Sir Launcelot lay down with the queen and they made love. At dawn Sir Launcelot departed silently, being careful to replace the bars in the window.

Later that morning Sir Mellyagraunce came to the queen's chamber and was told that the queen was still asleep, though neither she nor Sir Launcelot had slept during the night. Striding over to the bed, Sir Mellyagraunce drew aside the curtains and at once noticed the bloodstained sheets.

"So, Madam! I see now that you have betrayed your lord the king, for surely last night you lay with one of the wounded knights. Now I shall take this matter into my own hands."

"Sir, that is untrue; not one of these knights is guilty!"

Then one of the ten knights spoke up:

"Sir Mellyagraunce, how dare you defame our queen? Be sure that one of us shall champion her the moment our wounds are healed."

"My lords, forget your proud words and come and see the queen's bed," Sir Mellyagraunce replied.

The wounded knights limped over to the bed, looked, and were abashed, for none could deny the evidence of the blood-stained sheets. Sir Mellyagraunce rejoiced within himself, sure that he now had the queen at a disadvantage which would enable him to conceal his own treachery.

Then Sir Launcelot appeared. "My lords, what is this?" he asked.

Sir Mellyagraunce told him.

"Sir, it is not for you or any knight to search the queen's bed—such an action is altogether knavish. I do not suppose that the king himself would have the temerity to draw the curtains of his lady's bed unless he were about to enter it. Scurrilous as you are, you should hang your head in shame!"

"Sir Launcelot, what is plain is that the queen has acted treasonably, and by force of arms I shall prove it," Sir Mellyagraunce replied.

"Beware what you say, coward! Your challenge may be accepted."

"Sir Launcelot, for this cause I do not fear even you, great knight that you are; for it is just, and God will have a stroke in every battle."

"Sir Mellyagraunce, it is true that God is to be feared. But I will warrant that none of these ten knights lay with the queen last night. Therefore on behalf of the queen I accept your challenge."

"Sir, here is my gauntlet."

"Sir, I accept it. What day shall the battle be?"

"Eight days from now, on the field at Westminster."

"Agreed."

"Sir Launcelot, as you are an honorable knight I trust that you meditate no treason; myself likewise; and therefore until the day of battle let us be reconciled. We will go to dinner shortly; until then may I conduct you around the castle?"

"Sir, I have at no time in my life so far contemplated any treason. Lead on around the castle if you will."

Suspecting nothing, for only those who are themselves treacherous fear it in others, Sir Launcelot followed Sir Mellyagraunce from chamber to chamber until suddenly he fell through a trapdoor into a straw-filled cell thirty feet below.

Sir Mellyagraunce next gave orders for Sir Lavayne's horse to be hidden, and then, at dinner, feigned surprise at Sir Launcelot's absence, and suggested casually that since Sir

Lavayne's horse was missing, Sir Launcelot must have ridden off suddenly on some adventure, as he was wont to do.

After dinner, when Sir Lavayne had arranged horse litters for the wounded, the whole party rode back to the court at Westminster and Sir Mellyagraunce' charge was laid before the king.

"I wonder," said the king, "that Sir Mellyagraunce is bold enough to bear arms against Sir Launcelot! But where is Sir Launcelot?"

"Sire, we suppose that he rode off on some adventure, as he often does," one of the knights replied.

"Let him be, then; he will certainly appear for the battle, unless by some treason he is withheld."

Meanwhile Sir Launcelot languished in his cell, nearly overcome by chagrin. Every day his food and drink were brought to him by a young noblewoman who offered to release him if he would first become her lover, but he refused her.

"Sir, you are not wise; for not only will you never escape from here, but the queen will be burnt at the stake if you continue to refuse me."

"God forbid that I should be so persuaded! Understand, my lady, that if I fail to appear on the field, the queen will know that I am either sick or dead or have been treacherously withheld; and then, you may be sure, some good knight of my own blood, or another of my fellows of the Round Table, will fight for the queen's cause on my behalf. Furthermore, were you the only lady in the land, I should not be your lover."

"Sir Launcelot, you shall die shamefully here, in this prison."

"My lady, what suffering our Lord has to bestow I shall endure gladly."

The young noblewoman spoke again to Sir Launcelot on the day the battle was due.

"My lord Sir Launcelot, you are too hard-hearted. I pray you, kiss me but once and I shall release you."

"My lady, I will grant you that, since it does not dishonor me."

Sir Launcelot kissed the young noblewoman. Then she brought him his armor and, when he had armed, led him to the stables to take his choice from twelve coursers. Sir Launcelot chose a white mare, and when she was harnessed, mounted her, took up his spear and shield, and bade farewell to the young noblewoman:

"My lady, I thank you, and if it is ever in my power to serve you I shall do so."

Confident of his plans, Sir Mellyagraunce had insisted that a pyre be built on the field at Westminster for the burning of the queen in default of Sir Launcelot's appearance. Reluctantly the king gave the order, and as the time for the battle was already past, the fire was lit.

Then Sir Lavayne spoke to the king: "Sire, it is not possible that Sir Launcelot should have voluntarily forsaken the queen; some evil fate must have befallen him. Therefore, I pray you, allow me to fight for the queen on Sir Launcelot's behalf."

"Good Sir Lavayne, you shall do so. There is not one among the ten knights who has not sworn that were he healed he would take up the queen's cause, in complete confidence of its rightness."

"My liege, you give me leave to fight on behalf of Sir Launcelot?"

"Sir Lavayne, I do."

Sir Lavayne armed and rode to the end of the field, and the heralds had just cried, "Lechés les alere!" when Sir Launcelot galloped up and halted before King Arthur.

"Hold!" cried the king.

Sir Launcelot told the king the whole story of Sir Mellyagraunce' treachery, the queen was released and brought to the king, and then Sir Launcelot took up his position at the end of the field.

The two combatants thundered together and Sir Mellyagraunce was flung high over his horse's tail and landed on the ground with a crash. He leaped up, sword in hand. Sir Launcelot dismounted, also drew his sword, and they fought savagely for a short time. Then Sir Launcelot caught Sir Mellyagraunce a blow on the helmet which sent him reeling to the ground once more. Sir Mellyagraunce cried aloud:

"Most noble lord, as you are a knight of the Round Table, I pray you spare my life! I yield myself a prisoner to the king and to the queen."

Sir Launcelot looked up at the queen: he wished dearly to kill his opponent and he waited for some sign of assent. The queen nodded almost imperceptibly.

"Rise, coward! We fight to the death," said Sir Launcelot.

"My lord, I will not rise, except as your prisoner."

"I will make you an offer: I will remove my helmet and the armor on my left side, and my left hand shall be bound behind my back so that I may not use it. Will you fight me then?"

Sir Mellyagraunce started up and shouted:

"My lord King Arthur! Did you hear Sir Launcelot's offer? I accept."

"Sir Launcelot," said the king, "do you abide by your offer?"

"My liege, I do."

Sir Launcelot was prepared in accordance to his instructions: His helmet was removed, and the armor on his left side; then his left hand was bound securely behind him.

Once more the combatants faced each other. Sir Mellyagraunce raised his sword and made a sudden lunge at Sir Launcelot's left side. Sir Launcelot deflected the blow with his own sword and then struck Sir Mellyagraunce on the helmet. The blow cut clean through the helmet and split open the head down to the throat.

Sir Mellyagraunce was buried without further ado, and the manner of his death inscribed on his tomb.

And thereafter Sir Launcelot was more than ever loved by the king and by the queen.

5. THE HEALING OF SIR URRY

It is told that during the reign of King Arthur there was a Hungarian knight called Sir Urry, who, in search of adventure, roamed from country to country until he came to Spain, where he met Sir Alpheus, who was the son of an earl and a sorceress, and a knight no less hardy than himself. These two knights were jealous of each other and agreed to fight to the uttermost, with the result that Sir Alpheus was killed, and Sir Urry wounded in seven places: three on his head, two on his body, and two on his left hand.

In order to avenge her son Sir Alpheus' mother cast a spell over Sir Urry so that none of his wounds might heal until he had been touched by the greatest knight on earth. Sir Urry's mother devised a horse litter between two palfreys and then commanded her daughter, together with a page, to lead Sir Urry abroad until they met the knight who could cure him.

For seven years Fileloly wandered abroad with her brother,

throughout the length and breadth of Christendom, and eventually coming to Scotland, crossed the border into Carlisle, where King Arthur was holding his annual celebration of the Pentecost. Fileloly's announcement that she was searching for the greatest knight on earth came to the ears of King Arthur, and he summoned her to the court and questioned her.

"Most noble king," Fileloly answered him, "for seven years I have searched in vain for the greatest knight on earth, for only he can cure my brother; and this is a shame because he was one of the greatest knights himself before he was wounded."

"My lady, you are welcome to this realm, and here, I promise you, your brother shall be healed if there exists a knight capable of it. I do not myself presume to be the greatest knight on earth, but in order to encourage the nobles of my court, I shall offer first to probe Sir Urry's wounds."

Thereupon the king commanded that Sir Urry should be laid in the meadow with a cushion of gold cloth beside him, and that all the nobles present (of whom there were a hundred and ten of the Round Table knights) should be in attendance for the attempt to heal him. King Arthur himself then knelt on the cushion, and as he looked at Sir Urry thought what a fine-looking knight he was.

"Good knight, I pray you suffer me to touch your wounds, for I would cure you; and if I hurt you I pray you forgive me."

"Noble king, as God commands, do as you will. I most readily place myself in your hands," Sir Urry replied.

King Arthur gently touched the wounds, and as he did so they bled once more.

King Clarivaunce of Northumberland likewise attempted to heal Sir Urry and failed to do so, also Kings Barraunte of the Hundred Knights, Uryens of Gore, Angwyshaunce of Ireland, and Carados of Scotland; Sir Galahalte the High Prince, Prince Constantyne of Cornwall, Duke Chalens of Claraunce, and the Earls Ulbawys, Lambayle, and Arystanse.

Next to try were Sir Gawain, his three sons, Sir Gyngalyn, Sir Florence, and Sir Lovel, and his four brothers, Sir Gareth, Sir Gaheris, Sir Aggravayne, and Sir Modred; and they likewise failed.

Then came the knights of Sir Launcelot's kin: Sir Ector de Marys, Sir Lyonel, Sir Bors de Ganis, Sir Blamoure de Ganis, Sir Bleobris de Ganis, Sir Gahalantyne, Sir Galyhoden, Sir Menaduke, Sir Vyllyars the Valyaunte, Sir Hebes le Renowne.

And then Sir Sagramour le Desyrus, Sir Dodynas le Saveage, Sir Dynadan; Sir Brewnor le Noyre, named by Sir Kay La Cote

Male Tayle; Sir Kay the Seneschal, Sir Kay le Straunge, Sir Melyot de Logres, Sir Petipace of Winchelse, Sir Galleron of Galway, Sir Melyon of the Mountayne, Sir Cardoke, Sir Uwayne les Avoutres, Sir Ozanna le Cure Hardy, Sir Ascamour, Sir Grummor Grummorson, Sir Crosseleme, and Sir Severause le Brewse.

Sir Severause was a hardy knight but curious in that his courage was at its greatest when he encountered dragons, monsters, or wild beasts, but at its least when he encountered his fellow knights. In consequence, the Lady of the Lake, who at different times had entertained both Sir Severause and Sir Launcelot, had prevailed on each of them not to fight the other; and both had honored their vow.

But to continue with the knights of the Round Table. The next were King Pellinore's sons: Sir Agglovale, Sir Durnor, and Sir Tore, whom King Pellinore had got on the milkmaid before she married the cowherd Aryes. Sir Lamerok, the most renowned of King Pellinore's sons and the one who was second only to Sir Percivale and Sir Galahad (who died on the quest of the Holy Grail), had been treacherously killed by Sir Gawain and his kin.

Then Sir Gryfflet le Fyze de Du, Sir Lucas the Butler and his brother Sir Bedivere; Sir Brandiles, Sir Cador's son Sir Constantyne, who was to succeed to the throne when King Arthur died; Sir Clegis, Sir Sadoke, Sir Dynas the Seneschal of Cornwall, Sir Fergus, Sir Dryaunte, Sir Lambegus, Sir Clarryus of Cleremount, Sir Cloddrus, and Sir Gwyarte le Petite.

Then the three kinsmen, Sir Hectymere, Sir Edward of Carnarvon, and Sir Pryamus, the last of whom had been christened by Sir Tristram; Sir Helyn le Blanke, who was the illegitimate son of Sir Bors and the daughter of King Brandegoris of Strangore; Sir Bryan de Lystenoyse, Sir Gauter, and Sir Raynole, three brothers whom Sir Launcelot had won on a bridge while he was wearing the armor of Sir Kay.

Then Sir Bellengerus le Beuse, who had killed King Mark in order to avenge the deaths of his father, Sir Alexander the Orphan, and Sir Tristram. King Mark had killed both treacherously: Sir Tristram whilst he was playing the harp to his lover Iseult the Fair. Sir Tristram had been the most greatly loved and the most deeply mourned of all knights of his time, and his lover, Queen Iseult, had swooned on his grave. Sir Bellengerus had killed not only King Mark, but also his treacherous cousin Sir Andret, together with other of his evil-minded fellows.

After Sir Bellengerus came Sir Hebes, Sir Morganour, Sir Sentrayle, Sir Suppynabiles, and Sir Belyaunce le Orgulus, whom Sir Lamerok had won. Then Sir Neroveus and Sir Plenoryus, whom Sir Launcelot had won; Sir Darras, Sir Harry le Fyze Lake, and Sir Ermyne, who was brother to King Hermaunce, whom Sir Palomides had once championed at the Red City.

Then Sir Selyses of the Dolorous Tower, Sir Edward of Orkney, Sir Ironside of the Red Lands, who had been won by Sir Gareth when he championed the Lady Lyoness; Sir Arrok, Sir Degrevaunt, Sir Degrave Saunze Vylony, who fought with the giant of Blak Lowe; Sir Epynogres, Prince of Northumberland; Sir Pelleas, who would have died for the love of Lady Ettarde had not the good sorceress Nyneve, whom he later married, come to love and to rescue him.

Then Sir Lamyell of Cardiff, who was also a great lover; Sir Playne de Fors, Sir Melyas de Lyle, and King Arthur's son, Sir Boarte le Cure; Sir Madore de la Porte, Sir Collgrevaunce, Sir Hervyse de la Foreyst Saveage, and Sir Marrok, who was betrayed by his wife and had spent seven years as a werewolf. Then the three brothers, Sir Persaunte, Sir Pertolope, and Sir Perymones, all of whom Sir Gareth had won when he was called Beaumains.

These were the hundred and ten knights who tried and who failed to heal Sir Urry. Then Sir Launcelot was seen riding toward them.

"My lords," said the king, "I pray you, be silent and I will speak to Sir Launcelot."

"Dear brother," said Fileloly, "my heart warms to this knight."

"Dear sister, mine too—more so than to any who have so far tried."

"My lord Sir Launcelot," said the king, "you must now do as we have all done. . . ." And he explained how they had tried to heal Sir Urry.

"My liege, surely it could only be presumption on my part to suppose that I might succeed where so many noble knights have failed," Sir Launcelot replied.

"Sir Launcelot, it will not be presumption on your part because you try at my command; and I do not hesitate to add that I suppose that if any knight on earth has a chance of healing Sir Urry, you have."

"My liege, I may not disobey you, even though in my heart I still protest!"

King Arthur and the fellows of the Round Table all urged

Sir Launcelot not to hold back, and then Sir Urry himself spoke up:

"Good knight, I pray you, for the love of Jesu heal me! Already, by your very presence it seems that my wounds pain me less."

"My lord," Sir Launcelot responded, "I had never supposed myself worthy of so high an order!"

Then Sir Launcelot knelt by the wounded knight and prayed:

"Blessed Father and Son and Holy Ghost, I beseech You hear this prayer which comes from a simple and honest heart! Through Your grace, blessed Trinity, and not for my own honor, I pray You, let these hands heal the wounded knight."

Sir Launcelot touched Sir Urry first on the head, then on the body, and then on the left hand, and as he did so the wounds closed, and the flesh was renewed without trace of them. The whole company knelt down and gave thanks to God and to the Holy Mother, and Sir Launcelot wept like a child.

Sir Urry was conducted ceremoniously into Carlisle, accompanied by the priests and clerks who sang to the glory of God. The king appareled him in fine clothes, in which he appeared strong and handsome, and asked him how he did.

"Gracious king, I never felt so well!" he replied.

"Then I pray you, will you enter the field and joust?"

"Sire, nothing would please me better."

King Arthur ordained a tournament for the following morning, with a diamond for the prize, which was to be contested by two parties, each of a hundred knights, but excluding the most experienced knights.

Sir Urry and Sir Lavayne each overthrew thirty of their opponents and were acclaimed the winner. King Arthur then proposed, and it was agreed, that they should both be made knights of the Round Table. Thereafter they remained at the court in the service of Sir Launcelot, to whom they were both devoted, and Sir Lavayne married Fileloly and was granted a barony by King Arthur.

For a year after killing Sir Mellyagraunce in battle, Sir Launcelot, to spite his enemies, adventured forth in a cart as though he were about to be hanged. He became known as the Knight of the Cart and won for himself even greater renown than hitherto; but this material I* have lost, so we will come next to the Morte D'Arthur, which begins with Sir Aggravayne, who all this time was watching Sir Launcelot and Queen Gwynevere with evil in his heart.

---

* "I" refers to Malory; not to the present editor.

Le Morte d'Arthur

1. SLANDER AND STRIFE

It happened in the month of May—when most men and women rejoice in the fresh flowers, feel comfort in the season, and forget the winter months spent cowering by the fire—that two knights with malice in their hearts first plotted the downfall of Sir Launcelot and Queen Gwynevere; and by those plots brought about the entire destruction of King Arthur's court.

The two knights, Sir Aggravayne and Sir Modred, brothers to Sir Gawain, had for long been spying on Sir Launcelot and the queen, and then, one day when all their brothers were gathered in the king's chamber, they spoke openly to them.

"I marvel," said Sir Aggravayne, "that we are not all ashamed, both for ourselves and for King Arthur, to witness how Sir Launcelot consorts with the queen, during the day and at night."

"Sir Aggravayne, I am ashamed that you should bring such a charge before us," Sir Gawain replied. "Understand that for my part I will not listen to you."

"Nor will I!" said both Sir Gaheris and Sir Gareth.

"Then I will!" said Sir Modred.

"Sir Modred, I can believe you, as your only pleasure lies in the discomfort of others; but I warn you that more than you can foresee will come of your meddling," said Sir Gawain.

"Come what may, I shall inform the king!" said Sir Aggravayne.

"It is wrong that you should do so," said Sir Gawain. "A quarrel between Sir Launcelot and the king would disrupt the whole court, for Sir Launcelot has many supporters. Also you seem to forget that we are all beholden to him. Has he not rescued the king and the queen on several occasions? Me he saved from King Carados of the Dolorous Tower, for which I shall ever be grateful; and you and Sir Modred, together with threescore others, from Sir Tarquine. Therefore I say that you should be ashamed of your calumny."

"Think what you will, but I shall act," Sir Aggravayne replied.

At that moment King Arthur walked into the chamber.

"Good brothers, hold your peace!" said Sir Gawain.

"We shall not!" Sir Aggravayne and Sir Modred replied together.

"You will not? Then I shall take no part in it," said Sir Gawain.

"Nor shall we!" said Sir Gaheris and Sir Gareth.

The three knights departed and the king asked Sir Aggravayne what had happened.

"My liege, as we are your cousins, Sir Modred and I feel obliged to speak of a matter which our three brothers all shun. It is known to us, and to many others at this court, that Queen Gwynevere is Sir Launcelot's mistress. Need we say that this is a disgrace upon our family and upon the realm? And if you require proof, we are willing to furnish it."

"My lords, if this should be so, who at the court, man for man, could prove it against him? For Sir Launcelot is the greatest knight of us all."

The king had suspected for many years that his queen was unfaithful to him; but because of his love for Sir Launcelot and for her, he had never wished to prove it.

"My liege," said Sir Aggravayne, "if you will ride hunting tomorrow and send word that you will not be back overnight, Sir Modred and I will take Sir Launcelot with the queen."

"My lords, you will require many knights for your protection," said the king.

"Sire, we shall enlist the aid of twelve knights of the Round Table," said Sir Modred.

"Then try, but I warn you that Sir Launcelot is a peerless fighter."

"Sire, have no fear!" the brothers replied.

Sir Aggravayne and Sir Modred found the following knights to support them: Sir Collgrevaunce, Sir Madore de la Porte, Sir Gyngalyn, Sir Melyot de Logres, Sir Petipace of Winchelse, Sir Galleron of Galway, Sir Melyon of the Mountayne, Sir

Ascamour, Sir Gromoreson Rioure, Sir Curesalayne, Sir Florence, and Sir Lovel. These knights were their relations or sympathizers.

Sir Launcelot that night spoke with his cousin Sir Bors before obeying the queen's summons to go to her chamber.

"My lord," said Sir Bors, "do you not fear Sir Aggravayne and Sir Modred, who never cease to spy on you, and who I am sure must sooner or later contrive to betray you?"

"Good cousin, I do not fear them! And how could I refuse my queen when she has summoned me?"

"Sir Launcelot, I fear that disaster must befall you and the queen and all at this court."

"Sir Bors, have no fear; I shall not stay long!"

"Then God's speed!"

Wearing his mantle and armed only with a sword, Sir Launcelot went swiftly to the queen's chamber. Whether they made love that night or wished only to talk to each other is not known; but Sir Launcelot had not been with the queen for long when Sir Modred, Sir Aggravayne, and their supporters came crowding to the door of the chamber and, striking on it, cried out:

"Sir Launcelot, traitor! You are discovered."

"Alas," said the queen, "that this has happened!"

"My lady, have you any armor? If you have I shall soon silence them!" said Sir Launcelot.

"My lord, I have no single piece—helmet, armor, shield or spear—and I fear that our long love must come to an end. It seems that there are many knights outside, and doubtless armed, and that you can neither resist them nor escape them —if only you could! I know that you would soon come to my rescue when they dragged me out to be burnt!"

"Never in my life have I so needed my armor!" said Sir Launcelot.

"Traitor! come forth from the queen's chamber; you shall not escape us!" cried Sir Modred.

"Ah Jesu! it would be better to die," said Sir Launcelot, taking the queen into his arms and kissing her. "My beloved queen, have we not always been true lovers, from the very day that I was first knighted? Then I beseech you, if I have served you well, and constantly, and given you succor when it was within my poor power to do so, pray for my soul when I die! Then you must go to my cousin Sir Bors, who with his kin and with Sir Lavayne and Sir Urry will not fail to rescue you. They will take you to my castle and you shall rule my realm."

"My lord Sir Launcelot, it cannot be! Once you are killed I shall accept my own death meekly enough."

"Then, my queen, I shall sell my life dearly, not for my sake but for your own. And would I not barter the whole of Christendom for a suit of armor just now! I could then die honorably and men would speak of it."

"If they would take only me, and spare you!"

"For the love of Jesu, do not say so!"

Sir Aggravayne, Sir Modred and their accomplices had now found a bench and started ramming the door. Taking his sword firmly in his right hand and draping his mantle over his left arm, Sir Launcelot spoke to them:

"Hold, my lords! There is no need to batter open the door; you may come in and do what you will with me."

"Sir Launcelot, it is better so, for you have no chance against us."

Sir Launcelot unbolted the door and opened it, but only enough for one man to enter at a time. Sir Collgrevaunce strode in, and with one stroke of his sword Sir Launcelot killed him. Then, closing the door again, he swiftly stripped him of his armor and, with the aid of the queen, clad himself in it.

"Traitor! Open the door!" cried Sir Aggravayne and Sir Modred.

"My lords," Sir Launcelot replied, "enough of your noise, for you shall not take me prisoner tonight. I advise you to disperse to your chambers and in the morning lay your charge before the king. I will answer you and prove on my body that Queen Gwynevere and I are innocent of treason this night."

"You shall not do so! The king has empowered us to take you prisoner tonight, alive or dead as it pleases us."

"If nothing else pleases you, defend yourselves!" Sir Launcelot replied, and flung open the chamber door.

In the rush that followed Sir Launcelot struck down and killed every one of the thirteen knights but Sir Modred, who fled, sorely wounded. Then Sir Launcelot spoke to the queen again:

"My queen, what now? For the deaths of these knights King Arthur will become my mortal foe. Will you come with me and allow me to protect you, or will you remain here?"

"My lord, enough harm is already done. I shall remain here; but if I am charged with treason, come to my rescue."

"My lady, as you command!" Sir Launcelot replied.

Sir Bors and his kinsmen welcomed Sir Launcelot back to his quarters.

"My lord," said Sir Launcelot, "I see that you are all armed. What is the meaning of this?"

"Sir Launcelot, when you had left for the queen we all suddenly feared some treason and leaped for our arms, although some of us were already in bed and half asleep."

"My good cousin, you guessed the truth! I have never before been in such danger, and so I pray you stand by me. Soon there will be war." Sir Launcelot then related to his kinsmen all that had happened.

"Sir Launcelot," said Sir Bors, "in speaking for myself, I am sure that I speak also for my kinsmen, and I say that as we have ever loved and honored you, you can rely on us now for support. And we are knights who go in fear of none."

The assembled knights all assented, and then Sir Launcelot spoke:

"May God reward you for your love! Now, good cousin, I pray you, while it is yet night, search the castle for our friends. Otherwise we cannot know who are our friends and who our enemies."

"My lord, I shall see to it that your friends are all here by seven o'clock in the morning," Sir Bors replied.

First Sir Bors called on his kinsmen and proved friends, and they were twenty-two: Sir Lyonel, Sir Ector de Marys, Sir Blamoure, Sir Bleobris, Sir Gahalantyne, Sir Galyhoden, Sir Galyhud, Sir Menaduke, Sir Vyllyars, Sir Hebes, Sir Lavayne, Sir Urry, Sir Neroveus, Sir Plenoryus, Sir Harry, Sir Selyses, Sir Melyas, Sir Bellengerus, Sir Palomides, Sir Safere, Sir Clegis, Sir Sadoke, Sir Dynas, and Sir Clarrus of Cleremount.

Then Sir Bors discovered another hundred and twenty knights from Cornwall and West Britain, who in memory of Sir Tristram or Sir Lamerok swore allegiance to Sir Launcelot.

At dawn, when all were armed and mounted, Sir Launcelot spoke to his followers and described all that had happened in the queen's chamber that night. "My lords," he continued, "how the plot came about to implicate the queen and me I do not know; at all events I hold the queen innocent. But I fear that because I killed thirteen of his knights, King Arthur will declare himself my mortal enemy, and will not rest until they are avenged. Further, I fear that in the heat of the moment he will indict the queen for treason and sentence her to burning at the stake.

"This is what is likely to befall us, although to my knowledge I have honorably served the king and the queen since I first came to the court; howbeit my motives are now mistaken."

"My lord Sir Launcelot," said Sir Bors, "we must surely accept this change of the tide. I counsel you first to muster your forces for your rightful defense, and secondly to make it your charge to protect the queen; for with what ignominy would you not be regarded if you failed her whom you have hitherto championed, and who suffers this terrible indictment on your behalf!"

"Ah Jesu, defend me from such shame!" said Sir Launcelot. "Now, my lords, how will you be counseled?"

"As you will, Sir Launcelot!" they all shouted.

"And if the queen is to be burned at the stake tomorrow, what then?" said Sir Launcelot.

"Save her! Save her!" the whole assembly shouted.

"My lords," said Sir Launcelot, "if, as you counsel, we rescue the queen, and such seems the only honorable course, we must allow for the shedding of blood, not only of our enemies, but of those who are our friends, while yet under the king's command; and to hurt them I am loath, as I am to dishonor our name or to bring future misgivings. Also, if we win the queen, how then shall we keep her?"

"Sir Launcelot, that is the least of our cares," said Sir Bors. "We have only to recall how Sir Tristram, by your own advice, carried off Iseult the Fair and kept her at the Joyous Gard; and is not that castle yours to use when you will? Therefore, I counsel you, hold Queen Gwynevere there, and when King Arthur's anger has subsided, return her honorably, and I am sure that he will always be grateful to you."

"Sir Bors," Sir Launcelot replied, "should not we be warned by what happened to Sir Tristram when he returned to King Mark? how the king killed him treacherously with his sharp spear as he played on the harp for the queen. Even now to talk of his death fills me with grief."

"Sir Launcelot, that is what happened; but surely it is false to compare King Arthur to King Mark?"

So the discussion continued, but in the end it was agreed that they should rescue the queen if she was sentenced to burning, and Sir Launcelot accordingly disposed his followers in an ambush near to Carlisle.

When Sir Modred had escaped from the fury of Sir Launcelot, wounded as he was, he rode straight to the king, and told him all that had happened.

"Ah Jesu, Sir Launcelot is indeed a peerless knight!" said the king. "How sad it is that now he should be turned against me. And this must mean the end of the fellowship of the Round Table, for his kin are many and powerful. I suppose that to uphold my own dignity as king I must now suffer my queen to be burnt at the stake."

The queen was judged and sentence pronounced, for in those times summary trial and judgment were at the command of the king; the sentence for treason was invariably death, and for adultery, burning at the stake. However, when the trial was done, Sir Gawain spoke up:

"My liege, I pray you defer judgment on the queen. I believe that she is innocent, Sir Launcelot also. Consider: the queen probably summoned Sir Launcelot in secret only because she is aware that we have scandalmongers at this court; and her summons was probably for no other purpose than to reward Sir Launcelot for championing her cause when no other knight at this court would do so. Why not then permit Sir Launcelot to prove his innocence man for man? I am sure that he would not fail you."

"Sir Gawain, I do not doubt it! But Sir Launcelot must suffer the law as the queen must," the king replied.

"God forbid that I should witness such a thing!"

"How so? You surprise me, for has not Sir Launcelot killed your brother Sir Aggravayne and your two sons, Sir Florence and Sir Lovel, and wounded your half brother Sir Modred?"

"My lord, I repent their deaths, but I warned them not to meddle with Sir Launcelot; and I hold their calumny in abhorrence."

"Sir Gawain, I require you to make ready in your best armor to escort the queen to the pyre for burning."

"No, most noble king! I refuse. While this heart beats in my body I will not watch the queen burn, nor take any part in her death."

"Sir Gawain, you must then suffer your brothers Sir Gaheris and Sir Gareth to do so."

"My lord, they will be no less loath than myself; but they are too young to say 'nay.'"

Sir Gareth and Sir Gaheris came forward.

"Majesty, unless it is a command, in which case we would not dare to disobey, we beg to be excused; for in our hearts we hold you wrong. Whatsoever your will may be, we shall not bear arms."

"For the love of God! Sir Gaheris and Sir Gareth, I command you to escort the queen," said the king.

"Alas! that this day ever dawned!" said Sir Gawain, and weeping, made blindly for his chamber.

The queen was led from the castle of Carlisle into the field and stripped to her chemise for burning. Then she shrove to the priest, and her ladies wailed dismally. Few of the court were without tears in their eyes, and the guards, out of sympathy for her, were mostly without arms.

Meanwhile Sir Launcelot watched from his ambush, and just as they were leading the queen to the fire, shouted the word of command, charged with his followers through the spectators, and assaulted the guards.

In the tumult that followed many of the guards were killed, among them Sir Bellyas, Sir Segwarydes, Sir Grybblet, Sir Brandiles, Sir Agglovale, Sir Torre, Sir Gauter, Sir Gyllymere, Sir Raynolde, Sir Damas, Sir Pryamus, Sir Kay le Straunge, Sir Dryaunte, Sir Lambegus, Sir Hermynde, Sir Pertolope, Sir Perymones, and lastly Sir Gareth and Sir Gaheris, both of whom were unarmed, and whom Sir Launcelot killed without recognizing.

When this was done Sir Launcelot rode up to the queen, gave her a gown and girdle to put on, and then, telling her to be of good cheer, mounted her behind him and galloped away. The queen uttered a prayer of thanks to God and to Sir Launcelot.

Sir Launcelot and his comrades withdrew to the castle of the Joyous Gard, and there entertained the queen as befitted her rank. They were joined there by knights from all parts of the realm who sympathized with Sir Launcelot and the queen's cause.

2. THE VENGEANCE OF SIR GAWAIN

When King Arthur received the news of Sir Launcelot's rescue of the queen, and of the death of Sir Gaheris and Sir

Gareth and the twenty-four knights who had formed her escort, he fell faint for sorrow, and when at last he came to, spoke sadly:

"Alas! that I should have to remain your king! For now surely the fellowship of the Round Table is broken forever. In two days nearly forty knights have been killed, and the remainder are divided in their loyalty between Sir Launcelot and me.

"I charge you all: do not tell Sir Gawain of the death of his brothers, Sir Gaheris and Sir Gareth, at the hands of Sir Launcelot, for he will go out of his mind; and I myself fail to understand it, because I know that Sir Gareth especially was loved by Sir Launcelot."

"Majesty, it happened in the heat of battle, and Sir Launcelot killed them both unwittingly."

"My lords, our troubles will not end here. I know that Sir Gawain will not rest until Sir Launcelot and his kin are all destroyed, or else until we ourselves are destroyed. I regret less the loss of my queen, for of queens I had my choice, than of our fellowship, which was surely without equal in all Christendom. Alas! that Sir Aggravayne and Sir Modred, led by the evil in their hearts, should have brought us to this."

Thus the king complained to his counselors, but meanwhile one of the knights had run with the news to Sir Gawain.

"For the love of Jesu!" Sir Gawain exclaimed. "I knew that Sir Launcelot would rescue the queen; he was bound in honor to do so, and I should have done the same. But pray tell me, what of my brothers, Sir Gaheris and Sir Gareth?"

"My lord, they were both killed."

"For the love of the Holy Virgin, no! Who killed them?"

"Sir Launcelot, my lord."

"That I may not believe. Sir Gareth loved Sir Launcelot above all other knights, and I know would have taken his part against the king if Sir Launcelot had asked him to."

"My lord, Sir Gareth is dead."

"Do not say so! Now all my joy has gone!" said Sir Gawain, and fainted. When he came to he ran to the king.

"My lord, my brothers Sir Gaheris and Sir Gareth are killed," he said.

The king made no reply, but wept.

"My lord, I would see them."

"Dear nephew, you may not. I have buried them, for fear that if you should see them you would grieve too much."

"My lord, is it true that Sir Launcelot killed them and that they were not armed?"

"Sir Gawain, so I have been told."

"Majesty, as I am your subject and a knight, so I swear that I shall be revenged upon Sir Launcelot. I pray you muster your armies. In your cause and in mine we shall march against them; and even if we march through seven realms, I shall not stay until Sir Launcelot is dead, or I am."

"Sir Gawain, we have not far to march. Sir Launcelot holds the queen at the castle of the Joyous Gard, and there many knights have gathered in support of his cause."

"My lord, that I can believe."

"Very well, we shall march against him. I suppose that our armies are great enough to take the Joyous Gard."

The king let cry a call to arms, and those subjects who were loyal to him mustered beneath the royal flag. But many sympathized with Sir Launcelot and the queen, and when they met Sir Launcelot's couriers, hastened to them. Thus King Arthur's realm became once more divided.

Sir Launcelot provisioned his castle and town, and made sure that the defenses were well manned; then King Arthur arrived and with his armies laid siege to them for fifteen weeks. Apart from skirmishes both sides were reluctant to enter battle on the open field, for there was still love between them. Then, one day when Sir Launcelot had mounted the wall of his castle, a parley was held by him, King Arthur, and Sir Gawain.

"My lords," said Sir Launcelot, "why do you not abandon your siege? You must realize that if I were to lead my men out of the castle and offer battle, you would be defeated."

"Sir Launcelot, lead your men onto the field, and you will find that we are more than your match," the king replied.

"My lord, the only reason I do not do so is that I would not bear arms against my own king."

"For shame! Understand, Sir Launcelot, that I am your mortal enemy; for have you not killed many of my own loyal knights and, after consorting with the queen for many years, now abducted her by force?"

"My liege, you charge me with killing your knights, and I repent it! But I beg you to consider that I did so only in self-defense, and to save your queen. You charge me with consorting with the queen; and I answer you, has any knight, excluding yourself and Sir Gawain, come forward to prove it by force of arms? They have not, and if they did, the queen would be proved as innocent as any woman living. Finally you charge me with abducting the queen by force. Did I then steal her from you? No! I stole her from the fire to which you had consigned her.

"I beg you to recall that this is not the first time that I have saved the queen from burning, or championed her cause where no other knight at the court would do so. And yet you are surprised that she should favor me above all other knights? Surely your suspicions are misplaced, and formerly you have admitted that this was so, thanked me, and held me in high esteem.

"But I see that now you must mistake my every action, and those of the queen. Why is it? Because this time when I fight for the queen I fight for myself too, to protect my own name from calumny? Thus you reward me for my good services in the past; and yet even now, I would pray you to restore the queen to your favor, for she shall be proved both good and true."

"Recreant!" cried Sir Gawain, "the king has judged you both, and you shall live or die as he pleases."

"Sir Gawain, the queen and I are not yet won; and when I lead my knights from this castle, you may discover that we are not to be won."

"Proud words, my lord!" Sir Gawain replied. "Concerning the queen I will not quarrel; but what of my brothers, Sir Gaheris and Sir Gareth? Did you not kill them with your own hands, and when they were not armed? Could any but a murderer kill one whom he professed to love, and whom he himself had made a knight? Answer me that!"

"Sir Gawain, I swear by the love of Jesu that when I killed your brothers I knew them not! At that moment, when I fought by the fire to rescue the queen, I could as easily have killed my own cousin Sir Bors—yet God forbid!"

"Sir Launcelot, you lie! You killed them to spite me: and understand that while I live we are mortal enemies; and that soon one or the other of us must die."

"Sir Gawain, I am sorry to hear you say that. But for your chagrin the king and I might well be accorded."

"Not with one who murders innocent knights!"

"My lord, I am not guilty, as you are, of murdering innocent knights. I have ever fought only in self-defense, or in a righteous quarrel."

"Treacherous knight! You speak of Sir Lamerok? Why should I deny that I killed him?"

"Sir Gawain, you did not kill him man for man, no! He was too strong for you, so you killed him by treachery."

"Sir Launcelot, I defy you! And do not suppose that you, any more than Sir Lamerok did, will escape me."

"I understand well what mercy I should receive at your hands, now that you have the king to support you."

It is told that King Arthur would readily have received his queen again and been reconciled to Sir Launcelot, for he loved them both, but that Sir Gawain would have none of it, and incited his fellows to a state of uproarious abuse. And hearing these shouts of abuse, Sir Bors, Sir Ector, and Sir Lyonel called on their fellows, Sir Palomides, Sir Lavayne, Sir Urry, and several more, and interceded with Sir Launcelot:

"My lord, we have heard Sir Gawain's imprecations, and yet you stand meekly as though afraid! We charge you, lead us forth from this castle, and in open battle let us prove our cause. For never, while Sir Gawain lives, will you be reconciled to the king."

"Alas! you are right! And still I am reluctant to bear arms against my own liege," Sir Launcelot answered, and then, turning once more to Sir Gawain and the king:

"My lords, I am leading my men into battle; I beseech you both, avoid me on the field."

"How so?" shouted Sir Gawain. "Shall not the king fight his own quarrel, and I mine? Be sure I shall be there to avenge my brothers."

"My lords, you will repent this battle," said Sir Launcelot.

In the morning King Arthur drew up his three armies on the battlefield, and Sir Launcelot's army galloped out of the three gates of the castle, the first column led by Sir Lyonel, the center by Sir Launcelot, and the rear by Sir Bors. Sir Gawain had commanded his men to concentrate their attack on the person of Sir Launcelot, and Sir Launcelot had commanded his men to spare the persons of Sir Gawain and the king, at whatever cost.

A deadly battle ensued, with many killed on both sides, for the greatest knights in the realm were fighting each other. The first of Sir Launcelot's knights to encounter Sir Gawain was overthrown but not killed, and this was Sir Lyonel, and Sir Ector led him back to the castle.

The most formidable attack made on the king's army was led by six of Sir Launcelot's knights: Sir Bors, Sir Palomides, Sir Safere, Sir Blamoure, Sir Bleobris, and Sir Bellengerus. The king led attack after attack on Sir Launcelot himself, but Sir Launcelot did no more than rebuff him; then Sir Bors met one of the king's attacks and struck him to the ground.

"My lord," said Sir Bors to Sir Launcelot, "shall I make an end to this battle now?"

Sir Launcelot saw that he was about to behead the king.

"No," Sir Launcelot replied. "God forbid that I should watch my own liege killed!"

Thereupon Sir Launcelot dismounted and set the king on his horse again, saying as he did so:

"My liege, I pray you withdraw your armies! I fear that otherwise you will suffer an ignominious defeat. As it is, I have given the order that your own person and that of Sir Gawain are to be spared. And I would still protest that for my past services I am ill rewarded."

The king wept as he rode from the peerless Sir Launcelot, and sighed to himself: "Alas! that this war ever began!"

Both armies withdrew for the night, salved their wounded, and buried their dead. In the morning battle was joined once more, and began with a duel between Sir Gawain and Sir Bors, who was anxious to avenge his brother Sir Lyonel. They jousted, and each was deeply wounded and led from the field by his fellows.

The battle soon grew heated and many were wounded or killed on both sides; however, Sir Launcelot, after rescuing Sir Bors, fought only halfheartedly. Then Sir Lavayne and Sir Urry spoke to him:

"My lord, we see that you forbear from fighting as we do; and yet are not your followers falling thick and fast to the enemy? Surely you should go to their aid?"

"My lords, what you say is true, and yet my conscience ever forbids my fighting the king."

"My lords," said Sir Palomides who had just come up to them, "if the king himself were to capture you, you would be killed with little ado, also the queen. For while Sir Gawain lives this quarrel must proceed to the bitter end."

Thereafter Sir Launcelot renounced his scruples, and remembering that his favorite cousin, Sir Bors, lay wounded, led his men in a series of relentless attacks which by evening had all but crushed King Arthur's army. Then, for pure pity, Sir Launcelot allowed the king to withdraw.

Meanwhile news of the war between King Arthur and Sir Launcelot had spread swiftly from country to country; and when it reached Rome, the Pope, considering the virtue of King Arthur and the prowess of Sir Launcelot, issued a bull charging King Arthur, on pain of excommunication of the whole of Britain, to be reconciled to Sir Launcelot and to restore the queen without prejudice.

The bull was delivered to the king by the Bishop of Rochester. The king was completely willing to acquiesce, but Sir Gawain insisted that there could be no reconciliation with Sir Launcelot. Hence the bull was sent on to Sir Launcelot with the king's ruling that he would duly restore the queen without prejudice, but grant safe passage to Sir Launcelot only for the purpose of delivering her.

The bishop delivered the bull and the king's letters to Sir Launcelot, and explained briefly their contents.

"My lord," said Sir Launcelot, "it was ever my wish that the queen should be restored; and I shall take more pleasure in delivering her to the king than I did in abducting her. But I was obliged to do so in order to save her from burning at the stake. Provided I have safe passage and that no stigma shall attach to the queen, I will readily submit to the bull; but should the queen be in jeopardy I will not hesitate to rescue her as I did before."

"Sir Launcelot," the bishop replied, "you have here the king's undertaking that he too will be ruled by the bull. And indeed you will both do well to take heed of it, for failing that, the whole of Britain will be excommunicated."

Sir Launcelot read the bull and the king's letters.

"I see here," he said, "the king's seal and his own writing, and I have no reason to mistrust it; and certainly I do not doubt the king's promise. Therefore, I pray you, tell him that I will, given eight days' grace, restore the queen to him, as I am commanded."

The king received Sir Launcelot's undertaking and wept.

Sir Launcelot prepared to deliver the queen. When the day came they rode in magnificent array from the Joyous Gard to the castle of Carlisle. First rode a hundred knights all dressed in green velvet, with green trappings for their horses, and bearing olive branches. Then rode the queen and Sir Launcelot, accompanied by twenty-four ladies-in-waiting and twelve gentlemen-of-the-court. They were dressed in white velvet trimmed with gold cloth, as were the trappings on their horses, which were held by gold chains. The whole company was ornamented with jeweled clasps and rings—more than a thousand stones in all, sparkling in the light.

When they arrived at the castle Sir Launcelot helped the queen to dismount and led her to the king, who sat waiting with Sir Gawain and his counselors, and knelt before them. Many wept at the magnificence and humility of the supplicants. Then Sir Launcelot rose, and with great dignity addressed the king:

"Most redoubtable king, in accordance with the commands given by you and the Pope, I restore to you your queen. And if any knight present, excepting only you and Sir Gawain, will call her false, by force of arms I will prove it otherwise.

"Sire, I would now beg to remind you that on several occasions in the past when I fought for the queen or rescued her from the unjust sentence of burning, you were well pleased.

"How is it, then, that when I last came to rescue her from a sentence which was pronounced on my own behalf, you were constrained to regard me as your enemy? Is not the dissension between us the result only of the chicanery of Sir Modred and Sir Aggravayne? I put it to you that, with their twelve accomplices, it was their wish, not to vindicate your honor, but to inculpate the queen and plot the death of my person.

"And yet it can only have been by the grace of God that I, unarmed and unprepared, was given strength to endure and overthrow them all. To this day I do not know for what purpose the queen summoned me to her chamber, for I had hardly entered before Sir Aggravayne and Sir Modred began hammering on the door with cries of 'Traitor.'"

"Their cry was just!" said Sir Gawain.

"My lord, by force of arms they failed to prove their charge."

"Sir Launcelot, for what cause did you betray me?" said the king. "Have I not always in the past honored you and those of your house above all others?"

"Majesty, was not that honor our due? For have not my kinsmen and I always been to the forefront in battles, adventures, and tournaments, winning renown for your court, rescuing you or your knights from danger, giving succor when you were overwhelmed?

"For myself I would claim too that I have encountered the greatest knights of my time, such as Sir Tristram and Sir Lamerok, and that I have not failed to match them, and where I proved the stronger, was not found wanting in courtesy. Further, that I have at no time tried to rob a knight of his honor, but rather, when I saw one winning renown, have stood aside, glad to give him my praise.

"My lord, finally I beg to recall that it was I who rescued

Sir Gaheris from the formidable knight Sir Terquine, whom I killed man for man, and from whose prison I delivered some threescore of your knights. And that it was I who rescued Sir Gawain, who looked less proud when he was wounded and lashed beneath his horse's belly than he does now sitting above me as judge, and for him I fought and killed King Carados of the Dolorous Tower, a powerful knight if ever there was one.

"For all these things I beg to be remembered, because you who judge me have in the past been beholden to me for your honor and your lives."

"Sir Launcelot," Sir Gawain replied, "I do not speak for the king, but for myself. While you live and I live you cannot be forgiven for killing my two brothers when they were unarmed."

"So hear me God! I wish that Sir Gaheris and Sir Gareth had both been armed! While I live I shall repent their deaths, for did I not love them better almost than my own kin? Especially Sir Gareth, who was gentle and true, a noble knight, and one I made with my own hands. Also he was fearless— how could I not repent his death? both for himself, and for its consequence in turning Sir Gawain against me.

"My lords, hear me all! I offer to make a pilgrimage, on foot and wearing only my shirt, from Sandwich to Carlisle, and every ten miles to found a hermitage, complete with holy offices and appurtenances which I shall provide from my own estates, and in every one of those hermitages candles will be burned and prayers offered for Sir Gaheris and Sir Gareth.

"Surely this is more worthy of them than the persistence of a deadly war with King Arthur and Sir Gawain against me and my kinsmen?"

King Arthur, his counselors, and the ladies at the court were all deeply moved by Sir Launcelot's offer.

"Sir Launcelot," said Sir Gawain, "I have heard your large offer, and yet it does not remedy the charges against you; for you have been false to the king and to me. If the king accepts you, he must lose my service and that of my house."

"Sir Gawain, there is no man living but can remedy his life, and for your proud charges you must ask pardon. Otherwise, by the grace of God, with might of arms I shall answer you."

"Not so!" said Sir Gawain, "the time for dueling is not now. We are required by the Pope to grant you safe conduct, and you are required to restore the queen to the king. That is all.

"But when you have left this court you are banished, and

I give you fifteen days to leave the realm. Then I shall search you out, and the time will come for us to prove the quarrel between us body for body."

"Alas!" said Sir Launcelot, with tears in his eyes, "I am banished, without cause and without redress, from this realm where I have won my renown, and which I love above all others. Yet such, I know, have been the misfortunes of kings and conquerors—of the noble Hector of Troy, King Alexander of Greece, those in whom sovereignty was the most deeply rooted—and have I not myself added my sum of honor to this court?

"Hear me, Sir Gawain: I am a lord of my lands as much as any knight here, and if his majesty and you make war I shall defend my own realm as well I may. But I warn you, Sir Gawain, that you will have to answer the charges you make."

"Sir Launcelot, say what you will! You can be sure that we shall storm our way into the strongest castle in your possession."

"Sir Gawain, were I as vain as you I should offer battle on the open field."

"Enough! Sir Launcelot, deliver the queen and go hence."

"Sir Gawain, I repent that I honored the king's command in restoring the queen to this court. I have already proved with my armies that I have force enough to hold her for as long as I please; and if your charges had been true, that is what I should have done."

Then Sir Launcelot spoke openly to the queen:

"Madam, I must now depart from you and from this noble fellowship forever. And since this is so, I beseech you pray for me, and I will pray for you. If any knight at this court dares offer you the slightest affront, call on me and you shall be avenged.

"My lords all! If there is any one amongst you who dares to charge the queen with treason, speak now, and man for man I will prove her innocent."

Therewith Sir Launcelot led the queen to the king, and departed. Everyone at the court, with the exception of Sir Gawain, wept.

When he arrived at the Joyous Gard, which henceforth was to be renamed the Dolorous Gard, Sir Launcelot spoke to his kinsmen:

"My lords, I am banished from the realm. My honor and my renown are lost. I am shamed, and that is what I have feared more than anything else, otherwise I should never have parted from the queen."

"Sir Launcelot, why not remain? We of your blood will support you; and we have proved already that we are more than a match for the king."

"My lords, I thank you, but it cannot be. Instead I shall divide my lands equally among you, for what need have I of lands, beyond a bare livelihood, now that honor and fame are lost?"

"My lord Sir Launcelot, do not speak so! Surely you, more than any knight living, have brought honor to King Arthur's court, and with your departure the noble fellowship of the Round Table will come to an end. In the court there will be nothing but jealousy and strife. And now, do not suppose that we of your blood are going to desert you. No! rather will we go to the ends of the earth to be by you."

"My good brothers, I thank you from my heart! It is true that in the past, perhaps, I have helped to preserve the equanimity of the court, and that now, with the dealings of Sir Modred, they are faced with dissension."

A hundred of Sir Launcelot's kinsmen and knights pledged themselves to his following, and together, when all was prepared, they sailed from Cardiff to Benwick in France, where Sir Launcelot and his kin had long been rulers.

When they arrived people of all estates flocked to Sir Launcelot to pay him homage, and before long he called a parliament and conferred upon Sir Lyonel the title of King and Overlord of France. Sir Bors he made king of the realms which had been ruled by King Claudas; and Sir Ector, King of Benwick and Gyan. He then advanced his knights to earldoms and dukedoms:

Sir Blamoure	Duke of Lymosyn in Gyan
Sir Bleobris	Duke of Payters
Sir Gahalantyne	Duke of Overn
Sir Galyhoden	Duke of Sentong
Sir Galyhud	Earl of Perygot
Sir Menaduke	Earl of Roerge
Sir Vyllyars	Earl of Bearne
Sir Hebes	Earl of Comange
Sir Lavayne	Earl of Armynake
Sir Urry	Earl of Estrake
Sir Neroveus	Earl of Paryake
Sir Plenoryus	Earl of Foyse

Sir Selyses	Earl of Marsank
Sir Melyas	Earl of Tursank
Sir Bellengerus	Earl of Lawundis
Sir Palomides	Duke of Provynce
Sir Safere	Duke of Landok
Sir Clegis	Earl of Agente
Sir Sadoke	Earl of Sarlat
Sir Dynas	Duke of Angeoy
Sir Clarrus	Duke of Normandy

Besides these, Sir Launcelot made many other appointments which would take too long to tell.

3. THE SIEGE OF BENWICK

When Sir Launcelot had established dominion over France, he garrisoned the towns and settled with his army in the fortified city of Benwick, where his father King Ban had held court.

King Arthur, after appointing Sir Modred ruler in his absence, and instructing Queen Gwynevere to obey him, sailed to France with an army of sixty thousand men, and, on the advice of Sir Gawain, started laying waste all before him.

News of the invasion reached Sir Launcelot, and his counselors advised him. Sir Bors spoke first:

"My lord Sir Launcelot, is it wise to allow King Arthur to lay your lands waste when sooner or later he will oblige you to offer him battle?"

Sir Lyonel spoke next: "My lord, I would recommend that we remain within the walls of our city until the invaders are weakened by cold and hunger, and then let us sally forth and destroy them."

Next, King Bagdemagus: "Sir Launcelot, I understand that it is out of courtesy that you permit the king to ravage your lands, but where will this courtesy end? If you remain within the city, soon everything will be destroyed."

Then Sir Galyhud: "Sir, you command knights of royal blood; you cannot expect them to remain meekly within the city walls. I pray you, let us encounter the enemy on the open field, and they will soon repent of their expedition."

And to this the seven knights of West Britain all muttered their assent. Then Sir Launcelot spoke:

"My lords, I am reluctant to shed Christian blood in a war against my own liege; and yet I do know that these lands have already suffered depredation in the wars between King Claudas and my father and uncle, King Ban and King Bors. Therefore I will next send a messenger to King Arthur and sue for peace, for peace is always preferable to war."

Accordingly a young noblewoman accompanied by a dwarf was sent to King Arthur. They were received by the gentle knight Sir Lucas the Butler.

"My lady, you bring a message from Sir Launcelot?" he asked.

"My lord, I do. It is for the king."

"Alas! King Arthur would readily be reconciled to Sir Launcelot, but Sir Gawain forbids it; and it is a shame, because Sir Launcelot is certainly the greatest knight living."

The young noblewoman was brought before the king, and when he had heard Sir Launcelot's entreaties for peace he wept, and would readily have accepted them had not Sir Gawain spoken up:

"My liege, if we retreat now we will become a laughing-stock, in this land and in our own. Surely our honor demands that we pursue this war to its proper conclusion."

"Sir Gawain, I will do as you advise, although reluctantly, for Sir Launcelot's terms are generous and he is still dear to me. I beg you make a reply to him on my behalf."

Sir Gawain addressed the young noblewoman:

"Tell Sir Launcelot that we will not bandy words with him, and it is too late now to sue for peace. Further that I, Sir Gawain, shall not cease to strive against him until one of us is killed."

The young noblewoman was escorted back to Sir Launcelot, and when she had delivered Sir Gawain's message they both wept. Then Sir Bors spoke:

"My lord, we beseech you, do not look so dismayed! You have many trustworthy knights behind you; lead us onto the field and we will put an end to this quarrel."

"My lords, I do not doubt you, but I pray you, be ruled by me: I will not lead you against our liege until we ourselves are endangered; only then can we honorably sally forth and defeat him."

Sir Launcelot's nobles submitted; but the next day it was seen that King Arthur had laid siege to the city of Benwick. Then Sir Gawain rode before the city walls and shouted a challenge:

"My lord Sir Launcelot: have you no knight who will dare to ride forth and break spears with me? It is I, Sir Gawain."

Sir Bors accepted the challenge. He rode out of the castle gate, they encountered, and he was wounded and flung from his horse. His comrades helped him back to the castle, and then Sir Lyonel offered to joust. He too was overthrown and helped back to the castle.

Thereafter, every day for six months Sir Gawain rode before the city and overthrew whoever accepted his challenge. Meanwhile, as a result of skirmishes, numbers on both sides were beginning to dwindle. Then one day Sir Gawain challenged Sir Launcelot:

"My lord Sir Launcelot: traitor to the king and to me, come forth if you dare and meet your mortal foe, instead of lurking like a coward in your castle!"

Sir Launcelot heard the challenge, and one of his kinsmen spoke to him:

"My lord, you must accept the challenge, or be shamed forever."

"Alas, that I should have to fight Sir Gawain!" said Sir Launcelot. "But now I am obliged to."

Sir Launcelot gave orders for his most powerful courser to be harnessed, and when he had armed, rode to the tower and addressed King Arthur:

"My lord King Arthur, it is with a heavy heart that I set forth to do battle with one of your own blood; but now it is incumbent upon my honor to do so. For six months I have suffered your majesty to lay my lands waste and to besiege me in my own city. My courtesy is repaid with insults, so deadly and shameful that now I must by force of arms seek redress."

"Have done, Sir Launcelot, and let us to battle!" shouted Sir Gawain.

Sir Launcelot rode from the city at the head of his entire army. King Arthur was astonished at his strength and realized that Sir Launcelot had not been boasting when he claimed to have acted with forbearance. "Alas, that I should ever have come to war with him!" he said to himself.

It was agreed that the two combatants should fight to the death, with interference from none. Sir Launcelot and Sir Gawain then drew apart and galloped furiously together, and so great was their strength that their horses crashed to the ground and both riders were overthrown.

A terrible sword fight commenced, and each felt the might of the other as fresh wounds were inflicted with every blow. For three hours they fought with scarcely a pause, and the blood seeped out from their armor and trickled to the ground. Sir Launcelot found to his dismay that Sir Gawain, instead of weakening, seemed to increase in strength as they proceeded, and he began to fear that he was battling not with a knight but with a fiend incarnate. He decided to fight defensively and to conserve his strength.

It was a secret known only to King Arthur and to Sir Gawain himself that his strength increased for three hours in the morning, reaching its zenith at noon, and waning again. This was due to an enchantment that had been cast over him by a hermit when he was still a youth. Often in the past, as now, he had taken advantage of this.

Thus when the hour of noon had passed, Sir Launcelot felt Sir Gawain's strength return to normal, and knew that he could defeat him.

"Sir Gawain, I have endured many hard blows from you these last three hours, but now beware, for I see that you have weakened, and it is I who am the stronger."

Thereupon Sir Launcelot redoubled his blows, and with one, catching Sir Gawain sidelong on the helmet, sent him reeling to the ground. Then he courteously stood back.

"Sir Launcelot, I still defy you!" said Sir Gawain from the ground. "Why do you not kill me now? for I warn you that if ever I recover I shall challenge you again."

"Sir Gawain, by the grace of God I shall endure you again," Sir Launcelot replied, and then turned to the king:

"My liege, your expedition can find no honorable conclusion at these walls, so I pray you withdraw and spare your noble knights. Remember me with kindness and be guided, as ever, by the love of God."

"Alas!" said the king, "Sir Launcelot scruples to fight against me or those of my blood, and once more I am beholden to him."

Sir Launcelot withdrew to the city and Sir Gawain was taken to his pavilion, where his wounds were dressed. King Arthur was doubly grieved, by his quarrel with Sir Launcelot and by the seriousness of Sir Gawain's wounds.

For three weeks, while Sir Gawain was recovering, the siege was relaxed and both sides skirmished only halfheartedly. But once recovered, Sir Gawain rode up to the castle walls and challenged Sir Launcelot again:

"Sir Launcelot, traitor! Come forth, it is Sir Gawain who challenges you."

"Sir Gawain, why these insults? I have the measure of your strength and you can do me but little harm."

"Come forth, traitor, and this time I shall make good my revenge!" Sir Gawain shouted.

"Sir Gawain, I have once spared your life; should you not beware of meddling with me again?"

Sir Launcelot armed and rode out to meet him. They jousted and Sir Gawain broke his spear and was flung from his horse. He leaped up immediately, and putting his shield before him, called on Sir Launcelot to fight on foot.

"The issue of a mare has failed me; but I am the issue of a king and a queen and I shall not fail!" he exclaimed.

As before, Sir Launcelot felt Sir Gawain's strength increase until noon, during which period he defended himself, and then weaken again.

"Sir Gawain, you are a proved knight, and with the increase of your strength until noon you must have overcome many of your opponents, but now your strength has gone, and once more you are at my mercy."

Sir Launcelot struck out lustily and by chance reopened the wound he had made before. Sir Gawain fell to the ground in a faint, but when he came to he said weakly:

"Sir Launcelot, I still defy you. Make an end of me, or I shall fight you again!"

"Sir Gawain, while you stand on your two feet I will not gainsay you; but I will never strike a knight who has fallen. God defend me from such dishonor!"

Sir Launcelot walked away and Sir Gawain continued to call after him: "Traitor! Until one of us is dead I shall never give in!"

For a month Sir Gawain lay recovering from his wounds, and the siege remained; but then, as Sir Gawain was preparing to fight Sir Launcelot once more, King Arthur received news which caused him to strike camp and lead his army on a forced march to the coast, and thence to embark for Britain.

4. *THE DAY OF DESTINY*

During the absence of King Arthur from Britain, Sir Modred, already vested with sovereign powers, had decided to usurp the throne. Accordingly, he had false letters written—announcing the death of King Arthur in battle—and delivered to himself. Then, calling a parliament, he ordered the letters to be read and persuaded the nobility to elect him king. The coronation took place at Canterbury and was celebrated with a fifteen-day feast.

Sir Modred then settled in Camelot and made overtures to Queen Gwynevere to marry him. The queen seemingly acquiesced, but as soon as she had won his confidence, begged leave to make a journey to London in order to prepare her trousseau. Sir Modred consented, and the queen rode straight to the Tower which, with the aid of her loyal nobles, she manned and provisioned for her defense.

Sir Modred, outraged, at once marched against her, and laid siege to the Tower, but despite his large army, siege engines, and guns, was unable to effect a breach. He then tried to entice the queen from the Tower, first by guile and then by threats, but she would listen to neither. Finally the Archbishop of Canterbury came forward to protest:

"Sir Modred, do you not fear God's displeasure? First you have falsely made yourself king; now you, who were begotten by King Arthur on his aunt, try to marry your father's wife! If you do not revoke your evil deeds I shall curse you with bell, book, and candle."

"Fie on you! Do your worst!" Sir Modred replied.

"Sir Modred, I warn you take heed! or the wrath of the Lord will descend upon you."

"Away, false priest, or I shall behead you!"

The Archbishop withdrew, and after excommunicating Sir Modred, abandoned his office and fled to Glastonbury. There he took up his abode as a simple hermit, and by fasting and prayer sought divine intercession in the troubled affairs of his country.

Sir Modred tried to assassinate the Archbishop, but was too late. He continued to assail the queen with entreaties and threats, both of which failed, and then the news reached him that King Arthur was returning with his army from France in order to seek revenge.

Sir Modred now appealed to the barony to support him, and it has to be told that they came forward in large numbers to do so. Why? it will be asked. Was not King Arthur, the noblest sovereign Christendom had seen, now leading his armies in a righteous cause? The answer lies in the people of Britain, who, then as now, were fickle. Those who so readily transferred their allegiance to Sir Modred did so with the excuse that whereas King Arthur's reign had led them into war and strife, Sir Modred promised them peace and festivity.

Hence it was with an army of a hundred thousand that Sir Modred marched to Dover to battle against his own father, and to withhold from him his rightful crown.

As King Arthur with his fleet drew into the harbor, Sir Modred and his army launched forth in every available craft, and a bloody battle ensued in the ships and on the beach. If King Arthur's army were the smaller, their courage was the higher, confident as they were of the righteousness of their cause. Without stint they battled through the burning ships, the screaming wounded, and the corpses floating on the blood-stained waters. Once ashore they put Sir Modred's entire army to flight.

The battle over, King Arthur began a search for his casualties, and on peering into one of the ships found Sir Gawain, mortally wounded. Sir Gawain fainted when King Arthur lifted him in his arms; and when he came to, the king spoke:

"Alas! dear nephew, that you lie here thus, mortally wounded! What joy is now left to me on this earth? You must know it was you and Sir Launcelot I loved above all others, and it seems that I have lost you both."

"My good uncle, it was my pride and my stubbornness that brought all this about, for had I not urged you to war with Sir Launcelot your subjects would not now be in revolt. Alas, that Sir Launcelot is not here, for he would soon drive them out! And it is at Sir Launcelot's hands that I suffer my own death: the wound which he dealt me has reopened. I would not wish it otherwise, because is he not the greatest and gentlest of knights?

"I know that by noon I shall be dead, and I repent bitterly that I may not be reconciled to Sir Launcelot; therefore I pray you, good uncle, give me pen, paper, and ink so that I may write to him."

A priest was summoned and Sir Gawain confessed; then a clerk brought ink, pen, and paper, and Sir Gawain wrote to Sir Launcelot as follows:

"Sir Launcelot, flower of the knighthood: I, Sir Gawain, son of King Lot of Orkney and of King Arthur's sister, send you my greetings!

"I am about to die; the cause of my death is the wound I received from you outside the city of Benwick; and I would make it known that my death was of my own seeking, that I was moved by the spirit of revenge and spite to provoke you to battle.

"Therefore, Sir Launcelot, I beseech you to visit my tomb and offer what prayers you will on my behalf; and for myself, I am content to die at the hands of the noblest knight living.

"One more request: that you hasten with your armies across the sea and give succor to our noble king. Sir Modred, his bastard son, has usurped the throne and now holds against him with an army of a hundred thousand. He would have won the queen, too, but she fled to the Tower of London and there charged her loyal supporters with her defense.

"Today is the tenth of May, and at noon I shall give up the ghost; this letter is written partly with my blood. This morning we fought our way ashore, against the armies of Sir Modred, and that is how my wound came to be reopened. We won the day, but my lord King Arthur needs you, and I too, that on my tomb you may bestow your blessing."

Sir Gawain fainted when he had finished, and the king wept. When he came to he was given extreme unction, and died, as he had anticipated, at the hour of noon. The king buried him in the chapel at Dover Castle, and there many came to see him, and all noticed the wound on his head which he had received from Sir Launcelot.

Then the news reached Arthur that Sir Modred offered him battle on the field at Baron Down. Arthur hastened there with his army, they fought, and Sir Modred fled once more, this time to Canterbury.

When King Arthur had begun the search for his wounded and dead, many volunteers from all parts of the country came to fight under his flag, convinced now of the rightness of his cause. Arthur marched westward, and Sir Modred once more offered him battle. It was assigned for the Monday following Trinity Sunday, on Salisbury Down.

Sir Modred levied fresh troops from East Anglia and the places about London, and fresh volunteers came forward to help Arthur. Then, on the night of Trinity Sunday, Arthur was vouchsafed a strange dream:

He was appareled in gold cloth and seated in a chair which stood on a pivoted scaffold. Below him, many fathoms deep, was a dark well, and in the water swam serpents, dragons, and wild beasts. Suddenly the scaffold tilted and Arthur was flung into the water, where all the creatures struggled toward him and began tearing him limb from limb.

Arthur cried out in his sleep and his squires hastened to waken him. Later, as he lay between waking and sleeping, he thought he saw Sir Gawain, and with him a host of beautiful noblewomen. Arthur spoke:

"My sister's son! I thought you had died; but now I see you live, and I thank the lord Jesu! I pray you, tell me, who are these ladies?"

"My lord, these are the ladies I championed in righteous quarrels when I was on earth. Our lord God has vouchsafed that we visit you and plead with you not to give battle to Sir Modred tomorrow, for if you do, not only will you yourself be killed, but all your noble followers too. We beg you to be warned, and to make a treaty with Sir Modred, calling a truce for a month, and granting him whatever terms he may demand. In a month Sir Launcelot will be here, and he will defeat Sir Modred."

Thereupon Sir Gawain and the ladies vanished, and King Arthur once more summoned his squires and his counselors and told them his vision. Sir Lucas and Sir Bedivere were commissioned to make a treaty with Sir Modred. They were to be accompanied by two bishops and to grant, within reason, whatever terms he demanded.

The ambassadors found Sir Modred in command of an army of a hundred thousand and unwilling to listen to overtures of peace. However, the ambassadors eventually prevailed on him, and in return for the truce granted him suzerainty of Cornwall and Kent, and succession to the British throne when King Arthur died. The treaty was to be signed by King Arthur and Sir Modred the next day. They were to meet between the two armies, and each was to be accompanied by no more than fourteen knights.

Both King Arthur and Sir Modred suspected the other of treachery, and gave orders for their armies to attack at the sight of a naked sword. When they met at the appointed place the treaty was signed and both drank a glass of wine.

Then, by chance, one of the soldiers was bitten in the foot by an adder which had lain concealed in the brush. The soldier unthinkingly drew his sword to kill it, and at once, as the sword flashed in the light, the alarums were given, trumpets sounded, and both armies galloped into the attack.

"Alas for this fateful day!" exclaimed King Arthur, as both he and Sir Modred hastily mounted and galloped back to their armies. There followed one of those rare and heartless battles in which both armies fought until they were destroyed. King Arthur, with his customary valor, led squadron after squadron of cavalry into the attack, and Sir Modred encountered him unflinchingly. As the number of dead and wounded mounted on both sides, the active combatants continued dauntless until nightfall, when four men alone survived.

King Arthur wept with dismay to see his beloved followers fallen; then, struggling toward him, unhorsed and badly wounded, he saw Sir Lucas the Butler and his brother, Sir Bedivere.

"Alas!" said the king, "that the day should come when I see all my noble knights destroyed! I would prefer that I myself had fallen. But what has become of the traitor Sir Modred, whose evil ambition was responsible for this carnage?"

Looking about him King Arthur then noticed Sir Modred leaning with his sword on a heap of the dead.

"Sir Lucas, I pray you give me my spear, for I have seen Sir Modred."

"Sire, I entreat you, remember your vision—how Sir Gawain appeared with a heaven-sent message to dissuade you from fighting Sir Modred. Allow this fateful day to pass; it is ours, for we three hold the field, while the enemy is broken."

"My lords, I care nothing for my life now! And while Sir Modred is at large I must kill him: there may not be another chance."

"God speed you, then!" said Sir Bedivere.

When Sir Modred saw King Arthur advance with his spear, he rushed to meet him with drawn sword. Arthur caught Sir Modred below the shield and drove his spear through his body; Sir Modred, knowing that the wound was mortal, thrust himself up to the handle of the spear, and then, brandishing his sword in both hands, struck Arthur on the side of the helmet, cutting through it and into the skull beneath; then he crashed to the ground, gruesome and dead.

King Arthur fainted many times as Sir Lucas and Sir Bedivere struggled with him to a small chapel nearby, where they managed to ease his wounds a little. When Arthur came to, he thought he heard cries coming from the battlefield.

"Sir Lucas, I pray you, find out who cries on the battlefield," he said.

Wounded as he was, Sir Lucas hobbled painfully to the field, and there in the moonlight saw the camp followers stealing gold and jewels from the dead, and murdering the wounded. He returned to the king and reported to him what he had seen, and then added:

"My lord, it surely would be better to move you to the nearest town?"

"My wounds forbid it. But alas for the good Sir Launcelot! How sadly I have missed him today! And now I must die—as Sir Gawain warned me I would—repenting our quarrel with my last breath."

Sir Lucas and Sir Bedivere made one further attempt to lift the king. He fainted as they did so. Then Sir Lucas fainted as part of his intestines broke through a wound in the stomach. When the king came to, he saw Sir Lucas lying dead with foam at his mouth.

"Sweet Jesu, give him succor!" he said. "This noble knight has died trying to save my life—alas that this was so!"

Sir Bedivere wept for his brother.

"Sir Bedivere, weep no more," said King Arthur, "for you can save neither your brother nor me; and I would ask you to take my sword Excalibur to the shore of the lake and throw it in the water. Then return to me and tell me what you have seen."

"My lord, as you command, it shall be done."

Sir Bedivere took the sword, but when he came to the water's edge, it appeared so beautiful that he could not bring himself to throw it in, so instead he hid it by a tree, and then returned to the king.

"Sir Bedivere, what did you see?"

"My lord, I saw nothing but the wind upon the waves."

"Then you did not obey me; I pray you, go swiftly again, and this time fulfill my command."

Sir Bedivere went and returned again, but this time too he had failed to fulfil the king's command.

"Sir Bedivere, what did you see?"

"My lord, nothing but the lapping of the waves."

"Sir Bedivere, twice you have betrayed me! And for the sake only of my sword: it is unworthy of you! Now I pray you, do as I command, for I have not long to live."

This time Sir Bedivere wrapped the girdle around the sheath and hurled it as far as he could into the water. A hand appeared from below the surface, took the sword, waved it thrice, and disappeared again. Sir Bedivere returned to the king and told him what he had seen.

"Sir Bedivere, I pray you now help me hence, or I fear it will be too late."

Sir Bedivere carried the king to the water's edge, and there found a barge in which sat many beautiful ladies with their queen. All were wearing black hoods, and when they saw the king, they raised their voices in a piteous lament.

"I pray you, set me in the barge," said the king.

Sir Bedivere did so, and one of the ladies laid the king's head in her lap; then the queen spoke to him:

"My dear brother, you have stayed too long: I fear that the wound on your head is already cold."

Thereupon they rowed away from the land and Sir Bedivere wept to see them go.

"My lord King Arthur, you have deserted me! I am alone now, and among enemies."

"Sir Bedivere, take what comfort you may, for my time is passed, and now I must be taken to Avalon for my wound to be healed. If you hear of me no more, I beg you pray for my soul."

The barge slowly crossed the water and out of sight while the ladies wept. Sir Bedivere walked alone into the forest and there remained for the night.

In the morning he saw beyond the trees of a copse a small hermitage. He entered and found a hermit kneeling down by a fresh tomb. The hermit was weeping as he prayed, and then Sir Bedivere recognized him as the Archbishop of Canterbury, who had been banished by Sir Modred.

"Father, I pray you, tell me, whose tomb is this?"

"My son, I do not know. At midnight the body was brought here by a company of ladies. We buried it, they lit a hundred candles for the service, and rewarded me with a thousand bezants."

"Father, King Arthur lies buried in this tomb."

Sir Bedivere fainted when he had spoken, and when he came to he begged the Archbishop to allow him to remain at the hermitage and end his days in fasting and prayer.

"Father, I wish only to be near to my true liege."

"My son, you are welcome; and do I not recognize you as Sir Bedivere the Bold, brother to Sir Lucas the Butler?"

Thus the Archbishop and Sir Bedivere remained at the hermitage, wearing the habits of hermits and devoting themselves to the tomb with fasting and prayers of contrition.

Such was the death of King Arthur as written down by Sir Bedivere. By some it is told that there were three queens on the barge: Queen Morgan le Fay, the Queen of North Galys, and the Queen of the Waste Lands; and others include the name of Nyneve, the Lady of the Lake who had served King Arthur well in the past, and had married the good knight Sir Pelleas.

In many parts of Britain it is believed that King Arthur did not die and that he will return to us and win fresh glory and the Holy Cross of our Lord Jesu Christ; but for myself I do not believe this, and would leave him buried peacefully in his tomb at Glastonbury, where the Archbishop of Canterbury and Sir Bedivere humbled themselves, and with prayers and fasting honored his memory. And inscribed on his tomb, men say, is this legend:

HIC IACET ARTHURUS, REX QUONDAM REXQUE FUTURUS.

5. THE DOLOROUS DEATHS AND DEPARTING OUT OF THIS WORLD OF SIR LAUNCELOT AND QUEEN GWYNEVERE

When the news of King Arthur's death reached Queen Gwynevere in the Tower of London, she renounced all her worldly estates, and with five of her ladies entered the abbey at Amesbury. There she became abbess, and adopting the white-and-black cloth of the order, with fasting and prayer sought atonement for her long years of vain and carnal sin. And so great was the change wrought in her person by her repentance that all who witnessed it marveled.

Meanwhile Sir Launcelot at the City of Benwick had received Sir Gawain's letter with its piteous appeal to give aid to King Arthur and to offer a prayer on his own tomb. Sir Launcelot said to Sir Bors:

"Alas, good cousin, that I should have caused the deaths of Sir Gawain, Sir Gaheris, and Sir Gareth, three noble knights! And how it touches me that Sir Gawain should beg me to pray on his tomb! Certainly I shall. But this is not all. King Arthur's bastard son, Sir Modred, now leads a revolt against him with an army of a hundred thousand, and has even attempted to make the queen his own. Why could I not have killed the traitor Sir Modred instead of his gallant brothers?"

"My lord, enough of complaints! We will hasten to Britain

and there you shall offer your prayers on Sir Gawain's tomb, and then march against Sir Modred and avenge King Arthur."

"Good cousin, you are right; and I thank you."

In all haste Sir Launcelot led his huge army, and the seven kings who were his allies, to Britain. When they arrived at Dover Sir Launcelot learned that he was too late. He was told of the three battles between King Arthur and Sir Modred, of their deaths, and of Queen Gwynevere's retreat to the abbey at Amesbury.

"I pray you, lead me to Sir Gawain's tomb," said Sir Launcelot.

All day and all night Sir Launcelot knelt by the tomb and wept and prayed. In the morning he ordered a requiem to be sung, and offered fish, flesh, wine, and ale for all the town and country folk who would come to offer their prayers at the tomb; and to each he gave a shilling. When the requiem was over he offered a hundred pounds from his private purse for masses to be sung; the seven kings each offered forty pounds, and a thousand of the knights each one pound.

Sir Launcelot remained for another two days and nights by the tomb, and on the third day summoned his followers:

"My lords, I thank you all for accompanying me here. As you know, we have come too late: the king is dead, and against death none can rebel. I shall now seek Queen Gwynevere, who has suffered greatly. I pray you, remain here for fifteen days, and then, if I have not returned, take to your ships and sail for your own countries, for my journey will have reached its end."

"My lord," said Sir Bors, "you are beset by enemies in this realm. Will you not allow some of us to accompany you?"

"Sir Bors, I thank you, but I must now travel alone."

Sir Launcelot rode west for eight days, and then came to the abbey at Amesbury. Queen Gwynevere was walking in a cloister when she saw him. Three times she fainted, and three times her ladies lifted her up again.

"My ladies, you wonder why I fainted: it is because of yonder knight. I pray you summon him to our presence."

When Sir Launcelot was before the queen she spoke again:

"Because of the love that was between this man and me, my lord King Arthur and his noble knights now lie dead. Therefore, Sir Launcelot, I repent; and I would enter the kingdom of heaven, through the grace of the Passion of our Lord Jesu, and sit on His right side: for many who are now in heaven were on earth as sinful as we.

"And I charge you, for the love of Jesu, never to see me again, but to return with your doughty lords to your own realm, there to rule wisely and preserve the peace; lastly to take unto yourself a wife, to cherish her, and in your prayers to beseech pardon for my own misdeeds."

"Sweet lady, you would not have me marry; my vows to you are not to be broken! But as you do I shall do, and so I shall retreat to a monastery, and there with my poor prayers try to intercede for you with our Lord Jesu."

"My lord, hold to your promise if you will; but can I believe that you will not turn to the world again?"

"My lady, I have yet to make a false promise, and God forbid that I should fail to forsake the world when you have already done so. And was not my earthly pleasure all vested in you? and was I not castigated for loving you when I sought the Holy Grail? Otherwise I should have surpassed my fellows, all but my son Sir Galahad, in the quest.

"Surely now I may turn once again to holy things, for such would have been my ambition but for the blossom of our earthly love. So I pray you, good queen, let us kiss, and then, putting such love aside, we will part."

"My lord, we shall not kiss now, or ever; and I pray you depart," the queen replied.

Sir Launcelot took his leave of the queen. His heart was stung by her words, and when the nuns had led him to his chamber he fainted for pure sorrow. All the next day and the next night he rode through the forest, careless of direction, and the following morning came to a hermitage which had been built between two rocks.

He entered the chapel and there saw the tomb of King Arthur, where the Archbishop of Canterbury was saying mass. Both he and Sir Bedivere recognized Sir Launcelot, and when the service was over Sir Bedivere described to him the last battle and the death of the king. Sir Launcelot wept.

"Alas! who can trust this world?" he exclaimed.

Then he shrove to the Archbishop and begged to be admitted into the order of the house, and to spend the remainder of his days in repentance, fasting, and prayer. The Archbishop granted him his wish.

Meanwhile Sir Launcelot's cousin, Sir Lyonel, had ridden in search of him to London with six of his companions, and all had been killed. Sir Bors had then dismissed the army, and with Sir Ector, Sir Blamoure and Sir Bleobris, pledged himself to search for him throughout Britain.

Within six months not only Sir Bors, but also Sir Galyhud, Sir Blamoure, Sir Bleobris, Sir Vyllyars, Sir Clarrus, and Sir Gahalantyne had all found Sir Launcelot at the hermitage, and likewise become hermits.

For six years they lived thus, humbly assisting the Archbishop in his holy offices, ringing bells and singing the mass. From utter neglect their horses wandered away into the forest, for these seven hermits had renounced their earthly possessions. They grew lean and pale, and few would have recognized them for the lusty knights who had won fame for their feats at arms.

Then one night Sir Launcelot was vouchsafed a vision in which he was instructed to go with his six companions to Amesbury, where they would find the queen already dead, and to return with her for burial next to King Arthur. The same vision came to Sir Launcelot three times that night, and in the morning he consulted the Archbishop.

"My son, you must obey the vision," he was told.

Sir Launcelot and his companions set forth on foot from the hermitage, and in two days covered the thirty miles which lay between Glastonbury and the abbey at Amesbury. They were greeted by the nuns who told them that the queen had died half an hour before their arrival. Apparently she had known that Sir Launcelot would come to take her for burial next to the king, and her last words had been a prayer that she might never again see Sir Launcelot "with earthly eyes."

Sir Launcelot looked into the face of the queen and wept a little and then sighed. That night he read the service himself, and in the morning sang mass. With due ceremony he and his companions conveyed the body of the queen to Glastonbury. The body was laid on a horse bier, a hundred torches were lit, and frankincense burned while the knights sang or read the orisons.

At Glastonbury the body was wrapped in thirty folds of waxed cloth from Raynes, then in a sheet of lead, put into a marble coffin, and lowered into the tomb of King Arthur. Dirges were sung, the requiem conducted by the Archbishop, and then each of the knights, starting with Sir Launcelot, offered his prayers at the tomb. Once the ceremony was over, Sir Launcelot fell into a deathly faint. When he came to, the Archbishop spoke to him:

"My son, God forbids such sorrow over the death of the body."

"Father, I pray that my sorrow is not displeasing to God.

But when I recalled the peerless grace and beauty of the queen, and the great joy with which we all beheld her and the king at their court, my heart began to fail me. Then, seeing them together in the tomb, I fully understood for the first time how I had betrayed them and brought each to his death through my selfish love and pride; and so it is I feel that my spirit can no longer sustain my body."

Thereafter Sir Launcelot barely ate or drank, and slept but little. Most of the time he lay weeping and praying on the tomb. None could cheer him, and by the end of six weeks he was unrecognizable. Then, one night as he lay on his bed, he begged the Archbishop to give him extreme unction.

"My son, do not ask me; for, by the grace of God, you shall recover."

"My lords, I am warned that by morning I must be laid into the earth; therefore I pray you, give me the last rites."

The Archbishop did as Sir Launcelot wished; and when it was over, Sir Launcelot spoke once more:

"Now I pray you that I may be buried at the Joyous Gard, for that was my vow many years ago; and it would trouble me ever to break a vow."

The Archbishop and his companions wept bitterly and retired to the chamber where they all slept. Suddenly, in the middle of the night, the Archbishop startled his companions by laughing in his sleep. They hastily wakened him.

"My lords, why did you waken me? I was never so happy!" he exclaimed.

"Wherefore, good father?" asked Sir Bors.

"I watched Sir Launcelot borne by angels through the open gates of heaven, where he was welcomed—a blissful sight!"

"I fear that it was a mischievous dream!" said Sir Bors.

"It may have been so; let us go to him," the Archbishop replied.

They found Sir Launcelot already chilled in his death; but on his lips was a sweet smile, and from his body rose a sweet aroma. They all knelt down and wept as they prayed for him.

In the morning the Archbishop conducted the requiem, and then Sir Launcelot's body was conveyed, in the same fashion as Queen Gwynevere's had been, to the Joyous Gard, in accordance with his last wish.

They arrived at the Joyous Gard fifteen days after Sir Launcelot's death, and for a further fifteen days his body was kept in the open coffin. Many were the tears shed and prayers offered over the greatest of King Arthur's knights.

Then by chance Sir Ector rode by the castle, and observing the commotion therein, entered and found the body. However, he failed to recognize his brother, so greatly had Sir Launcelot changed during his six years as a hermit, during all of which time Sir Ector had been searching for him. Then Sir Bors recognized Sir Ector and told him who lay in the tomb. Sir Ector fainted, and when he came to, he spoke:

"Sir Launcelot, surely you were the greatest of all Christian knights: none could match you! You were the most formidable in battle and the most courteous in manners; in the company of warriors the most courageous, in the company of ladies the gentlest of men, and in a righteous cause implacable. And of great lovers surely you were the truest. So it is you shall be remembered."

The Archbishop buried Sir Launcelot with solemn ceremony, and then the mourners dispersed from the castle.

Sir Constantyne, son of Sir Cador of Cornwall, was elected King of Britain. He ruled wisely and justly, and restored the Archbishop to office.

Of the surviving knights: Sir Bedivere returned to Glastonbury, where he lived until the end of his days as a hermit, and Sir Gahalantyne, Sir Galyhoden, Sir Vyllyars, and Sir Clarrus, though King Constantyne invited them all to live at the court, returned each to his own country and lived as a hermit.

Sir Bors, Sir Ector, Sir Blamoure, and Sir Bleobris traveled to the Holy Land and there fought against the Saracens, in honor and love of their Lord Jesu—for this had been the wish of Sir Launcelot—and it happened that they all died together in a battle fought on Good Friday; so God rest them!

HERE IS THE ENDE OF THE HOOLE BOOK OF KYNG ARTHUR AND OF HIS NOBLE KNYGHTES OF THE ROUNDE TABLE, THAT WHAN THEY WERE HOLE TOGYDERS THERE WAS EVER AN HONDRED AND FORTY. AND HERE IS THE ENDE OF THE DETH OF ARTHUR.

I PRAYE YOU ALL JENTYLMEN AND JENTYLWYMMEN THAT REDETH THIS BOOK OF ARTHUR AND HIS KNYGHTES FROM THE BEGYNNYNG TO THE ENDYNGE, PRAYE FOR ME WHYLE I AM ON LYVE THAT GOD SENDE ME GOOD DELYVERAUNCE. AND WHAN I AM DEED, I PRAY YOU ALL PRAYE FOR MY SOULE.

FOR THIS BOOK WAS ENDED THE NINTH YERE OF THE REYGNE OF KING EDWARD THE FOURTH, BY SYR THOMAS MALEORE, KNYGHT, AS JESU HELPE HYM FOR HYS GRETE MYGHT, AS HE IS THE SERVAUNT OF JESU BOTHE DAY AND NYGHT.

Appendix

Synopsis of Principal Characters

MERLIN: Prophet and magician, son of the Devil. Arthur's mentor from his birth to his marriage with Gwynevere. Places Arthur as a baby under the care of Sir Ector and his wife, who bring him up with their own son Kay. Falls in love with the sorceress Nyneve, who imprisons him forever in an enchanted cave in Cornwall.

THE DUKE OF TINTAGIL: A rebellious Cornish duke. Married to Igraine and father of the sorceress Morgan le Fay. Defies King Uther and is killed in battle.

KING UTHER PENDRAGON: King of all Britain. With the aid of Merlin impersonates the Duke of Tintagil, seduces Igraine, and begets Arthur. Marries Igraine thirteen days later. Dies in bed when Arthur is aged two years.

QUEEN IGRAINE: Sister to Queens Margawse and Elayne. Married to the Duke of Tintagil, later to King Uther. Deprived of Arthur at birth by Merlin. Acknowledged by Arthur only after his coronation.

KING ARTHUR: King of all Britain. Conqueror of Rome. Founder of the Knights of the Round Table. Commits incest and adultery with his aunt Queen Margawse and begets the bastard Sir Modred, whom he tries to drown. Marries Gwynevere and, after the quest of the Holy Grail, sentences her to burning for adultery. Exiles her lover, Sir Launcelot, and besieges him at Benwick in France. His throne, meanwhile, is usurped by Sir Modred, who wounds him fatally in single combat after his return to Britain. Conveyed to the Isle of Avalon by the Lady of the Lake.

QUEEN GWYNEVERE: Daughter of King Lodegreaunce. Brings Round Table to Arthur as marriage gift. Championed by her lover Sir Launcelot, who twice rescues her from burning at the stake. Repents after Arthur's last battle, and dies a nun.

MORGAN LE FAY: A sorceress, half sister to Arthur. Marries King Uryens of Gore and bears him a son, Sir Uwayne. Plots with her lover, Sir Accolon, to destroy Arthur and her husband and to seize the throne; the plot is thwarted by Nyneve and Sir Uwayne. Subsequently captures and tries to seduce Sir Launcelot, Sir Tristram, and other knights of the Round Table.

KING LOT: Leader of the rebel kings of the North and West. Marries Margawse and begets Sir Gawain, Sir Aggravayne, Sir Gaheris, and Sir Gareth. Killed in the battle of Terrabyl by King Pellinore. His death is avenged by Sir Gawain.

QUEEN MARGAWSE: Sister to Queens Igraine and Elayne. Marries King Lot. While officially spying on Arthur, becomes his lover and bears him Sir Modred. Subsequent to King Lot's death, is murdered by her son Sir Gaheris, who surprises her in bed with her lover Sir Lamerok.

SIR GAWAIN: Eldest son of King Lot, and Arthur's favorite cousin. Avenges his father's death by killing King Pellinore, and his mother's dishonor by killing Sir Lamerok. Abandons quest of the Holy Grail after killing his cousin Sir Uwayne, being rebuked by a hermit, and wounded by Sir Galahad. Twice challenges Sir Launcelot at Benwick in order to avenge his brothers Sir Gareth and Sir Gaheris. Fatally wounded by Sir Launcelot and dies on his return to Britain. Writes letter of reconciliation to Sir Launcelot an hour before his death.

SIR GARETH: Youngest son of King Lot. Sir Launcelot's favorite. Serves for a year in the kitchen at Arthur's court under Sir Kay, who dubs him Beaumains. Accomplishes quest of the Lady Lyoness before revealing his identity to Arthur. Posted as guard when Queen Gwynevere is bound to the stake for burning and, together with his brother Sir Gaheris, is unwittingly killed by Sir Launcelot during the latter's rescue of the queen.

SIR MODRED: Bastard son of King Arthur and Queen Margawse. Escapes drowning by a miracle. Exposes adultery between Sir Launcelot and Gwynevere. Exploits dissension to usurp throne. Attempts to marry his stepmother, Gwynevere, while Arthur is in France. Delivers fatal wound to Arthur in single combat, and is killed by him.

KINGS BAN AND BORS OF BENWICK AND GAUL: Arthur's allies in the battle of Bedgrayne. Traditional enemies of King Claudas. King Ban is the father of Sir Launcelot, King Bors of Sir Ector de Marys, Sir Bors, and Sir Lyonel, and godfather to Sir Blamoure and Sir Bleobris—all of whom are knights of the Round Table but adopt Sir Launcelot's cause when he is exiled.

SIR LAUNCELOT DU LAKE: Son of King Ban of Benwick. King Arthur's favorite. Champion and lover of Queen Gwynevere. Begets Sir Galahad on King Pelles' daughter Elaine while under an enchantment. Driven to madness for two years by Gwynevere's jealousy. Punished for his adultery by being denied participation in the mystery of the Holy Grail. Kills forty knights, including Sir Gaheris and Sir Gareth, in defense of Gwynevere. Is exiled by Arthur and besieged by him at Benwick in France. Challenged to mortal combat by Sir Gawain, whom he wounds fatally. On return to Britain finds

Arthur dead and Gwynevere a nun. Becomes a monk, and dies of a broken heart shortly after Gwynevere. Is buried at his own castle, the Joyous Gard.

SIR GALAHAD: Bastard son of Sir Launcelot and Princess Elaine of Carbonek; last descendant of Joseph of Arimathea. Sinless and invincible. Occupies Siege Perelous at the Round Table. Heir to Sir Balan's sword and King Evelake's shield. Purges the Maidens' Castle and cools the waters in the Well of Lust. Wins the Sword of the Straunge Gurdyls. Purges Earl Hernox' castle of antichrists. Accomplishes quest of the Holy Grail. Crowned king of the city of Sarras. Dies after second experience of holy emanation and is buried in the Spiritual Palace.

SIR BORS: Son of King Bors of Gaul. Brother to Sir Lyonel and Sir Ector de Marys; kinsman to Sir Blamoure and Sir Bleobris. Begets Sir Helyn le Blank on the daughter of King Brandegoris of Strangore. On the quest of the Holy Grail defeats the Devil in various guises, and his brother Sir Lyonel. Accomplishes quest together with Sir Percivale and Sir Galahad, both of whom he buries at the Spiritual Palace before returning to Camelot. Together with his kinsmen, supports Sir Launcelot during his exile and during his sojourn as a monk. Together with his kinsmen, dies fighting the infidel on a Good Friday.

KING PELLINORE: Hunter of the Questing Beast. Begets Sir Lamerok, Sir Percivale, Sir Percivale's sister, Sir Agglovale, Sir Dornar, and, on a milkmaid, Sir Torre—all of whom become knights of the Round Table. Arthur's ally in the defeat of the rebel kings. Kills King Lot, their leader, and is subsequently killed by Sir Gawain.

SIR LAMEROK: Son of King Pellinore. Champion of tournaments at King Mark's court and at the Ile of Servage. Sends Testing Horn to King Mark to expose adultery of Sir Tristram—who has slighted him—and Queen Iseult. Defeats twelve renegade knights in the service of Morgan le Fay. Becomes Queen Margawse's lover and is assassinated by Sir Gawain and his brothers.

SIR PERCIVALE: Son of King Pellinore. A lifelong virgin. Knighted by Arthur and resolves not to return to court until he has won fame. Rescues Sir Tristram from prison and rebukes King Mark. On quest of the Holy Grail defeats the Devil as Stallion, Serpent, and Seductress. Accomplishes quest together with Sir Galahad and Sir Bors. Becomes a hermit and dies two years later. Buried at the Spiritual Palace at Sarras.

SIR PALOMIDES THE SARACEN: Son of King Asclabor. Brother to Sir Segwarydes and half brother to Sir Safere. Unsuccessful rival to Sir Tristram as champion and lover of Queen Iseult. Defeats the brothers Sir Helake and Sir Helyus at the Red City and is awarded suzerainty. Reconciled to Sir Tristram and baptized a Christian. Devotes himself to the pursuit of the Questing Beast, being next of kin to King Pellinore and his successor to this task.

KING ANGWYSHAUNCE OF IRELAND: One of the Rebel Kings defeated by Arthur at the battles of Bedgrayne and Terrabyl.

Claim to Cornish tribute championed by his brother-in-law Sir Marhaus and opposed by Sir Tristram—who defeats Sir Marhaus and subsequently appears at his court under the name of Tramtrist. On discovery of Sir Tristram's identity grants him safe-conduct. Championed by Sir Tristram when impeached for treason by the brothers Sir Bleobris and Sir Blamoure. Awards Sir Tristram charge of his daughter Iseult the Fair in return for his defeat of Sir Blamoure.

KING MELYODAS OF LYONESS: Marries King Mark's sister Elizabeth, who dies bearing him a son, Sir Tristram. Mourns her death for seven years and then marries a daughter of King Howell of France; she attempts to poison Sir Tristram in order that the inheritance may revert to her own sons. Prevailed upon by Sir Tristram to spare the queen from burning at the stake. Appoints a tutor, Governayle, for Sir Tristram and sends him to France and then to Cornwall to complete his education. On Sir Tristram's return at the age of eighteen, grants him a large part of his inheritance and permission to serve his uncle King Mark.

KING MARK OF CORNWALL: Uncle and liege to Sir Tristram, who delivers him from bondage to Ireland and wins for him the hand of Iseult the Fair. Plots to destroy Sir Tristram variously by ambush, hazardous charge, summary execution, imprisonment, and enchantment—finally succeeds by stabbing him in the back. Also murders, or attempts to murder: Sir Kay, Sir Uwayne, Sir Gaheris, Sir Amaunte, Sir Bersules, and his brother, Prince Bodwyn, together with Bodwyn's wife, Anglydes, and son, Sir Alexander. Is beaten by Sir Lamerok, ridiculed by Sir Dagonet, taken prisoner by Sir Launcelot, reproved by King Arthur, and lampooned by Sir Dynadan. Dies, together with his equally treacherous cousin, Sir Andret, at the hands of Sir Bellengerus, who is Sir Alexander's son.

ISEULT THE FAIR: Daughter of King Angwyshaunce of Ireland. Cures Sir Tristram of poisoned wound delivered by Sir Marhaus, and falls in love with him as he plays to her on the harp. Their love intensified by drinking love potion intended for her and King Mark, to whom Sir Tristram delivers her and whom she is obliged to marry. Undergoes many hazards in the course of her love for Sir Tristram before rescuing him from prison and taking refuge with him in Sir Launcelot's castle, the Joyous Gard. On their return to Cornwall, sees Sir Tristram stabbed in the back by King Mark while he plays to her on the harp. Falls prostrate upon his grave.

SIR TRISTRAM OF LYONESS: Son of King Melyodas and Queen Elizabeth. Defeats Sir Marhaus on behalf of King Mark, and Sir Blamoure on behalf of King Angwyshaunce—thereby winning Iseult, whom he delivers to King Mark. Escapes summary execution by making the Chantry leap; rescues Iseult from the Leper's Hut and takes refuge with her in the forest. When Iseult is recaptured, flees to the court of King Howell in France, defeats the king's enemies, and marries his daughter Isode—but does not consummate the marriage. Returns to Cornwall and, after a period of madness—due to his discovery of love letters between Sir Keyhydyns and Iseult—joins Arthur at Camelot and is made a knight of the Round Table.

In a series of tournaments proves himself the greatest knight in the realm, with the exception only of Sir Launcelot. Twice champions King Mark against his enemies and is rewarded by imprisonment and, after his return from the Joyous Gard, by assassination.

KING ARTHUR'S COURT: Principal dignitaries and nobles—Sir Kay: Royal Seneschal. Sir Lucas: Butler. Sir Bedivere. Sir Badouin: Constable. Sir Ulphius: Chamberlain. Sir Brastius: Warden of the North. Sir Dagonet: Fool. Sir Dynadan: Wit and Lampoonist. The Archbishop of Canterbury. King Pellinore and his sons. Sir Gawain and his brothers. Sir Launcelot and his kin. King Bagdemagus and his son Sir Mellyagraunce.

KING ARTHUR'S PRINCIPAL ENEMIES: The Roman Emperor Lucius. Kings Royns and Nero of the West. The Eleven Kings: King Lot, King Brandegoris, King Clarivaunce, King Morganoure, King Uryens, King Idres, King Cradilment, King Angwyshaunce, King Nentres, King Carados, the King of the Hundred Knights. Also the Five Kings of Denmark, Ireland, Sorlayse, the Vale, and the Isle of Lonteyse. Finally, Morgan le Fay and Sir Modred.

King Arthur defeats and either kills or wins allegiance from all his enemies with the exception of Morgan le Fay.

THE QUESTING BEAST: has the head of a serpent, the body of a leopard, the buttocks of a lion, and the feet of a hart. From its belly issues the sound of thirty pairs of yapping hounds. It is never brought to earth.

THE HOLY GRAIL (Sangreal): In Christian legend the silver dish or cup in which Joseph of Arimathea collected drops of blood and sweat from the wounds of Jesus Christ when He was crucified. Together with the lance with which He was pierced, was brought by Joseph to Glastonbury, where he founded the first Christian church in Britain.

In pagan legend the Caldron of Plenty—an attribute of the variously named Goddess of Fertility, and from which divine children might receive inspiration and knowledge. Alternatively, one in which those children might be stewed for the benefit of the goddess and her adorers.

The above remarks are not intended to be in any way conclusive: for a discussion of this very complex legend the reader is referred to the collaborative history edited by R. S. Loomis: *Arthurian Literature in the Middle Ages*. Oxford (The Clarendon Press), 1959.

398.2   Malory, Sir Thomas   756543
Mal   Le Morte d'Arthur

DATE DUE

FE 24			
NOV 10			
DEC 16			
OC 12 '82			
MR 23 '83			
NO 10 '83			
DE 1 '83			
JA 8 '86			